# The Bad Mother's Handbook
## and
## Swallowing Grandma

Kate Long lives in Shropshire.
She is the author of several novels
including the No. 1 bestseller
*The Bad Mother's Handbook*.

D0532603

Also by Kate Long

**QUEEN MUM**

# Kate Long

## The Bad Mother's Handbook

## and

## Swallowing Grandma

PAN BOOKS

*The Bad Mother's Handbook* first published 2004 by Picador.
First published in paperback 2005 by Picador.
*Swallowing Grandma* first published 2005 by Picador.
First published in paperback 2006 by Picador.

This omnibus first published 2008 by Pan Books
an imprint of Pan Macmillan Ltd
Pan Macmillan, 20 New Wharf Road, London N1 9RR
Basingstoke and Oxford
Associated companies throughout the world
www.panmacmillan.com

ISBN 978-0-330-45789-7

1 3 5 7 9 8 6 4 2

A CIP catalogue record for this book is available from
the British Library.

Typeset by SetSystems Ltd, Saffron Walden, Essex
Printed and bound in Great Britain by
Mackays of Chatham plc, Chatham, Kent

# The Bad Mother's Handbook

## Acknowledgements

For their encouragement and guidance:
David Rees, Kath Pilsbury, Ursula Doyle, Leslie Wilson,
Katherine Frank and Simon Long.

For helping to get the ball rolling:
Judith Magill, Adrian Johnson, Lynn Patrick
and Peter Straus.

For invaluable practical support:
the Headmaster and staff of Abbey Gate College.

For inspirational background material,
and a whole lot of Oldham Tinkers LPs:
Mum and Dad.

*For Lily*

I'll tell thee a tale
About a snail
That jumped in t' fire
And burnt its tail

I'll tell thee another
About its brother
Did t' same
Silly owd bugger.

In the battle between handbag strap and door handle,
far better to knacker your handbag
than let the door handle feel it's won.

# Chapter One

NAN DREAMS:

When I was twelve I fell and broke my elbow. It was election day 1929 and we were mucking about on top of the wall by the polling station. It was about six feet up and you were all right as long as you sat astride the coping stones, only I'd turned side-saddle so as to spot the people who'd voted Conservative, my dad said you could see it in their faces. Jimmy nudged me and we started singing:

> 'Vote! Vote! Vote for Alec Sharrock
> He is sure to win the day
> And we'll get a salmon tin
> And we'll put the Tory in
> And he'll never see his mother any more.'

I swung my legs to make the words come out better and the next thing I knew I was sprawled on the ground with my arm underneath me. Jimmy tried to make a sling out of the yellow muslin banners we'd been waving but I screamed and he started to cry in panic. It hurt so much I was afraid to get up in case I left my arm on the floor.

The following day, when we heard Labour'd got in, Dad got so drunk he couldn't open the back gate.

'I'll go and let him in,' Jimmy volunteered.

'Tha'll not!' said Mother. 'Leave him where he is.'

So I lay on the sofa with my arm all strapped up and watched him struggle. Finally he fell over and my mother drew the curtains on him.

It was funny, we'd never known him touch a drop before.

His vices lay in other directions.

## JANUARY 1997

**The day after** it happened everything seemed normal. Even from behind my bedroom door I could hear Mum going on at Nan. She tries not to get cross but it's the only emotion my mother does these days,

'Come on, Nan, it's time for your bath.'

'I can't. My arm hurts.'

'No, it doesn't. You've been dreaming again. Come on.'

Ours is a house of lost things; keys, hearing aids, identities. There was a row about sausages this morning. My mum had cooked two sausages for Nan's dinner and left them on a plate to cool. Then the window cleaner came to the door, and when she got back they'd gone.

'What have you done with them?' she asked Nan (patient voice).

'I han't touched 'em.'

'Yes, you have, you must have.'

'It were t' dog.'

'We haven't got a dog, Nan. Where are they? I just want to know, you're not in trouble. Have you eaten them?'

'Aye, I might have done. Yesterday. I had 'em for my tea.'

'How can you have had them yesterday when I've only just cooked them? God Almighty, it's every little thing.' My mother ran her hand wearily over her face and sighed. It's something she does a lot.

'By the Crin! There's no need to shout. You're a nowty woman. You're like my daughter Karen, she gets her hair off at nothing.'

'I am your daughter Karen.'

'Hmph.'

It was me who found the sausages next day, wrapped in two plastic bags inside the bread bin.

Not that Nan has the monopoly on confusion.

I know my name is Charlotte and that I'm seventeen, but on a bad day that's as far as it goes. 'Be yourself' people, older people, are always telling me: yeah, right. That's *so* easy. Sometimes I do those quizzes in *Most!* and *Scene Nineteen*. Are you a Cool Cat or a Desperate Dog and What's Your Seduction-Style, how to tell your personality type by your favourite colour, your favourite doodle, the hour of your birth. Do I

    a) believe this crap?
    b) treat it with the contempt it deserves?

Depends on my mood, really.

Sometimes my nan thinks I am her own childhood

reincarnated. 'Bless her,' she says, rooting for a Mintoe, 'her father beat her till she were sick on t' floor and then he beat her again. He ran off and her mother had to tek in washin'. Poor lamb. Have a toffee.'

This drives my mum up the wall, round the bend and back again. She doesn't like to see good sympathy going to waste, particularly in my direction, because she thinks I Live the Life of Riley.

'You have chances I never had,' she tells me. 'Education's everything. How much homework have you got tonight?' She bought me a personal organizer for Christmas but I lost it – I haven't had the balls to tell her yet. 'You must make something of your life. Don't make the mistake I made.'

Since I am part of the Mistake ('I was a mother by the age of sixteen, divorced at twenty-one') this leaves me in an unusual position: I am also her redeemer, the reassurance that her life has not in fact been wasted. My future successes will be hers and people will say to me, 'Your mother was a clever woman. She gave up a lot for you.'

Or so she hopes.

Actually I'm in a bit of a mess.

When Nan walked in on me and Paul Bentham having sex yesterday afternoon she didn't say a word. She's surprisingly mobile, despite the bag. The colostomy was done donkey's years ago, pre-me, to get rid of galloping cancer.

'THE QUEEN MOTHER HAS ONE, YOU KNOW,' the consultant had shouted.

'Ooh. Swanky,' replied Nan, impressed. 'Well, Ivy

4

Seddon reckons Cliff Richard has one an' he dances about all ovver.'

I thought she might let it slip that evening while we were watching *Coronation Street*. Suddenly she said: 'She were too young, she didn't know what she were doing. I towd her, tha maun fret, I'll tek care of it.' My mum, coming in with a cup of tea for her, banged the saucer down so that the tea spilt on the cloth, and gave me a look.

Christ, Nan, please don't say anything or I'm done for. ('A thirty-three-year-old woman was today formally accused of bludgeoning to death her teenage daughter with what police believe may have been a personal organizer. Neighbours reported hearing raised voices late into the night . . .')

It still hurts a bit. I didn't know it would hurt like that. I knew there'd be blood because I read somewhere about them hanging the bed sheets out of the window in olden days so that all and sundry could see the bride had been virgo intacta. I used an old T-shirt and rinsed it out afterwards; if she asks, I'll tell my mother it was a nosebleed.

I'm not a slag. It's just that there's not a lot to do round here. You can walk through Bank Top in fifteen minutes, a small dull village hunching along the ridge of a hill and sprawling down the sides in two big estates. From the highest point it affords panoramic views of industrial Lancashire; factories, warehouses and rows and rows of red-brick terraces, and on the horizon the faint grey-green line of millstone-grit moorland. To the south there's the television mast where a German plane is supposed to have come down fifty years ago; to the north there's Blackpool

Tower, just visible on the skyline. I used to spend hours squinting to see the illuminations, but they're too far away.

There are three types of housing in Bank Top. Victorian two-up two-downs line the main street, while on the fringes of the village it's all modern boxes with garages and uniform front lawns. None of the people in these Prestige Developments talk to each other but you can hear everything your neighbour's doing through the cardboard walls, apparently. Beneath these shiny new houses the foundations shift and grumble over defunct mine shafts – the last pit closed forty years ago – making Bank Top a sink village in every sense.

Then there's the council estate, thirties semis, where dogs roam free and shit on the pavement with impunity. This is where we live. We bought our house in the boom of '84 (also Divorce Year) and my mother celebrated by having a Georgian front door fitted and mock leaded lights on the windows. The front box room, which is mine and minute, looks out over the Working Men's Club car park; some rum things go on *there* of a Saturday night, I can tell you.

In the centre of the village is the church and the community centre and a rubbish row of shops, a newsagent, a launderette, a Spar. Two pubs, more or less opposite each other, battle it out but one is for old people and families off the new estates with quiz nites and chicken tikka pizza, and the other's rough as rats. I don't go in either. For kicks I get the bus to Wigan from a bus shelter smelling of pee. Fuck off, it says over the lintel, so I generally do.

I don't belong in this village at all. Actually, I don't know where I do belong. Another planet, maybe.

**So there I was,** on my back, entirely naked and rigid as a corpse, when Nan totters into my bedroom and says to Paul, 'A horse has just gone past the landing window.'

'Which way did it go?' asks Paul.

'*Which way did it go?*' I said later. 'What are you, mad as her?'

'I was only trying to make conversation.' He shrugged his bony shoulders under the sheets. 'What's up with her? Is she mental, like?'

'No more than a lot of people,' I said, a bit sharply. I get defensive about her, even though she is a bloody nuisance. 'Some days she's more with it than me. She's just old. You might be like that when you're old.'

'I'd shoot myself first.'

'No, you wouldn't. That's what everyone says, but they wouldn't.'

Part of the problem in this house is hormones. There are too many undiluted women for one small ex-council house. Huge clouds of supercharged oestrogen drift about and react sending showers of sparks into the atmosphere; the air prickles with it. Nan hasn't got any left, of course, although she hung onto hers longer than most (had my mum at forty-six! Didn't realize people even had sex at that age), but I've got more than I know what to do with. Certainly more than my mother knows what to do with. She suspects I have tart DNA (passed on from her, presumably). If she finds out I've been having sex she will kill me. Really.

This would be my worst nightmare:

BLOODY BLOODY bloody hell. Bloody Nan for making a mess on the bed. Again. Not her fault but I DON'T CARE, nobody cares about me. COME OFF, you bloody fitted sheet, bastard son of a sheet HELL. Trailing this armload off to the washing basket and HELL I've dropped a pair of tights HELL I've dropped a pair of knickers trying to pick up the tights, whole bloody lot's gone now all over the floor. Navy sock in with the whites, that was a close shave. Charlotte WILL NOT put her dirty clothes in the right baskets, what kind of a slut have I produced, you'd think she'd have more consideration. Dying for a cup of tea, cotton with pre-wash, heavily soiled, everything's heavily soiled in this house. Not Nan's fault, that bloody tape doesn't stick to her skin if she gets Nivea under it, what's this, what's this? What's just fallen out of the dirty pillowcase onto the floor?

Oh, Jesus, it's a condom. Charlotte's been having SEX.

I've known Paul Bentham since primary school. Funny to think of all the small events that lead up to a big one. Once, when I was about ten, we were down on the rec, watching the lads play five-a-side. Paul went for an extra big kick, got it wrong and smacked me really hard in the face with the football. The girls all marched off to tell on him and he thought he was in big trouble. Even his ears went red. But I didn't cry, even though I thought my nose had changed shape. I think he appreciated that.

Then there was the Valentine's Day before we moved schools. I knew he'd made a card for me, his friends had all been teasing me about it, and I waited; morning playtime, dinnertime, afternoon playtime. It wasn't till four o'clock he thrust it into my hand, and even then he'd changed the words on it:

| | |
|---|---|
| ~~Roses are red~~ | Vilots are blue |
| ~~Vilots are blue~~ | Roses are red |
| ~~If you go with me~~ | If I went with you |
| ~~I'll go with you~~ | I'd be off my head |

I wasn't that fussed, though. I knew it was Martin Hedges who'd made him do it.

I was more upset when he didn't dance with me at the leavers' disco. We knew we were off to different schools, him to the comp and me to the grammar, so I thought he might be up for a kiss, but he never came near me, just raced around hitting his mates with balloons and stuffing streamers down their backs. I told my mum about it afterwards (we got on in those days). She said, 'Well, what can you expect, he's a little boy.' It made me wonder when he'd be grown up.

Luckily it's impossible to avoid anyone on a place as small as Bank Top. We'd meet at the bus stop, blank each other out and sit as far apart as possible on the red leatherette seats, so I knew there was a chance he was interested. When he was with his friends he'd spread himself out over the back of the 214 to Wigan and talk loudly and swear a lot, writing on the windows and converting the sign EMERGENCY EXIT to VIRGIN EXIT by scratching off bits of the lettering. Then the boys would say to each other, 'That's *your* door, that is. That's the door *you* should use.' Such a stigma.

Now neither of us would be able to use it.

I thought it would make me feel different, not being a virgin, but mainly it's made me feel scared.

'Have you done this before?' he asked as he unzipped his jeans.

We knew what was going to happen. It was my New Year's resolution and I'd told him. I don't think he could believe his luck.

'No. Have you?'

'Does it matter?'

I didn't trust myself to answer so I took my skirt off. Like we were changing for PE; hand your valuables over. I was sure we should be undressing each other, or at least kissing, but that seemed too intimate. I started to shiver with nerves and the cold. 'Can you stick the heater on? You're nearest.'

CLICK went the thermostat and we got into bed.

Then time seemed to hang for a moment and I was back at last August's carnival, sitting on our front wall watching the streamered floats go past and waving at toddlers dressed as bees, when he came sauntering over with his bucket of coins. He was wearing a pirate costume and he'd drawn a black curly moustache over his soft top lip, but the skin only looked more smooth and bright, almost girlish. 'It wrecks, this eyepatch,' he said, peeling it off and rubbing at the red mark on his cheek. 'I'm sure I'm doing myself damage. And these boots are killing me, an' all.'

So he sat down and we chatted shyly, then we walked

to the field together to hear the judging and watch the endless teams of high-stepping knee-socked majorettes waving giant pompoms about. The megaphone squawked the names of princesses and queens. 'Why is there always a fat one in every troupe?' he'd said, and the brass band played 'Oh When the Saints' while the air glittered around us. Little children ran about screaming, teenage girls lay on the grass and exposed their midriffs to the sun. Before he went home he said, 'You'll have to come round some time and we'll listen to some CDs or summat.' The sun flashed on his dagger. 'Yeah,' I said. 'All right.'

CLICK.

He was fumbling between my legs and pushing a finger inside me then, Christ, two, stabbing and rotating clumsily. (Wasn't that what the boys boasted about, the girls at school said, how many *fingers* they'd managed?) No. I'd changed my mind. This was a bad idea. Stop. I looked for his gaze to tell him to slow down, to abandon the whole thing and go downstairs and watch *The Simpsons*. But the fierce desire in his eyes paralysed me. I'd heard of people's eyes burning, but I'd never seen it in real life. It was like all his maleness concentrated there, shocking.

Suddenly he paused and half turned away. My heart lurched, then I realized he was rolling on a condom. His vertebrae were clear through his skin and I followed their curve down to the shadow at the base of his spine. Were all men so angular?

CLICK.

Then he turned back to me, grasped his cock like he

11

. meant business and forced his way in. Ow ow OW it stung so much it was all I could do not to cry out. A football in the face was nothing compared to this. I held myself rigid and clung on to his back, wondering why something so universally billed as brilliant could be so awful. Why didn't they warn us at school? I'm sure if some teacher had said, 'Oh and by the way, it feels like someone sandpapering your cervix,' they needn't have bothered with all the Aids warnings and morality stuff. I'd certainly have thought twice. He came quickly with a series of great shudders and then collapsed into me, hiding his face against my neck.

It was at this point that Nan walked in, so all credit to him really that he managed anything coherent at all.

Afterwards it was embarrassing. Even though I ran over and locked the door I still felt the horror of Nan's blank stare and half-smile. Neither of us knew what to say and there was blood and we were still naked. Down the landing we could hear Nan singing:

> 'You know last night, well you know the night before
> Three little tom-cats come knockin' at the door
> One had a fiddle, another had a drum
> And the third had a pancake stuck to its bum.'

'Don't put that in the bin!' I shouted as he scooped up the condom and neatly tied a knot in it. 'Hell's bells, if my mother finds that in with the tissues . . .'

'So what am I supposed to do with it? Do you not want to keep it forever?'

He dangled it from his finger then made as if to throw it at me. I screamed and flinched. He lunged and we rolled about on the bed, then somehow it became a pillow fight. I bet that never happens in my mother's Aga Sagas. His ribs moved under his pale skin and his blue eyes shone, and I thought, He's still just a boy really. He was panting and smiling, and I knew then I'd done the right thing.

At last we rolled into the bedhead. He banged his chin and I knocked a picture off the wall which fell down the back.

'Aw, shit, sorry. I'll get it.'

He dived under the bed, all sharp shoulder bone, and brought out the photograph; two hand-tinted ginger kittens in a basket above the legend *Happy Hours!*.

> *Hoping always for a meeting*
> *With a friend I love so true*
> *Dear I send this simple greeting*
> *May the world deal well with you*

'The frame's a bit jiggered.'

He handed it over. The thin black wood was split at the corner and the glass was cracked.

'I can get a new one. Best not let my mother see, though.' I opened the bedside cupboard and slid the picture in under some magazines. 'I know it's naff but it's got sentimental value. It's one of Nan's birthday cards from when she was little, she used to have it in her room and I always wanted it. I nabbed it when her mind began to go. Sort of a way of preserving a piece of my childhood, do you know what I mean? Against all the change . . . She's never noticed.'

'Very nice. Do you want to come round on Saturday?

Everyone's out so, only I've got to get back to let Darren in now. Sooner he gets his own key the better.'

He was pulling on his sweater as he spoke.

'Can you not stay just a bit longer?'

'Sorry. Little brothers and all that. Have you seen my sock?'

I scrambled to put something on, we found the sock and then he went home. I lay on the bed wishing he'd kissed me goodbye instead of ruffling my hair. Should've asked. Or maybe that's not cool. What are the rules, anyway? Perhaps some men just aren't all that demonstrative; it doesn't necessarily mean anything, it's the way they are.

So there it is, the great seduction. I suppose I've made the whole thing sound pretty gross. Some of it was. But the point is, the point is, I'm a woman now, an adult. Perhaps people will be able to tell just by looking at me (God, I hope not! The girls at school used to say you walked funny afterwards). But the point is I have a life that is not my mother's and it is the beginning of some big changes round here.

I know things are going to be different from now on.

*

I'D MET Billy when he ran across the street to help me carry a basket of washing. It was blowing about, a great white sheet on the top, and I knew if it hit the ground and got dirty my mother would chow. It happened once before when I was little and Jimmy had hold of one handle and I had the other. We were staggering down the street to Dr Liptrot's with his week's wash when a big gust of wind took two or three shirts right off and they fell in t' road. We were two-double laughing as we picked 'em up, but when we got home and showed my mother she laid her head on the table and wept.

Billy had been courting a girl he'd met in the TB sanatorium, a bonny woman but it made no difference. We had ten for the wedding tea, then caught the train to Blackpool. At Chorley some lads got in and saw all t' confetti in my hair so they started singing, 'We have been married today, We are on our honeymoon all the way.' When we got to the bed and breakfast I gave a fish to the landlady so she could cook it for our supper. The next evening she said, 'Mrs Hesketh, are you ready for your fish now?' And I never took her on because I wasn't used to the name.

When I got back to the mill I had such a colour all the girls said I must be pregnant.

*

WHERE'S CHARLOTTE? Gone to Wigan for the afternoon, no doubt to spend money she hasn't got on crap she doesn't need. Nan? Asleep in the chair, legs apart, mouth slightly open. God, if I ever get like that. And why are there never any pens in this house? You put them down and they walk. Useful Drawer; what a flamin' mess, I don't know why we keep half this rubbish. Sandpaper, candles, napkin rings – like we're ever going to use *those* – Stain Devil's leaked all over the clothes brush now. Had a big row with the hoover and a table leg today; broke one of the attachments, so that'll be something else to sort out. Bingo! Black biro, bit fluffy round the nib, still, be all right. Here goes nothing.

# *Love 'n' stuff*

## *Finding You a Partner for Life's Adventure*

### *Outline Questionnaire*

*Please try to answer as honestly as possible*

**Name** Karen Cooper

**Status** *Very low actually.* Divorced.

**Address** 21, Brown Moss Road, Bank Top, Nr Wigan, Lancs WI24 5LS. *Moving in with my mother was supposed to be a fresh start.*

**Age** 33. *Feel about 60 sometimes.*

**Children** One. *17-year-old madam.*

**Occupation** ~~Teacher.~~ Part time classroom assistant. *At my old primary school! My life's just gone round in a big loop.*

**Educational Qualifications** 10 'O' levels. *Yes, 10. I could have had a degree if I'd wanted. What the hell does it matter anyway? I've been to the University of Life (though I had originally set my sights on Leeds).*

**Salary (approx)** Crap. *Funded this caper out of Nan's present (I just withdraw it from her savings account, Merry Xmas Happy Birthday etc, even buy my own damn card).*

**Do you consider yourself to be**

❑ working class ☑ middle class

❑ upper class ❑ not sure

**Political Persuasion** *If push came to shove I suppose I'd say Conservative. I mean, they're going to be in forever, aren't they? Anyway, if it wasn't for Maggie Thatcher we couldn't have bought this house (although I can't say I rate John Major much). Truth is, nothing ever changes for people like us, whoever's swanning about in Number 10.*

**Religion** None. *Mum'll put in a good word for us all when she gets to heaven.*

## Physical appearance

**Height** 5'9''. *That's going to put a lot of men off for a start.*

**Weight/dress size** 12/14. *Depends how bloody Nan's being. Some days I can eat a whole packet of gypsy creams at one sitting.*

**Hair colour** Brown. *Currently. I'm always looking for the perfect hairstyle, the one that'll solve my life for me. Growing out a perm in the meantime.*

**Eyes** Sort of grey. *Charlotte's got her dad's blue eyes. Nan's are brown. None of us bloody match in this house.*

**Special Interests** Reading, drinking, watching tv. *Doesn't sound too clever, does it? But believe me, when the alternatives are changing your mother's colostomy bag or arguing with your daughter, there's no contest. Always meant to take up something worthy, but there you go. Actually I do read quite a lot. Joanna Trollope, Rosamunde Pilcher, that kind of thing. It helps.*

## *Personality*

Do you consider yourself to be any of the following? (It may be useful to ask a friend or relative.) *You must be kidding. Charlotte would wet herself laughing if she saw this.*

❏ extrovert ❏ generous ❏ organised

❏ shy ❏ patient ❏ creative

❏ optimistic ❏ thoughtful ❏ spontaneous

❏ loyal ❏ down-to-earth ❏ understanding

*To be honest, none of these seems quite right.*

Please feel free to add your own ideas below:
*Knackered, bitter, unfulfilled, self-sabotaging. Hence this questionnaire.*

What kind of relationship are you hoping might develop out of our introductions?
*Christ. Just forget it.*

MY LAST DATE was a classic. We'd met in the Working Men's. It's a bit common, but I go there occasionally because it's cheap and local, and if Nan gets up to anything really mad Charlotte can nip across the road and let me know. Sometimes I need to get out of the house in a hurry.

Anyway I was sitting at the bar cradling a Bacardi Breezer and feeling bleak when he came over. Greyish – well, grey, but not balding; normal shape; about my height. He was wearing a check shirt with the sleeves rolled up, and jeans, which gave no clues. I clocked hairy forearms, no wedding ring, clean fingernails as he proffered his money to the bar man.

'Can I get you a drink while I'm here?'

That gave me licence to have a better look at his face. He just seemed ordinary, pleasant, not weird or anything.

'Thanks. I've not seen you in here.' It was true; it's always the same faces in the Working Men's.

'No. I used to live up Bolton way, I'm revisiting old haunts. What about you? Is this your regular?'

'Not really.' God, what a thought. 'I just drop in from time to time. When it all gets too much.' I laughed loudly but really I felt like banging my forehead against the bar. Stupid thing to say.

He only smiled, which made his face crinkle up. I wondered how old he was, not that it mattered. I get like that sometimes; desperate.

See, I know you shouldn't look for a man to solve your life for you, but it's easier said than done when you're out in the throng on your own. Sometimes it would be so nice for somebody else to take the flak for once, never mind have some decent sex. A hundred million sex acts a day worldwide, there are supposed to be; you'd think one of them might waft its way over in my direction. Nobody in our house understands that I have Needs as well, it's like Montel Williams says. He was on Channel 4 yesterday afternoon, a show called 'I Hate My Mom's New Boyfriend'. 'Doesn't Mom have a right to some happiness too?' he kept asking these sulky teenagers. The audience were all clapping. I nearly called Charlotte down but she was revising for her modules.

Six Breezers later and for all his grey hair I was out in the car park kissing him long and full, putting off the moment when I had to go home and change Nan and face

Charlotte's scowls. Even light rain and sweeping headlights weren't putting me off my stroke. It was so nice to be held, even for a few minutes. Then a car nearly reversed into us, which broke the mood slightly. I disentangled.

'I'd invite you back but my daughter's around . . . It's a bit difficult . . .'

'Can I see you again?'

Jackpot.

He fished in his back pocket and gave me His Card, very swish, and said there was no pressure but to give him a call. 'Soon.' I liked that, it seemed gentlemanly; also it meant I didn't have to sit around waiting for him to ring me. I should have known it was all looking too good.

The next day at school I was telling Sylv, the secretary.

'He wasn't sex on a stick but he was all right. I'd see him again.'

'*What* was his name?' she asked with a funny look on her face.

I gave her the card.

She studied it and pursed her lips. 'You do know this is Vicky's ex, don't you?' She handed it back smugly. I don't like Sylv any more, I never really liked her. She draws her eyebrows on and wears skirts that are too tight.

'Vicky? Deputy Head Vicky? Vicky Roberts?'

'Yep.'

'The one she divorced just before I started here?'

'The one who couldn't *get it up* unless he wore *special rubber knickers*.' Sylv dropped her voice and mouthed exaggeratedly.

'Jesus.'

'Wanted her to wear *some kind of mask*, too. That's when

she asked him to leave.' Sylv smacked her lips with satis-
faction. She'd be dining out on this for months, I could
tell. I am never going to tell her anything personal again.
I wanted to sink to my knees and beg her not to pass it on
but I knew it would be a waste of time; Rubber Man would
be all round the staff room by lunchtime. For once I was
glad I was on playground duty. So instead I said:

'Well, he was too old, anyway.'

'So you won't be seeing him again, then?' she called
after me as I swept out of the office.

It's just as well Sylv didn't catch me photocopying my
practice run at 'Love 'n' Stuff' in school. I reckon perhaps
I'm ready to do the questionnaire properly now.

NEVER LET IT be said that when things are looking their
grimmest, they can't get worse.

I was sound asleep when I heard the crash. I struggled
with the bedsheets, tangled from some overheated dream,
threw on a dressing gown in case it was an intruder,
although I knew it wasn't, and hurried downstairs.

It was completely dark in the lounge but there were
muffled sounds coming from the kitchen. I opened the
door and blinked in the light.

'What are you doing, Nan?'

Actually I could see what she was doing. She was
pulling out drawers and emptying Tupperware boxes onto
the floor. Six tins of salmon were stacked at her feet.

'Are you looking for something to eat?'

'I've lost my key.'

'Which key?'

'To t' back door. Bloody hell fire.' She wrestled with a

plastic lid and flung it across the tiles. Then she sat down wearily.

'You don't need a back door key. What would you want to go outside for? It's the middle of the night. And it's freezing.'

'I need to check the bins.'

'No, no you don't. You did them this morning. Don't you remember? Charlotte helped you.'

What it is, she worries if we put envelopes with our name and address into the wheeliebin, in case someone roots through and takes them. 'Then what, Nan? What would they do with the envelopes?' 'Ooh, all sorts,' says Nan mysteriously. 'There's some wicked people about.' It clearly worries her, so we let her rip them up into tiny pieces. It's one of our routines which has become normal. This nocturnal activity was something new, though.

'Come on, Nan, come to bed, you'll catch your death. I'll clear up in the morning.'

'The bins!'

'We did them. Tiny pieces. And the bin men come tomorrow.' And I'm bloody cold and Christ it's twenty past *three* in the morning and I've got to go to work in five hours and nobody cares that my life is a complete fuck-up.

'I'll just put this salmon back.'

'LEAVE IT! Just COME to BED and LEAVE this mess. Please.' I used to cry before the divorce but I don't seem able to any more. I get angry instead. She didn't move, so I lunged over and pulled her up roughly. She's only small and pretty light. We staggered together and I fell into the edge of the unit and banged my arm.

'Hell.'

Nan looked up with watery eyes.

'You'll want some knit-bone for that.'

'Shut up.' I was trying not to swear at her.

'Or Dr Cassell's Miracle Cure-All Tablets. They cured Uncle Jack and he had malaria. Caught it in Mesopotamia during the Great War. He always had to have the doors shut and a big fire. When he emigrated he sent us a lamb. My mother took it to t' butchers to be jointed up but she never got back what she should have done.'

'WILL YOU COME TO BED!'

She turned and stared at me, trying to focus. Then she put her face close to mine.

'I don't have to do what you tell me,' she said quietly. 'You're not my daughter. Your mother was called Jessie. Didn't you know? You're not mine.'

*

'**Did you have** an orgasm? I want to give you an orgasm, Charlotte.' Behind him David Beckham grinned confidently; no sexual hang-ups for him. We were lying under a Manchester United duvet and it was four weeks since we'd first done it. Outside children were screaming and an Alsatian barked from behind wire netting in next door's garden. His house is no quieter than ours. I glanced up at the window (Man U curtains).

'Is it snowing yet? It's cold enough. Snow's about the only thing that makes our estate look any better.'

'Did you hear what I said?'

'Sorry. Yeah. Well, no. It doesn't matter. It was nice.'

'Nice? Is that it?' Paul rolled away onto his back and gazed at the ceiling, hands behind his head. He had little tufts of hair under his arms that I loved to stroke. 'I want it to be fantastic for you, fireworks going off, that kind of stuff. I don't feel you're always . . .'

'What?' I leant up on an elbow and watched his face struggle.

'Sort of, I dunno, *with* me. Oh, I can't explain. It's not like it is on the telly, is it?'

'Nothing is. This is Life.' I lay back down and put my face close to his. 'It's loads better than it was, though.' This was true. It wasn't painful any more, for a start, especially now I'd sorted out the cystitis. And when we did it at his house it felt more relaxed; no leaping up and legging it afterwards, no fear of interruptions. Paul's mum left two years ago, and his dad was so laid back about his son's sex life I got the impression we could be having it off on the living-room carpet and he'd only complain if we got in the way of the TV screen.

'Yeah, well. Practice makes perfect, eh?' He reached over and ran his hand over my breasts. 'These are great.' He circled a nipple with his finger and watched it firm to a peak. 'Brilliant.' Then he moved sideways and put both palms flat over my chest. He sighed happily. 'You'll get me goin' again.'

It was thrilling, this power I never knew I had. I pushed the duvet back and watched his cock grow and twitch against his pale thigh; it wasn't scary any more. I felt like the goddess of sex. I wriggled against him and he groaned.

'Touch it.'

I still didn't know the proper technique but it didn't seem to matter. Whatever I did he rolled his eyes back as if he was having a fit, and panted. There was all this loose skin below the tight, shiny stalk. I fiddled experimentally and he began to swear quietly.

'Like that, yeah. Fuck. Fucking hell.'

When my hair fell forward and brushed his stomach he drew his breath in sharply.

'Wait a minute.'

He groped around on the bedside table and snatched up a condom, which he dropped with shock when I dipped my head and kissed his navel.

'I'll get it.' I leant over and retrieved the little foil packet from off the floor.

'Put it on for me. Go on. It'd be so sexy.'

I must have looked doubtful.

'I'll show you how.'

I thought, you have to learn these things if you're a woman, it'll be another string to my bow.

He tore off the packet end and squeezed out the slimy ring. I watched closely, the way I used to in science lessons when Bunsen burners were being demonstrated. Then he handed it to me. I tried not to flinch.

'Keep it this way up. Pull that pointy thing in the middle, just a bit, gently. Gently! It's my last one. Now, put it on the top like this – ' he guided my hands to his groin – 'and, that's it, roll it down – Jesus—'

And then he was on me, in me again, jerking his hips and burying his face against my shoulder.

'I'm going to make you come,' he whispered savagely. It sounded like a threat.

I moved my hips under his and he slowed his pace, adding a sort of grind to the thrust.

'What does that feel like?'

'Ni— fantastic,' I breathed. But I was panicking. I didn't know how to rise to the occasion. Perhaps I had come and didn't realize it. No, because the girls at school said you definitely knew when you'd had an orgasm. It was like a sneeze, Julia had said. A *sneeze*?

Meanwhile Paul ground on. 'Ooh, that's so good.'

'Mmm.'

Should I fake it? I tried panting heavily and moaning a bit, but I didn't have the confidence to pull it off. He would guess, and then it would be awful. But what to say?

He humped away and I stroked his back absently, gazing round the room at his collection of football programmes pinned to the walls, his red and white scarf draped over the lintel, the rosette stuck to his computer. The rhythm of his pelvis became a playground skipping song: *Keep* the kettle *boil*ing, *keep* the kettle *boil*ing—

Suddenly he stopped. 'Have you come yet?'

There was a brief pause then I smiled dazzlingly.

'No, but it was great. Have you?'

He looked hurt. 'Yeah. Ages ago. At the beginning. I was only keeping going for you. Do you think you might be close?'

'I don't know,' I said truthfully.

'Do you want to try a bit longer?'

I shook my head and tried not to shudder.

'Look, Paul, it really doesn't matter. It'll, it'll sort itself out. I probably just need to relax more. Don't worry about it. I'm not.' I smiled again, reassuring. 'It's great. You're great.'

'OK, then.' He grinned. 'God, I'm knackered.' He pulled away, then, 'Shit.'

'What's the matter?' He was looking down in a horrified sort of way. 'Have you hurt yourself? Have *I* hurt you?'

'The condom. It's . . .' he gestured at his limp and naked cock. 'It's still . . . Can you . . . ? Look, I think it's still inside you. Bloody hell. Do you want to, er, have a feel?'

I was seeing stars of panic but I did what he said. I leant flat on the bed, drew my knees up and put my fingers gingerly inside myself. 'Don't watch!' It felt raw and strange in there. I kept trying to take deep breaths and not clench up. 'I can't . . . Oh, God! Paul!'

'Let me have a try. I'm at a better angle.' He giggled nervously.

As he turned back to me I closed my eyes. It was like being at the doctors. Once there'd been a girl at school, in the first year, who'd got a tampon stuck up her and a teacher had had to fish it out: I remember the horror of simply being told. I wanted, now, at this very moment, to die with fear and shame. I opened my eyes a fraction as he probed and concentrated, and saw his tongue poking out slightly between his lips.

'Sorted!' He pulled out the slimy thing and held it up for inspection. Then he nodded. 'Phew! We're OK, it's not bursted or anything. I'll stick it in t' bin.' He threw it across the room. I hoped he wouldn't shout *Goal!* like he normally did, but he didn't. He just said, 'Christ, I can do without that!'

*You* can, I thought, rolling miserably up in the duvet.

That was, would be, without doubt, the worst moment of my entire adult life.

'Cheer up. It weren't nothin'.' He ruffled my hair. 'I'll go and get us a Wagon Wheel in a minute. I'll stick t' kettle on too. Do you want to play Tomb Raider when you've got dressed? I nicked it off Dan this morning.'

He was throwing on clothes as he spoke. So it must be all right, then. But why don't they tell you sex can be so bloody *embarrassing*? I have to admit, it isn't like I thought it would be. Perhaps I don't love Paul enough, or perhaps it's me. Either way, I need some answers and I think I know where to get them.

\*

THE QUESTION IS, is Nan telling the truth? And if she is, what then? I have to, *have to* find out.

# Chapter Two

BY GOD, Bill were a clever man. I don't know what he saw in me. Sometimes, when he was a lad, they sent him home early from school because he'd done all his work. Teacher used to say, 'Hesketh! Come out with your sums, an' if they're not finished, you're in trouble.' An' he'd go up to t' front and it'd all be done, all correct, and he'd be sent home at half-past three instead of four. He should have stayed on, he had a 'ead for learning, but he had to leave at thirteen for the wage, same as me.

So he went down the mines, like his father had, and hated it. He never got any proper rest. In the evenings he used to go to Bob Moss's grocer's shop and pack orders, then tek 'em round in a wheelbarrow. Then he started with TB and that was it, off to the Co-Op Convalescent Home at Blackpool, where he met his fiancée. Her name was Alice Fitton, she lived up Chorley way, and she was a bonny woman. She was broken-hearted when he finished with her to start courting me. I should have felt sorry but I didn't. I had what I wanted. I'd seen the way my mother suffered and I knew the value of a good man.

After we married he got a job at Cooks's paper mill, and took up with Bank Top Brass Band, playing tenor horn. He used to say they were one of the finest second-class amateur bands in the league. They practised every other day in a barn over the smithy, and paid a penny a week into funds. Once they played at the Winter Gardens at Southport in front of an audience of four thousand, and won a cup, it were t' first time ever. The conductor, Mr Platt, was overwhelmed. By the time they got back home it was past midnight but he insisted they play Souza's 'Semper Fidelis' as they walked through the main street. 'I don't think as we'd better. We'll wake everyone up,' Bill had said. 'Well, then,' Mr Platt told him, 'we'll tek our shoes and socks off.'

His chest stopped him playing in the finish; there was the TB, and he'd been smoking since he were thirteen. It kept him out o' t' war too, more or less; he stayed at home and was an ambulanceman for th' Home Guard. We were never short of crepe bandage in this house. But it were his lungs that killed him in th' end. He was only sixty-three. We'd been married forty-two years. And it was a happy marriage, oh it was. Except for the one thing.

*

**Where do you go** to get the answers when you're seventeen? Well, you start by pushing your way through the Enchanted Forest of people around you who *think* they know the answers: parents, teachers, solve-your-life-in-twenty-minutes-magazine-article writers. Mum thinks ballsing up her own life makes her an expert on mine (now where's the logic in *that*?), but what she fails to see is that I am about as much like her as she is like Nan, i.e. not at all. To look at us both you'd think I'd been found under a hedge. Bit of a relief if I had been, in some ways. It would certainly explain a lot.

Dad, of course, is conspicuous by his absence. Oh, I

*know* where he lives, and it's not so far away, but if I turned up on the doorstep and started asking for Advice about my personal life, he'd have kittens. It's not his field. Anyway, I think I scare him.

Teachers, they mean well, most of them, but they just see everything in terms of exam results, as if your 'A'-level grade print-out will have magically at the bottom a projected CV to tell you exactly where you're going next. 'A A B B, Accountancy at Bristol, followed by a meteoric career with Touche Ross, marriage at twenty-six, a nice house in Surrey and two healthy children by the time you're thirty (suggested names Annabel and Max).'

I suppose a normal girl would ask her friends, but I only have acquaintances, people I hang around with but never Talk to. Is it geography or psychology? John Donne wrote, 'No man is an island', but he didn't live in Bank Top. Lucky bastard.

Part of the problem is that the village is at the back of beyond and there's no one else from my form lives there. All the other kids from my class at primary school swarmed off to the Comp, sneering over their shoulders at me as they went: I see them around but they don't want anything much to do with me now I'm officially A Snob. Most of the people who go to the Grammar live on the other side of Bolton (in, it's got to be said, much bigger houses). I can't drive – no money for lessons and though Dad's promised faithfully to teach me I know this will *never* happen – and the buses stop running at 10.30. Mum can't be ferrying me about because she doesn't like to leave Nan unattended for fear of mad accidents. So here I am. It's never worried me till now.

Don't get me wrong, I'm not Billy No-mates, I know where to sit in the Common Room, I go out (and return early). I just don't seem to have that need for intimacy that some girls do. Strolling around the field at lunchtime, sharing confidences, not my thing. But maybe I'd be like that wherever I lived. I was always on the outside at St Mary's; the one helping Mrs Ainscough in the library at dinner break rather than playing Scott and Charlene by the bins. 'You spend too much time in your own head,' my mother once told me during a blazing row over nothing at all, and I hate to say it, but I think she was right.

So where was I going? Here, to this ordinary-looking modern semi on the outskirts of Bolton, a mere bus ride away from our house. Behind this front door with its glass panels of tulips, a figure moved.

'Hang on a sec. I'm trying not to let the cat out.' The door opened a fraction and a woman's plump face appeared, squashed against the crack. 'Can you – oh damn.' A grey shape squeezed past our feet in an oily movement and was gone. 'Never mind. Come in.'

I stepped into a white hallway full of swathed muslin and stippled walls, church candles and statuettes, *Changing Rooms* gone mad.

'Hiya, I'm Jackie. Is it Charlotte? Great. Come through. Mind the crystals.'

I dodged the swinging mobiles as she led me along to a room at the back. This was all black and red and stank of patchouli. On the walls were pictures of Jackie when she had been younger (and slimmer) together with framed testimonials and a poster of a unicorn rearing up under a rainbow. The table was covered with a scarlet chenille cloth. Jackie lit an incense burner in the corner.

'Now. Take a seat and we'll start with a palm reading.'

We sat with the corner of the dining table between us and she took my hand. The contact made me shiver and it was all I could do not to pull away.

'Relax,' she murmured, touching the soft pads of skin carefully. It felt really freaky. What the hell am I doing here, I thought. Jackie's blonde head was bent and I could see her dark roots. Her nails were immaculately manicured and her fat fingers full of rings.

'I bet you're wondering what you're doing here,' she said without looking up.

Shit shit shit. 'No, not at all.' I could feel myself blushing. 'You were recommended. A girl at school, you told her not to panic when suitcases appeared in the hall, and then her dad left home, but he came back again two weeks later. She was dead impressed. She's been telling everyone.'

'Right.' She shifted her bottom on the chair and leaned back, scrutinizing my face. 'Only a lot of people feel self-conscious consulting a psychic.'

'Yeah, well, I'll be honest . . . I don't know what to think. Does it matter? Am I going to interfere with the vibrations if I don't, er, completely believe . . . ?'

'No.' Very assured. 'What is it you want to know, Charlotte?'

'I, um, oh God, now you're asking. I think I need to know what to do with my life. I want somebody to tell me how to get out of Bank Top, 'cause it's a dump, and where I'd be happy. Is there, like, somewhere I should be headed? Point me in the right direction. Show me how to change things.' She was really listening, which unnerved me, I wasn't used to it. 'Because I thought I had, but everything's just the same . . . Does any of this make sense?'

Her lids and lashes were heavy with make-up as she frowned, leaned forward again and studied my hand. Then she began to talk quickly and confidently, her gaze still fixed on my palm.

'You're an independent person. You are surrounded by conflict. You have moments of confusion and at times you feel nobody understands you.'

Welcome to the World of the Average Teenager, I thought.

'There are a lot of choices coming up for you. You don't know which path to take. Difficult times are ahead but things will resolve themselves by the end of the year.'

Presumably I'd have sorted out my university application by then.

'You need to take particular care of your health over the next twelve months.'

'My mother's always on at me to eat fruit,' I joked. No reaction.

'Your love life will be complicated. Basically you have too soft a heart, but you try to hide it. You will find true love in the end, though.'

Yeah, well, I wouldn't have expected to hear anything else. She wasn't going to say, 'You'll shack up with a one-legged dwarf from Adlington and he'll beat you nightly.' My lips were forming a cynical smile when she pulled in her breath and whispered, 'There's somebody from the Other Side looking after you. He's here now.'

A faint sad cry, like a child, made me freeze.

'Oh, God.' I half turned round, appalled. 'A dead person?' But there was only my reflection in the patio doors and the grey cat mewing to be let in.

'A little boy.'

She waited for my response. I shrugged.

'About eight or nine I'd say, dressed in old-fashioned clothes, a cloth cap and short trousers. Big thick boots, like clogs. He won't tell me his name, he's too shy. But he's holding out forget-me-nots to you.' Jackie's face had gone blank-looking and she was focusing on a spot by my shoulder. It was beginning to spook me.

'I don't know any dead children. God, this is so weird.'

'He's very cold, very cold. He says you're lucky, you're a lucky person. He says you should make the most of your opportunities in life.'

The tension made me laugh. 'He's been talking to my mum. It's a conspiracy.'

Jackie glared at me and let go of my hand. 'He's gone now.' She made it sound as if it was my fault.

'Good.'

'But he's never far away.'

'Christ, don't say things like that, I'll never sleep at night.'

'He's a friend.'

'Right.'

She got up and pulled the curtains across roughly. I could tell she was annoyed with me and I smirked nervously in the gloom. Then she lit candles and brought over a Tarot pack.

'Do you want me to carry on with this?' She had a penetrating stare; I felt like I was back in the first year at school.

'Yeah, absolutely. Sorry.' Might as well get my money's worth.

'Pick a card, then,' she said.

**'Dirty little bugger,'** said Paul when I told him. 'Here, this'll shift him.' He aimed a trainer at the empty space by the end of my bed. 'Shoo. Go spy on someone else, kinky devil. Go back to your cloud and play with your harp or your pitchfork or whatever.'

'Do you think there could be anything in it?' I was sitting up with the duvet wrapped round me. I hadn't felt properly warm since I'd come home. 'Well, it's the middle of bloody winter, in't it?' had been Paul's response when I told him.

'Ghosts in cloth caps? Sounds like one of the Tetley Tea folk. Get a grip, Charlie.'

I giggled in spite of myself. 'I didn't believe her up till then. But she went sort of creepy after that. You'd have been rattled. You *would*. Stop laughing.'

'And how much did you pay this old hag?'

'Sod off. I only told you because I thought you'd be interested.'

'I am. Take off your bra.'

I unhooked resignedly. 'I know it was all just a load of rubbish . . .'

'So stop worrying.' He was kissing my neck and shoulders and his body heat was wonderful.

'Anyway, you're in the clear.'

'Mmm?'

'She told me a dark-haired boy would hurt me "more than I'd ever been hurt before". It was in the cards. So you're all right.'

'How do you mean? Because I'm blond?' He took his mouth away from my skin reluctantly.

'Yeah.'

'Smashing. Do you want to stop talking now?' he said.

**There wasn't** the usual mad scramble afterwards because Mum had taken Nan for a hospital appointment and the Metro had died so they'd gone by bus. The journey to hell and back, I'd have thought.

'Did you get that picture sorted?' Paul asked, his eyes roving round the room. We were getting better at the post-coital business. 'The one you broke that time.'

'The one you broke, you mean? While we were scaling the heights of passion? No. Although I did get as far as buying a new frame. I couldn't get the old one off so I gave up.'

'Bloody feeble girly. Do you want me to have a go? Give it here.'

I fished about in the bedside cabinet under the magazines and brought it out.

'Couldn't get it off? What is it, super-glued or summat?'

'Just you have a look.'

He turned the frame over in his hands and examined the back. 'Jesus. I see what you mean.'

Wires criss-crossed the thick cardboard; they had been stapled into the frame at irregular intervals. Blobs of ancient brown glue bulged from the corners. 'I took off another layer of card and Sellotape to get to that. I thought I'd damage the picture if I went any further. Does it need a screwdriver or something to lever the staples out? We have got one but I don't know where.'

'Nah, a penknife should do it. Pass us my jeans.'

He set to work, absorbed. I watched him and thought about my little ghost.

Finally the sections eased apart. 'There you go. Just needed the masculine touch.' I took the pieces in my hands and laid them on the covers. 'If you bung us the new frame I'll put that on for you an' all.'

'Hang on a minute.' I was taking off the layers of card. 'There's something in here. My God, look at that, it's a letter.' I unfolded two sheets of thin yellowing paper. 'It looks like . . . Shit, listen to this.' And I started to read.

Dear Miss Robinson,

<u>Re Sharon Pilkington.</u>

Thank you for your letter informing me that the Adoption Committee have accepted this little girl for a direct placing adoption. I am as certain as it is possible to be in these cases that the mother is quite definite about the adoption. She will not change her mind.

Yours sincerely,

P Davis

'Sharon Pilkington? Who's she when she's at home? Somebody's cut the top off so you can't see the address or date.' I turned the paper over but it was blank. 'Let's have a see what's on the other.'

Notes for the Information of the Case Committee

Name of child: Sharon Anne Pilkington
Weight at birth: 7lbs 2oz
Date of birth: 13.4.63
Present weight: 9lbs (at 3 weeks)
Child of: Miss Jessie Pilkington
Occupation of Mother: mill worker      Aged: 16 years
The Natural Father is:               Aged:
Whose occupation is:
Recommended by: Mrs P Davis
The Child is at present: with mother at
Mother and Baby Home, Hope Lodge, 46 Walls Road,
London N4

General Remarks

Jessie Pilkington is unable to keep and support her baby,
she is only 16 and has several young sisters and brothers
at home. She feels that it would be unfair on her parents
and particularly her mother to bring up another young
child. She is unwilling, or unable, to supply the identity of
the father, so there is no possibility of support from that
quarter. Therefore Jessie feels it is in the child's best
interests to be adopted and have the chance of being
brought up in a happy family atmosphere.

She has asked that the baby be placed with an
acquaintance of hers, a Mrs Nancy Hesketh, who is
unable to have children of her own. Jessie feels sure that
she has made the right decision to give her baby up and
will not go back on it.

Particulars of Mother

Character: good character and reputation

Appearance: good complexion, 5ft 7ins, grey eyes
Health: a strong and healthy family

Particulars of baby

Mrs Davis has seen this baby and she says she is a nice
little baby with light brown hair and grey eyes. Her skin is
very slightly dry in parts. She has a tendency to colic but a
lovely smile.

Additional notes

No history of mental illness, nervousness, alcoholism,
bad temper, brutality, delinquency, history of crime in the
mother's family.

'So what do you reckon to all that, then?' Paul was
busy fanning out all the blades on his penknife and admiring them. 'Charlie? Y' all right?'

I didn't know what to say for a minute so I read
the pages again. 'Oh, Paul . . . I don't believe this . . .'
I went back up to the date of birth at the top and my
throat went tight. 'Paul, stop a minute. I think this is
my mum.'

'Who?'

'This Sharon Pilkington. Because, because Nancy
Hesketh is Nan, and it's the right birthday, let me just
count on . . . 63, 73, 83, 93, 97, yeah. And, oh God, it all
makes sense, Nan was really old when she supposedly had
my mum and everyone said it was a miracle because she'd
tried for years. That's the word Nan used to use herself,
a miracle.' I'd put the letter down on the bed and was
holding my head between my hands. 'I can't take it in. She
doesn't know, surely? My mum, I mean. Oh, Jesus, Paul,

this is just amazing. It means Nan's not my nan. It's this Jessie woman. Whoever she is. Wherever she is.'

Paul shrugged. 'Well,' he said closing up his penknife with a click. 'There's summat your psychic didn't mention.'

\*

'THERE'S BLOOD in your shoe.' I spotted the smear on Nan's tights as she knelt to pick up half a Rich Tea she'd spotted under the table. Her joints really are amazing for the age, the doctor at the hospital couldn't believe it. Wouldn't believe me either when I told him how mad she gets, because Sod's law, she was on top form and completely coherent, chatting away as if she'd known him all her life. Even flirted with him. 'I feel champion today. Are you courtin'?' she asked him. 'You're a bonny lad. Have you a car?' He thought it was sweet; I thought it was monstrous. I wanted to hit her over the head with a bedpan, only that would probably have got me admitted instead. Maybe that wouldn't have been such a bad idea.

I spotted the blood in the morning as I was opening the post. Sylv reckoned – I know I said I'd never tell her anything again but she's got this *way* – Sylv reckoned I could just write off for a copy of my birth certificate and that would tell me who my mother was. So I'd been running to pick up the letters from off the mat ever since.

'Have you hurt yourself?'

'No. Where?' She turned her head this way and that, trying to see down her own body.

'Your leg, your ankle. Sit down a minute. Leave the biscuit. Sit, Mother.'

She sank down and pulled at her tights. 'Where? I can't see owt.'

Then I saw her heel was filled with blood.

'Oh, God, lift your foot up.' I squatted down and gently eased off the shoe.

'That's not my blood,' she said immediately.

'Well, who the hell's is it?' I didn't mean to shout so loudly.

'Eeh, you're nowt. I know what's up wi' you. What you want is another baby.'

'Jesus, Mum. You are so wrong. What would I want with a baby when I've got you, eh?'

In the end it was only a scab she'd knocked on her ankle and nothing like as bad as it first looked. But pulling her shoe on again I thought, Why am I doing this for you? Who are you, anyway? And when I went back to the post, there it was; my birth certificate. And she was right. I'm not her daughter. I'm Sharon Anne Pilkington, from London, from limbo.

| 1 | 2 | 3 | 4 | 5 |
|---|---|---|---|---|
| When and where born | Name, if any | Sex | Name and surname of father | Name, surname and maiden surname of mother |
| Thirteenth March 1963 Hope Lodge Mother and Baby Home 46 Walls Road East Finchley | Sharon Anne | Girl | ———— | Jessie Pilkington 56 Prentis Road Wigan |

So my mother – real mother, birth mother, whatever you call it – is from round here. What I was doing popping out in London, God only knows. She must have run away. I can understand that. Only it's funny I ended up back in the north. Perhaps it was policy then. Maybe they thought babies with northern genes needed weaning on cow heel and parkin. Or maybe they didn't want me polluting southern stock.

I'd like to say I still can't believe it, except that's not true. It kind of confirms a feeling I've always had, that I never fitted in. When I was little and Dad was still alive, on winter evenings we used to draw the curtains and all sit round watching rubbish: *Wheeltappers and Shunters*, or *Bullseye* (super-smashing-great!). Mum's favourite was *The Golden Shot*. I'd have a bottle of pop and a big bag of toffees to pass round, and there'd be this crackly telephone voice droning on: *left, left, stop, right a bit, down, stop, up a bit, up a bit, fire!* Silence, groans or the rattle of coins and cheers. Once Dad dropped his coconut mushrooms in the excitement and there were white flakes in the rug for weeks.

Happy times, sort of, but even then I used to feel I didn't really belong. Somewhere out there was a Beatrix Potter sort of a childhood that wasn't like mine, dandelion and burdock and Jim Bowen. I can remember thinking, Is this all there is? So perhaps I should have stayed in London. With my *mother*.

I imagine her looking like Julie Christie, swinging her bag and wearing a short belted mac and black eyeliner. I bet she sat in cafes and looked soulful when she was pregnant, with the rain lashing down outside and people hurrying past. Everyone's always in a hurry in London. Or maybe that's just an image from some film I've seen. It seems like a real memory, now I know the truth. Can you do that, tune into other people's memories?

The next step, apparently is to contact the Adoption Register. It's a list of people who want to trace each other, so if Jessie Pilkington wants to find me, she can.

I'm sure she'll want to. I can hardly wait.

\*

**People were moving** as if they were under water, ponderously. The air was thick and warm, you could tell it had just been in someone else's lungs. The beat of the music pummelled your chest, and then the strobe started up making everything look jerkily surreal. I closed my eyes but the light cut straight through the lids.

Fifty-five minutes to go till closing.

I was in Krystal's Nite Club in Wigan, and it was one of those times where you think, I should have stayed in.

Gilly Banks' birthday and at least half the lower sixth were there, maybe all of us; I hadn't exchanged two words with her since the beginning of term and I'd got an invite, so she wasn't being particularly discriminating with her guest list. '+ *friend*' it had said on the gold-coloured card, but I was on my own because I'd had a row with mine.

'Do you think we ought to try summat different?' Paul had said after the last session. When his hair's all ruffled from sex he looks almost too pretty, like something out of a Boy Band. That day, though, it was irritating, not cute.

'What, you mean like actually going out somewhere? Or talking to each other? That would be a novelty.' I'd been in a temper all week, what with the burden of the Nan revelation and the next History module coming up, and feeling sort of generally not myself. He'd also managed to locate the only Valentine card in the universe which didn't have the word Love on it.

'All right, there's no need to take my head off. We'll go to t' pictures if you're that bothered, bloody hell. I just meant we could try some new positions, I've been reading up on it.' He pulled out a magazine from under his bed and began to flick through. 'There's this one where you get on top but face my feet.'

'Sounds charming, what a view.'

'No, come on, don't be like that. It's supposed to mean you can, er, Control your own Pleasure. Or summat. I can't remember exactly. Oh, forget it.' He flung the magazine across the room and began feigning interest in a ragged fingernail. 'I just thought . . .'

'What?'

'Nothing.'

'It's this orgasm thing again, isn't it?' I reached for my knickers so I could argue with more dignity. 'Why do you keep going on about it? What's the big deal? It's not an issue. But I'm beginning to feel like there's something wrong with me.'

He opened his mouth and the words dropped out. 'Well, you could nip down the doctors and get yourself checked over. Check there's nothing . . . *amiss*.'

('YOU OK?' shouted Gilly over the racket. 'HAVING A GOOD TIME?' She was breezing past on her way to the bar, birthday girl, in combats and a little vest, bra strap showing. She's one of those people who doesn't give a toss. I bet she has loads of orgasms.

'OH, YES. EXCELLENT. NICE ONE.' I raised my glass through the smoke and smiled at her and Paul's voice said again in my ear, 'Get yourself checked over.' Bastard.)

'Bastard!' I'd shouted at him, before pulling on the rest of my clothes in a frenzy. 'I can't believe what you just said! What the hell are you suggesting? That I'm *abnormal*?'

He lay there chewing his nail and watched me struggle with my trousers. I'd got my toe caught in the hem and was pushing at the stitching, making it rip, wanting it to rip.

'You want to watch it, you'll tear 'em.'

'Jesus!' Some threads gave and my foot shot out. I staggered against the bed end.

'All I meant was, it's not been, oh, you know. Like you hear it's going to be.' He looked embarrassed, but resolute, like he was going to say his piece whatever. He held out his hand to me in a gesture that might have been meant to reassure. 'Did you not think the same though, really?'

'And could it not be,' I put my burning face close to his, 'and could it not perhaps be that it's *you* who's getting it wrong? That it's *your* amazing technique that's failing to deliver?' I nodded at his flaccid cock which lay across his thigh innocently. 'That your mighty equipment is not quite *up to the job*?'

He pulled the sheets across himself and flushed.

'No,' he snapped. ''T i'nt, actually.'

'Really?'

'No. An' I'll tell you why.'

'Go on.' I sensed what was coming.

'Because. Because Jeanette Piper never had any trouble, that's why.'

So I finished dressing and let myself out. Past next door's sad Alsatian, past the bench with no slats left, and the tyre-marked verges, past the shattered bus shelter and home to my room where I cried for half an hour.

It's true, he never actually said he was a virgin. But then again, he didn't say he wasn't. I should've kept asking, only, what do you do if you don't hear the answer you want? 'Stop, it's all off, put your underpants back on; I only sleep with the undefiled!' I don't think so. And it's not something he could have done anything about, you can't rewind time. Once It's gone, It's gone. I should bloody know.

No, it wasn't the fact that he was one step ahead, though to be honest it's not nice knowing he's dipped his wick elsewhere (thank God I don't even know this Jeanette Piper, I think she lives in Standish. He did say she was a bit of a dog before I slammed out, but that was probably only to make me feel better). No, it's what he said before. About me. My defective body. What if it turned out to be true?

'OVER THERE, BY THE BAR. I THINK YOU'VE GOT AN ADMIRER!' twinkled Gilly as she squeezed past, a pint glass in each hand.

I squinted across the room but it was all heads and bodies and there was a great fat man in front of me. I stepped backwards into a bit of a gap and immediately trod on someone's toe.

'Sorry. SORRY.'

It was Daniel Gale, recently arrived in our sixth form from somewhere down south and already dismissed as a boring swot. He swept a hand through his wild hair and grinned weirdly. What was someone like him doing here, for God's sake? He should have been at home chasing Internet porn.

'ACTUALLY,' he leaned closer, 'IT'S A PROS-THETIC.'

'A WHAT?' I was still trying to see over to the bar.

'GALVANIZED STEEL AND PLATINUM BONDED. BIONIC. I HAD IT FITTED AFTER A TERRIBLE FREAK ACCIDENT. YOU COULD DROP A MINI COOPER ON HERE AND I WOULDN'T FEEL A THING. IT'S FULLY MAGNETIZED TOO. IF YOU DROPPED ME IN THE SEA MY TOES WOULD POINT NORTH.'

'YOU WHAT?'

His shirt lit up dramatically as the ultraviolet came on: it made his head look disembodied and wobbly. I don't know what my face was doing but I don't think it was registering anything very positive. His glasses flashed reproachfully at me and he opened his mouth, then shut it again. 'JOKE,' he finished sadly and drifted away, shoulders hunched.

It was then I spotted him; a tall bloke leaning against a pillar, watching me. Black jacket slung over his shoulder like a catalogue model, dark curly hair, thin nose, might have been all right but it was difficult to tell from a distance. He waved. I looked away. I looked back. He started to come over, smiling. Bollocks, I thought. Then, well why the hell not? Teach that bastard Paul, wouldn't it?

It wasn't till he got really close that I could see the leather pants.

Now the only stuff I know about leather pants, not owning a pair myself, is what I heard some stand-up cockney comedian say once, that they turned your privates into a fiery furnace. As he got closer I could see he was quite nice-looking, but the thought of the turkey-neck testicle skin and the accordian-wrinkled penis cooking gently in there persisted and my brow furrowed.

'PENNY FOR THEM,' he said as he reached me.

I could hardly say I was thinking about his genitals.

'YOU LOOK LIKE YOU'RE IN ANOTHER WORLD. YOU DO. WITH YOUR BIG EYES. LIKE YOU'RE WAITING TO BE RESCUED. LIKE A PRINCESS.' He put his hand on my arm. I didn't move. 'SO WHERE *DO* YOU COME FROM?'

I couldn't think of an appropriate reply to this – there was no way I was going to utter the words 'Bank Top' – so I reached up and glued my lips to his. Out of the corner of my eye I could see Daniel Gale watching us, so I shifted round and put my back to him.

This guy knew how to kiss, that was for sure. No bits of escaping spit, no feats of ridiculous jaw-stretching or clashing front teeth, just a nice lazy action. I let myself go with it and after a while we found ourselves a corner and settled in for what was left of the night. The leather pants felt odd under my hands but also safe in a reinforced sort of way. You couldn't feel anything *personal* through them, just the lumps and bumps of folds where they creased. We had the last dance together, well we stood on the dance floor and snogged while slowly pivoting, then the lights came on and we were suddenly blinking at each other and looking sheepish. It was then I realized how much older he was.

**Outside in the** quiet cold air his pants squeaked.

'Can I see you again?' he murmured over the creaking. My ears were still ringing slightly and it took a moment to register what he'd said.

'How old are you?' I found myself asking. Around us crowds of people moved into knots and couples, shouting or embracing, slapping passing cars on the roof. Someone was throwing up in a shop doorway amid cheers.

He held up his palms to me, head on one side. I was sure I could see crow's feet in the lamplight. 'Hey. What's up? Does it matter?'

Does it matter? That's what Paul said when I asked him if he'd done it before. And yeah, it bloody well did, as it turned out. So not a great question, Rawhide.

'I'll take *your* number. I'll give you a call.'

He shrugged. Then, with difficulty, he extracted a pen from his back pocket and wrote it on my hand, held onto my fingers afterwards. He was staring into my eyes.

'I'm twenty-eight, if you must know. God.' He shook his head. 'Still don't see what the deal is. Why, how old are you?'

'Like I said, I'll give you a call.' I loosed my hand from his grip. 'See you.' And I joined Julia and Gilly on the taxi rank, feeling as if, somehow, I'd got one back. On some-body.

See the doctor. I should bloody cocoa.

\*

IT WERE summat an' nowt, only a dance at the Mechanics', but I got in a row over it. It were a regular thing when I was about sixteen. I'd throw my lace-up shoes and best frock out of the window, then tell my mother I was off to Maggie Fairbrother's. Her mother used go out drinkin' so we could do as we liked. So then we'd walk it into Harrop and go dancin'. The last time though it were t' Carnival Dance and when I got back home I had confetti all in my hair and cuffs. I kept brushin' it out but it sort of clung. My mother spotted some of it on the floor, and I got a good hiding and sent to bed. She was allus angry, and tired to death, bent over her dolly tub or her scrubbing board or her mangle. And shamed. You see she could never hold a man, never had a home of her own. I think she were terrified I might end up the same.

\*

I HAD A TRIP into Wigan to find out what I already knew.

There was a time, late sixties I suppose it'd be, when approaching the town was like driving through a war zone. Nan and I would get the bus in and I'd stare out of the windows at rows and rows of shattered terraces, brick shells, piles of rubble. Sometimes there'd be a square of waste ground with just a line of doorsteps along the edge of the pavement, or ragged garden flowers sprouting through the masonry or a tiny patch of floor tiling in the mud. On the horizon there would always be those huge swinging metal balls on cranes. It made me shudder to think what they could do. That was the progressive period when they were busy putting people into tower blocks (I don't know what they called the period when they moved everybody back out again).

The journey through all those ruins always unsettled me. We'd have reached the Market Hall by the time I felt right again. Nan would visit each stand, chatting and joking with the stallholder over every purchase, and I'd turn on my heel and gaze upwards at the steel rafters where pigeons fluttered, and escaped balloons dawdled tantalizingly. You could smell the sarsparilla from the health-food booth, and ginger and hot Vimto. If I was good I had a hair ribbon off the trimmings stall, and I got to choose the colour.

So now I drove through the outskirts of a reinvented Wigan with grassed-over areas and new, prestige estates with names like 'Swansmede' and 'Pheasant Rise'. Imaginative chaps, these developers. I got through Scholes and onto the one-way system, over the River Douglas, past the Rugby League ground, under Chapel Lane railway bridge. Huge hoardings promised faithfully to change my life if I bought a new car, cereal, shampoo: if only. Then I was out the other side, glancing over at the *A–Z* spread out on the passenger seat. Finally I was turning into Prentis Road.

Streets like this used to be cobbled, but the council tarmacked them over years ago. At the beginning of the road two short blocks of terraces nudged the pavement. I know these back-to-back houses, there's enough of them in Bank Top. The flat red fronts, the white doorsteps that nudge the pavement and, at the back of each house, a flagged yard walled round six foot high and a door opening onto a cinder track. The original outside privies would all have been demolished in the sixties, and little narrow kitchens built on to free up what had been the parlour. Then in the seventies everyone had to go Smokeless, so the coal sheds went. While they were at it, most people had the two downstairs rooms knocked through and folding screens put in (so much more versatile!). Anything so long as it didn't look Victorian. (You want to get them picture rails tekken off an' all.)

This was where my Real Mother grew up.

I parked the car and walked slowly along the pavement, this stupid song going through my head, the one we used to chant on school trips when I was in the juniors.

*We're goin' where the sun shines brightly (BLACKPOOL!)*
*We're goin' where the sea-hee is blue (RIVER DOUG-ER-LAS!)*
*We've seen it in the movies*
*Now let's see if it's true (IS IT BUGGERY!).*

Christ, I thought, I'm turning into Nan. But that should have been impossible. At least I wasn't singing out loud.

I started counting door numbers although I could see, ages before I got to the end, that I was going to run out. 28 was the last in the row, then there was a grassy space with a sign saying 'Hollins Industrial Park'. Past this was the first building, a sort of hangar, Naylor's Body Work Repairs. A row of courtesy cars was parked outside and one of those revolving signs turned sluggishly: OPEN/ SUNDAYS. A young lad in overalls came out, saw me staring and shouted over.

'Y' lookin' for summat? Boss is out the back.'

'It's OK,' I called.

He shrugged, climbed into one of the cars and started revving the engine with the door open. I walked a bit further, to where I reckoned 56 would have been, and silently blessed my mother. I knew she wouldn't be here. I'd known it all along. She was in London, with a Life.

Talking of which.

I'm supposed to be holding out for Mr Right, but what do you do in the meantime? I was prepared to settle for Mr Do For Now If You're Not That Fussed, while I was waiting. 'Love 'n' Stuff' had sent me Davy, looked a bit like that actor who played Jesus of Nazareth in the '70s, only not so holy. Same age as me but a completely different attitude to life. Dressed young, smoked roll-ups. Tall and lean. I'd seen him twice, once for a quick drink at the Wagon and Horses (he had an appointment with somebody), and once for an Italian meal in Bolton (we went Dutch, but that was OK, it is the nineties). Right from the word go he let it be known that he had a full and active social diary. Well, I thought, I bet you don't have a mother with a high-maintenance colostomy and a daughter ready to hurtle off the rails at any moment. I just smiled and said, 'Good on you. Hope you can fit me in somewhere,' which sounded naff and desperate (again).

At Luciano's he told me he was divorced, which I think even now was probably the truth, and that he'd been in a few different dating agencies but 'Love 'n' Stuff' was the best so far (he gave me a little wink when he said this line). Then he did some tricks with a bread-stick which I thought were screamingly funny, although in retrospect I'd had quite a lot to drink by then. He also said he was a rep and so the only way he could be contacted with any regularity was through his mobile. Yeah, well, I know it's the oldest trick in the book, but when you want to believe someone, you do.

I wouldn't have brought him back to the house but he claimed to be Mr I Might Be Able To Fix Your Metro too. Also it was Saturday afternoon, Nan's nap time, and I knew Charlotte had gone into town as usual, so the coast should have been clear. Hah. When is my coast ever bloody clear?

He'd not been under the car two minutes when Nan appeared at the front door. I motioned her to go back inside but she only waved back, put her hand to the jamb and lowered herself down the step. Then she waddled down the path holding some bit of paper aloft.

'I've won a Range Rover,' she said, pushing a letter in my face. 'Charlotte can have it, she can have it for school.'

I thought there hadn't been any post that morning, but Nan had been up before me.

'Let's have a look.' I whipped it off her and scanned the contents. 'Load of rubbish. No, you haven't, Mum. It's junk mail. And it's for me anyway.'

'It never is.' Nan looked cross.

'Look, what does that say?' I pointed at the address window. 'See?'

She peered forward and huffed at me. Then she spotted Davy, who had wriggled himself back out from under the chassis while we'd been talking. 'Who's this?'

'Davy, Mum.'

'Jamie? Eeh, you favour a German.' She reached down and touched his leg. 'Is he foreign?'

'No. Come on back inside and I'll make you some tea.'

She gave him a glazed smile before retreating. 'You want to watch them swanky pants,' was her parting shot. 'Don't get muck on 'em.'

We went back up the path, me holding her elbow to stop her escaping, and I got her ensconced in her chair and put the telly on. *Love Boat*, ideal. Then I came out again.

The Ribble bus went past and stopped at the corner. Charlotte got off, face like thunder.

When she got close enough she held up a carrier bag and snapped, 'They wouldn't take it back! Can you believe it! Just because I'd washed it! I tell you what, I'm never shopping there again, bunch of rip-off merchants.'

She stepped angrily over Davy's legs, then paused as she realized they were coming out from under my car.

'Bloody hell,' she said staring down. 'Mum? Mum, who is this?'

'It's Davy. A, er, friend of mine.'

She shot me a withering look.

Davy shuffled out, grin at the ready, wiping his hands on the oily rag. Then his face fell. There was a pause.

'Jesus, Mum; we've met, actually,' said Charlotte in icy tones. 'Last week, at Krystal's. I'm sure you remember, all those *teenage girls*. God, how disgusting. Twenty-eight, my arse! You're really wrinkly in the daylight, Mr Leather Pants. Don't you ever wear anything else? They must be beginning to *stink* by now.'

The penny was beginning to drop.

'You old, sick bastard,' she said, and turned on her heel. I gaped after her. *Charlotte?*

'Small world,' said Davy.

'I'll give you small world,' I snarled. My leg twitched with the effort of not kicking him. 'You want reporting. Get your hands off my car and leave my daughter alone, or I might do something vicious with that socket set.'

'You'll laugh about this one day,' I heard him saying as I walked away.

When I got inside Charlotte had stropped off upstairs, but Nan was still watching *Love Boat*. A soft-focused couple were embracing to a backdrop of blue sea, and from the bridge a little boy was watching them, a big smile on his face. The captain put his hand on the boy's shoulder and a tear twinkled in his eye. 'I guess your mom's found what she was looking for, Jimmy,' he said as the music swelled and the credits rolled.

'I forgot to tell you, I've won a Range Rover,' said Nan, pulling out an envelope from under the cushion.

'Jesus Christ,' I said, snatching it off her. But this time it wasn't junk mail. It was from Social Services Adoption Department.

# Chapter Three

**I didn't know** what to do.

If I contacted him first, would that make me look like a total Sad Act? Would it be reported to his mates that I was turning into some mad stalker, unable to accept the bleeding obvious, that her boyfriend had blown her out? Because he had, hadn't he? Or was it me who gave him the boot? Or was it neither?

*Or* what if I'd got it all wrong and he was sitting alone in his room, broken-hearted, too dispirited to pick up the phone? After the initial fog of anger had cleared I'd got to thinking we'd make it up, maybe sulk for a few days but then fall into each other's arms, and out of the ether he'd pull some magic words which would wipe my head clean forever of Jeanette Piper and her writhing limbs and panting cries.

But that had been two weeks ago. Oh WHY hadn't he been in touch? Even to finish it. You know, if you've shared bodily fluids with someone then they ought at least to tell you where you stand. Surely it's manners. It wasn't just my pride, there was my hymen too. Or perhaps best to forget about that.

Bloody Paul bloody Bentham, bloody men.

So in the end I went round to his house.

I practised all the stuff I was going to say before I went, and on the way as well, trying to get the inflections exactly right, the face, the body language. *I just want to get things cleared up*, I told my bedroom mirror, folding and unfolding my arms to assess the different effects.

Clothes had been a problem too. I didn't want to wear anything which implied I'd made an effort, only for him to give me the elbow, that would make me look really pathetic. On the other hand, I didn't want to look like something the cat dragged in, in case he had wanted to get back together but changed his mind when he saw the state I was in. God knows, I didn't want him to think I'd been *pining* for him. In the end I'd settled for washing my hair and worn my second-best jeans.

*I think it's best for both of us*, I told my friend the Alsatian, and it wagged its tail slowly and grinned. Then I marched up and rang Paul's doorbell, shaking. *Paul Bentham is no good, chop him up for firewood*, my head kept chanting, which wasn't exactly helpful. There was a funny metallic taste in my mouth.

Chimes echoed in the distance but no one stirred. I waited a long time, then turned to go, half relieved, only to hear the door open behind me.

'Sorry, love, I was on the toilet.' Mr Bentham, naked to the waist, bare-footed, embarrassed and embarrassing. I tried not to look at his pink rubbery nipples, and the line of wiry hair which came up from inside his trousers and touched his paunch. His face was shiny and he had too much forehead. You could tell he'd been pretty once, like Paul, but everything had begun to blur and slide. It made me think of my dad, about the same age, mid-thirties, but sharp-featured, built like a whippet, all his own hair – extra, actually, if you count the recent moustache. I hate it when old people let themselves go.

Mr Bentham stared at me for a moment. 'He's norrin. Went off to Bolton, I think. He'll be back about tea time. Shall I tell him you called?'

'Yeah.' My heart sank. I was going to have to go through all this palaver again. 'No. Actually, can I just scribble him a note? I won't be a minute.' I smiled nicely.

'Aye, awreet, love. Come in.' I followed him down the hall to the back kitchen. 'Want a cup of tea? There's one brewed.'

I glanced round the mess and took in the dish of gritty butter, the weeping Brown Sauce bottle, top askew, the open bag of sliced bread stuck on the table. I knew without looking what state the sink would be in. Even if it was clear of dirty pots there'd be Christ knows what clogging and breeding in the plughole. My mum has her faults, God, but at least our house is fairly clean. Three men living on their own: possibly even worse than three women.

'No, ta, you're all right.'

Mr Bentham followed my gaze. 'I work shifts,' he said simply. 'Oh, you'll need some paper.'

We doubled back and stopped at the telephone table, which stood under a rectangle of lighter-coloured wall-paper, a little hook still protruding at the top. 'Used to be their wedding photo,' Paul had pointed out on my very first visit. 'You'd have thought he'd have stuck something over it,' I'd said to Paul, who'd shrugged.

'Anyway, give me a shout when you've done. Like I said, he's gone off to t' shops. After some video or summat, I don't know.' He shook his head. 'He dun't talk to me you know, I don't have a clue what he's up to from one day to t' next. But that's lads for you.' He scratched his neck and dropped his gaze to the floor.

'Thanks.' I brandished the pen and pad. 'I won't be long.'

Mr Bentham wandered off into the lounge and *Grandstand* came on.

Dear Paul,
    I ~~came~~ popped round to say can I have my CDs back sometime? If you want we could ~~get together~~ meet up for a drink and a ~~talk~~ chat (but only if you've got time). I've got loads on at the minute and I bet you have too!! Give me a ring.
    Love ~~Charlie~~ Charlotte

This masterpiece of literature took me nearly ten minutes to draft; I kept thinking, at any point Mr Bentham's going to re-emerge to check I'm not up to anything dodgy, like rifling through his wallet. And what if Paul came back early and caught me off guard? An RNIB envelope came though the letter box and I jumped about a mile. 'Get a grip,' I remembered Paul saying, which irritated me so much I lost my thread even more. But finally it was finished.

'Shall I leave it in the hall?' I shouted towards the lounge.

Mr Bentham ambled out. 'No, give it here, we put them on a board in the kitchen. See?'

'Oh, yeah. Right.'

I thought that was a bit civilized, but then I registered the gingham frame round the cork and I realized it was just another bit of Mrs B that she'd left behind. He impaled the note with a map pin, underneath a take-away menu and next to, oh God, next to a note for Paul, written in childish handwriting, must be Darren's, saying 'Phone Chrissy about Sat eve!'

Of course, Chrissy could be a bloke. Or a friend. No need to panic yet.

\*

I WANTED TO get back so I could read the letter again, just in case I'd missed something, because I still hadn't decided what to do. But shopping with Nan takes forever because we have to stop and chat to all and sundry. Forty-five minutes it took us to walk back up from the butcher's; we could have done it in ten, and all the while the blood seeping out of the cold chops and pooling in the corner of the plastic bag. Little Jim by the Post Office, with his flat cap and muffler, wanted to know how Reenie Mather's operation had gone ('She were the colour of this envelope when th' ambulance men carried her out, she were, honest'). Then he detailed his own ailments for us (why should he think I want to know about his prostate? Nan was all ears, though).

Next it was Skippy, our local tramp, so called because he spends a lot of time ferreting about on the Corporation tip. He was turning on his heel outside the library, blagging change and spitting on the pavement.

'Awreet?' Nan asks, cheerful as anything. I can never

tell what Skippy says, so I left them to it and went in to see if the new Mary Wesley was in (it wasn't). When I came out Skippy was on his hands and knees making a sort of yipping noise and Nan was two-double, Christ knows what was going on there. I didn't stop to ask, just dragged Nan away. 'Eeh, he's a rum 'un,' she said, wiping her eyes with a hanky. 'Filthy old deviant, more like,' I muttered, but she was blowing her nose and didn't hear.

Then, when we were on the home stretch, up pops Mr Rowland, the newish vicar. Don't know what it is about vicars, they always make me feel guilty, then annoyed with myself for feeling guilty. I mean, I know I don't go to church but on the other hand, I'm not especially sinful either. Not on the world scale of evil, anyway.

'Lovely to see you,' he calls across the road like he means it. Nan beams, and he bounds over and starts to describe at length how the vicarage is shaping up and how Mrs Rowland's knee has been poorly because she fell off a stepladder trying to get to a cobweb and it's started an old hockey injury off again. Nan tuts and shakes her head sympathetically while I lean on the wall and look over his shoulder. Hanging baskets are going up in the High Street; they'll last all of two minutes.

He finally remembers some appointment and dashes off (where does he get his energy from? God, presumably). Nan watches him go fondly. 'Now *he's* a good man. Not like that Mr Shankland, playing guitars and tambourines, what have you. I'm not surprised he didn't last long. Clapping in church! He went off somewhere foreign i' th' end, didn't he?'

'Surrey, Mum. Mr Shankland went to form a Charismatic group in Farnham. You told *me* that.'

'Nay, I never did. Are you sure? Well, who was it went to Japan?'

'I've no idea.' I bundled her up the step and shut the door. I felt like I'd run the London Marathon. 'I'll get the kettle on. Give us your coat.'

I pulled the letter out of the table drawer and took it into the kitchen to scan it again while the water boiled.

In the past it was thought best for all concerned that an adopted child's break with his birth family should be total. Parents who placed a child for adoption were generally told that a child would not have access to his birth record. The current legislation reflects increased understanding of the wishes and needs of adopted people. It recognises that although adoption makes a child a full member of a new family, information about his or her origins may still be important to an adopted person.

People adopted before 12 November 1975 are required to see a counsellor before they can be given access to their records because in the years before 1975, some parents and adopters may have been led to believe that the children being adopted would never be able to find out their original names or the names of their parents. These arrangements were made in good faith and it is important that adopted people who want to find out more about their origins should understand what it may mean for them and others.

This means that *if you were adopted before 12*

*November 1975,* you will have to see an experienced social worker called a counsellor before you can obtain further information from your original birth record.

There was something in the phrasing that had made me pause. *What* might it mean for me? And who else was it going to affect if I began my search properly? The Adoption Contact Register had drawn a blank. All they'd said was that 'my details had been entered in Section 1', so that must mean there was nothing in Section 2 which matched up. But Jessie Pilkington probably didn't know the Register existed: why should she? She'd been told nobody could trace anybody, when she handed me over That was That. However you looked at it, I was going to be a bolt from the blue. Best not to over-analyse the situation, really. I mean, if you went through life examining the minute consequences of everything you were about to do, you'd end up so bloody paranoid you'd do nothing. We might as well all live under the table.

I shut the letter inside a Trex cookbook and shoved it to the back of the cupboard.

'Phyllis Heaton's had a hysterectomy, did I tell you?' Nan was playing with a piece of toast left over from breakfast; God knows where she'd stowed it.

'No, Mum. No, she hasn't. She's gone ex-directory. You mis-heard.'

'And she can't accept it.' Nan carried on as if I hadn't spoken. 'If you ask her, she denies it. Eeh, it's a shame for some folk. We don't know as what we'll come to, any on us.' She gnawed at the toast like a terrier.

It was then I noticed the amaryllis.

'God, Mum, what's happened to my flower?'

Instead of two brilliant red trumpets, a naked green spike rose two feet into the air, and stopped. The pot had been pushed back to the left of the windowsill, behind the curtain, so I knew who'd done it. I leaned across the table and slid it back out.

'Mum? Mum, look at me. Mum, what happened to the flowers on the end? Where have they gone?'

Nan laughed uncomfortably. 'I were closing t' curtains and I must have caught it. It came away in my hand. It'll be all right.'

'How can it be all right when you've knocked its head off? Honestly! I can't keep anything nice in this house, if it's not you it's Charlotte with her magazines and clothes all over the floor, I ask her and ask her to tidy them up but she takes no notice, neither of you do. What's the point of me reading *Homes and bloody Gardens* when you're busy mutilating my plants and hiding bits of food around the place?'

Nan glanced guiltily at the sofa.

'Oh, hell, you've not got butter on the cushions, have you?' I flipped them up angrily, one after the other. But it wasn't toast, it was the amaryllis, tattered and flaccid like a burst balloon, and sporting a little Sellotape collar round the base. I held it up, speechless.

'It'll be all right,' said Nan. 'We'll just stick it back on. It'll be all right.' But she didn't sound convinced.

'No, Mum. It won't be all right.' The flower heads came apart and I squashed them up hard in my palms, feeling the cool petals bruise and smear. When I opened my hands it was like the stigmata. Nan stared. I looked over to where the letter was hidden, waiting. 'There are some things you can't mend.'

\*

There is *no privacy* in this house. My mum, probably just to spite me, has the phone wall-mounted in the hall, which is just about big enough for two medium-sized people to stand chest to chest. Since there is no room even for a chair, let alone those swanky telephone seats she drools over in the catalogues, I have to sit on the stairs to have a conversation. It's bloody freezing, too, I don't know why we bother having a fridge. We could just keep the milk on the doormat. The letter box doesn't fit properly and she's never got round to fixing it (waiting for a man to sort it for her, dream on, Ma), so it blows open at the slightest breeze. You can, of course, hear everything that's going on in the next room and vice versa. So all in all, it's pretty crap. I'm *definitely* having a mobile for my birthday.

I could have sneaked out to the public phone box, but knowing my luck my money would jam or run out, or there'd be some pervo outside listening in. I needed this call to go well, I had to be on top of it. I didn't want to lay my heart on the line in a stinky glass box.

As I dialled the number I could hear Mum picking on Nan again, something to do with some stupid flower. Like it matters. I pulled Nan's scarf down from the hook above and wound it round my neck. It smelt of Coty L'Aimant.

*Ringing. Ringing. Click.*

*Paul:* Hello?

*Me:* Hello.

*Paul:* Hello?

*Me:* It's me, Charlotte. I was—

*Paul:* Oh yeah, right, Charlotte—

*Me:* Yeah . . .

*Paul:* I was going to give you a ring.

*Me:* Did you get what you were after?

*Paul:* You what?

*Me:* Your video. Your dad said you'd gone into Bolton.

*Paul:* Oh yeah, oh, I see what you mean. Yeah, *England's Pride*, top twenty goals of the decade. Narrated by David Beckham. I've not watched it yet.

*Me:* Sounds fantastic. Look, when you do, can I be the first to borrow it?

*Paul:* Ha bloody ha. It's better than a video on, I dunno, make-up or summat, girly stuff.

*Me:* Sod off. Look, did you want to meet up for a drink some time? Only . . .

*Paul:* Oh, yeah, right, that would be great. Em, yeah. I'll give you a ring . . . we'll get summat sorted. Maybe next week. If it's not too busy. All right?

*Me:* Yeah. All right. Well . . .

*Paul:* I'll call you.

*Me:* Paul?

*Paul:* What?

*Me:* Who's Chrissy?

*Pause, click, dialling tone.*

The door to the lounge opened and Nan wandered out. There were crumbs all down her front.

'Phyllis Heaton's had a hysterectomy,' she said sadly, and sat down on the step next to me.

I unwound the scarf and draped it round us both. I wanted to cry.

'There's some things as can't be mended,' she whispered.

*

'WELL, YOU WOULDN'T catch me even thinking about it,' said Sylv, swinging her knees to and fro on her swivel chair like she does; she'll come a cropper one of these days and unswivel herself completely. I was sitting in the office to cut out my thirty daffodil shapes because Year 6 were watching a science programme on TV and the classroom was too dark to see what I was doing, not that it was exactly taxing stuff. Sylv, however, had been delighted to see me. 'I *mean*, what if they want your bone marrow?'

'You what?'

Sylv looked at me as if I was stupid. 'Don't you watch the news? When these long-lost relatives meet up there's always someone wanting your bone marrow, or your kidneys or what have you, and then if you don't give it to them *you're* the villain. It's not on. I was reading about a case in *Woman's Own* last week. This woman didn't even know she had a twin brother until he turned up on the doorstep wanting her organs. It's a hell of a risk. No, Karen, I wouldn't touch it in your shoes.'

Thanks, Sylv, I thought, these heart-to-hearts we have are invaluable. You've helped me make up my mind. I'm going to find my birth mother if it kills me.

Just then the Head came into the office with a letter for typing. Sylv quivered like a pointer.

'What do you think, Mr Fairbrother?' She ignored my

desperate expression and plunged on. 'Do you think Karen should try to find her natural parents?'

Give him his due, Mr F didn't bat an eyelid. I suppose he's used to it, he sees Sylv all the time whereas the rest of us only consort with her at break times.

'I really couldn't give an opinion,' he said and put the letter down on the desk. 'Can you get this out to Gavin Crossley's parents by the end of the day? We'll have to have them in, it's no good. Daryl Makinson's had to have stitches.' Then he turned to me. 'A difficult decision for you. Not one I should like to be faced with.' He gave me a nice smile and left us to it.

'Such a shame,' said Sylv as soon as the door was shut. She means because he's past forty, possibly fifty, and still single, and used to live with his parents till they both died and now he lives on his own in that big house up Castleton Road, he must rattle around in it, why he doesn't buy a little bungalow, and maybe he's homosexual but doesn't realize it, not that it matters in this day and age. And he's losing his hair, poor chap. I've heard Sylv's musings on the subject more times than I can count. But he's actually a pleasant man and really quite OK as a boss, especially when you think the staff are all women: you'd think we'd drive him mad. He's great when I need to take time off for Nan, and he buys us all Christmas presents; just bits and pieces, but it's the thought. This year it was cacti. Sylv got a squat, spiky number. Mine was tall and sort of hairy, as if a gang of spiders had run amok over it. I don't like them as plants, I tend to think they're a bit common. You never see cacti on 'Inspector Morse'. So I put Mr F's effort on the back kitchen windowsill, behind the terracotta garlic jar, but I didn't throw it out, that would have been ungrateful.

The bell was about to go for break so Sylv tottered off to the ladies' to re-do her lipstick and rearrange her under-skirt, and I gathered up my daffodils and set off for the classroom. As I got to the corner some of them began to escape and flutter to the floor. Any minute now and they'd be stampeded by a bunch of ten-year-olds, so I put the rest of the pile on the Nature Table and got down on my hands and knees and began swishing up the little paper shapes with my hands.

'Let me help.' Mr F, with his clipboard and stock cup-board invoices under one arm, was stooping to pick at a lone petal which had welded itself to the grey vinyl floor tiles. 'Tricky customers, aren't they? Look, I'm sorry about earlier.'

I must have looked blank.

'In the office. Sylv.' He lowered his voice. 'Sometimes her enthusiasm to, ahm, *help* gets the better of her.'

'It's not your fault, you've nothing to apologize for.'

'Well. Rest assured, it won't go any further.' He handed me my daffodil. 'And if you'd like someone to talk it through with sometime, someone objective . . . I can see it must be a difficult situation, with your mother being as she is . . . Anyway, I'm usually in the Feathers of a Sunday lunchtime, the Fourgates Ramblers meet there. It's quite a nice atmosphere, I don't know if you've ever been in. No jukebox, which is a rarity these days.'

Before I had time to do anything other than smile vaguely we heard the click of heels behind us. Sylv's face, newly drawn on, was eager with news. 'You might like to know we're running short of paper towel in the ladies',' she said as she drew level. Mr F gave a small salute and walked off towards his room. 'He's very much on the short side for a headmaster, isn't he?'

*

**My dad always says,** 'As one door shuts, another one slams in your face.' Mind you, he's not nearly as bitter as my mum, because according to her, he didn't have anything like as much to lose. He was an apprentice with British Aerospace when she got caught, and he just carried on, finished his training and got a full-time job there. He's still on the machines, despite waves of redundancies and his appallingly casual attitude. 'He thinks it's beneath him,' my mum often says, and we know who to blame for that idea. A blue-collar worker? Nah. She wanted to land a professional, a doctor or a lawyer, that sort of league.

Anyway, he's wrong. About the doors. I was asked out by someone else the very next week.

I was in the senior library, because I often am. I love it in there. It smells of furniture polish, and the wicker-bottom chairs creak under you as you lean back against the radiator to chew your pen and think. On sunny days the light makes beams of sparkly dust that drifts like random thoughts. The calm is intoxicating. It's about as unlike our house as you can get.

The one thing my mum can't get at me for is, I do work. I'm after four As, mainly to get me away from her. Don't know if I'll get the grades, but it won't be for want of trying. There was another module coming up and an essay to get out of the way (what I want to know is, why can't teachers communicate with each other so you don't get about twenty deadlines at once?).

So I had my Keats out and my Brodie's Notes and my Oxford pad and I was just getting into my spider diagram when someone put an illegal cup of hot chocolate down on the desk next to me.

'Absolutely NO food and drink to be consumed in the library,' said Daniel Gale brightly. 'It's OK, the librarian's outside arguing with Mr Stevens over the budget. She'll be there for the duration. Cheers.' He produced a KitKat and snapped it in half. 'There you go. Eat up.'

Out of the corner of my eye I saw two Year 11 girls half turn to gawp.

'What's that for?'

He ran his hand through his wiry hair like he does and pushed his glasses against the bridge of his nose. 'You looked in need.'

'Of what, exactly?'

'Chocolate.'

'I think you ought to know I never accept sweets from strangers.' I bit into the KitKat and felt better. 'Thanks.'

'My big sister always swore by chocolate. Contains iron and antioxidants, boosts your immune system, relaxes your arterial walls making strokes less likely. Really. It ought to live in the medicine cabinet. And, most importantly, it lifts your mood through the mystic power of everyone's favourite chemical neurotransmitter, ta-daah, serotonin.'

The Year 11s were hunching their shoulders suspiciously and nudging each other. Girls that age are *so* immature.

'Right. Do I look like a miserable bugger, then?'

He had the grace to look uncomfortable. 'I overheard Julia telling Anya that you'd split with your boyfriend. Although, and I know I'm almost certainly going to regret saying this, he was somewhat lacking in sartorial discretion.' Daniel sat down opposite me and leaned forward across the desk. 'He dressed like a tosser.'

I was genuinely confused. He didn't even know Paul.

'Spooky leather trousers. Give you crotch-rot. Apparently. Not that I've ever worn them.'

'Oh, I get you. He – it wasn't—' I stopped. If I started to explain he'd think I was a right tart. Bloody hell. Why did I attract these weirdos? What bloody business was it of his anyway? 'It's not really your place to comment,' I snapped and stuffed the rest of the KitKat into my mouth.

For a moment he seemed crushed. 'No, fair enough. Scrub that bit. Foot in bloody mouth again. The Aztecs used cocoa beans as a simple form of currency, you know.' He snatched up the hot chocolate and took a deep swig. Then he put the plastic cup back down on my spider diagram and grinned hopefully. I scowled back. He took the scrap of silver foil and scrunched it deftly into a four-pointed star shape, which he stuck on the end of his finger and waved around. The star dropped off and skittered away, leaving a red dent in his skin. Finally he picked up my retractable biro and began clicking it on and off rapidly.

'Right, well, having fucked up big time I might as well go the whole hog.' He fixed his gaze on me. 'Would you – *go out* with me?'

And it seemed to me he shouted those words and they

went echoing round the ceiling, because the hum of chat suddenly dropped, like it always does exactly when you don't want it to.

I was completely amazed. It wasn't only that he looked a bit odd and talked posh bollocks, but it had been popularly assumed since he arrived at the school that he wasn't interested in girls. Electrical gadgets, maybe; human relationships, no. He'd been here a term and a half and never asked anyone out, never got off with anyone at a party, never even seemed to notice the opposite sex in any way. Julia had reckoned he might be one of these God-botherers. There was an intensity about him that made you feel fidgety. He certainly wasn't like anyone else in the year.

'Shit, shit, shit. I've done it wrong, haven't I? I ought to have said, "I've got two tickets for a gig," or "Do you fancy coming for a drink sometime." ' He threw down the biro and scrumpled up the KitKat paper in anguish. 'And then you'd say, "No, sorry, I'm bathing the dog that night," and I'd crawl off and die quietly in a corner somewhere. Much as I'm going to do now.' He flushed and rose to his feet, scraping the chair loudly on the parquet so that the Year 11s put their pens down and turned right round to watch the show. 'Don't know what I was thinking of. Sorry. Catch you later,' he muttered. Then he slunk off, banging the double swing doors behind him.

I slumped forward and bowed my head till my brow touched the wooden desk. Absolutely fucking marvellous. Just what I needed at the moment, to be responsible for someone else's misery.

That lunchtime I watched him in the common room.

He was sitting, as usual, with The Two Nerds (subjects: Maths, Further Maths, Maths With Knobs On, Complete Bastard Maths). One's tall, the other's short but they both have bad haircuts, crap clothes and look about forty. Daniel looked almost elegant beside them, with his good suit and expensive shoes (I don't think they're short of a bob or two in his house).

The Nerds were playing chess and Daniel was making a show of reading an Asterix book. There was this *aura* of unhappiness around him. I edged my chair closer to Julia and laughed loudly at something Anya said. The realization made the hairs on my neck prickle: he reminded me of myself.

*

I DIDN'T MIND school, on the whole. Now our Jimmy hated it. As soon as it were time to go, he'd want the toilet. He'd stay in, and when the factory whistle went at nine he'd come out. Of course it were no good then, 'cause you got the stick across your hand if you were five minutes late. He were worst on Monday mornings when his class had to go through the books of the Old Testament. **Gen**-esis, **Ex**-odus, Le**vit**-icus, **Num**-bers. He had a block, he said; he could do them at home. **First** and Second **Sam**-uels, **First** and Second **Kings**. You could hear him chanting it through the toilet wall. But the minute he got his bum on t' long wooden form with th' others, it went straight out of his head. So he'd get t' stick again.

One day there were a bit of excitement. The big lads in the top class – some of them were fourteen, and tall – turned on the headmaster, Mr Avis. He were a vicious man, he had it coming. He used to cane pupils for nowt, humiliate them, just to show who was boss. Nobody ever learned anything in his class, you were too frightened. Six of 'em carried him to the window, opened it up, pushed him out and held him over the sill by his ankles. It was his good luck that there were some workmen in the hall below who heard his shouts and came running. The pupils pulled him back in sharpish and sat down meek as you like at their desks, so by the time the workmen arrived the only evidence that summat had been going on was Mr Avis's red face and his broken suspender. He was far too embarrassed to admit the truth in front of them, it would have finished him in the village, and we weren't going t' say owt, so he picked up his cane, laid it across his desk and said he was going home because he felt unwell. He resigned t' same day. I think he went to teach at Lytham in the finish.

Startin' work wasn't much of an improvement. You still got the stick – well, you did at our place anyroad, and across your legs too. At thirteen I started in the cotton mill; it was that, or the bleachworks or pickin' coal at Pit Brow. You hadn't a right lot of choice in the matter. I had to clean under four looms before they started up, and you got sixpence extra for that, what they called your 'spender'. But it meant gettin' there early, and y' ad to walk it in all weathers. You got put wi' a woman as 'd learn you how to piece ends, that were called tentin', but if you were slow she'd rap your legs. They got paid by how much cloth they wove, you see, an' they didn't want to waste time on sortin' out such as me. And every mornin' the boss'd be waitin' outside, ready to knock money off if you were late, which was worse than any stick.

They say 'The Good Old Days', but they weren't nice times, not really.

*

**I think worries** are like Russian dolls; almost anything can be eclipsed by something worse. You think a terrible emergency is, say, a monster spot or a bad grade, but that would be nothing if your house burnt down, which would still not be as bad as if you found out you had incurable cancer. (I suppose the only calamity that could top that would be full-on nuclear war.) So it's a matter of scale.

I wondered, as I searched desperately for my completed Keats essay that Thursday night, why on earth I'd ever been concerned about a loon like Daniel Gale. I'd left the essay on my desk, in a blue Slimpick wallet, ready to hand in next day, which would leave the weekend free to do some last-minute revising for the exam. But it had vanished. I looked in all the pockets of my school bag, my course books, my Oxford pad; I got down on my hands and knees and peered under the bed, moved magazines, shoes, clothes; school bag course books Oxford pad under the bed again, then downstairs: house magazines, table drawer, letter rack, under the sofa, under the chairs, in the sideboard, kitchen surfaces, kitchen cupboards, bread crock, bin inside, bin outside (quickly, because it was dark and smelly), airing cupboard, bathroom cabinet, top of the cistern. There aren't that many places in a house the size of ours. Then I really started to panic.

'Mum. Mum! *Mum!*' I bounded back up the stairs and burst into her bedroom.

'God, Charlotte. Is there no privacy in this house?' she snapped, shutting the wardrobe mirror quickly. I vaguely took in the fact that she was wearing a black miniskirt and a shiny white blouse, like a waitress, and she'd been blow-drying her hair in a sad attempt at a Rachel. 'Do you think you might knock before you come barging into my room?' Crossly she pulled on her old grey sweater over the blouse; it was nearly as long as the skirt. She saw me staring. 'I'm only thirty-three. Look at Madonna.'

'Thirty-four tomorrow. What's Madonna got to do with it? Look, Mum, I'm desperate. Have you moved a blue folder from off my desk?'

She clocked the state I was in. 'Give me a minute,' she said reaching for her leggings.

We both knew it was Nan. 'Let me talk to her, you're too hyper.' She went into Nan's room and I heard low voices. Please God, let her remember where she's put it, I prayed as I hung outside the door biting my thumbnail. But Mum's face was glum as she came out.

'Oh, God, Mum! I spent *hours* on that essay! I haven't even got my notes any more! Can't you have another go at her?'

We could hear Nan singing, so I knew it was hopeless.

> '*Oh the moon shines bright on Charlie Chaplin*
> *His boots are crackin'*
> *For want of blackin'*
> *And his owd fustian coat is wantin' mendin'*
> *Before they send 'im*
> *To the Dardanelles.*'

'I know where we'll find it.' Mum's expression was suddenly bright and I noticed then she'd got lip gloss on.

'Go on.'

'The Tin.'

She slipped back into Nan's room and I heard the wardrobe door go, a scuffle as Mum shifted footwear aside, then the lid of the large biscuit tin Nan keeps full of Spam and canned baked beans in case of war. I twisted impatiently and peeped round the jamb. Nan was flat out on the bed, staring at the ceiling.

At last Mum stood up. 'Sorry, nothing. We'll try downstairs again.'

'Jesus! Why do I have to live in this bloody hole!' I exploded at her. 'You can't put *anything* down without someone interfering with it. I'm completely *sick* of this house! When I get my "A" levels, which I probably won't do at this rate, you'll not see me for dust. God Almighty! What am I going to tell them at school? My nan ate my homework?' I was close to tears. 'I *can't* do all that work again. I'm so tired, and what about my revision? I haven't *time* to do both, I'm just going to fail. I don't know why I *bother*.'

'You're hyperventilating. Calm down. We'll have another look and I'll write you a note.' She squeezed past me and began to go downstairs.

'A *note*?' I shouted over the banisters at the top of her head. 'Do you know how old I am? It's not like I need to be excused games! A *note* won't do any good.'

She turned her face up to me. 'Do you want me to help you or not?'

'Christ!' I turned on my heel and threw myself into my bedroom, slamming the door. Papers fluttered off the desk, but not the right ones. I sank onto the bed in a welter of self-pity. No one else had to put up with this continual family sabotage. Why hadn't I been born into a different life?

Except, I nearly was, wasn't I?

I'd been trying not to think about it, because the implications were too big and too scary. Only you can't *not* think of something, it's impossible. By making a conscious effort to blot it out, you give it life. Try *not* thinking of a blue elephant. See?

Later on, it must have been about 2 a.m., I crept in to see Nan. She looked awful without her teeth, her head lolling, little snores coming from the back of her throat. Close to you could see the pink scalp through her thin hair. One day she'll be dead, I thought, she'll be lying like this but there'll be no breathing and her skin will be cold. I took her small hand, loving and hating her at the same time. I'm here, in this house, in this life, because of you, I told her. She didn't stir.

Just before I went to sleep I remembered Mum's birthday present. *The Stately Semi: How To Achieve The Neo-Classical Look In The Suburban Home*. She's forever decorating, trying to paint out the council house, rag-roll away her roots. I supposed I ought to wrap it, so I tiptoed downstairs for some Sellotape and there, as I clicked on the light, sitting on the table were some narrow-ruled sheets covered with my handwriting. My heart leapt. But it wasn't the essay, it was only my notes. There was orange spaghetti bolognaise sauce on the top page which my mum had tried to wipe off. She must have trawled through the wheeliebin after I'd gone to bed. I wrapped the present quickly and left it for the morning.

\*

WHAT IS IT about kids? I'd lie down in front of a tram for Charlotte without a second thought, but most of the time

I want to beat her about the head with a blunt instrument. Do all mothers feel this way?

*

WHEN THEY laid her in my arms I thought I was going to die with happiness. I used to wheel her up the street in that big pram and old Mrs Moss used to be leaning on her gate, and she'd say every time, 'Whose babby's that? Wheer's tha getten' it?' And I'd say, 'She's mine.' Mrs Moss would suck her teeth. 'She never is.' I'd look down at the little fingers poking out over the top of the crocheted blanket. 'Oh, yes she is. She's mine. She's mine.'

*

'Not enough sex. That's what causes aggression in middle age.' Daniel Gale was twittering at me as I blew my nose into his enormous handkerchief. 'It's true. Those ones who write in to *Points of View* to complain about the pronunciation of "controversy", or constantly moan on to the council about their neighbour's Leyland hedges, those maniacs shouting their mouths off in restaurants and reducing the waitresses to tears, those are the types you know just don't get laid enough. You've got to feel sorry for them, really. I mean, Mrs Stokes must weigh about fifteen stone, and she's got that moustache. We know there's a Mr Stokes, but I don't suppose he's panting to exercise his conjugal rights of an evening. That's why she was such an A1 bitch. Nothing to do with you at all.' He hovered at my chair, not touching it, not sitting down. We were in the library; he'd followed after seeing me storm out of cow-bag Stokesy's office.

'But I've never been late with a piece of work for her, *ever*.' I was still crying with temper. 'She said, "Oh, I'm sorry, Charlotte, you're the fifth person today with an excuse. I can't make an exception for you. Monday, 9 a.m." So *I* get penalized because of someone else's laziness.' I put my head down on my arms. 'And I'm *so* tired. I want to sleep all the time.' I'd been too angry to be embarrassed with him at first so he got it all, blow by blow, from Nan downwards. Now I'd finished, though, I wanted him to go away. 'Here.' I lifted my head up and gave him back his handkerchief. I knew my mascara must have run, so it was imperative I get to a mirror as soon as possible.

'You can keep it, if you like.'

'No, really.'

'You've got a bit of . . .' He gestured to his own cheek. 'Do you want me to . . . ?' He was wrapping the hanky round his finger, the way mums do with mucky toddlers.

'No! Sorry, no, it's OK. I need to wash my face anyway.'

'Right.'

'I'm fine now. Nothing a hatpin and a voodoo doll won't cure.' I smiled feebly.

'Right.'

He hesitated.

'See you.'

'Yeah.'

'And thanks,' I called after him faintly. He didn't acknowledge me.

But on Monday, after I'd handed in my essay and before the exam started, he found me again.

'You been here all weekend? Sorry, stupid joke. I won't hold you up.' He nodded at my open textbook. 'I just wondered if this was any use.' He plonked a plastic bag down on the table. I peered in, and nearly swallowed my biro in shock.

'My God, Daniel, it's a laptop! You can't give me this!'

His hands went fluttery and he swept his hair back several times. 'No, no, it's simply a glorified typewriter. We've had it for ages. My dad was literally throwing it out, well, he was going to put it in the loft, anyway. He doesn't bother with it now he's got the PC. It's yours to borrow – indefinitely – if you think it'll help.'

'How do you mean?'

'You can save your essays on disk as you type them. That way it wouldn't matter if you lost a copy, you'd always have a backup. It's an absolute doddle to use. The instruction booklet's in there, and I've formatted a couple of disks for you so it's all ready to go. Just be careful not to pull the lead out while you're in the middle of something, that deletes it all. Best to save your text as you go along.' He was gabbling now. 'Oh, there's this as well.' He fished out a small cardboard box and flashed it at me before dropping it back into the bag. 'Iron tablets. You're probably a bit anaemic, that's why you're so tired. My sister used to take them, before she ran off to join the circus, well, read medicine at Birmingham. Not these actual tablets, obviously. I'm not trying to palm you off with drugs that are past their sell-by date.' He gave a high-pitched laugh. 'Anyway, give them a try – or not – as you like.'

He let go of the back of the chair he'd been gripping, and stalked off towards the doors.

Well, bugger me, I thought. You've got to give the lad credit for trying.

I picked up the bag and ran after him, squeak squeak across the parquet. Everyone looked.

I bundled him outside and held up the typewriter.

'I understand. You can't accept it. Say no more.' He sighed and made to take the handles of the bag off me.

'No, no, it's fab. I'm really grateful. Tell your dad thanks. And – if you want, if you're not doing anything on Saturday afternoon, I usually go to Tiggy's for a coffee about three. Do you know where I mean? So . . .'

'I'll see you there.' He grinned manically and all but ran off down the corridor.

Straight away I wished I hadn't done it. He was bound to get the wrong idea.

**In the event** it didn't matter. Not at all. That Saturday, at about three, Daniel, the essay, the exam were a million years ago. I was in my bedroom, amongst the posters and the pictures of impossibly beautiful women, staring at my naked body in the full-length mirror. Downstairs Mum was lecturing Nan at top volume, and through the chink of curtain I could see the light of a keen, bright spring afternoon.

I was trying to see if my breasts had got any bigger. I had to contort a bit because of the old Take That stickers which refused to peel off the glass properly. Robbie Williams leered at me unhelpfully but Gary Barlow looked sympathetic, even though the top of his head was missing. I turned side-on to check out my stomach. I grabbed some flesh and pinched. Impossible to tell. Then I let out my breath. That did look pregnant. I sucked in my muscles again quickly.

I heard Mum pounding up the stairs; thank God I'd locked the door. She was shouting down to Nan to stay where she was or she'd get it all over her clothes. There was the sound of drawers slamming, then footsteps on the stairs again. I blanked it out and continued gazing.

I wasn't sure where the idea had come from. I hadn't felt sick in the mornings, but my bra had definitely got tighter. If only I had X-ray vision. What would I see? A little fishy tadpole thing, wriggling its limbs and nodding its outsize head? Probably the length of a baked bean, if I was right about the dates. Oh, please let me not be right. Would it have *implanted* itself in me yet? Burrowed in? God.

It was paranoia. I looked exactly the same. There was no baby. I started to put my clothes back on and checked my knickers once more for blood. Virgin white, alas. Still, I'd been late before, that meant nothing. My jeans still fitted, so it was probably all right.

Suddenly there was a clattering noise from the hall. I pulled my fleece on, unlocked the door and ran across the landing to see. Mum was bending down to pick up the pile of CDs that had been posted hastily through the letter box. I saw her open the front door in puzzlement, and beyond her, Paul's retreating figure hurrying across the road.

Without a second thought I dashed down the stairs, whipped a pistol out the pocket of Nan's Welsh wool coat which was hanging in the hall, and fired. In the distance Paul crumpled into a denim heap.

'Nice shot,' said Mum admiringly.

No, not really. What actually happened was that together we craned to watch him disappear round the corner then I turned and ran back into my room, banging the door shut.

# Chapter Four

I stayed put for two hours and would ideally have spent the rest of my life there only the need to pee drove me downstairs.

The table was laid and tea was in progress, the TV blaring. Next to the pepper mill sat a neat tower of CDs.

'They catch seagulls off the rubbish tip and pass them off as chicken,' Nan was saying.

'Charles Darwin!' shouted my mother, oblivious to everything except *University Challenge*. '*The Magic Flute*!'

I hurried through and gained the bathroom. Nan had taken all the guest soaps out of their little pot and lined them up along the cistern, as she always does. Usually I put them back, it avoids another row, but this time the lavender perfume pushed right up my nostrils and made me feel queasy. I leaned forward and laid my forehead on the rim of the cold sink. There was still no blood.

At last I got myself together and went to face the inquisition.

'You tell me,' Nan was poking a drumstick round her plate and shivering theatrically. 'You tell me what chicken has four legs. It's never right, that. Four legs.'

'They came out of a bag of chicken pieces off the

market.' Mum was busy eyeing up Jeremy Paxman. 'There were three wings as well.'

'Good God.'

'Yours is in the fridge, Charlotte, under some cling-film.' Mum tore herself away from the screen. 'Oh! What's happened to your head?'

In the mirror over the fire I could see the red furrow left by the edge of the sink. Christ.

'Nothing!' I said venomously and plonked myself down in the armchair.

And waited.

*Bleak House*. A. A. Milne. The Dissolution of the Monasteries.

'Was that the boy you were seeing before Christmas?' she hazarded finally.

Hah, Mother! You know *nothing*! You have no idea how long it's been going on! You miss what's *right under your nose*. You'd have a *blue fit* if you even knew the half of it. I *never* tell you anything because you'd always con-struct the worst (and all right, in this case you'd be right, but that's *not the point*). It's none of your business, I'm an adult. Get yourself a life then you can stop interfering with mine!

I said, 'Yeah.'

'I take it . . . it's finished?'

I wanted to wrestle her to the ground and bang her skull repeatedly on her precious white marble hearth.

'What do *you* think?' I hunched my knees up under my fleece and pulled in my arms so that the sleeves hung empty. I waited for her to say, 'Take your feet off the chair,' but she didn't. I hated her so much I could hardly breathe.

'They eat frogs' legs in France,' said Nan jabbing a fork in the direction of the TV. 'The dirty buggers.'

'He's not French, Nan, I've told you before. He does *Newsnight*.'

'Of course he is. Look at his nose.'

How long would I have to live in this madhouse, I wondered, before my head caved in.

*

I WAS IN the bedroom trying on clothes again when the telephone rang.

I'd just been thinking, maybe I don't look so bad for my age, actually, you see a lot worse on reality TV. I haven't got those road-map veins you see some women with, and my teeth are all my own. You've got to be realistic. Anyway, I reckon we could all look like Jennifer Aniston if we had a few million in the bank and a personal trainer. I wasn't fat, not *fat* fat. Size 14 isn't fat. I pulled my stomach in and turned sideways on to the mirror. Now that didn't look bad at all. If I could stand in this pose for the rest of my life people might think I was quite slim. I did a film-star smile at myself and arched my eyebrows. Then I tilted my head and tried a wistful gaze; nice. If I ever released an album, this would be the covershot.

I fluffed my hair up – currently mid-length, lightened, Brauned to within an inch of its life – and slicked some shimmery lipstick on my pout. You see, I told myself, if you had the *time* you could look half-decent. But it's so hard with Charlotte and Mum. Sometimes it's like a conspiracy,

I only have to get the can of shaving foam out of the cupboard and there's some domestic crisis, so back it goes on the shelf, and I get hairier. Thank God for opaque tights.

Charlotte would have had a blue fit if she knew how much I'd just spent on the catalogues; thank God you get to pay by instalment. *So What If I'll Never See Thirty Again, I've Got Legs*, favourite outfit of the new batch, lay on the bed slinkily; I'd have to get the razor on my shins for that. You should have seen Charlotte's face when she saw me in it. Bit of a shock for her, seeing her mum look like a proper woman for a change. Serves her right for barging in.

She's a sly devil, though! Some daughters talk to their mothers, I've seen it on *Trisha*, but Charlotte's like a clam. I never know what's going on in her mind. Then again, if I'm being absolutely honest, I don't want to. It's not worth the row to ask, anyway. She'll snap your head off if you ask her what she wants on her toast, never mind how her love life's going.

You walk on eggshells in this house.

And this boy, nice-looking but cocky with it; I can't say I particularly liked him. I think he was called Paul, she used to go to St Mary's with him, years ago. I'd only met him twice and even then she whisked him away before I could say much to him. What would you say, though? Paws off my daughter till she's finished her education? She wouldn't thank me for that.

I wish I could have told her 'It doesn't matter, you're better off without him,' but that would have sounded pretty hollow coming from me. We might be about to enter a third millennium but a woman's still a non-person without a man in tow. At least that's been my experience.

Anyway the phone rang while I was still wearing *Semi-Casual Sunday Luncheon In A Pub With Mr Fairbrother*. No chance of Charlotte stirring her stumps at the moment, she's far too traumatized, and Nan can't hear through the receiver properly so she won't touch it: probably just as well. The ringing continued as I wrestled with the top button. 'Buggeration!' I yelled at my reflection. Album cover girl had vanished. My face was hard and cross and my hair had gone all staticky.

'Telephone!' Nan shrieked up the stairs.

I gave in, shoved my slippers on and nipped down to the hall. It was a woman from Bolton Social Services.

'We just need you to give us a couple more details. I think you missed a page out on the form. Have you got your National Insurance number at all?'

I ferreted it out of the Useful Drawer in front of Nan's glassy stare, then returned to the phone.

'I thought you were ringing to tell me you'd found my birth mother,' I said, knowing it was stupid. They'd only had the forms a week.

The woman gave a short laugh. 'We have to process the information first. Then you get assigned a social worker, and have an interview. It's the procedure.'

'Will it take long?'

'You should hear back from us in two to three months' time. Give us a call if you haven't heard anything by then.'

'Two to three *months*?'

'It's the procedure.'

'No sooner?'

'We're very overstretched at the moment.'

Aren't we all, love, I felt like saying.

Nan opened the door as I was hanging up. She was focusing again and gave me the once-over. 'Ooh, swanky. Turn round. You're a bonny woman when you want to be. I never see you in a dress.' She stroked the sleeve thoughtfully. 'You want a nice pair of courts with that. Did you know you've a button loose?'

'You're one to talk,' I said. 'If anyone's got a button loose, it's you. Now look, I'm off upstairs to reinvent myself. Stick the telly on and *don't* touch the kettle till I come down again.'

\*

A **miracle!** A *bloody* miracle! Well, two actually, although one's quite small-scale. And Fate can go stuff itself. Start the clocks again, open the champagne, exhale.

We were in the hall for the last assembly of term. We'd had the sermon, some gubbins about how all the people in hell have to eat with six-foot-long chopsticks, where do they get this bilge from? Then it was the hockey and football results, then some Year 7 kids got a road safety award then, finally, it was the dismissal prayer. The Head put his fingertips together in that way that always makes me want to give him a good kicking, bowed his oily head and began.

'Lord, thou knowest how busy I must be this day . . .'

I prayed: Oh, God, please make me not be pregnant, please please, I'll make such an effort with Mum and Nan and I'll revise really hard and never have sex again until I'm at least twenty-five, and then only with the pill, a condom and a cap as well, please, God. Amen.

Someone was digging me in the ribs.

'Get a move on, cloth ears,' Julia hissed, and I looked up and saw the line of upper sixth nearly out of the door and a big gap where I should have been following. I lurched forward and scuttled after them, aware that all the Year 11s behind were watching and sniggering. 'What's up?' asked Julia when we got outside.

'Nothing. Just . . . I've got to go somewhere.'

'Not coming into town with Anya and the twins?'

'Gotta go straight home, sorry. Thanks.'

I knew the bus was waiting, but first I had to go check the state of my knickers.

The cubicle was narrow and the lock put up a fight. I closed my eyes, pushed my underwear down quickly and stared. Blood. BLOOD. Thank Christ. My knees buckled and I sat down on the toilet rim, still staring. Not much blood, but that didn't matter. It was OK, everything was going to be OK. Outside girls came and went, cisterns flushed, then it all went quiet. I'd missed the bus but I didn't care. Catch another one. I could fly home, if it came to that.

Oh, the other little miracle, hardly worth mentioning really but one less thing to worry about. I'd been dreading seeing Daniel Gale and having to invent some lie about why I stood him up. Then, when he wasn't in on the Monday I began to wonder if he'd chucked himself off a motorway bridge or something, that'd be just my luck. Any minute now, I thought, the head of sixth is going to walk into the classroom with a stony face and ask us if we knew of any reason why he might have been feeling depressed. Then he was in registration on Tuesday, a tad paler than usual perhaps, but definitely not dead. He kept trying to catch my eye, and I kept staring at the floor. I tried for a quick getaway out of the common room but he beat me to the door and put his hand on my shoulder, all breathless and earnest. Here we go, I thought, clenching my teeth.

'I am *so* sorry,' he began, making my mouth drop open.

'What?'

'About Saturday. God! I hope you didn't wait for long. I know you must be really angry with me, I mean it's the most awful manners, you must think I'm unbelievably rude—'

'No! No, not at all—'

We were hustled through the door in the general scrum. Someone pushed between us with a large art folder then the bell went above our heads. We grimaced at each other until the din stopped.

'Look, I'll be quick.' He pushed his hair out of his eyes and blinked. 'I did try to contact you. I went through the directory but there were stacks of Coopers and my mum was on the phone most of the night anyway. The thing is, we heard on Friday night that my grandfather in Guildford had died. Mum wanted to go down straight away but Dad persuaded her to wait till Saturday morning—'

'Oh, God, I'm really sorry.'

'Yeah, well. Thanks. These things happen. He was a nice guy but pretty old. Mum's all over the place, though, and so is my grandmother. So you can imagine, it was all a bit hectic over the weekend, travelling down there and back. But I really am sorry about leaving you in the lurch like that.'

I tried not to seem joyful. 'Forget it. Honestly. It must have been awful for you.' I laid a hand on his arm and he looked down at it in surprise. I took it off again hastily.

'The thing is, I was really looking forward to it.'

'No bother. Some other time.'

'We're down there again this weekend. It's the funeral on Friday.'

'We'll catch up at some point. I'm in town most Saturdays.'

The corridor had gone worryingly quiet.

'So, what, the Saturday after?'

'Whatever, yeah. Look, we'd better get a move on, it's nearly twenty-five past. Last day or not, Stokesy's a complete git if you're late for any of her lessons, she keeps records, you know, and then makes sarky comments on your report.'

'And I should be in physics, which is right over the other side, which means it'll be half-past by the time I make an entrance. Hardly worth going, in fact.' He furrowed his brow. 'Do you fancy bunking off, just for this session?'

'You *what*?' Daniel was even more law-abiding than me.

'I don't mean leave the building or anything rash like that. We could just go back into the common room and have a coffee. Quite a minor crime. *I'll* be OK, I can say I was overcome with sudden grief, and I'll put on an innocent expression and swear to Mrs Stokes that I compelled you to stay and counsel me. You'd get away with it because you're normally so good. And they think I'm so weird they wouldn't like to pursue it for fear of sending me into a mad fit.'

I began a laugh, then looked away in embarrassment.

'Sorry. I shouldn't be so flippant about the grandfather situation. I'm not, honestly. He was a great guy and I'll miss him. Only it's so bloody serious at home, awful actually. Scary seeing your parents show their feelings.'

I thought of our house, where Feelings flowed like hot and icy water, constantly. I realized my mouth was open again, and shut it.

'So, what do you say?' He cocked his head and looked at me over his glasses.

'You're full of surprises, aren't you?'

'I like to think so.' He turned to go back through the door. 'Coming?'

'Nope. You might be a genius but I have to work my tail off to get a half-decent grade. She's going over past papers today and I need to be there. That's the trouble with me; I'm just so bloody conscientious.' I smiled and he smiled back. 'Enjoy the coffee, though. And I will use you as an alibi, if that's still OK.'

'I'll be ready to prostrate myself with misery at break time.'

And he did. And then I bled. Happy Easter.

\*

IT DIDN'T GET OFF to a particularly auspicious start, that Sunday. I'd downed a couple of gins for luck, and put the new dress on. Then I stood in front of the wardrobe mirror, trying to decide on earrings, studs or danglies. Downstairs

Nan was belting out 'Tell Me the Old, Old Story', presumably they'd had it at church that morning. From behind her bedroom door Charlotte was moaning like a cat in pain, which meant she must have her headphones on. And me? *Well, tonight, Matthew, I'm going to be . . .* I breathed on the glass and waited till the mist cleared: *Celine Dion!* (Sound of cheering, clapping, murmurs of amazement etc.) Pouting at my reflection I took a deep breath. I had to admit, the new highlights did look good.

'*Baby think twice, for the sake—*'

The smoke alarm began to go off in the kitchen.

'Fucking hell,' I said to Celine in the mirror, and legged it down the stairs. Nan met me at the bottom.

'Karen! The toaster's set afire. What do I do?'

I shouldered her aside and barged into the kitchen. Black smoke was rolling from the toaster slot. Nan appeared at my shoulder, wringing her hands.

'I were just mekkin' a bit o' dinner—'

'I was *going* to do it, if you'd just waited for two minutes!' I yelled and she shrank back into the lounge.

I wrenched the plug out of its socket and flung a dishcloth over the toaster. The smoke stopped. I opened the back door, put on oven gloves and carried the thing to the step, then stood looking at it. Thirty seconds later Charlotte came in, sniffing.

'What's that awful smell?' she said, then she spotted the trail of crumbs across the tiled floor, the dishcloth bundle. 'Oh, right, yeah. I bet Nan's been putting the cheese spread on again before the bread goes in, I caught her trying that one last week. She scrapes it on about an inch thick and it welds itself to the element.' She put on a sorrowful face. 'Poor old Nan. She doesn't understand, it's not her fault. Do you know she's crying on the sofa?'

I ignored her; it was that or stab her to death with a fork. I didn't know why she was being so bloody reasonable all of a sudden but I could do without it. The doorbell rang.

'That'll be Ivy. I'll go. By the way, you've got odd earrings in, Mum.'

'AND IVY IS?' Mr Fairbrother took a sip of his pint. He'd moved his chair a little off from the rest of the Fourgates Ramblers and we were sitting at the end of a long table in the lounge bar of the Feathers. Thank God he'd seemed pleased to see me: thank God he'd been there at all.

'One of Nan's friends from her Mothers' Union days. Ivy Seddon and Maud Eckersley take her up to church every Sunday, then Ivy comes and sits with her in the afternoon. They take her to the Over Seventies' Club on a Wednesday across at the Working Men's, and Maud visits on a Tuesday morning and stays for her dinner. And if one's ill, the other comes, they never let me down. Then I have a woman from Crossroads Carers on a Monday and a cleaner for three hours on Thursday, which I pay for out of the Allowance. I mean, I could leave her with Charlotte, and I do, sometimes, but I try not to. And anyway, Charlotte's at school most of the time, so I couldn't even do part-time work without some help. It's funny how these things creep up on you. Ten years ago, even five, Nan was fine, just a bit forgetful, then . . .'

Mr F looked sympathetic. 'Your mother's lucky to have that support network. That's the marvellous thing, though, about community. Our parents grew up in a time when everybody knew everybody else in this village. Times may have been hard, but they all helped each other out. There's too much isolation these days.'

I nodded, thinking of myself. Where was my little network of support, my social life? At fifteen there was a big group of us, out every weekend. More energy than we knew what to do with, on the phone all hours; it used to drive Nan mad. We all had plans, we were going to set the world on fire. Then Dee, my best friend, moved to Cheltenham, and then I got pregnant, and there was just this *gulf* between me and the other girls, even though they tried to be nice about it.

Some of it was not understanding. They got fed up of me moaning about always being tired, and they didn't see at all why I couldn't leave the baby and just go off places at the drop of a hat. And I couldn't confide about the horror of veins all over my boobs, peeing when I sneezed, the big jagged purple lines on my tummy.

Some of it was, too, they were scared it might happen to them, that they might 'catch' my pregnancy. I always remember one of them, Donna Marsden, coming to see me in hospital. She'd got a little rabbit suit for Charlotte and she'd come all prepared to coo. But she barely looked at the baby. What she couldn't keep her eyes off the whole visit was my saggy stomach, bursting out from under one of Nan's old nighties. She was clearly appalled. Finally she slinked off down the ward in her size-8 jeans and I sat in the metal-framed bed and cried my eyes out.

The bottom line was, I was going to be married with a baby while they were all buggering off to college to screw around and do things with their lives. And by the time some of them came back to Bank Top to settle down and do the family stuff, I was divorced, and they didn't much rate that either.

Mr F was still speaking, fortunately, and didn't notice the tears of self-pity pricking my eyes.

'Sorry?'

'And, of course, your mother's lucky to have you. Too many people walk away from their responsibilities these days.' He smiled at me approvingly and I thought his face looked nice, fatherly. He was wearing an Aran sweater, canvas trousers and hiking boots. It was odd to see him out of a suit. 'By the way, I take it you've had lunch?'

I glanced down the long table and took in the dirty plates and screwed up paper napkins. Bloody hell, him and his rambling mates had already eaten.

'Oh, yes. I had something before I came out,' I lied, praying my stomach wouldn't rumble.

'Then I'll get you another, what was it, vodka and orange?'

'Lovely.' I'd have to scoff some peanuts in the loo soon or I'd be drunk as a lord. Pace yourself, I thought. On the other hand, the quicker I drank this round, the sooner I'd get something to eat.

'So how long's your mum been a widow?' Mr F's brow furrowed as he handed me my glass and sat down again.

'God, let me . . . nearly twenty years it'll be. January 1978, my dad died.'

'I'm sorry.'

'Yeah, it was pretty grim in the end. Lung cancer. It seemed to go on forever, him being ill, but then I didn't really know all the details. I was only fourteen, and Nan kept a lot of it to herself.'

'She sounds like a strong woman.'

'Oh, she is. They built them tough in those days. Once, when she was a little girl, she broke her elbow and she never cried. Her brother did, though, had the screaming hab-dabs, apparently, and they all thought it was him that was hurt because he was in such a state he couldn't get the words out to explain.'

Mr F smiled. 'But you're strong in your own way.'

'Not really.' If only he knew the truth. But it was flattering all the same. *This* date I wasn't going to spend the whole time dissecting my own inadequacies, I'd done enough of that in the past. His niceness, and seeing him in these unfamiliar surroundings looking like a real person rather than a boss, made me ridiculously nervous. I swigged at the vodka like it was going out of fashion and grinned inanely.

'Yet to cope with losing your father at that age. It must have been traumatic.'

The grin fell off my face. 'Yeah. It was, actually. We were really, really close, he'd have done anything for me . . . At least he didn't live to see . . . But then he'd have loved Charlotte, he really would. I think it's what pulled Nan through in the end, having a baby around. She was, I have to admit it, brilliant with Charlotte. I used to walk out of those screaming rows with Steve, go round to Nan's and dump the baby in her arms. I don't know how I'd have coped otherwise.'

'And yet you still want to look for your biological mother?'

I paused, and Mr F looked concerned.

'I'm sorry, do tell me if I'm stepping out of line—'

'No, not at all. It's nice to have the chance to talk it over with someone. I was just thinking . . .' I drained my vodka and stood up. 'Ahm, while I'm up I'll get some more drinks in, you're on . . . ?' I glanced at his pint. Mr F had drunk about two inches. He tried not to look surprised.

'No, not for me, thanks.'

'Well, I'll just—'

I got two packets of dry roasted and headed off to the ladies'. Actually, peanuts take longer to eat than you think. I leant against the sink and munched madly like a demented hamster, then the door opened and I nipped into a cubicle. Several years later I finished the first packet, tore open the second, and poured them into my mouth. Next door the other person pulled the chain, and the shock sent a peanut nib down the wrong way. I started a choking fit, scattering bits of mashed-up nut and spit everywhere. Finally I got my breath back, but by then I'd totally gone off the whole peanut thing. I threw the plastic packets in the loo and flushed. They floated back up. I waited till the cistern filled, the theme tune to *Countdown* running through my head, then flushed again. When the bubbles cleared the packets had vanished but two stubborn peanuts still lurked in the bottom of the pan. Bugger it, that'd have to do.

I opened the door cautiously and saw my reflection in the mirror. My cheeks were bright red and my eyeliner had run. I moved over to the sink and started to repair the damage, trying not to catch the eye of the other woman who was making a right meal of washing her hands. Sod off, I told her silently. But she went on standing there, and, I thought, taking sneaky glances at me every so often. Then, just as I reckoned she was finished, she sidled over and murmured, 'You can get out of it, you know.'

'You what?' I hadn't a clue what she was on about.

'I used to be like you.' Since she was about ten years younger than me and a heck of a sight more glamorous, I wondered what she meant. She lowered her voice to a whisper. '*I used to have an eating disorder.*' She laid a comforting hand on my shoulder. 'You can break out of it, with help.'

Light dawned. She thinks I've been making myself sick.

'It's nothing to be ashamed of. Princess Diana . . .'

'Thanks, but you've got me wrong—'

She smiled and began rooting in her handbag. 'I always carry these. When you're ready, just give them a ring. Admitting you've got a problem is the first step.' She squeezed my elbow and placed a little card in my hand, then went out. *The Bulimia Helpline*, I read. *Together We Can Change Tomorrow.*

What about changing yesterday? Now that really would be worth ringing up about.

I got myself a spritzer and rejoined Mr F. Across the room the lady from the toilets gave me the thumbs up.

'You were saying?'

'About my mum? Yeah, well . . . It's difficult to explain, you probably won't have the foggiest what I'm warbling on about.'

He looked worried again. 'No, please . . .'

'Well, it's like – no, you'll think I'm mental.'

'Go on.'

'Well . . . well do you ever think you might be living the Wrong Life?'

He leant forward, as if getting his forehead closer to mine might help him understand.

'I mean, who we are, where we live, the jobs we do – everything, really – it's all just down to chance, isn't it? The lottery of where we were born, and who to. It's like, the same person could be born into two completely different homes, well not *really*, but imagine it.' I started shunting bar mats purposefully round the table. 'And in one home he might get loads of encouragement, go to a posh school, end up all confident and successful in some top job, while in another he might have awful scummy parents who don't care about him, and he might get in with a bad crowd and go to a rotten school and end up in prison or something . . . Am I making sense?'

'The Prince and the Pauper?'

'Yeah, that's it, sort of.' I leaned a pair of bar mats into a wigwam. 'And I don't mean I've been living like a pauper, God knows Nan did her best, but I've always felt like I belonged elsewhere. I mean, I'm nothing like her. She's never been that interested in my education, for one thing. As long as I behaved myself at school, that was enough for her. The comp was OK and I'd probably have done really well if, if—' I had a sudden flash of memory, Steve in school uniform leaning against the iron gates, arms folded: that was the afternoon before the First Time. I shook my head and the image cleared. 'But she'd never have even thought of the grammar, and I didn't because of my friends . . . And she's got, it's not her fault, it's the way she was brought up, oh, God, I sound like such a snob, but she's got terrible taste. In everything. Calendars with kittens in baskets, plastic flowers in miniature wheelbarrows. I knew what kitsch was before I ever realized there was a word for it. And I try and keep the house nice, you know, improve it, but no one else cares. I've got this vision of my real mother in a lovely drawing room somewhere, fresh flowers, long white curtains. Like the cover of a Mary Wesley novel. Because I think she'll be like me, she'll understand me. And then, then . . .' The wigwam slid apart and collapsed.

'What?'

'Then I can go on looking after Nan without hating her.'

I heard myself say it and I couldn't believe it.

'Oh God, I didn't mean that. I did not mean it, just pretend I never said it—'

But Mr F was putting his hand over mine.

'It's all right,' he said gently. 'You forget, I've been a carer too. I know what it's like. It's perfectly natural to feel as if you're at the end of your tether sometimes. When you love someone, that's when the other emotions are at their strongest. It's the most difficult job in the world. I know. But you do a marvellous job, keeping that house running, and your clever daughter . . .'

I started to fill up. This kindness was outfacing. 'I must nip to the loo again,' I said huskily, and went off to splash cold water on my face.

When I got back there was another vodka on the table for me.

'I got us some peanuts too,' said Mr F. 'Dry roasted all right?'

'Mmm. Then again,' I plonked myself down and carried straight on, unstoppable, 'it might be a real can of worms. I mean, she might hate me, my real mother, I mean. Or Nan. Nan might hate me for finding this other woman. Not to mention Charlotte. She's unstable enough at the moment. But who do you live your life for, in the end? You've got to take some risks, or you might as well be dead. Don't I owe it to myself? Don't I owe it to my birth mum? What if she sobs herself to sleep on my birthdays, or kisses my picture every bedtime? There's more than one sort of duty.'

By now I was talking quite fast. I made a conscious effort to stop, took a deep breath and asked; 'So was it very hard, caring for both your parents?'

Mr F began to talk in a low, sad voice and I let my eyes unfocus. I felt very tired and slightly sick. After a while I realized he'd stopped speaking.

'Sorry?'

'Are you all right?'

My eyes smarted from the effort to keep them open. 'Mm, yeah. Fine. Look, it's been really nice, it really has, to talk, but I'll probably have to make a move soon.' The idea of getting up and walking anywhere seemed impossible. I could have put my head down on the table top and gone straight to sleep. I let out an enormous yawn. 'Sorry.'

'Do you want me to walk you home? If you're not – if you're a bit tired.'

'I'll be fine, really.' I reached round the back of my

chair, then remembered I'd left my jacket in the hall; it had been a perfect spring day when I set out.

'Haven't you got a coat?'

'No. Well, it's gone so mild. You'd never think it was only April.'

The pub door swung open and a middle-aged couple came in, shaking snow out of their hair.

'Don't worry. I always carry a spare cagoule,' said Mr F, rummaging in his rucksack. He drew out a little package of bright blue material and began to unfold it. 'You'll need your hood up by the looks of things.'

I struggled into the shiny sleeves and he zipped me up. The other ramblers looked across and nodded at us.

'Do you think it's possible to love somebody and hate them at the same time?' I asked, as he pulled the toggles tight.

'Oh, yes. Very much so. Now, out into the frozen wastes.' He squeezed my hand briefly, then steered me to the exit.

'*This is getting serious,*' sang Celine, quite out of the blue. Mr F looked puzzled, but politely held the swing door ajar and ushered me through.

'I have to say—' I began, but then with the icy air a wave of nausea swept over me and I had to stop and press my hand against the wall.

'Do you feel faint? Best to put your head—'

I didn't hear the end of the sentence because I found I was throwing up peanutty vodka against a half-barrel of pansies. Mr F's arms were round me as I bent and heaved, and when I could right myself he offered me a hanky and turned away while I sorted myself out. 'It must be something I've eaten,' I mumbled.

He took my arm and we walked home mutely through the blizzard, my small circle of exposed face getting redder and redder and my wet fringe sticking to my forehead. My feet, in their unsuitable courts, were agony. At my gate he said briskly: 'So, I'll see you tomorrow,' and I thought, Not if I go upstairs now and slash my wrists, except I'm too bloody cold to hold the knife steady and my veins have all shrunk to nothing anyway. I just smiled weakly. He gave his half-salute and strode off into the swirling white like Captain Oates.

Ivy Seddon opened the front door as I trudged up the path. 'They're smashing, them pack-a-macs, aren't they?' she shouted. 'We saw you coming, be quick and get by t' fire. And can you check her bag, I think it's come away again. I'll mek a brew.'

\*

SHE'D ONLY been at the mill two weeks but I'd had her down as a hard-faced madam, sixteen or not. Then that Monday morning she went off for a break and didn't come back, and I found her crying out by the bins, nearly hysterical.

'T 'int fair!' she sobbed. 'He only has to hang his trousers ovver th' end o' t' bed and I catch on. Me mum'll kill him. She'd no idea it was still goin' on. An' she'll want me to see that foreign doctor in Salford again. I can't go through wi' it. I thought I were goin' t' die last time. They pull all your insides out, you're bleedin' for weeks and weeks after. I'll run away first. No one's layin' a finger on me, not this time!'

And I put my arm round her. 'You'll be awreet. Me an' Bill'll look after you,' I said.

*

**Mum had said** to take the washing in if it started to rain and I wouldn't normally have bothered, but my best jeans were out on the line. So when Ivy shouted up that it was snowing I crawled out from under the duvet and thumped downstairs. I'd forgotten about the toaster on the doorstep and, in my haste to get at the jeans, accidentally booted it, sending it skidding across the flags. Crumbs and what looked like bits of singed paper sprayed out of the slot. I ran across the lawn, tugged at the clothes in turn till they pinged off the washing line, pegs left swinging on the blue nylon rope or catapulted onto the lawn, I didn't care, then laid the bundle over my arm and scooted back to the house. It was bitterly cold. On the way I scooped up the toaster, American-football style, and carried it under the other arm. I slammed the back door behind me and dumped everything in a heap on the floor.

'Nan says you're getting a Range Rover,' Ivy called from the lounge.

'Yeah, right,' I shouted back. Total bloody nut-house. I started to examine the toaster.

Dear Mrs *charred bit*
    Imagine what you could do with a loan for £10,000! A new *charred bit* perhaps, *charred bit charred bit* or maybe the holiday you've been promising yourself.

I extracted the rest of the letter and flipped open the

pedal bin where it could go with all the other loan offers we'd had that week. Even Nan gets them. God knows what she'd spend £10,000 on. Pontefract cakes, maybe, except she's not allowed them because they play havoc with what's left of her bowels. Then I turned the toaster upside down and gave it a good shake. More flakes came out, devil's confetti, but there was something still wedged inside. I brought it over to the window and picked a table knife up off the draining board. I could definitely see folded paper when I tilted the slot towards the light. I fished around, got the blade underneath and eased the thing out.

'What's so funny?' asked Ivy from the doorway. She moved over to the pile of clothes and automatically began to pick them up one by one, smooth them out and stack them neatly on top of the fridge. 'Something's tickled you.'

'It'd take too long to explain,' I said, unfolding the ruined Keats essay and watching as it disintegrated in my hands. My shoulders shook uncontrollably and tears of laughter started to run down my face.

'Eeh, I like to hear her laugh,' called Nan. 'She's a bonny laugh but we never hear it these days.'

'Well, she's certainly laughing now,' commented Ivy as I lay down on the tiles, helpless, and put the essay over my face.

*

SHE WENT down to London first, the story was she was going to try for an actress, and I handed my notice in two weeks later. We'd found her a place at a Mother and Baby Home run by a charity, although they wouldn't tek her till she were six months. So we stayed down t' road wi' Bill's sister Annie in Finchley; she'd been widowed two years before, and she was glad o' t' company. She had a funny daughter, Theresa, face like a line of wet washin'. Now she must have been about sixteen too but very backward, and she kept asking why Jessie was so fat. I heard Annie telling her afterwards it was because Jessie had been a Bad Girl, and to watch herself or she'd end up t' same way. Except I don't think any man ever went near her, she were so sour.

Hope Lodge, they called the home. I'd heard about it through the Mothers' Union: never dreamt I'd ever have anything to do wi' it. It weren't a nice place, though. Big Victorian brick house, slippery floors, long dark corridors. I can smell the disinfectant now. They had their own rooms, the girls, but that made it worse apparently. You could hear 'em cryin' at night, Jessie said, behind the doors. She'd not been there above a fortnight when she announced, 'I'm not stoppin' here, Nance. Let me come back to Annie's wi' you. It's awful. We're not allowed to use t' front door, did you know? And they make you go to church on Sundays but you have to stand at t' back so none o' t' congregation can see you.' I talked her round. I said, 'You have to stay where there's nurses and doctors. They have to keep a special eye on such as you, with you being so young. You'll get t' best care here, love. I'll come every day, look after you.' I were terrified she'd change her mind, if you want to know. Or disappear, or do herself a mischief. I knew she hadn't thought it through.

When she went into labour, five weeks early, it was at night and I didn't know. It was quick, too, just over four hours. The nurses said she was mustard. 'I've never known such a foul-mouthed creature,' one of them told me, 'and we hear some things within these four walls, I can tell you.' She said they were cruel, wouldn't give her anything for the pain. 'It was unbelievable. I'm NEVER goin' through that again, I'll tell you that for nowt. An' the doctor, he came in near th' end and never spoke a word, not one word. I hope he rots in hell, I hope they all do.'

I couldn't think of anything except that baby. 'Do you still want me to take her?' I asked. My heart was in my mouth. 'Oh, yes,' she says straight away, 'you can have her. I don't want her.' And I went hot and cold all over.

Bill came down to bring me home, stayed a week, and when I got back everyone was agog. He'd put it about that I'd been nursing a sick relative. So then I told them that had been a white lie because, although I was thrilled to be expecting finally, I was worried it might go wrong, what with my age. I don't know if they believed me or not. It didn't matter. No one ever really asked, whatever they thought in private. A nine-day wonder, that's all it was. And that first Sunday they said prayers at church for me and t' little one, and I didn't feel a bit guilty. 'It's our secret,' I told the Lord. 'I won't say owt if you don't.'

*

We have no radiators in our house, of course, nothing so useful, so I had my jeans laid out on the bed with a hair-dryer nozzle up one leg. Downstairs the front door banged and I heard Ivy's voice, then Mum's (sounding strangely muffled). I transferred the nozzle to the other leg and thought about meeting up with Daniel, that it wasn't going to be the ordeal I'd first thought: I could almost say I liked him. Not *that* way, of course, he was too fucking weird. Funny, though. He seemed to understand me more than anyone else at school. Maybe I was the weirdo.

I switched off the hairdryer, and in the sudden silence heard Mum's bedroom door click shut. Ivy shouted up, 'I'll bring you some Milk of Magnesia in a sec, love, you get your head down for half an hour. I'll just hang your mac out on the maiden.' Another crisis, then.

When I felt at the ankle cuffs the denim was more or less dry, so I pulled down my trackie bottoms, eased the elastic over my feet, and stepped into my jeans.

I stopped. Looked at myself in the full-length mirror. Something wasn't right. Even as they got to my knees I knew they weren't going to do up over my rounded belly.

Fate had got me after all.

# Chapter Five

*THIIIINGS CAN ONLY get better.* It must be true, it was on TV. But you tell me what political party could sort out my problems. If I thought it would really make a difference I'd be down that polling booth at 7 a.m., but nobody really cares about people like us, stuck at home with only the insane for company.

We save this country a fortune and where does it all go? Bloody subsidies for bloody London opera houses and the like. I'd vote Monster Raving Loony if I could actually be bothered, but I haven't got the energy. It's all right them offering a lift to the polling station, but I bet none of them would be prepared to change Nan's bag while I was out exercising my democratic right.

Politicians, they want to try living in the real world.

*

'You'll have to do a test,' said Daniel, his face blurry through my tears. We were sitting in Tiggy's Italian coffee bar at a Formica-topped table covered with wet ring-marks. I hadn't meant to say anything, but it was all my head was full of, there wasn't room for anything else.

Besides, somehow I thought he'd know what to do. He seemed that sort.

'I *can't.*'

'Yes, you can. Look, it's probably a false alarm. I mean, you don't *look* pregnant, if it's any consolation. How far are you meant to be along?'

'About three and a half months, if I'm right.' I began to draw miserable lines in the sugar with the end of my spoon. 'God, I just can't be. Not me. Anyone else, but not *me.*'

'It might simply be too many Easter eggs. Or a hormonal imbalance; have you been sprouting hairs on your chin?'

'Oh, for God's sake, Daniel, it's not something to joke about!'

He drooped his head. 'Sorry.'

'Do you *promise* not to tell anyone about this? I couldn't bear the thought of the other girls . . .'

'As if I would.' He seemed really hurt. 'I don't do that sort of thing. Besides, who have I got to tell? Look, if it's not too personal a question, have your periods stopped?'

'*Daniel!* Honestly!'

'Well, it's a bit crucial, Charlotte. I mean, I'm only a mere male but even I can see there might be a connection.'

'Well, yes and no. Oh, I can't start going into details, it's too gross. And especially not with you. You don't talk about things like that, it's not polite.'

He shrugged. 'We talk about everything biological in our house. It's with my dad being a GP. No bodily function is taboo. They used to take us to a naturist beach in

Greece every year, until I started getting what my mother called "stirrings".'

'That's because you're Middle Class, probably. In our house everything's taboo, there are no safe subjects, so mostly we don't talk. Well, Nan does, but she doesn't count because none of it makes any sense.' The knowledge of why I was here settled on my shoulders again and I slumped forward. 'Oh, Daniel, what am I going to do?'

'Wait here,' he said, rising to his feet. 'Don't move a muscle.' And he dived out of the shop.

I waited and watched through the window. Shoppers crowded past, carefree. Every other figure was loaded with personal irony: the willowy pair of teenage girls with flat stomachs, laughing at some private joke; the smart brisk career woman whose life was clearly going places; the – oh, horror – hugely pregnant mum holding a toddler on reins and peering into the cafe, her hand shading her weary brow. I stared back. Surely it must hurt when your body got to that size? What happened to your skin? Might it not split, like a dropped tomato? How did her trousers not fall down? How could she see what she was doing when she went to the toilet?

'Give the woman a break,' said Daniel, sitting down again and sliding a Boots bag across at me. I realized I was gaping with horror, and looked away quickly.

'Is that what I think it is?'

'Uh-huh. Now, nip to the toilets, sort yourself out and then come with me.'

'Where?'

'Do as you're told. Come on.' He pulled me up and shepherded me to the back of the cafe.

Once in the cubicle I undid the cellophane, then opened the box. A white plastic felt-tip thing slid out. I had a good look at it, pulled the cap off, then fished out the instruction leaflet and unpleated it. So, you just peed on the end of the stick; two minutes later it was all over bar the shouting.

When I came out Daniel was waiting. 'Well?'

'I haven't looked yet.'

'Good.'

He grabbed my hand and pulled me out onto the street.

'Where are we going?' I shouted as he yanked me through the crowds.

'Just come on!'

We ran and ran, up Standishgate, down Market Street and Parson's Walk, into Mesnes Park Terrace and through to the park.

'Quick!' We dashed through the iron gates and dived for the grass. I sort of fell, then rolled over and lay back, gasping. 'It's not too wet, is it?' he asked, patting around with his palm.

'Yeah, it's bloody soaking but I don't care.' I was still panting like mad. 'What's going on?'

He squatted beside me. 'Unwrap the test. Go on.' He nodded encouragingly.

I sat up, drew the bag out of my jacket pocket and held up the box. My fingernail slid under the cardboard flap. 'I know what I'm looking for, I read the blurb. If the second window's empty, I'm in the clear . . . Oh, God, Daniel, oh, God. Oh, no.'

He leaned over to peer at the two blue lines. The air

felt still around us. It was one of those moments when the universe pivots and you know nothing's ever going to be the same again.

Daniel looked shattered. 'Oh, Charlotte, I'm sorry. I was so sure it was going to be OK. I was so sure.'

Don't touch me! I thought, but he didn't. He set his jaw and gazed out to the tree tops. I could tell he didn't have a clue what to say and I wished to God I could snap my fingers and make him vanish.

I don't know how long we sat there on the damp grass. I wasn't thinking proper thoughts, just giving in to a squeezing sensation round my ribcage and a feeling like my heart was going to explode. I just kept staring at the sun going in, out, flirting with the clouds, but there was no heat. I was chilled right through.

'Your teeth are chattering,' said Daniel, wrenching his focus back to me. 'Maybe we should go.'

I hate you, I thought. If it wasn't for you, I wouldn't have known. It's your fault, you speccy weirdo bastard. I was waiting for the sky to cave in, or one of those giant pointing fingers to come pushing out of the heavens. *It could be YOU – and it IS!* How could things be going on as normal around me, the woman walking the Airedale, the kid wobbling around on a bike, when my life was over? It wasn't fucking FAIR.

But then I thought, it could still be wrong, the test. It only said 98% accurate. That meant two in every hundred *weren't*. So, say they sold, I don't know, five hundred a week nationwide, somewhere in Britain ten women would be shitting themselves for nothing. And one of them might be me. After all, I had had a period, so that proved it. It was probably OK after all. I'd sneak one of my mum's water tablets when I got home, see if I could shift some of this pot belly. Because, at the end of the day, I was me, Me, and there was no way *I* could be pregnant. Encouraged, I began to hunt in my pocket for the instruction leaflet.

'I think,' said Daniel cautiously, 'your next step is probably to get checked out at the doctor's. You might need to act quite quickly, depending . . .' He trailed off.

I think I went a bit mental.

'What the FUCK is it to do with YOU?' I gave him a shove and he nearly toppled. His glasses fell off and landed in the wet grass, and that made me hate him even more. 'It's MY body! MY problem! You have NO idea about ANYTHING. Just, just,' my arms were waving pointlessly, 'get out of my HEAD!' As Daniel tried to wipe his spattered lenses on his sleeve I struggled up, clutching the white plastic stick with its parallel lines of doom. 'And you can FUCK OFF too!' I told it, ramming it into the soil like a tent peg and stamping it down. I turned and stalked off, towards the wobbly kid.

'I don't know why you're so cross with *me*,' I heard Daniel call, then mutter, 'I'm not the one who got you pregnant.'

I broke into a run.

\*

THE TRAINS IN my head came back again last night. Details change, but the dream's recurring in its basic plot: I'm trying to go somewhere (although the exact destination's always pretty vague) but the train I'm on never gets there. There's always some crisis; I'm on the wrong train, or it won't leave the station, or it turns into a wheelbarrow. Sometimes it never comes at all. I wake with a terrible sense of panic, and loss.

Not hard to interpret that particular sequence of symbols, any cod-psychologist could work it out. I wonder, though, if I ever got my life together, would the trains actually Get There, or would the dreams simply stop?

Sometimes in the morning, before I get up, I lie for a few seconds and my heart's strung out with nostalgia for something I can't even identify.

I got to school at 9.10 that Monday, even though I'm not technically paid till half-past: I wanted a clear field. It was eerily quiet. Everyone was in assembly (except for Sylv who's let off the daily spiritual injection to man the phones). I tiptoed past the main office, turned the corner and trotted quickly down the long corridor. That morning's hymn floated out to greet me.

> 'The trivial round, the common task
> Should furnish all we ought to ask'

sang the children flatly, northernly. And yes, when I peeped through the double doors Mr Fairbrother was standing at the front, hymn book aloft, a trumpet and a traffic cone at his feet (he likes his visual aids, does Mr F. 'I hear and I forget, I see and I remember,' he's always quoting at us). So I had about five minutes. I hurried back up to the reception area, peered round the corner, All Clear, and scuttled across to Mr F's office.

Once inside I dumped the carrier bag containing the

cagoule on his chair where he couldn't miss it. I'd wondered about a note with it, but what do you say? 'Sorry I
puked on your shoes'? My eyes travelled round the room
for a moment. Shelves of box files and books, union memos
and selected children's art-work displayed on a pinboard;
on the floor by the far wall a giant ammonite, an inflatable
hammer, a monkey puppet, a hamster cage, a devil mask
(as I said, he does like his props); in the corner a box of
confiscated footballs, cap guns, poking devices, etc. On
his desk was his parents' wedding photo and a selection of
horrible ornaments bought for him by various kids over
the years. It was the room of a kind man. Oh how, how,
how I had messed up.

Time to go. I listened at the door, then opened it
slowly.

'Everything all right?' Sylv's voice made me jump
about a mile in the air. She was standing across the corridor, lipsticked coffee cup in hand, waiting for me. 'He's in
assembly. But you know that.'

I could have told her. I could have beckoned her into
the office, closed the door and taken her through the whole
sad story, she'd have loved that. Sworn her to secrecy (a
slim chance but a chance nevertheless). But I couldn't do it.
I said, 'I was just checking Lost Property,' and she stared at
me so hard her eyebrows nearly disappeared into her hair-
line. 'Oh, piss off, you poisonous old witch,' I nearly said.
Nearly.

The morning seemed to last forever. By ten I was sitting
in the quiet corner with the remedial group helping them
fill in worksheets on Area. We'd all drawn round our
hands and agreed that mine was the biggest, and I was

trying to count away the recollections of Sunday with square centimetres.

'How old are you, Miss?' asked Dale. They do that, remedials, constantly try to distract you with personal chat.

'That's rude,' said Lisa promptly. 'You shouldn't ask a lady that.'

'I think she's about twenty-five,' persisted Dale. He had a long face with a large jaw, and chewed his pencils compulsively.

'No,' I smiled. 'I'm afraid I'm a bit older than that.'

'Fifty?' offered Lisa. 'You've a look of my gran, and she's just had her fiftieth birthday.'

'When's your birthday, Miss?' asked Dale, spitting splinters of mashed-up wood across the table.

'Mine's next week,' said fat Philip, waking up. 'I'm gettin' a Furby.'

'You big poof,' said Dale. 'You big girl.'

The groups moved round and I helped put up some backing paper for a display on Transport. Mr F's disappointed face and Sylv's peevish one were printed on every sheet of sugar paper. Each time I pulled the trigger on the staple gun it felt like I was driving staples into my own temples. Finally I asked Pauline if I could go and get a paracetamol.

'Then go and sit in the staff room,' she said. 'There's only ten minutes to break, I'll clear up here.' I must have looked really poorly.

Sylv's the guardian of the paracetamol unfortunately but, hooray, she wasn't in the office so I unlocked the cabinet and helped myself, swigging them down with a mug of cold water. From there I went straight to the staff room where I heard through the half-open door: '. . . *saw them embracing in the car park of the Feathers, apparently'*. So I did a smart U-turn and walked back along the corridor, and met Mr F coming in the opposite direction.

'Thanks for the, ahm, bag, ah . . .' he said as he drew near.

'Oh, no bother. Thanks.' I couldn't look him in the eye. Keep walking, I told him silently. He did, and I pushed out through the swing doors into the playground and breathed again. My whole body felt hot and I knew my cheeks were burning. Maybe it was the menopause, come early. That'd be just about my luck.

The bell went and children began to trickle out. I walked across the rec over the patches of slush and perched with the edge of my bottom on the low wall by the gates, wishing I had a coffee. 'Hey, Miss?' Dale appeared at my elbow. There were tiny flecks of red paint all over his lips off the crayon he'd been eating. 'Look! I did you a card. For your birthday. You can save it, like, and bring it out when it's time.' He handed me a folded piece of centimetre-squared paper with two pencil figures drawn on the front. One was lying down in what appeared to be a pool of blood. 'It's OK, he's a baddie,' explained Dale, pointing. 'The other's Gravekeeper, he saves the world.' He spread his arms out like wings, then let them flop to his sides.

'Nice trick if you can do it,' I said, opening the card up. *To a grat teasher*, it said. *Meny happy retuns.* You're not supposed to touch the pupils, the times being what they are, but I leant forward and gave him a hug. On these slender shafts of sunlight sanity seems to turn, at times. 'You've made my day,' I told him warmly. He stepped back slightly. 'No, really. You've redeemed the moment, you've given me the impetus to lurch forward into the next inevitable crisis. You've provided a tiny spark of light in a tunnel of gloom. Dale, you are a superhero within your own galaxy.'

'Steady on, Miss,' he said.

\*

I waited a week and did another test, also positive, so that was that. Then I sorted all my clothes out and ended up with a capsule wardrobe of fleeces and baggy jumpers and tube skirts and leggings. Standing naked before the mirror now there was no doubt. My whole body had started to change. It wasn't mine any more. It belonged to the thing inside.

At school I avoided Daniel, avoided everyone, really. Spent a lot of time in the library, books open, looking out the window. Well, how could I join in the common-room chit-chat about clothes, and boys, and weight, and fall-outs? In the smart corner it was all Tony Blair and his New Vision, but I couldn't engage with any of it. The very word *Labour* turned my insides to water. None of it seemed real; it was as if there was a big glass wall between me and the others. I'd realized in the park, nothing was going to be the same ever again, but it was taking time for the extent of it to sink in. I mean, I couldn't see further than the pregnancy. There was the immediate problem of trying not to look fat, and (more hazily) steeling myself up for the hoo-ha when everyone found out, not least my mother, who was definitely going to have some kind of breakdown. On the very far horizon was the prospect of giving birth, which I'd heard was quite painful, and I wasn't very good with pain. But after that? I knew there was going to be a baby at the end of it, but I couldn't get my head round it. Not *me*, not a *baby*.

Unless I decided there wasn't. But, as Daniel, damn him, had pointed out, I was going to have to get my skates on if I wanted to go down that route. I didn't even know what they did. Hoovered you out, a girl had once told me. It didn't sound too awful in that respect, but even I could see there was probably more to it than a quick trip to the Outpatients'.

I think it was the toes that were bothering me. We'd had a video on pregnancy, in Year 10. It showed the foetus wiggling about, sucking its thumb and kicking its skinny legs with their little splayed toes, then the narrator had said, *See if you can guess how old this baby is.* The teacher had paused the tape and we'd had a go, most of us thought about five months. Then she switched the video back on and the answer had been fourteen weeks. *See how the heart, with its four chambers, is already beating*, the narrator had continued. *In fact, a heart beat can be detected at just six weeks of development.* The miracle of creation. It was a sod.

So what a mature and sensible person would have been doing at this stage of the game was weighing things up, the fucked-up life versus the other, differently fucked-up life, and seeing which she thought she could honestly cope with. What a mature person would do was tell their mother, see a doctor, get a counsellor. Face up to it all, and pronto.

But I was frozen. Because it still couldn't be true; it couldn't be me who was going through this. I was going to slide the pregnancy under the lining paper of the chest of drawers in the spare room of my mind. Something would turn up, surely.

*

HE CAME STRIDING across the tarmac, kids buzzing round him like flies.

'Here,' he said. 'No sugar.' I took the steaming mug off him and studied the ground while he scanned the sky above my head. 'Don't worry about Sunday, anyway. These things happen. I was once very ill after a rogue sausage roll from a garage.' He nodded at my bare fore-arms; my coat was still in the staff room. 'Don't catch cold, will you?'

He walked away, and was immediately accosted by a very small Year 1 boy, tugging at his trouser leg and pointing over to the football pitch. Mr F bent down to hear the tale and it was like a scene from *Goodbye Mr Chips*, except that Mr F looks more like Syd Little than Robert Donat.

I'd give them breaktime to get it out of their system, then I was going back inside.

*

I was having a conversation with Daniel in my bedroom. He wasn't actually there, I'd just conjured him up for the purposes of rational debate.

'I know you *want* to see Paul again. But all I'm asking is, have you thought through the reasons behind it?' Daniel sat scrunched up in the beanbag chair, his knees to his chin. I was at the desk, doodling boxes and clouds on the flyleaf of *Sense and Sensibility*.

'He's got a right to know,' I said sulkily. I wanted to see Paul so much it was like toothache; I couldn't keep still, couldn't get comfortable. Today was Sunday, which always makes things worse. There's something about Sundays which makes you rattle around inside yourself, even in these exciting days of car boot sales and extended trading hours. Mum had gone to Do-It-All to get some polystyrene coving and Nan was downstairs playing dominoes with Ivy. I'd paced up and down my room so much I had a stitch in my groin; I thought I was going to go mad with indecision. Hence Daniel.

'He will know, sooner or later. You can't keep it a secret much longer. Unless you . . .'

'Yes, all right,' I said testily. 'I know the score.'

'What do you honestly expect his reaction to be?'

I wasn't ready to answer this question, even from myself. We tried again.

'In an ideal world,' Daniel pushed his imaginary glasses further up the bridge of his imaginary nose, 'what would you expect his reaction to be?'

That was better. 'Well, he'd be totally supportive, for a start. He'd say, "Whatever you want to do, Charlie, I'll stand by you." '

'And what *do* you want to do?'

'I want . . . I want not to be pregnant in the first place.' I heard my voice rise to a wail.

Daniel sighed heavily. 'Come on, Charlotte, grow up now. Are you saying you want an abortion?'

'I—' Suddenly, out of the corner of my eye, I saw the door handle turn and my heart jumped in horror. The door swung open and Nan shuffled in. 'Ivy's doin' some toasted teacakes, d' you want one?'

'Oh, Nan, thank God it's only you. I thought it was Mum.'

Nan smiled blankly. 'Toasted teacakes,' she said.

'Oh, no, you're OK. I'll wait till later. I'm not hungry.'

'Eeh, I don't know. Not hungry. I could eyt a buttered frog.' She chuckled at her own joke and retreated, pulling the door to after her. I waited till I heard it click, then turned my attention to Daniel again.

'Well, are you going to . . . ?'

'It depends what *he* wants. If he came with me while they did it, if he was really nice and we got back together and he let me talk about it afterwards, and he never mentioned Jeanette Piper or Chrissy . . .'

'If pigs went flying past the window.'

'Oh, ha-fucking-ha.' I vanished him, then sat in a temper drawing cartoon bombs and lightning bolts.

Julia and Anya materialized on the bed, unbidden.

'Isn't it the absolute worst thing you can think of, though,' Anya was saying.

'Oh, yeah. Well, cancer would be pretty bad, and losing both your parents in a car crash.'

'Or being permanently disfigured, with, like, acid or something. You know, having a glass eye or whatever.'

'Or being a quadriplegic.'

'Yeah.'

'But being pregnant's pretty horrendous. I mean, your whole life messed up. Can you imagine what your mum would say?'

They both pulled manic faces and Julia put her hands round her throat and made strangling noises. 'I'd just die. Wouldn't you?'

'Oh, God, yeah. Awful. Completely fucking awful.'

'What I don't understand, though,' Julia wound a strand of glossy hair round and round her finger, 'what I don't get is, how she let it happen. I mean, she's supposed to be so clever. She got an A in that last History module, the one she was supposed to have ballsed up.'

'Yeah, I know. And I tell you what, I didn't even really know she had a boyfriend. Actually, she can be a right miserable cow, she never tells you anything. To be honest, I still had her down as a virgin.'

'They say it's the quiet ones,' sniggered Julia. Anya began to giggle, then Julia started too. 'Oh, shit, we are awful. 'S not funny. Poor Charlotte.'

'Yeah, poor old Charlotte.'

**Three identical** culs-de-sac run off Barrow Road; Paul's house is down the second. Not much had changed since I last went, except the bus shelter now had no roof at all, and the form was completely slatless, just two thick concrete stands five feet apart rising out of the tyre-marked grass. I remembered when I was a little girl, three old men in caps and mufflers used to always be sitting there, smoking away, gossiping. They were sort of like custodians of the highway, Neighbourhood Watch. Nan knew who they all were, used to say howdo and get a nod. Then after a few years there were two, then only one old man, sitting on his own, clouded in blue smoke. One day there was no one at all, and after that the bench started to get taken apart. I think maybe Bank Top didn't used to be so crap, something went wrong with the people.

The Alsatian had gone too. The yard was bare except for a chewed rubber ball and a length of chain.

Mr Bentham let me in; I could tell he was surprised.

'Paul! Paul!' he shouted up the stairs. 'You've gorra visitor!'

Paul's face peered over the banister and he mouthed *'kin 'ell* when he saw me. But when he didn't move I climbed up after him.

By the time we got inside his room I was out of breath and sweating.

'What d'you want?' he asked gracelessly.

I saw with a pang that he was still as handsome, that the Man U duvet looked sex-rumpled, that someone had bought him a white teddy with heart-shaped paws which he'd stuck on top of his computer.

'Can I sit down?'

He just shrugged, so I stayed where I was, shoulder to shoulder with David Beckham. The moment twisted slowly on its long thread. I couldn't make my mouth work, though my brain was racing, until:

'Nice bear,' I said, like a pillock.

'Oh. Yeah.' He snickered awkwardly, looking all round the room, everywhere except at me. 'Shit, y' know, seems really weird—' He allowed himself a glance in my direction. *All those times I was here,* I was thinking, *and the last few weeks, we never knew, I had cells dividing inside me. 2, 4, 8, 16, an exponential time bomb. Cells all drifting to their allotted place like synchronized swimmers. Shape-shifting: amoeba to blackberry, to shrimp, alien, baby. There's a baby under this fleece. Hallo, Dad.*

'Hey, are you all right? You look a bit – funny.'

I took heart from what might have been concern in his voice and stepped forward. 'Paul, I – no, I'm not all right. I, I'm—' My hand dipped automatically to my stomach and his eyes followed it, then widened. Then his brows came down and his whole face went hard.

'Paul?'

'Oh, no. Oh, no, not that one. I do *not* want to hear this! I do not fucking want to hear this!' He turned right away and put his hands on the back of his neck, blocking me out. Any minute now, I thought, he's going to put his fingers in his ears and start humming.

'Paul, you've got to know—'

'Fuck OFF!' he shouted over me. 'Don't try and put this one on me. This is your fault. Christ! You stupid, stupid bitch!' He thumped the wall, then leant on it, shoulders hunched, still with his back to me. He looked like a three-year-old whose mum has refused to let him go on the Tigger ride outside Tesco's.

There was silence while I fought the urge to run down the stairs, through the door and across the Continent; run for ever, run the pregnancy away.

'I'm sorry, Paul, it's true.'

'Aw, Jesus.' He groaned and finally turned back round to face me. 'You've gotta be wrong. It weren't like we didn't use owt. Loads of girls have scares, it dun't mean a thing. You've just got yourself in a state.'

'I did a test.'

He put his hand over his mouth and swore behind it. 'It is yours.'

He took his hand away from his chin and stared at me. 'No, Charlotte. That's where you're wrong. It's yours. It's all yours. I don't want fuck all to do wi' it.'

**At least you know** where you stand. At least you know where you stand.

I don't remember walking back home but here I was under the duvet in my bedroom, so I suppose I must have done. Maybe I'd been asleep, because I was very hot and my mouth was dry. Maybe it had been a dream. – Maybe it had *all* been a dream! – But no, my hand strayed down over my bump, and Paul's parting shot still rang in my ears. I'd put my Walkman on but it'd made no difference, Paul was louder. That exact intonation would be etched into my brain all my life, long after his features had become vague. I'd probably die with that last sentence replaying itself.

I snuggled down further into the bed. When I was very little and Mum and I still got on, she used to let me make a Nest at bedtime out of the duvet. Then she'd peer in and pretend she couldn't see me and that she was going. I'd shoot out from underneath, all flushed and ruffled, and shriek, 'Story!' and she'd pretend to be incredibly surprised. She used to read to me every night, long after I could read myself. If only I could be little again. You don't appreciate it at the time.

I must have drifted off again because the tape was on side two and Nan was shaking me gently.

'A shut mouth keeps flies out,' she was saying when I lifted up the earphones.

'You what?'

Nan settled on the bed and leant over to stroke my hair. Normally I'd have had to fight the urge to squirm away; not that I don't love her, I just get really touchy about my personal space sometimes. But this time I lay there quietly, glad of the sympathy. After a while she said; 'You're havin' a baby, then.'

I nearly jumped out of my skin.

'*Nan!*'

'Don't you worry, it'll be awreet. We'll see you through.' She fished under the duvet for my hand and took it in her gnarled fingers. The flesh moved loosely over the bones, as if it was ready to come away. I shuddered and closed my eyes, tears brimming out from between the lashes.

'Oh, Nan.'

'Charlotte, love.' She gripped my hand tighter.

'*Please* don't tell Mum. Not yet. I can't face her.'

She half-smiled. 'I know all sorts as I've never towd.' (Of course you do, I thought.) 'Tha maun fret, I'll not say owt till you're ready.'

Beside my ear the Walkman played:

> *You walk out of trouble*
> *Into trouble*
> *Out of trouble*
> *Into trouble*
> *And this is your life*
> *This is your life*

'Oh, Nan, why is everything such a mess? Why me?'

'Eeh, lamb,' she said. 'You'll be awreet, you'll see. God's good.'

'How *can* I be?'

But she just shook her head and carried on stroking my hair. I closed my eyes, let the earphones fall back.

\*

MY MOTHER was eighteen when she had me, Jimmy was born two years later. But she couldn't hold my father. Harold Fenton was a restless soul, his own mother couldn't make moss nor sand of him. I think he loved us, though. He wouldn't marry my mother, but he gave us his surname for a middle name, so's everyone would know who we were. Nancy Fenton Marsh. I hated it, still hate it today. Fillin' in forms and such; whose business is it anyway? Because in them days, the sin fell on the childer as well as the mother. But there was a lot of it about.

She were allus short of money, that's why she had to tek in washin', an' it were a right palaver in them days; two dolly tubs, a coal boiler, scrubbing board, mangle, it took for ever. She never had a home of her own either. The summer before I was born she'd sit out every evenin' in her parents' back yard wearing her nightie and her dad's overcoat, there were nowt else as'd fit. She said it was a terrible labour: when they held me up and said, 'Polly, it's a girl,' she told them she didn't care if it was a brass monkey so long as it was out.

Once, when I was about six and Jimmy four, we were waitin' at a bus stop to go to Wigan an' a smartish woman came and stood alongside us. There was a bus comin' and my mother just bundled us on. I said, 'Mam, this in't our bus, where are we goin'?' 'Never you mind,' she said. It turned out this woman was my father's latest fancy piece. We went all the way to Worsley before my mother came to herself. He had a lot of women, she told me before she died, but she said he was her man and that was that. 'At least he never drank,' she used to say.

She'd be thinkin' of her father, Peter Marsh. Her mother, Florrie, had a grim time of it even though she had a husband. They'd married because she was expectin' and then after, she had three children die in their first year. The doctor told her not to risk any more or she'd damage her own health – all she could think about was that at last she could sleep in the front bedroom with Polly, away from him. He were mean, you see; she allus struggled to get money out of him because he spent it all on drink. She used send Polly to the colliery gates to try to get some of his wages off him before he went in t' pub (he never came straight home when there was brass to spend) but then that would get him in a rage. I think she were relieved when he went to join the Loyal North Lancashires in 1917, except when he got there, there were so few on 'em left he had to join up with the East Surreys. He sent some beautiful silk postcards though, 'Greetings from France', all embroidered with flags and flowers, and his slow big pencil writing on the back. Then he was hit by a shell, or at least he jumped into a hole to avoid one, and got buried by a wave of mud. They'd just been wondering how to break it to him about the baby, me, when they got the telegram. He was only forty-two.'

My father tried to join up as well at seventeen, but it'd finished by the time he got there, typically. I don't suppose he were too bothered. My mother's big fear was that she'd be made a widow too, but never being married she wouldn't have qualified anyway. She lost him young, though; two days after his thirty-first birthday he was knocked down in Manchester, outside the Corn Exchange. And I did miss him, even though he'd been in and out of our house like a cat. We both cried over him. He was my dad. And you need your dad when you're growing up. Well, I think you do, anyroad. Family's everythin' when it comes down to it.

*

I woke with a jolt. The tape had finished and my earphones were hissing. I unhooked myself and struggled out of the duvet.

'I can't have this baby, Nan. I've decided.'

From the end of the bed Nan snored gently. I folded the covers over her and tiptoed out of the room.

# Chapter Six

I WENT ON a blind date with Pauline's brother's friend from tai kwon-do class. 'He's got a smashin' personality,' Pauline had said. Ugly as sin, then, I thought. But it was worse than that. When I walked into the Working Men's and saw him propped against the bar it was like that old music hall joke, Don't stand up, oh I see you already have. He came about level with my nose. That wouldn't necessarily have been a problem, only he looked like Ken Dodd and talked like Roy Chubby Brown. I sat through fifty minutes of filth, then he said, 'I've got good manners, me. Tits before fanny,' and laughed uproariously. 'Wanker,' I hissed, picking up my bag. 'Ah, get away, you love it really, you ladies,' he grinned. 'Have you ever actually *had* sex with anyone?' I asked nastily. That shut him up.

'His twin brother's on a kidney machine, you have to make allowances,' said Pauline the next day.

I gave her a hard stare. 'Why? Why should I? No one does for me.'

She just turned away and started counting Tesco's computer vouchers. Cow.

\*

'My God, you're here!'

Daniel was sitting in the window of Tiggy's, looking anxious.

'Did you think I wouldn't be?' he asked.

'Well, under the circumstances . . . I'd have stood me up, without a doubt.' I slumped down beside him. My bulge nearly came up to the edge of the table. 'I don't know what to say. I've been such a bitch.'

'No, no, well yes, actually.'

We laughed nervously.

'Sorry.'

'Hormones under the bridge. This thing's too important to fall out over.' Fingers through hair, worried frown. 'So, you really have decided, then?'

'Oh, yeah.' I kept my voice low. 'It's not practical. I could no more look after a baby than fly to the moon. Think about it. Mum's life would be in tatters, I'd have to throw in my university place and stay, God, stay at home for *years*, it doesn't bear thinking about. And I know I'd make a terrible mother, I'm just not the sort. I've been really stupid, I should just have got on with sorting things out. I mean, the father . . .'

My voice began to quaver and my eyes pricked.

'Say no more.'

An enormously fat chef carrying a tray of dirty cups squeezed past our table, his apron straining over his stomach. 'Keep your hair on, we're short-staffed,' he barked at an old biddy in the corner. Everyone turned to see. The biddy stuck two fingers up at his back, then swept all the sachets of salt and pepper into her handbag.

'Now *he* looks pregnant. You're a positive sylph

compared to him. Look, I'll get you a milkshake while you cast your eye over these.' Daniel began pulling some folded sheets of paper out of the pocket of his jeans.

While he was at the counter I looked through the pages he'd printed off the Internet. *An abortion is legal until the 24th week of pregnancy*, I read. *There is an initial consultation with a doctor, but the woman can also see a counsellor if she wishes.* Hmm. Now there was an idea. I didn't want my head screwed up any more than it was already. On the other hand, they might try to persuade me to change my mind, and now I'd made the decision there was no way I was going back on it. Toes or not.

'Banana,' said Daniel putting the tall glass down on the table. 'They're all out of chocolate. Drink up, anyway, you need your calcium or your teeth will fall out. And you don't want to be toothless on top of everything else, do you?'

I tried to smile.

*In order to qualify for a same-day procedure, the woman must be under 19 weeks pregnant. If she is more than 19 weeks, she must stay overnight at the hospital or health care centre.*

Same-day procedure!

*It is generally accepted that there is very little risk associated with abortion.*

Toes.

'How far are you on?' asked Daniel gently.

I thought back and counted. 'I'm fairly sure. Eighteen weeks, I think. So I might be just in time. I could go to the clinic in the morning and be back by teatime, tell my mum I'd been to Manchester shopping.'

Buy some extra-large pads, pretend I had flu and rest up for a day or so. Maybe it wouldn't be so bad after all.

Daniel looked uncomfortable. 'Yeah, you might just about be OK. Only, they have this funny way of calculating.'

'What do you mean?' My heart began to thump.

'It's something I've heard my dad mention. They don't calculate from the actual date of, er, conception.' He dropped his gaze. 'They take it from the start of your last period. So—'

'You *what*?'

'So, well, that means you're not actually pregnant for the first two weeks or so of your pregnancy. As it were.'

'You've got to be wrong about that. That's ridiculous, it doesn't even make sense. I've never heard that one before.'

'Forget it. I'm probably wrong.'

As soon as he said it I knew he was probably right. 'So what you're saying is, that would make me nearer twenty.' I put my hands over my face and dragged them down over the skin. What a fucking mess.

Fat chef came out from behind the counter again and began shouting at two boys for breathing on the window and drawing pictures of willies. 'If yours looks like that you need to see a doctor,' he bellowed. 'I'll be phoning your headmaster. Which school d'you go to, when you're not playin' truant?' 'Best go before he sits on us!' one of them shouted, and they slid out of their seats and barged past us, colliding with the table and sending the sauce bottle spinning on its axis. We watched it lurch and fall. Tomato ketchup blobbed out slowly, mesmerizingly.

Stupid I may be, but I'm not daft. I knew that nineteen-week cut-off point must be there for a good reason, that a later operation was going to be a lot more traumatic than an early procedure. I'd been really ill having a wisdom tooth out once, vomiting everywhere and swollen up like a hamster. My insides still scrunched up when I thought about it.

Did they use a general anaesthetic? It would be best if they just put you under so you didn't know what was going on, but what if they didn't? What if it really, really hurt and you *saw what came out* and it lived in your head for ever and ever?

'Do you know what they do, exactly?' I made myself ask.

'No. The website didn't go into details. Just what's on those pages.'

I couldn't tell if he was lying or not. We looked at each other for a long time but he held his gaze steady. Panic rose suddenly up my throat like nausea, catching me off-guard. *Not me! This can't be happening to me! I can't cope, there has to be another way!*

I struggled to get a grip. My mum has these breathing exercises, they use them on anger-management courses; she does them if we have a big row. She doesn't know I use them too. In through the nose, count five, out through the mouth. I had – breathe – to stop the scary thoughts – breathe – and face up to – breathe – the practicalities – breathe. There was no other way. Breathe. It was going to be all right if I kept my head.

'What you could do,' Daniel was saying, 'is tell your

mum you're staying over at a friend's, a girlfriend's obviously . . .'

'Which is something I never do.'

'Work with me, Charlotte. You could tell her it was a special occasion, an eighteenth or something . . .'

'I'd have to bunk off school, they'd want a note.'

'It's half-term the week after next.'

'What if she rung up my friend's house to check?'

'Take your mobile.'

'I haven't got one!'

'Take mine, for God's sake!' Daniel sounded exasperated. 'You could tell her your friend lent it you so you'd always be contactable, even if you got in from clubbing very late. And give her a false number for the home telephone, then when you get back say, if she's tried it, that you must have made a mistake.'

Once again I looked at him with respect. 'God, you're a good liar.'

'Sign of intelligence.' He cocked his head, eyebrows raised. 'So, are we sorted?'

I closed my eyes and took another long deep breath. 'You are so . . . God, I don't know what to say.'

'It's no big deal. Just providing information.' He drained his cappuccino and leaned back.

'Well, yeah, then, I think I am, er, *sorted*. Bloody funny word for it, though.' I scanned the papers again while I waited for my insides to settle down. It looked as though everything might work out OK. Outside the two rude boys had returned and were busy writing FAT BASTAЯD on the steamed-up glass.

Then something on the papers caught my eye.

*For details of our tariff please click on our homepage.*

'Hey, Daniel, is this a private clinic?'

He nodded.

'Well, I can't afford it, how much is it going to be?'

'About five or six hundred pounds.'

The milkshake straw pinged out from under my fingers. 'You're joking.'

'It's no big deal—'

'Pardon me, it bloody is!'

'If you'd *listen* for a minute. I was going to say, my grandfather left me a few thou, it's sitting in a savings account doing nothing.'

'Oh, God! No way. I am *not* taking your money for this. No way. That's final.'

He put his hand out to me across the table but I didn't touch him. 'Charlotte, what choice do you have? You can pay me back when you get your student loan, whatever, if it'll make you feel better.'

'NHS?'

'If you want to start from scratch and find out all about that route, it's up to you. But to be honest, you're leaving it all a bit late.'

I wanted someone just to sort it out for me, take it all out of my hands. I felt utterly weary.

'Can you book me in, then?'

'I'll telephone as soon as I get home.'

Like he said, what choice did I have?

*

THIS IS THE WAY my world collapsed.

I'd gone on a mug-hunt. Opened the kitchen cupboard

and there was only Nan's china cup with roses, and an egg-cup with Blackpool Tower on it. Ridiculous, as we have about twenty mugs in this house.

I knew where they'd all be so I steamed upstairs and rapped on Charlotte's door. No answer. I didn't seem to have seen her properly for weeks, she kept disappearing off to her room with sandwiches and endless bloody yoghurts. She reckoned to be revising but I'd thought she might be brooding over that boy, so I'd left well alone.

I stood and listened: nothing. I hadn't heard her go out but she obviously wasn't in her bedroom. (Can I just say I don't normally go barging in; for one thing, I'm always frightened of what I might find – justifiably, as it's turned out. Oh WHY did I have to be RIGHT?)

I opened the door slowly, sniffing the fuggy teenage air, and looked round. Mugs, yes, several, dirty, dotted about; her fleece on the floor in a heap; Charlotte, *Charlotte* on the bed, half-sitting up against the headboard with her Walkman on and a book on her lap.

Her lap.

Through the thin T-shirt I saw, for the first time, the outline of her belly rising in an unmistakable swell. The paperback was perched on top and it looked like she was using one of those beanbag trays for the elderly. Her head whipped up and she stared. And the look in her eyes was mine, eighteen years ago.

\*

**Out of the corner** of my eye something moved and my whole body jolted with shock. I was *sure* I'd locked the door, but there she was, like Nosferatu only with permed hair, pointing a sharp fingernail at my belly. OhGod-ohgodohgod, worstnightmarescenario, major panic for about five seconds, then, weirdly, something else. Something else taking over.

The guitar solo on my Walkman faded out and a voice in my head spoke over it, *Don't panic. This is the worst it gets. What can she do to you, other than shout? And you're well used to that, it's water off a duck's back, isn't it? And, listen, you're her equal now, in this situation. You're one woman talking to another. She can't accuse you of anything she hasn't done herself. Keep calm and say what comes into your mind.*

\*

EIGHTEEN YEARS AGO, sitting at the table in tears and Nan kneeling at my side trying to hold my hand, except I kept pulling it away. Nan saying over and over again, 'Tha'll be awreet, we'll sort it out.' Me saying, shouting, 'How CAN it be, for God's sake?' She was frightened – I think I bullied her a bit after Dad died – but very sure. Very sure.

\*

**Then I was ready,** and from then on it wasn't like me speaking at all.

\*

'You STUPID—'

Charlotte wrenched her earphones off. Her face was twisted with some emotion, but it didn't look like shame.

'Oh, Christ, don't start—'

'What do you mean, *don't start*? I cannot *believe* what I'm seeing – ' I pointed in fury at her stomach – 'that my own daughter could have been so bloody bloody stupid – and, and *loose!*'

She put the book down deliberately on the duvet and shuffled herself more upright.

'What, like you, you mean? Exactly like you, Mum, or had you forgotten?'

She was too cool by half. I wanted to strangle her with my bare hands.

'Oh, no. How could I *possibly* forget? That's the point. All that sacrifice and now this slap in the face.' I clenched my fists so hard my nails dug into the palms. 'You should have taken notice of me, of my mistake! I thought, Jesus wept, if there was one thing I'd taught you, it was not to throw your life away—'

'Like you did.'

'Exactly!'

Her eyes were flashing anger back at me, as if *I'd* done something wrong.

'So, in fact, you wish I'd never been born? Isn't that what you've been burning to tell me for the past seventeen years?'

All that sacrifice.

'Well, you said it.'

'Well, then. That makes two of us, doesn't it?'

The words flew out and collided in midair. There was a moment of deafening silence.

Then Charlotte threw her book against the wall and it dropped down on top of her pot of pens, scattering them across the desk. At the same moment Nan walked in, wide-eyed with fear. She pushed past me and tottered over to the bed.

'Eeh, love,' she said, putting her hand on Charlotte's shoulder.

Rage boiled up inside me at the gesture. Just who should be getting the sympathy here?

'Get OFF her!' I shouted, and they both flinched but stayed where they were. 'YOU,' I barked at Nan, 'it's YOUR fault, all this. We wouldn't be in this mess if it wasn't for you. Get out and leave us to it.'

They moved closer together and Nan lowered herself down on the edge of the bed. She put her arm round Charlotte's bulk.

'Talk sense, Karen,' Nan muttered.

I thought I was going to hit her.

'Talk sense? Talk sense? That's the pot calling the bloody kettle, isn't it? There's no one comes out with as much rubbish as you, and it's me who has to put up with it on a daily basis, it's a wonder I'm not off my head.'

'Are you sure you're not? Anyway it's not Nan's fault, Mum. Whatever else, it's nothing to do with her.' Charlotte's face looked small under her fringe, but very fierce.

'Oh, isn't it? *Isn't it?* Well, I'll tell you something you don't know, lady.'

'Karen,' said Nan faintly.

I didn't even look at her.

'For a start, it was Nan who made me keep you. Just hang on, she told me. Have the baby, and then if you're still not suited, put it up for adoption, there's plenty of women who'd jump at the chance. Of course when I'd had you she knew I'd never be able to give you up. She said she'd look after you—'

'She *did*!'

'Only some of the time. And that's not the point. She *changed my mind*, ruined my life. I had such plans . . .'

'Oh,' said Charlotte tartly, 'put another record on. Come on, Mum, we all know it was *you* who fucked up. You can't blame it on anyone else. Not even Dad.'

'A lot you know. You're not even eighteen. You wait till you get to my age and the best years of your life are behind you and you know there's no redeeming them, see how you feel then about *decisions that got made for you*.' It was true what they said about a red mist coming down in front of your eyes. There was a buzzing sound too, and my heart was leaping with extra surges of boiling-hot blood. I stepped forward shakily and pointed down at Nan. 'She isn't even my real mother.'

Nan turned her face into Charlotte's shoulder and I waited for the thunderclap. She just stared back, cool as you like.

'Did you hear what I said? I'm adopted. *Nan isn't my mother.*'

'Well,' said Charlotte, 'same difference. She brought you up, didn't she? What's that make her, then?' She was breathing fast and clinging on to Nan, who had her eyes shut. 'At least she wanted you, which is more than I can say for *my* mother. From where I'm standing it looks like you got a pretty good deal. Now, would you get out of my room, please; I'm supposed to be watching my blood pressure.'

*

**To my amazement** Mum turned on her heel and swept out. I'd thought she was going to hit me at one point, or have a heart attack. Her cheeks had gone really pink and her eyes all stary. My own heart was pounding in my chest and my throat was dry.

After a minute Nan and I untangled ourselves. She fished a hanky from her sleeve, wiped her eyes and blew her nose. Then she began rooting in her cardigan pockets.

'Have a Mintoe,' she said, offering one up in a shaking hand. 'She dun't mean it. She loves you. That's why she could never give you up.' She wrestled with the cellophane wrapper.

'I don't care,' I said, and at that moment it was true. My insides were churning but my head was clear. I gripped the Mintoe in triumph. 'Oh, Nan. I can't believe I said all those things to her face, they've wanted saying for so long. It feels brilliant. How did I manage it? It was like I was possessed.'

Nan turned to me and smacked her minty lips. Her bottom dentures jumped forward suddenly and she popped them back in with her index finger. 'Pardon,' she said. We both began to giggle with nerves.

Then the door flung open and Mum was there again.

'How *dare* you laugh at a time like this!' she shouted. She held up a photo frame in front of her face. It was the one she keeps on her dressing table; me on a stretch of mud at Morecambe in a white sun-hat and knickers, hair blowing across my face. 'Look! You were five when this was taken and just *look* at you! Picture of innocence! And it turns out in the end you haven't the sense you were born with. All those times I've warned you!'

Nan and I sat and watched as she tossed the photo onto the desk where it sent more pens clattering off and knocked over my clay elephant I'd made in Year 7.

'Bloody hell, Mum. You've broken its trunk off.'

'You're having an abortion.'

I could have said, 'Yeah actually, I am, in two days' time. You can come along and cheer if you like.' But at that very moment two things happened. Nan drew in her breath and put her hand over my bump; and I felt the baby move.

It wasn't the first time, I realized now; there'd been flutterings before, like when a nerve twitches, only deep inside. But I hadn't clocked what they were, until this moment.

'You're having an abortion,' Mum said again.

If it had been a request; if she'd sat down and held me like Nan was doing; if we hadn't said those awful things to each other five minutes ago. But Fate gets decided on littler things than that every day.

'You're wrong, Mum.' Flutter flutter. 'I'm keeping this baby.'

Nan's arms tightened around me.

'Don't talk soft. You're not fit.' Mum leaned forward and spat the words at me. And if I hadn't decided by then, that would have swung me.

'Well, I'm a damn sight *fitter* than you. At least I won't make this baby feel guilty all its life,' flutter flutter, 'at least I won't try and make it Responsible for my own shortcomings. If you didn't want me, eighteen years ago, that's fine. But I'm not going to do to this baby what you did to me. Poor bugger. It deserves a better chance than I had.'

Can foetuses clap? I was sure I could feel a round of applause down in the left side of my pelvis. Washed in adrenaline, the thing was going berserk.

Mum's face had gone that nasty colour again and her legs were trembling.

'You'll change your mind. Or I'll never speak to you again.'

'There's worse things than babies,' said Nan. 'They're nice, babies are.'

'Damn you both,' said Mum.

\*

THERE'S worse things than babies, dear God in heaven there are.

It was all drinkin' i' th' owden days, an' feights all t' time. The children used come runnin' across the fields shoutin', 'Harry Carter's feightin' again,' an' we'd all go an' watch. He lived at t' top o' t' brow, an' he were allus after the women even though he was married. His little lads would be pushin' through t' crowds an' shoutin', 'Don't feight, Daddy,' but he never took any notice. He was forever askin' Herbert Harrison's wife for t' go wi' him, an' she'd allus tell her husband on him, it were like a game. They just wanted an excuse. One time I was stood wi' a big crowd watchin' them stagger about the street and Dr Liptrot came up alongside me. He didn't see me, though, he were glued to th' action. Finally Herbert Harrison knocked Harry Carter down, then he turned an' walked off. Harry got up, rubbed his chin an' stumbled towards us. I ducked away, but as he drew level Dr Liptrot patted him on the shoulder and said, 'Now, then, let that be a lesson. Feightin' dogs come limpin' whoam.' Harry stopped for a second, looked at the doctor, then hit him so hard he knocked out both his front top teeth.

It weren't just the men who drank, neither. My grand-mother Florrie used to have a big oak sideboard with a long dark patch on the top. Once she caught me an' Jimmy playin' wi' matches outside on the flags and she dragged us in and pushed us reight up again' the drawers of this sideboard. 'Do you know what made that mark?' she said. I shook my head; I'd only have been about seven and she could be very fierce. 'A neighbour set herself afire with an oil lamp,' she told us. 'She were dead drunk, an' she came running out into t' yard and staggered in here, all i' flames. She laid her arm along this side-board, an that's why there's a mark.' She put her face close to ours. 'So think on.' 'Did she die?' Jimmy asked. 'Of course she did,' said my grandmother, and she clipped us both hard round the ear.

I never saw it happen myself, but as soon as I knew the story it was in every dream I had for months. Jimmy never said owt, but I know he dreamt it too.

There was a lot of drunkenness in them days. My grand-father was allus on t' spree, my mother said. He used to knock his beer ovver and lap it up off table top like a dog, he were terrible. And when he'd spent up he'd go and stand outside the pub and wait for people to treat him, he had no shame. Even as a little girl my mother was sent wi' a jug to t' Waggon an' Horses for him, when he was too idle to get his own ale.

His friends laughed an' called him a 'character', but Florrie had another word for it. At his funeral do, when they'd had a bit, some of 'em were singin';

> *'Me father was an 'ero*
> *'Is brav'ry med me blush*
> *They were givin' free beer up at Bogle*
> *An' me father got killed i' t' crush.'*

My mother said it was disgustin', an' they were all tarred wi' t' same brush.

Then after, two of his mates from t' colliery were tellin' tales about him, how he'd gone to t' pictures once to see a Charlie Chaplin. He'd not been gone above an hour an' he was back in t' pub, an' they said, 'What's up, Peter, were it not a good show?' An' he said, 'They turned all t' lights out, so I got up an' came whoam.' They were all two-double laughin'.

'Aye,' said another man, 'an' there were a time when we went to see the Minstrels at Southport, an' a chap came on and sang "Danny Boy" an' he were really good, so all th' audience started shouting, "Encore! Encore!". An' Peter called out at t' top of his voice, "Never mind bloody Encore, let bloody man sing again!" '

Someone else said they remembered Peter Marsh coming out of the polling booth once, very pleased because he'd said to himself, 'Well I'm not voting for 'IM' – an' put a great big cross next to t' candidate's name. Was he soft i' th' head, or was it just the drink? No one seemed to care, it didn't matter, 'cause he was such a Character.

Florrie wasn't laughing, though. She had twenty-two years of his meanness wi' money and his not bothering about the babies she'd lost. She never married again; I think she'd had enough of men. So she lived with her daughter Polly, and then me when I came along, and it became my dad who had us all on a piece of string wi' his antics.

There were times as Jimmy hated his father, hated his comings and goings and the fact he would never marry our mother. 'He loves you, in his own way,' Mam used say. 'He gave you his name.' 'That just meks it worse!' said Jimmy. She had no answer to that, 'cause it was true. I think she felt it was her fault she couldn't keep him.

So as he got older Jimmy started to go wanderin', all ovver t' fields an' down by t' canal. He'd walk an' walk, as if he were lookin' for summat. An' he ran errands for people an' made a bit o' money that way. He used to see a lot of Mrs Crooks at Hayfield House; she was a widow and had never had children of her own. 'I'll pay thee Friday,' she'd say to him, an' she allus did. Then one day, he should have been at school, Harry Poxon saw him at t' side of t' canal, leanin' ovver wi' a stick. 'Tha'll faw in,' he said. That were t' last time he were seen alive. They were five days wi' a grapplin' hook before they found him, under t' bridge at Ambley. Mrs Crooks sent forget-me-nots for his coffin and all the school lined up an' sang 'There's a Friend for Little Children'.

He were only ten when he died.

*

THREE O'CLOCK in the morning and there's somebody standing at the bedroom door.

'I can't sleep. The baby's kicking.'

'Go back to bed, Charlotte,' I mumble, still only half out of a dream.

But it isn't Charlotte, it's Nan.

# Chapter Seven

**All night** I'd been dreaming I was drowning; now I'd wakened to the image of the baby lying face up, motionless, under water, and a terrible chill of knowing it was somehow my fault.

Then as my head cleared I thought about how its body was actually floating inside me now, this very minute, hair flowing round its huge head, and how everything would all gush out—

I couldn't face school. I lay in bed till eleven staring at the ceiling.

'I'll tell them I've had flu,' I said to Mum when I finally made it downstairs.

'Say what you damn well please,' she replied.

So I walked out through the front door, down Brown Moss Road, Gunners Lane and out onto the Wigan road. I was going to walk until I dropped off the edge of the world.

By the Cock Inn I turned right and started down the public footpath to Ambley, past the golf course and Hayfield House behind its screen of trees. I didn't know where I was going, didn't care. Rooks cawed overhead and sparrows flirted in the dust on the rutted track. Elderflower and dog roses were still thick among the hedgerows; you could smell the fertility in the warm air.

I turned off the track, scrambled down the canal bank and began to make my way along the towpath. A barge chugged past, castles and roses round the door, Jack Russell perched on the roof. The middle-aged woman steering smiled and nodded. Now there was an idea; I could always go and live on a boat, sail off up the Manchester Ship Canal and start a new life. A blackbird ran across my path chuck-chucking, and the baby fluttered. You daft tart, I told myself. That's exactly why you're in this mess now, starting a New Life.

As I drew level with the Fly and Tackle I realized I was thirsty. I fished in my pocket to see if I had any money and extracted £3.30 in loose change. I climbed up the worn stone steps onto road level, checked for traffic and crossed over.

After the brightness outside, the interior of the pub was dark and I had to blink a few times before I could get my bearings. I'd passed the place enough times on the bus, but I'd not been in before; it was a bit of an old gimmers' place, popular for Sunday lunches and real ale. Squinting, I made out movement behind the bar. A fat bald man was drying glasses and singing 'Born in the USA' over the jukebox. There were sweat stains under the armpits of his shirt.

'Have you got a telephone?' I asked, hovering by the door.

He pointed to an annexe by the ladies' and carried on being Bruce.

Inside the booth I checked my watch and dialled

Daniel's mobile number. 'Please have it switched on,' I prayed. There was a click.

'*Hell*-o.'

'Daniel! It's me! Hey! – What's that moaning sound?'

'Hey. Just a minute, I'll move somewhere a bit quieter. That's better. They're doing some sort of charity karaoke at one end of the common room. Just what you need after a hard morning's physics, some boil-ridden Year 10 apeing Noel Gallagher at top volume. Are you all right? I saw you weren't in registration this morning—'

'Yeah, I'm fine, just not feeling very schooly today. Look, have you got any frees this afternoon?'

'Surely you mean *Study Periods*? Actually I have one genuine, and one by default because Mr Chisnall's away at a conference so he's set us work to do in the library. I do hope you're not going to suggest bunking off.'

'Too right I am. Can you get away at all?'

'What, now?'

'Yes, please. It's a bit of a crisis. Another one. Sorry.'

'No problem, I'm on my way. Are you at home?'

'God, no. Do you know the Fly and Tackle?'

'At Ambley? We went there two Sundays ago for my mum's birthday. Nice line in pies, dire jukebox. OK, I'll be with you in . . . twenty minutes. Don't do anything foolish.'

He rang off. I got two halves of cider and went outside to wait.

I sat at one of the wooden tables and watched the glinting cars hunching over the little stone bridge, and the water sliding under it. The banks were lush and the trees bent low with green fruits. Two swans glided past sending a V of ripples behind them that broke the reflection of a perfect sky. If only I'd had a camera. The scene was idyllic, something like the picture on the front of Nan's old toffee tin she uses for storing buttons. I'd come back here, I promised myself, and take a picture of this place; maybe even do a painting, and give it to Nan. She'd like that.

At last Daniel's shiny red Ka, last term's present for passing his driving test, bobbed over the bridge and disappeared into the car park. Thirty seconds later he emerged through the back door into the beer garden, blinking. If only he'd do something about his hair, I thought meanly.

'There's a man in there auditioning for *Stars in their Eyes*,' he said lifting his long legs over the bench and laying his jacket down carefully.

'I know. *Nuts in their Head*, more like. They'd have to strap him into some corset to get him to look like Bruce Springsteen. And put a paper bag over his face. Here.' I slid his glass over.

'Cheers.' He took a long drink. 'Now, this crisis. You've not changed your mind again?'

'God, no. I still want the baby.'

'Thank Christ for that. I cancelled the clinic when you phoned, and anyway, being realistic, you're probably too late.'

'I know. I've done it now, haven't I?'

'Yep. So, I brought you this.' He reached into his jacket pocket and pulled out a banana.

'What is it with you and fruit? I've had two apples today already. You're turning into a food fascist.'

'No, it's not to eat, well you can if you want, I suppose. This is your baby.'

We both looked at it, lying on the table. It was mottled brown and there was a fingernail scar at the stalk end.

'I hope to God it's not.'

'I don't mean it's banana *shaped*, I mean it's about that size. I looked it up on the Internet.'

'Oh, my God, really?' I put out a hand and stroked the clammy skin, then picked it up and held it against my stomach. 'Wow, weird.'

'You still don't look particularly pregnant, you know,' said Daniel peering at my bump. 'A bit fat, maybe. I wouldn't guess, just seeing you.'

'Yes, well, that's why I wanted to talk to you. I want to, now I've decided, there's no point in hiding any more, I want to tell them at school. And I'm terrified, and I don't know how to go about it. I mean, I could just walk in wearing my T-shirt, that'd be a dead giveaway, you know, no fleece or anything to cover it. They all think I'm mental still wearing winter stuff anyway, I'm nearly passing out with heat exhaustion in some lessons and I have to keep saying I'm cold. Or I could take Julia aside and ask her to tell everyone, she'd love that, all the drama. Then I'd be waiting for the summons, Mrs Lever poking her head round the classroom door, lips pursed, asking ever so politely if I could pop along to the Head's office, while everyone looks at each other and whispers. *Or* I could go straight to the Head, or some other teacher maybe, and ask them to handle things. They could have, you know, a special assembly on it and I could be shuffling about outside the hall listening. Oh, God, either way is going to be completely awful.' I put my head in my hands. 'What am I going to *do*, Daniel? How, *how* am I going to cope with all the fallout?'

'You will. You're that sort,' he said confidently.

'What do you mean?' I asked through my fingers.

'Well, ahm . . .' His hands fluttered. 'Hmm . . . OK, have you ever smoked?'

'No. Never even tried a cigarette.'

'Why?'

I took my hands away from my face and considered. 'Well, I weighed up the pros and cons. Stinky breath, needless expense, appalling health risks, grief from adults, looking like a slag, versus maybe losing two pounds and joining in with everyone. I decided it wasn't worth it. Why d'you ask?'

He grinned and slapped the table top. 'Have you any idea how few people think that way? You are *so* unusual.'

'I am?'

'You know you are. Most people want to fit in at any cost, whatever the risks; you, you don't give a monkey's.'

I was staring at him.

'Can I be totally honest with you?' He looked straight into my eyes.

'Be my guest.' I wondered what the hell was coming.

'I think you're driven by bloody-mindedness.'

A vision of my mum flashed up, and for a second I thought I was furious. Then I started to laugh. 'Go on.'

'Well, you're incredibly self-contained, aren't you?'

'I – oh, I wouldn't say . . . In some respects maybe.'

'Oh, come off it, you know you are. You've got friends,

yeah, but you don't care whether you sit with a group in the common room or on your own.'

'That's not true! You make me sound like some kind of freak-girl. Honestly, Daniel, I'm just a normal teenager – apart from being up the duff, obviously.'

'No, that's not it. What I mean is you're not afraid to swim against the tide. You're an *individual*. That's why—' He broke off and studied the canal for a while. 'Anyway, I'm not saying you're in for a picnic, but if anyone can cope with it, it's you.'

He really did know how to make you feel better.

'Damn you for being right.'

'My pleasure. Can I get you another drink?'

'Lemonade, I suppose. Have to think of the banana's welfare. Don't want the little thing pickled.'

When he came back I said, 'Don't suppose I'll have much time to be self-contained after the baby's born.'

'I don't suppose you will. Have you thought of any names yet? You could start talking to it, you know, it can hear you in there.'

'Honestly? God, that's so spooky.' I looked down at my stomach and spoke to the bump. 'Chiquita if it's a girl, Fyffes if it's a boy. What do you think of that, then?' No response. 'Too disgusted to reply. Oh, Daniel, it's so nice to be able to *talk* to someone about all this. Mum can't even bear to look at me; half-term was hell. Mind you, I did get a lot of revision done . . . Do you think I should tell a teacher, then?'

'If you can find one you like. Mrs Stokes?'

'Oh, ha ha. No, I was thinking of Mrs Carlisle, she was my form tutor in Year 10 and 11. She's a bit of an old hippy so she won't be too shocked. She always gave me nice pastoral reports.'

'She could even have a word with your mother,' suggested Daniel, under the impression that Mum was in a rational enough state to be spoken to.

'Well. Let's not get too carried away. One step at a time. Eh, Chiquita?'

'So you'll be in Tuesday?'

'I've an appointment at the hospital tomorrow, so it'll be Wednesday. God forbid I should miss the exams.'

'I'll have chocolate and Kleenex ready.'

**He really got me** thinking. Was I not normal?

I remember seeing Charlotte Church on telly last Sunday, hair shining with cleanliness. 'I'm just an ordinary teenager,' she kept saying. Yeah, right. So what's an Ordinary Teenager? I can't see she has a right lot in common with, for instance, Gary Whittle who I went to primary school with and who I remember once tied a firework to a cat's tail. He's in a Young Offenders' Institution now. And she's certainly nothing like me and my ever-expanding bulge of shame. The only thing I can see teenagers have in common is that they've waved twelve goodbye and they haven't reached twenty yet.

Imagine:

**General Studies Paper 1: Section 1, Arts and Society**

*Q 1: How normal are you?*

Intro: need for both individuals & society (esp media) to stereotype across age range, class, ethnic group, occupation etc; usually collection of negative characteristics; allows person to feel superior and in possession of all significant facts on basis of flimsiest evidence.

Para 1: teenagers pigeonholed by jealous middle-aged & elderly. Threatened not by teenagers themselves but by reminder of their own mortality & wasted chances. Unflattering characteristics projected onto young include:

Para 2: moodiness. Unfair accusation; not confined to any specific age group. My Mother = Queen of the moods. If sulking an Olympic sport, she'd get row of perfect 10s. A grown woman who can out-strop any adolescent.

Para 3: materialism. Unfair again. Rife throughout society – Ikea on a Sunday! No point *my* being materialistic anyway as we have no money.

Para 4: vanity. Unfair. Self-obsession an insecurity thing, not age-related. In fact, older you get, more you focus on looks eg Grecian 2000, Playtex corsets, super-strength Dentu-fix etc. Teenagers aren't the ones spending £70 a pot on La Prairie face cream.

Para 5: habitual drunkenness. Inaccurate! 1/4 of our 6th form = Muslim for a start. Also Dave Harman = Jehovah's Witness & Alison Gill teetotal ∴ mother killed by drunk driver last yr. To judge by what staggers out of Working Men's every Sat night, worst offenders are 50+.

Para 6: spottiness. Even this boring old chestnut wrong. Supply teacher in Science labs this term has spots *and* wrinkles, must be at least 40 poor cow. I only get them on my back & shoulders, so doesn't count.

Conc: can't stereotype teenagers way you can old people. No such thing as typical teenager. ∴ if no such creature, I can't be judged as either normal or abnormal. QED.

*

I WAS SITTING IN a council office overlooking the Town Hall Square, sulking. Across the desk sat Mrs Joyce Fitton, my social worker; I'd already written her off as a waste of time.

'What have you found out?' I'd asked as soon as I'd sat down.

'Nothing yet. That's not why you're here. This is a counselling session. So we can be sure of where you want to go.' Mrs Fitton wore glasses on a chain and had a big motherly bust. She talked slowly and kept stopping to smile. I wanted to smack her.

'This place could do with a good clean. Those Venetian blinds are thick with dust,' I said rudely. I was so disappointed.

'I can see you're very angry, Karen. With your birth parents?'

No, with you, you daft old bat. I took a deep breath.

'I just can't cope with all these delays. I thought today you'd have some information for me.' I thought today you'd have found my mother and solved my life for me. I imagined you handing over a big thick file containing photos of my real mum, a résumé of her life so far (including the empty hole I left in it), pictures of her lovely house (polished wood floor, French windows, field with ponies at the bottom of the garden) and a beautifully written letter on Basildon Bond saying how much she wanted to see me.

'You need to have a clear idea of what you hope to get out of any contact you might make. And be sure you can handle the possibility of rejection and disappointment.'

'Oh, I'm good on those.' God, I sounded bitter.

Mrs Fitton took her glasses off and gave me a long look.

'Of course we may decide, after careful discussion, that you don't in fact want to find your birth parents,' she said. 'Some of these situations are potentially quite damaging, you know. I would say,' she put her glasses back on and began to sort pieces of paper on the desk, 'that unless you have the right, ahm, approach, you're laying yourself open to a lot of harm. Not that I want to be negative.'

I took the hint.

'Yes, absolutely. You're just doing your job. So, do you think you can find her?'

'I think there's a very good chance, yes. And your father, if you want.'

'To be honest, I haven't really thought that much about him. It's my mum I feel drawn to.'

She smiled again. 'That's usually the case, Karen. Even with men. There's something very special about the person who carried you for nine months, then went through labour for you. Most people assume there's going to be a special bond.'

'Isn't there always?'

'Usually. Now, have you discussed this issue with other members of your family?'

'Oh, yes.'

'And what have their reactions been?'

'Everyone's totally behind me. I have a very close relationship with my adopted mother, we can talk about anything.' So long as it's bollocks. 'And my daughter and I are more like friends, sisters, sort of thing.'

'So you anticipate them welcoming your birth mother into their circle?'

'Oh, absolutely.' I won't let them anywhere near her.

Mrs Fitton wrote some notes in a small hand.

'And what do you expect to get out of finding your birth mother, Karen?'

Ah ha, I'd been expecting this question somewhere along the line, and I was ready.

'I just want to ask her about her experiences, tell her about mine. Talk to her as one woman to another. I'm not trying to, ha ha, replace my own mum, God forbid. I'm not looking to her to solve my problems or anything mad like that.' I rolled my eyes. Crazy idea.

'Have you got problems at the moment, then?'

Damn and blast.

'No, nothing to speak of, you know. Only ordinary, everyday, little problems, like everybody has. The washing machine breaking down, the bin men not coming, that sort of thing.'

She nodded sympathetically. 'Someone keeps taking our wheeliebin, would you credit it? We've had to paint our number on the side.'

I tutted.

'Well, you sound as if you've given this whole business a lot of thought.'

'Oh, yes.' That bit was true, at any rate.

'Are you happy then if I go ahead and contact the mother and baby home on your birth certificate?'

'They've closed down.' It slipped out. 'I, I tried there first, phoning, but it's a business school now.'

She didn't even blink. 'Yes, they relocated. We've dealt with them before. They should have all your records. Then we can make another appointment and go over the papers, and see where we go from there. Maybe think about your dad too.'

'How long will that take?'

'Couple of weeks, not long.' She smiled once more. 'You seem like a level-headed young woman, Karen. I'm sure you'll cope with whatever we turn up.'

Level-headed? Didn't these people take psychology exams? Gullible old trout. Still, I wasn't going to own up to being a bag of neuroses. I watched her fill in a Post-it note and stick it onto her computer, next to a small orange gonk with goggle eyes. Fancy getting to that age and still believing the best of people. Bloody odd.

We shook hands and as I was going out I said, 'I'm sorry I was so rude about your blinds.'

Mrs Fitton smiled.

'We get a lot worse than that here, believe you me,' she said.

*

**I'd have liked** Nan to go with me to the hospital only she wasn't fit. I could just imagine the consultation with the midwife: 'So, Charlotte, how many weeks pregnant are you?'

Nan: 'Do *you* believe they've sent a man to the moon? Load o' rubbish.'

I'd have liked to take Daniel, but it was too much of an imposition. The potential for embarrassment was colossal ('No, this isn't actually the father, he's only come along to hold my urine sample') and besides, he had a Maths exam that day.

I suppose I could have taken Mum, if she wasn't still a quivering mass of rage. We nearly came to blows last week when she gatecrashed my doctor's appointment.

'Folic acid? Never mind bloody vitamin pills, tell her what a stupid girl she's been. Tell her, Doctor. Did you know she was supposed to be going to university?'

Fortunately Mum's fairly scared of health professionals so when he told her to shut up, she did. In fact she hasn't spoken to me since.

**The midwife** I saw at the hospital was really nice. Dead young, not much older than me I think, and that helped. The first thing I asked her was: 'How can you have a period and still be pregnant?'

She sketched me a little womb on a notepad and a little egg implanting itself.

'As the egg burrows in it sometimes breaks a few blood vessels. That'll be what you had. Not much blood, just spotting, is that right?'

I nodded glumly. The things grown women keep quiet!

'I bet you didn't know whether you were coming or

going,' she smiled. I think she must have guessed, looking at my birth date and the absence of a partner, but she didn't say anything at first. It came out when she was strapping the black Velcro sleeve round my arm to take my blood pressure.

'My mum's on the way,' I lied. 'She must have been held up.'

'And your partner?'

The sleeve tightened and the blood pulsed in my fingers.

'Is a grade-A bastard. He's history.'

There was a hiss as the air seeped out and the sleeve went slack.

'I see. We do get a few of those.' She unstrapped me briskly. 'Do we know anything about this bastard's health? His blood group, any serious illnesses in the family, that kind of thing? I only ask because of this form we have to fill in.'

'Nope.'

'OK, then, not to worry.'

Like I said, she was really nice.

After she'd filled in pages and pages on my diet and progress, we listened to the baby's heartbeat, *pyow-pyow-pyow-pyow* through a special microphone. Then it was time to go and drink a pint of water and wait for the scan.

The scan. Night after night I'd had that scan, and always there was something wrong. The baby had no head, or it looked like an octopus, or it was too small—

Outside in the waiting room were a whole lot of bloated women. Some of them were reading magazines, some were trying to amuse hyperactive toddlers; nearly all of them were with someone. I sat down near a lone black lady with a football-up-the-jumper type profile and tried to catch her eye. She smiled when she noticed me, that secret club smile pregnant women pass round between themselves.

'Have you been waiting long?' I said.

'About half an hour.'

'How far are you on?'

'Thirty-seven weeks. The baby's turned the wrong way round, they're going to see if they can persuade him to do a somersault. Otherwise I might have to have—'

She broke off as a tall man in a suit came and sat down next to her. He put a hot drink down on the table, kissed her cheek, then reached over and patted her stomach. I edged away, feeling miserable. It was important not to think about the nightmares.

I rooted in my bag for the funky little paperback I'd been given by the doctor; *Emma's Diary*, a week-by-week guide to pregnancy. I wanted to see what it said about birth defects. As I pulled the book out a scrap of paper fluttered down onto the tiles. I got down on my hands and knees to pick it up, and recognized Nan's swirly writing.

> *Don't think you're of little importance*
> *You're somebody, somebody fine*
> *However you tumble, and get up and stumble*
> *You're part of a vision Divine*

A vision Divine. My eyes blurred with tears and I scrambled back onto my seat. Oh, Nan.

Forty minutes later, just as my bladder had passed from painful to critical, a little grey-haired nurse called me into a dim room, hoisted me onto a table, and pulled my shirt up and my leggings down to my pubic bone. I stared down at the slightly flattened bump as she squirted cold gel on my skin and then stood back for the doctor to get in there with his probe thing.

'Look at the screen,' whispered the nurse, beaming.

And there, in flickering white profile, was a head and an arm.

'It's sucking its thumb,' she said.

My God. So there was a baby in there after all. It was all true. The foetus squirmed about as the doctor pressed hard into my flesh for what seemed like ages.

'Don't hurt it!' I called out in alarm.

'It's fine,' he murmured and carried on methodically, taking down measurements every time the machine went *beep*. 'Sorry, when was the date of your last period?'

'I told the midwife, I don't know.' Who keeps track of these things?

He moved the probe around and two waving legs came into view. 'And you haven't had a dating scan . . . Well . . .'

The image froze.

'What's the matter?' I felt panic rise. Next to my hip the machine made a sinister whirring noise.

The nurse leaned over. 'It's OK, he's just taking a nice picture for your notes. You can take a copy home if you want.'

'Is there something wrong, though? Is my baby all right?'

The doctor flicked a switch and the screen froze again, then the overhead lights came on. 'You're fine, your baby's fine. I'd say you were about – ' he glanced over at my notes – 'about twenty-six weeks. So I'm going to put your due date down as the sixteenth of October.'

'Oh my God, that's my Nan's birthday!'

The nurse grinned and helped me up off the table, but the doctor was busy writing on my file.

'Can I ask a question?'

'Sure,' he said without turning round.

'Can you tell whether it's a boy or a girl? I'd really like to know. For the names and stuff.'

He glanced over his shoulder at me.

'It's not hospital policy to disclose the sex,' he said briefly, and turned back again. I wondered how he could be so unmoved by the miracle he'd just revealed.

'You'll have to knit lots of lovely white things,' twittered the nurse, squeezing my arm. I'd have liked her as a mother, I decided. 'Now, I'll bet you're desperate for a pee. I'll show you where the toilet is.'

And then I was on the bus going home, the grainy flimsy photo clutched in my hands. There was another universe-upside-down moment, when for the duration of that ride I and my baby were at the centre of creation, and the feeling that we two were all evolution had been working towards for millions of years overwhelmed me. Nobody on the 416 seemed to notice my fantastic revelation, but that's the way the world works, isn't it? We miss amazing things every day, right under our noses. Maybe it's for the best. If we went round being amazed all the time we'd never get anything done.

I bounced into the house and went in search of Nan, but there was only Mrs Crowther from Crossroads reading last night's *Bolton Evening News*. 'She's having a nap in her room,' she told me. 'At long last. She's been up and down like I don't know what. Something's mitherin' her.'

I shrugged and went to find something to eat. In the kitchen I smoothed out the little picture again and drank in the detail. Just its top half, the face in profile, a big forehead. I wondered who it looked like and a pang of memory, Paul's shining face and floppy hair, skewered me where I stood. Would he not like, would he not want to see . . . ? But that was not Paul I remembered, not the real Paul, who was scum. This baby didn't need a fantasy father.

I wanted to phone Daniel, but a glance at my watch told me he'd still be doing his sums so I made a giant cheese sandwich and went upstairs to do some more thinking.

When I opened the door and saw what was on the bed I couldn't believe my eyes.

*

ONE OF THE THINGS that's bothering me most about this baby business is that it means I'm on my way to being old. Thirty-four, it's no age is it? You see TV presenters older than me (occasionally). I want to throw out my jumpers and leggings and start again, wear spaghetti straps and combat trousers and little butterfly clips in my hair. Would I really look like mutton? How *can* I be a grandma? Yet once this baby's born I'll feel as if I've started down the slippery slope which ends with Werther's Originals, *The People's Friend* and Death. I didn't think I was even middle-aged really, but look, here I am, Grannie Karen. So even less chance of finding a man. I mean, it's not exactly an alluring chat-up gambit: Why don't you come back and see my grandchild? I bet Charlotte never thought of that, did she. How did I ever manage to produce such a selfish daughter?

*

**Laid neatly across** the bed were three blouses, a pair of jeans and a long floaty skirt. I went over and had a closer look. *MUM-2B* said all the labels. It was maternity wear! My first set of decent clothes for six months. I tore off the saggy size-16 leggings I'd bought off Wigan market and pulled on the jeans. They were really clever, sort of stretchy round the top and then skinny on the legs like real jeans. It was brilliant to have something that felt comfortable again. I struggled out of the T-shirt and put on the nicest blouse, a floral job, and all right, I looked a bit mumsy, but what could you expect in the circumstances? The point was everything fitted in the right places and didn't feel like it was going to fall down or cut me in half. Next I tried the skirt, also brilliant, with the same blouse then another, then the third, then I took off the skirt and put the jeans back on and it was then that the front door went and I heard Mum's voice in the hall.

'Mum!' I shouted down.

'Just a minute,' she called back. I heard her talking to Mrs Crowther, then the door going again. Finally her footsteps on the stairs, and she was in my room.

'Well?' She sounded sharp and I faltered.

'All these clothes . . .'

'Yes?'

'Did you buy them?'

'How else do you think they got there?'

'Oh, Mum, thanks so much—'

She cut me short. 'I ordered them from the catalogue. If you don't like them, don't pull the labels out and I'll return them. You can pay me back in instalments, we'll have to work it out.'

Even the news that they weren't a gift didn't dampen my gratitude.

'It's so nice of you . . .'

'Well, let's be honest, you were beginning to look a complete sight in that other stuff.' She turned to go and I stepped forward and grabbed her arm.

'Oh, Mum, I've got to show you something—' I picked up the scan photo from the pillow and held it out shyly.

She took one glance and then her eyes flicked away. She wrenched her arm free and walked out, slamming the door.

\*

SOMETIMES it's hard to see what a woman sees in a feller. I loved my dad 'cause he were my dad; we didn't see him so often, but when we did he were grand wi' us. He made Jimmy a boat out of wood wi' a mousetrap inside it, so's when you pressed a button at t' side it flew apart. We used play wi' it for hours out on t' flags at t' back. For me he made a little chair – I have it now – wi' spindles an' turned legs. When I got too big for it, it did for my dolls. An' although he could be sharp-tongued, he only twice laid a finger on me an' that was for sayin' 'Good shuttons' to the milkman – I didn't know it was rude – and for mouthin' 'What a face our cat's got' at my mother; she saw me in the mirror. He would never have touched our Jimmy, he thought the sun shone out of him; we all did. He had his father's charm wi' none of the arrogance.

But when I grew up, an' especially when I got married, I began to see what a terrible time he'd given my mother. Grandma Florrie hated him; hated the way he'd turn up at the house an' expect to stop the night, but she never said no because Polly'd be beside herself wantin' him to stay and so would we. Sometimes his mother, Grandma Fenton, would come round an' the two owd women would sit on the horsehair sofa and moan about his behaviour.

We felt sorry for Grandma Fenton. Fancy havin' produced a son who hated women. She'd been in service when she got caught and she'd never say who the father was, although it was pretty obvious it was the chap who employed her; he wouldn't have owt to do wi' it, I suppose. So when Harold was young she had a poor time of it, no benefits in them days, of course. She used have a stall again' the Victoria where she sold nettle beer, brandy snaps and treacle toffee. An' she were a nice woman, it was a shame. She'd have done anything for Polly. She never got much love from her son.

I know I've been lucky. Bill were a wonderful husband and father. And the more I see of the world, the more I think there aren't so many on 'em about.

\*

I'D BEEN putting it off – frankly I'd rather have driven six-inch nails into my kneecaps – but it had to be done. Steve had got to be told about the situation.

I wouldn't say we were on bad terms; he's too bone-idle to harbour a grudge. For him the past is the past, he's not fussed about the way our marriage turned out. He always seems quite pleased to see me (which is about once a year) and quite pleased when I leave.

He lives in Harrop, at the bottom of the Brow; you could walk it, but it'd be a heck of a climb back up. I took the Metro and parked it up the entry at the end of the terrace.

'Hey up.'

He'd seen the car and was standing at the door in his stocking feet. He'd grown a moustache since I'd last seen him and it made him look older. Still as lean as a whippet, though, still that sharp-featured face and the cheeky grin.

I walked up the overgrown path and went through the dark hall, picking my way past cardboard boxes, to the back sitting room.

'Have a seat. Kettle's just boiled.'

There were more boxes and some bundles of news-paper on the floor, lots of used crockery dotted about, a pair of jeans folded over a wire maiden by the unlit gas fire. When we'd first split up I'd been appalled at the way he lived, but now I just left him to it. A bit of peeling wall-paper border never hurt anyone, I suppose. As long as it wasn't in my house, obviously.

'So what's this all about? You sounded a bit rattled on the phone. Is it summat to do with Charlotte?' He handed me a mug with a picture of Linda Lusardi on it and sat down opposite.

'Yeah. God, there's no easy way to say it. She's got herself into trouble.'

'Wha', at school? I thought she were a gold-star pupil.'

'No, you great lummox, *into trouble*. She's pregnant.'

'Oh, bleedin' 'ell.' Steve put his cup down on the carpet and shot me a twisted grin. 'Not our Charlie. I thought she had more sense.'

'Apparently not.'

Steve shook his head. 'I can't believe it. Not our Charlie. She's such a clever girl. Cleverer than us, anyroad, I thought. What did she think she were doin'?'

I shrugged and lay back against the sofa wearily. 'It's not like I haven't warned her a thousand times. But you know what she's like, so deep. So difficult to talk to. I wasn't even absolutely sure she had a boyfriend for ages, she's so secretive. And she's well on, it's too late for an abortion. She hid it from everyone.' It wasn't my fault, I wanted to add, but then Steve would never have thought like that anyway. I was justifying to myself, not him.

'An' this lad, what's he got to say about it all?' Unconsciously he drew himself up and squared his jaw.

There was a pause.

'I've not really pursued that line,' I said awkwardly.

'What do you mean? Haven't you been round to his house, had a talk with his parents? Because it seems to me he's got some explaining to do.'

I couldn't tell him I'd been too wrapped up in blaming Charlotte and my own inadequacies to dream of doing anything other than getting rid of the pregnancy. When this plan had failed I was so drunk with fury I couldn't think straight. I couldn't even bring myself to say good morning to Charlotte, let alone have a rational discussion about the role of the baby's father. In any case, I secretly didn't blame him, I blamed her, because whatever they say, there'll never be equality of the sexes till men can get pregnant; she was bright enough to know she'd be the one to get caught, so she ought to have sorted it. Men'll just try for what they can get where sex is concerned, they don't think it through; that's for us women to do. So as far as I was concerned it was her fault.

But Steve had scented a villain and his blue eyes were bright.

'What's this little bugger's name and where's he live?'

'Paul. Paul Bentham. He lives round the corner, off Barrow Road, apparently. He used to go to school with Charlotte when she was in the juniors. Cocky so and so. He dumped her about three months ago, and that's why I thought she was so moody, still pining for him. I never dreamt . . .'

'Well, I'm going to pay this Paul Bentham a visit and tell him exactly what the state of play is. He can't just walk away; I didn't, did I? You've got to face up to your responsibilities even at that age. Little shit.' He thumped the arm of the chair. 'Upsetting our Charlie like that and then doing a runner. Poor lass. Is she all right?'

What about me? I wanted to shout. I'm not all right! I want to jump on the next bus to Manchester airport and flee the country, except the whole house would collapse without me. Christ, I can't even pop down the shops without checking Nan's bag or Charlotte's sanity; I feel like that Greek bloke who had to hold the world up on his shoulders.

But I hadn't come round to moan. There's no point with Steve, he blocks it out, which is partly why we used to have such God-awful rows. He never understood that women like to complain for the sake of it, to get things off their chest, and they don't *want* to be fobbed off with practical solutions and courses of action. They just want sympathetic attention, and lots of it.

So I said, 'She's fine. I'm not worried about her at the moment, she's – ' a bitter laugh escaped – 'really into the pregnancy now and pretty up-beat. Though I think it'll all go pear-shaped when the baby's born.'

'Well, it does, dun't it?'

'Exactly.'

There was a silence while we both remembered the unholy fuck-up we'd made of the post-natal months.

'Well, she's got you to look after her,' said Steve and a big spear of guilt ran through me. 'So what d'you want me to do? I'm no good at talking to her . . . She scares me a bit, if you want to know.' He laughed sheepishly. 'She's so bloody clever, and she's taller than me an' all . . .' He ran his hand through his hair. 'I don't know her well enough.'

I could have made a nasty remark here but I was too conscious that the feelings Steve was trying to articulate were basically my own. In any case, I needed more aggro like I needed a hole in the head.

'I could probably find some extra cash,' he continued. He gestured vaguely at the cardboard boxes. 'I'm looking after some stuff for a chap at work, and there'll be a few quid in it at the end for me. I don't mind passing it Charlotte's way.'

'I can't pretend it wouldn't be welcome. Money doesn't buy you happiness—'

'But at least you can be miserable in comfort,' he

finished and we grinned briefly together. 'Right-oh. 'S not a problem.'

'I didn't come round here to scrounge, though.'

'I know you didn't.'

'I thought you needed putting in the picture. She might – she might still want to come round and talk it over with you.'

A look of panic crossed Steve's face. 'Oh, bloody hell. Look, I'll tell you what I'll do. I'll go round to see this lad and I'll see if I can sort summat out. I mean, I can't make things any worse, can I?'

I gazed at my cup and considered. Linda Lusardi simpered out at me from under a film of tannin.

'Probably not. Just make sure you don't lose your temper,' I said.

*

**I bottled it,** the big school revelation. At four o'clock Scan Tuesday I phoned Mrs Carlisle and told her the whole sorry story. She said to give her half an hour to have a think, then she rang back and said what they'd do was let me sit my exams up in Mrs Duke's office, out of the way, and I could come and go during lesson time so nobody would see me. So that's what I did, sloping in and out of the building like a bulky shadow. For the external papers I had to have a teacher sit in with me, but for the internal ones I was just left alone to get on with it; me, a bottle of Evian, a packet of Polos and my little curly photo. I've never felt so focused.

At the end of the last exam Mrs Carlisle came and had a long chat with me. She'd brought me a syrupy mug of real coffee, unaware that even the smell of instant made me heave. Still, it was something to do with my hands while she went on about deferred university places and childcare options for next year. She'd done a lot of research. 'You mustn't let go of your dreams,' she said, twice. I didn't even know what my dreams were any more.

On the last day of term she gathered the lower sixth girls together and told them the score. I'd had every intention of going in and saying goodbye; Daniel thought I should. But when it came to it I couldn't face the glare of publicity and spent the morning down the canal bank at Ambley again, throwing leaves in the water and watching them float off to freedom.

That was on the Wednesday; on Thursday I had a phone call from Julia asking me to meet her in town for lunch and I thought I owed it to her, so I went.

The thing about Julia is that she's brimming with social aplomb. She must get it from her mother, a girlish woman with a bright, lipsticked smile who can talk to anyone. I remember last Open Day there was a woman with no hair, I think she must have had cancer, and Julia's mum just breezed up to her and started chatting away. I was on the refreshment stall and I'd been dreading this woman coming over in case I said something like, 'Do you need a wig?' instead of 'Do you need a tray?' So, I have to admit, if the boot had been on the other foot and it was Julia who'd been pregnant, I'd have been struck dumb with embarrassment.

No such problems for Julia. She came rushing over to my table and gave me an enormous hug round my neck and then said, 'Look at *you*! You look *amazing*! Your hair's really glossy and your skin's absolutely *glowing*! Fantastic!'

She sat down and ordered, then produced a plastic bag containing a fluffy toy from Anya, a card signed by the sixth-form girls, and a book on pregnancy month by month from Mrs Carlisle. I was completely over-whelmed.

'Anya wanted to come too, but we thought it might outface you seeing us both together. But she says she'll ring you next week. We'd have been in touch before but Mrs Carlisle told us when you were first off you'd got sus-pected glandular fever and didn't want to get out of bed. But, wow, you're doing great. Everyone's really excited, and they all send their best wishes.' She sat Anya's little fluffy rabbit-thing up on its hind paws. 'Sweet! So, how you doing?'

I'd been feeling not too bad until the presents, but the unexpected kindness slew me. My face went red and my voice strangled with the effort of not crying.

'It's really nice—' was all I managed.

'Say no more.' Julia was brisk. The drinks arrived and a plate of cakes. 'God, don't you just *love* these chocolate muffins? I could literally eat them till all my buttons popped off. Fantastic. Oh, you missed some major gossip over the last few weeks. Did you know Denny's been suspended for selling funny cigarettes to Year 9s? One of them nearly set fire to the toilets, apparently, trying to light one of his home-made fags. God knows what was in them, because it wasn't tobacco. Martin Ainsworth reckons it was dried seaweed. Some of the kiddies lost their voices, that's how the teachers knew something was going on, they'd all come back in after break croaking like frogs. Anyway, at least it wasn't proper dope because he'd have been out on his ear, you know how twitchy the Head is over drugs.'

It was relaxing to have her rattle on like this. It made me pretend I could be normal again, with the usual teenage concerns and excitements. She made me laugh in spite of myself, and the baby inside me jumped and squirmed.

'. . . So then Jimbo told Simon that he'd seen Abby and Dom eating each other's faces in Fatty Arbuckle's, and Simon went absolutely ballistic and told Abby she was a tart in front of everyone in the dinner queue, so Dom jumped on him and there was this huge fight, tables everywhere, and Mr Barry had to drag them apart and make them go to separate rooms to cool off and their parents were called in. It was really hectic.' Julia stopped to draw breath. 'So you can see you've missed loads. I don't know how anyone's got any work done. I certainly didn't. My report was a disaster. Like I really care.' She took a big bite of cake and winked at me.

'Mine was brilliant,' I said gloomily. Mum had been in a terrible temper when it came through the post. It was one of those no-win situations, like every year when the GCSE results improve and the press go, 'Oh, standards must be slipping.' But if ever the results were down on last year's, it would be, 'Oh, we see standards are slipping,' and the *Daily Telegraph* would commission a special shock report on how thick today's teenagers truly are. So if my exam marks had been bad Mum would have been beside herself because I was throwing away my chances. The fact that they were better than I could ever have expected made the pregnancy even more of a disaster because I was clearly destined for great things. Or would have been.

'Julia,' I said, 'what happened when Mrs Carlisle told you about me?'

She paused for a fraction of a second only. 'Well, we were all really surprised, and a few people looked at me because they must've thought I knew about it—'

'You can understand why I couldn't say anything?'

'Yeah, yeah, of course. A big thing like that, you need to get your own head round it before it becomes public property. Then the twins asked if they could send you a card and Mrs Carlisle said she thought that'd be very nice. That was it, to be honest. Oh, a few people have asked me whether you'll be around next year. Will you?'

'I dunno. I don't know what it's like having a baby around. If it's not too much hassle I could put it in a crèche or something and come back in January. Maybe sooner. I don't want to have to repeat the year, not with all those bozos from Year 11 coming up. The teachers could send me work and I could get Special Consideration for the exams. Oh, I don't know. It goes round and round in my mind. We'll have to see.'

Julia was nodding, then she said, 'And of course, somebody asked me who the father was . . . I told them I didn't know, but I don't know if they believed me. Obviously you don't have to say anything if you don't want to.'

I could tell she'd been burning to get this question out.

Well, she'd been pretty good with me so far. It would be a relief to say something at last.

'I don't think it's anyone you'd know. A lad I used to go to school with years ago. Paul. But we're not together any more. He didn't want anything to do with me once he'd found out. I got it *so* wrong. You'd think, if you'd . . . if you'd slept with someone – that you'd know them pretty well. That's what I'd thought anyway, more fool me. I hope – I hope he gets run over by a lorry, very slowly, so his ribs crack one by one and you can hear his screams all the way to Blackpool. I hope he moves to the other side of the world and I never see him again. Oh—'

A pain shot through my groin.

Julia was on her feet at once.

'Charlotte! Are you all right? Do you want me to get someone? Shall I phone for a doctor?'

I shifted on the chair. 'It's OK, stop flapping. I think it was a one-off. Ooh!' This twinge bent me over and made me gasp.

'Stay where you are, I'll get an ambulance.'

'Come back!' I shouted as Julia shoved her chair out of the way and prepared to do a mercy dash. 'I'm not going into labour. At least, I don't think I am. The pain's in the wrong place. It's down here. Ow.'

Heads were beginning to turn and the panic that always overtakes me if I inadvertently become the centre of attention began to well up. There was another twinge. I had to get out, and quickly.

'I need to go home,' I said. 'Can you walk me to the bus stop?'

'To the bus stop? You must be kidding. I'm driving

you home. But don't you dare give birth on my mother's new seat covers, we'd never hear the last of it.'

Julia drove me back from town with exaggerated care, glancing over at me continually. Was the seat belt too tight? Were the pains coming every three minutes? Did I want her to turn the car round and go to the Royal Bolton? I kept saying no and gradually the pains went off. She began telling me about her holiday plans and her new bedroom, and then we were pulling into Brown Moss Road, both of us heaving a sigh of relief.

She stopped the car. 'You gave me a fright, missus. Are you OK now?'

I nodded.

'You're not just saying that?'

'No. Honestly. Thanks.'

'Do you want me to walk you to the door?'

'No, really. I feel fine now, it must just have been . . .'

We both caught sight of him at the same time. Julia turned to me puzzled.

'Who's that man bleeding onto your doorstep?'

'Oh God,' I said. 'Oh God oh God. This is why I never bring anyone home.'

# Chapter Eight

'Id wed a bid wrog,' my dad said through his hanky.
'I'b sorry, Charlie.' Mum had got him sitting on the sofa
leaning forwards and pinching his nose; she has to deal
with nosebleeds all the time at school.

'Don't keep swallowing,' snapped Mum, 'it'll make
you sick. Spit into this if you have to.' She thrust a Pyrex
bowl under his chin.

'I can't believe you went round there. Why didn't you
say anything to me first? What was he like? Was he really
angry?'

Part of me was horrified that Dad had crashed my private life like this, after years of sitting on the sidelines. But
part of me was grateful that someone should finally have
thought to give Paul a good bollocking, it was about time.
If that's what had happened. It didn't look too promising.

'Aggry? He were brickid hisself when he realized who
I was. I told hib the score. Dobody walks away from
subbat like that. Be a ban, I said. Face up to your responsibilities.'

'Is that when he hit you?' said my mum. I knew what
she was thinking because I was thinking it too. He looked
pathetic, with his red hanky and his head bowed, a

button hanging off his shirt. Beaten up by a seventeen-year-old, nice going, Dad.

Through the muffles of clotting blood we finally got the tale, though how much he'd brushed it up I wouldn't like to say.

He'd gone round late afternoon when he knew Paul would probably be in (and I guess hoping his old man wouldn't). A 'little lad' opened the door and then shouted for Paul who came down the stairs unsuspecting. Dad started his speech which quickly turned into a slanging match, during which Paul maintained first that the baby wasn't his, and then that since it was my decision to keep it against his wishes, he couldn't be called to account. (I broke in to argue at this point but my mother shut me up.) After a few minutes of hurling insults at each other, Paul had turned to go back upstairs and my dad had completely lost it, lunged forward and grabbed Paul round his legs. Paul fell face-first onto the step – 'He'll have a beltin' black eye tomorrow' – and in the struggle to get away kicked out, making contact with Dad's nose – 'it were nowt, a lucky blow'. At this point Mr Bentham appeared on the landing, bleary with sleep and taking out his earplugs – 'though he soon looked sharp when he saw me'. He ran down and hoisted Paul upright, checked him over briefly and propped him against the banisters. Meanwhile Dad had been shouting the odds about his son's behaviour, and despite Paul's denials, the finer details of the situation had begun to dawn on Mr Bentham. He'd apparently turned to take a swipe, seen Dad's berserk blue eyes and his bloody nostrils and let his arm drop to his side. (I suspect this bit is true. Mr

Bentham goes in for a quiet life.) Then he'd told Dad to get out of his house and if he wanted to take it further to get a blood test done. 'I will, don't worry. We'll have the CSA on you. An' you want to see that lad of yours gets a good hidin',' my dad had told him, and stormed out.

'So, full of sound and fury and signifying nothing,' I muttered. My mother leaned over and cuffed me round the ear.

'Less of that, madam. A thank you would be nice, after what your dad's been through. Even if it was a waste of time.'

Dad shot us a despairing glance and I immediately felt sorry. A proper daughter would have got up off her backside and given him a hug, but of course that was impossible, so I just gave him a thin smile instead. 'Thanks, anyway. Hope your nose doesn't hurt too much.'

He took the hanky away experimentally.

'I was trying to help.'

'I know you were. He's a total git.'

'Well, I must admit, I don't know what you ever saw in him, love. I thought he were an arrogant little gob-shite.'

The baby elbowed me sharply and I thought, You poor bugger, that's your father we're talking about. What an inheritance.

'Do you mind if I go upstairs and have a lie-down?'

Mum and Dad shook their heads and I dragged myself up to my room. Next door Nan was snoring and mumbling. I flopped onto the bed. The baby kicked on.

'It's probably something called "round ligament pain",' said Dr Gale. 'Nothing to worry about. Your muscles are having to hold up a tremendous weight, it's not surprising they're putting up a bit of a protest.' We were in the back garden of Daniel's enormous house enjoying the sunshine. They'd installed me in a sun-lounger in the shade of a beech tree; later on, under that same beech tree, Daniel would try to kiss me and I would refuse, so spoiling a perfect day.

'That's what the midwife reckoned. All the joints are under such pressure I'm bound to get some aches and pains. It was really scary, though. My friend thought I was about to give birth.'

'You'll be fine,' smiled Mr Gale. 'You look perfectly healthy to me, anyway.'

He was nice, Daniel's father. Tall, like his son, but more assured, quite distinguished. Lovely newsreader accent. I bet all his menopausal women patients harboured fantasies about him. He made me feel relaxed despite the fact that I'd never met him before and I was seven months pregnant and I didn't know what he'd been told about me. I suppose he sees all sorts in his surgery. The sun shone warm on us both and bees crooned among the lavender at our feet.

Inside I could hear Mrs Gale and Daniel preparing the evening meal. I'd have called it tea, but here it was dinner and it happened at seven not five. I remembered Mum trying that one out on us a few years ago; Nan was nearly eating the tablecloth in frustration, and I kept sneaking Custard Creams so by the time the food was on the table I didn't want it. 'Eeh, I can't be doin' with this caper every night,' Nan had said. Big row.

I wondered what Mum would make of the Gales'

Edwardian villa. Actually she'd be struck dumb with envy and inadequacy as she ticked off their Minton floor, the polished staircase, the quality art prints on the walls. By the time we reached the dream kitchen her jaw would be on the floor, as mine was. Kitchens aren't my thing, I tend just to breeze through on the scrounge, but even I could see this one was like a show-home. It was huge, for a start, with a quarry-tiled floor and immaculate units and – yes, Mum would have died – an Aga *and* a conventional high-tech built-in oven. Then there were all those little tasteful touches that I've seen on the front of Mum's house magazines; bunches of dried herbs hanging from the ceiling, gleaming copper pans, a hotchpotch of Victorian tiles along the back wall.

'Mum does cake decorating for weddings and parties,' said Daniel dismissively. 'She works for Relate too.'

He'd taken me out through French windows into the lovely garden and introduced me to his father, brought us drinks, then left us alone to have a chat.

'So, have I set your mind at rest?' asked Dr Gale. 'You don't want to be brooding and worrying just now, especially over something that's perfectly normal. Try to keep yourself calm. Calm mums-to-be make calm babies, so the research has it.'

'Really?'

'Oh, yes. You think about it. There are all sorts of chemicals passing between you, including all the ones your body releases when you're under stress. In the later stages of pregnancy it could have an effect on the foetus's eventual personality. And at this point, well, you've got a viable baby in there now.'

'What do you mean?'

'I mean that if you went into labour tomorrow there'd be a good chance the baby would survive. Provided it got immediate and proper care. It'd be a skinny little chap but it would have all its parts, more or less.'

I laughed and stroked my bump. 'It's certainly pretty active.'

'Good.' Dr Gale took a sip of his drink and looked out over the lawn.

I wish I could move in here with you for the next three months, I thought.

Dinner was grilled trout and salad and, guess what, Mrs Gale had grown all the parsley and dill herself. I thought of Mum's Herb Garden two summers ago, a row of pots along the back windowsill. Most of the herbs grew fantastically tall and then fell over; some of them didn't grow at all. Nan kept putting her used teabags in the pot nearest the drainer, which didn't help.

'Daniel tells me you're hoping to read English at university,' said Mrs Gale pleasantly. I say pleasantly, but really she was gritting her teeth to stay nice. I had some sympathy. There was her precious son bringing home some pregnant slapper who clearly didn't know which knife to use and, having wrecked her own life, was hatching God knows what plan to wreck his.

'I'd like to go to Oxford,' I said through a mouthful of fish.

'We wanted Tasha to apply, but she had her head set on Birmingham, for some reason.' Grimace. 'Still. Daniel'll probably apply to Lincoln. David went there.' Mrs Gale nodded at her husband.

'Smashing. Is that a nice university, then? Isn't it very hilly?'

Dr Gale coughed politely. 'I think you've misunderstood. I went to Lincoln *College*, Oxford.'

How we all laughed. I gave up the battle with the fish and put my cutlery down. I'd begun to feel sick if I ate too much at one go.

'Gillian went to St Hilda's. We met at a May Ball.'

'How romantic,' I said, meaning it. These were people who'd got everything right, done their lives in the right order.

'Yes, she was with a chap I detested. Ended up punching him in the mouth.' He smiled at his wife and raised his glass. 'Marvellous days.'

'And you were with Elise Osborne, owner of the most irritating laugh in Oxford,' replied Mrs Gale smartly. 'Finished with that plate, Charlotte?'

I helped clear away and we finished with fruit, which is also something which never makes an appearance in our house due to it generally sitting in a bowl till it goes mouldy and then getting thrown out. Poor Mum. She'd love to do this: Italian bread, wine, five cheeses, grapes. She used to try us with different foods but she's given up now. Nan's preferred dish is belly pork, two disgusting bow-shaped pieces of meat covered in a thick layer of fat which Nan eats with her fingers; she'd have it for breakfast, dinner and tea if Mum'd let her. Alternatives are a nice bit of tripe, Fray Bentos steak pudding, Greenhalgh's whist pies or potted shrimps. Oh, and tinned salmon. Should Mum ever be foolish enough to serve up something mad like rice or pasta, it ends up in the bin, untouched. How Nan got through the war I'll never know.

I'm a grazer and don't like sitting down to meals. I eat yoghurts by piercing the lid with my thumbnail and drinking them down in the light of the fridge door. Makes no mess, you see. You'd think Mum would be grateful for this low-maintenance approach, but no. If I want a biscuit I have to go through all the palaver of extracting a plate from under a tower of cups or bowls – quite often I'll have scoffed the biscuit by the time I've got the plate down – and then there's the washing up and putting away again for what would have been a twenty-second eating experience. As if a few crumbs mattered. If she had a life, then they wouldn't.

So we all sat round and ate fruit nicely. And apart from a few sly looks from elegant Mrs Gale, the meal was great.

'Coffee?' she asked at the end.

'Not for Charlotte, she's gone off it.'

'It's true.' I didn't tell her what I'd told Daniel, though, that I thought it tasted of piss. 'I'll have another grape juice, though, if that's OK.'

Daniel moved round to pull my chair out for me. 'And I'll have some more of that wine. We'll take it outside.'

It was still nearly as light as day but cooler out on the patio. I breathed in the evening and felt rejuvenated. Banana-baby rolled and wriggled inside me, making strange shapes I could feel under my palms. The greens of the lawn seemed to glow under the evening sky and my eyes fixed and unfocused on a cloud of midges swaying over the pond near the hedge. It must be so much less stressful being this far up the social scale, to have the space and the cash and the knowledge about the world. I thought of Mum and wished I didn't have to go back home.

'It's a lovely garden. God, that heady scent . . . Makes me think of Keats: *I cannot see what flowers are at my feet*. Although presumably that wasn't because he was straining to see over an enormous bloated belly.' Baby heaved, a blackbird began singing near us and for a moment I felt as though I was on a film set. 'You're so lucky, you know.'

Daniel helped lower me onto the steps and sat down beside me. 'Yeah, I suppose so.'

'No supposing about it.' I wondered whether to count his blessings for him – nuclear family, pots of money, social poise – but decided it might be in bad taste. In the end I said: 'Your house is incredibly calm.'

'Is it?'

I looked at him but he was gazing at the horizon.

'Oh, yeah, amazingly. Well, compared with my place, it is. So is Beirut, probably.' The bird finished singing and flew away, a cut-out black shape across the streaky sky. 'Don't you like it here?'

'Not much.' He rested his chin in his hand. 'Actually I was quite happy in Guildford.'

'Why did you move?'

He sighed. 'Dad got an offer he couldn't refuse from an old university chum. He wanted to start up a practice with my dad as a partner. Dad said it was Fate and went off to see, and liked the place. So we all upped sticks and followed. If it had been one year earlier or later we probably wouldn't have gone, they wouldn't have wanted to disrupt my education, but I'd just finished GCSEs. Conveniently.' There was a bitter note to his voice. 'I'd chosen my options for Year 12 and I was looking forward to a great year dossing with my mates – I had some, down there. Miles and Toby. We used to have some great laughs. And they weren't like those geeks I sit with in the common room; God, they're so boring they even bore themselves.'

I moved away slightly and stared at him.

'I had no idea you were so fed up.'

'We email each other, but Miles has got a girlfriend now so I don't expect I'll be hearing much from him for a while. Anyway, it's not the same.'

'Maybe you'll move back there,' I said, 'if your dad's job doesn't work out.'

'I don't think so.' He picked up a piece of gravel and flicked it out over the grass. 'You see my mum was having an affair, so we won't ever go back.'

I drew in my breath. 'God.'

'He was one of her Relate clients. She broke every rule in the book. She'd have been chucked out pronto, but luckily for her everyone involved decided to keep their mouths shut. He went back to his wife. We had a family conference about what to do, not that anyone was very interested in what I wanted. Then this job offer came up. Dad reckoned it was the only way to keep the family together. But he's still really angry, and so's she, for different reasons. Mad! In some ways it might have been better if they'd split up. I don't know. It hacks me off the way we pretend, like this evening.'

It was shocking to see him like this. I'd not thought of

him having his own problems, he was just someone who supported me through mine. I edged nearer again and put my arm round his shoulders.

'It's the wine talking. No, it's not the wine talking, it's me.'

'Oh, Daniel.'

'You're the only thing that keeps me sane, I think,' he said, and in a swift movement turned his head and kissed me on the mouth.

I didn't stop to consider, it wasn't a conscious decision, but I pushed him away and put the back of my hand to my lips. The sour tang of wine and guilt. He jerked backwards and stared, then dropped his head down so I couldn't see his face.

'Sorry, sorry, sorry. Stupid—'

I couldn't make out the rest.

'No, I'm sorry, Daniel. I really am. Sorry.'

Behind us the French windows slid open, then we heard the click of his mother's heels on the patio. A chill breeze passed over my shoulders and at the end of the garden the leaves of the beech tree stirred suddenly.

'Have you two finished with your glasses?'

'Oh, yes,' said Daniel. 'We've definitely finished.'

\*

THEY PHONED ME at work, on the last day of term. The kids were all high as kites, clearing display boards and turning out drawers. Year 6 were running round the building trying to find drawing pins to prise off the walls because Mr F had promised a Mars Bar to the child who brought him the most.

Sylv took the message, so she was beside herself with importance by the time I hit the office at morning break.

'Social services have been on. They want you to make an appointment to see a Joyce Fitton as soon as you can. Here's the number. Is it about your adoption?'

'Yes,' I said. I didn't have the energy to lie.

'Oh, Mr Fairbrother, Karen's found her birth mother.'

Mr F, who had just popped his head round the door to ask for the stapler, looked at me in surprise.

'No,' I corrected. 'Sylv's a little ahead of herself. I've got an appointment with social services, that's all. They might have some information, then again they might not. A lot of it's talking, you know, assessing.'

'Assessing what?' asked Sylv.

'Can I break in here and ask you to find a file on the computer?' said Mr F. 'Only it's quite urgent. See you later, Karen.'

I backed out gratefully and went to ring from the staff room.

I HADN'T SPOKEN to Joyce on the phone, it was another woman who took down my name in the diary, so I didn't know what she'd found out. Surely, this time, she'd have the address of my mother. The desk was a sea of papers and there was a plastic carrot stuck on the computer next to the gonk. It didn't look very professional to me. Someone had had a go at the blinds, though.

Joyce put her glasses on and opened a cardboard folder with my name on the front.

'I'm not able to disclose the address of your birth mother today, Karen,' she began.

'Fucking hell! What do we pay our fucking taxes for?' I felt like shouting. Fucking social workers! What do you do all day, sit round and drink coffee? 'Cause you don't do any fucking work, that's obvious.

'What's the delay?' I managed.

'Are you disappointed?' Joyce inclined her head sympathetically.

'I seem to have been waiting for ever.'

'It's hard, isn't it. Well, what I can give you now is a contact for your mother, someone who does know where she is and, if you like, can act as an intermediary.'

'Why? Doesn't she want to be found?'

'It's a little complicated.' Joyce put the file down and leaned forward, elbows on the desk, hands clasped. 'After she left the mother and baby home she went to stay with this lady, who was like a kind of foster-carer. She offered the girls who didn't have any support in the area a halfway house, until they'd got themselves set up with a job and lodgings, or decided to go back home. When your mother left she kept in touch over the years – I don't believe she had anything more to do with her own family back in Wigan. She settled in London and, er, changed her name.'

'You mean she married?'

'You need to speak to our contact, Mrs Beattie, Mary Beattie. She's expecting you to call and arrange something.'

'Right, well. You'd better give me her address.'

Joyce handed over a sheet of paper.

'What you can do, as I said, is use her simply as an intermediary; you don't have to meet your mother at all if you don't want to. You could just exchange letters through Mary without giving your own address.'

'Why would I want to do that?'

'I'm only telling you your options, Karen.' Joyce folded her hands over the closed file. 'And obviously I'm here if you feel you want to talk it through afterwards.'

All this bloody mystery, what a fuss over nothing. They make a job for themselves, social workers. Still, at least I could sort things out myself now, and we'd get on a damn sight faster too.

'Thanks,' I said, standing up and putting the paper in my handbag. 'I'll have to run, I've got a date.'

'Good luck,' said Joyce.

I walked out under a grey sky and hurried off to the municipal gallery to meet Mr F.

It was a collection called Dogs In Art.

'I like paintings to look like something recognizable, not a chaos of splodges. I don't know if that makes me old-fashioned.' Mr F, Leo-Since-We're-Not-At-Work, was standing in front of a large picture featuring a woman in a white nightie holding a cocker spaniel. 'I don't particularly care, either. Have you seen this little fellow? We used to have a spaniel when I was a boy.'

'What was it called?'

'Kipling. My father named him.'

'We had a black cat called Chalkie. My dad named him too. The funny thing was, he went missing the week my dad went into hospital for the last time. Neither of them came back. Chalkie wouldn't have known what to do with himself without my dad for company anyway; he used to sit on the workbench while Dad tinkered about in the shed.

Dad used to say he was teaching him how to hold a nail in his paws.'

'He sounds like a nice man.'

'Oh, he was. He really was.'

We walked on in silence and saw a dachshund on a riverbank and a gundog lying next to a pile of pheasants.

'And how did the interview with social services go? If you want to talk about it.'

'Oh, yeah, there's no problem. Well, at least I think there's no problem. They're being a bit cloak-and-dagger about making actual contact, but I've got the address of a woman who knows her so it's up to me now.'

'So you'll be off down to London?'

'Ah, well . . .'

We walked on past a St Bernard standing silhouetted on a mountain ridge and a medieval whippet sitting at the feet of a knight.

'It's weird, but I feel . . . almost scared now the end's in sight. No, maybe not *scared*, but kind of reluctant to take that final step. I keep thinking about my childhood; memories I thought I'd forgotten have started popping into my head, some of them in dreams. Nan on a picnic with a caterpillar stuck to her tights. The time she helped me win the Easter bonnet competition at school. I wonder if – if I'm kind of rejecting all that by looking for my real mother. Because they weren't all unhappy times.' We stopped in front of a Great Dane standing over a tiny baby. 'In fact, the more I think about it, I actually had quite a nice child-hood. Before Dad became ill, the most frightening event I experienced was Dr Who fighting the Sea-devils. The only betrayal I can remember was finding out the label on my teddy bear's blanket said Pure New Wool and not Mr Fuzzy's. It only went sour between me and Mum after Dad died. And some of that was probably my fault. See, within her limitations she's been a good mother. We just weren't matched, that's all.'

'Are you feeling disloyal?'

'Yes.'

'Come and have a cup of tea and a bun.'

Leo led me out of the gallery – 'Unashamedly populist but very enjoyable nevertheless,' he told the woman at the desk – and across the road to the Octagon.

'This is something I remember.' I stirred the sugar round in the bowl with a teaspoon. 'Did you believe in sugar stealers when you were little?'

'I'm not sure what you mean.'

I started to smooth out the granules with the back of the spoon. 'Those floaty seeds – dandelion clocks and such – we all thought at primary school that they were insects, or something, and they lived on sugar. I was always finding them in our larder. I really thought it was true for ages.'

Leo laughed. 'No, I can't say I've heard that one. Tell me another.'

I chopped patterns in the smoothed-out grains while I thought.

'OK, what about those green glass chips you get on graves.'

'What about them?'

'Well, if you take even one of them home with you, the ghost of the person whose grave it is will come and haunt you in your bedroom until you put it back.'

'Did you ever try it?'

'No way. Too scary. But a boy in our class did and he swore he was woken in the night by an evil old woman. He lived with his grandma, though, so that was probably it.'

Leo was chuckling and wiping his eyes. 'Stop, stop. You'll have me choking on my bun.'

'And there was a big craze for giving yourself love bites on the arm, of course we were only eight, we didn't know what they were. Some lads had completely purple forearms. I'm amazed nobody contacted the NSPCC. Then a girl called Sharon Dawes said her mother had caught her doing it and told her it would give her cancer, so we all stopped overnight. Except for Christopher Flint, but he was mad. He got sent to a special school in Little Lever.'

We were both giggling now.

'Sounds like Gavin Crossley,' said Leo. 'I can't see him being with us much longer, the rate he's going.'

'Oh, he was much worse than that. He pushed a wardrobe on top of his brother once, and fired an airgun at Mrs Porter from the newsagent's when she refused to give him a paper round.'

'Village characters.'

'Happy times.'

'So do you think you'll go to London or not?'

'God knows. I'll toss a coin. No, I won't; I'll count the currants in my bun. Evens says I go, odds I stay.' I took a knife and began to saw. 'I can always change my mind later.'

\*

I NEVER had no new clothes when I was a girl except for the lace-up shoes I wore on a Sunday, it was all hand-me-downs. So at Field Days, Walkin' Days they're called now, I used have to go at t' back o' t' line even though the only time I ever missed church was when I broke my arm. I'll tell you who allus walked under the banner, it was Annie Catterall in her fancy white frock, an' she never went to Sunday school nor nothin'. It was only 'cause her parents could afford to kit her out. One time my friend Lily Alker was on a ribbon off a banner, I don't know how she managed it 'cause her father was an invalid. She'd perhaps lent a frock off someone. Anyroad, they were gettin' to th' end of the procession and this ribbon broke. Annie pocketed it, took it home an' made hair braids out of it. When she got found out she was stripped and sent to bed, besides gettin' a good hidin'. So perhaps I was best off marchin' at the back.

The worst whippin' I ever got was when I took all my mother's buttons to play in t' street. We used make a circle in t' dirt an' try an' flirt these buttons in, an' if you got a button inside you could have your pick of all the others. I got in a row many a time for it, but you don't think when you're young. They used play piggy too, an' cock-on-big-or-little. Piggy were t' best, though I don't think they play it now. You used put your piggy, which were a fat peg of wood with a whittled end, on a brick on t' floor so as snout was hangin' ovver th' end. Then you got a stick and you walloped it so it flew i' th' air. Some big lads could mek it go right along t' street. They used guess how many strides away it was. Sometimes the Co-Op held races down the Chantry, but I never won owt. I could never run, me. I got a doll once, but that was only 'cause everyone did; I still finished last.

But they were poor days. When times were good Grandma Florrie made parkin an' barm cakes, steak puddings and cow heel with a crust on top. A tripe man used come round t' streets too, shoutin'. But in the years after the war, when I was still only little, my mother had to go to the church for charity loaves, you could have two a week. An' there were allus people singin' in the streets, beggin', an' miners squattin' at street corners 'cause they had no work.

My mother was marvellous, now I think about it, because me an' Jimmy never felt it, all that poverty, not really. I wish I could have known her longer.

*

**Anya had** phoned up to say she was going into school for her module results and did I want to meet her there.

'The twins are going for a picnic in the park after, if it's not raining. They're dying to see you. So am I. Come on, shift yourself.'

I thought I was too miserable to lift my head off the pillow, but I went in the end. Missing Daniel was like a pain; worse than splitting up with Paul, which had been a series of stabs to the chest. This feeling was a deep, dull ache all over, as if I was about to come down with flu.

I wondered if I was going to bump into him at the office. Theoretically students come between 10 and 12 to pick up their slips, but in practice there's a seething crowd of hysterical teenagers round the front door by 9.50 and a mad rush when the head of sixth comes down to open it. I slid in with the general melee at 10.03 so I didn't have to wait around being gawped at. Generally the students who come later are the ones who know they've either done really well or really badly. A lot of posturing goes on, class jokers pretending to be amazed they didn't do even worse; huddles of girls patting and hugging tearful friends in an agony of embarrassment at their own success.

The teachers stand around and offer congratulations where appropriate, and avoid eye contact where it's not. The air is electric. I hated it last year, hated it again now.

For those few minutes my pregnancy was completely forgotten. Anya and I stood in isolated pools of agony, tearing open the slips, gazing, absorbing, then shrieking at each other, at anyone who'd listen.

'I got an A!'

'Oh my God, so did I!'

Anya put her arm round me, no mean feat, and we tottered out onto the drive like two drunks. Mrs Carlisle hurried after us.

'Well done, both of you. Looking forward to next year.' She smiled at me. 'This is for you, my home phone number. You can call me at any time and we can get together to talk about how things stand.' She passed me a sealed envelope. 'Don't let it fall into the wrong hands. I don't want obscene calls all summer!'

'She is *so* nice,' said Anya as we walked slowly out of the gates towards the park. We passed the twins on their way in, mad with nerves, but there was still no sign of Daniel. It occurred to me he might be away or have arranged for them to be posted. But I couldn't stop scanning the faces as one car after another drove past us over the ramp and crawled round the quad.

'Do you want to talk about the baby?' asked Anya unexpectedly. 'Now, I mean, before the twins come out. Because we weren't sure whether you'd like to or not, and we didn't want to get it wrong.'

Poor Anya. It must have cost her an effort to say that.

I shook my head. 'Thanks. No, I don't, not this after-noon. I think I'd like to just be me, not Mrs Pregnant. Do you mind?'

'No, not at all.' There was relief in her voice. I wished then, so keenly, that I could have shed the pregnancy for a few hours, unstrapped the bulge and hung it up in the wardrobe. I wanted a break, time off for good behaviour, one last good laugh with the girls and then I'd be ready to go back to it in the evening. It was so *part of me*. I looked awful now and felt breathless most of the time, couldn't bend down, constantly needed to pee . . . You're a big parasite, I'd told the baby in the bath. Let it hear, I didn't care.

When the twins caught up ('two Cs') we strolled to the park and sat round the sunken garden, eating. And although there was this great black hole in the conversa-tion, everyone including me trying to avoid the topic that was screaming in our faces, it was good because there were so many other things to talk about. Teenage things, trivia, plans, gossip. I couldn't exactly join in, but I could listen and laugh and tease.

An ice-cream van rolled up and Anya and I went to get 99s for us all. The sun was pretty hot now and there was a shimmer over the grass. As I cast my eyes over the red and white flower beds sloping up to the entrance I spotted Daniel walking quickly towards us. I didn't know what to do, and anyway I had an ice-cream cone in each hand so I was a bit restricted. I smiled, then looked away in case that was too much. One of the ice-creams began to melt and drip over my fingers, so I twisted my hand round and tried to lick it off. Daniel broke into a run.

'No!' he shouted.

'What's up with him?' I turned to Anya but she only shrugged.

Without losing speed he charged at me and, like a jousting knight, knocked the 99 from my grasp. It splatted onto the floor, cone upended, and began to merge with the gravel.

He overshot, blasted through a flower bed and staggered to a halt several metres away, panting. Anya pulled a Loony face at me.

'What the bloody hell do you think you're doing?' I asked. This was some bizarre revenge for rejecting him.

He came up to us, wild haired and grinning.

'That was a close one. Didn't your midwife tell you about listeria?'

'Yeah. Deadly bug. It's in blue cheese and pâté and I don't like either. So?'

'And in soft ice-cream from vans, if you're unlucky. Can't be too careful. Can I treat you to a choc ice?'

'Jesus.' I turned to Anya with a despairing look. What would you do with him?

'I'll leave you to it,' she said, sniggering, and joined the goggle-eyed twins back on the bench.

What could I do? 'I'll have a Zoom,' I said grimly.

We must have made an odd couple from a distance, me like a barrel on legs and him a tall streak of nothing. When he gave me my lolly he flourished his hand and bowed. I could have kicked him.

'Listen, Prince Charming, do you want me to stick this up your nose?' I hissed.

We went over and joined the others but there were a lot of meaningful looks going on behind our backs and stifled giggles. I'll give them the benefit of the doubt and say they were still a bit hysterical from the exam results.

'Well,' said Anya after about thirty seconds, 'we must be off if we're going to hit the shops. Are you coming into town with us?'

'Not a lot of point me trailing round the Arndale at the moment. I'll have to be getting back soon, anyway.'

I knew they couldn't wait to be on their own. They'd probably phone Julia from town and give her a blow-by-blow account of the Madman in Queen's Park.

We said goodbye with lots of hugging and promises to ring and good lucks, then they scarpered. Daniel was lying along a bench chewing his lolly stick.

'Waiting for the E numbers to kick in,' he said.

'I think they already have. Did you take your Ritalin today?'

'The only problem I've got is Grade Deficit Disorder,' he said sitting up and shading his eyes.

'Really? What did you get?'

'B and a C. My parents will be scandalized. Still, serves them right for moving me at a critical period of my development.'

I went and sat at the other end of the bench.

'B C isn't too bad. They're only modules. You can retake, can't you?'

'Yeah, yeah. It's OK, I've got all the spiel worked out in my head for when I get home. You got an A, didn't you?'

'More trouble at home; my mother'll make me wear it round my neck like the albatross. How did you know?'

'Lucky guess. Well done. My dad'll be delighted, he thinks you're wonderful.'

'It was nice of him to drive me back last week.'

'No problem. He enjoyed talking to you. He says you're intelligent. I got a bollocking though for being too pissed to drive you myself.'

'Were you? Pissed?'

'Oh, yes.' He inspected his lolly stick and read out the joke. 'What zooms along the river bed at 100 m.p.h.?'

'I dunno.'

'A motor pike and a side carp. Nice one.' He pock-eted the stick and got up. 'I'll give you a lift back now, if you want.'

'I won't say no.'

And so, just like that, we fell back into step as if nothing had happened. Maybe both of us had too much to lose.

'Do you mind if I don't ask you in? Only I'm dead tired, I really need to lie down.'

'I've got to get home myself. Face the music.' Daniel grimaced. 'Bloody parents, they're a liability. See you!'

He bibbed his horn and I trailed up the front path feeling suddenly depressed. Reaction, I suppose. I struggled with the door, tossed the results slip on the table and collapsed on the sofa. Nan came out of the kitchen, beaming.

'Eeh, it's our Charlotte. You're looking bonny, love. Get your feet up and Debbie'll make you a cup of tea. She's brought a little present for you.'

I blew her a kiss.

'I do love you, Nan,' I said.

\*

WHEN I GOT IN Milady was lying on the sofa admiring a tiny sleepsuit, Nan was massaging Charlotte's feet and Debbie the cleaner was holding a needle and thread over her tummy.

'I can't tell whether it's swinging in a circle or not,' Debbie was saying. 'And I can't remember which way round it is, anyway. Can you, Nan? Is it a circle for a boy and a straight line for a girl?'

'Perhaps it's a hermaphrodite,' quipped Charlotte. I know for a fact neither of them know what that is, but they both laughed.

I picked up the scrap of paper on the table and winced. It was the report fiasco all over again. Shame she didn't get an A in Doing as you're Damn Well Told.

'You do know you're throwing your life away,' I snapped as I went past. She never even turned her head.

'Ooh, I just saw the baby move!' exclaimed Debbie. 'Bless it.'

'Can I have a feel?' said Nan.

THREE DAYS later I walked out.

# Chapter Nine

THE DAY STARTED as per usual, with Nan wandering in and announcing it was morning. Up with the lark, that's my mother. Back in her bedroom I changed her bag then she stumped downstairs and had a wash. Meanwhile I threw on leggings and shirt. Nan returned to her room to get dressed and I trailed down to the kitchen to make breakfast. It's a kind of ballet sequence we've refined over the years, and the only one who ever throws a spanner in the works is Charlotte, rising unexpectedly early or locking herself in the bathroom for a pre-school hair crisis.

But this morning I'd finished my toast and Nan still hadn't made an appearance, so I went back upstairs to see what the matter was. She was sitting on the bed in her underslip glowering at the chair.

'What's up now?' I asked. 'Your Weetabix is going cold.'

'I'm not wearing that.' She pointed to the dress slung over the chair back.

'Why ever not?'

'It's not red.'

'Oh, for God's sake. It's a lovely frock, Mum. You wore it last week.'

She glared at me.

'I tell you what, why don't you put that little maroon cardigan over the top? That's reddish.'

No answer.

'Well, you can't go to church in your underslip. Maud and Ivy'll be here soon, you don't want to hold them up.' I opened the wardrobe door and rifled through her clothes. 'Wait a minute, what about this?' I pulled out a grey dress with scarlet flowers on the skirt. 'This is a nice one.'

'It's not red enough.'

With enormous control I put the grey dress back and walked out onto the landing to check the laundry basket. Maybe her red wool two-piece could be redeemed with a squirt of Febreze and a good shake. I rooted about and found it, but there was a soup stain down the front. I flung it back in and stood there thinking. I had four choices. I could throw myself over the banisters now, this very minute. Then they'd all be sorry. I could burst into noisy tears which no one would take any notice of. I could go into Mum's room and slap her across the face – oh, I know it's a terrible thought, I'm supposed to be her carer and it's not her fault etc. etc., but believe me, there are times when I come so close I have to walk away and count ten. Or, and this was the plan resolving itself before my eyes as being the most reasonable course of action under the circumstances, I could run away.

I went back into Mum's room and pulled out all the spare bags and tape she needs for changing and put them on the dressing table. Then I got out the little scissors from her jewellery box and cut the right size openings in the top of every bag.

'I'm old enough to do as I like,' she snapped suddenly.

'No, Mum, you're not old *enough*, you're *too* old, that's the point.'

I got the overnight case from the top of her wardrobe and took it into my room. (*We're off! We're off!*) My head started to sing a stupid song of Nan's to the rhythm of my breathing. I packed a smart suit and a pair of courts, two pairs of leggings and assorted tops, knickers, travel wash, make-up and curling tongs. (*We're off in a motor car!*) Walking past Mum's bedroom I could see she'd lain down on the bed and closed her eyes. I carried straight on downstairs to the bathroom where I topped up my sponge bag, then in the hall I checked my handbag and address book. (*Sixty bobbies are after us and we don't know where we are!*) Finally I scribbled a note to Charlotte saying I'd gone to stay with a friend for a few days but I'd give her a ring that evening and if she needed help to contact her dad or social services. It was completely irresponsible of me. I imagined the expressions of horror when Charlotte finally roused herself to let Maud and Ivy in and they discovered the truth together. Well, they'd just have to sort it out.

I slammed the Metro door so hard the hinges all but fell off, then stuck a Madonna tape on full blast. All the way to Manchester I justified myself to the music. 'Rescue Me'. 'Secret'. 'Bad Girl'. I couldn't believe what I'd done.

Then, as I drew into the half-empty car park, the tape came to an end and a man on the radio said Princess Diana was dead.

I sat in the car for a few minutes, listening; a car crash, France, early hours of the morning, a high-speed chase. 'The phone lines are open now for your calls,' the presenter said. 'Please do dial and let us know how you're feeling about this terribly sad, this shocking tragedy; hello, Gemma from Radcliffe.' Gemma, quavering: 'I just can't believe it, she was so young—' I switched the radio off and got quietly out of the car.

I walked up to the station, past the screaming headlines on the newspaper stand, past a huge chalk-heart someone had scrawled on the wall near the cafe, *R.I.P. DI.* Unreal. I bought my ticket on autopilot and went to stand on the platform where a little group was talking to each other animatedly. Tight-faced fifty-something woman, nasty claw-shaped brooch on her coat; very thin man freezing in shirt sleeves; young lass in salwar kameez and anorak, towing meek child: normally they'd all be busy maintaining personal space. But this morning was different.

'In a tunnel,' claw woman was saying, 'awful.' 'Those boys,' murmured the young mum, shaking her head while her tiny daughter stood with her face upturned, watching pigeons fly between the metal rafters above our heads. The thin man balled his fists: 'Bloody journalists. They want locking up. They've no bloody scruples.'

'It said in our paper she was just Very Badly Injured,' claw woman piped up, 'I thought she was still alive till I put the telly on. I can't believe it.'

Thin man saw me staring at his *Observer* and handed it to me without a word. I held it up, saw the pictures and read the words, so it was true.

Then the train to Euston slid in.

As the coach lurched out of the station I sat alone in my corner by the window and thought about Diana, and about me. I remembered all the royal wedding celebrations, all that hope and happiness in the midst of my own messed-up life, her lovely smiling face and that rumpled fairytale dress. Everyone had seemed united, you'd felt like the whole nation was with you as you sat in front of the telly watching that balcony kiss. I'd kept the souvenir issue of the *Radio Times* and even copied the haircut, briefly. I thought she was charmed, then it turned out she'd been duped just like the rest of us. Confessing and crying on prime-time TV; I'd squirmed for her. And now after so much unhappiness she was dead, shocking proof that money and elegance and class and beauty, none of them mean anything in the face of Fate.

Sadness tightened on my chest, and guilt. If she couldn't get it right, what chance had the rest of us? Then my own failings and inadequacies seemed to rise up like a cold mist around me so that I suddenly found myself in tears and had to stare out of the window at the blurred countryside. I didn't even know her, I thought, so why am I crying?

\*

**It was turning into** a surreal kind of day. No Mum, Dad in the kitchen unloading frozen ready-meals and tins of Nan food, and all the TV stations awash with the Diana story, whichever channel you flicked to.

'I know it's a shame, but I don't know why there's all these women in tears,' I muttered. 'You'd think she'd been personal best friend to a hundred thousand people. I reckon they're putting it on for the cameras.'

'I got you six of these mini pizzas 'cause they were

on special offer,' said Dad. He was well pissed off, you could tell. 'What a flamin' carry-on. I have to be at work tomorrow, you know. I've had that much time off the boss has given me a warning. But Ivy Seddon says they're organizing a rota at the Over Seventies', and I've been on the phone to social services and there's a nurse coming round every morning for an hour. That Crossroads woman's here tomorrow and then there's that cleaner you have. It'll be like Paddy's market. You certainly won't be on your own, love. I'll come round every evening after I've had my tea. Anyroad, your mum might not be away so long, she could be back in a day or two.'

'I'm not bothered, Dad.' I wasn't either. In some ways it was a relief to have her out the house. 'She's done it before, remember. That time she found a lump in her breast and took herself off to Fleetwood for a long weekend.'

'Aye. And it were nowt in t' finish. Do you think she really has gone to stay with a friend?'

'I wouldn't have thought so. She doesn't have any.'

'It's norra man, then?'

'Nah.'

'I just wondered.'

'She's been horrible about the baby, you know. She wanted me to get rid of it.'

Dad became very busy stacking the freezer compartment.

'Well, she was only thinking of you. She thought it would be for t' best. You know, your education and that.'

'I don't think I'll ever forgive her.'

Nan wandered in.

'Where's our Karen?'

Dad and I exchanged glances.

'She's had to pop out for a while. Do you fancy a brew?' Dad unplugged the kettle and held it under the cold tap.

'I need my bag changing,' she sighed.

'Over to you,' said Dad.

*

As soon as I got off the train I found a mobile phone place, threw my credit card at the assistant and emerged with a Nokia, a charger and twenty quid's worth of vouchers. 'You've one blob left on your battery,' the smart lad in the shop had said. 'You're telling me,' I joked, but he'd lost interest. Then I went outside onto a grass verge, away from all the bustle, and read the instruction booklet. At last I felt ready to dial.

Unluckily it was Steve who answered, so the first few seconds were him calling me every name under the sun. When I could get a word in edgeways, I told him my number and got him to write it down and read it back; it's not that he's thick, far from it, but he's careless. I asked after Charlotte and Nan and got another mouthful of abuse, then I heard Charlotte's voice in the background asking to speak to me. I knew if I let her I'd fall apart; I'd turn straight back to the station and climb on the next available train home. So I said quickly, 'Tell her I'll be home in a day or two. Battery's flat. Got to go.' Then I pressed *End* and switched off for half an hour. If I was going to do this right I needed to clear my head.

I retraced my steps into the station, bought a street

map off a stall and went down the escalator to the Underground. I stood in front of the Tube map for ages, trying to work it out while people barged into me and sighed with impatience over the top of my head. I reached forward and tried to trace the route with my finger, like a slow reader. Northern line, change at King's Cross to the Piccadilly. That was OK. But which *zone* was I in and how much would that make the ticket? There was a massive queue at the ticket office so I spent ages studying one of the machines to a background of irritated tuttings from the woman behind me. At last I pressed the right button and a bit of card dropped into my palm. Now, which escalator? I stood like a rock in the middle of a swirling river. An oriental man with a briefcase stood on my foot. 'Sorry,' I said. He disappeared into the crowds without looking back.

I made my decision, glided down past the adverts for theatres and museums, and found myself in a windy tunnel that smelt of burning rubber. Did I want platform 1 or 2? How should I bloody know? A quick check of my pocket diary and down the tiled walkway, then finally out onto a platform with a lot of bored-looking people. Almost instantly there was a terrific noise and the train shot out and slowed to a halt in front of us. The doors hissed open. I stood back politely and was nearly knocked over in the rush to get on.

The last time I was in London was a school trip to coincide with the Silver Jubilee. We'd worn school uniform and our commemorative badges because, our form mistress had said, that's what the Queen would want, not jeans and Kickers. We'd gone to stand outside Buckingham Palace and someone had said the Queen was definitely in because of the way the flag was flying, so she might have looked out of the window and seen us.

The train came into King's Cross, where there was a teenage girl begging with a baby on her hip. I thought of Charlotte and pulled out my purse. The girl's top lip was covered in sores, but her eyes were pretty. Where was *her* mum, I wondered.

'What's his name?' I asked smiling at the round-eyed snotty baby.

'Ellie,' she said and pocketed the note neatly.

I thought about her all the way to Arnos Grove.

At last I came up the steps into the sunlight, feeling bruised. I pulled out my street map and started walking. I was looking for Hemmington Grove and Mrs Mary Beattie.

*

**Actually it's** no big deal, changing Nan (after all, I'll be doing nappies soon). It used to freak me out at first, but now it just makes me sad. Nan lies meekly on the bed with a towel under her, her dress pulled up and her knickers and tights round her thighs. There are poor little white hairs between her legs and the skin is loose round her belly. You peel off the old micropore tape and the used bag and put them in something like a nappy sack. Then you wipe round the weird, amazingly clean hole in Nan's flesh with a sterile tissue. You take the backing strip off the new bag, stick it down with the opening against Nan's stomach, and Mum likes to make extra sure with some tape on top. Sometimes, if the skin's red, we use Nivea but you have to be careful not to get it under the tape or nothing sticks and it's a disaster. Nan remains glassy-eyed throughout, then switches back into life the minute you pull her dress back down. So there you are. Nothing to it.

I was heading towards the bin after the lunchtime change when the doorbell rang. Dad was right, it was like Paddy's market. I thought it was another of Ivy's volunteers, but it turned out to be Daniel clutching a Moses basket.

'One of my father's patients asked if he could find a home for it. It needs a new mattress but it's got a stand and some frilly gubbins to go round the sides.'

'Brilliant.' I took it off him and laid it on the sofa while he went to get the rest from the car. Maud and Nan crowded round to see.

'Eeh, in't it lovely?' said Nan.

'Better than a drawer,' said Maud, peering inside. 'That's where me mother put me when I were born.'

'Well, they did in them days,' said Nan. 'In't it lovely, though.'

'Where's it going to go?' asked Maud.

Nan shrugged.

'It can come in my room,' I said. 'It'll have to. Be easier, anyway, if I'm getting up at night.' I glanced out of the window and saw Daniel struggling with a stack of books and a froth of broderie anglaise. 'Hang on.'

I waddled down the path and opened the gate for him.

'Come here, you daft 'aporth. Let me have some of the books, at least.'

'They're from Mrs Carlise. She thought you could be doing some reading before term starts. Don't take too many now, just these from the top.'

'Oh, God, I must phone her. I've been meaning—' I

broke off with a cry and the paperbacks fell on the pavement.

'What's the matter?' Daniel threw his stuff back on the seat and put his arm round me.

'Get me in. Get me in, Dan.'

We staggered inside and I sat down breathlessly.

'What is it, Charlotte? Have you got a pain?'

Nan and Maud were hovering anxiously.

'Shall I make her a cup of tea?' asked Maud.

'Yes, that would be excellent. Thank you.' Daniel came and sat next to me and fluttered his hands. 'What is it, Charlotte?'

I groaned. 'It was Paul. Across the road, you didn't see him. He was walking past with a Spar bag. He saw me—' Oh Christ, the humiliation. He'd seen me and stared, then deliberately looked the other way till he was round the corner. He'd have run if he could. Bastard.

'Paul.'

'Yes.'

'Dirty bugger,' said Nan miming a spit. 'He'll come to his cake and milk.'

'I'm not terrifically good at that sort of thing, but I'll go after him and hit him if it would make you feel better,' said Daniel. 'All you have to do is tell me where he lives.'

Even in the midst of my personal hell I couldn't help but smile at the image. 'Excuse me,' Daniel would probably say first, 'do you mind if I punch you in the mouth?' Then Paul would knock seven bells out of him.

'No, it's OK. My dad's tried that one. Silly sod.'

Daniel let out a sigh of relief and Maud came in with the tea.

'Look, are you definitely all right? Do I need to get you to a doctor?'

'No, really, I'm fine. Just mortified, that's all.' I took a sip of tea. 'Thanks, Mrs Eckersley. I could do with a lie-down, though.'

'Good idea. Get your feet up.' Daniel rose to his feet. 'I must be going, anyway.'

'Please stay,' I said. 'Come up to my room so we can talk.'

Maud gave me a funny look and I nearly said to her, 'For God's sake, I can't get any *more* pregnant, can I?'

'**I'm sorry** the room's so small,' I said as Daniel folded himself into the beanbag chair.

'What are you smiling at?'

'Nothing. It seems strange you being here, that's all.' I was reclining on the bed with Nan's V-shaped pillow behind my head, trying to find the right way to lie. 'The trouble with being this size is you can never get comfortable.'

'I suspect you're going to get even bigger before you've finished.'

'It's all right for you, Slim-Jim.' I lay back.

'Shall I put some music on?'

'Yeah, will you? The tapes are on that shelf by your head. Pick what you like, so long as it's chilled. Actually, that one on the top is good, it's what Julia did for me. Supposed to be my labour tape. Soundtrack to my agony.'

'Everything's very . . . to hand in this room.' Daniel switched on the cassette player by leaning to one side and stretching across the shelf. The music started and we listened for a few minutes without speaking.

> *What sense does love make?*
> *Your brain's turned inside out*
> *A chemical illusion*
> *That makes you want to shout*

It was me who began. 'The thing about Paul is, I hate him but in a way I still love him. No, not *him*, but the person I thought he was. He seemed great at first because he was so happy-go-lucky and I'm so serious; I actually thought he was *good for me*. Mad. Even now I can't totally shake off the promise of those initial few weeks. My brain still hasn't caught up with recent events. I *know* he's a shit but he's the baby's father too.'

'Not if he doesn't want to be. You can't force him to have anything to do with the child if he doesn't want to. You might be able to extract a few quid out of him after the birth, but that's about all.'

'I know. But biologically . . .'

'Biology's nothing. Inserting your knob at an opportune moment.'

We both blushed. The song finished and another one began.

> *You are the star–sun–moon that guides me*
> *My lightship in the storm*
> *You keep me safe from harm*
> *Safe and warm*
> *Through the storm*

'The other problem is he's practically on the doorstep,

as demonstrated today. We'll always be bumping into each other, it'll be awful.'

Daniel chewed his fingernail. 'All the more reason to get your university place sorted, you can always defer it. Put that wanker behind you and get on with your life.'

'I know, I know. You are right.' I heaved myself up slightly and grinned feebly at him. 'Actually, now I think about it, he was a wanker at primary school. He was one of those lads who used to set up trouble and then walk away. It was never him who got shouted at. But he was funny and good at football so he had a lot of mates. He knew all these rude songs.'

' "My Uncle Billy had a three foot willy", that sort of thing?'

I smirked. 'It was four foot round here. You were obviously suffering from shrinkage down south.'

'Huh,' said Daniel.

'Then there was the classic: "Ooh, aah, I lost my bra, I left my knickers in my boyfriend's car", and "Jesus Christ superstar, wears plastic knickers and a Playtex bra", "All the girls in Spain wash their knickers in the rain". It was all underwear.'

'The knickers-knackers-knockers school of comedy.'

'If you say so. He had this joke too; he'd go up to you and he'd say, "Are you a PLP?" If you said no, he'd say, "Are you not a Proper Living Person, then?" If you said yes he'd go, "You're a Public Leaning Post, then," and barge into you.'

'Sounds like a genius.'

'And once we had this student teacher in, a really nice bloke, actually. He was always changing in and out of his tracksuit like Superman or something, and one time when he left his shoes in the classroom Paul wrote WAN KER on the bottoms with Tipp-Ex. Or at least, that's what he meant to write. But he got the shoes mixed up, so when this teacher sat on the floor with us at storytime with his legs out in front of him and his feet together, it actually said KERWAN on his soles. Everyone still thought it was dead funny, though.'

'I suspect there's a lot of inbreeding in this village,' said Daniel.

\*

NUMBER 80 WAS a neat Edwardian semi with white-painted sills, a black front door and two giant terracotta pots on either side of the step. I could see swagged Sanderson curtains at the bay window and a fern in a Wedgwood planter. I must have stood for ten minutes just staring; I suppose I was hoping someone would come out, but no one did. Eventually I picked up my case and carried on down the road, swinging my head from right to left as I searched for B & B signs. I turned right at the bottom of the road into a street where the houses were smaller and terraced and found a bed and breakfast place at once.

The hall smelt of elderly dog and the wallpaper was grubby but I wasn't too fussed. It was only a base. The wheezing old lady who led me up to my room asked lots of questions but then didn't give me any time to answer, which suited me. I shut the door on her and took off my shoes; it was time to phone Mrs Beattie. Where was my mobile?

I psyched myself up to press the on button, but this

time the battery really was flat. Now that was Fate. I threw the phone down on the bed in relief. Then I had second thoughts and put it on to charge while I unpacked and had a wash in the poky little sink. Looking at myself in the mirror I wondered what my mother would make of me after all this time. I wanted her to be impressed, to think I'd grown up to be a stylish, together sort of woman. I wasn't in bad nick, on the whole. My skin was quite good for my age – a few lines round the mouth, that was all – and my hair was in between cuts which is when it looks its best. I'd wear my suit and courts, and paint my nails if I had time. I lay back down on the bed and caught my breath with the enormity of it all.

My mother.

After an hour I tried the phone again. The screen lit up; it was time.

A posh woman answered.

'Am I speaking to Mrs Mary Beattie?'

'Yes, you are. Can I help you?' She sounded cool and professional, like a consultant's receptionist: I'm sorry I can't give you your test results over the phone.

'Er, my name's Karen Cooper. Mrs Fitton from Bolton Social Services might have rung about me. I think – she said you might be able to – can you help me find my birth mother? Her name was Jessie Pilkington. She stayed with you once, a long time ago.'

'Yes, yes . . . Joyce Fitton did ring.' She paused and I could hear my own breathing in the receiver. 'Yes, well, what we thought you could do was come down and see me sometime and I'd talk you through—'

'I'm here.'

'Are you actually in London?'

'Yeah. I'm staying with a friend. I'd like to, if it's not too much trouble, I'd like to come and see you.'

'Let me check my diary,' she said.

I wandered over to the window and gazed down at the back yard. It wasn't so different from a two-up, two-down in Wigan. It was more the *feel* of the place; it had to be London, somehow. It just didn't feel northern.

'Right.' She was back on. 'Can you manage tomorrow morning? Say, ten? Or is that too early? Where are you coming from?'

'Ten's fine. I'll be there.'

'I'll look forward to seeing you,' she said, and my heart dropped like a stone with terror.

*

**That night** it was antenatal class. I plonked myself at the back and tried to look older than I was, also as if I'd just left my loving husband at home instead of an angry dad and a mad grannie.

The midwife held up a plastic pelvis and forced a doll's head through it. I sat there, thirty-four weeks pregnant and still thinking: *This isn't me, this is not going to happen to me. I'm not ready. I can't do it.*

'Burned your bridges now, girl, haven't you?' I heard my mother's voice say.

*

I SAT ON the chaise longue, waiting for Mrs Beattie to make tea, feeling exhausted. All night long I'd been running after trains. One was going to America and I said to John Noakes (because he was with me), 'How can it go across the sea?' and he said, 'Oh, anything's possible.' I got up far too early, felt cold, got back in bed again and painted my fingernails. I turned on the radio but it was all still Diana's death. I had a little weep – half of it was nerves – and then went down to breakfast which I couldn't eat. My landlady was clearly a big Elvis fan and all through the meal I kept my eyes fixed on the Love Me Tender wall clock whose hour hand was the neck of a guitar. Time moved so slowly I thought the thing was broken. Then I got dressed and was all ready to go by nine twenty, so I had to walk up and down the road several times. Even though Mrs Beattie wasn't my mother I'd put on the suit.

'Here we are,' she said, passing me a china cup and saucer. I looked in vain for a safe place to put it down. If I spilt tea over this nice chintz! I perched the cup on my lap and took in the room.

'This is such a lovely house,' I said. It was too. Everything I'd seen, I wanted.

'It's rather big for me now I'm on my own. The stairs are becoming difficult too.'

I wondered how old she was. Seventy? Very elegant, though. Nothing like Mum. 'You could get one of those stairlifts.'

'It might come to that.'

We sipped our tea. What was she thinking? Inscrutable, that's what she was.

'Well, about my birth mother,' I announced.

She pressed her lips together and put down the cup on the slate hearth. 'Yes. There are some documents on the bureau, if you'd like to fetch them over. Bring the side table and we can have it between us. I need to take you through this.'

My heart thumped as she separated the sheets of paper one by one.

'Do I take it you know nothing about your mother at all?'

'Only that she was very young and she wasn't married. Oh, I knew she'd stayed in London. Probably couldn't wait to escape!' I squeaked with nervous laughter. My voice was too loud in that quiet room.

'Right,' said Mrs Beattie carefully. She pushed a piece of photocopied paper towards me. 'I want you to read this.'

It was a newspaper report dated April 1971. A man and a woman living in Croydon had been charged with manslaughter after a child had died in their care. The six-year-old's body showed signs of serious malnourishment and was covered in bruises and sores. She – it was a little girl – was described as looking like a child two years younger because of her small frame. Neighbours had become suspicious after seeing the girl foraging in dustbins and reported what they had seen to social services, but somehow the messages hadn't got through. School noticed nothing because she was never there. She hadn't even been on the At Risk register when she died.

The little girl's name was Emma and Jessie Pilkington had been her mother.

I read it and read it and read it and it still didn't make sense. Mrs Beattie reached out and took my hand. I was shaking.

'Would she have been my sister?' I whispered.

'Half-sister.'

'Oh, God. My little sister.' I started to cry. Mrs Beattie sat back and let me, patting my hand. The clock ticked and traffic swooshed past the window; I wasn't aware of anything else. We stayed like that for a long time.

At last she said, 'I have a photograph, but you may not want to see it.'

I wiped my eyes. 'Of Emma?'

'Of all of them. Taken from a newspaper.'

'I think it might break my heart.'

She put her arms round me and I felt like I was a child again, Nan holding me the first time we knew Dad was ill. There was a ticking clock then as well, and the radio in the kitchen playing 'Bridge Over Troubled Water'.

I'm on your side.

'Did Mrs Fitton know all this?'

'Yes.' Mrs Beattie wiped her eyes. 'But because I'm a trained counsellor and I used to work for social services she thought I'd be the most suitable person to talk to you about it. And, of course, I knew your mother.'

'How could she do something so *awful*? I mean, your *own child*?' Charlotte, baby Charlotte crying in her cot, toddler Charlotte throwing porridge on the floor, wetting the bed; beautiful Charlotte.

'She became involved with a violent man, as a lot of women do, you'd be surprised by how many, all walks of life. She was a very . . . needy person, not at all able to stand up for herself, despite the big talk. So she stayed with this man even after he began to abuse her daughter – it wasn't his child, she'd got pregnant by another man, which didn't help matters. She always maintained she never actually hurt Emma herself. I don't know if that was true or not. There certainly wasn't enough evidence to convict her of direct cruelty; her defence claimed the only reason she hadn't acted to save her daughter was that she was frightened he might start beating her as well. It may have been true. She got four years; he got fifteen, but he died of cancer before he was released.'

'Good.'

'Then when Jessie came out of prison she changed her name and moved. There was terribly bad feeling towards her from the public, as there always is in these cases, though I don't think the press was as intrusive then as it is now. She'd had hate mail, death threats, so she tried to walk away from what she'd done and reinvent herself. By and large she succeeded.'

I put my hands to my temples. 'I still can't take it in.'

'It must be a great shock for you. Can I get you anything, a glass of brandy?'

'No. I'll take a couple of paracetamol, I've some in my handbag.' But I knew paracetamol would never take away the cold clamping sensation in my heart, or stop me reliving those horrific phrases from the report.

Mrs Beattie went off to get a glass of water and I found myself opening the file again, scanning for those pictures. Don't do it! part of me was screaming, but I had to know. And there she was, a fine-featured little girl in a check dress and a cardigan, smiling away and looking as if she didn't have a care in the world. I closed the file quickly. My heart felt as if it was going to burst with grief and fury.

'So my m— Jessie Pilkington's still alive?' I asked when Mrs Beattie came back.

'Yes, she is. I have a contact address for her, even though I haven't spoken to her for many years now. She sends a card at Christmas, that's all.'

How could a child-killer send Christmas cards? 'Don't you hate her?'

'It's difficult . . . I hate what she did, certainly, but there are other factors. She's been punished, of course, she's served her time. You have to remember too that she was a victim herself in many ways. Her own father . . .'

I put my hands over my ears. 'Stop. Oh, please stop.'

Mrs Beattie took the file and slid it under her chair. I wished I could have done that with the new knowledge in my head.

'I feel like a different person,' I said. 'Nothing will ever be the same again.' She nodded. 'I need to go away now and think about this. Can I have Jessie Pilkington's address?'

'I have no right to withhold it from you.'

'But you don't believe I should have it?'

Mrs Beattie pulled her cuff straight and smoothed her skirt. 'I'm not sure you could do anything very constructive.'

'All the same.'

She went back into the file and pulled out an envelope. 'It's in there. Think carefully about how you want to handle this situation tonight, and come and see me tomorrow. We'll talk it over together.' She clasped my hand again. 'You've been very brave. Whatever your life has been like, it's made you a strong person.'

'I don't feel strong.'

'Well, you are.'

Then she hugged me again and I left.

I DON'T KNOW why I did it. I should have gone straight home but I knew I'd never settle till I'd seen Jessie Pilkington, or whatever her name was, and talked to her face to face. I trailed back to the B & B, collected my stuff and set off for the Underground.

Back on the Tube everything seemed squalid and threatening. People looked at each other out of the corner of their eyes; hardly anyone spoke. Even the beautiful young couple strap-hanging seemed like they were mocking the rest of us when they laughed together. The diversity was frightening too; every race, language, class and sub-class seemed to be on our train and it made my head spin. I unfolded the envelope and checked the address for the umpteenth time. Lewisham. What was that like, then? You hear the names of these London boroughs they don't mean a right lot. Certain ones have memory-tags attached – Brixton (riots), Peckham (Del Boy), Lambeth (Walk) – but mostly it's all pretty vague. Well, how many Londoners know the difference between Worsley and Whalley Range?

Maybe she'd make it all right. She might say something that would explain and make it not so bad. It couldn't be any worse. In any case it was what I needed to do.

It didn't take me long to suss out that Lewisham isn't a top-class area full of millionaires. There were a lot of boarded-up windows, for one thing, and metal grilles on some of the shops. Big difference to Hemmington Grove. I got the feeling terracotta pots wouldn't survive that long here. A filthy man with a droopy eye came up to me as I stood turning my street map round, and shouted something in my face. I put my head down and started walking.

It took me nearly twenty minutes to find her street, Bewely Road, and it was grubby and depressing. I followed the numbers down until I came to a sixties block of flats, two storeys high, with coloured panels, orange and blue, stuck to the bricks under the windows. There are some flats like that in Wigan, just as you get near the town centre. They smack to me of desperate mothers caged up with screaming toddlers, and teenagers pissing in the stairwells. Maybe I was being a snob; your house doesn't make you who you are, I should know that. But I didn't feel sure of anything much any more.

She lived on the ground floor. I rang the bell – by now I was so nauseous and swimmy I had to lean against the jamb – and waited. The plain front door swung open and there she was.

It was the toes I noticed first; she was wearing sandals and her toenails were painted red, but dirty underneath. Leggings, a baggy T-shirt, much like I knock about in when I'm at home, and a face that was mine but old and twisted with sourness.

'I know who you are,' she snapped in an accent that was still northern. 'Mary phoned me. She warned me you might turn up.'

'Can I come in?' My mouth was very dry and the words sounded odd as I said them. 'I've come a long way.' Behind her I could hear a television going but I couldn't see past her into the hall.

'I don't care how far you've come. You've to go away. I never asked to see you. What do you want to come rooting round and stirring up trouble for? Haven't you got a life of your own?'

'That's what I wanted to talk to you about, tell you what I've done with myself over the years. I thought you'd like to know. There's things I need to ask you.'

She pushed her greying hair behind her ears and lowered her voice. 'Look, I just want you to sod off. If I didn't want you when you were a sweet little baby I'm hardly likely to want you now you're a bitter-faced thirty-year-old, am I? For God's sake. I owe you nothing.'

'I'm thirty-four, actually.'

She made to shut the door.

'Wait!' I wedged my shoulder painfully into the gap and forced it open again. A smell of chip pan floated out. 'Tell me about my dad at least. He might want to see me even if you don't.'

'You'll have a job. He's dead.' She laughed meanly. 'And a bloody good job an' all.'

'Well, who was he? I've a right to know.'

'Oh, *Rights*, is it? We've all got Rights, love. Well, I'll tell you, since you're burning to hear the truth. He was an evil bastard. He just wanted rid of you. He'd have done it hisself if I'd let him, he did it to another lass. D'you get me?' I must have looked blank. '*With a –* ' her face screwed up and she made a kind of clawing movement with her hand – '*coat hanger.*'

I clapped my palm to my mouth and took a step back,

and she slammed the door. I noticed my suit had a black mark all the way down the front.

*

**Daniel had** come round again and we were watching children's TV prior to our frozen pizzas. It was so relaxing without Mum there.

'You won't believe this but I need to pee *again*,' I said heaving myself up off the sofa. There was a sudden rush of water between my legs. 'Oh, my God.' We both stared at the dark stain spreading over my skirt. 'I think I've wet myself.'

'That's not wee,' said Daniel.

*

I was standing on the platform at Euston when my mobile rang. I nearly had kittens when it went off.

'Hello?' I was expecting another ear-bashing from Steve.

'Hello,' said a polite young man. 'I don't believe we've ever met, but I'm just ringing to tell you your daughter's in labour.'

# Chapter Ten

'Shall I phone the hospital or your father first?' Daniel asked as I struggled with the bath towel he'd brought me to mop up the mess.

'God, *I* don't know,' I snapped. I was really frightened.

'OK. I'm going to ring for an ambulance. Lie down and try to relax.'

I stretched out on the sofa and willed the baby to keep moving. 'My antenatal notes are on the sideboard. You might need to give them some details.'

'Fine.'

Daniel disappeared into the hall. I started to pray.

When he came back he looked cheerful. 'They'll be here in ten minutes. Now, what do you need to take?'

'There's a sports bag upstairs. I'll come with you.' I started to haul myself up.

'No. Stay horizontal. I'll sort it.'

'There are some extra things written on a Post-it note stuck to the handle,' I shouted after him. 'Don't forget my Walkman. And try not to wake Nan. I can't cope with her as well.'

I lay there for about ten seconds, then got up. 'Oh,

little banana, hang on,' I whispered. I shuffled to the phone, still holding the towel between my legs, and dialled Dad's number. Thank Christ; he was back.

'Yep?' he said with his mouth full.

'Dad? Can you come over right now? I've got to go to hospital.'

'Charlotte? Are y'awreet, love? What's up?'

'We think the baby's coming.'

There was a choking noise followed by coughing. 'I thought it weren't due till October.'

I started to cry.

'I'll be round straight away,' he said. 'Damn and blast your mother.' He hung up.

'Get back on that sofa,' hissed Daniel over the banisters.

When the ambulance came I wanted Daniel to come with me.

'No, Charlotte, that doesn't make sense. I'll stay till your dad arrives, then I'll follow in the car. That way I can come and go from the hospital; otherwise my car'll be stranded here and I'll have no transport.'

I started to sob even though we were standing in the road with all the curtains twitching. '*Don't* make me go on my own. *Please* come. I'm so *scared*.' I grabbed his hand and squeezed the fingers desperately.

'Has your father got a key?'

'Yeah,' I sniffed.

'Fuck it, then. Come on, let's get this show on the road.' And he lifted his long legs and climbed into the back of the ambulance.

*

'**I'm going to** strap this round your tummy so we can hear your baby's heartbeat,' said the Irish midwife. 'You'll need to lie fairly still. Do you think you're having contractions?'

They'd met me with a wheelchair, which was pretty freaky – did they think the baby might drop out if I walked up to the ward? – and pushed me along the shiny corridors at speed, Daniel trotting alongside. Now he was lurking at the foot of the bed. I wouldn't let him out of my sight. Mum was on her way; he'd telephoned her from the hospital foyer, but she thought it would be about another five hours.

I didn't know if I was having contractions or not. 'There's a funny feeling low down every so often but it doesn't hurt.'

The nurse nodded and pointed to a slip of paper hanging out of the monitor like a long white tongue. 'This will tell us if you're in the early stages of labour,' she said. There was a black wavy line drawn along the centre.

'It looks like a lie detector,' said Daniel.

*Pyow-pyow-pyow-pyow* went the baby. The midwife left the room.

'Your mother thought I was Paul.' Daniel grinned.

'Oh, God, what did you say?'

' "I certainly am not." Then she decided I must be a doctor.'

'It's the posh accent. My mum's a sucker for BBC English.'

'Look, I could wheel the telephone in here, there's one outside, if you want to speak to her. She sounded fairly frantic. She said she'd never have gone if she'd realized, but that first babies usually came late.' He fished in his jeans pocket. 'I've got about a pound in silver.'

'Put it away,' I said grimly. He didn't ask again.

Ten minutes later a doctor arrived to Do An Internal.

'I'll pop outside,' said Daniel and slunk away. Poor bugger, neither fish nor flesh nor good red herring.

'My name is Dr Battyani,' said the smily gentleman in the white coat. 'I will try not to hurt you. Now, will you put your heels down, your ankles together and let your knees fall apart.' He poked about for a minute or so while I stared up at the air vents in the ceiling, and it did hurt, quite a lot. 'You are only two centimetres dilated,' he announced, pulling the sheet back over my shame. 'But I can see from the monitor you are having mild contractions. Although your baby is early we will not try to stop your labour because of the risk of infection. What we might do is administer a steroid injection to help your baby's lungs cope better.'

My heart cringed with fear. 'Will my baby be all right?'

'You are in the best place,' he said, and left.

**The contractions** started properly about half an hour later.

'It hurts but it's not too bad,' I said to Daniel, who was reading out the *Times* crossword to me. 'I have to say, so far labour's been quite boring.'

'I wouldn't complain, if I were you,' he muttered, chewing his biro thoughtfully. 'Whenever I've seen women on TV giving birth it always looks grim. Loads of gripping onto brass bedsteads and rolling about screaming. Maybe you've got a high pain threshold. Now, what about "seed pod", five letters?'

But an hour later, when the midwife was examining me again, I was sick as a dog. Daniel melted away again as I retched into a kidney basin and moaned. 'It's really hurting now. Can I have something for the pain?'

'Well, you're getting there. Six centimetres.' She pointed to the chart by the bed which showed circles of increasing diameter. The biggest one was like a fucking dinner plate. I was never going to make it to ten, that was just plain ridiculous; what the bloody hell did they think I was made of, latex?

'OhhhhhhhhhhhhhhhhhhHHHHHHHHHHHHhhhhhh hhhhhhhhhhh,' I panted miserably, overtaken by a wave of agony. My God, it was wonderful when it stopped, but it was like being in the eye of the hurricane. You knew it was only a temporary respite.

'We can give you some gas and air. But you need to try and work with the pain.' She was all happy and brisk, I hated her.

'What do you mean?' Why did they talk such bollocks? I really couldn't be doing with it.

'Keep on top of your breathing. Deep, controlled breath *as soon* as you feel a contraction coming on, then *slowly* out with the pain. Hum if it helps.'

'But what about the drugs? I want drugs.'

'Well, pethidine isn't a good idea with you being a wee bit prem, it can make the baby a little woozy and we need him nice and alert. I'll sort you out with the gas and air.'

'I want an epidural. It says so on my birth plan – ohhhhhhhhhhhhhhHHHHHHHHHHHHHHHHHHHHHHH Hhhhhhhhhhhhhhhhhhhhhhhh. Jesus. Oh, I can't do this. I can't.'

She gave my hand a squeeze. 'Of course you can. You're doing great.'

Fucking five-star liar.

'The epidural!'

'Ah, the anaesthetist's with another lady at the moment. We'll bring him in as soon as he's free.' She nipped out sharpish.

My wail brought Daniel scuttling back in. 'Charlotte, what is it?'

'What's the good of writing a *fucking* birth plan if nobody takes any *fucking* notice of it?' I shouted at the top of my voice. Let the evil bitch hear. Far off someone else was yelling too.

'Medieval women used to chew willow bark, I gather. Contains natural aspirin. Sorry. I'll shut up.' He dabbed at my neck and forehead with a cold flannel. His expression, wide nervous eyes and fixed mouth, made me think of a cod trying to smile. I could nearly have laughed.

Mrs Happy trundled the tank of nitrous oxide in and invited me to bite on the mouthpiece. 'Like the breathing, start inhaling the second you feel the pain beginning.'

I took a huge great lungful and nearly fainted. Another contraction hit me.

'Is it any good?' asked Daniel, trying to read the writing on the side of the container.

'Bloody rubbish,' I said when I'd stopped groaning.

\*

IT WAS LIKE being in prison, sitting on that train. All I had with me was my own thoughts, one dreadful memory after another layering themselves on top of each other, and uppermost, fear. There was no relief. Wherever I turned my gaze there was an awful image imprinted on my mind's eye, like the mad stain on your vision after you've looked too long at a lightbulb. The pictures, some of them from the past, some from the future, blotted out the placid faces and the countryside around me. As we neared Manchester night was falling and all I could see when I stared out of the window was my own scared white face.

\*

'I want to get up,' I raved.

'We need to keep the monitor pads round your tum. Concentrate on your breathing now. Not much longer.' The midwife wrote some notes and checked her watch.

'Well, I need to take this off, then.' I'd managed to get myself all tangled up in the T-shirt I'd brought. Why was it so fucking hot in here?

'Er.' Daniel was hovering at the edge of my vision. 'Look, Charlotte, would this be a good time to go? My dad's here and he's going to drive me back to get the car. But I'll stay if you want me to. You know I won't leave if you need me.' He reached out for my hand just as another contraction swept over me.

'Charlotte? Charlotte?'

'It's fine,' I managed to gasp. 'Yeah, go.' I needed to concentrate on the rhythm of the pain. I could see now why animals crept off on their own to have their litters in bushes. I couldn't cope with his concern, his anxious questions, that bloody flannel.

'Sure?'

I closed my eyes; perhaps he'd think I'd fainted.

'I'd go if I were you,' whispered the midwife. 'You can come back tomorrow, bring her a nice big bunch of flowers.' I saw her wink at him.

'He's not the father, you knowooooooooWWWWWWW WWWWWWWWWWooooooooooooo,' I howled. Her smile never slipped.

'See you then,' he muttered and waved limply. It felt better when he'd gone.

\*

'THE 10.05 TO BOLTON is running . . .' The TV screen over my head flickered for a second . . . 'thirty-five minutes late. We apologize for any inconvenience.'

'But I NEED to get to my daughter!' I shouted up at it, my voice echoing slightly under the iron rafters. No one on the platform took much notice; after all, there are a lot of nutters around these days.

\*

'Now, Charlotte, I need you to listen to me.' The voice was coming as if from under water. 'Charlotte, I can see the top of the baby's head when you push. Lots of lovely dark hair. What I need you to do is to push as hard as you can with each contraction. Yes? Tuck your chin down and push through your bottom.'

I was beyond speaking now but I tried to do as I was told. There aren't the words to describe the sensations, I was only a heaving mass of muscle and pain, all control gone.

'Keep on top of it now. Down through your bottom.'

I pushed with all my might but I was getting exhausted. 'I can't do it,' I managed to gasp.

'Yes, you can. Come on now. You want to get this baby out, don't you?'

Stupid fucking question.

I pushed till I thought my eyes would pop but we didn't seem to be making much progress. I thought of all the women in history who'd had babies. Why did you never hear what it was really like? Had it been this bad for all of them? Some women had loads. Mrs Shankland at the post office had *seven*; had she been through this every time?

'Charlotte.' This was a man's voice. 'It's Dr Battyani again. How are you doing?' Sensibly he didn't wait for a reply. 'I've had a little look at you and I think we need to make a small cut.' He didn't say where, but I knew. We'd done it at antenatal class and I thought then, Whatever happens, I do *not* want one of those, no way. 'It's OK,' he consulted his clipboard, 'we will numb the area with an anaesthetic first.'

Oh, so you've *got* fucking anaesthetics *now*, have you? I thought. 'Nyerhhhhhh,' I managed. He took this as a yes; well maybe it was. I was so desperate to get the baby out by now they could have threatened to use a blow-torch and I'd have agreed.

The next part is confused because I was waiting for the cut, and an Irish voice said, 'There's somebody here to see you,' and 'Come in round this side and hold her hand.'

Then a huge wave came over me and I began to push again. 'That's it, Charlotte, you're doing so well, the head's nearly out.' There was somebody crying near my face and when I opened my eyes it was my mum, my mum, and she held my hand tight then the head was out, and with a great slither and a gush the whole baby plopped onto the bed in a slimy mess. I was sobbing and panting and my mum looked like she'd been dragged through a hedge backwards with tears running down her cheeks.

I collapsed against her while they took the baby and checked it over. 'Time of birth, 23.42,' I heard a woman's voice say. The baby squalled when they put it on the cold scales.

'Bless it,' choked Mum. 'I've no hanky.' She wiped her eyes on her coat sleeve leaving a smudge of mascara on the beige cuff.

The midwife brought the baby over and laid it on my chest where it squirmed and hiccupped.

'You've got a little boy, five pounds ten,' she beamed.

'Oh, a boy. I thought it would be a girl.' I stared down at it, him, in bewilderment, with his matted black hair and his screwed-up, puffy eyes. I'd made that. He was mine.

Everything was quiet for a moment; somehow I'd expected a fanfare of trumpets or exploding fireworks, but there was nothing except the sounds of the midwife clearing away. Dr Battyani leant over me and lifted the purple baby up in his large brown hands.

'We need to check him over again,' he said and took him over to a table on the other side of the room.

Mum hugged me and kissed my hair while a new midwife appeared and began fiddling about down below. 'I'm just after your placenta,' she said cheerfully. 'Then we're all done and dusted.'

Together Mum and the first midwife tidied me up and put my nightie on from out of the case, combed my hair and sponged me down.

'Can I have my baby now?' I asked, still feeling like I was floating.

'He needs to pop down to the SCBU to have a spot of oxygen,' said Dr Battyani. 'Just to help his breathing.'

Mum and I looked at each other in horror.

'Is he going to die?'

Dr Battyani tutted and shook his head. 'He is a strong healthy baby for thirty-four weeks. But he will be more comfortable during the night if we give his lungs a little assistance. Have you got a name for him so we can write it on his tag?'

'No.' I thought briefly of Fyffes. 'Oh, God, Mum, I've no name for him . . .'

'Do not panic. We can put your name on.' The doctor came over to my bed and spoke to Mum. 'She needs to get a good night's rest. You can stay with her for a little while.'

My limbs began to tremble with fatigue. I closed my eyes and snuggled against her, something I hadn't done since I was tiny. 'Oh, Mum, I'm so glad you're here.'

She leant over me, stroking my arm.

'My father and I just wanted to say well done,' said Daniel emerging from the shadows.

'Are you a hallucination?' I asked reasonably. He

laughed. Mr Gale stood behind him. I could see Mum eyeing them up and down. 'I thought you were going home?'

'Dad said I could hang around till midnight. And you
got there in the nick of time.'

'Didn't we all,' muttered Mum.

\*

HOW OFTEN DO PARENTS say sorry? (Well, most of
them don't listen, for a start, so they never even realize
they've done anything wrong.) In the struggle to take on
the mantle of parenthood, and it is like a mantle, a big
padded-shouldered superhero costume, you fall into this
trap of arrogance. It starts early on when you're outside a
supermarket and your toddler is screaming for something
totally unsuitable they've spotted on the shelves and
taken a fancy to, e.g. a box of After Eights. You have to be
firm, obviously. You have to look as though you know
what you're doing because there's always this fear that if
you don't some passing shopper will spot your deficiencies
and report you as a fraud, someone who's only playing at
being a parent. Then your children will be taken into care
and your life will be in ruins.

Also you have to convince your child that you're in
charge, because this is what kids are supposed to like,
firm boundaries and what have you. But listen, I don't
believe they ever do think you're in charge. They know all
along that what you're doing is simply steam-rollering
your opinions through because you're bigger and can
smack harder and shout louder, and that's not really the
same thing as being in charge. But you're so caught up in
the role you convince yourself that whatever the situation,

you're right and if your child disagrees they must therefore be wrong: the After Eights come to symbolize your
superior understanding of the way the world works. And
this is true up to the point where you die, so that there are
even now seventy-year-olds being berated by parents in
their nineties for being wasteful with money, deficient
in visiting duties, slatternly round the house, etc.

Larkin wrote that famous poem about your mum and
dad fucking you up; notice he didn't go on to say, 'And
afterwards, when you're all mature adults, they can appreciate all their mistakes and apologize wholeheartedly over
drinks on the patio.'

I was going to break the mould. I was going to tell
Charlotte I was sorry, and watch the sky crack and the
earth split apart.

'I THINK THEY'VE forgotten about us,' she murmured,
resting her head on my arm. 'They were pretty busy
earlier on. I'm not bothered. It's nice, this, just us two.
Do I look a right state?'

'You've just given birth, it doesn't matter what you
look like. Was that your new boyfriend, the lad with all the
hair?'

'No. He's a friend . . . from school.'

'Some friend to come with you and hold your hand
like that. He deserves a medal.' I shifted round on the
bed and gazed at her damp hair and her red eyes. She
seemed so young, as if she'd woken up from a bad dream
and sneaked into my room for a cuddle like she used to
after Steve left. 'Oh Charlotte . . .'

She let out a huge yawn. 'What, Mum?'

'I'm so sorry.'

Her blue eyes flicked onto me and her brow furrowed. 'What for? You were here, weren't you, in the end. I was all right. You know, they reckon that gas and air is only a temporary effect but I think it stays in your system. I could rise off this bed and drift round the ceiling.' She stared up at the dirty tiles as if they were the most beautiful things she'd ever seen.

'No, I didn't mean going away. I shouldn't have done that either—'

'Where did you go?'

'Lyme Regis,' I blurted out. *The French Lieutenant's Woman* had been on Granada last week.

'Mmm. Dig up any skeletons?'

'What do you mean?'

'Any old fossils. Ammonites, that sort of stuff. I know I'm talking rubbish, ignore me.' She closed her eyes again.

'Oh, I see. No, it was very quiet, really. I had to do some thinking. But I should never have walked out like that, without any warning. It wasn't fair. Sometimes I feel like I've been following some sort of manual, *The Guide to Being a Bad Mother*; actually there've been times when I feel I could have *written* it.'

'God, Mum, there are plenty worse than you.'

I pictured for a moment a door slamming in my face and, further back, a little shabby figure cowering in a corner, nobody there to protect her. Tears spilled over my cheeks again.

'I've been rotten to you over this pregnancy,' I sniffed. 'I only wanted you to have a happy life.'

'I know, Mum. But let's not argue all the time from now

on, eh? I hate it when we argue, the air turns all . . . spiky. Nan hates it too.' She stretched and tried to roll onto her side. 'You know, I used to be jealous of Nan when I was younger, 'cause of all the time you spent looking after her. You once said to me, "Love isn't a cake, you can't divide it up into slices." And I said, "No, but time is. A clock even looks like a cake." Do you remember?'

'No.' God, I had got it wrong. 'I'm sorry for that as well, if you felt neglected.'

'It was my problem, selfish adolescent; you were just trying to do your best. I can see that now. I can see a lot of things. I really love her, you know.' She sighed and there was a long pause. I thought she'd dropped off to sleep and I was wondering about slipping over and dimming the lights over on the other side of the room. Suddenly she said, 'Tell me what it was like when you had me. I've never asked.'

I settled back against the metal bars.

'Well, some of it's still very clear. It was the best and worst day of my life, I think. I remember, I was in labour for nearly twenty-seven hours and they had to use forceps, which is why you've got that tiny dent over your left cheekbone. The midwife was absolutely horrible. When I told her how much agony I was in she said, "You should have thought of that before you got yourself into this mess." Honestly. You'd report them today. Steve wasn't with me because he said he couldn't face seeing me in pain, lame excuse. And Nan was beside herself with worry; she was terrified of losing me, or you, because she hadn't long been a widow, so by the time you were born she was like a wet rag. She held you first – I think she may even have cut the cord, I'll have to ask her – and then she put you in my arms. All the nurses commented on your blue eyes, and you fixed me with this fierce gaze, as if to say, You're *mine*; don't even think about giving me away. It made my insides melt, because it was the first time in all the pregnancy that I'd realized you were an actual person.'

I glanced down, proud of my speech, but Charlotte was fast asleep with her thumb in her mouth.

*

**I woke with** a shock when the breakfast trolley rattled past the door. My first thought was, The baby's died in the night and they daren't tell me. I pressed the buzzer and a young nurse came in carrying some charts.

'How's my baby?'

'Oh, he had a very good night. You're both going up to the ward today. You can have a shower first, make you feel more human; I expect you'll be feeling a bit bruised and battered, but that soon passes. I just need to do your obs while I'm here.'

She took my temperature and blood pressure and all the time I was trying to get my head round the fact that I had a baby, I was a mother. Surely it was all a mistake. I couldn't really have a baby, not *really*.

Up on the ward there were lots of real mothers all with their babies next to them in clear plastic cribs. The space by my bed was empty. I lay there, the biggest fraud in the world, while the woman opposite picked her child up, put her hand inside her nightdress and fished out a breast. Then she clamped the baby to her nipple and started to flick through a magazine with her free hand. It was pretty impressive. To my right a girl about the same age as me was changing a nappy, like she knew what she was doing. I tried to peer over her shoulder but it looked a bloody complicated arrangement and the baby kept wriggling. When she'd parcelled up its tiny bottom she put its sleepsuit back on, bending the minute limbs carefully, poking inside the sleeve openings with her finger to extract the curled fists. Finally she picked it up, her hand behind its floppy head, and called the nurse who brought a bottle which the baby drank with its eyes closed. I knew for certain I'd never be able to do any of this. I'd drop him, sure as eggs is eggs, or break his arm trying to dress him. I'd better tell them now I wasn't fit to be a mum.

Just then they wheeled him in.

'Here we are,' said the nurse parking him expertly and flipping on the brake. 'Here's your mummy.' There was no response from the swaddled heap. 'He's still asleep.' She leant over the side of the crib and touched his head. 'What a lot of lovely hair.'

'Is that normal, to sleep so long?' I could feel myself panicking again.

'Oh, yes. Labour's a very tiring experience and not just for the mum. He'll wake up when he's ready. My goodness, you'll be praying for him to go to sleep before he's much older!'

I leant over and watched his crumpled face. There was absolutely no movement. I looked for signs of breathing but there were too many blankets round him so I gingerly swung my legs out of bed *ow ow ow ow* and started to unwrap his body. At last his chest was uncovered and I could see it rising and falling. Thank

God. I got back into bed and lay there watching that small movement, up and down, because if I didn't it might stop.

He didn't wake properly until after dinner and by then I was convinced he was going to starve to death. 'Help me feed him,' I said to the nurse pathetically.

I'd just got my boobs out when Mum walked in.

'Oh, Christ, you've not brought anyone with you? Imagine if my dad saw me like this, or Daniel!'

Mum rolled her eyes and drew the curtains round. 'How are you getting on?'

'I can't seem to make him open his mouth wide enough.' I looked down at the feeble scrap rooting about blindly. 'See, he hasn't a clue. I thought it was instinct.'

The midwife manoeuvred him around and pushed another pillow under my arm. 'Stroke his cheek, that makes him open his mouth.' She took hold of my breast and sort of stuffed it between the baby's lips. It was a shock having another woman touch me like that.

I shivered. 'I don't like this. It feels funny.' The baby tugged at my nipple and broke away. He started to cry at a pitch that went right through you.

'I don't think you're going to be able to do this, Charlotte, it's very difficult you know. You might be better off bottle-feeding,' said Mum.

I pulled my head up, annoyed. 'Give me a chance. We've not been at it two minutes. Anyway, what did you do with me?'

Mum looked smug. 'Oh, you were entirely breastfed for four months.'

I frowned. 'Well, so's he going to be. Come on, matey.

Put some effort into it.' I pulled his face against me and again felt that questing mouth on my skin.

'Here,' said the midwife. She pulled my shoulder forward and turned his head. He shifted in my arms, latched himself on and relaxed. 'That's right.' She stood back to admire the composition. 'Now, can you see him swallowing? That's what you need to watch for. It's a slightly tricky technique at first, you need to persevere, that's all. Give me a shout if you need me again.' Mum gave her a wink and I knew I'd been had. I didn't care.

I sat up like a queen, like a mummy, while he suckled on. 'Well,' I said after we'd sat in reverent silence for a while, 'pigs can do it, and cows and sheep.'

'Dogs and cats.'

'Mice and rats.'

And we both started to laugh.

*

IT WAS THE first time in all the pregnancy I'd realized you were an actual person, and although you'd got your dad's blue eyes, the expression behind them was mine. Stubborn. Perhaps that's why we've argued so much, being so alike. I knew you'd be trouble though, even then, but there was nothing at all I could do about it because I'd just fallen down a big well of love.

*

Baby Jesus had the Three Wise Men: I had Dad, Daniel and Nan. Dad came first, shuffling in as if he had a poker up his bum.

'What's up with you?' I asked, amused.

'I 'ate hospitals, me. Brrrrrr. Even the smell of 'em makes the hairs on my neck prickle.' He sat down in the easy chair by the bed but kept his back straight, alert for any sign of attack. 'How are we, then? Oh, I see him. He's a grand little chap, in't he? Very nice. Well done.'

'How have you been getting on? What did you do about Nan's bag?'

He grinned. 'Oh, I phoned that woman from Crossroads and pleaded with her to send someone, I said it were an emergency, like. I told her to send a nice young nurse, preferably a blonde.'

'And did she?'

'Aye. His name were Simon.'

I sniggered. 'Serves you right.'

'P'raps it does. Hey, before I forget I brought you a book. I know you can't get enough on 'em.' He pulled out a carrier bag from under the chair and extracted a Penguin Classic. 'There you are. I looked at the cover an' I thought, That'll be right up our Charlotte's street. I got it off a bloke at work, he has whole van full of 'em.'

I picked it up off the bedspread. *Tess of the D'Urbervilles,* I read. 'Oh, Dad, you are priceless!' I gave him a hug.

'What's up? You've not read it, have you? I dunno what it's about but it looks like the sort of thing you like.'

I muffled my laughter on his shoulder.

He didn't stop long but before he went he gave me something else.

'Come here an' I'll tell you summat you'll bless me for over the next few weeks. It'll be t' best piece of advice anyone gives you. Come closer, I'll have to whisper it.'

I moved closer, intrigued.

'When that baby of yours cries you'll want to run to it right away. And that's fine, most o' t' time. But there'll be some days as you can't cope and he's screaming away and you think you might throw him out the window. Well, at times like that you change his nappy, try him with a bottle, get him burped and then you leave him. You close the door, go downstairs and have a cup of tea. Nobody phones the police, God dun't strike you dead with a thunderbolt; you give yourself five minutes and then you go back. And if you're really lucky, little bugger'll have gone to sleep.'

'Thanks, Dad.'

'No problem.'

**Next came** Daniel, bearing a huge bunch of flowers. There was also a book on babycare by Miriam Stoppard.

'I don't know if you've got this already, but my father says it's a definitive work.' He tossed it on the bed and lounged in the chair. 'I can't believe how normal you look after all that trauma.'

'Get away, I look like a dog. And I feel as I'd been run over. Just as well he's so good.' I nodded at the cot.

Daniel rose and peered across. 'Skinny little chap, isn't he? Dad says he wouldn't have had a chance to lay down all his fat stores but that he's a good weight for his age.' He poked the baby experimentally but it didn't stir. 'Does he do any tricks?'

'None at all. Very disappointing. Oh, yeah, he does black poo.'

'Lovely.' He sat back down again. 'Decided what to call him yet?'

'Nope. I was going to have a chat with Mum about it. She might know some family names I could use.' I looked across at the cot again and got another electric shock of disbelief. 'It feels so weird having him here.'

'Yeah, I know what you mean.' Daniel took his glasses off and began to clean them on his shirt. 'I'm sorry I was so crap towards the end.'

I turned to him in surprise. 'You weren't. You were great. I'd never have got through the first few hours on my own.'

'Yeah, but when you started having those terrible pains . . . I didn't know what to do, and it was awful watching you like that and not being able to do anything. Plus, I think in retrospect I should have worn a placard round my neck saying NO, I'M NOT THE FATHER. There were one or two embarrassing moments with nursing staff. One of them asked me whether . . .' He gave an awkward laugh. 'I'll tell you some other time. Hey, did you ever actually use Julia's birthing tape?'

'Oh, that. No, I forgot all about it. Actually being strapped to the monitor was bad enough, I couldn't have coped with headphones as well.'

'You can listen to it now; it might help you relax.'

'Good idea,' I said. But even as he was digging in my suitcase I realized that I couldn't put my phones on *and* listen for the baby. It was going to be a very long time before I wore my Walkman again.

**Nan came** in the evening. She looked smart, as if she was going to church, in a red two-piece and pearls. You could tell she was worked up, though.

'Where's little thing,' she quavered. Mum guided her round to the cot and she gazed at the baby in total adoration. 'Eeh, little lamb. It's like our Jimmy, safe and sound. In't he beautiful? Eeh. How can they hurt 'em, honest? Oh, Charlotte love, he's beautiful.' She gave me a perfumy kiss and Mum installed her in the best chair. Her whole attention was focused on the cot. 'They're all as matters really, babies. Han't he got a lot of hair? He does favour our Jimmy.'

'Who's Jimmy? He can't favour anyone, can he?' I mouthed at Mum.

'No,' she whispered, 'but don't say anything.'

I watched Mum watch Nan and I thought she seemed different with her, somehow. Nothing I could put my finger on, but sort of calmer towards her. I might have been imagining it of course; I was brimming with hormones.

'Can I hold him?' asked Nan, her face shining.

I glanced at Mum. 'Will she be all right?'

'She'll be fine. I'll keep my arm round him. Let her, Charlotte, it'll mean such a lot.'

Mum scooped him up and laid him gently across Nan's lap so that his head was cradled in the crook of her elbow. He was coming round and his blue eyes were peeping. Nan sat stiffly as if she hardly dared breathe.

'Have you got any further with names yet?' asked Mum.

'No. I keep thinking, who does he look like, but then getting depressed . . . I don't *think* he looks like Paul, do you?'

'I only ever saw him twice, if you remember, and that was nearly a year ago. But it doesn't matter, even if he does. Who you are is the way you were brought up, it's nothing to do with your genes. I'm sure of that.' She pulled a strange expression.

'If you say so. But you'd better tell the scientists so they don't waste any more time on research. Anyway, I hope to God he isn't like Paul, I hope he's a nicer person than that.'

'We'll bring him up right,' said Mum. 'He'll know the difference between right and wrong.'

'And if he doesn't we'll smack his bottom.'

'No, we won't,' said Mum quickly. 'We'll find other ways. You shouldn't hit children, not for any reason.'

It took a second for this revelation to sink in. 'Bloody hell, Mum,' I said outraged, 'I wish you'd thought like that when I was small. You never had any problem slapping *my* legs. My God, there was that time in Stead and Simpson's . . .'

'I know, I know. I'm sorry.' Her mouth had gone all funny, as if she was going to cry, so I left it. Maybe these hormones were infectious.

Nan began to sing to the baby in a wobbly voice.

*'How can I be poor*
*When there's gold in your darling curls?*
*How can I be poor*
*When your dear little teeth are like so many pearls?*
*Your lips to me are rubies*
*Your eyes are diamonds rare*

*So while I have you, my baby,*
*I'm as rich as a millionaire.'*

'Oh, Nan, that's lovely. He hasn't got golden curls, though.'

'He hasn't got teeth, either, but I don't suppose he's going to put in a complaint.'

'What should we call him, Nan?'

'Eeh, tha'll soon be spittin' in t' fire,' she told the baby. 'Tha will. Yes tha will.' He stared up with round unfocused eyes as she waggled her head at him.

Mum opened her handbag and pulled out her diary. 'I made a note of some family names for you.' She flicked through the gilt-edged pages to find the scrap of ribbon. 'Here we are. There's Bill, of course; William if you like. It'd make Nan's day if you called him that.' She smiled over at Nan but got no response; Nan was too wrapped up in a baby bubble to notice. 'Harold; you could shorten that to Harry; that was Nan's father's name. Jimmy, or James of course; that was Nan's little brother.'

'I didn't know she had a brother.'

'Oh, he died very young. I think he was knocked down by a tram. Or that might have been her dad, I'm not sure. She's had a tragic life, really, because her mum died when Nan was only in her thirties, and she lost her father when she was a teenager.'

'Like you.'

'Yes, like me. He'd have loved that baby, you know.' I saw her eyes flick over Nan's pink-and-white head and over the tiny black-haired scalp inches below. The baby's skin was still dark purply-mottled; Nan's was pale and blue-veined and liver-spotted. Mum heaved a great sigh which turned into a yawn. 'Sorry, love, I'm done in.'

'*You* are?'

'I know, I know, I remember what it's like.' She peered in the diary again. 'Oh and then there's Peter, that was her grandad, so your great-great-grandad.'

I shifted my bra strap and winced.

'They're a bit like icebergs, families; all that hidden history.'

'I don't think icebergs are anything like as hazardous, though,' said Mum closing the book.

*

MY VERY first memory is rocking our Jimmy in his cradle by the fire and gazing into that terrible red glow deep down in the coals, while Grandma Marsh sang to lull 'im to sleep.

> *'Th' art welcome little Bonny Brid*
> *But shouldn't ha' come just when tha did.'*

She allus called him Bonny Brid; well he were, a little angel. I were never jealous; I just couldn't wait for 'im to grow up so's we could play together. By eight he were t' best in our street at spittin'; he'd fortify himself wi' pop beforehand then give t' others monkey nuts, casual like, so when it came to it they were dried out; he won all sorts that way. An' if I were feeling down he'd sing 'Tickle me Timothy, Tickle me do' till I cheered up; he were allus full o' fun. That time he got under t' table playin' Pirates and pulled t' leg so th' end dropped down, I told me mother it was me even though her best cup were broken. An'

I ought to have tekken more care of him. If I'd been with him that day down by the canal—

*

**Out of the corner** of my eye I became aware of movement. 'Nan?'

Nan was slowly slumping forward, the baby sliding down her lap. My heart thumped with fright but Mum made a grab for him and caught him as he began to roll. I saw a thread of saliva hang from the corner of Nan's mouth and stain her red top.

'Quick, Charlotte,' said Mum, dropping the baby back in his cot and rushing to Nan's side. 'Press that buzzer of yours and get a nurse.' I hesitated for a second, stunned at the sight of Nan deflating like a balloon. 'Do it!' she shouted. 'I think Nan's having a stroke.'

THEY SAY as it's a tunnel wi' a light at th' end, but I found mysen on t' canal bank at Ambley, wi' Jimmy.

'Awreet?' he says, big grin on his face.

'You're looking well,' I say, 'considering.' He just laughs and puts his arm through mine.

He tugs me over in the direction of the bridge – it's a beautiful day, all reflections in the water, very peaceful, and as we get near I can see all sorts of folk sitting on the opposite bank having a picnic. They've a blanket and some bottles of ale, a basket full of barm cakes and pies and things. There's a lot of babies lying on t' ground, waving their legs in the air or sitting up and patting the grass round them, chuckling to themselves the way babies do – and the queer thing is, there's not one on 'em skrikin'. One's crawled ovver an' cadged itssen a barm cake and it's chewin' away, must have a tooth coming. There's a little girl laid out on her front in a summer frock and cardigan, blowing bubbles at them out of a basin of soapy water, she's got a bit of wire bent in a loop. Jimmy's arm tightens on mine and I squeeze back, all warm. I'm dying, I think, and it's lovely.

'Look,' says Jimmy, pointing under the trees, and it's Grandma Marsh and Grandma Fenton; Grandma Marsh is holding up a skein of red wool while Grandma Fenton winds it into a ball. They're nattering so much neither of them take me on. Jimmy digs me in the ribs and makes a face, so I give him a hug.

'You han't changed,' I tell him. He shrugs. I want to ask him about our mum and dad but something tells me to wait.

There's a tenor horn starts up and I know it's Bill before I spot him. He's at the water's edge standing very still and straight. He doesn't wave, never takes the horn away from his lips, but he's playing for me. 'Stranger in Paradise'; the notes dance across the water like light, like a language. There's such love in the air, you could get drunk on it. There's no rush. He'll wait for me.

We're nearly at the bridge.

'Come on,' says Jimmy, 'only a cock-stride now.' He pulls me along by the hand and his eyes are shining. I want to run, because suddenly I've all this energy, maybe I could just jump the canal, but as I put my fingers on the coping stones darkness comes up round the side of my vision and everything falls away. And while I watch, there is a pin-point of light, tiny, getting bigger. It's coming towards me very fast, very fast

# Chapter Eleven

'MRS HESKETH! Nancy! Can you hear us?'

You've to go away. It's hurting my eyes. I'm dead.

*

I SAT IN that hospital corridor for hours. Might as well have moved in, the amount of time I was spending there. One floor up in another wing I'd sat with Charlotte while she gave birth; now I was waiting to see whether my mother was dying. Sorrow and joy a few hundred yards from each other. Turn left, up the stairs and through the double doors.

Over my head the strip light hummed. My eyes were sore with lack of sleep. Even when I'd managed to snatch a few hours it had all been trains again, exhausting, only this time I'd known where I was headed; I was trying to get back home. I would have done too if that bloody platform hadn't turned into Chorley market.

I kept having to blink to stop the reflections in the night-sky window from flickering. Every time a trolley went past it felt like the rubber wheels were trundling right over my heart, the rattling and clanking dislodging bits of my brain. I wondered whether Emma had been to hospital, sat in Casualty while nurses tended broken bones and exchanged glances over bruises. *Why* hadn't anyone done anything? Why hadn't *Jessie*? Every time I tried to think about that a gulf of incomprehension opened up in my mind and instead I saw again her face, hard, sour, in the crack of the door. It was fear in her eyes at the end, not anger; she'd been afraid of me. She'd always be running away from the past, there'd be no rest. Nor should there be.

I wondered if he'd suffered at the end, that man. I hoped he had. I hoped he'd had terrible pain for a long time, and then gone to hell. I could understand now these stories of ordinary people hiring hitmen. In the face of such evil, what else is there to do but wipe it off the face of the earth?

You try not to think about life's darkest things, but sometimes they just flood into your head and you can't stop them. In a place like this, in this no-man's-land of time, you've no chance. Because being in a hospital reminds you how every second sees someone off or ushers someone in, souls squeezing in from the dark or flitting out into it. There are supposed to be ten ghosts behind every living person, aren't there? And what about the ones waiting to be conceived, baby-ghosts of the future? If they knew what pain was waiting for them, how many would choose not to be born? Awful images were flying into my mind one after another. War reports on the news, Diana in a hospice with a little bald lad, NSPCC posters, even that mocked-up TV ad for immunizations where the tiny baby rolls about on the edge of a cliff. Curtains closing on Dad's coffin. A strange sea in front of Buckingham Palace.

The hospital clock ticked on taking lives with it and the

dead queued up to be remembered. I'd been waiting for ever. I ached to hold Emma and make it all right; she was there, surely, just by me, I could feel her; and behind Emma all those other children who cry at night from fear or pain or loneliness crowded round and reached out little hands to me until I thought I was going to scream—

'Could I have a word?' The doctor was a young Indian woman, very pretty, slightly beaky nose. I looked up at her gormlessly and struggled to my feet. My handbag dropped down my arm onto the floor but I was too tired to bother. We stood facing each other and I searched her expression, trying to guess. There was a lash on her cheek and a stray hair coming down over her forehead. I wondered if she ever wore one of those red spots on her brow. All this in a fraction of a second. Make eye contact, I pleaded, because if you don't, I'll know it's bad news.

\*

**Nan was in** a room off the main ward on her own when we went. I wondered if that was a bad sign. She certainly had enough wires and tubes coming out of her.

'They won't know what damage has been done to her brain until she comes round,' Mum had told me. 'But she might be able to hear us, they say it's the last sense to go. So watch what you say. She's no teeth in so she looks a bit grim, anyway.'

I'd forgotten she was so small. There didn't seem to be anything of her under the covers, and her hands resting on top were like little turkey claws.

'Mum?' I whimpered, but she shushed me and patted me forwards.

'Let's get his lordship installed first.' She hoisted the baby's car seat onto a chair – he was sparko from the journey – and drew one up for me. Then she sat down herself and started unpacking all the goodies people had sent. 'I thought I'd tell her about them even if she couldn't see them, something might filter through, and she'd be so pleased everyone was thinking about her. Now. Mum?' She leaned over the bed and raised her voice. 'Mum, Charlotte and the baby are here, they've come to see you. And I've brought some presents and cards. They're all asking at church after you, your name was read out for special prayers, apparently. The vicar sends his love.' She fished in a Morrison's carrier bag. 'I've all sorts in here for you, shall I put them on the bed? No, best not, they might interfere with one of these tubes. Anyway, Ivy's given you some lemon-scented tissues, they'll be useful.' She plonked them on the bedside table. 'I've brought a stack of *Woman's Weeklies* from Maud, and a cologne stick. Mrs Waters from the library's sent you a big bag of Mintoes, here, and Reenie's given me a pot of honeysuckle hand cream for you. I could put a bit on for you now if you like.'

There was absolutely no response, it was awful, but Mum just chattered on.

'There's all sorts of cards too, I'll read them out in a minute. Oh, there's a bottle of Lucozade from Debbie, and Nina from Greenhalgh's brought round a tin of Uncle Joe's Mintballs . . .'

I sniggered with nerves.

'What?'

'Sorry. It's the name. It always makes me laugh.'

'What, Uncle Joe's Mintballs?'

'Yeah.' I was fighting giggles; it was that or tears.

Mum smirked; I think she was on the verge too. 'Well, you know what they say about Uncle Joe's Mintballs, don't you?'

'No.'

Mum lowered her voice. '*Uncle Joe's Mintballs keep you all aglow, Give 'em to your granny and watch the bugger go.*'

We stared at each other for a second and then burst into hysterics. I laughed until my ribs hurt, we laughed so much Mum went red and I got hiccups, then she knocked the tin off her lap and it rolled all the way to the door, which was hilarious, and the baby woke up and Mum tried to pick him up but she couldn't undo the straps which was also incredibly funny.

And then Nan opened her eyes and said, 'Blast id.'

*

I SCREWED my eyes up tight. If I didn't open them happen I could get back. I could almost feel that warm stone under my palm still. When I'd looked down at Jimmy he'd got dandelion seeds stuck in his fringe and I wanted to brush them out with my fingers and feel his bonny hair again. But a wall of black had come up between us and I knew he was gone, Bill was gone, all of 'em. I'd missed the boat. I couldn't stand it.

*

'**Wake up, Nan,** and give my little boy a name. We're waiting on you to christen him. We can't go on calling him Banana-baby for ever, he'll get teased at school.' I chafed her small cold fingers under their tape while Mum went to call for a nurse. My mouth was dry as I watched her eyelids flicker and wince. 'Nan? Nan!' She sighed deeply but made no other movement. If she dies now they might think it's my fault, I thought. 'Come on,' I hissed. The baby suddenly sneezed twice and I felt Nan's body twitch. I put my face close to hers on the pillow and saw the lashes flutter and a huge tear roll out and pause, then spread into the wrinkles of her cheek. Her lips pursed and I could see she was trying to say something. The lines round her mouth deepened.

'What, Nan, what?'

The breath came out of her in little pants but no words. I dropped her hand and ran for Mum.

*

LET ME get back, I wanted to say. Give me summat, quick, while I still remember how to get there. If I can just go to sleep and if they'd just turn this blasted light out. I tried and tried but I couldn't make my mouth work.

*

'What's she saying?' Mum asked me as the nurse held Nan's wrist, counting.

'I couldn't tell. Her teeth . . .'

The nurse adjusted some machines and wiggled tubes, then unhooked the chart at the end of the bed and made some notes. Nan snorted a little and moaned. The nurse put down the chart and bent lower, putting her ear to Nan's lips, frowning. We waited. She straightened up.

'Apparently she's won a holiday. For two. I'll just fetch the doctor.'

*

THAT wasn't what I wanted to say at all.

*

**It was baby's** naming day and Nan's birthday. The nurses stood round the bed clapping while I took a photo with one of those disposable cameras; Nan in a new bed-jacket holding a cake on her lap. The walking frame was just visible in the corner but to cut it out of the picture I'd have had to chop Nan's arm off. I told her this.

'Might as well chop it off, all the use it is,' was her comment. 'Do you know why they clap when someone old says their age? It's because you're not dead yet, that's all.'

'I see it hasn't affected her speech, then,' muttered Dad to me.

'No. She's been lucky, really. If you call not being able to walk properly or feed herself without stuff going every-where "lucky". She's getting very frustrated though, stuck in bed. She used to be so active. How many eighty-one-year-olds do you know who can still touch their toes?'

'Aye, well, she's short. She dun't have so far to bend down.'

'Stop it. I think she's really depressed.'

Dad looked chastened. To be fair, he's not good at tragedy. He only came because Mum put the screws on, how it might be her last birthday and she'd always thought so much of him.

'So how's she going to go on when they turf her out of here? I mean, Karen's got her hands full with you and the baby, never mind hauling miniature pensioners about. What's she going to do?'

'It were t' best place for her t' 'ave a stroke,' said Ivy loudly, grasping Dad's arm. She nodded at Nan. 'I were sayin', it were t' best place for you. You've some beautiful flowers.'

'Blood and bandages.' Nan pulled a face at a vase of red and white carnations. 'They're bad luck. I've told the nurses but they don't do owt.'

'Let's have one of you, William and me on the bed with her,' said Mum. 'Steve,' she handed him the camera, 'if you'll do the honours.' Mum and I settled on the metal-framed bed either side of Nan, with Will like a fat white grub on her lap. 'Ready.'

'Right-oh. Say Hard Cheese.'

'Eh, it's a poor do,' said Nan closing her eyes.

*

IF THE TIMES had been different I'd have felt completely disorientated by Nan's uncharacteristic gloominess, but you've got to be realistic. It was chaos in our house, and you can only take on board so much at a time. I was going all out to be a Better Mother in the most trying of circumstances, I mean the house looked like several bombs had hit it. Nan was out of the way for the time being, true, but I was trailing off to visit nearly every day and Charlotte had me going up and down those stairs like a demented yo-yo.

—Mum, Mum, my jeans still won't do up!

—That's because you had a baby six weeks ago. Your figure'll come back, give it time. Dry your eyes and we'll have a cup of tea.

—Mum, Mum, his stump's fallen off!

—Well, they do. Wipe round his tummy carefully and watch you don't catch it when you're changing his nappy.

—Mum, Mum, there's all bits in his poo!

—That's normal. Come on now, Charlotte, stop worrying about *every little thing*.

—Mum, Mum! *Mum!* I've forgotten how to bath him!

—Oh, for Christ's sake, Charlotte, just have a go! His head's not going to drop off! Five minutes' bloody peace with the *Bolton Evening News*, that's all I wanted.

Etc.

I can't believe how she's changed; she used to be so damned independent and now she's on my back all the time. Secretly, though, it's quite nice. I like being able to tell her what to do and have her listen for once. She hangs on every word, asks me constantly about when she was a baby. We talk like we haven't done for years. When the baby blues hit she went down like a rag doll, completely useless. He'd got jaundice, and I *told* her it was very common and not serious but she kept yammering on about him turning into a banana; I thought she was going mental. Then she came out of it and two days after we were joking about the size of her boobs. 'Look at this, Mum,' she said, holding up one of her old bras against her massive chest. 'It's like a fairy bra.' We were two double laughing. She's doing ever so well, really. There'll always be rows, the habit's too ingrained, but

I really do feel as if I'd been given a second chance with her.

*

**People think** I'm coping but I'm not.

All these secrets women keep. Actually, I can understand why; after you've given birth you feel as if your body's been turned inside out and left hanging on the line for a week. If word got out what it was really like, nobody would get pregnant ever again. I'm certainly not up for it a second time, no way, Will'll have to resign himself to being an only child. I'm such a mess down there it's horrific. I can feel these knobbly stitches; they're supposed to dissolve on their own but I'm not convinced. I touch myself in the bath and it's not my body any more.

My breasts aren't mine. They've changed into tender, meaty bags of milk and they go knobbly too if Will sleeps through a feed. Then I have to go and milk myself into the bathroom sink like a big cow. It sprays out in tiny jets, it's just weird.

The baby's weird, too. He's got pathetic scrunched-up little legs and a huge tummy now, and eyes that scan your face as if they're going right inside your head; I hope to God they're not. His willy's funny, a tiny soft teapot-spout of a thing. When you're cleaning the poo off it you think it's impossible that one day it'll be this huge hard veiny stalk with wiry hairs all round it. Mum says he's a good baby to what I was, he only wakes once or twice in the night and goes back down after a feed, but it's killing me getting up to him at all hours. How do people manage without sleep? Sometimes I lie awake in the dark, waiting for him to cry, and I wonder if he can read my thoughts and whether that starts him off.

Once, and I haven't told anyone this, he was crying and crying in his cot and it was half-past three in the morning. He had wind but I didn't know, I thought he was doing it to spite me. I picked him up and he carried on screaming into my ear and my whole body started to tremble because of the urge to shake him hard. A good shake will show him, make him stop, I thought. Then I came out of it and remembered what Dad had said, but as I went to put Will back down he let out a huge burp and stopped crying immediately. I went down and had a cup of tea anyway.

He is a sweet baby. I call him Will, Mum calls him William, to Nan he's Bill or sometimes 'Bonny Brid'. Dad refers to him as 't' little belter'. I can change his nappy now no problem, I sing him songs by Oasis; he's gaining weight and he might have smiled for the first time today. Mum said it was a smile, anyway.

But I'm still a fraud. I put him to the breast and look down at his fragile skull and I think: I don't love you yet. I wouldn't want any harm to come to you, I'd fight off a tiger with my bare hands if you were in danger. And yet there's a gap inside me where I'm sure I should be feeling something more. You shouldn't just be *fond* of your baby, should you?

What have I done?

*

THE HOUSE is full of cards and people troop up the path almost daily with bits and pieces for the baby. Mr F sent a book of lullabies from around the world; Debbie's sister brought a bag of clothes, 3–6 months, she'd finished with. All Mum's friends from the Over Seventies' have given something, knitted cardigans and teddies and what have you. Mrs Katechi from the Spar gave us a scrapbook entitled 'Baby's First Year'; Pauline came with a bag of gifts from the staff and kids, even a couple of parents had chipped in. A lot of it's second-hand but that doesn't matter, William's not going to complain, is he?

Charlotte wanted to know why everyone was being so nice.

'I don't know half these people. Why have they bought me presents?'

I was writing thank-you notes at the table but I stopped and put my pen down. 'Do you know, it's funny, I remember thinking exactly the same, but I can understand it now. It's because a new baby's a blank sheet, it's not made any mistakes like an adult has. People want to get in on that innocence and celebrate it while it's there. It's very attractive, that unspoilt life, sort of magical. It gives us all hope. The baby's got a chance of getting it right where we've failed.'

Charlotte snickered. 'Steady on, Mum. Isn't it just that babies are cute?'

William, who was lying naked on his changing mat with his chubby legs kicking, snorted and sneezed.

'Maybe. That's only my take on it. Hey, you'd best put his nappy on before he wees. It goes a long way with boys, I've discovered.'

'I know, it's like a fountain.' Charlotte knelt – she's getting so capable with him – and started to strap him up.

'Yeah, I can understand people being nice with *him*, who wouldn't be? But I thought some of them might be a bit off with me, you know, not being married and that. The older ones, anyway.'

'Oh, love, there probably isn't a woman alive who doesn't think, There but for the Grace of God. The older ones especially, I shouldn't be surprised, because when they were young it was a lot easier to get caught.'

Charlotte snapped the last popper on William's suit. 'Oh, God, imagine, Mum, imagine Ivy Seddon . . . and Maud Eckersley . . . on their backs, in the grass!'

'Stop that now, madam, you've a nasty mind. I've got to give them both a lift to the hospital this afternoon. I think all those hormones must have affected your head. Hell's teeth, what an image, though.'

'But they must have been young once. They must have courted and that . . .'

I put the last card in its envelope.

'Oh, I don't think so. Sex wasn't invented until the 1960s, you know. Before that everybody behaved themselves.'

'Did they? Did they really?'

'What do you think?'

\*

**When Mum** asked me what I wanted for my birthday I said, 'Sleep.' It was true. Key of the door or not, all I wanted was to get my head down for a few hours. You could stick your parties and your presents. I thought she'd roll her eyes and suggest a gold locket, but she only said, 'You'd best get expressing some milk, then.'

So on the morning of my eighteenth birthday the fairies came and spirited Will away and I slept on in a tangle of sheets. I slept till noon, woke up and went back out again. This second time, though, I started to have a very strange dream. I was on the London Underground and a dwarf with a black beard was crushed up next to me. He kept looking at me and licking his lips so I tried to move away but the crowd was packed too tight. Then he reached up and started squeezing my breasts hard. Harder and harder he squeezed until it really hurt, then I woke up.

I was lying in a pool of my own milk. It had soaked right through my bra, my T-shirt and the bottom sheet. My breasts were so hard I could have lain on top of them and been a foot off the mattress. 'Bloody hell,' I said, in some pain, and stumbled out of bed. I staggered to the landing, blinking in the light, desperate to find my baby and have him relieve some of the pressure before I exploded.

'God, Mum!' I shouted as I reached the bottom of the stairs. 'Where's Will? I've got to give him a feed, my boobs are like two rocks. And I've got milk all down me.'

I opened the door to the lounge and in my thick-headedness took in a small crowd: Daniel, Julia, Anya, Mum, Ivy and Maud, Mum's boss (?), Debbie, Dad, a banner, balloons, cocktail sausages. 'Happy birthday,' I heard Daniel say weakly.

I turned and fled upstairs, locking the bedroom door behind me. Ten seconds later Daniel knocked.

'Come on, Charlotte, I'm sorry, we're sorry, let me in.'

'Go away!' I shouted. 'I want Mum.'

She came, with fat-chops Will slumped against her shoulder. 'Here you are.' She handed him over and he started rooting immediately. 'Get yourself settled first.' He latched himself on and began to gulp. 'He's missed his mummy, haven't you? He's been fine, though, good as gold all morning,' she added hastily. 'Now, are you all right? I'm *ever* so sorry—'

'What do *you* think? Standing there like I'm in a wet T-shirt competition in front of all and sundry, no make-up on, my hair like a bird's nest, how would you like it? God, Mum, how *could* you?'

'It was meant to be a surprise.'

'Yes, well, it was that all right. Stop smiling! It's not funny, it's *not*. Christ Almighty. *Why* didn't you come up and warn me? It was awful. I don't think I'll ever set foot outside this bedroom again. I'll get agoraphobia and it'll be totally your fault.'

Mum patted my knee. 'Come on, nobody minds. I did keep coming up to check on you, every fifteen minutes. I was going to let you come round then say Daniel was here, so you could get your lipstick on. But last time I looked in on you, you seemed to be sound asleep and it didn't seem fair to wake you, then Maud wanted to know how long to put the vol-au-vents in for and I got waylaid. We only caught a glimpse, for Heaven's sake. Nobody minds, honestly.'

'I do.'

'I was trying to do something nice for you, Charlotte; give me a break.' Mum looked weary suddenly. 'I get tired too, you know. In fact, with having to take care of miladdo here all morning *and* sort out a buffet, I'm absolutely jiggered. But I wanted it to be nice for you because it's your eighteenth, it's special. I think I'll take your present back to Argos, you don't deserve it.'

'What is it?'

'You'll have to come downstairs and find out.'

Will put his palm on my bare chest and spread his fingers ecstatically. I put my hand out to meet his and he caught and gripped my thumb. His hair was still thick and dark and none of it had dropped out as Maud had predicted.

'You funny monkey,' I said to him. 'You don't care what state I'm in, do you? You haven't a clue. Oh, hell. All right, I give in.'

'Don't put yourself out or anything! Honestly! Everybody in that room just wants to wish you a happy birthday, stop being so horrible.' She took wriggling Will off me while I hunted around for clean clothes.

'It's not my fault I'm bad-tempered, you know, it's the hormones.'

'Rubbish. You can't go on using that excuse for ever. Now, I've brought you up your toothbrush and I've even filled Nan's jug and basin next door for you so you don't have to trail through the lounge to the bathroom, you can make yourself decent up here.'

'Am I a miserable cow?'

'At times.'

'Why can't we have an upstairs bathroom like normal people?'

'When we win the lottery. Now get a move on.'

Actually it was Daniel who gave me the best birthday present, although Mum's was pretty amazing.

She wheeled it in on the hostess trolley. 'We thought you'd had enough things for the baby. This is just for you.'

'For your studies,' said Dad shyly.

'It's a good package.' Daniel handed me the scissors and I started to undo the Sellotape. 'Though you might want to upgrade at some point.'

So I knew it was a computer before I'd got all the paper off. 'Oh, God, how did you . . . ?'

'Your Dad put some money towards it, and Nan. We don't want you to forget your plans for the future.'

I circled the huge boxes in awe. 'But you already got me the car seat. I don't deserve this.'

'Yes, you do,' said Dad and Daniel in unison: 'No, you don't,' said Mum.

'Where's it going to go?' I thought of my room, the tiny desk, the two square metres of floor space.

'We can maybe move the display cabinet out of that corner. We'll have a chat about it later.' Mum went into the kitchen and came back with a bin liner. 'Help me get that polystyrene into here before it goes all over.'

'When's this cake going to get etten, then?' asked Dad.

**Julia and Anya** (box of goodies from The Body Shop) stayed till Dad left for his next shift, then Debbie (photo album) had to catch the bus. Maud and Ivy (book token and arnica cream) tottered off to an evening service at church which left Mr Fairbrother (*The Little Book of Calm*) and Daniel (nothing as yet). Mum started to ferry crockery through to the kitchen and Daniel jumped out of his chair as if he'd been stung by a wasp.

'I'll do that, Mrs Cooper, you sit down.'

Mum flushed with pleasure. 'Well, that would be very nice. Just leave everything out on the drainer and I'll put it away tomorrow.'

'I'll pour us all some wine,' said Mr Fairbrother.

I sat in the kitchen to keep Daniel company and rocked Will, who went to sleep.

'I wonder if everybody's life turns so weird after having a baby, or if it's just mine. I feel as if all the things I was certain of before have been blown away.'

'Such as?' Daniel groped in the water for the dishcloth.

'Mum; she's almost human these days, that break must have done her some good. Nan not being around, that's *really* strange, I mean she's *always* been there. Part of me misses her like mad and part of me's dreading her coming home. I mean, a two-month-old baby *and* Nan under the same roof. Chaos. Mum'll go all ratty again, it's a shame, and there's every chance Nan'll get ratty back now she's on this new medication.' Will mewed unexpectedly, then settled again. 'Then there's Dad being around so often, that's pretty unnerving. He doesn't change though, he's still charming and useless. And this bloke, Mr Fairbrother—'

'He wants us to call him Leo, he said earlier.'

'Leo, then. What's he doing buzzing about the place? He's too old for Mum, surely. Not her sort at all.'

'I thought he seemed OK. I don't think your dad liked him, though.'

'No, well, they're like chalk and cheese. And then Julia and Anya coming; I was really touched. Did you arrange that?'

Daniel tried to push his glasses up and got foam on his nose. 'Might have done.' He blew the bubbles off and they floated down like snow to settle on the tiles. 'I was going to take you out to Pizza Hut and ask them to come along, then your mum phoned and told me about this—'

'She phoned your house?'

'She was chatting to my dad for ages before he put me on.'

'Oh, God. I am sorry.'

Daniel shrugged. 'I wouldn't worry, he's a natural flirt, it doesn't mean anything. My mother calls it his Bedside Manner.' He emptied the bowl and filled it up again ready for the pans. 'She'd like this Belfast sink. Thirties, isn't it? She'd probably kill for these original black and white tiles too.'

'She wouldn't like having to traipse through the kitchen to have a bath, though.'

'I was wondering about that. I suppose the bathroom was added on after the house was built.'

'I know Nan and Grandad moved in here just before the war but I don't know if they used a tin bath and the outside privy or whether the council had updated it by then. I'll have to ask her. Mum remembers there being a range in the front room, where the gas fire is now, but that went in the seventies.'

'It's full of character, your house. Full of history.'

'Get away. You can say that because you don't have to live here. I'd swap you any day.'

Call-me-Leo appeared in the doorway holding two glasses. 'Are you having your wine in here?'

'Stick it on top of the fridge for now.' I got up carefully; Will was totally out. I carried him through into the living room and laid him in his bouncy chair. With his head thrown back and his turned-up nose he looked like a piglet in a Babygro.

'Bless him,' said Mum. I could see the bottle of wine was well down.

'Can you look after him for a bit longer? Birthday treat?'

She nodded. I went back to the kitchen and picked up my glass. 'Leave that now, Daniel. Come on.'

'I was hoping you'd say that,' he smiled.

Up in my room he turned all serious. 'I've been waiting to give you this,' he said, putting his hand in his jacket pocket. 'I didn't want to do it in front of everyone.' He pulled out a small black cube, about the size of, well, a ring box. Oh, hell, I thought. 'Take it,' he said, placing it in the palm of my hand. Any minute now he was going to sink to his knees and ruin everything. I swallowed and opened the lid.

'Oh, Daniel.'

'They're your birthstones. You have got pierced ears, haven't you? I forgot to check.'

I was laughing with relief. 'Oh, they're lovely. Brilliant. I'll put them in now.' I stood in front of the wardrobe and fitted the tiny pins through my lobes. The blue gems glittered as they swung in the light. 'I like my ears. One part of me that hasn't changed shape recently.'

Behind me Daniel glowed with pride. 'You look fantastic,' he said.

I turned round and since we were standing so close together it wasn't much of a stretch to reach over and kiss him. He put his arms round me and we fused together, lips, hips and toes. If this was a film, I thought, music would be swelling and the camera would be circling us in a long close-up. He kissed really well, surprisingly well. Maybe he'd left more than friends behind in Guildford; I'd never thought to ask.

'Come and lie on the bed,' I said quietly.

'If you're absolutely sure.' He looked into my eyes. 'Are you?'

'Yes.'

We lay for a long time snogging and writhing against each other. He ran his fingers down my back and neck, seemed to know instinctively not to touch my breasts. His kisses on my skin were light and shivery, but he scrupulously avoided contact below my waist, even though I was grinding my hips against his crotch like a complete floozy. Suddenly I wanted him to touch me, really touch me. I didn't care about the flab or what the stitches looked like, I just needed his fingers. I guided his hand down, past the waistband of my skirt, under the hem of my knickers, an electric path. I thought I was going to die with lust.

All the time he was gazing into my eyes and moving his hand really gently, so gently. I knew I was soaking wet; I knew too that the sensation was better than anything I'd ever felt with Paul. No thrusting or stabbing, no jagged nails, just his feathery fingertips slicking over and over the exact spot it felt most good. The pleasure got more and more intense, became a different feeling altogether, he had to keep going, he mustn't stop, I closed my eyes and came, came, came on his hand, in waves of the most exquisite, fantastic, glorious—

'Are you all right?'

I opened my eyes. 'Oh my God. That was unbeliev-able. I never knew what it was like. Oh, God.' I collapsed back onto the pillow. 'You're brilliant. You knew exactly what to do.'

'I've been reading up on it,' he said modestly.

I buried my face in his chest. 'You and your bloody Internet.'

'Ashley Carter, actually, historical novelist. One of my mother's dodgy paperbacks. She keeps them in the bottom of the wardrobe; she thinks I don't know. It might all be crinolines and fans on the front but it's hot stuff between the covers, I can tell you. They've been quite an education to me over the years.' His face was pink and he'd taken his glasses off which made him look different and vulner-able. I had a sort of leap of love for him then and reached over to snog him again. I felt the hardness at his crotch against my belly.

'Is there, is there anything I can do for you?' I asked.

'I should think *so*,' he sighed, lying back as I unzipped his trousers.

\*

I HAVEN'T DREAMT about the London visit at all, and I was expecting nightmares. Maybe it's because I think about it all the time so there's no need for my subconscious to drag it out at night. Emma haunts me like a little ghost, her big eyes, her wispy hair. I see her everywhere, as a child in the kids at school, as the adult she never had a chance to be. There's a weathergirl on GMTV who reminds me of her for some reason, something about the arch of her brows. My heart does a stupid jump when Judy Finnegan announces her.

What can I do, Emma? I ask her, but she just looks sad and frightened. She's become my imaginary friend; any day now I'll find myself setting a place for her at the table. And sometimes in the night my heart bulges against the mattress with emotion, and I feel as if the love in me could flow out like a huge sea and bathe all those children no one wants, their little limbs, if only I could get to them. What can I do?

As for *her*, she's a bad sensation that crawls over my memory from time to time; often unexpectedly. The gaps between flashbacks are getting longer though. Maybe, some time in the future, a whole day will go past and I won't picture her at all. Did Nan ever actually know Jessie Pilkington? It seems impossible; such goodness meeting such evil. In any case, I found my real mother. Surprise, surprise, she turned out to be Nan after all.

I was thinking through all this again while I sat in the consultant's waiting room, ready for him to deliver her long-term assessment. I was all set up for an argument: *Don't you dismiss my mother as a bed-blocker! She's paid her National Insurance contributions all her life, she's only asking for what she's entitled to. If it takes her a long time to recuperate, then so be it, you'll just have to make arrangements. Don't we care about old people in this country any more?* No consultant was going to walk all over me.

And yet, when I met him, Mr Hammond turned out to be perfectly reasonable.

'Take a seat. Now, Mrs Coper.'

I laughed out loud. 'Oh, I wish! It's *Cooper*, actually.'

'Oh, dear, that wasn't a very good start, was it?' He amended his notes. 'I see you've been looking after your mother, Mrs Hesketh, for thirteen years, is it?'

'Yes, I suppose it will be . . . Although to be honest, she looked after me for a while. I suffered from mild post-natal depression, then it came back when I got divorced so when I moved into Mum's I was a bit of a mess. She was marvellous with my daughter, got her in clean clothes every day, made her her packed lunch for school when I couldn't manage; it's not a time I like to think about, I'm not very proud of myself.'

Sudden mental image of me sitting at the table with tears running down my face and Charlotte's paintbrush in my hand. Nan's patting my shoulder and saying, 'Nay, they don't put children into care just because their mother's done a bit of painting.' From upstairs we can both hear Charlotte thumping about, furious with me because during the night when I had more energy than I knew what to do with, I've filled in every damn page of that magic painting book I bought her, she's not even got to do one tiny bit. 'I couldn't stop myself,' I keep saying, 'it was like a compulsion.' And Nan keeps patting, and Charlotte keeps thumping. Oh, I did weirder stuff than that; don't know why that incident popped into my head.

When I came back to myself Mr Hammond's eyebrows were raised above the steel frame of his glasses and I realized my mouth was open, God knows what he thought of me. I pulled myself together and carried on.

'So it's only in the last, oh, I don't know, five or six years she's been bad. It's difficult to pin down exactly when the balance tipped from caring to being cared for. For ages she was just forgetful; we put it down to old age. I can't really leave her on her own now in case she sets the grill pan on fire or floods the sink, but then again some days you wouldn't credit it, she's as right as rain and you wouldn't guess there was anything wrong with her. I gather that's pretty normal, is it, with dementia?'

Mr Hammond gave a slight nod. 'It can be.'

'Weird, isn't it? You never know which side of her you're going to get, is she putting it on or not; sometimes, you know, I could—' I clenched my fists in front of my face, then laughed to show it was just a joke. Wonder if he was fooled? I suppose he's seen enough carers to know the score. He kept nodding anyway, didn't call the police. 'But I've been able to manage because she's been so independent physically. She can get in and out of a bath no trouble, climb the stairs, dress herself; marvellous, really.'

Mr Hammond clasped his hands and looked sympathetic. 'I'm afraid things are on a different footing now,' he said.

'I guessed so.'

'You have to understand that for the foreseeable future Mrs Hesketh is going to be significantly disabled. At the moment nurses are helping to feed, dress and toilet her. She's going to need a lot of care.'

There was a silence while I took this in.

'What about physiotherapy?'

'That may have some long-term benefits, but it isn't going to work miracles.'

'Will she be able to climb the stairs?'

Mr Hammond shook his head. 'She won't be able to *walk* without assistance. She was quite severely affected by the stroke. So what we have to decide, together, is how to provide the level of care that your mother needs to achieve the best possible quality of life.'

So this was my penance for rejecting her and trying to find something better. I was going to have to fireman's lift her every time she needed a wee, for the rest of her life; spoon-feed William with one hand and her with the other. My heart sank to my boots.

'She wants to come home. She'll have to come home eventually, but can you not keep her another month or two? My daughter had a baby eight weeks ago and the house is upside down, as you can imagine, and we're going to need more help from social services . . . Can you see to that for me or do I have to contact them myself?'

'I'm still not sure you understand the full picture,' he said gently. 'I don't see how you can cope on your own. Your mum will need a *lot* of care.'

I thought of her bedroom, of carrying her downstairs to the toilet in the night, or of trying to fit a bed in the living room, then where would the table go, where would we eat? Maybe if we shifted the sideboard – but where? Could we make Nan's room into a study-cum-dining room for Charlotte to work in? It would be funny eating upstairs, and taking food all the way from the kitchen and then the dishes back again . . .

'Do you work?' asked Mr Hammond.

'Part time. Why?'

But he didn't have to say anything. My life was telescoping before my eyes.

'I think you should consider a nursing home,' he said.

'Oh, I'm sorry, that's out of the question. We'll find a way of managing,' I replied. I knew that however grim the situation was, there was no way I could hurt Nan any more than she was already. It was an impossible idea, Nan not being around.

As I got up to leave an idea I'd been trying to suppress for a long time rose to the surface. Mr Hammond seemed a kind man. 'Can I ask you something?'

'Go ahead.'

'Do you think my getting divorced all those years back might have triggered the dementia? She was really cut up about it; family's everything to her.'

'No.'

'Oh. Thank you.' I got as far as the door. 'And, er, is there any chance that her stroke might have happened because I had a few days away on holiday the week before?'

'No.'

'Oh. I thought I'd ask.'

'Goodbye, Mrs *Coper*,' I heard him say as I closed the door. I didn't know what to make of that.

I walked through the hospital building, past the maternity unit with its soft colours and posters of happy breastfeeders, past the children's ward with its giant Tigger mural, to the shop where I bought a family size bar of chocolate. I wolfed it down unhappily, then I went to see Nan. She was trying to turn over a page of *Woman's Weekly*, licking her thumb and index finger and fiddling with the corner. 'Damn useless,' she was muttering. But her face lit up when she saw me, and that was something. 'Eh, it's our Karen. You look bonny. Have you brought that baby today? He's so lovely, little thing.'

'No, Mum, I'll bring him tomorrow.'

She looked vacant for a second, then she was back again.

'Ooh, it is lovely to see you, I can't be doing with hospitals, everyone talks rubbish. And you look bonny; have you a new frock on?'

'No, Mum. It's C&A, I got it when we went to Chester that time. Do you remember? It poured down so all we did was go in shops.'

'Aye. No, not really. Have you brought that little baby, then?'

AFTER THAT I went back to Steve's and accidentally slept with him.

'You're full of surprises, you.' Steve shifted so he was leaning up on his elbow. 'I'd have changed t' sheets if I'd known.'

'Oh God.' I closed my eyes in irritation. 'Why do you have to be so disgusting! You're never any different.'

'It's part of me charm.'

When I left the hospital I was too upset to go home so I went shopping. After an hour wandering round Debenhams I still didn't feel like going back, so I stopped off at his house. I was hoping for a cup of tea and half an hour to get my head round things before I talked to Charlotte. What I got was Steve fresh out the bath, clean shaven again and slightly tipsy still from the night before. 'I'd best sober up, I'm back at work in two hours. I hate these evening shifts. I could do wi' workin' part time.'

'You could do with packing up altogether,' I laughed. 'I've never known anyone as lazy.'

He scratched his head amiably. 'Aye, well, life's too short. So, what can I do you for? Everything all right with our little belter?'

I told him about the consultant. 'You see, Nan's so trusting, she's like a baby herself. I couldn't put her in a home, it would be cruel.'

Steve pulled at the belt of his dressing gown. 'Aye, it's a poser. Can social services not sort summat out for you?'

'I don't know. They'll have to, won't they? Oh, the thought of having to go through all those different departments again and fill in all those assessments.' I didn't want to have to go near their offices again either in case I bumped into Joyce Fitton and had to face the look of pity in her eyes. 'It's been one thing after another this year. I must have broken a mirror or run over a black cat.'

'I've been thinking,' said Steve (and he moved chairs to sit next to me), 'this in't the drink talking, you know, this has been on my mind for a while.'

'What has?'

'All it is, I've enjoyed helping out a bit more, you know, being around, involved. It's nice to see more of Charlotte now she's not so hoity-toity all the time, it's done her good to roll her sleeves up and change a few nappies. I'm not much of a one for babies—'

'You can say that again.'

'No, fair enough, but the lad'll need someone to play

footie with him as he grows up and I'd quite like to be, well, around.'

'You are. You've been quite helpful at times. What are you trying to say, Steve?' I was aware of his arm pressing against mine and the smell of his aftershave.

'Are you seeing that feller?'

'Who? Leo Fairbrother?'

'Yeah, th' headmaster.' He rubbed his lip where the moustache had been. 'Is he your boyfriend?'

'No.' This was true; absolutely nothing had happened between us and it didn't look as though anything was ever going to. I had no idea what Leo was up to, but it didn't seem as though a great seduction was on the horizon. I'd more or less given up. 'What about you? What about that woman from Turton, that one who ran the London Marathon?'

'Oh, her? She were nowt.'

'Nowt as in Nothing or Nowt as in Bad-tempered?'

'Both, really. She wanted me to go jogging, can you imagine? I said, the only way you'll get me to jog is to put a pub at t' finishing line. She weren't amused.'

'What are you like.' I nudged him good-humouredly, he nudged me back and it turned into a clumsy embrace. His face loomed into mine, his lips hit my cheek then my mouth, and my face went into shock. 'Bloody hell, Steve, what are we doing?'

He stopped. 'Why? Do you not like it?' He had a point; it was very nice. I'd not slept with anyone for over a year; some of the men at the Over Seventies were beginning to look pretty tasty. 'No strings, come on. It'll do us both good.'

'I can't sleep with you, don't be ridiculous.'

'You know your trouble?' said Steve kissing my neck where he knew I liked it. 'You look for problems. Sometimes you just have to go with the moment. Stop analysing everything.' His hand dipped under my collar and eased down my bra strap, making my nipples tingle with anticipation. His dressing gown fell open. 'You don't know what you do to me.'

'I've a fair idea,' I mumbled as he unbuttoned my top.

# Chapter Twelve

'DOES THIS MEAN I'm back in, then?' Steve pulled his jeans on and fastened them round his skinny waist.

'Back in where? Have you seen my tights?'

'They're here, stuck on this lampshade.' He threw them over. 'Back in the bosom of me family.'

I wriggled my hand down inside each leg to turn the tights right-side out. 'Get off. It's not like you live in Australia, is it? You are part of the family, whether I like it or not; you're Charlotte's dad and she needs you around at the moment.'

'I were thinking, though.' He sat down on the edge of the bed. 'We could have another go, couldn't we? I don't mean move back or anything mad like that, but we could meet up for a drink sometimes and, and . . .'

I located my shoes, slipped them on and stood looking down at him. 'No, Steve, no way. It would be too complicated.'

'Complicated? I'm about the least complicated chap you could have. There's nowt complicated about me, now is there? Go on, admit it.'

I sighed. 'That's not what I meant. The answer's no.'

'Ahwww. I've got you a smashin' Christmas present, an' all.'

'Bribery won't get you anywhere. We haven't bought each other Christmas presents for thirteen years. I'm not going to start now.' I picked up his mucky hairbrush and tried to smooth my hair without actually touching the bristles. 'Let's quit while we're ahead, eh? You can come round when you want, but no more of this malarky.'

He put his face under mine and grinned. 'It were good though, weren't it?'

*

The first place we went to was at the bottom of the village: Bishop House. The air had been freezing, the sky looked like tracing paper and the tarmac drive was slippery under the pram wheels. The light was failing too, even though it was only mid-afternoon. As far as I was concerned Bishop House had just been a big Victorian pile behind some conker trees on the bus route to Bolton, but now there was every chance it could be Nan's new home.

'You see,' Mum had said over breakfast, 'I'm not sure I can give her the care she needs. She's been really poorly and she's never going to get completely better. That's what the doctors say. She needs qualified nurses round her twenty-four hours a day.'

I stared out of the window trying to take in the news. The Ribble bus went past and I remembered the trips with Nan to Wigan on the top deck, and the Pick 'n' Mix from Woolworth's we always used to choose together. I really enjoyed going shopping with Nan as a child because there was never a row *and* I got my own way and a bag to put it in. She loved my company, and I loved hers, simple. Then, as I got older, things changed; I changed. For all those hours she'd spent cutting pictures out of catalogues for me and helping me make pastry animals, suddenly I never had the time for her any more. God, I'd let her down.

'I could help out. Can we not get the council to put in one of those stairlifts Thora Hird's always chuntering on about? They do walk-in baths too, I've seen them advertised during *Countdown*. If the two of us work together . . .'

Mum shook her head. 'You've more than enough on your plate. It's all you can do at the moment to wash your armpits in a morning and put your sweater on right-side out. Well, isn't it? You don't understand the level of attention she'll need, *I* didn't at first. You're thinking of the old Nan, Nan as she was. She's a different person now.' She was speaking in a slow, sort of rehearsed way that made me think she'd been over the arguments again and again.

'I feel as if she'd died, it's horrible, Mum.'

'You mustn't think like that, Charlotte.' Mum stirred her coffee rapidly, but she didn't elaborate.

We sat in gloomy silence while Will watched us seriously from the hearthrug. I tried to get some cornflakes down but they stuck in my throat. I'd really thought, once Nan was out of danger, it was simply a matter of time and she'd be out of hospital, back home and making a nuisance of herself. I mean, here we were on the verge of the twenty-first century, they could send cameras to Jupiter and Saturn, so why couldn't medical science sort out her wayward limbs? It was unbelievable that Nan wasn't coming home.

'We'll find somewhere nice with some young male nurses she can flirt with. Everyone'll love her, she'll be happy as Larry once she settles in.'

I was still wondering about this as the huge front door of Bishop House opened and a smell of pee hit us. I noticed Mum had got baby sick all down the back of her sleeve, but I knew she was so keyed up it was probably better not to mention it. We pushed Will up the wheel-chair ramp and parked him in the hall while the young girl who had let us in went to fetch the Matron.

'God, it's hot in here,' said Mum, unwinding her scarf. 'You'd better unwrap William before he cooks.'

As I was fiddling with the baby's blankets a tiny old man came out of the TV lounge and moved shakily towards us. He fixed on my mother and snapped: 'I need to go to the toilet!'

Mum raised her eyebrows at me. 'I'll see if I can find a nurse.'

'You don't understand, I need to go *now*.' His eyes were watery and desperate; he made me want to throw up.

'Hang on, Mum.' I popped Will back down and ran along the hall, round the corner (only four old ladies play-ing cards in a side room), doubled back and checked up the stairs to the landing, but there were no staff in sight. 'Nurse!' I shouted. 'Nu-urse!' a white-haired biddy in a blue dressing gown sang back at me cheerfully. She waved at me over the banisters till I got to the bottom. 'You'd think they'd have a bell or something . . .' I called as I stalked crossly back to the pram, but Mum and the old man had vanished. I hoisted Will out again and went to sit on the stairs to wait. Finally she reappeared, frowning.

'Honestly! That poor man.'

'You didn't—?'

'Well, of course I did, once we'd found where the toilet actually was. He was terribly upset. Did you manage to find a nurse?'

'Nope. So, did you have to, *wipe his bum*?' I couldn't believe what she'd just done. I was full of appalled respect.

'*No*, only his willy.' Mum checked her watch. 'What can that woman be doing? Don't look so funny, it's only what I have to do at school sometimes only on a bigger scale, Reception are forever having toilet incidents. If it had been Nan you'd have wanted someone to help her, wouldn't you?'

That shut me up. We waited for another five minutes under the feeble Christmas decorations stuck to the light fittings, then the young girl came back.

'Mrs Street says she's very sorry but she's been delayed.' She lowered her voice. 'A resident passed away this morning and she's with the daughter now. But I can be showing you around till she's free.'

We walked along behind the girl whose hair needed washing. It was a sad route. Every door opened like a blighted Advent calendar: a lady on her own, slumped in an easy chair, watching *Bodger and Badger* on children's TV; three old women all asleep where they sat, sticks laid on the floor; a bald, hunched man sitting looking out of a bay window at the gathering dark. The furniture was cheap and nasty, house-clearance stuff in white melamine or black ash and the carpet was that rough, corded type; some of it was stained. In one room we passed a lady was lying in her bed shouting, 'Help! Help!'

'Do you not need to go in to her?' asked Mum.

The girl smiled. 'No, she's all right, our Mrs Wallis. She always does that, then when you go in and ask her what's up she says, "Was I shouting?" She's fine, really.' She shut the door on Mrs Wallis' cries. 'It's a lovely place for them, they get their meals laid on and their own rooms, and there's always company for them. We do bingo and concerts too. The children are coming from St Peter's next week to do carols in the dining room. It's a nice home, this one.'

I searched for irony in her face but there was none. I grasped Will to me and he rooted against my shoulder and whimpered.

By the time we got outside we were nearly hysterical with the horror of it all. I could see the relief on my mum's face in the security floodlights. Her breath came out in a frosty cloud.

'We can't send her there!'

'Oh, thank God, Mum. It was *awful*. The thought of her in with that lot . . .'

'I know. And yet, do you know, I think the staff were trying their best. It's just so sad . . .' She shook her head. 'That commode, though!' She started to giggle.

'Well, *I* didn't know what it was, I thought it was just a seat. I was tired; you try carting Fatso here round for forty minutes, I thought my legs were going to give way.'

'It wouldn't have been so bad if it had been empty . . . Your face!'

'All right.' I was laughing too, it was the nerves. 'But we're not sending Nan there, are we?'

'No.'

'Good. Merry Christmas.'

'Merry Christmas, Charlotte. Incidentally, did you know you've got baby sick on your shoulder?'

From inside the depths of the pram, Will's eyes glittered.

'You little soiler,' I told him.

*

I'D MADE UP my mind, to be honest, or at least I thought I had; come hell or high water there was no way my mother was going in a home. But it was Leo who said, 'Have you investigated Mayfield?' Apparently his father had had a couple of weeks' respite care there and they'd both been impressed. 'More like your four-star hotel,' he told me in the Octagon bar after we'd been to see *An Inspector Calls*. 'Very upbeat, not at all depressing even though some of the residents are pretty laid-up. I know it's further away than you'd want, ideally, but you've always got the car, it's only fifteen minutes or so. Worth a recce, anyway, I'd have thought. I'll come with you if you like.'

So I took his advice but went with Charlotte. It was a family thing, after all.

Mayfield was modern orange brick and overlooked a superstore, but inside it was clean and airy. The only detectable smells were furniture polish and dog. *Blossom*

*Where Ye Are Planted* proclaimed a tapestry over the vestibule door.

'Mum, have you seen this?' Charlotte pointed to a six-foot-high cage full of budgies all going berserk because a tortoiseshell cat was lounging across the top and dangling a paw over the side.

'They're the best of friends, really,' said the Matron, a smart woman in navy who met us in the hall. 'They just enjoy scolding her, but she's too well-fed and lazy to do any harm, even if she could get at them. Aren't you, madam?' The cat flicked an ear at her but otherwise made no movement. 'Oh, and there's Bertie as well.' Bertie was a yellow Labrador who came up to the pram and laid his head on William's blanket. 'Everyone loves Bertie.' Matron patted his flank. 'I have such a job trying to stop our guests from over-feeding him.'

Charlotte stroked the dog and it wagged its tail so hard its back end nearly went over. 'Nan would like him,' she mouthed at me.

I don't know what it was, whether the paint they used was brighter or the windows were bigger, or perhaps it was because we were seeing the place in the morning rather than at dusk, but it was a different world to Bishop House. There were still some very poorly old people there but there seemed to be more activity. Even the television watchers were arguing amongst themselves. How Old is Too Old to Give Birth?

'We like Mr Kilroy in here, don't we?' said Matron. 'What is it today? "I Had A Baby At 60"? Good God. What do you think about that, Enid?'

'I reckon she's mental,' said a lady in a pink cardigan.

'I put the flags out when I had my last one, and I were only twenty-six. Teks me all my time t' look after mysen, never mind a babby.'

They all went mad over William, though. Enid wanted him on her bony knee.

'See the doggy? Can you see that nice doggy? That's my Bella, that is.'

Bertie trotted up to each outstretched hand in turn before exiting.

'Off on his rounds again,' said Matron. 'He's everyone's pal. So, what else can I show you?'

'I think we've seen enough, haven't we, Charlotte? Thanks for the tour, we're very grateful. And you do have a place available?'

'At the moment.' She touched my arm gently. 'These decisions are never easy, but sometimes it really is for the best. Have a think and get back to me.'

Bertie raced past us pursued by a woman with a zimmer frame.

'Honey! Honey! Come back here!' she was shouting. 'Damn dog's got my paper,' she complained as she passed Matron.

'Never mind, Irene, gets you your daily exercise, doesn't it?'

She let us out and we stood on the porch for a while looking out over Morrison's.

'What do you think?' Charlotte asked me.

'I think . . . it wouldn't be so bad,' I said. We walked slowly down the path onto the main road to where the Metro was parked. 'I only hope Nan agrees.'

You wait for years to overtake your parents and then when you do it's no kind of victory. When I was little and being told off, I'd think, Just you wait, when I'm grown up I'll show you. Sometimes Dad used to pull rank on me, *Because I Say So*, and I hated it. But nothing prepares you for the day when you realize your parents are weaker than you. It's like having the ground fall away from under your feet.

I sat by Mum's bed holding her hand for a long time before I spoke. I was talking to her, though.

*Mum,* I said, *I wanted to tell you something, a secret you should know.* She breathed evenly in her sleep. *It's something I've only just found out.* The funny thing was, in profile she did look a bit like me. We had some of the same lines and wrinkles, anyway. *Listen, Mum, you know when I got pregnant? I think* – the idea formed itself properly into actual words – *it might have been Freudian.* The way she was lying made her skin smooth out and she seemed years younger lying there next to my face. *Do you understand what that means? What I'm trying to say is, deep down, part of me was too scared to take exams and go off to university, start a new life away from everything I'd ever known. I didn't know it then, it wasn't conscious, but I can see quite clearly now. I think falling pregnant was a way of avoiding all that risk. So I would never have got rid of Charlotte, for all I moaned on at the time. And I don't blame you. I don't blame anyone. It's the way life works out.*

When she woke up I was going to tell her about Mayfield.

*

**There were** little yellow chicks all over the house suddenly.

'What're these in aid of?' I asked Mum, who was producing them at fantastic speed. 'I didn't even know you could knit.'

'Nan taught me years ago, you don't forget. You can knock these off in an hour. Ivy showed me. Then they fit over a Cadbury's Creme Egg, can you see?' She put her fingers inside the chick's body and filled it out. 'If you're not doing anything you could sew some eyes on those two over there. There's black wool in the basket.'

'I've got to change Will, he stinks. Anyway, what are you making them for?'

'The NSPCC. I talked it over with Leo, we're going to have a big drive at school next term and see how much we can raise with lots of different events. I thought we could have an Easter fair and sell these, say, a pound a time? Or could we get away with charging more, what do you think?'

'I think you're bonkers,' I said, hoisting Will onto his plastic mat and undoing his poppers. 'We're in the middle of Christmas, never mind Easter. I don't know how you've got the time.' I undid the nappy. 'Oh, God, look at that. It's gone up his back.'

'Well, I thought if I did two or three a week from now till March, and buy a couple of eggs every time we go shopping . . .'

Will chortled with delight as I wiped him down. 'It's not funny and it's not clever,' I told him. He grabbed his genitals and grinned. 'Perv,' I said and strapped him back up.

'Then I was wondering about a duck race on the canal at Ambley, and a sponsored walk, and maybe cake sales every Friday by the back doors, because if we have them outside then the cleaners won't complain about crumbs . . .' Mum's needles clicked busily.

'You're turning into Nan, you are,' I joked.

'Don't even think it,' she said.

I presume it's her way of coping. Apparently it was really hard to get through to Nan about not coming back here, and whenever Mum thought she'd finally broken the awful truth, Nan would gaze up at her and say something like, 'I can't wait to get home to that baby.' In the end she gave up.

Oh, another funny thing I found: talk about turning into Nan, she left some papers on the cistern, of all places; a pack from the DFEE about Returning to Education. I wonder what's going on there, and if Leo Fairbrother put her up to it. He seems to be behind a lot of stuff these days. I won't say anything, though, I don't think I was meant to see it. I left the pack where it was and it was gone next time I looked, anyway.

**On Christmas Eve** Daniel came round to have A Talk.

'What's going on here?' he said, surveying the chaos in my bedroom. 'Is this really the best time for a major clear-out?'

'Mum's idea. She wanted me to move into Nan's room, but I don't want to, so we're setting it up as a study-cum-nursery type thing. If you think it's bad in here you should see next door. Come and have a look, it's so weird.'

Mum had pushed Nan's wardrobe against the chest of drawers to clear a wall, and the bed was piled high with old-lady underclothes and spare bedding. The carpet was darker in an oblong where the wardrobe had been and there were some spectacular cobwebs across the newly revealed wallpaper. God knows what kind of tarantula hybrid had been sharing Nan's room for the last few years.

'The desk's going along there, and the bookcase. And Will's moving in the New Year, I thought he could have his cot under the window.' I squeezed round the bed and looked out over the frosted Working Men's. It would have been nearly beautiful, but for the fact that two lads were going from one vehicle to another inscribing rude messages on the sparkling windscreens. I opened the window catch and shouted down, 'There's two Gs in BUGGER, you know. What's Santa Claus bringing you? Lobotomies?' They whipped their heads up, saw me and gave me the finger. I gave it back and shut the window again. 'Nice to see community spirit's alive and well. Christ, it's bloody freezing out.' I pulled the curtains shut quickly and hugged myself warm. 'Don't know what's going to happen to the bed, though. It seems really disrespectful to start messing about with Nan's stuff when she doesn't even know she's not coming back. Like she was dead, only she's not.'

'Maybe your mum could put it in storage.'

'Maybe.' I perched on one side of the mattress and Daniel perched on the other. 'It's what we're doing to Nan, after all.'

He reached across and squeezed my hand. 'Hey up,' he grinned, in a pathetic attempt at a northern accent.

'Watch it, you.'

'By 'eck.'

'Bugger *off*.'

He pursed his lips and fluttered his eyelashes. 'Ooh, Mr 'Igginbottom, is that a ferret down your trousers or are you just pleased to see me?'

I picked up some big ecru knickers and threw them at him. 'Stop it, will you? I want to be miserable for a minute. You don't understand, Nan's always been here.'

'You said.'

He held out his arms and I crawled across the bed-spread to him. He pulled me against his chest and I found I was shivering.

'Well, she has. And I never really took her on. I thought she was a nuisance half the time. It's too late.' I sagged my shoulders and exhaled slowly. 'I've been a rubbish granddaughter. Why don't we ever say the things we should to the people we care about?'

'Like you said, she's not dead yet. Sort it out, if that's the way you feel. Look, I'm not trying to be unsympathetic, but simply by producing Will you've probably done as much for her as any doctor. Go and see her. Talk to her.' He gave me a squeeze, then took my face between his hands. 'And listen, there's one thing you should know that's more important than anything else right now.'

I searched his eyes. 'What?'

'That there's a damn great spider on your shoulder.'

I yelped and shot off the bed, pulling at my jumper and staggering into the wall.

'Hold it!' shouted Daniel and launched forward, clapping his hand over the dark shape that squatted between the tufts of the candlewick bedspread. 'Gotcha!' He held it up as if for inspection. 'Oh no, it's got away!' he yelled as the black blob leapt out of his hands and at my feet. I screamed at the top of my voice and threw myself against the wardrobe. The hairy mass flopped onto the floor. And lay still.

'You total bastard,' I said, and picked it up.

Mum appeared in the doorway, the old cross expression back on her face, like it had never been away. She wears it well.

'Will you two make a bit less noise? I've just this minute got the baby down—' She wiped her brow with the back of hand like a poor woman in a Victorian melodrama.

'Sorry—'

'Sorry, Mrs Cooper.' Daniel cocked his head on one side and raised his eyebrows earnestly; it made him look about twelve.

Mum huffed.

'It's all my fault I'm afraid, Mrs Cooper, I was being very immature.' Daniel's neck craned into an even more humble posture.

'Yeah, he was, Mum, actually, it was his fault, he threw this – God, it's not funny! – fake moustache at me.' I held it up for her to see. 'What's it doing in here? I don't remember having any pirate costumes as a kid.'

'Let me see.' She held out her hand and I placed it in

her palm. 'Oh.' She smiled, turning the moustache over in her fingers so it was tape-up. 'You'd never believe it, this was Nan's.'

Daniel's eyebrows shot up. I snorted. 'Get away.'

'No, honestly. She used to do a lot of plays for the Mothers' Union, comedy ones, in dialect. She was always the man, for some reason.'

'But she's such a midget!'

'I think that was part of the joke. She'd be paired up with some hefty woman as the wife; hen-pecked husband, that sort of thing. Seaside postcard couple. They used to perform over at the Working Men's, in the days when it wasn't quite so seedy.'

'God, really? Did you ever see her?' It was fascinating, this Nan I never knew.

'Oh, no; it was only when I was very little. Apparently she was very good, though. Had the audience in tears a time or two, with laughter. Ask Maud, she'll remember.' She passed the moustache back to Daniel like she was offering him a canape. 'Here you go, lad, try it for size.'

Daniel took it politely and pressed it against his lip. 'What do you think?' he tried to say, turning to me, but the moustache fell off and dropped down between his legs in a spider-type action. I half expected it to scuttle off across the rug.

'Gerrross! You look like the love-child of Professor Winston and Cher. Don't *ever* grow one of your own, promise?' I bent double and fished it off the floor. 'If you do, you're dumped, OK?' I put the moustache to my lip; it smelt of must. 'Imagine Nan dressed as a man, though.'

'Wherever did it come from?' asked Mum, stepping

forward to shift some of the ancient pillowcases and sheets. Some of them still had the cellophane wrappers on. 'Did it drop out of these? Oh, wait a minute, what's this?'

She lifted some linen and nestled in between the layers was a pink raffia knitting bag with wooden handles. It had been squashed under the sheets so long it had left its shape imprinted in them, top and bottom, like a fossil. A ginger moustache was sticking out of the top, and as Mum picked the bag up, a thick wooden peg fell out and rolled against my thigh.

'And this is?'

Mum frowned. 'A piggy, probably.'

'You what?'

'Some game they used to play in the olden days.'

The ghosts of Nan's past crowded round to see.

'I wonder what they did with it,' said Daniel, attempting to spin it on the bedspread.

'Hit it with a bat and ran after it, I think.' Mum rummaged in the bag and brought out a little plaster figure with a flat white triangle where its nose should have been. She held it out for us to see.

'They called these kewpie dolls, with their pot-bellies and moulded hair. This'll be old, you know.'

'Worth anything?'

'Wouldn't have thought so. Seen better days, haven't you, love? Never mind, so have we all.' Mum put the doll on the bed and emptied the bag carefully between me and Daniel, then she knelt down so she was on a level with it all. Papers, cards, odds and ends had spilled out. A pair of pink baby bootees caught my eye.

'Oh, sweet! Were these mine?'

'No. They were mine. And the lamb rattle.' Mum looked sad as she touched them.

'These must be from World War One,' said Daniel flicking carefully through a bundle of postcards with embroidered fronts. 'Amazing. This is real social history.'

Mum handed me a letter to Santa she'd written when she was about six or seven.

'Purple felt tip? Bit sloppy, that. And what's that zombie-thing in the corner?'

'Zombie?' Mum imitated outrage. 'That's a drawing of Barbie. My whole happiness hung on that doll, you know, I thought it would complete my life. Even though it was in the days before she had all these poseable limbs and bum-length hair, what have you. It's all gone completely mad now, of course; they do Barbie Penthouse Apartments and camper vans, and beauty salons, discos . . . Takes all the fun out of it. I used to cut up shoe boxes and line them with wallpaper, stop sniggering, Charlotte. And you couldn't get Ken outside the States, nobody would import him, so I made do with an Action Man I got from a jumble sale. His gripping hands came in useful many a time.' Mum smoothed out the letter wistfully. 'Tell you what, though, I wish I'd kept that doll, it would have been really collectable. Nothing like those interchangeable pink-and-blonde bimbos you had when you were tiny. This one had black hair cut in a fringe and an op-art dress, à la Mary Quant. Quite scary, actually, but it could have been an heirloom.'

'Cool,' I said, then laughed. 'God, Mum, how sad are we?'

'Do you realize, these cards have seen actual bloodshed,' Daniel broke in. 'This thumb-print here, it might even be blood. Wow. You should take them into school, Mrs Carlisle would love it.' He turned one over and started to read it.

'No.' Mum took it gently out of his hand. 'Sorry. I want to look through them first. They might be personal. Nan's grandad was killed out there, you know.'

The light in the room shifted and the air in the chimney sighed. Daniel gazed at his knees in embarrassment, so to make him feel better I undid the safety pin on the crepe bandage I'd found and began to wind it round his wrist. He didn't seem to object so I carried on up his arm, tying a neat knot at the shoulder. After a minute he shook himself out of his mood and started a retaliatory action with a bobbin of thin pink ribbon. His fingers wove the satin in and out between my fingers, his long bony fingers mixed up with my thin girly ones, and I thought, I love you, you daft sod.

*

AND THEN EMMA was leaning into me, I could almost hear her breathing at my shoulder. So I reached under the papers and there was a New Testament with a black cover, very plain, but with a gap in the gold edged pages like a half-closed eye. I opened it up a fraction and caught a glimpse of a pink slip of paper, *Certified copy of an entry . . . General Register Office . . . caution.* My adoption certificate. They didn't see anything, the pair on the bed; too busy mucking about with ribbons. Well, let them. It didn't matter anyway. I closed the book and pushed it back in the bag. Next to me, Emma sighed again.

\*

**Mum came over** all moony suddenly and said she wanted to be on her own for a while, so I took Daniel back to my bedroom. There was even less space than usual but he managed to wedge himself into the corner nearest the door; I didn't tell him that at the bottom of the bin bag by his elbow was all the memorabilia from six months with Paul. I'd squirted hair mousse over the handful of cards, notes, photos and tickets before dumping them; now the room smelt like a cheap salon – The First Cut, perhaps. Daniel's nose wrinkled but he didn't say anything. I picked up a dog-eared magazine article entitled 'Perfect 10: Nails to Die For'. 'God, look at this! Imagine having *time* to paint your fingernails!' I dropped it in the plastic sack. 'A lot of this seems totally out of date now. From another era.'

'I can see what you mean. Oh, this is no good; if I don't move soon I'll seize up.' Daniel uncurled himself awkwardly and picked his way over the mess on the floor to install himself on the bed. He lay down and put his hands behind his head, very at home. 'So, now the dust has settled, what are you going to do with your life?'

I shrugged. 'There's only so much dust *can* settle with a baby. Mum still wants me to go off to uni but it seems impossible at the moment. Mrs Carlisle thinks I should have a year out to retake the modules I missed; she has this idea that she can send me assignments through the post and I could just come in for a few lessons a week. Apparently the Head's OK with that.'

'And you?'

'I really want those As. I worked hard enough for them. But it's going to be a bloody funny year.' He caught my rueful gaze and held out his hand. I stepped over and sat next to him.

'Come here.' He pulled me down, wrapped me in his long arms and kissed my hair. 'Listen. I won't go, I've decided. I'm not leaving you, Charlotte.'

'Don't be daft,' I mumbled into his chest. 'You had your heart set on Oxford.'

He snorted. 'Some chance. With an offer of three As it's not very likely. Dad can pull all the strings he wants, it's not going to get me in unless my papers get mixed up with some other poor sod's. Anyway, that's not important any more. You and Will are what matter.'

I moved away and touched his face. 'It *is*, Daniel. If you don't get into Oxford, somewhere else'll take you, you're too bloody clever. I bet Durham or Manchester accept you. You've got to go and get that degree. *I'd* go if it was the other way round.'

'Would you?' He looked surprised.

'Oh, I don't know.' Faintly from downstairs we heard Will begin to cry. I tensed to go to him, but then he stopped; Mum must have nipped down and picked him up. I let my muscles relax again, but my mind was racing. 'It's all too difficult. My brain's not what it used to be.'

'How about I defer my place and take a year out? I

might be able to swing some sort of job at the engineering works; could your dad put in a good word for me?'

I laughed. 'My dad? That really would blight your chances. No, don't. We'd still have to part at the end of the year, unless I got in at the same uni and there's no guarantee of that.' Daniel looked mournful. 'Come on, it's only what happens to thousands of couples every year. And in the end they either make it or they don't—'

'We will.'

'Yes.'

'I don't want to leave you.'

This was getting out of hand, I felt.

'Daniel!' I shook him by the shoulders, pushed him against the mattress and climbed astride him. His eyes were wide and miserable. I blew in his face but he only turned away. 'Right, you!' I growled, putting my mouth close to his ear, 'Stop being such a silly bugger. It's not till next September, anyway! You might meet some fancy piece and run off with her long before then. Snap out of it! Lighten up! Because if you don't I'm going to have to take your trousers down and interfere with you.'

There was a pause.

'Did I tell you how depressed I've been?' he said.


**Afterwards** we lay quietly and I combed his hair with my fingers.

'You really should get this chopped, you know.'

'Do you think? I've always thought of it as my finest feature.'

'Get off.' I ruffled his mop. 'You look like Young Einstein.'

He gripped my wrist and kissed it. 'I know you think I was being over the top before, but this is the first time in my life, well certainly the first time since I left Guildford, that I feel like I belong with someone. Does that sound mad?'

'No, 'cause I think I feel like that too. It's . . . trying to find out where you fit in. I've never felt very good at that. Mind you, this household hasn't been exactly conducive to forming settled relationships. It's been such a battle-ground, and with the three of us it was always two against one, different combinations. You won't have had that with there being four of you.'

'No, but I know what you mean about the rows.' We shuffled into spoons and he put his arm across me and talked into the back of my neck. 'About a year before we left Surrey there were shouting matches every night, and actually there were just the three of us then because my sister had left home. Then, after the rows came the freez-ing silences and the "Tell your mother that I won't be in for dinner" and "Tell your father that he'll have to cook his own, then" routine, with me in the middle. I never want to go through that again. If they ever start up I shall leave, I'm old enough now.'

'Move in here. See how the other half live.' I reached back and dug him in the ribs.

He sighed. 'All us damaged adolescents, all over the country, trying to create our own families. I hope to God we succeed.'

*

THE FEELING hit quite suddenly; perhaps post-natal depression's catching. I'd spent a long time going through Nan's bag, although I didn't look at the certificate again. There were four suspender ends, and seven Robinson's Golly vouchers bulldog-clipped together, and an empty cotton reel with nails hammered in for French knitting (Nan had drawn a smiley face in biro on the side); an award for long service at the paper mill with my dad's name on it; there was a Temperance Society newsletter dated 1899, God knows whose that was; there was my first baby tooth folded in greaseproof paper in a BunnyBons tin; and a scraggy binker mat I'd made in the juniors, all lumpy knots underneath.

I thought of Nan as a young woman, a girl, then as she was now. The present didn't wipe out the past, she had been those other, young, people.

Then Will began to cry again so I gathered it all together and took the bag downstairs with me. And as I hoisted him up and held his squirmy bulk to my chest, it seemed to me that time split clearly down the middle and I realized what I'd so nearly done.

Once, when I was about seven, I'd found a sparrow's nest in one of the bust-up garages on the edge of the estate. There were three blue eggs, perfect as a painting, against some white fluff and grey-brown feathers. The mother bird was going frantic, chip-chipping at me from the rafters above, so at first I just looked, but finally the urge to cradle the smooth warm shells against my palm became too much and I picked them up. They felt precious and thrilling. I carried them carefully back home and took them straight to Dad. I assumed he'd be as excited as I was.

His face went angry, then sad when he saw what I had. Deep lines came from his nose to the corners of his mouth; it was much, much worse than if he'd shouted at me. He marched me back in silence to the nest and made me roll them gently back in, then we stood for a while waiting to see if the mother bird would come. 'You see,' he'd whispered, 'she might be able to smell you on 'em, then she'd be too frittened to come near.'

'Does that mean the babies'll die?' It had only just dawned on me that that's what the eggs were; I mean, you buy eggs in the supermarket like a packet of biscuits, don't you? Then when you eat them it's yellow and white goo inside, not tiny birds. I felt terrible. Dad nodded almost imperceptibly and I burst into tears. We waited a good thirty minutes but no mummy bird appeared.

'Don't give up hope,' he said comfortingly, as he took my hand to lead me home, but I wasn't daft. I knew eggs had to be kept warm. I knew what I'd done.

'Thing is,' he explained as we got past the church, 'if you take even one egg you're not killing one bird, you're killing millions.'

'How come?' I'd been wiping my nose on my cardigan sleeve all the way but he didn't tell me off for it.

'Because that bird would have had babies, and those babies babies of their own, and so on and so on, down the generations. Ad in-fin-i-tum.'

It wasn't like him to heap coals of fire on my head, so I knew he thought it was serious. All the rest of that summer I trailed back and forth to the garage in the hope that I could deliver some good news and wipe the slate clean, but each visit the eggs were still there, proof of my guilt. At the beginning of autumn the whole nest disappeared, I don't know whether it was lads or gales or a fox maybe; do they eat rotten eggs? I stopped going, anyway.

To make it up, Dad bought me a pair of binoculars for my birthday the next year and took me up the Pike to see if we could spot the albino jackdaw (we did!), only the effort of climbing winded him and it took us a long, long time to stagger back down again. I think maybe that was the very beginning of him getting ill. I can still remember Nan's face as he finally tottered in through the front door. So all things considered, I never really got into bird-watching.

But baby Will lying so trusting in my arms, delicate flaring nostrils, little screwed-up yawn; I so nearly destroyed you. I was so nearly *such* a bad mother. I can't believe what I almost did with your life and your mother's. Every time I look at you, I'll feel the weight of what might have happened; all that future wiped out. Your first tooth, your first step, your first word, your first day at school. And so I should. I'll make it up to you, Will; I'll be such a good grandma, I really shall, really.

*

**Strange thing:** I heard Mum crying in the night when I got up to do Will's feed. She was sobbing and it sounded like she was talking to herself too. Anyway, I didn't go in. I was knackered, and I wouldn't have known what else to say. She'll just have to work the Nan thing through.

*

I'VE KEPT thinking of summat the vicar said at Bill's funeral: the Door is Always Open. It is Never Closed. I wish I'd asked him what he meant but he's dead now, Mr Speakman.

What did he mean?

*

IT TURNED OUT to be a weird Christmas, all right, even though it started off fairly normal. It was the first Christmas with Emma, for a start. Throughout the morning she hung at my elbow, round-eyed. 'You're never going away, are you?' I asked her silently, and she shook her head.

Nan came home for Christmas dinner, thank God, or I'd have spent the day under a cloud of guilt. I cut the food up for her while the plate was still in the kitchen; Matron had tipped me off about that. Then I chopped Charlotte's up too, so she could eat with grizzly Will on her knee. So we got through that all right, although pulling the crackers proved to be a bit of a challenge and the snaps made Will bawl. He worked himself into such a foul temper Charlotte finally took him upstairs where he went to sleep at once. Then Steve arrived with his Brilliant Present.

'I'm not stoppin', my sister's expectin' me. I wanted to drop these off, though.'

There were some CD-Roms for Charlotte, a bottle of dodgy perfume for Nan, a ridiculously large teddy for William and a spiral-bound notebook for me.

'What's this?' I asked, turning it over and finding only a W. H. Smiths price label on the back. True, it had a nice picture of Lake Windermere on the front but I didn't see that was anything to get excited about.

'Take a look inside. There's twenty of 'em. Took me ages.'

I flipped a few pages over.

1 *voucher for*
1 *hours babysitting*
*signed*
*Steve*

'Good, in't it? A chap at work saw it on Oprah Winfrey an' he said it had gone down a treat.' He stood back and waited for the applause.

'Thanks. Really, that's a great present. I appreciate it.'

Steve beamed. 'I thought so. Only don't make it a Saturday afternoon 'cause of the footie. An' I'm out Tuesday and Thursday evenings. Fridays can be tricky, too. But apart from that . . . I'm all yours! Hey by the way, how much did you pay for that tree? 'Cause I know a chap at work selling 'em for a pound a foot. He gets 'em off motorway reservations, digs 'em up at night, 's not like it's stealing or anything. I'll sort you one out next year.'

When he'd gone Charlotte wanted to know what the deal was.

'It's just a way of getting back in with me, I know what he's up to. But don't look a gift horse in the mouth, eh? I don't suppose he knows what he's letting himself in for.' We looked at each other and sniggered. 'I'd like to be a fly on the wall when he has to change one of William's demon nappies.'

'Or when Will pukes all down Dad's back.'

'Quite.'

'This scent smells of toilet cleaner,' said Nan. 'Put it under t' sink wi' t' Vim.'

Daniel arrived shortly afterwards like some kind of rogue Santa, bringing with him an entirely new future.

I could tell he was on pins from the word go.

'I got all these for Will,' he said breathlessly, unpacking a stack of garish toys from the Early Learning Centre. 'Dad says a baby's brain carries on developing for months after birth, so he needs plenty to stimulate him.' He pressed a plastic cow in the stomach and it mooed. 'That'll get those neurons sparking.'

'Have you been running?' I asked.

He only gave a nervous giggle and handed me a huge poinsettia. 'For your table,' he explained. 'Although I have to say it looks extremely nice already.'

We all turned to the scene of devastation that was the remains of the turkey dinner. A trail of gravy bisected the white cloth, and Nan had wiped her hands on her paper hat and screwed it up in the sauce boat. Dead jokes lay curled next to a set of jacks, a metal puzzle and a fish key-ring.

'Yeah, right,' said Charlotte. 'We did have a centrepiece but I set it alight and melted the robin.'

'Jolly good. Now, take these; I haven't finished yet,' said Daniel producing more parcels with the flourish of a conjurer. I began to wonder if he was drunk.

There was talc for Nan and a snakeskin belt for Charlotte to match some boots she had. She was made up.

'Are you taking your coat off or what?' I laughed.

'Yeah, sit down, for God's sake, Fidget Britches,' said Charlotte. 'And while you're here you can settle a debate.'

She pointed at the silver tinsel tree with folding arms we bring out every year. 'Is that or is that not a Middle-Class Christmas tree?'

'Be quiet,' I said without much hope. 'I've got to go and strip the turkey.'

'Hang on a minute. What do you say, Dan?'

He shuffled himself backwards into the settee and shrugged. 'I'm not entirely sure what you mean.'

'Well,' said Miss Clever, 'Mum thinks we should start having a real tree because it's posher, even though it's loads more hassle.'

'I *like* them,' I said. 'I like the smell, it's atmospheric. We'd have had one this year but what with one thing and another I never got round to it.'

'Only,' she went on, 'I told her that in real Middle-Class homes they care about the environment too much to cut down trees on a whim, so it's actually cooler to have an artificial one.'

'I think they're both rather fun,' he said, 'if you have to have a pagan anachronism in your front room.'

'Well, what sort of tree do your parents have, Daniel?' I asked, rising to tackle the mess on the table.

'Norway spruce. But my father has a synthetic one at the surgery, I don't know if that counts.'

'See,' said Charlotte, but actually I thought *I'd* won that one.

*

'What was all that about trees?' asked Daniel when Mum was in the kitchen sawing the last bits off the turkey.

'You're a bonny lad,' said Nan attempting to lean over and pat his knee. 'I'm nearly ninety, you know.'

'Splendid.'

'They think as 'cause you're owd you're not so gradely reet.' Nan sat back with a satisfied look on her face.

'Do they? Do they really?' He turned to me.

'Oh, yeah, well, I was winding her up. She's such a daft bat at times. Listen.'

> *While shepherds washed their socks by night*
> *All watching ITV*
> *The angel of the Lord came down*
> *And switched to BBC,*

sang Mum over the noise of the radio, then, *'Bugger bugger bugger!'* Evidently the turkey was putting up a fight this year.

'Have a toffee,' said Nan brightly. But I knew she couldn't open her handbag so I got down on the rug, fished some out for her and began unwrapping the cellophane.

'It's Mum's fixation about being Middle Class. It's stupid, I keep telling her we're probably all Middle Class these days.'

'I wouldn't have thought it mattered.'

'Ah, well, that's because you're Real Middle Class. It's the half-and-halves, caught in between, who obsess about it. Nan knew where she was, working in the mill and proud of it; I'll probably go off and get my degree – eventually – and earn my twenty-thousand-plus a year, so I'll be all right.' Daniel's eyebrows moved up and down rapidly. 'Yeah, well, if everything goes to plan, that is. Sorry, didn't mean to sound so smug. But Mum's in the land of the class-dispossessed; part-time school assistant living in an ex-council house. She's Aspirant Something, but I don't know what.'

Daniel squirmed and opened his mouth to say something, then changed his mind.

'The irony is, she's become Middle Class and she doesn't even know it.' I placed the naked Mintoes on Nan's lap and clambered back on the sofa. 'Shall I tell you why?'

'I'm utterly intrigued.'

'It's the fact that, instead of spending her energy moaning about things, she's now getting up and actually doing something to make them better. As long as I can remember she's droned on about how life ought to be different and I always thought, "Well, why not see if you can change it, then?" And I never had a satisfactory answer, unless you count, "We don't do that kind of thing", "That's the way it is", "We put our heads down and slog on". But your Middle-Class person says, I'm going to write to my MP, organize a rota, lobby the council, hold a meeting. Middle-Class people *act*, they don't suffer.'

'Too much of a generalization,' said Daniel hugging himself like a man who's been accidentally shut in a freezer. 'I know plenty of whinging Middle-Class. Half my father's patients probably fall into that category.'

'Huh. It's my theory and I'm sticking to it.'

'Mrs Waters is fed up 'cause she's having a hip op,' Nan piped up.

'No. She said she's fed up with her son playing hip-hop.' I sniggered, then felt mean when she looked confused. 'He plays his music loud,' I explained.

'Well, they do, young 'uns. You do.'

'I don't—'

There was an extra loud clatter and a yelp from the kitchen. I got up to investigate.

'Do you think your mother's going to be long in there? Because there's something I want you all to hear,' he blurted out. 'Together. I think.'

Radar Ears was back in like a shot.

*

IT WAS LIKE an old-fashioned film. 'Mrs Cooper, may I have the honour of asking Charlotte to be my bride?' A shock, but quite a nice one. I mean, a doctor's son. I came through wiping my bleeding thumb on my apron, all ready to play Understanding Mother.

*

He stood up as soon as Mum walked in.

'Eeh, are you going?' mumbled Nan through a mouthful of toffee. 'You'll want a coat on, it's bitter out.'

He shook his head, embarrassed, and moved so that his back was to the fire. Me and Mum sat in front of him like an interview panel while he straightened his fingers, spread them out and put his palms together. Then his hands dropped to his sides and I thought, Oh God, what's coming now? Because I really hadn't a clue. He raised his head and began.

'I should have said this earlier, when I first came, but

333

I didn't know how – I have something I need to tell you both. At least, I think I should tell you – I mean, there's no question whether I should tell you, it's whether I should tell you both together, or just you, Mrs Cooper, or maybe you, Charlotte, and get you to speak to your mother.'

'Maureen Tickle had a broken ankle for six weeks before they X-rayed it,' said Nan. 'She'd been walking on it an' all. Exercise, the doctor told her, honest to God.' Her lips snapped shut and she stared at Daniel's knees.

'Go on,' Mum prompted him. She was gripping her thumb so tightly the tip had gone white.

'Right, well. The thing is, I may have been out of order, acting behind your back, in fact I probably was, and you're going to be very cross. My father will be furious with me when he finds out, he'll say I did it all wrong.'

'*What*, for Heaven's sake?' I tried to catch his eye but he was looking over the tops of our heads.

'They've a new woman at the Post Office, great big teeth like a rabbit.'

'Shut up, Nan, just a sec.'

'It was meant to be a surprise. I've been doing some research on the Internet. I thought you had a right to know—' Daniel pulled out an envelope from his jeans pocket and made as if to offer it to Mum, then pulled it back and held it to his chest. 'But I can see now I should have gone to you first because it was to do with your family, no business of mine—'

'Please, Daniel, tell us.' I rose from the settee and he let me take the envelope out of his hands. I started to unfold the contents, a printout from some website or other, an envelope paper-clipped to the back, and for a moment I thought, Christ, he's found Mum's birth mother, bloody hell what a can of worms that'd be. I sat back down quickly, not sure what to do. But then my eyes focused properly. www.nationalsavings.co.uk, the footer read. A photo of a smiling woman with her arms in the air, over the legend *Congratulations!*.

Mum leaned against my arm, scanning the page. 'Is it Ernie?' she asked, and swallowed. She undid the paper clip.

'Don't get too excited, chaps.' Daniel grimaced with emotion. 'It's not the jackpot. But it's better than a poke in the eye with a blunt stick. Tax-free, as well.' He was rocking on his feet; I think he'd have liked to run for the door and take off down the street.

'I'm sorry to disappoint you, Daniel, but I don't think we have any premium bonds. You must have typed in the wrong letters or something.' Mum's voice was quavering because, like me, she'd spotted the line where it said £10,000!. 'This is somebody else's prize.'

'Lucky bastards,' I said with a feeble laugh.

'No, no. That's what I was trying to tell you. It was absolutely the wrong thing to do, to go behind your back. When I spotted the bonds I should have handed them straight to you—'

'What bonds?' Mum's hand was really shaking as she undid the flap of the envelope.

'The ones out of that old bag. In Charlotte's grandma's room. It was in with all those silk postcards.' Daniel's face was flaming, his hair spectacularly on end where he'd pushed his fingers through it over and over again. 'Oh, hell, I can't believe I behaved so crassly; I should have just handed them over at once. I had this idea it would make a nice surprise.'

'Is there a James Bond on this afternoon?' asked Nan. 'He's a swanky chap.' Everyone ignored her and she closed her eyes. Mum spread the yellowed bonds out on the sofa between us. *Issued by the Lords Commissioners of HM Treasury*, the one nearest me said. *£1*.

'So Nan's won £10,000?' I laughed. It was a hysterical thought. 'My God, she'll be able to buy cartloads of belly pork!'

Nan opened her eyes and started to giggle too, though I don't think she had a clue what was going on.

'No, hang on a minute,' said Mum waving the page and breathing hard.

'What now?'

Mum frowned. 'Well, there's no name on the bonds themselves . . . but it says Miss *Karen* Hesketh on the card that's with them. Does that mean . . .'

'Oh, my God! I bet Nan and Grandad bought you these when you were a baby! How many are there?'

Nan was smiling broadly.

'Twenty pounds' worth. That would have been a fortune in those days.' Mum got up slowly and knelt in front of Nan, holding up the scraps of paper under her nose in a fan. They looked a bit like bank notes. 'Did you? Did you buy these for me when I was born?' Nan carried on smiling but said nothing. 'It's very important, Mother. Do you understand me? Did you buy these – for *me*?'

'They're dated-stamped April 1963, if that's any help,' murmured Daniel politely.

Mum put the bonds into the dip of Nan's skirt and took Nan's hands in hers. 'Oh . . .'

Nan patted her daughter's head absently, sighed, then closed her eyes again. 'It were a good big turkey,' she muttered. Her lips parted and she was asleep immediately, head lolling onto the antimacassar. How do they do that, old people, just drop straight off? Mum rocked back onto her haunches and Daniel helped her to her feet.

'OK, Mrs Cooper?'

She looked him in the eye. 'Are you absolutely sure this money's ours? Because I don't think I could stand it now, you know, if you were wrong.'

He stared right back. 'Mrs Cooper, I wouldn't have said a word till I was one hundred per cent positive.'

'No, you wouldn't, would you?'

'No.'

So Mum cracked open a foul bottle of wine one of the kids at school had given her at the end of term, and Daniel had one glass and then went because he said we had a lot to talk about. After I closed the door on him I went back into the room and Mum and I looked at each other and burst out laughing. 'Oh, my God,' Mum kept saying. 'Oh, my God.'

\*

I KNEW CHARLOTTE had in her mind a huge shopping spree; she'd have blown the whole lot on clothes *easily*, might have taken a few months but she'd have done it. But it was my money. I told her that straight off. Her face fell.

'Well, can we at least have the bathroom done, then? You said you would.'

I shook my head.

'Well, *what*, then?' She was brewing a strop, it was quite funny to watch. Well, all that tension had to go somewhere. 'You're not going to stick it all in the bank for a "rainy day", surely? Come on, Mum, life's too short.'

Emma nodded at me.

'I will share this money with you. In fact I'll split it down the middle, fifty-fifty.' Her eyes lit up. £5,000 to spend in Top Shop! 'But listen, we need this money to do something very important.'

'What?'

'It's going to get us both through university.'

You could see the cogs going round.

'Both? Are you . . . ? D'you know, I *thought* there was something going on with you and college. Bloody hell.' She was shaking her head. 'Will they take people so . . . people like you?'

'Get away.' I made to give her a kick. 'I'll be a mature student. Yes, all right, stop pulling faces, it's not that funny. There are thousands like me, apparently, I've been looking into it. I just never thought it was really on, what with the cost. But as soon as Daniel told us. . . . Oh, Charlotte! I still can't believe . . . There are debts to be sorted, quite a few of those, store cards, catalogues . . .'

'My computer.'

'Your computer. But the rest is going to pay for a teacher training course for me at Manchester Metropolitan, and your English degree, wherever you decide to do it. Because you must go on and do it now, Charlotte.'

I felt so full of energy, like I really was ready to step into this new millennium everyone kept going on about.

'I never had any intention of not applying,' she said, a bit haughty. 'But I can always get a loan.'

'I could throw this glass of wine over you. Don't be so daft! Why get in hock when there's a big lump of cash sitting there for the purpose? *And* it'll help fund a place for Will at the best nursery we can find. If you're all right with that.'

'Course it is; God, don't ask me. You'll be lumbered with the little star while I'm away, it's for you to decide.' She combed her fingers through her hair and sighed. 'Bloody hell, Mum, it sounds mental, but £10,000's hardly going to be enough, is it?'

I took a swig of wine. 'It won't cover everything, no, but it'll give us a damn good start.'

'You going to tell Dad? He gave us some out of that bogus compensation claim that time.'

'He didn't, actually. Although it wasn't his fault; he was supposed to get thousands but the claims company took most of it in fees. Serves him right, painting on bruises with eyeshadow. So, no, I think we'll keep quiet for now. Not that he'd begrudge it going on your education, he really wouldn't. He's proud of you.' Even if he does find you scary.

She kicked off her mules, stretched out on the sofa and put her feet in my lap like she used to do when she was very young. It was such an ordinary, intimate gesture, but she'd never have done that six months ago; when we hated each other. I looked down at her neat young toes and for a second remembered her as a baby, a startling memory of fat feet pressing into my naked thighs as I held her up, giggling, by her baby armpits. All that clean, innocent skin, this little piggy.

I came out of the dream and tuned back in.

'What I don't understand, though,' she was saying, 'is why the Premium Bond people didn't contact us. Is it like the lottery, it's up to you to check your numbers?'

I took her toes between my palms and she squeaked and wriggled; what a shock that we could be like this again. I was overwhelmed with the desire to bend right over and give her an enormous hug, thank her for having once been such a beautiful baby, but she'd have thought I was unhinged. Instead I just said; 'Yes, I was thinking about that. They're supposed to write. We should have had at least one letter the October, November before last. I wonder what happened to it.'

From the armchair, Nan smacked her lips and muttered. Charlotte turned her head round to look, then made a despairing face at me.

'Oh, God. She could have done anything with it, Mum. Toasted it, pushed it under a carpet, stuck it behind a pic—' She gave a funny sort of giggle. 'Well, who knows. They could have sent us a whole load of *Congratulations!* and she'd have snaffled them one after the other. Like having a vicious dog lurking behind the letter box. Who knows *what* vital communications we've lost over the last couple of years. But then, you'd think they'd have used the telephone . . .'

'Which she won't ever answer.'

Charlotte clapped her hand to her brow. 'And if we were tied up and missed the call . . .'

'They don't keep trying for ever. There are thousands in unclaimed prizes, apparently, Daniel said.'

'Thousands of people with grannies who eat the post?'

'Maybe.' I thought of what the New Year was to bring, the bed waiting for Nan at Mayfield. Remembering was like having a family Bible settle on your chest. 'Anyway, that's one problem we won't have to deal with any more.'

LEO CAME in the evening, after Nan had gone back. I told him about the money; I wasn't going to at first, but then it just came out. He was delighted for us, as I knew he would be. He *is* a nice man.

\*

**There are** a lot of things money can't touch, of course.

It was so weird leaving Nan in that home. We got her set up in her room – a pleasant one with a bay window and a tree outside that hid most of the car park – put her slippers by the bed, her underclothes in the drawers, her knick-knacks out on the shelves. She didn't have much with her. Big photo of Will on one side of the bed, Mum's wedding on the other, but pride of place went to a blown-up print of her and Grandad sitting on a form, they look about twenty, having a cuddle. She's got white stockings on and black shoes with a bar across and her hair is straight and shoulder-length. She's looking into the camera, only half-smiling, as if she has something on her mind. He's looking at her, his arms tight round her shoulders, shy grin. His legs are out in front of him and you can see four little studs at the front of each sole. They are so *young*.

'You'll be able to watch the birds, Mum.'

'Aye.'

When we walked away she was sitting on the bed like a lost child. Matron was chatting away to her but she wasn't taking much notice.

'I don't think I can stand it,' said Mum clinging to the door jamb.

'Come on. Quick, before you bottle it. If she's really unhappy after a few weeks, you can think again, but you've got to give it a try. The doctor said it was the best place.' I took Mum's sleeve and pulled her away, down the corridor. Bertie trotted past us, tail beating. I watched with my fingers crossed, and he disappeared into Nan's room.

'I need a drink,' said Mum.

'Do we not need to get back for Debbie?'

'I told her half three and it's not half two yet. She's got my mobile if William plays up.'

So we found a wine bar, and sat there for nearly an hour, just two women sharing a bottle of Chardonnay.

\*

CHARLOTTE HAD BEEN moth-eating me about filling in the family tree at the front of William's Baby Record book. I'd drawn a blank after three generations, so I told her to ask Nan. 'Take those old photos in the shoe box while you're at it, I've been meaning to get them labelled up for ages. And leave William here with me or you'll never get anything done.'

When she came back she was bubbling with excitement.

'God, it was mad, Mum! They had a full-scale emergency on when I got there because this old biddy reckoned she'd seen her friend eat a bit off a firelighter. They had an ambulance out, the doctor, everyone running round looking for the First Aid book, do you induce vomiting or not. Then in the end it turned out to be a chunk off a Thornton's nougat casket. Matron had to have a sit down after. Never a dull moment at Mayfield, she says.'

'And how was Nan?'

Charlotte started unpacking the carrier bag of photos. 'Amazing. It was like switching a light on, Mum; she just came to life. We talked for hours and it was dead interesting.'

She pulled some photos out of an envelope and laid them on the table. I stuck William under his baby gym and came to see.

'That one's their wedding day.'

'I guessed that.'

'Yeah, but check out that hat! You can hardly see her face. Is that the locket she still wears?'

'Probably. Gosh, doesn't my dad look dapper with his buttonhole . . . He was no age when he died, it was such a shame.' I picked up the picture and held it to the light. The dad I'd known had always been tired and short of breath; here was a young, happy, vigorous man starting out in life.

'And did you know he'd been engaged to someone else when she met him?'

I put the photo back down, surprised. 'No. She never said anything.'

'Yes, really. She snaffled him! Can you imagine Nan doing something like that? I reckon she was a bit of a minx when she was a girl.' Charlotte shook her head in mock disapproval.

'She must have really been in love.' I thought of my own wedding album, stuck underneath the wardrobe in shame. 'And she was right too, they were devoted to each other for over forty years.'

'My God, that's fantastic.' Charlotte picked out another; Nan in a gaberdine-type coat and a group of young girls in pinafores. They were standing, along with a big, stern man wearing a watch and chain, in front of a vintage bus. 'Nan said that was a charabanc. They called it Whistling Rufus and they went on trips to Blackpool and Southport in it. She couldn't remember who those people were, though.'

'Looks like a school party. Unless, no, she's about eighteen there so she'd have left school. It must be mill workers. She always said she had some good times at Jarrod's, but they don't seem so happy there, do they? Maybe good times are relative . . .'

But Charlotte wasn't listening. 'Have you seen this one, Mum?' In her hand was a very faded, creased and yellow photograph of four people: from left to right, a little girl, standing, with ringlets, hands folded in front of her; sitting, a grim old lady in black silk and wearing clogs with their curved-up soles; a boy, younger than the girl, standing awkwardly in a dark outfit with a large white collar, something like a sailor suit; and a pretty, anxious woman in her twenties, perched on a straight-backed chair, an oval locket against her white blouse. 'Do you know who they are?'

We huddled together and gazed at the four solemn

faces. Only the boy was smiling, as if he couldn't keep his energy and youth from spilling out.

'Well, that's Nan,' I said, pointing to the girl. 'And that'll be her grandma next to her.'

'Florrie Marsh, that's right. I've written it on the back. She looks a right old battle-axe, doesn't she? The other woman's Nan's mother, Polly. She's sad there because Nan's father kept leaving them, apparently, then coming back again. He was living with some trollop in Chorley when that picture was taken.'

I thought Polly looked tired to death. 'Poor thing. Awful not to know where you stand, so humiliating. Especially in those days. Nan would never tell me much about it, too ashamed, but I knew there was something funny about the set-up. Well, well.' I put my finger gently to the boy. 'I can guess who he is, what a little angel.' His dark suit was spoilt by a white crease in the paper running the length of his body. 'Terrible to die so young.'

'Nan's brother Jimmy. Aww, see, one of his socks is coming down.'

'Did she say anything about him?'

'He drowned in the canal.'

'Really? Poor lamb.'

'She cried when she told me, I think they were pretty close. But she was all right after,' she added hastily. 'I started telling her about Will puking into Ivy's shopping bag and she cheered right up.'

We shuffled the pictures together and Charlotte slid them back in their envelope.

'I tell you what, Mum,' she said as she put the lid back on the shoe box, 'I'm going to take that portable tape deck and record some of Nan's stories because they're really interesting, How We Used to Live and all that. I could keep the cassettes for Will when he's older, his family history.'

(My family history, I thought.)

'It's like . . .' Charlotte put the box at the bottom of the stairs and came back in. 'You know when the TV's on but you're recording a different channel to the one you're watching? It's like that with Nan. What you see on the surface isn't what's going on inside. We think she's mad half the time, but it's just that she sort of lives in a different dimension to the rest of us.' She rescued Will from where he had wedged himself against the hearth and held his face up to hers. He laughed and tried to swipe at her hair. 'Well, her time frame's different, anyway. Nan's past *is* her present. I mean, there's not much this decade has to offer her, is there? You know, if someone in their twenties was widowed and then disabled, everyone would be going on about how tragic it was, but because Nan's old she'd expected to get on with it. She's a really amazing woman actually. I reckon there's more going on with Nan than anyone ever realized.'

*

**I was listening** to Radio 4 and they were interviewing Kate Adie about what it was like to report on the conflict in Bosnia. She said what made it difficult sometimes was that the people there had no concept of an incident being the result of a single moment's action; when something happened it was because of an accumulation of events, sometimes stretching back for decades. She was sent to cover a massacre that had taken place in a small town near the main fighting.

'What happened here yesterday?' she asked an eye-witness.

'In 1943 . . .' the man began.

Everyone's history is the product of someone else's; what we think of as our own experience is only what's been bestowed on us by others and you can't walk away from that.

And why should you?

# SNAPSHOTS FROM THE FUTURE

**Will stands up** on his own for the first time, falls over and bangs his head on the marble hearth. For ten seconds I think he might be dead, and in that gulf of horror I realize then that I do love him after all. It must have sneaked up on me when I wasn't looking.

**Mum comes home** from school with the news that Leo Fairbrother's getting married, shock announcement. Some well-to-do fifty-something he's met in Italy, Maria Callas lookalike, though she actually comes from Oldham. How will Mum take this terrible blow? To be honest she seems fine about it; maybe they were only ever good friends. In the event Mrs F provides Mum with twice the social life (teaches her bridge, invites her to wine-tastings) and passes on her old Aquascutum and Jacques Vert, all contributions gratefully received. Now they go to the Octagon as a threesome (though I think it stops there).

**I come in** quietly through the back door. It's Reading Week at university, and no one's expecting me. I can hear voices before I get inside.

Mum is sitting on the toilet with the door open, blowing up a balloon, while Will rushes around the kitchen shrieking. 'Mummee!' he yells when he sees me.

'Good God, is there no privacy in this place?' she moans, her voice echoing off the tiles.

I put my bags on top of the fridge and lie down on the floor so that my son can climb all over me, giggling. It's good to be home, but only because I don't live here. Maybe I'm a bad mother for not being around all the time, but, hey, I'm doing the best I can. What more can any of us do?

**It's a Friday** teatime in November and I'm phoning home as usual.

'Shall I put Nan on?' asks Mum. 'She's been to a funeral today so I brought her back for tea.'

'Go on, then.'

There's a scuffling and someone says, 'Bloody hell fire,' then the sound of heavy breathing.

'Hello? Hello?' ('There's nobody there,' she tells Mum. 'Yes, there is,' snaps Mum, 'have some patience, for God's sake.')

'HELLO, NAN.'

'It's dark here. Is it dark where you are?'

'YES. I'M ONLY IN YORK.'

'They've a big bonfire at the Working Men's. Are you having a bonfire?'

'WE'VE GOT SOME FIREWORKS FOR LATER.'

'Are they?'

'NAN?'

'It were a beautiful sermon.'

'NAN.'

'What?'

'I LOVE YOU.'

'I love you too.' ('Here, Karen, I've got myself fast with this wire all round me.')

# sWallowing grandMa

## Acknowledgements

For help with research:
Mollie Thompson, Jennifer Leeming, Judith Magill,
Deborah Kelsall, Jane Smellie, Ruby Parr,
John and Margaret Green, and Graham Dixon of
http://www.btinternet.com/~troubleatmill/speak.htm.

For editorial and other assistance:
David Rees, Kath Pilsbury,
Peter Straus and the team at RCW,
Simon Long, Ursula Doyle and
my friends at Picador.

*For Mum and Dad*

# Chapter One

Dogman turned up on our doorstep at nine o'clock sharp, wolfhound in tow.

'You'll love me,' he said. 'I've brought you a crevice tool.'

'Let him in!' yelled Poll from the kitchen.

He rustled past in his grubby mac and I pressed my back to the wall in case he brushed against me. The dog sniffed my crotch, then trotted on.

'Here you are,' he said, rooting in one of his plastic bags and pulling out the crevice tool for me to admire. It's true, I had been wanting one for about six months. Ours had disappeared; probably Poll threw it out by accident, we lose a lot of stuff that way.

Poll marched in and snatched it out of Dogman's hand. She felt it carefully all over, then took it over to the standard lamp to peer at it in the light. 'Well, aren't you lucky, Katherine Millar? She's always moaning about dog hairs. Winston sheds all summer and all winter, it's a wonder he in't bald. Say thank you. Where did you get it, Dickie? Car boot?'

Dogman grinned. 'I found it.'

Nicked it, more like.

Poll handed it over to me and I squinted at the maker's

mark. 'But it's the wrong brand,' I said. 'This is off a Dyson, we have a Lervia. It won't fit.'

'Get away,' said Dogman. 'Bit of duct tape on the end of your tube, it'll be fine.'

I could have inserted the tool into his mouth, Tom and Jerry style.

'Are you seriously expecting me to start mauling with duct tape every time I want to use the thing? Putting it on and taking it off? I'm not going through that performance.' I dropped the tool onto the settee. If Poll wanted to claim it, she could do the hoovering herself.

Poll tutted and Dogman shook his head sorrowfully.

'Young people today,' said Poll, 'they want life gift-wrapped, they do. Tek no notice of her, Dickie. She's on t' crest of a rebellion all t' time. I think it's hormones. At least, I hope that's all it is.' She raised her eyebrows at him.

Piss off, I nearly said.

*

'One day I'll die,' Poll's always going, 'and then you'll be sorry, my girl.'

No I won't. I'll put the bloody flags out. I'll tie a red-satin bow round Winston's neck, dance stark naked up and down Mesnes Park, and put an ad in the 'Celebrations' column of the *Wigan Observer*.

> *She always had a lot to say*
> *She had a tongue sharp as a knife*
> *But now my grandma's passed away*
> *I'm off to start a whole new life.*
> In remembrance of Pollyanna Millar,
> evil-minded shrew and dog-botherer

That night, after Poll had groped her way along the landing from the bathroom, I wrote in my diary:

### New Year's Resolutions

1. *Stop eating (lose 10 kg by Valentine's Day)*

2. *Get everyone at school to call me Kat, not Katherine, as sounds cooler*

3. *Try to make friends with Donna French X X X lush lush*

4. *Decide what to do about My Future*

Then I lay down on the bed, under Dad's old posters of Blondie, and tried to block out the bad thoughts that always gather about this time by doing A-level essay plans in my head. Finally I turned out the light and blew Dad a kiss, like I always do. It might be mad, but it helps.

I share my room with two dead people. As well as Dad, in his jar on the windowsill, there's Great-grandma Florence, who was Poll's mother, in the bottom of the wardrobe inside a black and gold tin. I never think about her, to be honest, except when I'm hunting for shoes.

The rest of Poll's family are buried in Bank Top cemetery, a sloping field down which the gravestones are moving imperceptibly, along with the wall that's supposed to keep them in. If you climb up on the war memorial in the middle you get a good view, a clear view anyway, of the dirty brick town of Harrop below, with its derelict paper mill and defunct loco works. Surely this can't be where the occupants of the cemetery are headed? I can't see the attraction myself.

My big dream is to be normal. I need to ditch the socks

and frocks and be more like other girls, but it's not easy with a grandma like mine.

'Make-up? What do you want to wear make-up for? You'll ruin your skin. You'll end up looking like a clown or a prostitute, one or t' other. Smear some Vaseline on your face, that's all you need at your age. I were a married woman before I owned a lipstick.'

We have this bollocks continually.

It's dawning on me, now I'm reaching my eighteenth birthday, that actually a lot of things Poll says are rubbish, e.g. that mending your socks while you're still wearing them brings on terrible bad luck. 'It's sewing sorrow to your heart,' she always moans. 'You'll rue.' She also reckons that washing your hair while you're having a period sends you mad, and that sleeping with a potato prevents cramp.

When I was younger I believed her, so therefore all the other kids assumed I was mad too and wouldn't have anything to do with me. I couldn't catch a ball either, and I wore a hand-knitted school cardigan instead of a bought one from Littlewoods. I pretended I didn't care.

'Not everyone has a mother and a father,' I would recite when they cornered me on the rec. 'Me and my grandma are a family too.'

'Piss off, Fatso,' they'd say. 'You don't even call her grandma. How weird is that?'

'She doesn't like it.'

'She doesn't like you. You're mental. Your mum killed your dad and then ran off. Weirdy-weirdo.' Then they'd run away screaming and screwing their index fingers into their temples. Weirdy-weirdo would skulk by the bins for a bit and then go and stand by the teacher till the bell went.

The trouble with Bank Top is that everyone knows everyone else's history.

*

Poll doesn't want people to feel sorry for her – which is lucky, because in general they don't. She's as blind as she wants to be: some days, you'd hardly know she had a problem; others, she's all but bed-ridden. 'It's like having a black spot pasted on the front of your eyeball,' she says. 'If I look at your head, now, all I can see is an empty space.' She's got peripheral vision, though, so you'd be unwise to try anything sneaky.

The Rehab Officer likes to stay upbeat. 'Here, we prefer the term *partially sighted*,' she says when Poll goes to be assessed for extras e.g. hand-rails, magnifiers, large-button phones. Not that she bothers with most of these aids; after all, it's what I'm there for. I'm just a two-legged guide dog.

When she first began to lose her sight she was given this handy booklet, *Coping With Age-Related Macular Degeneration*. It's full of top tips for someone with a reasonable take on life:

• *Use strong lighting throughout the house, particularly on stairs.*

Poll says, 'If you think I'm getting an electrician in you've another think coming. Pass us that flashlight.' Our sockets are loaded to buggery and we have nine table lamps in the living room alone.

• *Tell others clearly what you need.*

No problems with this one. It's all I get, all day and every day. I shop, cook, clean, wash, iron after a fashion, lay her clothes out for her every night and put her eye drops in. She doesn't need the eye drops, she just likes the idea. She needs the ICaps dietary supplement pills, but she won't take them, of course.

- *Use your cane as a signal that you need help.*

Or a weapon. She may only have limited vision but she can always locate an ankle bone from a good height.

- *Don't dwell on your difficulties. Treat your visual impairment as a challenge to be overcome.*

To be fair, she isn't much into self-pity. Anger, petty-mindedness, pig-headedness; now those she does a treat.

- *Get to know your neighbours; build up a community around you.*

Don't know if Dickie the Dogman counts as community; he certainly hangs round our place enough. Poll thinks he's marvellous because he's always posting tat he's got off the market through our dog-flap; loaves with big holes all through them, unperforated toilet roll, bacon that's about 90% fat. And they have these long gossip sessions in the kitchen while Wolfie lolls about on the flags and tries to chew his own paws off.

'You know that woman up Nettle Fold who did Maggie's daughter's wedding dress?'

'Oh, aye?'

'She's a medium.'

'A medium what?'

'No, she talks to spirits.'

'Oh, right. What, part-time?'

'I suppose so. Maggie said she's snowed under with alterations for people.'

'So can she tell the future?'

'Maggie says she can.'

'It's a pity she didn't let on about the groom knocking off the chief bridesmaid, then, in't it?'

I never used to mind Dickie Dogman, in fact I thought he was quite funny when I first knew him. He came on the scene when I was about five, after he knocked on the door and offered us some sand he'd found. 'Mek a nice sandpit for t' littlun,' he'd said. 'Oh, go on, then,' Poll had said, unexpectedly. The pit was a disaster; it stained my arms orange and was a total cat-magnet. But somehow Dickie stayed on the scene. He knew a lot of jokes, and he could do tricks with matches. Sometimes I'd go with him over the fields while he walked Wolfie, or the other dogs he had then. In the spring he'd help me catch tadpoles which would go in a jar on the kitchen top for about two weeks, then Poll would knock them over, or pour melted fat on them, or swill them with bleach. In the autumn Dogman enjoyed identifying fungus, then smashing it up. 'That's fly agaric, that is. We'll have that bastard for a start.' I have a really clear memory of him sitting on a stile once and a red admiral butterfly landing on his coat sleeve. 'Look at that,' he said, watching it dip its wings and unfurl its tongue briefly. 'The miracle of Nature. Oh, it's fucked off.' But his favourite crop was dirty magazines, which grew all along the hedgerows near the lay-by. For a long time I thought he was just litter-picking.

As I hit puberty, I began to see Dogman for what he was; a dirty old man. I kept catching him staring at my breasts and licking his lips. From the time I was fourteen, I never had a cold without him offering to rub Vicks on my chest.

Then, one day last year, something really horrible happened.

I came out of the library to find him sitting on the form outside, talking to someone on his mobile. He had his back to me and he didn't know I was there. Wolfie wagged his tail at me but still Dogman didn't notice. He was engrossed in conversation.

'Well, you know me,' he was saying, 'I like 'em big. Yeah, completely topless, nips and all.' His shoulders shook with laughter. 'She didn't know I were there, it were first thing in t' morning. Yeah, massive. Round the back, through t' kitchen window. Hey, hang on, it's not my fault if she parades round wi' no bra on. I was just standing innocently by the back door, me.'

As he was sniggering down the phone, I remembered Saturday and how I'd run down at half-eight to let Winston out for a wee in the garden. I'd not finished getting dressed, but you don't hang about with Winston because his Westie bladder's old and unreliable. Not ten minutes later, Dogman had appeared at the back door with the glad tidings that Lidl were selling off dirt-cheap TVs, and did we want him to get us one. I thought he seemed agitated at the time, but I put it down to the amazingly low price deal.

So ever since then, I've tried to avoid him, he gives me the krills. But it's not easy; he virtually lives here. He's Poll's number-one best friend.

Dogman's not the only pervert round here, either. I've seen a penis, and I was only about eight. This elderly gent stopped me in the street near Flaxton's Chemist and asked me to help him get his puppy out of a drainpipe. 'I know wheer 'e is. I can hear 'im whimpering. What's your name love? Katherine? Well you've lickle 'ands, Katherine, you'll be able to reach in an' cotch 'im reahnd 'is collar.'

'I'll be late for school,' I'd said. Because I *thought* it sounded suspicious.

But he'd taken my arm and hustled me down the ginnel to the yard behind the shop, a scruffy walled area full of rubbish bags and cardboard boxes, and indeed there was a drainpipe sticking out of a mound of earth in the corner.

I stood there straining my ears for the sound of distressed dog and he told me to get down and put my face right up to the pipe. 'Call his name. Go on.' So there I am, down on my hands and knees, shouting, Beaver, Beaver, all the time peering into the dark anticipating the scrabble of tiny claws. When nothing happened I turned my head to ask what he thought we should do next and blow me, he had his tackle out. It looked exactly like he was yanking a plucked chicken head-first out of his flies. ''Ave a shufti at this, Katherine,' he leered. I was out of that yard like a pinball off a spring. I still can't go into a butcher's round Christmas time.

I ran straight back home in tears, and Poll was the nicest she's ever been to me. She made hot chocolate and got the biscuit barrel down and we cleared the whole stack of Dogman's Kit-Kat misshapes between us. I didn't even have to go back to school that day, which was a major coup.

'I keep telling you it's a dangerous world out there,' said Poll through a mouthful of wafer. 'Let's get that packet of Jammy Dodgers open an' all.'

One time we had someone keep ringing up then putting the phone down. You'd go, Who is it? Who is it? And there'd be silence, it was dead eerie. Then a few weeks later the nasty language started; I never heard it myself but Poll told me bits and pieces, stuff to do with underwear mainly. She's not one to bother normally, hard as nails our Poll, but it did shake her up. She used to tense when the phone rang. A few times she said, Don't answer it, so I didn't. But one time she picked up and went white, must have been more than knickers. She put the receiver to my mouth but with her fingers over the earpiece, and told me what to say: I had to shout, 'Leave us alone and get a life!' I enjoyed that. Most excitement I'd had in ages. And the best thing was, the calls stopped.

So Bank Top becomes the world in miniature, except it's even worse Outside with serial killers and exploding skylines and famine and anthrax-in-a-bottle.

'Yes, it's a sad world,' Maggie, Poll's bingo-friend, was saying last week over dinner. 'All our age are dropping like flies. I went to three funerals last month. And May Powell died last week, it was in t' paper.'

'May Powell? May Powell as we were at school with?' Poll looked up from her soup.

'That's the one. Th' undertaker's daughter. She was right snooty at school, do you remember? Not that I'd wish her dead. Does anyone want that last crumpet?'

Poll shoved the plate across the cloth towards her. 'She used say her father put her in one of his coffins if she'd been nowty, and closed the lid on top of her.'

Dogman snorted his tea, as if this was the funniest thing he'd ever heard.

'Eeh, and they'd go complaining to Social Services these days for summat like that.' Poll shook her head despairingly. 'You're not allowed to punish your child at all without somebody poking their nose in. Then they wonder why the kids are running wild. In them days, a parent had some authority. And really, it didn't do the children any lasting harm, did it?'

'No, said Maggie. 'Of course it didn't.'

'So how did May die?'

'Committed suicide.'

'My life's been full of tragedy too,' Dogman piped up. 'Hang about.' He pulled out a hanky and blew his nose hard to clear out all the tea, deliberately making a trumpet noise.

'Has it, love?'

'Oh, aye.' He wiped his eyes. 'I lost my father really young, in an accident.'

Maggie looked at Poll in surprise. 'What happened, Dickie?'

'It was terrible. You know he used to work at the brewery?'

'I didn't, no.'

'Well, he did. He were in charge of one of t' vats. Anyroad, the big paddle they use for stirring got stuck, so he climbed up to see if he could free it. And he fell in.'

Poll put her hand to her mouth. 'Oh, Dickie. I never knew that.'

Dogman nodded glumly. 'My mother was distraught. She said to t' foreman, "Were it at least a quick death?" And the foreman said, "Well it would have been, but he got out three times to go to t' toilet." '

'Ooh, Dickie,' chuckled Poll. 'You're a caution.'

I tell you, we have some hilarious times in this house. Life seems to be particularly dangerous for our family around the time of our coming of age. We get the key of the door and the hammer of doom at the same time.

The week after his twenty-first birthday, Poll's father lost his arm up to the elbow in a nasty bleach-works accident. We have the photographic evidence; a mild-looking man with sunken eyes and one flat sleeve stuffed into his pocket. The hand he still has is resting on a little table and there's a roll of paper poking out of his fist. 'His Certificate in Textile Technology,' Poll pronounces as if it were a Nobel Prize.

Then of course there was Roger, my dad, eighteen and smashed to pieces in the car that was his very special birthday present, a scarlet Mini Metro Vanden Plas. We all know whose fault that was. (Well, actually we don't, because although it was mostly my mad evil mother having a fit and grabbing the wheel just as a juggernaut was coming in the opposite direction, there's also the school of thought that if he hadn't been bought the car in the first place – which was Vince's bright idea – then the accident could never have happened.) So cars are deadly too and that's why I can never, ever have driving lessons because I will either kill myself or some other bugger, in fact best to stay off the roads altogether if possible (Poll once saw a schoolboy run over by a Selnec bus).

Poll's Aunty Cissie lost her fiancé in the war a fortnight before she came of age; she and her sister were actually cutting up old sheets to make streamers when they got the telegram. She's in her eighties now and she never had another sweetheart, so that was her life over with.

Poll herself got through her twenty-second year unscathed but only, she reckons, because she had a premonition that she'd drown, a recurring dream from childhood that she was stranded on a bare rock with a towering wave about to engulf her. She went to a clairvoyant in Blackpool who confirmed it, so she's made sure she's always stayed well away from water, and thus has cheated Fate.

And therefore because I'm almost eighteen now, and I've had no helpful dreams about avoiding accidents, I ought to be particularly nervous. I could leave Bank Top if I wanted to, I have somewhere to go. But is it a trick? Maybe Destiny has got something unpleasant lined up for me. Sometimes I lie awake at nights gripped with a fear I can't put a name to.

I don't know which is worse; fear or boredom.

Funnily enough Poll thinks she's going to die this year as well. 'Threescore and ten I am. Living on Borrowed Time.'

Yes, well, I think. Play your cards right. It could be arranged.

*

There are nights I wake up having dreamed about her and wonder then if maybe in those same hours she dreamed about me too. But the detail is never very positive. I'm always crying. Sometimes I'm covered in blood. Once I had her father's head in a holdall that I couldn't put down.

The need to let her know is a physical pull. It's a constant battle. But I have no substance in her life. I'm useless, as useless as a ghost.

# Chapter Two

What I really wanted for my eighteenth birthday:

- two parents
- a less stupid-sounding voice
- social aplomb
- the tiny bottom half of Courtney Cox

I don't look for a card from my mother any more, haven't done since I was fourteen, in fact I make a conscious effort *not* to. Which is quite mature of me because Poll still checks for one from my dad and he died in 1984.

There were seven cards, plus a small victory, on the table when I came down in the morning.

*On Your 18th* from Poll and Winston. Picture of a yacht on the front, a design Hallmark clearly intended for a male, although Poll's sight being what it is I suppose I should be grateful I didn't get *With Deepest Sympathy*. The victory was attached to the back of the card by a hinge of Sellotape: two packets of tan tights, reinforced panty, about forty denier by the look of them. 'Well, now you're eighteen,' sighed Poll.

Getting her to admit my real age is an achievement in itself. In Poll's benighted world, it's the Fifties and I've been eleven for the past seven years. I have a print frock for best that's like a sack with arm-holes cut in it, and the rest of the time it's A-line polyester skirts and bargain knitwear. On my legs I've been wearing navy knee socks, pulling them up and over my knee-joints trying to make them look like they might be tights, holding them in place with a double elastic band. In the summer it's white ankle socks which is worse because I've got the calves of a rugby player, hairs and all. Some nights when I can't sleep I've sat up snipping the wiriest hairs off with my nail clippers but they only grow back, twice as fierce. I even have a hair that grows out of my belly, and two on my right nipple. Deformed. Sometimes I think I'm too revolting to live.

I'd been asking for tights since I started in the sixth form. 'What d'you want them things for?' said Poll the first time I raised the possibility. 'You'll only put your fingernails through them, you'll have them laddered in five minutes. Do you think I'm made of money?' No, I nearly said, I think you're made of horse-fly bites and Parazone.

*Have a COOL birthday* – Card two was a Winston-type Westie wearing a party hat and sunglasses. Aunty Cissie's a complete sucker for anthropomorphism. You should see the walls of her room at the Home, doggies and kittens done up in all manner of garb. No children, see. Sad but vomit-inducing nevertheless.

*Birthday Girl!* – Dogman's was a flimsy market-job, cartoon of a blonde with a Barbie waist-span and orange minidress.

*On Your Special Day* – Maggie had left a card with a plastic gold key stuck to the front. 'She's having one of them cameras up her bum next Tuesday,' Poll reminded me, 'so it was good of her to remember.'

*Across the Miles I Send to You Happy Thoughts, Good Wishes too* – said Great-Auntie Jean in a fancy embossed affair with a silk tassel down the back. 'We have a beautiful new granddaughter, a little Sagittarian,' I read out to Poll.

'I know. I saw.' Poll gestured at her magnifier propped up against the mantel clock. 'And do you know what they've called it? Fat Louse. They've some daft ideas, these Australians.'

The baby's actually *FAY LOUISE* but I didn't reckon it was worth the argument. Jean never forgets my birthday, even though she escaped to another hemisphere before I was born. Far too good for us, says Poll. But I've seen an old photo of a plump little girl, cardigan, print frock and sandals, sitting on a stone wall feeding chaffinches. 'Inverness 1947' is written on the back. Little Jean has a beaming face, and she doesn't look stuck-up at all.

*Happy Birthday and here's hoping for a question on Tragic Heroines!!* – Rebecca-my-only-mate-from-school clearly did not want me to forget the Modules next week, as if I would, climbing the walls with fear.

*Congratulations on your coming-of-age* – Lastly a postcard of the Brontës, from Miss Dragon and Miss Mouse at the library; I was really touched.

Cissie and Poll had included money in their cards, although I knew that would have to go straight in my savings account, blink and you miss it. Dogman had dropped off a brown-paper bag containing a pair of 'gold' heart-shaped earrings, though they were for pierced ears and I'm not allowed those in case I get septicaemia and die. There was a pen set from Maggie, and a book token from the librarians.

But the best present was waiting on the doorstep.

I cleared the torn wrapping paper away and went to get my anorak from the hall.

'If you're goin' out, tek the dog. He's beside hisself,' shouted Poll from the living room where she was standing, skirt up, toasting the backs of her legs purple against the gas fire.

So I zipped up my anorak, clipped Winston's lead onto his collar, opened the door and nearly went sprawling over the black binbag that was on the step.

'Have you got your scarf?' Poll again. 'And you'll need a hat an' all. It cuts right through you, that wind.'

'Good idea,' I said, thinking fast because I'd spotted the envelope stuck to the side: FOR KATHERINE – A SECRET BIRTHDAY SURPRISE. 'I'll get my grey cardi too. Hang on, Winston.'

I grabbed the bag by the ears and shut the door in Winston's snout. Then I galloped up the stairs before Poll could see me and threw the bag on my bed. I ripped open the plastic and gaped.

Clothes. Not old jumble; freshly laundered by the smell of them, one or two items on hangers even. I drew out a tunic top in maroon, with one of those keyhole necks and a silver border to the sleeves. The label was sticking out at the back: XL. Heart beating, I pulled open the wardrobe door so I could see myself in the full-length mirror, and held the silky fabric against me. It looked amazing. I was a different person.

I laid it carefully on the bed, and pulled out a matching pair of wide-legged trousers. They formed the sort of suit you'd probably wear to, I don't know, an awards evening, or a posh dinner or something. Next there was a red velvet basque – God, a basque. I'd seen one like it on a poster for *Moulin Rouge*. It wasn't really underwear, more a party top. (Some party like I'd never been to, obviously.) Then I found a stretchy black tube skirt, very long, very vampish. Lastly there was a sexy purple V-neck sweater, again in my size. I was sweating with excitement by the time the bag was empty, and my fingers left prints on the note as I read it again and turned it over to check the back. No clue. The flap had been stuck down, but when I tore it open, the white envelope was empty.

'Are you goin' or what?' Poll yelled up the stairs. 'Because this dog's all set to soil the carpet. I thought you were only gettin' your cardigan. You could have bloody knitted one by now.'

There was a wheezing scuffling sound as Winston tried to start up the stairs, followed by a choke as Poll dragged him back again.

'*Coming!*' I said and scooped the clothes up into a bundle. I threw them to the back of the wardrobe and closed the door on them; I'd see to them later. Poll was waiting by the newel post.

'So where's your cardigan, then, after all that? Honest to God.'

I muttered at her and did a sharp U-turn.

'You mek some noise, you do,' she grumbled as I thumped back up the stairs.

We were nearly out the door when I had my second shock of the day: Dogman, nose to nose with me. He must have been standing on the step, under the impression the bell had rung.

I tried to get past but he blocked my way, holding his arms out.

'Stand and deliver,' he said.

Fuck *off*, I thought, and barged him to one side. It didn't stop him grinning.

'Your money or your life?' he shouted into the living room.

Poll came out with her hands up. 'My life, I'm saving up.'

Dogman pretended to shoot her, and they fell about laughing. 'I've brought a couple of tins of this bathroom mousse,' I heard him say. 'Big 'uns. They were just sitting there, on t' skip near t' council offices. There's no propellant so they don't squirt, but they're full. I bet you could get the fluid out if you stuck a knife in 'em, though.' He raised his voice. 'And I've summat for Katherine too.'

'Wait up!' said Poll, but I was already at the gate and I didn't stop. 'Dickie's brought you a beautiful calendar. It's all pictures of Stratford, and that Shakespeare. Aren't you going to say thank you?'

I knew without looking it would be last year's. 'Get a move on,' I said to the dog.

We inched up the hill to the main road. In my mind's eye I'd arranged all the new clothes on one of those rotary washing lines, and I was gloating over each outfit as it came round. Not that I'd ever get to wear any of them; if I swanned up the village to Spar wearing a bright red basque, Poll would have some kind of Attack. Ambulance men would find her frothing on the front-room floor and clinging pitifully to my grey cardigan. 'It were them tights as started it,' she'd gasp before she pegged out.

Who on God's earth would leave a present like that for

me? I gave Winston a tug and replayed the moment when I'd opened the front door. There it had been, my present, sitting on the mat. Maybe one of the neighbours had seen something. Maybe it was one of the neighbours. That wasn't very likely, though, because Poll's fallen out with both sides and I can tell they think I'm just odd. Whenever any of them do speak to me they do it s-l-o-w-l-y, as if I'm backward. Usually I don't bother answering.

Might have been Maggie. But she'd no money, and it wasn't her style, and she'd already given me the pen set. The timing suggested it was a gift from Dogman, but why not say? If it was him, then the level of literacy was higher than usual. Two years ago he'd sent me a Valentine card. *GESS HOW?* he'd printed inside. I'd binned it immediately.

At the top of the Brow we turned onto the high street, the village proper. 'An example of Ribbon Development,' I remember writing in my Y7 geography project. 'Bank Top grew up around the mining and cotton industries, but today is primarily a dormer village for the surrounding urban areas.' It's just a road that runs along the crest of a long flat-topped hill. Exit one direction and you're on the way to Bolton; exit the other and you're Wigan-bound.

Very historical, is Bank Top. General Julius Agricola used it as a vantage point to spy out Britons skulking in the forest below. Panicked Elizabethans lit a beacon here to warn of the approaching Armada, and Samuel Crompton invented his spinning mule just up the road. But time's moved on and, at the start of the third millennium, Bank Top's past its best. It's all very well the local papers publishing quaint photos of children playing on the cobbles; anything remotely picturesque was cleared away years ago.

The rows of stone cottages built for the handloom weavers, the Georgian horse trough, the worn granite mounting-block three hundred years old outside the church, were demolished half a century back and the oldest buildings you get now are Victorian terraces. The rest is post-war bland, with some Sixties eyesores thrown in at random.

Bank Top teenagers moan there's nothing to do here, except try and sneak into pubs. (I could go in a pub if I wanted: I don't.) The activity of choice for the underage seems to be to go down the bottom of the Brow of an evening and set fire to a garage. But it's not a bad place, really, there's worse. It's got the library, and it's where my dad is.

Right outside the cemetery gates there's a bus stop. That always used to strike me as funny, imagine the dead queuing up to go off to Bolton, but today it was a damn nuisance because two of Poll's Over Seventies chums were there having a natter.

'It's shocking, it is, honest, they've had all the lead flashing off his roof while he was away – Oh, hello, love. Birthday girl. I've a card for you.' That was Mrs Batley, thickly wrapped against the cold. She rooted in her bag and pulled out a mauve envelope and, bloody hell, a tube of Smarties. She clearly thinks I'm still about six. 'Here y'are, love. How's your grandma?'

I put my head down and looked through my hair. 'OK, thanks. Thanks.' I shoved the Smarties in my pocket and shifted away.

'Will you ask her, love, if she's had a letter about her heating allowance?' Mrs Threlfall, posher coat, furry hat as opposed to headscarf. 'Because we're all supposed to have had one, all them as is on benefit, and if you've not, you've to phone the council—'

I mumbled and nodded, squeezing through the gates onto the gravel path that leads up to the war memorial and Winston now pulling ahead, God knows what he'd seen or smelt. As I walked away I heard them murmuring together. Poor lass, poor Poll, she's a big girl, it's a shame. I bet that was the gist of it. I didn't care. They were going to die before me.

We crunched past the chapel then I bent down and let Winston off the lead. I found my perch on the memorial steps and watched him totter around for a minute till he disappeared behind a gravestone.

I leaned my head back against the granite and stared up to heaven. The sky was perfect winter blue with white clouds streaming across it. My eyes scanned back and forth for the message.

'Are you there, Dad?' I said out loud.

*

They were playing 'Land of Make Believe' on the radio at the actual moment he penetrated me.

I'd seen Bucks Fizz win the Eurovision Song Contest, watched the girls whip their skirts off for the finale. Never dreamt they'd be the soundtrack to my undoing. He said it would be OK, he kept saying that all the time, till he stopped talking altogether and started jerking around and biting my neck.

He was clever, string of O-levels already, predicted top grades for his A-levels – which he got, despite everything. But the clincher was he said he knew, he'd studied women's bodies and there was a cycle and it was an impossibility that an egg could be fertilized during that particular window. He had a textbook with a diagram in it; we had it open on the bed as he took his trainers off.

Mum was in hospital dying by inches, I had no one I could ask. Trust me, he said, I'm nearly a doctor.

# Chapter Three

My dad left me:

- – his posters, LP records and cassette tapes
- – a collection of stringy ties
- – a pair of nail clippers decorated on the front
  with an enamel violin
- – some medical textbooks
- – a stack of science-fiction novels
- – a gold ring set with a sovereign

He didn't specifically leave this stuff to me, but Poll's never said I couldn't have it. She threw everything else away after the crash. 'Why did you keep his ties?' I asked her one time she was in a better mood. 'He looked so bonny in a tie,' she said, then locked herself in the bathroom for an hour afterwards. Neither of us can get the ring on, Poll with her super-size knuckles and me with my sausage fingers, so it lives in my jewellery box, on a velvet hummock.

My mother left me: a single 6"x4" photograph. I found it in between the pages of *An Illustrated Biology Course*. It was under Symbiosis, although I don't think that's significant. I've left it there because that way it's safe from Poll. When I first came across it, at thirteen, I looked at it every day.

She's blonde and plump, and *young*; but then she'd only have been my age. Her hair's flicked into two wings at the sides of her face and she's wearing blue eye-shadow, a black T-shirt and a knee-length floral skirt. You can't see her feet because they've been cut off the bottom of the picture, so I don't know what kind of shoes she favoured. She's resting her hands protectively on her big bump of a stomach – me – as she leans against the bonnet of the deadly Metro. I'd say she looks fairly happy. She doesn't look like someone who's about to abandon their baby.

I can't place the house behind her. It's certainly not this one, because the window to her right has little octagonal leaded lights. We used to have two small stained-glass panels at the front, but when it came time for replacing them, Poll made Dogman cart them off to the tip to save on repairs. Although I bet he sold them to a reclamation yard, thinking about it.

Pictures of Dad are easier to come by. Poll's got dozens, charting his progress from babyhood to A-levels. He goes from a cute, cheeky-looking boy to a really handsome man, with dark brown hair swept across his brow, an intense gaze, and evidence of a slight mullet at the collar. He reminds me of the drawings in Auntie Jean's old *Dr Kildare* annuals.

I know Dad's back at the house in his jar, what's left of him. But for some reason I feel closest to him in the cemetery. It's so still, a space to think, and you're up on the highest point of the village so it's closer to the sky.

The year I was finally booted out of primary school for spooking the normal kids, I used to come up here a lot. If I wasn't holed up in the library, this is where I'd be. It was that summer, just when things were getting desperate, that Dad sent me his kiss. Some people might have said it was two aeroplane trails cutting across each other, but I knew it was a giant white kiss he'd scrawled across the ether.

So I look to the sky for messages; and sometimes they're there, and sometimes not. Usually, if you search hard enough, you'll see something significant in the cloud formations. I'm sure, for instance, that a Westie-faced cumulus told me Winston was going to be OK after his op six years ago. And going further back, when I was waiting to see if I'd got into the grammar, I came up here convinced I'd failed and there was a flat grey ceiling of nimbostratus. Then, as I watched, the sky broke open and a thin shaft of sunlight beamed down over Bolton. I don't know if it was shining precisely on the grammar school, but the next day I got the letter offering me a place. Last spring I was convinced I'd messed up a French module, but a band of cirrocumulus showed me a row of ticks. I got an A.

It was cirrocumulus again today, making a fantastic curving spine right above me, anatomically correct down to the number of vertebrae and the little tail of a coccyx; now that had to be Dad. I took my mile-high backbone to mean How were the resolutions going.

Well, first off, I'd kicked the diet into touch. They're rubbish, diets. I've tried them before. You start off hungry and virtuous, the next stage is light-headed and high, then ravenous and unreasonable with a blinding headache, as if someone has attached a couple of jumbo bulldog clips to your eyebrows. That's where the diet begins to fall apart. Eating is my top pleasure, it even beats reading;

also, food's not just food in our house. It's sugar-coated guilt, full-fat reproach, high-sodium defiance.

'What's going on? Why have you left your chips?' Poll said last time I tried to cut down.

'I was full.'

'Full? Full? You normally have twice this number, and a steak pie on top. And afters.'

'I was trying to lose a couple of pounds.'

Poll rolled her sleeves up crossly, then leaned over to pick up the plates. 'I've told you before, you're wasting your time. Your shape's genetic. Off your mother. There's no way you can change what you are. You were just born fat.'

'People aren't born fat. It's what you eat,' I said, without much hope.

She patted her rounded stomach. 'No, it's inescapable. Look at me. Legs like sticks and a great pot belly. It's the Southworth Stomach. Cissie's got it too, all the woman down that line have. You got Castle genes: big all over. You can't fight your heritage. Thank your lucky stars that's *all* she passed on. You might have been certifiable. Now, are you having a vanilla slice?'

Far above me, the spine had melted into long wispy fingers, ghost fingers pointing to the south. I stepped back up onto the memorial. 'Dad? If you're still there – I really could do with some help. About the future. Can you give me a sign?'

I watched my breath mist in front of my face, and waited. A helicopter chopped faintly in the distance. Two metres away from where I stood a wren flittered onto a hawthorn branch, bobbed about, took off again.

Winston chose that moment to reappear with something

hideous in his mouth. I bent down to prise the thing from his jaws but he was too quick for me; he threw his head back and bolted whatever it was down, gagging and snorting. Probably he'd be bringing it back up later, on the living-room carpet. 'Come on, mutt; home,' I scolded. 'You always have to ruin the atmosphere, don't you?'

I thought again of the backbone when I got in. The TV was blasting out of the lounge, *House-Strip-Neighbour-Swap-Challenge*. Still in the porch, bending to unhook Winston's collar, I called; 'I've been having a think about things, Poll, and I want you to call me Kat.' I said it quite loudly, partly because there was this bouncy theme tune to contend with, and partly because I wanted her to understand right from the word go that I was serious about it.

Poll's frowning face appeared round the door. 'You want me to call you a cat?'

'No,' said Dogman's voice from behind her. 'Don't be daft. She wants you to call her a cab.'

Winston walked stiffly off and I hung his lead up. The urge to impale myself on one of the coat hooks was tremendous. Instead I wrenched my mac off and pulled it down over the hook so hard that the collar ripped. Poll didn't see this, luckily.

'Come in here and tell us a proper tale,' she said.

'Can you turn the TV down?'

'I'll put it on mute,' said Dogman.

I wish I could put you on mute, I thought.

'So what do you need a cab for?' asked Poll, bristling at the thought of any extravagance.

I sat down heavily on the settee. 'I don't. I *don't*. Want a cab. I just had an idea.'

'We're not having any more pets, if that's what you're after. It wouldn't be fair on Winston. And I'm not keen on cats, they bring in dead things.'

'Aye, that's right, they do.' Dogman shook his bristly head. 'Or sometimes things that are still alive. My mother had an infestation of mice once after her Bruno brought in a pregnant one and it got away under t' cooker. I said to her, I thought cats were supposed to get rid of vermin, not attract it . . . ' His voice trailed away as, on screen, a busty woman in a T-shirt bent forwards over a workbench.

'Not cats, not cabs. Just listen, will you? All it was, I wanted to change my name slightly.'

'What for?' Poll shifted her weight onto one foot and started fiddling with the leg of her panty girdle. 'What's wrong wi' t' one you've got?'

'Nothing.'

'So? What's there to change?'

'It'd be easier.'

'How?'

'Well, Kat, it's shorter than Katherine.'

They were both staring at me.

Poll said slowly, as if she was humouring a mad person, 'You want us to call you "Kat"?'

I nodded.

'And shall we get you a collar wi' a bell on it, an' a little dish for your milk?' She started chuckling, and Dogman joined in. Laughter all the way. 'Kat? By, you come out wi' some stuff, you really do. Kat. I mean. Whale, more like. Elephant. Tell you what, we'll call you Ellie, if you like.'

I got up to go and pushed past them both, treading on Poll's slipper as heavily as I could.

'Ooh, bloody hell, watch where you're going,' she gasped.

'Pussy,' I distinctly heard Dogman mutter before I could get to the stairs.

*

That midnight found me basqued up and buzzing. On the other side of my bedroom wall, Poll slept the untroubled sleep of one who has no conscience. We'd had another row after tea because it was nearly a month since I'd gone to see Auntie Cissie, and because I wanted to read a book instead of listen to how ill the butcher's daughter's neighbour had been after eating squid on holiday. Before she'd gone up I'd mentioned casually about some new outfits, maybe, with the birthday money. She paused at the bottom of the stairs and checked me up and down while I was standing under the hall light.

'You are a bit scruffy at the minute, it's true.' She peered forwards, frowning. 'Your jumper's hanging funny; that's you pulling at the cuffs. Still, you've had your wear out of it.' She nodded. 'I'll have word with Dickie. He says there's some Marks and Spencer's seconds coming on Munawar Noor's stall next week. Munawar told him he could have first pick.'

'What like?'

'I don't know. Knitwear, I should think. That's what he mainly sells, in't it?' She turned away and started to pull herself up the steps. Behind her back, I stuck my tongue out as if I was being sick. 'He'd some nice embroidered cardies last time, do you remember? But they'd none in your size. I'll ask Dickie to watch out for them coming again.'

'Could I not have something a bit more, a bit more, young? Like, I don't know – ' as if the idea had just that second occurred – 'a trouser suit?'

'Trouser suit?' She paused in her tracks and half-turned, clutching the banister with a freckled hand. 'What would you want a *trouser suit* for? You look like the side of a house as it is. Backside like yours, you're best off in skirts. Trouser suit? You'll be wanting jeans next. And a sight you'd look in those an' all. There's more to life than fitting in with the crowd.'

I should bloody well hope so, I thought. 'Palazzo pants are quite flattering if you're curvy.'

'Palazzo pants? Are they them long trousers where you walk on the hems and get them all dirty? You're not having any of them, they'll be in holes in no time, I haven't the money to—'

'No, listen, they're sort of loose—'

'Oh, I know, them ones like they wear in the army with about fifty little pockets in all your nooks and crannies—'

'No, they're wide-legged trousers—'

'Yes, well they'd have to be wide-legged for you to fit in 'em—'

Bitch! Bitch! I wanted to scream at her, but the air had gone out of my lungs like it does in a nightmare and left me with a helium whimper.

'You *never* treat me— Oh, forget it,' I squeaked, and flounced off to the kitchen.

'You've got to be realistic, I'm only saying,' Poll called after me. 'You can't get away with such as these slim 'uns. You don't want to make a fool of yourself. Have you forgotten that time you walked around in a strappy top? And

31

you weren't as big then as you are now. You cried your eyes out, after. I could have told you.'

Pause.

*Die, you old witch. Do it now. Lose your footing and crack your skull against the skirting board. Lie there pleading for help. In agony.*

Creak creak up the stairs.

I stood in the moonlight, burning. It helps, times like this, to press my fingers into my scalp, very hard. One day I might push too hard and my fingers'll go *splot* into my brain.

Far-off flush of the toilet. Hiss of the pipes. I conjured Dad up for an out-loud moan; had him sitting at the kitchen table, looking sympathetic.

'It wasn't a proper top, that was why the other kids laughed.' He nodded at me encouragingly, like he does in these interviews. 'It was a thermal vest that Poll made me wear under my jumper, even though it was July. She said, "You'll be outside a lot, seeing the animals. Stop complaining. We never had any school trips when I was your age." '

I imagined Dad smiling. He'd have known what she was like.

'On the coach no one would sit next to me, so I got a book out and pretended to read while the other girls swapped bits of packed lunch. Julie Berry kept kneeling up on her seat to chat to Clare Greenhalgh behind, and Mrs Kirtlan kept turning round and shouting at her to sit down and put her belt on. Everyone was drawing love-hearts on the windows, then shrieking and rubbing the initials out. Part of me really, really wanted to join in but I just lifted my book up higher, like I was too gripped by the story to bother with anyone.'

'I've done it myself,' Dad said silently.

'And it struck me then, how do people know what to wear? Because when I looked round, all the girls seemed to be in on some great clothing conspiracy which meant friendship bracelets, and tiny twin plaits framing your face, and turned-up jeans were de rigueur. And yet if I'd dared to appear that morning wearing any one of those items, it would have gone out of fashion *the night before*.'

'It's a lot easier being male,' said Dad.

'All the girls had these little vest-tops on as well, even Sally Ralphs who was the other fatty in the class and should, by rights, have been a target too. She's got a boyfriend now, I saw them in the bus shelter before Christmas.'

'You'll get a boyfriend.'

'Don't want one. They're too much trouble. Anyway, halfway round the zoo, when I was nearly dead from heat-exhaustion, I thought it might be an idea to strip off the jumper and tie it round my waist. I thought I could get away with it.'

'You were more developed than the other girls, even at ten. They were probably jealous.'

'No, I think they just thought I was a blob in bad underwear. They were whooping so loud Mrs Kirtlan had to blow her whistle.'

'I'd have sorted them out.' I imagined my dad making a fist on the tabletop and scowling.

Above the kitchen, Poll's bedroom door clunked shut, vanishing Dad. I opened the cupboard over the sink, drew out a box of Frosties and ate a dozen handfuls while the moonlight streamed in, bright parallelograms on the specked lino. I was thinking about Sally Ralphs' big arms.

Once the house was quiet and the sugar had kicked in, I tiptoed upstairs and listened at Poll's door. Then I crept into my room, put a chair under the handle like they do in films, and pulled the rustly binbag from the back of the wardrobe.

It was amazing to get all the clothes out again and look them over in detail, like Christmas to the power of ten. The sweater and skirt were obviously brand new because they still had their tags in and I had to snip them out with my violin nail clippers. The basque I think had been worn before, because it had a tiny black bow at the front that was coming loose. I just clipped it off and the neckline was as good as new.

Then I set to trying all the outfits on, one after another. The clothes themselves looked fantastic. My stupid face stuck on the top spoilt the effect a bit.

I combed my long hair over my face, like Esther in *Bleak House* does the first time she looks in the mirror after her terrible disfigurement. Peeping through the strands, I thought maybe I didn't look too bad. Yes I was big, but I went in and out, I had a waist, and the flesh was pretty firm. Poll's arms are thin, but the muscle's all slack and hangs and swings under her biceps in a truly repulsive way. I gather there are men who find big girls attractive (Dogman, apparently).

I felt drunk on possibility. Perhaps I had an admirer. A secret lover had spotted my potential from afar, and left me these clothes as a token. I wondered what shoes you wore with an outfit like this. Not the brown sandals I had on now, that was for sure. A mum would know such things, but I didn't have one handy.

I so wanted Dad. Handsome, clever, sitting on the bed; I could nearly see him. Chatting about my plans, my escape; giving crucial advice. I wanted the life that went with these clothes.

Why couldn't I have a normal, alive father instead of a bloody dead one?

*

I put the stained sheets in a binbag and dumped that in next door's garden. Mum might have noticed, but I knew Dad wouldn't. Blood for blood, as it turned out.

# Chapter Four

'I was up all night,' sighed Maggie, clicking sweeteners into her tea.

Poll shook her head and tutted. 'Me an' all. Couldn't get off. Two o'clock, three o'clock. I kept thinking, What are the Gothic elements in Charlotte Brontë's *Jane Eyre*? And to what extent do they help shape the narrative structure?'

'It's the ending that bothers me,' said Maggie.

'Oh, me too. Have another biscuit, go on.' She nodded at the flowered plate.

'Ta, I will thanks. No, it's the religious parallel with the story of Saul, and the whole redemption angle I'm uncomfortable with. To me, the plot's too didactic, too bound up in biblical teaching; the emotional force of the novel becomes, ultimately, diluted. A Romantic writer like Brontë should never have confined her artistic scope within the narrow boundaries of Victorian Protestantism. The two elements are, by definition, diametrically opposed.'

'Dickie thinks the same.' Poll screwed up her face. 'He reckons it's like serving custard with bacon.'

Actually, this never happens.

*

36

When Maggie and Poll do get together they talk about illness or the good old days or crime rates. They like to sit with the local paper divided up between them, picking out the shock horror reports about elderly ladies getting beaten senseless for tuppence. If I'm in the room with them, I'm either part of society's decadence or, if Poll's in a good mood, a shining exception. Youth as it should be when it's been properly brought up. 'She's a whizz at *Countdown*,' Poll will often remark. 'Even the conundrum at th' end, no problem.' I keep quiet. It doesn't do to be too clever round here.

Sometimes we play Scrabble with a giant board, but even that's problematical. If I win, it's, 'Well, no wonder, you're studying English. I never had a proper education, me.' If I lose; 'Eeh, and you with all your brains, fancy.' Meanwhile, Dogman cheats for England. FUNT, he puts down. YESKER. NONING. When I challenge this shite, he claims they're dialect words and Poll tells me to stop picking on him.

If only life were an exam.

In real life, for instance, I can never think of anything to say, plus I hate the sound of my own draggy voice. Somebody says, 'Hiya, cocker, how's tricks?' and I panic, even if it's someone I know; especially if it's someone I know. I died a thousand deaths last month when Mrs Threlfall asked if I was courting yet.

I spend a lot of time smirking dumbly at the floor. But on paper I'm as articulate as anyone. (*In a sense, Mrs Threlfall, your question, though innocently meant, is redundant, for you should know that I have decided to shun the twenty-first-century mating rituals in which the majority of my peers are engaged.*

37

*In today's Britain, women can lead happily independent lives, unencumbered by the erroneous expectations of a patriarchal society. So put that in your Ty-Phoo and sup it.)*

They're underrated as a pastime, exams. There's something about the adrenaline rush, the legitimate isolation, the whole regulated nature of the exam experience that makes me feel the school hall is my natural element. I don't enjoy exams like, say, I enjoy a box of Maltesers, but I am fantastic at them whereas I seem to be crap at everything else. Ten A-stars, me; you'd never guess it if you didn't know. Some days I wear them round my brow like a crown, but mostly they form a constellation called the Sad Act.

When I walked out of that last English module, I felt elated. I'd been pulling *Sons and Lovers* to bits, brilliantly, because of course I am an expert on Destructive, Stifling Relationships, and Frustration generally.

Halfway through a wasp landed on the paper. It crawled onto the first question I'd answered, sat for a moment waving its feelers, wandered onto the second question, then took off to bother Lissa Hargreaves in front of me. She had a fit, of course, because it wasn't her wasp. It was my wasp and it had come to tell me that I was going to Oxford. Eventually Mrs Wills came over and shooed it away with a copy of Rules for Candidates.

I finished with five minutes to spare, had a quick read through, tingling; then, as Mrs Wills was cruising the aisles with treasury tags, I took all my hair-grips out and checked all the tops on my highlighters. I was high as a kite. When she said to us all, You may go now, I pulled my cardigan on, grabbed my little plastic bag and half-ran for the door. Rebecca caught me up and we fell into step, comparing notes. Really though I was thinking of the bacon bap I would shortly be ordering in the canteen.

'I was *so* not prepared for that Lawrence question. I've made a total mess of the ending, I ran out of time. I just hadn't revised enough,' she gabbled.

We both knew this wasn't true. It was something you said, schoolgirl etiquette. 'Me neither,' I said.

We made our way down the stone steps and past the gallery of school photographs, all those glossy Head Girls and Prefects, and on the bottom row a decade of guide dogs bought with silver foil.

'Don't you wish you could have your essays back for another hour, sort them all out?' Rebecca glanced back at the office with a convincing expression of longing. Maybe she had cocked up. 'Which Hardy question did you do?'

Now we were walking through the undercroft, nearly at the canteen. The wind blew Rebecca's short straight hair up off her high forehead. Her plainness annoys me at odd moments, and I know it's unreasonable, people in glass houses and all that. At least she wears better clothes than me. And if she's got no bust to speak of, it seems a small price to pay for not having a vast backside.

'The one on landscape.' I grimaced. 'Aren't we all just flies crawling across the giant tablecloth of fate?'

'Plus, we'd gone over it in class. Yeah, I think I did OK on that question.' She held the door open with a slender arm, then a frown creased her brow. 'God, I don't know, though. I might go and see Mrs Clements about it after dinner, get her to talk me through it. Do you want to come?'

'What's the point?' I ducked past her into the canteen; the smell was wonderful. 'It's finished now. Try and forget it.' I nudged her into the back of the dinner queue and we leant against the wall while Year Sevens dithered at the front. 'Listen, while I remember, I want to ask you something. I've been thinking of changing my name.'

'Your name?' Rebecca looked at me as though I was mad. 'To what?'

'Kat. I want you to call me Kat from now on.'

'Why?'

'Well, I like it. I think it's more *me*.'

'Kat?'

'Yeah.' I soldiered on. 'Haven't you ever wanted to change your name? Becky, Bekka, Bex, Beckham? You know, for fun?'

Rebecca shook her head. 'Actually, I hate it when people shorten my name.' You would, I thought. 'But if you really want me to call you Kat, I'll try not to forget.' There was just that hint of disapproval in her voice. Kat? *Kat?* What next? Tattoos and class-A drugs? The line shuffled forward and she started to get her money out.

Suddenly I slapped my sides with a sensation of panic. 'Bloody hell.'

'What's up?'

'Oh, *hell*, I've gone and left my purse in the exam room.' I knew exactly where it was. I'd got up and walked out with it draped over the back of my chair. It's another pre-exam ritual I have, the removal of the purse. Besides, it digs in when I lean over.

'Do you mean your belt thingy?' Rebecca began to rummage through her bag. 'I might have enough change, well, if you just wanted a snack. I could lend you—'

'No, it's all right. I'll have to go and get it, I can't leave it there for somebody to nick.'

This would, in fact, have been unlikely. For a start there was hardly more than a couple of quid in there, and more importantly, the belt itself was gruesome. Maggie's niece had made it for me back in Year 9, when the official school purse belt – a freaky item worn only by the socially inept – became too small even on its longest setting. We had a row about it. Poll said it was safest to carry your money on your person. I said what about pockets, but she pointed out that I was always poking my fingers through mine till they were all in holes. So Maggie had this mega-belt run up for me in navy, a school colour, and I've been wearing it ever since. Glamorous it is not, but it is handy, though I'd rather have pulled my own tongue out than admit this to Poll.

I panted back along the undercroft and up the wide stairs to the hall. I plunged in through the swing doors and stopped dead. The details of the scene flashed up and burned themselves on my brain forever.

At the far end of the hall the gigantic red and gold organ pipes rising in asymmetrical slopes to the hammer-beam ceiling. In front of them, the wooden stage with its lonely lectern, and formal seating at each side for visitors. Then, below and stretching towards me, ranks of wicker-bottomed chairs that squeaked on the parquet when you sat down.

All of it I knew, I'd seen before in a thousand years' worth of assemblies and speech days: but never with this detail in the window.

Unbelievable, at first. Two girls framed in the tall stone-arched window on my immediate right, where the chairs gave way to the rows of candidates' desks. Donna French, *Donna French* and Nicky Hunter, in slim profile, touching. They were standing face to face, belly to belly, in what looked like an embrace; laughing in a stifled, secret way.

They jumped in shock at my entrance and again at the bang of the door behind me, but, weirdly, they remained clinging together.

'Oh!' cried Donna, her face a mixture of dismay and hilarity.

Nicky let out a shriek and turned her head away towards the windowpane. Donna put her arms behind her back and dropped her eyes to the floor. I saw them arch their backs simultaneously, their willowy bodies curve apart like an Art Nouveau design, but I still didn't understand. Then there was a small thud and my purse belt, which had been around the two of them, hit the wooden floor.

Released, the two girls moved apart, Nicky giggling with embarrassment. She still had her face turned from me but I could clearly see her reflection in the glass. Her eyes were wide with horror and she was grinning stupidly.

I just stood there like a lump. Donna moved first, bent down and picked up the belt. Nicky took this as her cue to slide out and make a run for it.

'Sorry,' mumbled Donna, holding the belt out to me. She was trying not to snigger though at least she'd had the grace to blush. 'I was going to hand it—'

We both heard Nicky's far-off snort of laughter, and Donna's self-control dissolved. She flung the belt on the table nearest and stalked out. As the door bumped shut behind her, the belt slithered off the varnished surface, buckle end first, and fell in a coil. It lay there like a dead snake, with me hating it.

\*

He'd first spoken to me half a year before, under the horse-chestnut trees. A day like summer, although it wasn't. We were the new Upper Sixth; lords of the playing fields, monarchs of the benches. 'Come and see this,' he shouted as I walked past, nose in a book. When I looked up he was perched on the back of the Wasserman Memorial Seat, huge shoes planted on the slats. Even as I swooned I thought, someone'll sit there, in all that mud he's wiped across it.

I approached warily, in case he hadn't meant me at all.

'What are you reading?' He took the book out of my grip and scanned the cover. '*Mansfield Park*? Looks a bit old.' He shaded his eyes and smiled, though it wasn't a straight smile, if you know what I mean. I thought he was making fun. 'You can read too much, you know. Books aren't life. You have to live. Catch.'

I managed to grab a corner as it flopped down, drew it back up, hugged the novel against my chest. I wanted to defend it or, failing that, I wanted it to defend me. 'It's good,' I said lamely. I didn't dare mention the heroine was called Fanny. Behind his back a conker thudded to the ground but he never even flinched.

'No,' he said, 'this is good. Here.'

He held out his hand and showed me a conker-case, green mottled with brown. I could see where the little dark spikes had dug into his palm.

'Here.'

I took it off him gingerly, held it in my fingertips. Some joke, probably, this was. In half an hour he'd be back in the common room, laughing with his mates about me.

'Open it. Go on.'

'Why?'

He sighed and took it back. 'I'll do it, then.' He squeezed the sides and a dark crack appeared in the green. Then the crack opened like a mouth and a segment of the casing fell away and tumbled into the grass. With his long fingers he eased the other two pieces apart and let them rock slightly on the cushion of his left hand. The conker lay in the centre like a precious bead. 'There.'

I leaned forward to inspect the pattern, beautiful fingerprint whirls, and the shy nude underbelly of pale skin peeping out on one side. It was so glossy it looked almost liquid; a bubble of molten wood. When I poked it, its back was waxy, glossy, like something alive. I drew back. There was another thud inches from my right foot.

'Do you know what's special about that?'

He placed the bits of shell down on the bench by his feet and began to roll the conker between his hands.

'It'll grow into a mighty tree one day?' I clung hard on to my book. I was going to fail this test, whatever it turned out to be.

'No. Can you not see?'

I shook my head, wishing I was back in the library doing an essay.

'It's brand new. Never been seen before. You and I were the first people ever to lay eyes on that conker.' He tossed it high into the air and caught it neatly between two palms. 'So it's special, in't it?'

'Yeah, I suppose so.'

'Feel that.' He passed me one of the spiky casings and I took it more confidently. 'Not the outside, that bit's a bastard. The white stuff inside.'

I had to lay *Mansfield Park* on the arm of the bench to follow his instruction. Then I cradled the piece of shell and stroked the lining. 'It's really soft. It's like, like silk; no, suede.' He had made me marvel.

He nodded. 'Fantastic, in't it?'

I stretched out my arm to give it back but he clapped his hand quickly up under mine and the shell went sailing into the lower branches and disappeared. My heart nearly stopped with shock.

He laughed at my expression and I laughed with him.

'Tell me something,' I said. 'How come you're sitting under this tree with conkers falling all around you all the time, and you've never been hit?'

He pretended to inspect his head, rubbing his fingers across his scalp, then grinned. 'No, no it's true, no injuries to speak of. It's me, I'm magic. I'm charmed.'

I thought, It's me that's charmed.

# Chapter Five

The day had begun badly.

Dogman had appeared after breakfast, looking terrible. 'Wolfie's dead,' he'd announced, and collapsed onto the settee. I'd had to go and make him a cup of tea for the shock, although it turned out Wolfie had joined the dog-angels yesterday evening. 'He rolled over and gazed at me wi' his big eyes, as if he were saying, I've had enough.' Poll sat on the chair opposite with her hand to her cheek. 'He'd been on his last legs a while. But I knew this were summat different. And the vet said his kidneys had failed, that was why his breath smelt, and it would be a kindness to put him to sleep.'

Poll was in tears. 'Nobody loves you the way a dog does,' she sniffed.

'Aye, that's true,' Dogman sighed.

I left the scene before they drowned in grief; before I lost my temper and told Dogman it was just as well they didn't put humans down for having bad breath. I should have felt sorry for him, dogless Dogman, but I didn't.

I was too hungry. The sky above me was filled with clumps of mashed potato and clotted cream. By the time I got to Cissie's I was feeling faint; I could have dug up and eaten the daffodil bulbs by the front gate. Only the thought of the purse belt got me past the vending machine in the entrance.

'So they put in a catheter and drew out *two pints* of black . . . Yes?' They know me at reception, but this was a new woman, pie-crust collar, big pearl earrings.

'Cissie Southworth.'

'Sign in the book, if you would.' She slid the page at me through the glass hatch. I caught the biro-on-a-string as it swung past my stomach and scrawled my name, then checked as usual for any other visitors Cissie might have had since I last came. Just her ex-hairdresser, Edith – she must be in her sixties herself – and the vicar. Well, who else is there left?

Apart from the tragic fiancé lost in the war there's her sister, my great-grandma Florence, whose ashes live in my wardrobe: died of a stroke over twenty years ago. Poll's one-armed dad, who would have been Cissie's brother-in-law, came down with fatal peritonitis about the same time as the Coronation, so he's out of the picture too. Of her three nieces, Mary died in childhood, Jean's alive and well but in Australia, and Poll has to be dragged here because they always fall out whenever they meet up. I sometimes look in the visitor's book for Vince's name, but I don't really expect to see it.

I don't mind visiting Cissie. She's at least someone I can talk to without bursting into flames of embarrassment. I can sound off to her about Poll and get a sympathetic hearing. Also, she – ha ha, this is really mad – believes I have a life. If I could ask anyone (not dead) about leaving Poll, it would be Cissie.

She was sitting in the TV lounge watching *Watercolour Challenge* with a shrunken, oddly shaped woman. 'He's made a right dog's breakfast of that, now han't he?' Cissie was saying. 'You can't tell which way up it's meant to be.' Then she spotted me and her face lit up.

'Ooh,' she said, grasping my hand, 'our Katherine, what a treat. You're looking bonny, love. Come next door.'

I hoisted her to her feet and she cast a smug smile at the woman left behind with just Hannah Gordon for company. 'It's a shame,' she whispered to me. 'She's nobody.' I wondered whether Cissie meant she has nobody or she *is* nobody. Maybe they're one and the same.

We walked slowly along the corridor to her room and picked our way through her soft-toy collection. 'I've a few more since you were here last,' she said cheerfully. 'Edith brings them me, oh, and I won that pink 'un in a raffle for Heart Disease.'

'Don't the staff bother? I mean, it's all very nice—' I scooped a brace of dog-creatures off the armchair and looked round for somewhere to lose them. 'I'll just lie them down here,' I said, shooing them under the bed with my foot. 'Having so much stuff must make it difficult to clean round. Do they not mind?'

'I suppose so; they're very good wi' me. But we're not allowed pets, and you get to my age, you need summat to stroke.' She gave the dog a pat, as if it was alive, and I watched as a hank of white fur detached itself and floated to the floor. 'This is new. I'm going to call him Dulux.' It lay splayed across her thigh like road-kill.

Ally from the kitchens put her head round the door. 'D'you want a drink, you two? I'm just coming round with the trolley now.' Ally gave me the creeps. I used to think she was about fifty, but one day she was talking about the time she left school and I realized she was only ten years older than me. It's true her skin was unlined and her permed hair was brown, not grey. But she was enormous. Biceps like giant hams, hips that barely made it through the door frame. The sort of fat that makes strangers stop and stare in the street; morbid obesity. I should have felt some kind of solidarity with her, fatties united, but I just found her repulsive. That's the way you're heading, a voice in my head warned whenever any of Ally's flesh was on display.

'My Cuddly Carer,' said Cissie. 'We'll have two teas and a Penguin each. Forget your figures, eh?'

Ally winked roguishly. 'Coming right up.'

Everybody loved Ally.

'No sugar in mine,' I shouted after her massive back.

Ally handed out rations, beaming, and lumbered out of the room. Cissie checked over each shoulder, careless talk costs lives, and lowered her voice. 'So how's your secret boyfriend?'

A tricky one, this. 'Give us your biscuit here, I'll do it.' I tore open the plastic and my stomach rumbled as I caught the scent of chocolate. (Imagine that, went my head, imagine that in your mouth right now.) I handed it back.

'We've had a row,' I said decisively.

'Aw, love. What a shame. What happened?'

'He was too possessive. I needed my independence.' I thought of Donna silhouetted in the tall window and felt a stab of physical pain in my chest. 'And he didn't respect me enough. He wasn't as nice as I thought he was.'

Cissie tutted and looked sad. 'I tek it Poll still doesn't

know? Very wise.' She bit her biscuit and chewed thoughtfully. 'A fall-out, eh. And can you not make it up?'

'No. I need my own space for a while. I've got my
exams . . . '

'Aye, well, you've got to concentrate on your exams,
that's true. Are you not having your Penguin?'

'I had a huge breakfast.' (Weeny tub of diet yoghurt.
Took me about thirty seconds to eat.) 'I'll save it for later,
smashing. Cissie, I was wondering, is Poll really poor? I
don't mean starving or anything; obviously she gets by day
to day. I mean, has she any savings that you know about?
Or antiques to sell, that sort of thing? Long-term nest eggs?'

Cissie wiped the chocolate off her mouth with a tissue.
'It's not really any of my business, love. I don't think she
has, she's never mentioned anything.' She screwed up the
tissue in her fingers. 'You know I've nowt to leave. I've
already given her that mantel clock of Florence's, not that I
had much choice in the matter. I've a tiny bit in the Abbey
National, that's all, and that's coming to you, with my mother's rings—'

'Oh,' I said, embarrassed, 'I wasn't thinking of that.
Anyway, you're not going anywhere for a good while, are
you?'

'I should hope not.' She laughed, but what she said next
was drowned out.

'Hello, playmates.' It was shiny-head Mr Poole, ex-Bank
Top butcher. 'And how are we today? Excuse me while I
park here a mo.' He steadied his Zimmer frame against
the door jamb. 'Mind my bike! I'm en route for reception,
but I needed a breather. So I thought, why not drop in on
the lovely Mrs S?'

Cissie was all smiles. 'It's that man again.'

'Testing, testing.' Mr Poole tapped his hearing aid. 'Can y' hear me, Mother?'

'Can I do you now, sir?'

'I don't meynd if I do.'

They're worse than kids when they get going.

'An' how's your Poll?' Mr Poole said to me when he'd got his breath back. 'Still a rum 'un?'

I saw Cissie nodding out of the corner of my eye.

'Pollyanna Millar, terror of the playground sixty year ago. Our John's still got t' scar wheer she kicked him to mek him join th' Ovaltineys. After a gold badge, she reckoned. She all but crippled 'im for months.'

'She got one in t' finish,' said Cissie. 'Wore it to school every day, I remember Florence pinning it on. But there were a lot of blood spilt ovver it. She went round all t' littleuns, mekkin' 'em sign up. An' a lot o' t' juniors were frittened of her an' all.'

'He's the scar on his shin *till this day*.'

I looked from one to the other. 'Yeah, but, sixty years ago. You wouldn't still have a scar, not after all that time.'

'You would if you'd been clouted wi' a clog.' Mr Poole wagged a knobbly finger at me. 'Vicious things. They'd a' iron band all round t' sole. She cut our John's shin reight oppen. She were a nowty wench, your grandmother, when she were younger.' He glanced at Cissie. 'I'm not speykin' out o' turn, am I?'

Cissie shook her head. 'You're not, no. She deafened an American serviceman with a liquorice stick. Perforated his eardrum.' I started to giggle. 'It's not funny. Poor lad. They were our allies.'

'That wasn't Poll's fault, though, was it? She's always told me it was because he was interfering with her. She was only a schoolgirl. He said some rude words and she took fright; that's the version she told me.'

'Did he 'eck as like. That's what she told everyone so's not to get into bother. Does she hit you?'

'Nah.' I laughed at the idea. 'Not since I was tiny. I'm twice her size these days. I'd just dodge, if she ever did.'

'She's an evil tongue on her, though, there's more than one way to skin a cat. You forget,' Cissie concluded, 'I've known her longer than you, and I've seen you in tears often enough. She can be really sharp when she wants.'

I felt my cheeks flush and put my face down till it passed.

Mr Poole nodded. 'Mustard. She nearly took Eric Benson's finger off wi' a home-med firework, do you remember? Collecting cartridge cases and filling 'em' wi' gunpowder she'd filched out of t' quarry. She thought she were a boy, that was half the trouble.' Then, after an awkward pause, he went on, 'Still, we all do things as we're not proud of when we're young.'

'Oh aye, that's true,' said Cissie.

'Anyways, I'd best be off. People to see, pills to tek.' He patted his chest. 'Leave you two ladies to your gossip.'

'TTFN,' said Cissie, blowing a kiss. Dulux slid away and dropped on the floor but she didn't notice.

The rubber tips on Mr Poole's Zimmer made a squeaky noise that got fainter and fainter as we listened. Cissie seemed subdued.

'I suppose we're all a bit nowty, once in a while. I remember throwing all our Florence's make-up out of an upstairs window. I were angry with her because her husband was still alive. Velouty de Dixor all ovver t' flags. It meks no sense, I can see that now. You do some daft tricks when you're young.'

I couldn't think what to say, so I bent down and retrieved the sheepdog for her.

'Here you go. He was making a bid for freedom.'

'Eeh, y'are a love. So, tell me again about this boyfriend. Donny, in't it? Tell me again what happened. Are you *sure* as you can't patch things up?'

I came away feeling strung out. I'm not a natural liar, despite all the practice I get fending off Poll's incessant probing. I only invented the boyfriend for Cissie. I thought it would cheer her up, give us something to talk about. I didn't invent him for myself. I'm not that sad. Maybe I could kill him off, a drugs overdose or a drunken stroll up the railway line after closing time. Mind you, then she'd be scouring the *Bolton Evening News* every night and there'd be a whole new load of questions to answer.

As I walked up to the entrance I caught sight of Mr Poole sitting half-hidden in a winged chair behind a weeping fig. He had a tea towel over his lap and his hand beneath it was jerking up and down, up and down. Christ, I thought. Even in here it's full of pervs.

I veered slightly so that I would pass near him, and hissed, 'You're disgusting,' at the top of his head. He looked up, surprised. His face seemed odd and naked. As I glared at him the cloth fell away across his knee and I could see that he was holding a pair of glasses in his lap. His flies, I noted, were completely closed.

'Just a sec,' he said, sliding his glasses onto his nose.

'That's better. Couldn't see a blessed thing before.' He peered up at me. 'Now, what's tha sayin'?'

'It needs dusting. This place.'

He tipped his head to one side. 'Does it? I corn't tell.'

'That's probably why your glasses were so dirty.'

'Aye,' he said.

'So what's happened,' the woman at reception was saying down the phone, 'is she's fallen on top of her umbrella and the spoke's gone in her eye.'

I fled the place, cramming the Penguin down my throat as I went.

*

Dad let me have Radio One on as we drove in that last morning. Goody goody two-shoes. I was busy making deals in my head. All the songs had messages in them, but none of them mentioned death, so I thought we'd be all right.

My dad spent ages with the doctor while I read a magazine article about the glory of Venice. Then a nurse came. She took me into a side room and said, 'You know your mum was very sick. She's been really brave but she was a very poorly woman. Sometimes you can't fight illness. Sometimes the body's just too badly damaged.'

I looked at her.

'Your mum died during the night. She wasn't in any pain.'

I said, 'Well, she bloody should have been. I am.' And all the time, this song kept going round and round my head, getting so loud I couldn't think. It was as if my brain was broken. 'Where's Dad?' I managed to ask. 'I need to see him.'

'Give him a few minutes, love,' said the nurse. 'I'll take you to your mum.'

'What's the point?' I shouted.

'I'll leave you for a minute, then,' she said.

I stood totally still for a few seconds, then I lay down on the lino floor and started punching my stomach as hard as I could. I never even saw the doctor come in.

# Chapter Six

For all his evil nature, Vince sorted out a lot of household jobs before he left. He re-papered the chimney breast around the new gas fire, he laid lino over the chipped tiles in the porch, and he took out the hedge and replaced it with a larch-lap fence so it'd be less bother to maintain. He even creosoted it afterwards. He was quite thoughtful, as cheating love-rats go.

But that was nearly two decades ago, and although the flowery wallpaper and the lino were still good, the fence was now collapsing in the middle and several of the laps had dropped off. Dogman had been drafted in to help replace a couple of critical panels.

'You don't want to go paying garden-centre prices for stakes,' he'd told Poll. 'They charge silly money. I can get 'em for you. I've a mate.'

So on this sunny morning, Poll was in the garden holding a sharpened pole upright while Dickie hammered it into the soil with a mallet, and I stayed out of the way. They were singing advertising jingles to each other and laughing in a stupid way. I could have snatched that mallet and seen them both off with one good swipe. I was trying to watch a programme that would change my life.

*So the next time you visit your grocer*
*Tell him no other sausage will do*
*And to all his replies tell him, 'No, sir,*
*It's Donnelly's sausage for you.'*

I strained to hear over Dickie's yodelling.

'I was a mess,' the young woman with maroon hair was saying. 'I really was. A total wreck. My skin was, like, yellow, and I had these great bags under my eyes. And my teeth were a state, all the enamel coming off, the dentist used to go mad so I stopped going. But the worst was the sore throats, I always had a sore throat. I always felt like sh—, like a wreck.'

'And you were "hung up on control", you said before.' The presenter pointed the microphone back at her face.

'Well, it was like, I can't control that side of things, you know, the eating, so I wanted to control everything else. Smacking the kids for tipping their toys out because I couldn't, you know, cope with the clutter. Do you get me?'

'I'll come back to you, Elaine,' said the presenter, leaping lightly up an aisle to kneel at the side of a middle-aged woman in a red suit. 'What was it you wanted to say—?

'Jo.'

'Jo. Have you a question for Elaine?'

Jo leaned in close towards the microphone. 'Same thing with me. Five, six times a day. I got through a load of toothbrushes. And air freshener. Our upstairs stank like a harem.' She gave a short laugh, and the audience joined in supportively.

'And your husband never knew?'

'Never.'

'He didn't have his suspicions, when you disappeared

57

off to the toilet after every meal, and came down reeking of freshmint and perfume?' Close-up of presenter looking surprised.

'No. You see, you get very, erm, cunning; you do these tricks, scams. You might say, "I'm going to have a nice hot bath" – and do it while the taps are running to cover the noise. Or have the radio on. And when you've been doing it for a few months, you get so you can, you can be really quick. And you can hide your empty packets and till receipts, stick them at the bottom of the bin or whatever; I used to burn ours on the fire.'

There was a muffled shout from across the studio; the presenter sprang to his feet and jogged back to Elaine. 'Yeah, plus, there's a lot of husbands and boyfriends who don't *want* to know. Even if they suspect. It's easy to block out what you can't face.' Much nodding. 'I mean, how do you come out and say it? To your, to the person you so-called love and trust? How do you say, "Oh, darling, are you making – deliberately making – yourself sick all the time?" I mean, it's just disgusting, isn't it, to say that?'

The camera lingered on Elaine's expression while someone said something else in the background. The presenter put his hand on her shoulder for a moment.

Then the shot changed to a dowdy woman, fiftyish, sitting in the front row. Some doctor or other, written a book. Get off, you fat cow, I snapped at the screen. She droned on about levels of electrolytes and long-term damage to the oesophagus while I cursed myself for not having switched on sooner. Poll wandered in and asked if I wanted a hot-cross bun because she was doing one for Dickie. I said yes just to get her out of the room.

I'd actually put weight on. Would you believe it. Six days of starving, really going for it, then it was as though something snapped inside me and I ate and ate. You can't diet when you're the one in charge of cooking and shopping. How can I sit down to a bowl of soup and a couple of slices of Nimble when Poll's across the table tucking into toad in the hole? It's no contest. Poll was delighted when I started eating again. 'I thought as you were sickening for summat,' she said, ladling out the custard. 'You've been miserable as sin. Do you want to finish it off?' I did, I had. Then I went up to my room and tried the basque on and it barely did up.

For a minute or two I was so angry I could have scraped my cheeks raw with my fingernails or banged my head against the wall until I saw stars. In the end I went downstairs, opened the kitchen drawer and got out the big scissors. Then I went back up and cut my grey cardigan to tiny pieces. Poll would be furious when she found out, but she could stuff herself. My thumb was burning by the time I'd finished and I had a red welt coming where the scissor handle had rubbed. That was good.

Stupid to get upset in one sense because I'd never, ever wear the basque; but still. It had looked nice before. Like I could have had another life.

The credits were rolling as Poll came in with the hot-cross buns, a whole plate of them. 'There you go. I might have put too much butter on 'em, I don't know.'

She'd cut her hand too with the bread knife, I saw, so there was also blood on some of the buns. I snatched a clean one and focused my attention back on the TV.

'If you've been affected by the issues raised in this programme, then you can ring our helpline, or visit our

Web site at www.talkinghelps.co.uk.' Even though you couldn't see him, the presenter's voice was full of concern. I could imagine lonely women all over the country rushing to the phone to ask him how to sort out their lives. Then the credits finished and his tone changed to something more upbeat. 'Have you experienced a holiday romance? Did you meet your other half on exotic shores? Or did your sloe-eyed lover turn out to be nothing but a foreign cheat? If you're interested in appearing on a future show about long-distance love-affairs, why not contact us . . .'

'Bloody beltin', these,' Dogman mumbled. I tried not to look but I could see the mashed-up bun and butter in his mouth.

'Bloody being the operative word.'

'I sometimes reckon you've swallowed a dictionary,' he quipped, spitting bun on me as he passed.

'In that case you must have swallowed *Spot the Dog*,' I snapped. 'You've the vocabulary of a four-year-old.'

He grinned and showed more gluey bun.

'Watch your mouth, you,' said Poll. 'Dickie's never had your advantages. His dad used t' beat him if he saw him reading so much as a comic. He never had a bedroom of his own, neither, used t' have to sleep on t' landing, didn't you?' Dogman nodded tragically. 'So. Think on. And shift up. He's come to watch the racing.'

Time to move.

'I'm off to the library, then. I'm not taking Winston either, he can go in the back. I've revision to do.'

Poll didn't think much of libraries. 'Waste of a good building,' was her verdict. Apparently when she was young, the school library was a seven-foot cupboard that opened right out, and it served the whole village too. 'It was plenty big enough for a place like this,' she told me many times; usually as I was putting my coat on, books ready by the door. 'I don't know what you want to keep trailing all the way up there for. It's good telly tonight.'

Since its days as a cupboard, Bank Top Library's come a long way. The front elevation is modern smoked glass and breezeblock while inside it's cosy with its orange carpets and blue beanbag chairs, a fish tank, posters, funky mobiles. Best of all, in the far corner, there are three computer screens, because Bank Top Library is at last hooked up to the Internet.

'Let me know if it cuts you off,' said Miss Dragon, peering at the home page suspiciously. 'It's been misbehaving. I'm going to have to ring up. See how you go on, and come and get me if it disconnects itself.'

I watched her stride off. I almost love Miss Dragon, Miss Stockley to her face. She's a stone-faced woman, traditional, solid. Everything about her says, I'm not here to be liked, I'm here to run a good library. Large-print Western, drugged-up political rant, historical passion; Miss Dragon knows instantly where to locate it. She stands behind the front desk and frowns as punters rifle through the books with their grubby fingers. She wears her grey hair bobbed, and always a print blouse under a long knitted waistcoat. You'd think she was a right old misery, but you'd be wrong.

The time blind Poll knocked *Pride and Prejudice* into a full washing-up bowl, she was lovely with me. 'It's the sort of thing I do myself,' she said when I explained I'd had it propped open behind the taps because I couldn't bear to put it down. She said it was nice to come across a youngster who appreciated the classics, and had I read any Dickens? I told her I'd once started *David Copperfield* and given up, and she led me to the D shelf and found me *Bleak House* instead. She said, 'I shall ask you what you thought of this next time you come in.' I was back in three days.

'Well?' she asked. 'Didn't you enjoy it?'

'No,' I said, 'it made me cry.'

'Do you wish you hadn't read it?'

I thought about it. 'No.'

She seemed pleased.

One month after that conversation, I was expelled from Bank Top Primary in disgrace and it was Miss Dragon who helped pick up the pieces. She even offered to come to my first parents' evening at the grammar school, when she heard Poll wasn't going. I sometimes look at Miss Dragon and I think, she wouldn't have given up a baby and swanned off into the blue.

Nowadays she lets me have first pick of any books they're selling off, and asks my opinion on the ones they order in new. My opinion; fancy. And when I mentioned to her about calling me Kat, she didn't laugh.

'Kath?' She put a hand behind her ear.

'No. Kat. With a K.'

'Kategorically?'

'Katastrophically.'

'I hope not. I'll katalogue it in my brain, though it may take a while for my mouth to make the switch.'

I knew Miss Dragon wouldn't disturb my research, and if anyone else asked, it was a school project. I typed in the Talking Helps address and waited for the page to load. Scrolled up and down, found the right link, and clicked.

Here we go, I thought.

Bulimics (people who make themselves sick after eating)
often have LOW SELF ESTEEM. They may have
experienced A MAJOR STRESSFUL EVENT in their lives.
They may have difficulty dealing with NEGATIVE
EMOTIONS such as ANGER or LONELINESS. Some people
who suffer from bulimia say they feel an overwhelming
NEED TO BE IN CONTROL of their lives by strictly
monitoring what they eat. Almost all say they are under
SOCIAL PRESSURE to be thin from TV, magazines, peers
etc.

The site had clearly been put together by a panel of
doom-merchants.

<u>Physical Dangers associated with self-induced vomiting:</u>
dizziness, weakness, confusion, temperature sensitivity,
low blood pressure, high blood pressure, low platelet
count, hyperactivity, chronic fatigue syndrome, brittle
nails, hair loss, swollen legs, muscle wasting, cramps,
bloating, constipation, diarrhoea, incontinence, coeliac
disease, osteoporosis, arthritis, degeneration of the jaw
hinge, loss of periods, infertility, tooth erosion, easily
bruising skin, hypoglycaemia, hyperglycaemia, diabetes,
anaemia, respiratory infections, hairiness, temporary
paralysis, peptic ulcers, tearing of the oesophagus,
gastric rupture, gastrointestinal bleeding, cancer of the
oesophagus, cancer of the larynx, seizures, kidney failure,
liver failure, brain damage, blindness, stroke, arrhythmia,
heart failure, death.

Well, OK, but the main thing was you'd be losing weight.

I clicked onto the next page, but it was all about breaking out of the cycle and loving and valuing yourself, absolutely nothing about what to stick down your throat. So I called up a search engine and started looking for Eating Disorders. What I wanted was a sort of user's manual.

I caught a movement out of the corner of my vision. Miss Mouse, Miss Ollerton, was wandering over, clutching a stack of books and looking sad. She always looks sad. She's very nervous too, never looks you in the eye. I couldn't imagine her doing any other job than this, living anywhere other than in this castle of words. I leaned over the screen casually, blocking out what was loading; occasionally it's useful being so wide. Miss Mouse drifted past in her long droopy clothes, gave me a half-smile, and disappeared into the Hobbies and Crafts section. I could hear the gentle thump thump through the back of the shelves as she slid each volume into its correct place. Her skin and hair are so pale I think she sleeps inside a book cupboard.

When I sat back, the computer was displaying a blue sky bisected by a rainbow, and a sparkly waterfall in the bottom left-hand corner. Welcome to *Cherry's Home Page*, it twinkled. It didn't look like a site about making yourself sick.

Cherry-not-her-real-name was twenty, and at college in Wisconsin. Her hobbies were collecting buttons, horse-riding, and bulimia. She'd been bulimic since she was seventeen, and it was a *load of bull* that it made you ill. Her friends thought she looked great, and in any case it was her life and her body and if that's how she wanted to run the show, who had the right to tell her otherwise?

There were links to *My Button Collection* and *Some Great Pics of Horses*, and *Cherry's Guest Book*. In spite of myself, I had to check out the button page. Possibly what we had here was somebody even sadder than myself. I mean, buttons? Poll's got about five hundred of them in a tin under the stairs, mainly boring old shirt ones of Vince's.

Turned out she meant badges, which wasn't quite so nerdy. *I have over 2,000 buttons! I have catalogued them as follows: Animals, Brand-Names, Drugs, Humor, Miscellaneous, Music, Places, Political, Portraits, Religious, Vintage.*

I skipped to the Guest Book.

*Congrats, Cherry, on your great site. You tell it like it is. I use a toothbrush!* was the first entry I read, from The Kookie Monster. Cherry had replied: *Yeah, I tried that one time, but it scratched my throat.*

*You weren't using the bristle end were you?!!!* The Kookie Monster had typed.

*Doh!* Was Cherry's response. *Trust me to get it wrong! Ha-ha, only joking, stay Cool!* There was an emoticon of a laughing face next to some kisses.

In the next thread, Genius-Girl was tickling her tonsils with a ruler because she didn't like to smell vomit on her hands afterwards. *Kind of appropriate as I'm a math grad.*

Anni86 was still living at home with her parents, but she'd come up with a brilliant excuse for hogging the bathroom. *I say I'm using a face-pack and don't like to be disturbed for twenty minutes. Then I turn up the radio real loud. I always make sure I dab a little of the face pack round the sink or on the taps before I come out, and sometimes I leave a smear round my hair-line or jaw.*

*That is so smart.* – Cherry

*I'll try that one myself.* – Forestsprite

*Has anyone here used a proprietary emetic?* – Deepsouth

*Too risky. You have no control over where you puke. People start asking questions. – Genius-Girl.*

*Wanna swap some buttons? Mail me with your wants list. – Maddyfan.*

I unrolled the messages slowly, taking in the good bits. It was true what they said about the Internet, how it opened whole new worlds.

*Thanks a bunch, girls,* I could have added. *It's been a real eye-opener. – Barm-cake.*

I closed the site and heaved myself out of the swivel seat. With luck, racing from Chepstow would still be on for another hour.

*

Sometimes think I lost my virginity under a horse-chestnut tree, by moonlight. That there was moss under my head, and the leaves rustled as we moved together. Shadows played across his closed eyelids; I couldn't stop looking at his beautiful sad face. 'Your hair's the colour of conkers,' he whispered. The rain began to patter on the leaves as he entered me, but I didn't feel it on my skin till afterwards. He whirled the stars around the sky the way a child waves a sparkler. There was no pain. 'I shan't go to university,' he said. 'I couldn't bear to leave you now.'

# Chapter Seven

I reckon Poll's got an eating disorder, of sorts. That larder's stocked for a siege, terrorist attack, deadly virus outbreak, asteroid collision, economic collapse, etc. Cissie says it's to do with the war and being forced to make three square meals a day out of potato peelings and thin air. She tells tales of having to make tea-substitute (grate a pile of carrot onto a baking tray and dry it out on a low heat) and jam-substitute (mix in a pint of appropriate-coloured jelly and re-pot) or almond substitute (crack open a prune stone and dig out the kernel). She's cooked with blackcurrant leaves, onion skins, dandelions and nettles; she knows a recipe for fatless pastry, can bottle fruit without sugar, and scramble one egg to feed two people (add half an ounce of cornflour in with your butter).

'What's for tea?' the infant Poll used to ask her mother. 'Three jumps at t' cupboard an' a bite at t' knob,' Florence would reply, flicking through her Ministry of Food leaflets. Desperate times all round.

It's from these lean years, Cissie says, that Poll's developed her skewed relationship with food. So we have *two* bread bins, one for bread, and the other for sticky no-brand cakes with lurid icing and foreign writing on the packet.

She buys these off Chorley market, or they get brought along in tribute by the Dogman, and they don't last two minutes. 'It's a shame to let 'em go stale,' she'll say, licking hundreds and thousands off her fingertips. For breakfasts we have tram-scotcher toast – slices two inches thick – and condensed milk sandwiches for suppers. In between it's compulsive chain-snacking. The only reason Poll's not built like a sumo is she's Queen Fidget.

My trouble is, I spend too much time sitting on my bum and reading.

My trouble is, having Poll around.

\*

'It's in your best interests,' I remember them saying. They said it when they took my clothes off, and when they put me in a dim room and when they tried to show me the screen. I wouldn't look.

'There's no damage,' I heard the doctor say to the nurse.

There is. There is! I wanted to shout. There's damage in my head. How can that thing be alive when Mum's not?

But I didn't say a word, just bit the side of my hand hard.

In the end they switched the scanner off because I just kept my eyes tight shut and my head turned away. In the darkness I saw:

Him, holding a spray of lilac to my face. Close your eyes, he told me.

I did.

Open your mouth, he whispered.

I parted my lips and he placed something cool and moist and flat against my tongue.

Now eat it.

I chewed, carefully.

Keep smelling the lilac as you eat, he said.

I opened my eyes and saw him holding the apple and the penknife apart, then bringing them together and smoothly cutting another thin slice of white flesh. He passed it to me on the blade.

Do it again, he said.

Why? I asked.

Because I want you to, he said. I want you to experience life.

When they turned the lights back on, there was a crescent of purple teeth marks across the edge of my palm. I put my hand quickly behind my back, but the doctor saw. 'Have you any questions at this stage?' he asked me, picking up his notes. The nurse behind him had a face that would have soured milk.

'Yes,' I said. 'How did I get to where I am now?'

'I don't understand what you mean,' he said.

'I mean, this shouldn't be happening. I want to go backwards. Rewind. Six months ago, I was happy. Now I'm stuck in here and you're telling me a pack of lies. You can't keep me here, you know.'

I thought they'd give me my clothes then, but they didn't. They brought Dad through instead.

'They're wrong, Dad,' I cried. 'There's no baby. There can't be, I've not even had sex yet. Honest. They're making it up.'

But his eyes had gone like glass and he shook his head at me. It was about that time they were wheeling my mother down to the basement.

\*

It hadn't been too hard to conceal my new hobby from Poll, although Maggie caught me once just after a session in the bathroom and gave me a few searching looks. I stayed to ear-wig on the stairs.

'What's up with your Katherine?' I heard her ask.

'What do you mean?'

'She looks as though she's been skrikin'.' Poll probably shrugged because she didn't reply. 'Has Dickie said summat daft?'

I nipped back down and wandered in all innocent, blowing my nose noisily into one of Vince's large hankies. 'I tell you what,' I said, 'my hayfever's been terrible since old Rowlands planted all that rape at the bottom of the Brow.'

'Ah,' said Maggie. She was sitting by the gas fire drinking her tea from a sugar basin. She's not one to complain, isn't Maggie. 'Now, I've summat for you, if you'll howd on a minute. Fetch my shopping bag from t' kitchen, will you?'

I brought it in, trying not to snag my tights on the vicious raffia decoration.

'Here. Try this on for size. I spotted it in Scope and I thought, I know who that'll do for.'

She handed me a plain brown leather purse with a length of thong wrapped round and round it.

'What is it?' Poll squinted and reached for her magnifier. I unwound the long strap and passed it over to her. 'Hmm. Very nice.' She mauled it between her fingers, undid the top and sniffed inside. 'Leather. What do you say?'

'Thank you.'

'Well, I still think it's awful, them rough boys taking your purse belt and throwing it out of the bus window. You did report them, didn't you?'

I nodded. 'There wasn't any money in it.'

'That's not the point. You'd think you'd be safe on a bus

in the daytime. It's getting so you can't go out. Bolton's becoming a war zone. Over here, love.' She motioned me to bow my head so she could slip the purse on. 'You wear it round your neck. And I've a picture, see. It was in a magazine at th' hairdresser's.' She unzipped the purse and drew out an A4 page folded into squares. It showed a hippyish model with half a dozen scarves on, plus this purse dangling below her neck, and all sorts of jewellery hanging against her red hair. She looked gorgeous. Maybe it was a magic purse that would make me look like that. 'You can be really with-it, wearing this. And it's plenty big enough to fit your bus pass, your keys, all sorts. Kitchen sink, if you want.'

'Thanks,' I said.

'You suit your hair back, though, we can see your bonny face. She's a pretty girl, in't she, Poll? Hiding behind all that hair. How d'you expect the lads to see your bonny smile if you brush your hair all down like that?'

'I'm not interested in boys,' I said, pulling out the elastic on purpose and shaking my head like the girl in the Pantene advert.

Poll tutted. 'Tek no notice, Maggie. She's a lost cause. I've given up botherin', me. Now. Are you stoppin' for your dinner, cause I've a prayta pie and some pickled cabbage as wants eatin' up.'

'Hmm.' Maggie patted her belly. 'I s'll be awreet wi' t' pie but I might have to pass on the cabbage.'

I buzzed off back up to my room, purse swinging. Boys? Yeah. Right.

*

'I've lost my wife and my daughter on the same day,' I heard him say as he walked out of the room.

\*

Nothing ever turns out exactly like you imagine it. That's what allows you to play Cheat-Fate, where, for instance, you *imagine* unwrapping your exam results and getting a line of U grades then, because you've imagined it, it can't happen. I play this game all the time, but sometimes I can't stop myself fantasizing about good things, which is stupid because simply predicting them will prevent them from happening.

What I'd role-played for months was that I'd get put in a General Studies group with Donna French and that, being forced into close proximity to me, she'd suddenly realize that I was OK really and just needed bringing out of myself. Then she'd invite me on a few one-to-one shopping trips or meetings in coffee bars, and she'd quickly come to like me so much she'd decide to have me as her best mate. Rebecca would leave the school, or get herself a new friend, basically find some way of disappearing, as would all the rest of Donna's gang.

Under Donna's influence I'd become slimmer and smarter, because she'd find me the right clothes to wear and teach me make-up, and also tell me what music to listen to (at the moment I mainly play Dad's old 80s cassette tapes, hiss hiss, wurp wurp. All Rebecca ever listens to is classical).

Then, one day, Donna would invite me back to her lovely house, and it would look like a page of *Hello!* magazine. And, in the privacy of her super-cool bedroom, something would occur. A kiss, maybe. An embrace, endearments. Possibly some hair-stroking.

But now it was too late because we would be leaving school in half a term, and I hated her anyway because of the Belt Incident. I'd had Donna killed several times since; once on a ski trip, some kind of collision with a rock; once by a jealous ex-boyfriend who'd waited till she came out of a pub and then run her over in his sports car; and once a good old-fashioned tumble down the stairs in her high heels. The same for Nicky Hunter, too, only perhaps with just the sustaining of major injuries because I hadn't been in love with her.

Yet there we were on this Wednesday morning, Donna and me sitting at opposite ends of the common room during a midday free, and she was still alive and I was still fat. She was at the far end, half-hidden by the drinks machine, plugged into her Discman, and apparently engrossed in highlighting pages of notes. I was in a corner, covering my face with a book. There were only half a dozen other people around and I thought, if it ends up just me and her left on our own, I shall get up and walk out.

The door swung open and there was Mrs Law. You don't mess with Mrs Law; she's Psychology *and* Acting Deputy Head *and* Careers. If she decides she doesn't like you, that's your UCAS form down the pan. The Lower Sixth call her Judge Dredd, and she knows, and likes it.

'I'm looking for volunteers,' she announced.

Everyone shuffled but no one made any positive movement.

Mrs Law did her lighthouse-flash gaze round the room. 'Jenny? Lissa? What about you?' They got to their feet, frowning suspiciously at each other. 'And you, Sita? Come along; Alex as well. Just a quick job, helping out your fellow students in the sports hall. Won't take five minutes of your valuable time. Jasmine and Zoe, surely you're not hiding behind that curtain? That's it, out you come, a break will do you good.'

I saw Donna glance round and register alarm at the emptying common room. She unplugged her headphones swiftly. 'I'll come too, Mrs Law.'

Mrs Law smiled in a surprised way as Donna half-ran across to join her. Then she turned to go and, at the last moment, spotted me. 'And Katherine.' *I thought you liked me*, I wanted to say. But she only fixed me with her death-ray eyes and held open the door. I laid the book down and got up as slowly as I could, hoping she might walk on ahead and I could peel off and take sanctuary in the toilets till the coast was clear. No such luck. She ushered us all out, then brought up the rear like a collie.

'God, if we have to do circuit training or something, I'm going to tell her to get stuffed,' muttered Lissa.

'She can't *make* us do PE.' Alex swivelled her bracelet as she walked. 'I mean, we're out of this place in six weeks, forever. What can she do to us, really? Give us lines? I'd like to see her try.'

'She could stop us sitting our exams,' said Jenny.

'What, for saying no to this lark, whatever it is? I *don't* think so.'

Jenny shrugged.

We did as we were told.

When we got to the sports hall we saw there were four sets of equipment waiting for us. In each corner there was a short row of chairs, a stack of clipboards, a crash mat, a pile of newspapers, a roll of parcel tape, a ruler and a small polythene bag containing strips of black plastic. It looked as if we might be going to play some sort of hideous party game. A little group of Lower Sixth came forward to greet us.

'This is my psychology class,' said Mrs Law. 'They need you to help them with an experiment.' I saw Alex roll her eyes and slump against the wall bars, arms folded. Mrs Law mustn't have seen because she carried straight on. 'Emily, do you want to explain?'

A stocky girl stepped forward. 'Hiya, thanks. Thanks for helping out.' There were no answering smiles. 'Yeah, well, what it is, is we want to set you a competitive task. We're going to observe the different strategies people use to deal with it, the task, and evaluate which one is the most successful.'

Bollocks, I thought. Psychologists *never* tell you what they're observing.

'So we need you to get into pairs.'

No one moved.

'Chop chop,' said Mrs Law.

Alex sighed and slouched forward, pulling Sita by the hand. 'Sooner we get this started, sooner we can get back. To our A LEVEL REVISION,' she finished, glancing back over her shoulder at Mrs Law. Jasmine nodded at Zoe and I thought, oh fuck, I can see where this is headed.

'Jenny, do you want to go with me?' I asked, in an utterly crap, pathetic way. But Jenny and Lissa were already turning to go, together, which left –

Donna's head was well down. 'I feel sick, Mrs Law,' she mumbled. 'Need to go and get some Paracetamol.'

'Paracetamol won't help with nausea,' said Mrs Law briskly. 'What you need is to take your mind off it. Get cracking now; you're holding the others up and I don't believe they'll thank you for that.'

Donna and I trudged across the slippery gym to where our knot of Lower Sixths were seated, holding on to their clipboards. Donna flopped down onto the crash mat and lay full length on her front, as if she was sunbathing, while I stood above her, chewing my nail and feeling like hell.

'Right,' said Emily. 'I need you all to watch this carefully.'

She peeled a page of newspaper off the pile nearest and began to roll it up diagonally so it formed a long, thin tube. A Lower Sixth assistant handed her a bit of parcel tape and she stuck the final corner down so the tube couldn't unravel itself. Then she took the ruler, held it against the middle, and bent the tube down at both ends. 'You need to make each central strut exactly thirty centimetres long,' she explained. 'Do you see? Mand, can I have those ones I did earlier?'

Assistant Mand scrabbled under the wall bars and pulled out a bundle of other tubes, all with their ends bent over.

'Now, what you're going to do is use these struts to build three regular solids. A tetrahedron, a cube, and a dodecahedron.' Mand started rooting in some binbags that she'd hauled out from behind the benches.

'Come again?' said Alex. 'I quit maths after Year Eleven, you know.'

Emily wasn't fazed. 'Like this.' She held out her arms and Mand handed her two finished shapes, well-jointed with parcel tape and plastic ties. They were pretty rigid considering they'd been made from paper. 'Can you all see?

A tetrahedron, like this, is a *four*-faced solid, and a cube,
here, has *six* faces, and a dodecahedron, that's what Mand's
holding, has got *twelve*.' Silence. 'OK? Great. And because
this is a competition, we don't want you to talk to any of
the other couples, or ask us anything either. We're here to
observe. Ignore us. We're invisible.'

'Is there a prize?' Alex again, just this side of insolent.

'Yes,' said Mrs Law. 'A beautiful box of Belgian chocolates for the winning couple.'

'Oh my God, really?'

'No. Emily?'

Emily shouted, '3-2-1-*go*,' as if it was a proper race.
The competitors exchanged disgusted glances, but started
anyway.

Two minutes in and it looked as if Donna and I were
going to be winning a category all of our own; the only team
to complete the task without actually speaking. We sat at
opposite edges of the crash mat with our backs to each other,
while the clipboard girls scribbled away. I started rolling up
tubes and taping them, because I'd worked out we only
needed six to make up the tetrahedron and it seemed sensible to start with the easiest. Then, when I got to the fifth,
Donna said, '*Shit*,' under her breath. 'Shit shit shit.'

I moved aside my curtain of hair and peeped out.
Donna's shoulders were jerking oddly but I couldn't see
what she was doing.

'All right?'

'Shit,' she said, without looking at me.

I turned back to my rolling.

'Katherine?' she said in a tight voice. 'How do you get
these bloody things off?'

When I looked again she'd turned round and was holding her arm away from her body, and it was all stripy red round her cuff with scratching. A black cable tie bit into the skin just below the bone of her wrist and you could see the purple flush as the blood built up.

'I can't get it *off*,' she hissed. '*Fucking* thing. The more I try, the tighter I make it. It's agony. How do you undo it?'

'I'll ask those girls.' I glanced over. Still writing.

'No, don't! I feel such a div.'

'Well, you can't undo them once they're on, they've these little notches, can you see—'

'My hand's about to drop off—'

'Hang about.' I felt around in my purse and drew out my nail clippers between two fingers. 'You might be able to use these to shear through the plastic.'

She took them off me and I saw her hands were trembling. She squeezed them experimentally near the flesh but she couldn't get the angle. 'Oh! Shit.' The clippers flirted onto the crash mat, then bounced onto my shoe. I scooped them up and handed them back. She had another go and this time nicked herself properly. 'Ow, fuck, look at that. Hey,' she said with an effort, 'can you do it?'

Putting my skin on hers, even though it was only fingertips on a wrist, made me want to die. I concentrated totally on the cable tie, and she might even have closed her eyes. Any moment now, I thought, Mrs Law's going to glide over and ask us what we're playing at. I wondered what the observation team were putting in their notes: *Subjects went into what at first appeared to be a consultation huddle but within minutes had developed into lesbian-style groping. They made very little progress with their polyhedra.*

The tie pinged off and Donna yelped with relief. 'Christ. Thanks,' she said, rubbing the dark line where the notches had dug right in. 'God, I'm so stupid. What a bloody bloody stupid thing to do. I'm always doing stupid things. Mum calls me Little Miss Dizzy. I just dive in, I never stop to think—'

'Have you got any struts made yet?' I asked quickly.

'Too busy mutilating myself. Sorry. What can I be doing?'

'Well, I'm nearly ready to make the pyramid. I might need you to hold some pieces in place while I tape the others together.'

We got into a kind of rhythm: peel, roll, stick, bend-bend, and I sneaked glances at her while we worked. Her hair was so sleek; different shades of blonde fell across each other, then back into place when she moved her head. Her thighs were so slender that even when she sat on her haunches, they hardly spread at all. There were light freckles on her heart-shaped face. I watched her till it hurt.

Donna had started talking like a radio DJ, rattling off questions and laughing a lot. 'That's such a neat pair of clippers, where d'you get them? I've never seen ones with a violin on the front. Cute. Hey, look at Lissa's group, they're making hexagons. Should we be making hexagons? Don't you need hexagons for the dodecawhatsit? No? Shall I tell them? Won't it be funny when they realize they've done it wrong. Hey, you could use those tie things if you were a criminal, bind your hostages up, they'd never escape. Shall I tear off some pieces of tape for speed? Oh, ow, *ow*. My God, look at that, I've taken all the hairs off my forearm. I bet you could use this stuff instead of waxing, bloody painful though. Mind you, so's waxing. Can you believe there's women who pull their own hair out, for kicks? I mean, on their heads, so they go bald? Mental.'

We got two shapes completed before the bell went for dinner, so technically we beat everyone, although none of the Lower Sixth said that. They didn't even tell us what they'd been observing.

As we filed out of the gym, Donna was saying, 'We won, didn't we? Didn't we win?'

'You are so sad, Donna French,' said Alex, but in that way which means it's only a friendly thing to say and not bullying.

'Sad yourself, loser. Look, I've made myself a victory wreath.' She was stringing cable ties together into a large-looped chain. 'Smart, eh? Might wear it tonight, essential clubwear.'

'Looks a bit spiky to me,' said Lissa. 'You'd have somebody's eye out if they came up for a snog.'

I was hanging at the back of the group when Donna turned to me. 'You are so fucking clever, though. You deserve this.' She draped the plastic chain over my hair. 'Honest,' she turned back to the others. 'You should have seen her. Dead organized, worked out how many struts we needed for each shape before we started, had a proper strategy, no, stop laughing, to finish each shape before we started the next because that was quicker—'

I was half-smiling in case it was a piss-take, to show I was in on the joke.

'No, seriously,' Donna went on. 'If you're ever in desperate need of a paper polyhedron and time is of the essence, Katherine's your girl.' She raised her palm to me.

I gawped for a second, then it clicked what she wanted and I slapped her hand. 'Yo,' she said.

'Actually, it's Kat,' I said. 'My name. Kat. I've changed it.'

'Miaow,' said Alex.

Nicky appeared round the corner and Donna let out a squeak of joy. 'Nicks, Nicks, wait up.' She broke into a run. Nicky held her arms open for Big Hugs.

'See you then, Kat,' Donna shouted over her shoulder.

*

I don't know how long I was there. Time's different in hospitals. I don't even know if it was another part of the same building, or a different place altogether. There was still that giveaway smell of cleaning fluid and canteen. There was still nowhere to be private, people asking you questions constantly and putting needles in your arm. I didn't take much notice. I kept my eyes closed a lot of the time because it was better in my head.

The night before we did it, he took me to a playground and sat me on a swing. He swung himself like a maniac.

'You could launch yourself off into the sky, it'd be easy. Lose yourself in all them stars,' he shouted as he swished past me. 'Go higher. See if you can go right over the top bar. I bet you could if you got enough momentum up.' His hair flowed round his face, then back, blown tight away from his hairline. I slowed down to watch, saw the chain links shift, heard the creak of the giant bolts.

Then, without warning, he jumped right off in mid-swing, legs flailing. He landed hard and staggered, but didn't fall. 'Hit the ground running, that's what they say. That's the secret,' he called across the darkness.

He strolled over and stood close in front of me, gripping the chains near my hips. 'There's no need to be scared. I'll show you something.' He drew the swing seat towards him and held it for a moment, then let me fall away. 'Come on.'

I remember scuffing my shoes hard into the grass to stop myself, and the whole metal frame shuddering around me. He took my hand and led me over to the roundabout.

'We're at the centre of the universe, you and me,' he said.

I laughed.

'No, we are. I can prove it. Hop on.'

The roundabout was a solid cylinder shape with bright tube handles intersecting the top into cake-slices. We each sat in a slice and he pushed hard on the ground with his foot to start us moving.

'Lie back. Go on.'

I rested my neck on a cold handle.

'No, don't close your eyes. Look up.'

Orion whizzed round, Ursa Major wheeled from one edge of my vision to the other.

'I told you. The stars revolve around you. You're the centre of everything. We are. Us.'

A nurse came in. 'You've got visitors,' she said brightly. 'Shall we have these curtains open, let a bit of sunshine in?'

I wriggled myself up in bed, heart beating in case one of them was Roger, or Dad. I knew it wouldn't be Dad, though, really. 'You'd have broken your mother's heart with all this,' he said, the last time I saw him. 'You were everything to her. Whatever made you do it?'

'Love,' I told him.

'You don't know the meaning of the word,' he said, and started crying.

'I do!' I shouted. 'Roger loves me. He wants this baby.'

'Does he heck. He wants shut of you.'

'He says he'll look after me.'

'He's too busy looking after himself. Drunk on his own charm. Well, you go your own way from now on, it's nowt to do with me. You've made your choice as far as I can see.'

'Are you decent now?' asked the nurse. 'Come here and let me put a comb through your hair. Have you any cologne?'

The door opened and an elderly woman in a black and purple shell suit walked in, followed by a grey-haired man in a patterned sweater and baggy pants. I turned to the nurse in confusion.

'Who are they?' Because I didn't like the look of them at all. Especially her.

'I'm your rescuer, that's who I am. I'm family. My name's Pollyanna Millar, and this is Vince. We've come to tek you home.'

# Chapter Eight

The invitation was in my pigeonhole on the last day of term.

Skool's Out
Summer's Here
and Donna's 18!!!
Come and get slaughtered before the results!!!
The time: 7th August, 9pm –1am
The place: Steem
Dress: Bad Girl!!!

I checked Rebecca's pigeonhole to see if she had one too, but it was empty, spotless. Everyone was clearing out. Lockers were being moved, ancient pieces of food and forgotten books being unearthed, while Mrs Law barked instructions across the common room and handed out binbags.

'We want *no trace* of you by twelve o'clock,' she yelled above the noise of the radio. 'Anything left at the end of the day will be *thrown out*.'

I stuffed the invite in my purse. Obviously I wouldn't be going, but it was nice to have got one. The last party invitation I'd had was completely bogus. It had come a week after my birthday and had looked like a proper card from a real person. *PULSE invites you to rave the nite away with your mates,* the gold ticket said. 'It's a con. They get your name off th' electoral roll,' said Poll, destroying my last vestige of hope. 'It's a computer as sends 'em out.'

'Oh, that,' sniffed Rebecca when I showed her Donna's card. 'I heard them twittering on about it yesterday. Her dad's paying for the whole lot, you know. Club hire, drinks, everything.'

'Are you going?' I asked, madly.

'No, of course not.' Her eyes bulged at the idea. 'Anyway, I didn't get an invite.'

A little thrill of mean pleasure went through me.

'She probably thought you wouldn't like it.'

'Which I wouldn't.'

'Hey, you could come as my guest, though. It might be a laugh.' I tried to keep my voice light, as if I might be joking.

'You're not really going, are you?' She stopped ramming folders into carrier bags for a moment and goggled at me.

I considered for a second or two, and this is what went through my head:

1. Aerial shot of Ibiza-type rave crowd, lots of happy faces and bare shoulders.
2. Me, squeezed into the middle of it, flushed and petrified, in my basque.
3. Outside the front of my primary school, me standing crying in front of a felt-tip poster announcing COME AND GROOVE AT OUR DICO.
4. Donna and Nicky, joined at the hip.

'I've got a recital that evening, anyway. You're welcome to come to that if you've nothing else on.'

'I'll have to check,' I said, which was polite speak for

Even if Poll allowed me out after dark, I'd rather watch Maggie knit dishcloths.

*

'I've been invited to a party,' I told Cissie, for something to say.

We were tucking into crumpets and jam and I'd crammed down four, on the grounds that they'd be making a reappearance later.

'Ooh, how lovely. Whose is it?'

'A girl at school. I don't know her so well, she's inviting all sorts. Loads of people. She's in Badminton Club and Choir and Dram Soc, one of those types with a hundred close friends.'

'And will it be at her house?' Cissie's always keen to hear reports on how other people keep their homes.

I shook my head. 'It's going to be at Steem.'

Cissie looked blank.

'That big building opposite W. H. Smiths. The one that got set on fire.'

'Used to be Ethel Austin? I'm with you.' Cissie was disappointed. 'Funny place for a party. I tek it they've put a roof on now. You'll need to watch your purse, there's thieves everywhere.'

'I'm not going.'

'Why ever not?'

I let a huge lump of jam drop off the spoon and kept my eyes on it while I answered.

'It wouldn't be fair to leave Poll on her own at night. She's not been well.'

'First I've heard of it. What's up wi' her?'

I took a bite of crumpet while I thought of something. Do you ever wish you'd not started a conversation?

'She's had pains.'

'Where?'

'In her legs.'

'Pains in her legs?'

'Her feet, really. She's having trouble with her ankles swelling. And she gets bad headaches from straining to see.'

Cissie narrowed her eyes. 'She's had those a while. She teks her tablets and they soon shift. Are you sure she's not trying it on? I mean, we all get swollen ankles at our age. Look at that.' She pulled her pleated skirt over her knee and twitched a slipper at me. 'I used t' have beautiful ankles, me.'

'You still do, love,' shouted Ally from the door. 'Put 'em away or you'll cause a stampede.' She waddled in, chuckling. 'She's a minx, your aunty. We have to watch her, you know.'

'Great-great-aunt,' I muttered, seeing the sleeves strain across Ally's upper arms as she stacked crockery. I stuffed the rest of the crumpet in quickly to clear the last plate. Then I sat for a minute with my jaw working like a cow because you have to chew stuff well, otherwise it's hell to coax back up.

Cissie was admiring Ally's new ring.

'It's a belter, in't it?' said Ally. 'Alan give it me last time I was in Leeds.' She lowered her lashes and put her head to one side as if she was posing for a photograph: the Thoughtful Bride.

Cissie gasped dramatically. 'He's never asked you to marry him?'

'Yeah. It was brilliant. I din't have a clue. I was in t' kitchen and he shouts, "Oh, just fetch my tool bag in here, will you?" So I carried it into t' living room an' he says, "Open it up for me." ' Ally was growing pinker. 'So I said, "Do it yourself" – 'cause, to be honest with you, I have trouble bending right down – and he said, "No, go on, I've a surprise for you." So I did, and there it was.'

'How lovely,' said Cissie warmly. 'Is it a diamond?'

'Yeah. And that's white gold, not silver. He said he wanted summat a bit different.' She stretched her hand out and tilted the ring experimentally. 'We've not set a date yet, he's waiting for his mother's hip replacement.'

'And how long have you been seeing him now?'

'Only three months, I know, mad in't it? But we'd been emailing since before Christmas.' Ally winked at me. 'I got him off th' Internet, Webhearts it's called. It's dead easy, and there's photos. You should give it a go, Katherine. There's someone for everyone. You should get yourself logged on.'

You should try sticking your fingers down your throat, I thought.

'I'm not interested in boys,' I said.

'She's exams,' said Cissie. She reached over and patted Ally's hand. 'Eeh, I am pleased for you, love. When is it his divorce comes through?'

I went home in a terrible temper. The sky was just clouds, and it started to rain as I got off the bus. I don't know why I was so furious. What had Sad Ally's life got to do with me?

'Poll? Poll?' I shouted from the porch. Silence. She must be round at Dogman's. I stomped upstairs into the bathroom and locked the door. Then I threw myself on my knees, whacking the toilet seat up so it clapped against the cistern, and jabbed my fingers at the back of my mouth. A surge of relief came up along with the crumpet; anger and tension poured down the pan. I retched till my stomach hurt, then laid the side of my head on the edge of the bowl.

'Get Dickie in to sit wi' Poll if she's mekkin' a fuss about being left. They can watch the telly, he does a great running commentary,' Cissie had said. I told her I'd think about it, which I would, endlessly; only I knew I'd reach the same conclusion every time. I was more likely to win the Bogle Stroll than walk into a nightclub on my own.

Another home improvement was under way when I came back downstairs. Poll had returned with Dogman and they were carrying a biggish cardboard box between them.

'Careful now,' said Dogman. 'You don't want to chip them.'

'It's not heavy but it's awkward. There.' Poll slid her end of the box onto the table, then spotted me. 'Come and look. Dickie's been busy.'

I edged over as Poll undid the flaps and drew out a two-foot garden gnome.

'Jesus,' I said.

'I know, aren't they smashing? Look at this one, he's sitting down. And this one's got a hedgehog on his shoe.'

'A squirrel. The mould didn't tek so well there. If I can do some more, I'm going to flog them at car boots,' said Dogman, stroking one of the gnome's heads as though it were a newborn.

I picked one up gingerly. 'Why has it got pock marks all over it? It looks like it's got a disease.'

Poll tutted. 'You're allus finding fault, you are.'

'Air bubbles. I'm working on that one. I maybe should have med the mixture with more water. If you put the paint on thick enough, it fills up a lot of the dents.'

I stood my gnome back up on the table, and saw that my palms had gone red. 'God, have you seen this? The paint's coming off. The paint's dissolving, Dickie. What the hell did you use?'

Dogman looked upset. 'They were out of a kit.'

'Slap some varnish on, they'll come up a treat,' said Poll. 'And don't wipe it off on the sofa, Katherine; I saw that. Go and get a dishcloth.'

Poll was arranging the gnomes in a tableau when I came back from scrubbing my hands under the kitchen tap. 'Don't they look smart? That one favours Patrick Moore.'

'Dickie,' I said, 'what did you make them out of? Because they're very light.'

'Plaster of Paris.'

'So what'll happen when it rains?'

'I did wonder about that.'

'Fantastic. What next, birdbaths carved out of soap? Chocolate sundials?'

'Tek no notice of her, Dickie.' Poll stood back to admire the overall effect. 'They're great. I shall put them in our back, near the fence. I bet next door'll want one when they see them.'

'It might be an idea to wait till I get them varnished,' said Dickie, frowning.

'Nonsense. They'll be fine.'

I could tell she was livid with me. Those gnomes were being planted or she'd die in the attempt.

I prayed for rain, and when it hadn't come by 9 p.m., I filled a watering can and went off to imitate a monsoon. Poll finally found me in the dark, dousing the gnomes.

'Look at that,' I pointed gleefully at their melting heads. 'They've lost some weight, haven't they?'

'You know your trouble?' she said. 'You can't bear anybody else to succeed at something. It always has to be you on top. You're seriously disturbed, you are.'

\*

She installed me in the front bedroom in the middle of a lot of dark pre-war furniture. I never want to see another lozenge motif as long as I live. Roger's books were everywhere and I was growing fatter by the day.

'There'll be more space when he goes off to Sheffield. He'll be tekkin' all his clothes and papers with him,' said the Poll-woman. 'I suggest you stay here and rest up for now. There's nowt to go out for, and it's piddling down anyway. Get yourself settled.'

'I've got to go to school,' I said. 'I think I've got exams. Have I got exams?'

'Put your feet up, I'll bring you some Ovaltine. Roger gets through a tin a week.'

'I need my books. I've got to revise.'

'Look,' said Poll, 'you've missed 'em. Th' exams are finished. You weren't fit to do 'em. It's no good crying, that chapter's over. Do you tek sugar, or not?'

When Roger came back from town he'd bought me a bunch of pinks.

'That's bad luck, that is,' said Poll.

Roger laughed in her face. 'How are pinks bad luck? You're soft, Mum.'

'Pink's for a girl,' she said darkly. I swear she looked more pregnant than me.

Vince sat at the dinner table and studied the coaching inn on his place mat. He had thin cheeks and comb-over hair, Brylcreemed down.

'Is your dad a mute?' I asked Roger that night, after Poll and Vince had gone up.

'No. He's just lost the will to live,' said Roger.

'You won't leave me here, with them, will you?' I said.

'We've got to think in the long term now,' he said, which was ironic really as he only had another seven months to live.

# Chapter Nine

'I'm going to get a summer job,' I announced to Poll across the bed we were making.

'Ooh, hark at her,' said Poll, even though there was nobody else in the house.

'Well, I need some money, and you've none to spare, so I don't see any alternative.'

I snatched the sheet out of her hands viciously and pulled her off balance. She toppled forwards onto the mattress, swearing.

'Oops, sorry,' I chirped. 'I thought you had hold of it. Are you all right?'

'No thanks to you.' She struggled to her feet again and glared. 'If I didn't know better, I'd say you did that on purpose. I don't know what's got into you recently; you used to be so meek and mild. Bad blood coming out. What sort of a job had you in mind?'

'Whatever I can get, after the exams have finished. Secretary, maybe.'

'You can't type.'

'Shop assistant.'

'You'd never manage. All them strangers, you'd have a fit. You've to look people in the eye when you serve 'em.'

I took in a good breath and let it out again, slowly. 'There's girls at school have got jobs selling tickets in a booth. You just sit there, take the money and hand over the ticket. It's a piece of cake. You'd be able to sit there with a book, read all day if you wanted to.' I thought I could cope with that.

'What sort of tickets?'

'Charity. Registered, all legit. You don't get much for it but it's cash in hand, the girls say.'

Poll pulled a face. 'Oh aye, and think how vulnerable you'd be. In a booth on your own; you'd be a sitting duck for all kinds of funny characters. You attract that sort, you know you do. You'd have hooked yourself a stalker before you could say *Prime Suspect*.'

One of these days, one of these days Poll'll say to me, Oh, that's a good idea, I agree. Then I'll faint dead away. In fact I'll be in a coma for weeks and they'll have to play tapes of Carol Ann Duffy's poetry to bring me round.

I stood up straight while I rammed a pillow down into a clean pillowcase. 'I'm going to have to do *something*, at *some* point. In three weeks the exams'll be over. Then what am I going to do with my life?'

Poll opened her mouth to speak and I waited. 'You've years yet—' she began, but suddenly there was a terrible squeak of pain down by her feet. 'Oh, hell fire,' she gasped, 'I've trod on Winston.'

I crawled across the mattress and hoiked him up. He weighs nothing these days.

'Did I tread on your paw? Eeh, poor love, are y' awreet?' Poll stroked his yellowing head tenderly while I lifted one paw for inspection after another. There didn't seem to be any damage. 'He were in among t' dirty sheets. He mustn't have seen me. Poor thing.' She put her hand under his chin and lifted his muzzle. 'Oh, see his little face, his eyes are all glazed.'

He didn't look particularly bothered to me but I left her to her fussing. I straightened the pillows, finished tucking the sheets in both sides, and pulled the duvet and bedspread up on my own while Poll sat in the Lloyd Loom chair nursing the dog on her lap. They'd have made a good study for one of those collector's plates, *The Faithful Pal: see the fine detail of the matted sheepskin slipper, admire the workmanship needed to capture the tiny bobbles on the inside-out cardigan.* After a while she raised her head and said, 'He's gettin' owd.'

'Right,' I said. We were both thinking about Winston dying, and I didn't want to. 'I'll make some dinner, shall I? Will that gala pie be all right still, or does it want binning?'

She left Winston on the bed and came down after me. While I was cutting slices of pie with the huge sharp knife she came into the kitchen and slapped her hand down on the worktop next to me.

'Here,' she said ungraciously. 'If it's that big a deal. Of course, we may not be able to heat the house this winter.'

Like bollocks we won't, I thought, unrolling the five-pound notes. Thirty quid! 'Thanks,' I muttered. It was probably my child benefit anyway.

'I say, I don't know what you want it for. You've everything here. Young 'uns today, they expect everything on a plate. My best blouse when I was little was med out of a pair of bloomers my mother never wore. Pink silk.

And very smart it was too. I never had a dress as a girl that didn't have a flaw somewhere in t'material.'

One quick thrust with the knife and we'd have had an instant end to all these stories of wartime hardship. I could wipe the blade on the Bailey's tea towel and carry on cutting pie. No jury in the land would convict me.

*

By September, I felt like a whale.

'Ger away. You've a long way to go yet,' said Poll, Job's Comforter in tracksuit bottoms. 'It gets so's you can barely move. And if you go overdue, like I did wi' Roger, well. I can't tell you. It's terrible, that last six week.'

Late that night Roger took me outside to get cool. We perched on the low front wall, me facing the house opposite and him side-on with his back against the gatepost. You could barely see the stars. I was looking for Orion.

'Hey,' I said, I thought he'd be pleased with this, 'I've just noticed something. If I look straight at that tiny star to the left of Orion's belt, I can't see it. It disappears. But if I turn my head and squint at it out of the corner of my eye, it comes back again. It's magic. Is it magic? A magic star?'

He was using a pair of nail scissors to unpick a badge from the knee of his jeans. 'No,' he said flatly. 'It's to do with the receptors in your eyes.' The badge was coming away, thread by thread. 'The ones at the corner of your eye are better at distinguishing variations in light, the ones in the middle work best at picking up colour. So if you want to see something faint but monochrome, you look sideways at it.'

'That's fascinating,' I said.

'It's only science,' he said. The badge peeled off completely and he threw it over his shoulder into Poll's rose bushes. 'I'm going Tuesday. You do know, don't you?'

I nodded.

'Are you coming with us?'

For a second I thought he was asking me to go and live with him in Sheffield. Hope leapt up inside me like a spurt of blood.

'Vince is driving over to help me unpack. You can come up in the Metro with me, and go back with him in the Manta.' He said 'the Metro' like it was the most sacred phrase in the English language. Vince had taken him to see it on his birthday, at the start of August, put the deposit down, and they'd picked it up from the garage on Results day.

'I don't know if I want to or not,' I whimpered, the tears starting.

'For God's sake, don't lay this guilt on me now,' he shouted, throwing up his hands in a way I'd seen Poll do.

With a tremendous effort of will, I stopped crying. 'I'm all right. I'm fine. Shall I take out those loose threads for you?' There was the ghost of a rectangle fringed with orange cotton across his kneecap.

He shrugged. I leaned across and began to pinch out the threads one by one.

'Don't get in a state, though,' he said when he saw I'd got myself under control. I tried to smile. 'Because we need to look after this baby.'

Notice he didn't say anything about looking after me.

After Vince and I came back, that Tuesday, I fled upstairs to Roger's room to have a good weep. But the door was locked, and I could hear Poll sobbing her little shrew heart out behind it.

*

So I took the money sharpish, and went off to Bolton to spend it on normal-girl clothes. Half at the back of my mind, and slimmer than a shadow on a cloudy day, was the idea that maybe, if I found the right outfit, I would go to Donna's do.

I wasn't allowed to go into town by myself till I was sixteen. Poll thought it was too risky and I wasn't bothered enough to argue. If I wanted something from the shops, e.g. chocolate or books, I could walk up the hill into the village, or down into Harrop, which is the smallest town in the universe probably. Serious catch-a-bus shopping I associated with crashing boredom; trailing after Poll while she held packets, boxes, labels up to the light and demanded to know what was in the small print. Selecting the right coins for her out of her tatty old purse. Flashing looks of apology at the staff she was rude to.

'Can't you see I'm partially blind?'

'Yes, madam, but you still can't bring back soap if you've used it.'

'It's not on, this, it in't. I'm nearly seventy, you know.'

But once I'd got my GCSEs it mysteriously became safe to get on the 214 alone, as long as I didn't sit next to any men. This sudden change might have had something to do with the fact that Poll urgently needed me to go and see about a new gas cooker, but she was laid up with flu at the time and Dogman had gone to Barmouth for a week. 'Stop mithering,' she'd croaked through the big white hanky. 'I've written it all down for you.' Huge biro capitals dancing between the lines on my jotter. 'What can possibly go wrong?' And even though that afternoon there'd been a bomb scare and all round Boots was cordoned off, and then

I'd got stuck in a crowd of Bolton Wanderers supporters singing swear-songs, I came home in one piece.

You can't get much new for thirty quid, but there's good pickings to be had in charity shops. I found another ankle-length stretchy skirt, black with grey flowers on it, and a long black blouse with white collar and cuffs. 'That suits you,' the woman behind the counter said unexpectedly when I stepped out of the cubicle to get a better view in the mirror. I went scarlet and dragged the curtain back across. Beneath the hem of the skirt my brown school shoes stuck out. It's hard work, reinventing yourself.

Next I went to Debenhams to see what they had in their footwear department, just on the off-chance they were giving away the ultimate pair of solve-your-wardrobe shoes for twenty-one pounds.

I wandered past the make-up and perfume counters, and noticed how many cosmetics are named after things you eat. Grape, candy, toffee, vanilla, I counted off. Cherry, fudge, cinnamon. Clever marketing, that; your teenage girl's so busy trying to avoid real food she'll run a mile from a proper toffee, but she's still greedy for the idea of one. I've seen these girls, thin as whippets, inhaling choc-mint lipgloss like it was cocaine.

Even the mascara was called Liquorice. I picked one up and read the blurb along the side. *2000 CALORIES*, it said. That was never right. How could a mascara have two thousand calories in it? That made it as fattening as an entire Black Forest gateau. Presuming you ate it. Surely to God you didn't eat it?

'Can I help you?' said the assistant.

I had a quick look. Smooth oval face, neat arched brows, mouth in, I'd say, Frosted Ginger. Not much older than me.

'Oh. I'm sorry. I was only . . . I don't wear . . . '

'It's pretty daunting, in't it, all these colours, knowing what suits you. We see some women come in here, well, I shouldn't say really, but some of 'em look like clowns. You'd think they'd used wax crayon instead of make-up, honest. The old ones are the worst.' She giggled and leaned towards me. 'I'll not last two minutes here, will I? It's only my first week. I bet I'm not here by Sat'day.'

I couldn't think how to reply. I smiled back for politeness, but began to edge away.

'Tell you what.' She stepped out from behind the counter. 'Shall I give you a mini-makeover? We're really quiet. I could show you which colour spectrum suited you. You're an Olive Tones, so you'd look fantastic in some of these eyeshadows over here, and we could even you out with this base, take out some of the redness in your cheeks, I know this stuff looks funny being green but I swear it really works, and you've lovely strong brows, we could bring those out with a dark pencil, give them more definition and balance your features . . . '

I shook my head. 'No thanks. I don't wear make-up. My grandma says it's bad for your skin.'

'OK.' Her face fell ever so slightly. 'Do you want a free sample of foundation, though? You could try it at home, it's dermatologically tested, it's actually good for your skin 'cause it contains sunscreen, filters out harmful UVA and UVB rays, and then if you like it, you can come back some time and I can show you how to blend it with some of the cream blusher, which'd really bring your cheekbones out.'

I reached out for the sachet, thinking it might be worth a go with when I got home, just to see, and then I spotted her hand. It was odd somehow; very small and boiled red beneath the smart white cuff of her overall. I didn't stare but it looked, in that split-second flash, as if at least two of the fingers were missing. Her other hand, fluttering over the display counter, was beautiful, with long white-tipped nails. A burn? A birth thing? Her eyes met mine but there wasn't a flicker of anything, only eagerness.

'Go on. You know you want to.' She grinned. 'And if I make you look like Liz Hurley, tell my supervisor, will you?'

'All right,' I said.

'Come round, then, sit in the chair.'

I did as I was told, although my heart was thumping with shyness. 'Bet you won't find any cheekbones.'

'Bet I will,' she said.

After she'd finished and swivelled me round to see in the mirror, she smoothed my hair away from my brow.

'I'm not a hairdresser,' she said, 'but I reckon if you used some straighteners on this, and had a wispy fringe cut in, it'd really, really suit you. The way your hair is now, no one can see your face.'

My strange reflection made me giggle with nerves. The assistant laughed too, only in a non-hysterical way.

'I look like somebody else. It's like, like turning from black and white to colour.' I couldn't take my eyes off myself. I knew I wasn't beautiful, but I was, kind of, tidied up. Drawn-in. More *there*.

She was busy pulling out drawers and tipping up miniature cartons.

'I've found you some extra samples.' She handed me a

smart little paper bag with string handles. 'There's more or less everything here that's on your face, not the same lipstick but close, and we've no mini-eyeshadows at the moment, but your blusher crème's there, I already put you in a foundation didn't I, oh and we've a vial of scent going begging, I'll stick that in an' all.'

In my head I heard Poll say, She only did it 'cause she likes a challenge. I drowned her out by asking to buy a full-size mascara, then nearly had a fit when it was fourteen pounds. *Fourteen pounds.* I paid up, though.

'It's a lot, in't it? But you get what you pay for, it's really good quality, dun't flake or anything, you buy these cheap ones and they're halfway down your cheeks by the time you've got to t' bus stop.'

She shut the till and gave me a huge smile. 'Go an' knock 'em dead. And don't forget about the straighteners.'

What do you think you look like? said Poll's voice as I walked out into the fresh air where everyone could see me. I wanted to touch my tacky lips, but I knew if I started mauling I'd ruin the effect.

On the way back to the bus station I spotted a pair of black ankle books with low spiked heels in a charity shop window. SHOE EVENT said a banner above. I went in, checked the soles and, call me Cinders, they were my size. Four pounds I paid for them, and I don't think they'd been worn.

No perverts sat near me on the bus. I got a window seat so I could check out my reflection when we went past anything dark. There'd never be a day as good as this again.

As we got to my stop, I wondered whether to wipe some of the slap off in case Dogman made a song and dance about it and alerted Poll. Poll might even spot it all on her own if I was standing near a window. I knew the sort of thing she'd say. She'd go, Do you want to attract sexual deviants? Or; Is that what you spent my heating money on? Or; At the end of the day, you're still like the side of a house, there's no make-up'll hide that.

I could feel my insides winding themselves up as I stepped down from the bus and my body stiffened as I walked away, imagining her face. Just as I was getting into a big mental argument with her, I became aware of someone staring.

He was my height, my age, about. Thick dark hair, slightly wavy; white shirt with a granddad collar, and a black waistcoat over the top, like a gypsy. You'd call him handsome, although his neck was on the thick side. He was leaning against the wall of the Feathers, smoking; drugs, I shouldn't be surprised.

I put my head down and walked past him.

'Hey,' he called after me. 'Hey, wait!'

I quickened my pace, exactly like they say not to on *Crimewatch*, and made to cross the road.

'Wait,' he shouted again. 'Katherine.'

I stopped in my tracks.

'Katherine Millar. Wait for me. I only want a word.'

It was daylight and we were near a busy road junction. If he dragged me into the bushes and slit my throat before perpetrating a dreadful sexual assault, there'd be loads of witnesses. I turned round and glowered.

'Hi,' he said, flicking his tab-end into the hedge and hooking his thumbs into his belt loops. 'Do you mind if I walk you home?'

'You what?'

'I want to talk to you.'

'What about?' I gripped my keys in my fist so that the Yale was poking out through my fingers. This is a very effective weapon if you jab it in the eyes, and you can't be prosecuted the way you can if you carry Mace around with you.

He took a step towards me. 'I can't tell you in one sentence. Let me walk with you, a little way. Up to the timber merchant's.' I couldn't place his accent but it wasn't local.

'How do you know which way I'm going?'

'Oh,' he said calmly. 'I know where you live.'

\*

I'll always associate Phil Collins with extreme pain. Every DJ who came on played 'You Can't Hurry Love', it was number one. I'd rather have had silence, but Poll said the radio would take my mind off the contractions.

'When is it time to go to the hospital?' I kept asking. Phil went ching-ching-ching, ching-ching-a-ching.

'You've ages to go yet, I was hours with Roger. They get nowty at th' hospital if you turn up too early. Walk about a bit. Keep active.'

It didn't matter whether I sat, lay or stood.

'When's Roger coming?'

'We've left a message. It's an hour and a half from Sheffield. He'll come as soon as he can. He's a good lad. I only hope he teks care, there's some maniacs on t' motorway.'

He rang at teatime. That's it, I thought, time for action. When Poll put the phone down and turned round, I was waving her china beggar-girl high in the air. 'I'll smash this on the hearth NOW if you don't run me to hospital,' I shouted.

She rushed outside to where Vince was building an impromptu rockery. He'd started at lunchtime. A lot of it was broken bricks, I could see. Poll made a screwing motion with her finger against her temple, then saw me looking through the window and pretended she was scratching her head. I still had the beggar-girl in my hand. Vince came in at once and I handed him the car keys.

When we got to hospital they examined me straight away. 'You're well on,' said the midwife. 'Goodness, I should say this baby's more or less ready to be born. You left it till the last minute, didn't you? Try not to push till we get you to the delivery suite.' I was wheeled off at top speed, Phil-in-my-head sang, 'No, you'll just have to wait.' The best bit was leaving Poll standing, furious, in the corridor.

The best bit was when the pain was over and I could flop back and close my eyes.

The best bit was when they handed me the baby, wrapped in a white blanket.

The best bit was when Roger opened the door, even though he was followed immediately by Poll and Vince.

'God,' he said. 'I've thrashed that car to death. I swear the engine nearly jumped out of the bonnet. They posted a note up in the hall foyer, but I was in the library and I didn't see it till I got back in. I wish somebody would invent a phone you could carry about.'

'It's a girl,' said Poll bleakly behind him. Then she went out again, pulling Vince by his sweater sleeve.

'Still,' said Roger, 'it's pretty cool. Hey, I'm a dad.' He had a quick peer into the blanket, but the baby was just lying there with its eyes half shut. Its skin was red and flaky, like bad sunburn.

He sat down on the edge of the bed. I really wanted him to kiss me. 'You look grim,' he said. 'Did you have a rough time? Why didn't you let my mother in?'

I thought having the baby would make him forget about Sheffield. I thought once it was born, he'd stay with us.

I've never been too good at predicting the future.

# Chapter Ten

If you're a fatherless lesbian, chances are you don't know a huge amount about penises. This was all the information I'd garnered so far:

- they could be extremely dangerous
- they looked quite like a plucked chicken
- they featured on Greek vases a lot, pointing forwards like little signposts
- they worked on a hydraulic principle
- there were several components to the wobbly mass down there, although I still wasn't totally sure how many. Obviously I've seen giant willies spray-painted on bus shelters, and side-on most of them look like sports whistles. In these diagrams, the geography of testicles and phallus seemed fairly straightforward. But on the occasions I'd been flashed at, the confusion of slack pink danglies was less clear. When I was seven and innocent, I thought men had one thing in their trousers, and one thing only. Then, what happened to me behind the chemist's when I was eight showed me there were in fact two attachments hanging down between a man's

legs. Straight after, an unreliable boy at school tells me there are supposed to be three. Three? He used the phrase Meat and Two Veg. So then I thought, maybe I'd misheard and it was tentacles, and not testicles, and it was possible there was a whole clutch of wobbly bits, bunched together like a squid. Later, at secondary school, the diagrams in our biology textbook clarified the Two Veg part of the story, sort of. But even at eighteen, I wasn't clear whether the balls were arranged in separate little sacs, or one squashy cushion.

– Unless he's been the victim of a terrible accident, every man has one.

I remember the day that particular truth dawned on me; about a week after the non-existent-dog chase. The idea sent me into shock and I could barely cross the doorstep for weeks in case I bumped into a man we knew, e.g. Mr Porter at the newsagent's, Mr Rowland the vicar, the paperboy. Worst of all, that year at school I had a male class teacher called Mr Walker. So when he was settling on the carpet at storytime, I could see his penis flopping about with my X-ray imagination. And when he stood up to write the date on the board, I saw it again, swinging gently against the leg of his pants. I made it worse for myself by checking the back page of the Ladybird book Your Body every damn night and I think I'd have gone mad if it hadn't been for the summer holidays, and the promise of dry old Mrs Kirtlan next term.

It all came back to me, that time of horror, as I started to run away from the gypsy boy towards the brow. He wasn't going to rape me, I got that, but he kept shouting out for me to stop and talk, and that he knew me. He damn well didn't. I'd have remembered someone like him. It was a scam, maybe for money, maybe just to make mock. I was too wise and also too out of breath to reply. How the fuck though did he know my name and my address? Part of me wanted to turn round and see how close he was, but I was too focused on making it up the hill.

At last, when my lungs were ready to rupture and I was seeing blood-pressure stars, I let myself pause and look behind. He was still there but a long way away now. He hadn't made any attempt to pursue me at all, just stood there staring. As I watched, he raised his arm and waved. I turned and puffed on. But even as I gained the hall and slammed the front door, I thought, he still knows where to find me, any time he wants.

*

He read poetry when the pain got bad, and held my hand as she was being born.

'I wouldn't have missed this for anything,' he said as we cradled the baby together. 'Look at her. Our love meets in her tiny heartbeat.'

When I started crying for my mum, he wiped my tears away and said, 'We have to suffer loss so that new love can come into the world. It's the circle of Life.'

He always knew what to say.

*

He appeared again three weeks later, in the library. I was in the research corner, supposedly leafing through Job Opportunities in the *Bolton Evening News*, but really making a list of my all-time top-ten Emily Dickinson poems. I'd got 'I Felt a Funeral in my Brain' down at number one and I was debating which was better, 'Heaven Is What I Cannot Reach' or 'I Heard a Fly Buzz when I Died'. Then, out of all the voices, internal and external, my brain picked out someone saying 'Millar'. I jerked my head up and there he was, by the front desk.

He was standing chatting to Miss Dragon, and what was weird about it was her body language. Normally she's very stiff and brisk, and she likes to hug a bundle of books to her bosom like a breastplate. But even though gipsy boy was casual in the extreme, with his longish hair and pierced lobes, his combats and his leather wrist bands, she was leaning towards him as though she'd known him for years. And she was smiling. At one point she touched her fringe, like I've seen the girls at school do when they're talking to someone they fancy.

I tuned in more and heard her say, 'It's an unusual spelling,' and 'I had an aunt who lived in Nantwich. A beautiful church, I remember, with a square or a green in front of it.'

'We're not big church-goers,' he said. 'Mum's a pagan, if she's anything. But it is pretty nice, yeah. I like churches, they've got power. Specially the Gothic ones.'

As I watched, his eyes met mine and I started in my seat. I could have crawled under the desk, but too late, Miss Dragon was turning my way and nodding her head, then coming out from behind the desk in a purposeful way. He stood back for her politely and she noticed, and gave a tiny twitch of her lips.

'Kath-Kat,' she said, as she came up close. 'I have a young man here who'd like to meet you.'

We could all have been at a cocktail party.

'Hello,' he said, standing at a careful distance. 'My name's Callum. Callum Turner.' Big grin, eyebrows well up. I noticed he'd got a necklace or something peeping out of his collar.

'Callum's been doing some research into his family tree,' said Miss Dragon, looking down at me kindly. 'He's been travelling round the country searching out distant relatives.'

'Well, I'm going to. This is my, you know, first stop.'

I turned to Miss Dragon, excluding him. 'I don't know anyone called Turner, Poll's never mentioned any Turners.'

Miss Dragon inclined her head, inviting him to speak.

He said; 'I might be your cousin. I think, and obviously I could be wrong, but I think my mum was your mum's sister.'

I had a hot flush while his words sunk in. I must have gone a funny colour because Miss Dragon said, 'Come in the back office. You'll be private there for half an hour or so.' I didn't move. 'Come on. It's not an offer open to everyone.' She went behind me and took the back of the chair in her hands. I got to my feet.

'My mother isn't here,' I said, swallowing. 'We don't know where she is. She ran off eighteen years ago. When I was a baby— Oh Christ, do *you* know where she's living?'

'No,' said Callum. 'God. Sorry about that. Bummer.' Miss Dragon glanced from me to him, and ushered us towards the Private door.

When we were nearly there, Miss Dragon put her hand on my arm and drew me away. 'Excuse us for a moment,' she told Callum. Then she lowered her voice. 'If you don't want to speak with him, Kat, say. I thought you'd be excited to meet someone who knew some more about your family, but I didn't realize he was going to come out with something of that magnitude. I had absolutely no idea. I may have acted precipitately. So please don't feel you have to talk to him.'

'No, I do.'

'It might be, well, disturbing if you don't hear good news. You don't know what he's going to tell you. Or he might not tell you anything.'

'I know.'

Miss Dragon nodded. 'Would you like me to stay, then?'

'You can't, can you? You need to be on the desk.'

'Miss Ollerton could . . . No, you're right. I do need to be out front. But I'm only just outside if you need me. Yes?'

'Don't tell anyone what he just said, will you? No one *at all*.' I heard the tremor in my own voice.

'Of course I won't. It's not my secret to tell.' She showed us through the door, and scanned round the room quickly. 'Make a coffee if you want one, the kettle's in this corner, and there are some chocolate digestives in the Ryvita tin. Don't touch that bag of bananas, though, they're Miss Ollerton's. Shift those catalogues, that's it. I'll pop back in twenty minutes or so.' Then the door was closed behind her, and we were on our own.

'This is a big privilege,' I heard myself say.

'What, talking to you? I know it is. I'm honoured.'

'No!' I was gabbling. 'I mean being in here. It's Miss Stockley's territory. The whole library belongs to her, well not really, but she thinks it does. So being in here's like the Inner Sanctum.'

'Procul, o procul este, profani,' said Callum.

'You know Latin?'

'My mum taught it me. That's from Virgil. I know some Greek too. Are we having a drink, or what?'

He got up and put the kettle on, while I thought about clashing rocks and whirlpools. If the situation got out of hand, all I had to do was open the door and walk out.

'OK, me. I'm seventeen, and I'm in the sixth form at Crewe College.' He was moving round the room, opening the coffee jar, rattling spoons, teasing open milk cartons. 'I live in Nantwich, which is in Cheshire, with my mum Jude. Our flat's above a book shop where I sometimes do casual work, although mostly I sit and read the stock instead of serving customers. Luckily the owner fancies my mum, although she doesn't fancy him because he's so old. My dad exited the scene when I was still little, and I don't care because my mum's so cool about everything. She doesn't bother much with men, it's me and her, we're pretty close. My best friend's called Sam Haslam, my favourite film of all time is *Reservoir Dogs*, I hate McDonald's and my ambition is to buy a croft in north-west Scotland.' He picked up the kettle to pour and paused. 'That's about everything. My life in fifteen seconds. What you see is what you get; I'm the straightforward type.'

My heart rate was slowing a little. It was a small, safe room we were in. Install a bed and I could have lived here quite happily. You could tell everything was in its right place; the marker pens snug in their plastic wallet, the files on the shelves in alphabetical order with their fronts all flush, even the row of pencils had been arranged in order of height. This was the kind of environment I could imagine working in, one day, maybe, with Miss Dragon to watch over me.

'I'm sorry I ran off, before.'

He gave a short laugh. 'Christ, no, don't apologize, Kat. That was my fault, I did it all wrong, what a dickhead. You must have thought I'd escaped from somewhere. I'm amazed you didn't ring the police. The trouble with me is I just jump in.'

'You were quite scary.'

''What, me? Ha ha, I like it.' He waved a teaspoon triumphantly in the air. 'My mates would piss themselves if they heard you say that. My nickname's Mary at college. My motto is, if there's any trouble, leg it. Anyway, I'm sorry for frightening you. I just really wanted to speak to you about the family. Do you take sugar? Oh, there isn't any. Here you go.'

He placed the mug down in front of me, slid into his seat opposite and then pushed the tin of biscuits into the middle of the table. I shook my head. Even one would have choked me now. Up close I could see the dark bristles on his chin and the hairs on his forearms, the way the necklace chain rolled across his throat when he spoke. What was he seeing when he looked at me? Was he disappointed? He didn't seem it. I tried hard to sit still and not keep shifting in my chair.

'So your mum's a teacher?' I asked, more to break the silence than because I wanted to know.

'You must be kidding. Well, except in the sense she taught me. I got six GCSEs and I never set foot in secondary school. But I'm at college now just to see if I can bag a couple of A2s at the end of next year. Mum doesn't believe in formal education, she reckons it stifles individuality. School stifled her; she spent all her time rebelling against the system. Then she went off to uni and totally went off the rails.'

'What did she do?'

'Well, she had me, for a start.' He laughed. 'Big surprise for everyone.'

I shivered at the coincidence. 'Is she older than my mother? Why aren't they still in touch?'

'I don't know anything about her, not a thing. Sorry. Mum won't say a word. I managed to get out of her about your mother being involved with a man called Roger Millar, and his mum's name being Pollyanna – there aren't many Pollyannas around. That's how I tracked you down. But I guess they had some kind of major row before that because Mum won't even talk about their childhood together. It's like a closed book. I don't think she's got any idea her sister disappeared, what did you say, eighteen years ago?'

'Will you tell her?'

'I don't know. This family tree is something I'm doing for myself and I don't want to go upsetting Mum unnecessarily. There's something really hectic in the past that she just won't discuss.'

A sepia Philip Pullman looked kindly down at the back of Callum's head. You know, I'm normally dead shy with strangers, I felt like saying. But the situation here was so extraordinary. My heart was beginning to slow, I felt ready to tell him something back.

'Well, we don't talk about Elizabeth in our house 'cause

my grandma hates her. Loathes her. Won't have her name mentioned.' How to convey to him the emotions attached to my mother.

'Because she ran away and left you?'

'That, and . . . Poll – my grandma – feels Elizabeth was responsible for my father's death.'

Callum's jaw dropped. 'Shit. That's terrible. Was she?'

'Yes, basically. God, do you really want to hear this?'

'If you want to tell me.'

Through the pane of glass in the door I saw Miss Dragon give me a little wave. I felt a surge of excitement that he was going to listen to every word I said. For once I'd be in control of the narrative.

'Yeah, it's all right. I mean, if you're family, I suppose you should know. It's not like it's a big secret, everyone in this village knows the bare bones. But we don't ever discuss it now at home. Poll told me the once what happened, then whenever I asked again she'd just clam up. My great-aunt Cissie's filled in some of the details.'

I took a deep breath.

'They were in his car, coming back from Sheffield, when they started arguing. I don't know what about; Poll says they were always at it. Elizabeth was very bitter about having to give up university and stay at home with a baby. Because *she* got pregnant while she was still at school, which is weird – and she resented Dad his freedom, so it was probably that they were rowing about.'

Callum was leaning forwards, frowning. 'So what happened? Did they crash?'

'Yes. She grabbed the steering wheel and a lorry was coming the other way . . . She admitted it all at the inquest.

She didn't try and hide her guilt. Apparently she wasn't injured at all, not one scratch. And luckily I was at home in my cot, with Poll. I was only a few months old.'

'My God,' Callum breathed. 'So your dad was killed outright?'

'I think so. In his new car that he'd got for his eighteenth. Poll's world more or less fell apart, and she took it out on her husband Vince, and on Elizabeth.'

'Why on Vince?'

'Because he'd bought the car, I suppose. I expect she hated everybody. Mostly she hated my mother. I'm not surprised Elizabeth ran off, rather than live in that house of venom, but you'd think she'd have taken me with her, wouldn't you? What sort of sick mind leaves her baby in the care of a woman she detests? Anyway, sorry, she's your aunt, maybe you can see a better side to it.'

Callum was looking dazed. 'I don't know what to think,' he said.

'Then Vince went too, pretty much at the same time, so that left me and Poll, and that's been the household ever since. She made it legal by adopting me when I was about four, although sometimes I think it was just so she could avoid having a Castle around, that was my mother's name; your mother's name, obviously. I wish I could say we were as close as you and your mum, but we're not. I look after my grandma because she's disabled and she needs me, but at the same time she hates relying on me so she's usually in a foul temper. I can't ever call her Grandma to her face 'cause that's too cuddly a name. She's not a cuddly sort.'

'Sounds grim. So where did Vince go? Is he still in touch?'

'God, no. Poll would have him shot if he ever turned up on our doorstep. He didn't just leave, he ran away with a fancy-woman; I heard that part from Cissie. And we've not heard a dicky bird from him since. Alien abduction, emigration, the Foreign Legion; take your pick. He's not coming home again though, that's for sure. Not unless he wants a bullet through his neck.'

'Jeez,' said Callum, swirling his coffee mug round and staring into it. 'Hey, you don't think they're together, do you? Elizabeth and Vince? Love on the run?' He smirked in a way that made me cross.

'No I bloody don't. He was old enough to be her dad, for a start.' I wondered then if I'd told him too much. Just because he knew some Latin didn't necessarily mean he wasn't up to something. 'By the way, how come you're not called Castle, Callum Castle?'

He laughed easily and drained his cup. 'My mum married my dad. David Turner. They may only have been together for a year but she kept the name. Couldn't be bothered to change it, probably. Any more questions?' He put his head on one side, and his earring glinted in a way that made me think of the Ladybird book of *Pirates*. You'd suit a bandanna, I nearly said.

'Yeah. How come you didn't go to your maternal grandparents first if you had questions about your aunt? They'd be the ones with the info, surely?'

He sighed and folded his hands on the table in front of him.

'They'd have been my first port of call. But my gran's got Alzheimer's, doesn't know me from a root vegetable, and my grandad, ahm, passed away eighteen months ago. At

Christmas. Not a good time to lose someone. We knew he'd been ill, although my grandma was having trouble taking it in, Alzheimer's makes you totally selfish, you know. Then she wouldn't believe he'd died. Mum was on anti-depressants. It was—'

He broke off.

'Sorry. I wasn't casting doubt. I was interested in the process of finding someone.'

He got to his feet, scooped up the mugs by their handles and placed them on the draining board. 'Sure, of course.'

I stood up automatically to rinse the cups clean and, for a moment, I almost put my hand on his arm. I didn't, because a zillionth of a second later I came to my senses and turned the movement into a stretch towards the tea towel.

'All right?' he asked, turning round suddenly.

Through the glass, Miss Dragon raised her eyebrows at me. I gave her a smile but she carried on watching until old Mr Gardner tapped her on the arm and thrust a newspaper clipping under her nose. She led him away to the photo-copier and I heard myself saying, 'I've got a photo of her, of Elizabeth, if you want to see it sometime.'

'Cool. I could get to meet the one and only Pollyanna.'

I was pulling the door open as he spoke, but I turned back to stare at him. 'Haven't you understood what I've been saying? Don't you get it at all? She hated your aunt and she'll hate you on sight. She'll probably attack you with her stick. No way are you seeing her. *No way.*'

He shrugged. 'Whatever. I don't mind. I'd really like to see this picture, though.' He took hold of the door and held it for me, and as he raised his arm I smelt a sharp tang of, not sweat, but maleness. His forearms stretched showed the shape of muscles under the tanned skin. His face was close to mine. 'It would mean,' he said, 'an awful lot.'

*

Part of the problem was my weight. I thought the weight got expelled along with the baby. I'd never been fat before in my life, but I was now, just when it really mattered. I took his Debbie Harry poster down in the end, I couldn't stand to see her tiny thighs. When he complained, I burst into tears. I said to him, 'This isn't me, you know. This is not my body.' Not my baby either, it felt like.

This is what I felt for that baby: zero, zip, zilch, nothing, nowt. 'That's normal,' said the health visitor, the nasty big liar. You look at the front of all the parenting magazines and what you don't see is photos of bloated mum sulking in the background while the baby cries its lonely lungs out a few feet away. New motherhood was meant to be a naked pastel heaven, smiley smiley hormones, and little gums clamped on your breasts. I thought that was gross and I said so.

When he came home that Easter, I was miserable. It had been just me and the girl-baby, stuck in his bedroom. Poll clattered about downstairs, beating up the furniture it sounded like, and Vince hung around the garden, prodding at the frozen soil. I couldn't go out. At first I'd wanted to, before the baby was born, but Poll kept saying everyone would stare. So I tried, and they did. Village of the Damned. Everyone stopped to gawp but no one spoke to me. I don't know how Roger stuck living here for so long. So then I used to sneak into the fields where you hardly met anyone, and that was better. Poll didn't like it, though. 'Don't go so far. What if that baby comes and you can't get to a phone? Max Jolley across t' road were only in his back yard when he had a heart attack and died.' I took no notice; I'd have gone just to spite her. But then, after the baby was born, I stopped wanting to go out. I don't know why. I stopped wanting to wash and get dressed as well.

I made an effort when Roger came home, though. 'Blimey, you've put some meat on,' he said when he first saw me. In the back of the car, Poll smiled; I caught her in the mirror.

The first few hours he seemed pretty cheerful, but he got twitchy towards the evening. He went up the village for a breath of fresh air and he palmed a stack of ten-pence pieces before he went. When he got back, they were gone, I checked his pockets.

That night he became furious with the baby. 'Haven't you got her into a routine yet?' he snapped. 'She shouldn't be waking all through the night. You're doing it wrong.' He took a blanket out of the wardrobe and stomped off downstairs, and I've never come so close to hurting Katherine as I did during those next few hours. I didn't, though, and I'm proud of that.

I'd looked forward so long to him coming home, and yet it all went wrong. I knew there was something on his mind, it wasn't just dealing with the baby. 'Can't you shut her up?' he kept saying. Whenever Poll had her, Katherine went quiet as a lamb. 'You have to know how to handle them,' she said smugly, 'I've never had a peep out of her.' But a month after the accident, I found out she'd been slipping her sugar lumps to suck on, and teaspoons of brandy. So no bloody wonder.

Even Poll noticed something was up with Roger. 'You've ants in your pants,' she said, patting his hair as she walked round the back of the settee. 'Are you missing your pals in Sheffield? I bet y' are.'

All I could think of was that song, Please please tell me now.

Except I didn't want to know, and if he hadn't told me, he might still have been alive.

This is how the last few minutes of his life went:

Roger   I'm glad you're coming back with me for the weekend. It'll give us a chance to catch up.

Me   Yeah, on sleep.

Roger   Yeah. And I can show you where I hang out. I know you've seen my room but you've not been to the Students' Union yet. I thought we might go up to the Mandela bar this evening.

Me   Let's not stay too late, though, I'm really tired.

Roger   Aw, don't be a drag. How old are you, about forty? Anyway, I want you to meet a friend.

Me   Who?

Roger   She's called Judith.

Me   Oh.

Roger   Yeah, she's really nice. You'll have loads in common. I think you'll be soul-sisters.

Me   You just jumped a red light there, you know.

Roger   Did I? Oh well, we're still here to tell the tale. Yeah, she's really, really great, you'll really like her. And she loves babies. You'll have loads to talk about.

Me   I didn't want to talk about babies this weekend.

Roger   No, well, there's other things you've got in common, I'm sure. Are you all right?

Me   Just resting my eyes.

Roger   Right. Right. It's a funny thing, though, modern culture. You know, the way we have rules for everything. You know, like, say, marriage and relationships.

Me    Mm.

Roger    Yeah. I was reading a book on it before I came
         back. Fascinating stuff. There's love, this timeless,
         er, thing, and then every hundred years or so, a
         new set of conventions attached to it by the
         so-called moral guardians of society. I mean, the
         Ancient Greeks were much more fluid about love.
         They didn't have this rule, this arbitrary rule about
         how if you love one person then you can't love
         another. They said that the more you loved, the
         more love there was to go around. That trying to
         use up love was like trying to empty the sea with a
         cup. And that trying to put a fence round your love
         was like tying a rope around a beam of moonlight.
         Couldn't be done. Because love, particularly sexual
         love, you know, passion, is an elemental force. You
         can no more govern it than you can command the
         tides. It's too powerful.

Me    Mm.

Roger    And, if you think about it, no one who has more
         than one child is ever seen as betraying their
         firstborn by making it share its parents' love with
         someone else. Society accepts the sharing of love in
         that context, no problem. Which is right. Love isn't
         finite. Love feeds on love. Love begets love.

Me    Mm?

Roger    So, this twentieth-century fashion for monogamy
         is really unnatural, and actually spiritually stifling. It's
         really unhealthy. For instance, if you said you loved
         someone else, another man, I wouldn't be fussed.
         I wouldn't. Because that wouldn't necessarily mean

you loved me any less. It might mean you loved me
more, because your life had been, what, enriched,
and you'd grown emotionally. You see, the more
you love someone, the more you want to give
them their freedom. That's the mark of a really
strong relationship. And there aren't many people
who'd be . . . advanced enough to accept that.
That's why I'm glad I've got someone like you.

Me     You what?

Roger     Because I know you'll accept the situation with
Judith for the reasons I've just outlined.

Me     The situation with Judith?

Roger     You can help each other. Judith's a lot like you, she's
a clever girl. She's reading classics, you should hear
her talk. Really interesting. You'll like her. And what
I'll do is, I'll set you up in Sheffield together, find a
little terrace. 'Cause I know things are tough with
my mum; well you can move out and come and be
near to me. That's what you wanted, isn't it? And
there's no need to worry, Judith knows all about
you and Katherine. She's very interested in your
situation, supportive—

Me     Are you having an affair with her?

Roger     That's a very bourgeois term. I didn't think you'd be
so judgemental, I've always admired you for your
independent thinking—

Me     Shit. Is she pregnant? Is she? She is, isn't she,
I can tell by your face. Answer me. Oh for Christ's
sake, look at me, at least bloody look at me when
you're pulling my world down around my ears.

## Swallowing Grandma

Stop driving, pull over now and LOOK AT ME!
LOOK AT ME!

It's true, I did want to kill him at that precise moment but I'd never have had the wherewithal to do it on my own. It was his bad luck about the lorry on the other carriageway.

# Chapter Eleven

We met again in the library, with Miss Dragon as unofficial chaperone. I wasn't ready to have him in the house, I couldn't be doing with the subterfuge just yet.

'Is it not a bother to keep coming all the way up from Nantwich?' I asked as we settled ourselves into the study corner.

He pulled off his backpack and shoved it under the table. 'Soon as I pass my test I'm getting a Micra, Mum's promised she'll go halves with me. In the meantime she runs me into Crewe and there's a train goes straight through, although I seem to be the only one that ever gets off at Bank Top. I think it carries on to Blackpool. One day I might stay on it. I've never been, have you?'

'Not since I was about ten. My dad used to go a lot, to see the waxworks. Apparently there was a fantastic display of diseases there.'

'How do you mean?'

'Wax models of an arm covered in the measles rash, a foot with gangrene, various degrees of burns on flesh. You were supposed to be over eighteen to view them, but he used to march in long before that and no one ever challenged him.' Poll had told me she thought this display had been responsible for making Roger want to go into medicine. 'He used to pore over them cases,' she said. 'All the other children wanted to see the famous murderers, but not my Roger.' There were some terrible venereal diseases on display too. It was from Poll I learned that syphilis can eat away your nose and make you mad. She didn't tell me there was a cure. Sex was dangerous, all heartache and humiliation, she said; and a waste of time for women. Think on.

'Tell me about him, Kat.'

'Who, my dad?'

'Yeah. He sounds really interesting.'

'I've hardly said anything about him.'

'But his story's so tragic. Really sad. And I'm interested in the whole family.' He smiled at me the way Errol Flynn smiles at Olivia de Havilland in *Captain Blood*. I'd never seen such eyelashes on a man.

Across the room a grandma-type sat engrossed in *Peepo* while her toddler pulled out the contents of her handbag, one by one, and stuffed what would fit behind the nearest bookcase. Miss Mouse was returning videos to the carousel stand by the door, and glancing at the wall clock every ten seconds.

'I thought you wanted to see this photo?' I said, pulling it out of my carrier bag. I'd stuck it between the pages of my Emily Dickinson.

'Yeah, I do, I do. Pass it over.'

I slid it across the polished table and he caught it with his fingertips and twirled it round so it was the right way up. The effect on him was extraordinary.

First he stared, sort of shook his head, then stared again. Next he flipped the photo over to look at the back, but there's nothing there at all, it's completely blank. He turned it over once more and I could see his gaze sweeping up and down it, from one side to the other. He leant right over it, peering, and when he raised his head, his cheeks were flushed.

'Haven't you seen a picture of your aunty before?' I asked, surprised by the level of emotion he seemed to be feeling.

He was silent for a moment, then said, 'This is your mum?'

'Yeah,' I said. 'It was in the pages of my dad's textbook. That's why it survived; Poll threw everything else out after my mother left. She must've missed this.'

'Right,' said Callum, his colour fading a little. 'Only, it's a shock. To see her after all this time. Put a face to her.' I thought his hand might be trembling slightly, but then he laid the picture down, grinned broadly, and leant back in his chair.

'Does she look like your mum?' I craned to see the figure again, even though it had been etched on my brain for years; in case seeing it here, now, might somehow have changed the detail.

'Hmm. A bit.' He still had this massive smile on his face. 'It's so nice to have found you, and this branch of the family. You know? Can you understand? It's always been the two of us, Mum and me, so it's amazing to discover all these other people in the bloodline.'

'I can understand that.' The tiny pale woman still leant against the scarlet Metro, still held her bump shyly. 'I must get my dark hair from Dad, although Poll says I was blonde at birth and it all dropped out, typical. I wonder how many months pregnant she was there. It's so strange both our mums, both sisters getting caught the same way.' Except your mum kept you, lucky bugger.

'Yeah, and both not having dads; I know. We're sort of, linked.' He rubbed his hands over his face as if he was washing, then dragged his fingers through his hair at the sides. 'Look, Kat, I know I can't take this—' He held up the photo between his thumb and forefinger, and I thought his gaze would scorch the paper.

'It's my only one,' I said. 'I haven't the negative or anything.'

'Of course, yeah. Here. But I wondered, since we're in a library, can I have a photocopy? A black-and-white one'll do.'

'I suppose so.' I wondered if it was all right to let him share the picture that no one else in the world knew about. 'You're very serious about all this, aren't you?'

'It's family,' he said simply. 'It's important to me to know where I come from. And I honestly *don't* know where your mum's living, if that's what you're thinking. You have to trust me, I'm not about to track her down. Unless—'

'What?'

He leaned towards me and spoke quietly. 'Unless you want me to. I could have a go. Electoral rolls, the Internet; it's how I found your grandma. I couldn't promise anything, but there are Web sites where people leave messages . . . '

For five seconds I felt as dizzy as I did when Callum first presented himself. My God: to ask her, to tell her, to see what she was like, see where I came from. But then anger flashed through me like a fireball and burnt every other emotion away. It always does. My mother *is* anger. To remember her existence, and what she did to me, is to throw me into instant rage. 'God, no. *She* left *me*, why should I go running after her? I don't care where she is. She stopped mattering to me the day she walked out.'

I paused and lowered my voice again to a more normal, appropriate-for-a-library pitch. 'Sorry. I actually don't care, she's nothing. I only keep this photo to spite Poll. Do you want two copies, one extra for your mum? Or aren't you going to show her?'

'Haven't decided,' he said, retrieving his backpack. 'Play it by ear.'

No one is allowed to even breathe near Bank Top Library photocopier, much less lift the lid and press the red button. Terrible catastrophe will ensue if a member of the general public runs amok and attempts his own copying. Besides, it's 5p a sheet and Miss Dragon won't have anyone swindling the system. She likes to be there to count you down. But Miss Dragon was now with the computers, helping a young man type out a letter of application; we went and hovered by his machine but she was pretty engrossed. We had a hunt round for Miss Mouse, and tracked her to the office.

'Shall we knock?' asked Callum.

'I don't think we should, no. She might be on her lunch break.'

'Some lunch,' said Callum, blocking the glass square with his head. 'That is well odd. Oops. Come away.'

'Why? Let me see.'

'No. Shift.'

I let him lead me back to the photocopier. 'What was that in aid of?'

'Because she saw me looking in and she seemed a bit pissed off about it. Have you ever seen anyone eat a banana with a teaspoon?'

'A teaspoon?'

'Yeah, cutting teeny weeny slivers and sipping them off the end of the spoon. Like this. Really dainty. She must be sweltering as well, a long-sleeved jumper in this weather.'

It was true; even I had a blouse on. 'I've never seen her in anything other than baggy tops and long skirts, now you mention it. I get the impression she'd like a big shell, along the lines of a tortoise, that she could creep into when threatened. She always looks happiest in a cowl neck—' But I got no further because Miss Dragon was marching over, a nasty frown disfiguring her face. Surely it couldn't be for us?

'I'd rather you *didn't* spy on my staff when they're on their break,' she snapped, using the scary voice she uses with ordinary customers. 'What is it you want that's so urgent?'

'Photocopy.'

Callum tried a dazzling smile on her, but she took no notice, just whipped up the lid of the machine and slapped the picture face down.

'Two, please.' My voice was nearly a whisper.

She sighed heavily and pressed reset, then dip-dip for Number, then Start. The machine whirred, lit up, and two sheets skimmed out into Callum's waiting hand. His attention captured once more by the grainy lady, he could only hold out a ten-pence piece in Miss Dragon's general direction. She snatched the coin out of his open palm and stalked off to the till.

'That was awful,' I said. Out of all proportion I felt lousy.

Poll could carp round the clock and it all rolled off me, by and large; but Miss Dragon was special. *I* was special. 'She's never cross with me. Why's she in such a mood?'

Callum didn't care about Miss Dragon. 'She's just an old bat. Never mind her. Bad day at Menopause City.' He folded the pages carefully so the crease went around the edges of the image and not through it, then pushed it into a pocket of his backpack. 'Right, come on, I've had enough of this place. Stop moping now and tell me where I can get a proper coffee. Because you were going to tell me about your dad, if you remember.'

'Was I?' I said miserably. 'I'll need to get my carrier bag.'

'Go on then,' he said. 'Scoot.'

*

One day they'll invent a drug that can locate and destroy specific memories. Or they'll learn to shave bad times off your brain with a scalpel like slices of truffle.

I could have taken a chainsaw to my head. 'That's shock,' the doctor said somewhere in my subconscious. 'Or maybe concussion.' Total shut-down, I'd have called it; walking around the ward, blank-eyed. Two days later they shone a light in my face and I came to screaming. Tak-tak-tak went the doctor's shoes on the lino as he came to see me. He was pleased with the tears. 'That's healthy,' he said. 'We might be able to let you go before too long. Maybe when your hand's healed. We'll see.' Clang went the chart at the end of the metal bed. Tak-tak-tak.

I looked at my hand, which was bound up in a fat white bandage. I remember that, I thought. I put out my hand to grab the steering wheel back and pull us back out of the way. Something sharp cut me. I did try to save him.

A nurse came later to change the dressing. 'We've disconnected that hot drinks machine now,' she said. 'We don't want any more patients sticking their fingers under boiling water. Whatever were you thinking of?'

Then Vince turned up, looking like a corpse.

*

As we walked out of the library I glanced up at the sky, and directly above us was a cloud-placenta with a trailing umbilical cord. Callum said, 'Look at that cloud up there. It's exactly like a tree, isn't it? Freaky.'

'My dad,' I said, 'was handsome and clever. He'd have been a doctor if he hadn't died.'

'I fancy being a doctor,' said Callum. 'Bit late now, though. Have you any pictures of him?'

I laughed. 'No shortage there. We've got about two hundred stashed away in albums, and we'd have them all out on display if Poll's eyesight was up to scratch. The best one's in my room, him in his suit before he went up to uni for his interview. It makes Poll cry if she looks at it for long enough.'

'And you? Does it make you cry?'

'It's not the same for me, I never knew him. But I wish nearly every day he was still around. He'd know what to do, about . . . the future and things. Do you fancy beinga Methodist for half an hour?'

'A Methodist?'

'Their coffee's only instant, but they do make exceedingly good cakes.' I pointed at the poster outside the church. 'In aid of Lifeboats, 10.30 till 12.30. We're just in time.'

Callum looked doubtful. 'Don't you have to be religious to go in there?'

'Don't be daft, they only want your money. Just *look* holy. Don't start swearing at the top of your voice.'

It's a modern building, square and functional, with thin grilles over the windows to stop kids chucking bricks through the panes. There used to be a lovely old Gothic chapel, built in the 1800s, further down the main street; there are prints of it in the library. But the chapel got knocked down in the seventies to make way for a mini housing estate.

The new place was light, full of blond wood, and the metal grilles didn't stop the sun from flooding into the large foyer. Through a glass-panelled door you could see the church proper, a wall-hanging of a dove vomiting a rainbow, pews, a small plain altar covered with a white cloth. Here in the entrance there were children's drawings, posters and leaflets advertising community events, and small tables dotted around with plastic stacking chairs. Most of the tables were now empty but there was a tray piled with dirty crockery in the corner.

'Two coffees and two pieces of sponge cake,' I said to the old bid behind the table.

'My mother's favourite hymn's "For Those in Peril on the Sea",' said Callum piously behind me.

'Go and sit down,' I hissed. 'I'll get these.'

*Beautiful World* said a poster behind the counter, featuring two little girls, one black, one white, picking buttercups in a field. Old Bid collected all the components slowly, but did the sum in her head like lightning. 'Two pounds forty, and you're Pollyanna Millar's granddaughter, aren't you? Little Katherine.'

I dropped my head and spoke to my shoes. 'Yeah.'

'You'll not remember me, will you?'

'No.'

'Janey Marshall. I used to come round collecting catalogue money, d' you not remember? And you once fell while I was there and split your lip on t' step, and I gave you my hanky till it stopped bleeding? Are you sure you don't remember? Mind, you'd only have been about six. You were in a state. And you're getting a big girl now, aren't you? A big bonny girl. How's your grandma?'

'Fine.' I turned rudely away with the coffee but she came after me, passing *Let there be no strife For we be brethren*: picture of a happy football crowd, some wearing red, some wearing blue.

'I'll bring these plates for you, save your legs. And oh, who's this young man?'

It's at times like this I resolve to go and live in Australia. I'd write to Aunty Jean tonight about citizenship.

'I'm—' began Callum.

For a moment my heart stopped.

' – a friend from school.'

Old Bid Marshall put the plates down and looked at him over her glasses. 'I thowt as you went to a girls' school. Have they gone co-educational now?'

You cunning old bag, I thought. 'Only a bit in the Sixth Form. But he's my best friend's brother.'

'Kat's helping me do a history project,' said Callum. 'Do you want to see?' He started to pull open his backpack. Old Bid Marshall stepped forward. 'It's about prostitutes in nineteenth-century Lancashire,' he explained, drawing out a folder and making as if to open it. 'We've uncovered some fascinating facts. Here, take a look.'

'Well, well. Eeh, very good.' She stepped back with the expression of a woman who's been handed a cobra to nurse. 'They do some stuff in schools now. Eh, I don't know.'

'Go on,' urged Callum, pushing the folder towards her. 'Really. Be my guest.'

She gave an unhappy chuckle. 'I've no time to be looking at projects. That won't get the washing-up done, will it?' And she scooted off back to the counter and started putting cups into towers.

'What the hell did you say that for? God. That'll be all round the Over Seventies by teatime. Why prostitutes?'

Callum pushed his chair back so he could tip it against the wall. 'Why not? It came into my head and I said it. Got rid of her, didn't it?' *I shall light a candle of understanding in thine heart*, said the poster behind him: photo of candle.

'What'll I say if it gets back to Poll? What if she asks who you are?'

'Say what I did. Friend's brother. You bumped into me at the library and you were only being polite. You had no idea what my project was about when you agreed to help.' He put his hands behind his head and looked pleased with himself.

I huffed a bit and ate my cake while he rolled a cigarette for later.

'So go on, tell us about your dad. He looked like you, you said?'

I gave a hollow laugh. 'I said he had dark hair like mine.

Although he started off blondish in the baby photos. I'll bring some along next time. My grandma was enthusiastic but terrible when it came to taking photographs, so a lot of the pictures we have are out of focus or too dark, or he's missing body parts. And a lot of them are from the seventies so he's got this girly hairdo. But there's a nice clear close-up of him on the beach when he was ten, in a Cresta T-shirt; it's good because he doesn't know it's being taken, he's watching a crab die, so he looks serious. In every other photo we have he's flashing his teeth and striking a pose.'

'I'd like to see him.'

'Yeah, well, we'll sort something out. I wish I could tell you more about your aunt.'

'Hmm,' said Callum. 'Never mind.' He opened his folder and took a biro out of a side pocket in his backpack. 'Do you mind if I jot some of what you say down? I'll forget it otherwise, and it's important.'

I felt a bit shifty about that, but what could I say? 'If you really want to. What's actually in this notorious folder? Apart from prostitutes.'

He held it out across the table and flicked some pages quickly in front of my eyes.

'Mainly private stuff. Me. Some poems I wrote, my top-ten films and books, fantasy governments, a letter to my MP I once drafted. The start of a novel. A few diary entries. I take this folder around with me in case I have an idea for something. I'm going to stick that photocopy of – your mum into it, and I'd like to make a list of things about your family. Like, say, your mum's birthday and your dad's favourite bands; just, you know, trivia.'

I picked up the black ring binder and turned it over to

see the front. 'Oh, wow.' Callum had covered it with photographs of clouds, some of them really dramatic. There were wispy cirrus, stripy cirrocumulus, glowering cumulonimbus, plus two fantastic sunsets that could have been scenes from heaven, or hell. 'Did you take these?'

'Uh-huh. I love skies. Mum does too. She likes the sky at night best though. She reads the stars. She can draw up charts and things; it's not rubbish. People come to her for readings.'

I was still studying the photos, trying to make them out as picture-messages. 'Why did you take these particular clouds, though?'

'Dunno.' He tipped his chair back onto solid ground. "Cause they're interesting. No reason, really; sky appreciation. Everyone goes round looking downwards when they should be looking up. Do you ever look at the sky through Polaroid lenses? Fantastic definition of all the light and dark, like an oil painting or something.' He paused, half-turning the folder on the table, admiring his own work. 'These ones are all enhanced with filters. You don't ever get proper lavender skies. That sunset, it wasn't so amazing in real life. You can do all sorts with filters; every sky can be a sunset, if you want; you can turn a summer day into a thunderstorm just by fitting the right attachment over the lens. You feel like God.' He pulled the folder back and opened it again, leafing through for a blank page. 'OK.' He clicked his biro into action. 'Hey, I tell you what, though, I'm getting desperate for a fag now. Another five minutes and we'll make a move, shall we?'

I shrugged.

'I'll make these notes first.' He scribbled for a while and I finished my coffee. I could have taken the cup back to the counter in a helpful way, but I didn't. 'What sort of music did your parents like?' he asked finally.

'I don't know anything about my mother, I said. I'm not interested, and Poll wouldn't tell me if I was. Now Dad liked classic eighties stuff, the Jam, Pretenders, Debbie Harry, Adam Ant. I've got all his tapes and LPs; some of them are really good. I reckon one of his favourite albums was *Dare* by The Human League, because the cover's so scruffy. It looks like it's been played to death, and he's given some of the songs on it star ratings in red pen. 'Love Action' gets the highest, he's written 'I believe in the truth though I lie a lot' along the top, and 'You know I believe in love' on the flyleaf of his chemistry textbook. It's a great song. Do you know it?'

'No. But I'd like a copy. Can you get me one?'

There was no way he was borrowing the original. 'I don't know.'

'Give us a list and I'll download them off the Internet. Do you know what films he liked?'

'Haven't a clue. Poll's keen on Ronald Coleman, Errol Flynn, David Niven, anyone with a tiny 'tache. I quite like some of those old black-and-whites myself, although having to explain to Poll what's going on all the time's a pain.'

Callum had stopped taking notes. 'Listen,' he said, not meeting my eye properly, 'I don't suppose your dad left any letters, did he, in with the photographs?'

'Letters? Who to?'

He turned in his chair and began lengthening the straps on his backpack. 'I don't know; your mum, maybe. Or her letters to him.' He cleared his throat. 'All it is, I reckon you find out people's true personality in letters.'

My heart started to beat fast. 'I don't get you. You're asking me about private letters, to see private letters? Even if there were any, I wouldn't show you. I wouldn't read them myself. They'd be love letters.'

He had the grace to look ashamed. 'Sorry, you're right. Don't know what I was thinking of.'

No, neither do I, I thought.

'I need a fag,' he said. 'Come on.'

\*

We were in a house that was Poll's, and not Poll's. The same porch, leaded windows, stairwell, back kitchen, but none of the detail right. Hardly any furniture. I wondered at first if they'd decorated, but this was all old with dirty carpets and marks on the walls. Vince took me up to the bedroom and I thought, aye-aye, but all he did was show me the camp bed with one of Poll's bedspreads on it. He'd brought some books and a radio. 'I thowt as you'd want to come reahnd a bit, befoore I fetch y' 'ome,' he said.

I slept and slept.

Next day when he came he stood and looked at me for a long time, then he hauled me up and steered me through to the bathroom. He started taking my sweater off, lifting my arms up like a child. I remember my heart plummeting, but not being able to resist.

'Can you wesh yoursen?' he said. I didn't say a word. So he went back to the bedroom and brought a sponge bag. First he cleaned my teeth. Then he wet a flannel. 'Tek your blouse off, love. Come on.' I unbuttoned slowly. 'Now, lass, what hev you bin doin' to your arms?' he said when he saw the marks. He shook his head as though it was very heavy on his shoulders, and went out of the room. I heard his steps on the stairs, and the front door shut, but I didn't move.

'I don't know,' he muttered when he returned. He smeared the little oval wounds with Savlon and then papered me over with plasters. 'This'll hev to stop.'

He left me alone to wash my bottom half and when I came out of the bathroom, he'd gone. There were some jam sandwiches on the floor and a flask of tea. He'd left some of my clothes too, clean. The nail clippers had disappeared, though.

# Chapter Twelve

Poll was swanning about covered in fence mould. I didn't enlighten her. It was right down the back of her blouse, a great green smear on the white polyester. I saw from the kitchen window, first thing, but I didn't say anything. Her bed sheets are often marked all over from the washing line. So what, I say. She's damn lucky I launder them at all.

I was in her bad books already that day because she reckoned I'd broken her toe with a packet of fish fingers. It was true I had stacked the freezer in a rush, but it was her own fault for going in there, especially in her stockinged feet. Unluckily, you can't die from a squashed toe. 'What did you think you were after?' I said. 'You can't see the labels.'

'I just wanted summat cowd to put on my head where I bumped it,' she snapped.

Now that was my fault; I had left the kitchen cupboard open. I'd been selecting goodies for a binge later on, because the thing about bulimia is that you can actually plan round it. This is what bulimia looks like as a mathematical model:

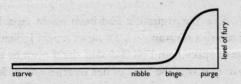

So it's easy to fit into even a busy lifestyle. I felt in total control, for once, and as a bonus, my teeth were the cleanest they'd ever been. Poll shouted of me one evening in a panic. 'What's Winston got fast round his mouth?' We watched as the dog did a good imitation of a rabies victim, rolling around on the carpet and spitting. I bent down to peer between his black lips.

'Hell, it's my dental floss,' I said, holding his head while he wriggled insanely. 'You get his back end.' So Poll got his haunches in a wrestler's grip while I unwrapped his muzzle. It's just as well he's a nice nature. 'Christ knows how he got hold of it,' I said as the last length came free. I traced the line back. 'Look, he's trailed it down the stairs like the Andrex puppy. Yuk. You wouldn't think he'd like the minty taste.'

'He eats the bread we put out for the birds even when it's gone blue,' Poll reminded me. 'And cowpats.'

For a moment there, grandmother and granddaughter were nearly getting on, but by bedtime it had all gone sour again. The same mathematical model can also be used to demonstrate why Poll and I will always essentially be at war.

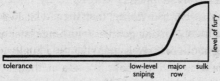

This time the argument had been about hair. I'd happened to say a woman on a TV news report looked a sight with short spiky hair. Poll had said she'd been in an earthquake so that was the least of her worries and at least you could see this woman's face when she talked. I said the reason my hair was so bushy at the moment was because it had been raining, so whatever else evil I was responsible for, Poll couldn't hold me accountable for that. Poll said, 'Yes, but you could wear a rain-hood. Why don't you wear a rain-hood? Maggie's given you dozens over the years. Slip one in your purse. You carry on like you're still seven. Why can't you act like a grown-up?' So I'd gone to the top drawer of the sideboard and got a rain-hood out and made as if I was going to garrotte Poll with it, but she turned and saw me, and twigged what I was doing. 'You're going all wrong, you are,' she shouted. 'You're going twisted like your mother.' Then she snatched the rain-hood off me and told me it was too good for me, and I grabbed it back off her and shredded the plastic in front of her face. I threw it on the floor and she screamed, 'Pick that up. Pick that up, lady!' But I just walked off and slammed the door.

Afterwards I sat in my room and thought about Callum. I didn't even know whether I was going to see him again. Being with him was like a sort of dance; when we met up I'd start off cool and awkward, then he'd say something which would make me feel as if he really understood me and I could tell him anything; then there'd be a split second when I suddenly lost confidence in him and became uncomfortable. Because who was he? What did I know about him, actually?

'I still feel terrible about Miss Dragon having a go at us,' I'd said as we walked towards the station. 'I don't even know what we did that was so wrong. Did Miss Mouse seem angry too?'

Callum took a drag of his cigarette, held the smoke in his

lungs, then breathed it out smoothly through his nose. 'Forget about it. You want to stop worrying about that pair. Couple of old lesbos.'

'What?'

'Lezzies. Ladies of the Sapphic persuasion.'

'My God, do you think so?'

'For definite. They're neither of them married. That Miss Mouse never wears make-up, has her hair short like a boy. And Miss Dragon's your archetypal bull-dyke.'

Behind him, a bank of rosebay willowherb waved in the breeze; far off I heard the hoot of a train.

'I'm surprised you never noticed,' he said.

\*

We sat in rows and you could smell the polish. I wanted to lean forward and bite the wooden back of the seat in front; instead I chewed at the inside of my cheek. I thought there'd be a jury like you see on Crown Court, but there was only a handful of us and the coroner in his dark blue gown.

'An inquest is not about establishing blame,' the coroner's clerk had said before we went in. The coroner was saying it again now from the bench. Tell Poll, I nearly shouted out. She wants me strung up.

The coroner went first with Name of the deceased and Time of death, then the pathologist gave the Cause of death which was trauma to the head and then we sang 'There is a Heavenly Land' while Poll choked and sobbed into her service sheet. The place was packed with people from the village and students.

I had to go up and swear on the Bible.

'Try to answer as clearly as you can,' said the coroner to me.

I wanted to tell him, straight out. I killed Roger. It was my fault.

I jerked the steering wheel in temper and pulled us across the road. I did try to say that but he asked me lots of questions about what I said and even as I was talking I could hear I didn't make sense. At this point, he said, I should warn you that you do not have to answer any question which you are asked in this courtroom by me or by any other party if you feel that the answer to the question would implicate you in a criminal offence. Do you understand?

I told him maybe I didn't touch the wheel, maybe I only hit the glove compartment with my fist.

After me, the lorry driver gave evidence. He was a Welshman, and thin as a rake. His eyes behind his black-framed glasses bulged with stress. 'The car just drifted across into my lane,' he whispered.

'I'm sorry,' said the coroner, 'but you'll have to raise your voice a little.'

The lorry driver wiped his glasses with a handkerchief and went on, clutching the sides of his chair. 'He was drifting. I saw what was going on and I tried to move out of the way, but I just wasn't quick enough. Lorries are heavy in the handling, they're not as responsive as cars are.'

'There was no sudden swerve on the part of the other vehicle?'

'No.'

'Are you sure?'

The lorry driver closed his eyes. 'Totally sure, good God.'

I kept quiet and watched the coffin which was pale wood with a huge wreath on the front in the shape of a heart. I thought, what did they do with his head in the end? Did they try and wrap it up in something? All that silk lining spoiled.

Another man, elderly, took the oath and said he'd been behind us at the scene of the crash and he'd seen the car drift in the same way. 'He'd been weaving for a while, a good few miles. To be honest, I thought he might be drunk.'

'Man that is born of a woman is of a few days and full of trouble,' said the coroner. 'He cometh forth like a flower, and is cut down. PC Whittle, could you give us your report on the crash scene now, please.'

PC Whittle talked about the pattern of tyre marks on the road, and the damage to the front and side wings of the car. The policeman said the physical evidence of the crash was consistent with the car having been struck a high-speed glancing blow to the extreme front offside wing, then having spun round on the road so that it was next hit squarely on the driver's door, which had caved in to some considerable degree. This suggested, he said, that the car had not swerved wildly into the lorry's path, but had been moving gradually over to the point where it was first clipped.

I imagined the coroner asking me again if I'd really grabbed the wheel. This time I'd say no, for definite. It made no difference. Roger was still dead. In my head we would always be crashing and he would always be dying; there would never be any room for anything else.

But the coroner didn't ask me again. He climbed up behind the lectern and gave his verdict. 'Without doubt, as we have heard from the pathologist, a contributory factor to Roger Millar's death was his failure to wear a seat belt. I note that his girlfriend, Elizabeth Castle, who was wearing hers and sitting alongside him, avoided sustaining any serious injury. Miss Castle feels she may have been personally to blame for the accident, but I have heard the evidence of Miss Castle and rejected it, because I believe she is confused about the details of those last few crucial seconds. She seems consumed by guilt, to a degree where her reliability as a witness is actually undermined. If she had really pulled the top of the steering wheel as she thinks she might have done, then the car would have swerved the other way, onto the left-hand verge. The weight of evidence from witnesses at the scene and from the Greater Manchester Police Traffic Department clearly suggests that Mr Millar allowed his concentration to wander during the discussion with Miss Castle, and it was this that led to the fatal collision. I therefore record a verdict of accidental death. Will the congregation now rise.'

The coffin began to move forward on the conveyor belt and the theme from *Chariots of Fire* was piped through the speakers. My mouth was so full of blood I had to swallow. The curtains closed and he was gone.

Outside the crematorium, Poll's friend Maggie was holding Katherine in her arms and jigging her up and down. She was singing, 'Andy is waving goodbye, goodbye,' under her breath. When she saw me she smiled and held Katherine out for me to take. But as soon as I touched her, the baby began to cry and I knew then she hated me.

*

I was skulking about outside the library, trying to decide whether or not to go in, when Miss Dragon pushed open the swing door and beckoned to me.

'I've got something for you.'

Bloody hell, I thought. I followed her past the video rack and the Books for Sale table to the counter.

'Here,' she said, bringing a postcard out from the shelf underneath. 'It's from your friend. He sent it here.'

The picture on the front was Glastonbury Tor by sunset, and on the back Callum had written: 'Staying with Mum's mates for two weeks in their Mediaeval barn. When I get back, I've got a present for you. Wednesday 28th OK? Late am, among the books. Cheers, Call.' Any other time I'd have been tickled by 'Kat Millar, Care Of the Library', but Miss Dragon wasn't smiling.

'There's no contact number,' I said, half to myself. 'So how can I let him know either way?'

Miss Dragon pursed her lips. 'You watch yourself. Timmy O, Danny S,' she said sternly, tapping the card with her finger. Then the phone rang and she turned away to answer it.

Timmy O? Danny S? Who where they? I hung around for a few seconds to ask, then decided I didn't care anyway and wandered back outside. I felt so lonely I almost went home and phoned Rebecca, but after a mooch round the newsagent's and a flick through some glossies, I came up with a better plan. Twenty minutes later I was on a bus to Bolton, nose in a fashion mag, a tenner filched from Poll's purse in my pocket.

*De-Fuzz for Summer Fun*, I read. *Nothing ruins a beach babe's look like a couple of coconut-style shins sticking out from under her sarong. You can forget the golden tan, the toned abs, the hot-label bikini. Furry legs say you just can't be bothered.*

*And the guys agree. 'If there's one thing that puts me off a woman's body, it's little black hairs poking out everywhere,' says Dave, 22. 'It may be OK for the Continentals, but it makes me feel sick. I wouldn't touch a hairy girl with a bargepole.'*

*Mind you, boys, it's only fair to tell you, we all loathe bristly backs on men, so if you're thinking about stripping your shirt off this holiday, you'd better sort yourselves out too!*

*Stubble Trouble*

*But with the vast range of depilatories now on the market, what is the best way to get those crucial bits smooth, sexy and strokeable? The Chique team have been road-testing the top brands and gadgets that promise no-fuss silky skin, and they've come up with some surprising results . . .*

In Boots, I took so long assessing all the products that I attracted myself a store detective, or it might have been another pervert, I'm not sure. He was definitely having a good look at my bottom. I went to stare at the tampons for a while – that got rid of him – and then came back and bought a box of wax strips. Donna used wax strips; what had she said about them? I found where the electric straighteners lived, but they were way too dear. Then I went along the hair-dye aisle and imagined what life would be like if you looked like some of these women on the boxes.

I paid for the strips and went to check out clothes.

Our whole sixth form was out that sunny Saturday. In Dorothy Perkins I saw Emma Pearson from my English set, and Surinder Badat from general studies in Woolworth's. Lissa Hargreaves was in the ladies' at Debenhams, wetting down a new perm and cursing. Serving behind the counter in W. H. Smith's was Nicky Hunter, while Donna French was pretending to browse DVDs next to her and sighing every time a customer interrupted their chat.

'Hiya,' cried Donna when she saw me. 'Hey, Nicky, it's Kat.'

Nicky looked a bit sick but managed a smile. 'Hey.'

Someone came up and asked for stamps, so Donna waltzed over to me. 'Whatcha got there, then?' I opened the bag slightly for her to peer in. 'Ooh, yikes, rather you than me. Not going for a Brazilian, are you? Yow-ow-ow.

Nasty. I'm saving up for laser treatment. For my legs, I mean.'

'Right,' I said.

'Nicky's being boring,' she said loudly over her shoulder. 'Working.'

'Earning money,' said Nicky.

'It's a drag. Anyway. You're coming, aren't you? To my do?'

'Oh, yeah.' Poll had taught me it was simplest to lie about these things.

'See?' Donna called over to Nicky. 'Kat's coming. Everyone's coming in the world, except you.'

Nicky was giving an old man some change, but when he'd gone she said, 'It's not my fault my stepdad's booked us a fortnight in Florence. I don't want to go.'

'Well, don't, then.'

'It's not as simple as that.' Nicky broke off to direct a woman to the printer cartridges. Her face was like thunder.

'Come on,' said Donna to me. 'Nicky's too busy. Let's go and have a coffee, or something.'

I didn't look in Nicky's direction as we walked away.

Anyone watching us trailing round the shops, picking clothes off the racks and holding them up against ourselves might have thought we were proper friends. She looked completely fantastic in everything she chose. I wanted to tell her that, but I couldn't because it would have sounded crap. I just looked like a barrel. At last, in Blayz, we found a really good Plus section and she pulled items off the rack for me to examine, and tutted when I rejected them.

'I don't know why you won't try that one on, it wouldn't half show off your cleavage.' She passed over a scoop-necked white top with a ruffle down the front. 'You've got bosoms to die for. You'd be causing traffic accidents if you wore this in the high street. See.' She stepped close and unbuttoned the top of my high-necked pale blue blouse and pulled the collar apart. My heart was beating somewhere up in my throat. 'Undo a few more yourself. Loosen up. That's it. Till you can see a bit of lace off the top of your bra. That looks loads better.'

We stood in front of the mirror together, then she did a neat side-step out of the reflection. I knew why she'd done that; so I wouldn't compare our figures. She's only being nice to you out of guilt, said Poll's voice, why else would she be bothering?

'Thing is,' Donna was saying, 'we've all got bits of our bodies we hate. Everyone. I've got this stupid scar on my belly button from an op I had when I was a kid. I can't stand anyone seeing it; not unless I know them very well, if you know what I mean.'

I was smoothing the white top against myself and squinting, trying to imagine it on.

'So I wear stuff that covers it up. Like, I'd never wear crop-tops with hipsters. Which is a fucking drag, actually. I never used to bother about it when I was little, until a girl at my primary school said it gave her nightmares. Katie Ainsworth, evil little cow. When we went swimming she made sicky noises in the changing rooms at me.'

I hung the top back on its rail. 'God, that's awful.'

'I got her back. Majorly.'

'How?'

Donna pursed her lips as if considering. 'Well . . . promise you won't be grossed-out by this? Because it is *pret*ty gross.'

'Go on.'

'OK. What I did was, I secretly dropped a handful of aniseed balls into the swimming pool at the shallow end where she always was, 'cause she couldn't actually swim for toffee, just mucked about with a float all the time and hung onto the edge. Within about two minutes there was a red slick all round her, it looked exactly like blood. I knew it would because a little boy in Greece last year had done the same thing in the hotel pool, and the lifeguards went mental trying to find the swimmer with the terrible injury.

'The instructor got us all out and sent us off back to the changing rooms, and while we were there I told everyone it had been Katie's period. All the other girls started screaming and trying to get under the showers, and she ran into a cubicle and wouldn't come out. The more she denied it, the more everyone believed me. By the time the instructor came in, she was hysterical. And it became one of those school legends, you know, so that whenever anyone mentioned Katie Ainsworth, it was, "Oh, she's the one who had her period in the swimming pool." '

I had my mouth open and my hand to my lips. 'Wow.'

'Told you it was gross. I don't care though, she deserved it.'

'Oh, she did.' I was so happy, to be here, in this normal clothes shop, talking about periods with Donna French..

'Are you going to buy this groovy garment, or what? For the record, I think you should.'

I shook my head. 'I haven't got enough money left.' That was true. I was relieved too, because although the top was really nice, I couldn't have faced the thought of going into a communal changing room with Donna.

'Don't be wet. Open an account,' said Donna airily, biting at a hangnail and managing to make the action look cool and provocative.

'I don't know how you do that.'

'Go over to that counter there, tell them you want to apply for a Blayz card, and I guarantee they'll be doing triple somersaults around you. Take the top. You get ten per cent off, it says on that sign.'

I wanted to say, I don't know what size I am any more, but I didn't dare. I wanted her to say, Give it to me, I'll take it for you, I'll sort you out a card. I wanted to drop the top on the carpet and run away.

She came up to me as I was still queuing. 'Are you sorted? Because I've got to go now, got to meet Nicks while she's on her lunch break. If she's speaking to me. Yeah? So, see you around? See you at my party, won't I? And on results day, oh God.' She made an unhappy mouth. 'See you.'

'Yeah,' I said, feeling suddenly flat. I looked down at the top again. There was no way I was going to be taking it home with me.

*

'She's going to have to come back with us,' I heard Vince say to Poll, over Katherine's squalling. 'She's its mother. Where else would she go?'

'Hell fire,' said Poll.

The baby carried on screaming.

*

I did it. I bought the white top, spoke to the scary girl behind the counter even though she had black nail varnish on and looked as if she could have gobbled me up for dinner. I had my library card on me, plus my Oxford letter I always carry, so that was two forms of ID. I thought everyone was watching me while I was standing at the counter, but when I turned round, they weren't. After I'd signed everything I went and tried the top on in Evans' changing rooms, which I know is a cock-eyed way to go about it, but it did fit so I didn't have to take it back. Came home to Poll's with the promise of unhairy legs and a killer cleavage, and even Dogman perched on one of the kitchen tops didn't dampen my spirits.

Poll was sitting with her elbows on the table, troughing her way through a pack of party rings. 'Dickie's brought you summat.'

'I've fetched you some chocolates,' he said. 'They've a bit of a bloom on but they taste OK.' He was drinking a bottle of cider and making a performance out of it, sticking his lips out to the neck, tonguing the rim, gasping after each swig.

'Gee, thanks,' I said as sarcastically as I could get away with.

'He's good to you, is Dickie.'

'I am,' said Dogman, and belched.

There's a pay-off, though, I felt like saying. These rubbishy gifts all came at a price. I had to put up with his weaselly eyes doing a constant body-search on me, his pathetic stream of innuendo and no-brain political commentaries, his smell. And the fact he was always in our house, winding up Poll against me, making me feel like the interloper. Mouldy chocolates were no kind of compensation.

In my head I heard Miss Dragon's voice again. 'Timeo Danaos,' she was saying. Timeo Danaos. Not Timmy O, Danny S. Timeo Danaos et dona ferentes.

'Beware of Greeks,' I said out loud, very pleased with myself.

'Beware of Greeks?' said Dogman, wiping his mouth on the back of his hand. 'I should bloody well think so. They had my wallet off me when I was in Cyprus two year ago.'

*

For days I sat like an old lady, looking out of the window in Roger's room. I shall die in this chair, I thought. Vince brought meals up, and sometimes my baby, though I don't think it did either of us any good, me or her. One of us would be in tears within minutes. No one tells you how much screaming there is, do they? You expect newborns to scream sometimes, but Katherine never stopped. For God's sake! I shouted at her. Once I tried screaming back. That brought Vince running. Afterwards he came up with a brandy. 'I don't want that,' I snapped at him. He drank it straight down and left.

Sometimes, when Poll and Vince went out, I shuffled downstairs and prowled around. I brought back books, Reader's Digests and tatty, old-fashioned children's stories. *The Inquisitive Harvest Mouse* was the best one. I wanted to climb into the pages and make friends with the little girls, swap daisy chains. I wanted to share their sunny, Fifties picnic. It looked like a warm world.

Poll's house was like ice. Most evenings there'd be shouting and thumping coming up from below. Then Vince would go out the back and chop wood with a big axe.

I knew this other girl would turn up, it was just a matter of when.

I spotted her before anyone. A brown Triumph Toledo drew up, and after a few minutes, a fair, plumpish woman got out. I pressed my face right against the glass to get a good view. She had on a denim skirt and a high-necked white blouse with a pink cardigan over the top. Nothing special. I wondered if I'd seen her before.

She stood and looked at the house, then turned and opened up the passenger-side back door. Her head disappeared as she bent to something – I knew what that was going to be – and the bottom fell out of my stomach when she straightened up and there it was, this baby. This baby in blue shorts.

Then, instead of walking up Poll's path, she started off along the pavement, towards the top of the hill. I went dizzy with relief. After a hundred yards, she turned round and came back again.

Now the wind was getting up and the clouds were rolling across the sky like speeded-up film. It was spitting with rain as well. She shivered and I saw the baby wriggle in her arms and open its mouth to cry. She opened the car door again, peered inside, then slammed it, crossly. I watched her take off her cardigan and swaddle the baby tightly up, so only its head was poking out, and kiss it, and hold it close. She looked perished. I'd never do that for Katherine, I thought. I'd hang on to my cardi and let her freeze.

I knew that next she would come through the front gate.

I went over to the bedroom door as the bell was ringing. I heard: 'Oh, hello, my name's Jude and I've come all the way from Wrenbury.'

'Oh aye, wheer's that, love?' – Vince's voice.

'Who is it?' – from Poll.

'I've come to see you about Roger.'

The front door slammed shut. I slid down the wall till I was sitting with my back against it, and waited.

It didn't take long; about ninety seconds. I heard Poll shout, and a crash like broken glass. A scraping noise, like furniture moving, a yelp of protest. I came out of the bedroom and started down the stairs.

'I'm not having it, get out! I'm not having another one in the house. You can't prove owt, we've only your word. You're after money? Well, you've come to t' wrong house. Can't you see this is a house of sorrow? What do you think them drawn curtains mean? How dare you.'

I ran back up and got to the window in time to see the girl stumbling down the path. The rain spattered hard against the pane now, distorting the detail, but I still saw Poll's Negro-lady money box smash on the brick behind her heels. The cast iron shattered apart like a bomb.

'I'll lame you!' screamed Poll, her voice almost unrecognizable. 'You've no respect – filthy liar – you ever come back here again—'

The girl almost threw her baby into the back seat. When she turned to get in the car herself, there was dark on her forehead, could've been blood, could just have been a shadow. I hoped it was blood.

As the car pulled away, tyres squealing, Katherine started to cry again.

# Chapter Thirteen

I waited till the day I was supposed to meet Callum to do the wax business.

*SILKEE Sensitive with Aloe Vera. The gentle and effective way to remove unwanted hair. Do Not use on ears, nose, eyebrows, breasts, genitals or perianal areas. Not suitable for the elderly.*

What you had to do was rub the strips of paper between your palms, as if you were praying. Then you peeled the layers of paper apart and there was a coating of what looked like earwax on each one. You pressed this to your skin, did a bit more rubbing, then dragged it off, yelping. It left a clearing of baldness in amongst the forest of shin-hair, together with some patches of scabby yellow wax. It looked as if my leg was going septic.

I tried again round the back, on my calf. Yaargh. Another smooth bit. But now I saw that if I wasn't careful I'd end up with a sort of patchwork effect, hedgerows of fuzz. So, despite the pain, I set to and pursued those remaining clumps of hair. They got smaller and smaller, till I was using a whole strip for about three of the buggers. Finally I was done. One leg was completely depilated. Then I realized I'd run out of strips.

They made it look like fun-fun-fun on the TV advert,

group of model types falling on the bed together, laughing, stroking each other's limbs. Nowhere in the proceedings does anyone cry with pain, howl, sweat or pee themselves in agony. 'With practice,' the leaflet said, 'the technique becomes easy and painless.' I could not *believe* they had been allowed to print that.

I swore a bit, then hunted out the instructions. *Each strip can be used up to three times*, it said. But when I checked the pile of discarded ones, a load were stuck to the carpet where I'd thrown them, and the ones that had made it into the bin were now covered in pencil shavings and hole-punchings. There were about four usable ones left. I picked up the bin and chucked it at the wall in temper, daft really because it would be me who'd have to clear the mess up.

It was at this point someone knocked on the bedroom door.

'Go away,' I shouted, assuming it was Poll.

The door opened a crack and Maggie peeped round. 'I'm sorry, love. I just wanted to check you was OK. I thought I heard you crying. And then there was that thud, and I wondered if you'd fallen down, or summat. But I'll leave you in peace. Sorry to disturb you.'

Now why couldn't she have been my grandma?

When I got downstairs, Maggie and Poll were getting ready to go out, Maggie discreetly removing a truly disgusting hanky from the table and swapping it for a clean one from her own pocket. She nodded at me, and I hooked the thing with the kitchen tongs and dropped it in the washer.

'Bingo,' said Poll as she wrestled to find the arm hole of

her raincoat. Luckily they've started using huge cards that even her mole-eyes can see.

'So we'll be back about four. And we're having our dinner at the Working Men's. What are you going to do with yourself?'

'Dunno,' I said, kicking the washing machine with my toe. Bugger off and leave me alone, I wanted to say. 'Might go down the library.'

'That cupboard under the sink wants clearing, if you've nowt else to do,' said Poll, stuffing the clean hanky in her bag. She made a face at Maggie. 'We had a leak, you know.'

'Oh, heck, was it your pipes?'

'No, it were one of these pouches of washing liquid. It bursted, and we didn't know till it had gone all ovver. I kept coming in here an' sniffing. Spring Fresh; by God, it did pong. Then Katherine went to get some bleach an' t' bottle were stuck to t' bottom of t' cupboard. It all needs swilling out properly.'

'That's my day sorted, then,' I muttered.

'I'll give you a hand if you wait till we get back,' said Maggie. 'You get yourself off out. You're only young, you don't want to be stuck indoors at your age. Go to the library and have some fun. Ooh, look, your belt's twisted. You must be in love.'

'That'll be the day,' grunted Poll. 'Love. Pigs might fly. Are we going, or what?'

Maggie gave me a cheeky pinch on the arm as she went past and tapped the side of her nose.

'Bloody hell,' I said under my breath.

After they'd gone I let Winston out for a totter round the garden and went to put some lipstick on. It felt peculiar, as if I'd not wiped my mouth after eating a cream cake, but I resisted the urge to rub it straight off. I brushed my hair and tied it back in a low ponytail. Then, at the last minute, I noticed through my tights that my legs had come out all spotty, so I changed into the birthday tunic top and pants. A check in the mirror showed I looked quite smart. The effect was almost ruined by a wax strip which had attached itself sneakily to my heel, but Winston saved the day by limping back in and trying to eat it.

Up at the library Miss Dragon and Miss Mouse were busy dealing with the holiday influx of schoolchildren, and I couldn't see Callum anywhere. I took myself over to the Returned Today section and was just about to start trawling through when I spotted him in Newspapers, reading the *Guardian* Media supplement.

'You look different,' I said.

'So do you.'

'No, I mean you look *really* different. Why did you cut your hair?' He'd had a clipper cut, not skinhead-short, but short. He was wearing black framed glasses and a light coloured jacket.

'Felt like a change. And it's cooler on my scalp.' He ran his hand over the top of his head, feeling the fuzz.

'And the glasses?'

'Got sick of contacts. I'll go back to them, sometime. When I get bored with specs.'

'You're like Sherlock Holmes, master of disguise.'

He pretended to be peering at me through a magnifying glass. 'The Mysterious Case of the Missing Mother. Where did Elizabeth Castle run off to when she ducked out of Bank Top?'

'That's not funny.'

'Sorry. Hey, cheer up, I've brought you some stuff you might like.'

He pulled his backpack out from under the table and flipped it open.

'Here you go.' There was a small paper bag and a brown envelope. 'This one first; this is the proper present. From my holidays. She makes them, Mum's friend, the one in the barn. Shona. She used to live on a boat in France but somebody tried to set fire to it, so she came home.'

I unpleated the top and put my hand inside. I touched something cold. It slid out into my hand like a coin.

'A wasp?'

'No, you noggin, it's a bee. She does them in enamel. You can put it on a chain if you don't like the thong.'

I was staring at it. 'Are you sure it's not a wasp? It's on the skinny side for a bee.' The back was blank metal.

'Don't be silly, that's just the style. Who'd make wasp jewellery? Bees are cool, they make honey and royal jelly, they pollinate fruit trees. And they don't sting you unless they absolutely have to. Wasps, on the other hand, are pure evil. They live in litter bins and eat carrion.'

'They're not all bad. I'll tell you something really important about wasps.'

'What?'

'Not now. Later. Maybe.'

Callum scratched his head and frowned at me. 'You're being very enigmatic today.'

Miss Dragon walked past, scanning our table as she went. 'Everything all right?'

We nodded. I held up the necklace for her to see.

'Hmm,' she said. 'A median wasp.'

'It's a *bee*, for God's sake,' laughed Callum.

'Wrong shape,' said Miss Dragon. 'The abdomen's too narrow. And the bands of black are too wide.'

'Oh, have it your own way. It's two against one. Clearly I'm in the wrong.'

Miss Dragon gave him a searching look, then went away to deal with the queue at the desk.

'God, I wouldn't like to be late returning a book here, I tell you. Scaree. Anyway, these photos, I thought you might like to see them too.' Callum nudged the envelope over towards me. 'It's written on the back who they are.'

The first was a blurry picture of what looked like a horrid red doll with an oversize head. Its legs stuck out like a frog's.

'That's me,' said Callum proudly. 'I was really premature. Mum was so ill before I was born, they thought she might die. She had pre-eclampsia and the doctors had to get me out before I died too. She wasn't allowed to move for weeks. She just had to lie flat all the time.'

There were four others of Callum; one as a toddler in a hooded suit with ears; one in his school uniform, aged about four ('I only went for two or three years, it was rubbish'); one where he was sitting on a motorbike dressed as a Cavalier and one with him standing in front of a huge unframed painting. 'I did that,' he said. 'It's in oils. It was exhibited in Nantwich museum for a couple of months 'cause it won a competition. Mum's got it in her bedroom now. It's clouds.'

'Yeah, I can see that,' I lied. 'Wow. Really good.'

'And this one's Mum.' He pointed to a photograph of a middle-aged woman with longish dull blonde hair and a round, friendly face. She was wearing a black top with an embroidered neckline, and dangly earrings. 'One of her would-be boyfriends took that last year. She doesn't like it because you can see some wrinkles, but I think it's a good likeness.'

'She has a look of her sister.'

'Yeah, I thought so. Now this one, this is the first cloud picture I ever took. No filters or anything fancy, I just pointed the lens and snapped. But the strange thing is, I took the photo because I thought it looked like a dolphin leaping out of the water, only when I got it developed, it had changed and now, can you see, it's a face. Look. Turn it round. The eyes there, and that's the mouth. A sad face.'

His finger traced the outline for me.

'Then there's this one I took at Avebury, which is through an orange filter. It's as though there's a giant finger point- ing to the tallest standing stone. Like the finger of God, except it was really an aeroplane trail.

'This next one's a place called Mow Cop, a sort of folly, and when you stand on the top you can see for miles. What I did here was to frame the section of cloud I wanted to highlight inside the stone arch, can you see? And I used a filter to give a kind of subtle rainbow effect.'

'Like petrol in a puddle.'

'Yeah, exactly. And these last two, I took them over water, Lake Coniston, so you got the light reflecting back up to the clouds and kind of illuminating them from under- neath. The filters here add some depth to the shadows, that's all.'

He changes when he talks about his photographs, I thought.

'I like this one the best.' I put my fingertips on the Mow Cop one.

'Do you? I'll make you a copy. You know, you could come down some time and see the place for yourself, bring your own camera. I might even be able to drive by then.'

'Yeah, that'd be good,' I said, knowing it would never happen but really pleased he'd asked. I could imagine us up there, staring out across the fields and towns under a lowering sky. Suddenly my empty stomach dipped, gathered itself up, then let out the most enormous whine. I froze, mid-cringe.

Callum turned his head from side to side, brows furrowed in confusion. 'That's strange. I could've sworn I heard a cat. Did you hear a cat mew?' He bent to look under the table. 'Here, puss puss. Tch-tch-tch. Nope, can't see anything.' He sat upright again and his grin started me giggling.

'Stop it.'

'It must have nipped behind the desk. Probably after a vole. Oh, wait, did you see its tail poking out then?'

'*Stop* it.'

'I think we'd better get some lunch before we both starve to death. Any minute now our intestines are going to break out into a duet, and I tell you, mine sings a lot louder than yours.'

I nodded gratefully. 'Right, well, we could get a sandwich at . . . ' My fingers touched the pendant's leather thong and I drew my wasp towards me. I would wear this. 'We could go home. Poll's not in.' I felt myself blush, but carried on. 'So she can't get cross, she needn't know. Come and see our house.'

'I thought you'd never ask,' he said.

As we walked the mile down the village to Poll's end, I pointed out Bank Top's invisible highlights. 'That's the site of a Tudor tithe barn.'

'What, that hardware shop?'

'Yeah. They bulldozed the barn in the Fifties. And across the road, all down that side, there used to be a row of stone cottages that dated from 1585. The walls were two feet thick and they had flagstones on the roof instead of slates.'

'Where those Sixties bungalows are? God, what a waste. How do you know all this?'

'School projects, and also they have some pictures in the library, have a look next time. Miss Dragon's a big fan of local history. Now, coming up, on our side, there used to be a pub called the Brickman's Arms, and when they demolished that in the early Seventies they found a wattle-and-daub wall which dated from the end of the twelfth century. And there used to be a cock-fighting pit at the back too, although I'm glad that's gone. Oh, mind that sick on the pavement.'

As we pulled level with the big council estate, I nodded towards the road leading onto it. 'That used to be called Four Lanes, but it's been renamed School Road because they built a new primary school at the end.'

Callum crossed over and walked a few paces along the pavement, trying to make out the detail of the grey Eighties building with its red tarmac playground.

I followed him across the road, even though I didn't want to, and stood next to him. 'It still makes me feel ill, just looking at the place. The number of times I've willed a bomb to drop on it.'

There was dog shit and fag ends mixed in with the grass at the edge of the pavement, just as there had been nine years ago, when some girls had bent me over this metal street sign one afternoon, and told me I was in the stocks. Then they'd pulled up my skirt so everyone could see my knickers and Julie Berry shouted out that they were dirty, which wasn't true. Then Clare Greenhalgh had whacked me on the backside with a tennis racquet, really hard, so it left a bruise along the top of my legs. When they'd got me crying, they ran off. Obviously I wasn't going to tell Callum about that.

He turned back, and we walked slowly on. 'So is that where your dad – and your mum went?'

I shook my head. 'Don't know where my mother went. Somewhere in Bolton, I think. And Dad was at the old Victorian school, we passed where it used to be a while back. Do you remember that cluster of orange semis near the church?'

'Not really.'

'Well, that's where it stood, originally, I should've said while we were walking past. It was stone, with a nice gable in the middle of the roof. I've seen it in the background of Dad's Year 6 photograph. I can show you, if you're interested.'

It was a bright day and warm; above us, cumulus clouds lay on their backs like dogs waiting to be tickled. I felt so confident I was doing the right thing, taking him home. 'There's the cemetery. I'll take you in there one day.'

'Is it where your dad's buried?'

'No, but it's a good place, quiet. There are these fantastic red-hot pokers all along the front in June but they've gone over now.'

We reached the bottom end of the village, the top of the Brow. 'Nearly there,' I told him. 'The council put a Christmas tree up every year, on that traffic island. Then there's this village tradition called Stoning the Lights. All the youngsters from miles around join in. The bulbs last, oh, three days maximum. Last year some of the kids got ambitious and stoned the Rotary Santa as he went round the council estate. He's said he's not coming next time.'

And I could swap all this soon for Gothic quadrangles and spires, if I wanted, I thought.

I couldn't read Callum's expression as we finally stopped outside Poll's house. I tried to see it through his eyes; the low wall and the tiny patch of grass too small for a mower, that Dogman has to clipper into a rectangle for us; the stone windowsill marked streaky green; the peeling black door.

'Nice fanlight,' he said, looking up at the last piece of leaded light above the door frame. 'I notice next door's have had theirs taken out. Big mistake. Some people have no soul.'

I hurried him through the front room with its nasty wallpaper and swirly carpet, and into the back where Poll and I eat, watch TV, argue and sulk.

'You've a lot of lamps,' he said, looking round. 'It's like a lighting shop in here.'

'Has to be,' I replied, thinking of Poll squinting through her super-magnifier at her large-print thrillers. 'They could probably spot this house glowing from outer space.' I saw, now, the sheen on the walls where Poll trails her hand as she navigates the room. I'd never spotted it before. Ditto the cobwebs up above the picture rail, and the layer of grey fluff on the carpet underneath the gas fire. I do clean, but there's no point in running yourself ragged when Poll can't make out the dirt and Dogman doesn't care. Suddenly the house looked a tip.

'Come upstairs,' I said quickly, before I got too shy to say the words.

He was still gazing round like he was at some sort of an exhibition. 'OK. Great. Lead on.'

\*

That last night, Poll hit Vince. There'd been shouting, but that was normal. I'd gone downstairs for some milk and I saw it happen. I don't know what the lead-up had been, she just went for him with the iron. He grabbed her hand and shoved her over so she fell against the sofa. The iron dropped out of her hand, hit the wall, and the base came away from the plastic casing.

She scrambled straight up again and ran at him. It was like watching a dog or something, she was wild. He got hold of one of her wrists but she clapped the other down hard over his ear. I could see it hurt from the expression on his face.

She started slapping him repeatedly round his head and he was trying to hold her off. I'd have belted her back. After a minute, she stopped struggling and threw herself face down on the sofa. She pulled a cushion over her head and held it there. I tiptoed back up the stairs. Katherine was screaming so I sat on the landing for a while.

Later that night, it must have been around two, I woke up and Vince was in my room. He came over to the bed and looked at me. It was too late to pretend I was still asleep. I thought, this is it, he's going to rape me.

He leaned over and touched the covers. 'I don't know about you, lass, but I've hed enough. I'm flittin',' he said. 'Are you comin'?'

# Chapter Fourteen

Winston was snoring on my candlewick bedspread, so I scooped him up, carried him across the landing and dropped him on Poll's. 'Pee there, if you want,' I told him.

Then I nipped back down to the kitchen and stuck the kettle on. While the water was boiling I made some inelegant cheese butties, but trimming off the blue-mould edges which is more than I do for Poll. I shoved the sandwiches on two Royal Albert side plates, brewed up, and plonked everything on a tray to take upstairs.

When I returned, Callum had taken his jacket off and was fiddling with something in the inside pocket. I'd have thought nothing of it but for the way he jerked his head up guiltily as I came through the door.

'Dinner is served,' I said, pretending not to notice. 'I've had to sack the butler.'

'Oh, excellent.' He left his jacket alone and took the tea off me. 'I am so ready for this.'

I settled myself on the floor with my back against the wardrobe, because there was obviously no way I could sit next to him on the bed, but he got up then, sandwich in hand, and started wandering round the room touching things. He traced the diamond shapes on the bed frame with his fingers, set the little drop-handles on the chest of drawers quivering, bent sideways to check out more book spines. Then he stopped near the photos and stood for ages, while I tried to wipe some dust surreptitiously off the bookcase with my sleeve.

'Are all these your dad?'

'Yeah. Can you see the school in that one? Wasn't it a nice building? Poll went there too, when she was young. She says there were stuffed birds in cases on the wall, and a platform for the teacher's desk. And she got the cane for being naughty, although when Dad was there the Head just used a slipper.'

'He hit the pupils with a slipper? Sicko.'

'Weapon of choice for Primary headmasters in the Seventies. Dad got the slipper every other week.' Cissie had told me that, not Poll. 'He used to make a lot of stuff up, and they didn't like it. Nowadays you'd say he was being creative, using his imagination.'

'That's school for you, bunch of Fascists,' said Callum, kneeling to flick through Dad's old LPs. 'I more or less got chucked out in the end. They could have slippered me into oblivion and it wouldn't have made any difference. I wouldn't do what the others were doing. I didn't see why there had to be set times for painting, and set times for maths, set times for Plasticine play and sand expression. I mean, why not let the kids follow their impulses? That way, you'll get real impetus behind each individual child's work.'

'You told them all that when you were seven?'

'Oh yeah. Well, my mum did. They kept calling her in, for "interviews". She got more and more defensive, 'cause basically they were calling her a bad parent, inadequate single mother, till one day she marched me out of the building and said, "You're not going back there again." And I never did. It was great.' He eased out a record spine with his finger nail. 'Hey, here's that Human League album you were telling me about.' He rose, walked backwards to the bed and sat down, still holding the LP. 'And Mum was such a great teacher. She made learning fun, and if it was sunny we'd go outside, or take the day off. My dad sent us some money so she didn't have to work, although we were always a bit strapped for cash. It didn't matter, though, because we got by.'

I felt a pang of jealousy, hearing him talk about his mum like that. That kind of support must make a difference.

'Well, my Grandma took me out of school because I was being bullied,' I said. It was true; Poll had saved me from God knows what. Ritual burning, probably.

'Girls can be bitches,' said Callum, his eyes scanning the lyric sheet. 'They all have to dress the same, like the same music, that sort of thing. There's a girl at college, Lizzo, really funky, bit Goth, and she said she'd had a terrible time in Year 9 because she stood out and wouldn't join in with all the trends.'

'They thought I was a witch.'

'What?' Callum put the album down and blinked at me.

'The other kids in my class. First they thought I was weird because of living with my grandma and having no mum or dad. And because I, because I didn't look like they did.' (*Oi, Pavarotti, Fatty-bum-bum. Look, she's got tits already!*) 'Then something happened. They thought I'd caused it, so I became a witch.'

There was a split second where I thought, Christ, I shouldn't have told him. Why did I have to fuck everything up by telling him what a crap person I really was?

'Oh my God,' said Callum. 'How cool is that?'

'Not cool at all, actually. A right pain.'

'No, no it is cool. Wow. A witch.' He leaned forward, encouragingly. 'So what was it exactly that you did?'

I thought of Donna's aniseed balls. 'Hell. I wish I'd never said. Look, you've got to promise not to make fun of me after, if I tell you.'

Callum offered up his palms. High above his head, a long furry cobweb wagged in the breeze. 'As if,' he said.

How could I not believe him? He'd come here, to this room from last century, with Vince's pictures of warplanes still up and dead people stashed away in corners, and he'd never flinched. He must have seen other girls' bedrooms, normal bedrooms, but he hadn't scoffed or made smart comments. Dad's jar was on the windowsill behind his head. I knew Callum was OK.

'Right, then, are you sitting comfortably? Because it's a long story, if you include all the build-up.'

'You have to have the build-up.' Callum grinned.

'You do, don't you? OK, well, there was this boy. I mean, a lot of them used to hassle me and muck about with my books, my coat and stuff, but there was this one boy, Jason Roper, who was a year old for our class. I suppose they kept him back so he'd catch up or something. He was big and mouthy and he'd shout things from the climbing frame, and spit as you walked past.' (*You big fat cow, you're mental, you are, you still wear nappies and your grandma gets your clothes off the tip.*) 'So one day he was really having a go, about me not having a dad and my mum running off, and he was so into it all he overbalanced and fell right off, head-first. I was just standing there while he was writhing about and spitting blood; some moron had left their skateboard on the ground and he'd smashed his mouth against the edge of it. Then one of the girls suddenly screamed, "It was her, she did it. Katherine Millar hexed him." He pulled some strange faces, then looked at me and splurted, "Where's my tooth?" The dickhead had swallowed it. But I heard myself say, in this spooky voice, "I've made it disappear. You'll never get it back." ' (*You fucking evil witch. I'll have you, you're dead.*) 'I thought he'd try to hit me, but he ran off to the toilets, trailing blood down his shirt front.'

'Do it again, that spooky voice, it was really good. Really witchy.'

'Get away, you're putting me off. Where was I, oh yeah; I don't know why I came out with something like that, you know, against myself, because after that the other kids wouldn't leave me alone. I was Witchy-poo all afternoon and the next day too.

'Before, I'd been teased about my family and – stuff – but suddenly it got more serious. A friend of Jason's, Christopher Horton, wouldn't stop making evil-eyes at me, and he tried to throw salt at me in the dinner queue because he reckoned that it killed a witch's powers. That could've been the end of it, a two-day wonder, because within forty-eight hours Jason had passed the tooth and seen it go down the toilet. But then Christopher had an Accident.'

Callum's mouth hung open. 'Shit, what happened?'

'He got clipped by a bus, playing chicken. He wasn't

badly hurt, just shaken up and bruised. But everyone blamed it on me, they said it was a curse I'd put on him.'

'Hang on, what's chicken?'

'You know, where you run out in front of a moving vehicle at the very last minute. Did they not play that round your way?'

'No, they didn't. So, let me get this straight, he blamed you for nearly getting run over while he was playing a game where the object is to nearly get run over? Durr. Was he as thick as his friend?'

I laughed. 'It wasn't a class full of geniuses, no. I started getting pictures of pentangles left in my desk, or I assume they were meant to be pentangles, a lot of them were those Jewish six-pointed stars because they're not so tricky to draw. One girl, Julie Berry, used to ask where my broomstick was every bloody playtime, it became a major nuisance. Then one day, while the teacher was round the other side of the building breaking up a fight, this Julie announced to her friends that witches should be stoned and she threw a pebble at me.' (*Next time it'll be a brick, Witchy-poo. You better watch your back.*) 'So I lost my temper, 'cause it was just going on and on, and I shouted that Something Terrible would happen to her within fourteen days.'

Callum looked impressed. 'I bet that put the wind up them.'

'Yeah. They all went dead quiet. It's quite funny now, looking back, but it wasn't at the time.'

'Do you know, I'm seeing a whole new side to you. So go on, did she die horribly?'

'I wish. She had a rotten fortnight, though. I took in a

doll I'd made out of bits of cloth, with some hair attached, and let her friend catch a glimpse of it. You know, like it was by mistake. I made sure she saw there was a big darning needle stuck through its middle.'

'And was it Julie's hair?'

'God, no, how would I have got hold of that? She never came within six feet of me. No, it was off Dogman's spaniel, Kylie. She had ears more or less the same colour as Julie's plait. And so there was a great debate raging amongst the girls, about how Julie should tell a teacher or her mum, or whether that would make the curse more potent, and whether it was worth looking up counter-curses on the Internet, and I had two of her mates come to me and plead with me to take the spell off. But I said that once a spell had been cast, there was no way of cancelling it out. It had its own momentum, I told them, like the laws of physics. I remember saying to them, "This isn't Mildred bloody Hubble you know, this is for real." They nearly wet themselves. If Julie herself had come and apologized for being such a cow, I might have pretended to sort it for her, but she hated me too much.' My heart was thudding as I thought myself back to that time. It was strange how fresh the feelings still were after eight years. 'The sad thing was, I was beginning to think I actually was a witch.'

Callum laid himself back on the bed with his feet hanging over the end. 'You and about a million others.'

'What do you mean?'

'How many people carry lucky charms round with them, or touch wood to ward off evil? Or have a special rhyme they use if they spot a hearse? Or walk round, instead of under, ladders? Personally speaking, I get spooked by magpies; never pass a magpie without greeting it politely, or you're asking for trouble, Mum taught me that. Everybody believes in witchcraft, to a degree.'

'You don't think I was being – abnormal?'

'I think you sound like the most normal person in your class,' said Callum calmly. I flushed with pleasure. 'Yeah, I really do. I thought my school was bad. What a bunch of fuckwits. What happened to Julie in the end?'

'Nothing much. It got to day thirteen and she was really wound up, and then day fourteen arrived and she was like, "Ha ha, I knew it was a con, let's get Witchy-poo Weirdo." When I realized how truly pissed off she was I scarpered, left the premises even though we hadn't even had morning assembly yet, and ran home. I told Poll I was ill, and she fed me cake and let me watch TV for a while before handing me the mop and telling me to wash the flags. She's always thought education's overrated. I thought what I'd do was, I'd stay off the rest of the week, then go back on the Monday when maybe Julie would have cooled down. Only, that very evening, her chinchilla died.'

'Dah-dah-daaaah.' Callum put his hands to his face and rolled his head about, imitating extreme horror. 'Oh, Christ, not her chinchilla.'

'No, stop laughing, it was a tragedy as far as she was concerned. She'd had it for years and she loved it more than her granny, she always said. She was way too distressed to come to school. I heard she made her family hold a funeral for him in the garden. And the fact that he was ten had nothing to do with his death, it was clearly my evil spell that had stopped his little heart beating. You can imagine how welcome I was at school, come the Monday.'

'Katherine Millar, chinchilla-killer?'

'Got it in one.'

'Jesus. And so you left school.'

'No, not then. No, you haven't heard the worst of it yet.'

Callum hauled himself up on one elbow. 'Bloody hell, what did you do? Set the place on fire?'

'Credit me with a bit more imagination,' I said, waving my hands at him in a witchy way.

He put his index fingers into a cross-shape and raised them in front of his brow. 'Oh no, you don't get me like that, you fiend. I am immune to your supernatural powers.'

'That's what you think. Listen, I only got the entire school banned from Chester Zoo. *And* they had to draft in an educational psychologist to deal with the fall-out.'

'I'll sit up for this,' he said. 'Go on.'

'Well, I got the idea from Dogman, he was my mate in those days. I used to go for walks with him and his dogs, he had three then. One of them was an ex-rescue greyhound bitch, Mollie, very nervy, she never stopped barking. He said the neighbours were getting sick of her and he was going to have to do something before they contacted Environmental Health. So he bought a dog-dazer.' I held up my hand. 'Before you ask, it's a little electronic device about the size of a matchbox that you use to subdue troublesome mutts. Press a button and it emits an ultra-high-pitched sound that only doggies can hear. They hate it, it must be like nails down a blackboard, and you use it to train them out of bad habits. You know, woof – zap. Or chew – zap.'

'Or hump – zap.'

'Dunno, probably. I had charge of the dog-dazer and I trained Mollie myself, although she had to be put down in the end because she kept attacking men in uniform. Afterwards Dogman let me borrow it so I could stop Winston eating the fence, and that's when I decided it would be a laugh to take it on a school trip.

'The girls at school were being totally horrible now and they were particularly shitty that day. I wanted to go round on my own but the teacher reckoned we had to stay in groups. All the bitchiest kids were in with me, Julie, Clare, Christopher, Jason, the whole brigade. I'm sure the teacher did it deliberately. Because she could hear them going on at me but she never stopped them. So we did the elephants and giraffes, the boring stuff, then we all trooped over to the Bat Zone. It's a huge mock cave containing the largest collection of bats in Britain, and you had to push your way into it through some heavy plastic bat-proof strips hanging down like creepers, which kind of slithered over your neck and shoulders. That alone was freaking some of the girls out, that and the darkness inside.

'Jason said to me as we walked through the entrance, "This should be right up your street, Witchy-poo." So I said, "Yeah, I love bats, actually." And he said, "Yeah, well, you are a bat. Fat bat," and I said, "I can control these bats. I can make these bats do whatever I command." Just as I was speaking, a bat flew low over him and he didn't half jump. Clare, who was standing next to him, gave a little scream and we all began to realize just how many bats were in there; you can't make them out at first till your eyes adjust to the gloom, then they're everywhere. I took the dog-dazer out of my pocket but slyly, so no one saw, then I turned to Jason and said, "Right, are you watching? I'm going to say a magic spell and *all the bats will take flight simultaneously.*"

Jason goes, "Like fuck they will. Who do you think you are, Vampira?" but he sounded worried. Clare said, "Oh, don't, Katherine, wait till I get out, please." I laughed in her face like a madwoman and she screamed again, then she tried to make a dash for the exit but you couldn't run because there were so many people there and the pathways were too narrow. That's when I pressed the dog-dazer.

'Maybe it was coincidence, I don't know; maybe the bats picked up the scent of human hysteria, but suddenly it was like a black storm. Every bat in that cave left its perch and began swooping round. The air was thick with bats in an instant, I swear there must have been two hundred, and some of the tropical ones were the size of briefcases. All the kids and most of the adults were totally spooked; a lot of them were standing still with their heads bowed, but a lot were struggling to get out of the cave. I spotted Julie cowering in a rock crevice, her eyes closed, so I went up and ruffled her hair, shouting, "Oh my God, there's a giant bat on your head. Look out, it's biting your neck." She went ballistic and started hyperventilating. After a minute, an alarm sounded and some extra doors were opened to one side, and zoo staff rushed in to try to get everyone out and calm the bats.

'When we got outside everyone was in a state. Christopher was squirting Ventolin down his throat and Clare had wet her nice turned-up jeans. But Jason was a burning flame of indignation because, for once, it wasn't him in trouble. He was literally jumping up and down and pointing at me, shouting, "It was *her*. *She* did it. It's her fault." Some of the other kids joined in, those that weren't weeping or traumatized into silence. Mrs Kirtlan hauled me off to the side and looked me straight in the eye; I mean, I was smirking from ear to ear while everybody else was in shock. She said, "Are you in some way responsible for this mayhem?" And I said, "Yes," because at that moment I felt really proud of myself. "How?" she asked. So I showed her the dog-dazer.

'I had to spend an hour in the zoo office explaining what I'd done – I think they were worried I'd start a trend, because they'd had some trouble with sickos pointing laser pens at the big cats' eyes. I kept saying I was sorry if I'd hurt the bats but I don't think anyone believed me. Then the Deputy Head arrived in her car to take me home separately.

'And that was it. On the Monday, the Headmaster had my grandma in for a "chat" and told her the other parents were up in arms about me, Clare couldn't sleep for nightmares, Julie had hung garlic all round her bedroom, that sort of thing. He probably wanted to say a lot more but Poll never let him finish. The funny thing is, she criticizes me herself all the time, but she wasn't going to take it from him; at one point she threw a paperweight at him. I wish I'd been there. And the result was that I had a year off.'

'Fucking hell. So Poll tutored you?'

I laughed out loud. 'Poll? You must be kidding. I taught myself, more or less.'

'What, and Social Services let you?' Callum looked incredulous. ''Cause they were always on my mum's case, checking up.'

'Well, Miss Dragon helped me draw up a programme of work for the Support Officer to see, and provided me with some answers-in-the-back-type textbooks. She set me a few projects and did a spot of marking here and there. Mainly, though, I cribbed up on old Ladybirds.' I pulled *The Public*

*Services: Water Supply* out of the bookcase and passed it to him. 'By the end of the year I'd the History series off by heart, all of Nature and Conservation, and my knowledge of Sixties technology was second to none. The Support Officer who interviewed me had his doubts, but I reckon what clinched it was when we went out into the back garden to look at my home-made rain gauge, and he commented on the spectacular mackerel sky there was that day. I said, "I think you'll find they're cirrocumulus clouds, actually." He scribbled something down on his clipboard and left. The next year I started at the grammar school where, I can honestly say, I haven't touched a bat since.'

Callum rose to his feet and applauded. 'Jesus. Kat Millar, that is one hell of a story. You are so . . . ' He didn't finish, just shook his head at me, smiling, and sat down again. 'I take my hat off to you for sheer surreal inventiveness. Dog-dazer! The only times I've tried to get revenge on someone it's been pathetic, small-scale stuff. Pritt-stick on a chair, dropping someone's folder down the back of a cupboard. A rank amateur. Though I did once leave a king prawn in a glove box.'

'A prawn? What kind of cruel bastard does that to an innocent shellfish?' I felt so high now I'd told him and he'd been OK.

'It was *dead*. It was supposed to smell terrible after a while and send the owner of the car crazy. But he found it immediately and threw it out the window. Then I got called Prawn-balls for a while, but it wasn't serious, he was a mate.'

'*Prawn-balls?*'

'Uh-huh. Mary Prawn-balls. It doesn't do much for a guy's image.'

'I can imagine.'

'You've gone all pink.'

'I know, I do. After you with that hanky.'

When we'd sobered up slightly, I decided I knew him well enough to ask whether he wanted to help clear out the sink cupboard.

'Well, shit, you sure know how to show a lad a good time,' he said, starting to laugh again. 'OK, then. On one condition.'

'What's that?'

'That I'm invited to this birthday do next week.' He pointed to Donna's invite, which I'd stuck in the wooden frame of the oval mirror that hangs above the chest of drawers.

He completely threw me. 'Oh, that. I didn't know what you – I'm not going, to be honest . . . ' A happy thought struck me. 'And even if I was, how would you get back to Nantwich? It goes on till one in the morning.'

'Oh, yeah. You've got a point. Forget it, then. I'll still help you do your sticky cupboard, though.'

'Good man.'

'I might have to have a slash first. It was a big mug of tea.'

'Straight across the landing, the door without the disgusting ceramic Westie plaque on it.'

The second the toilet door shut, I stopped grinning and made a dive for Callum's jacket. In the inside pocket, carefully folded into a tiny square, was one of Dad's early biology drawings: *Cockroach: A) Dorsal View B) Ventral View*

*1. Head 2. Thorax 3. Abdomen 4. Antenna 5. Wings 6. Veins* or
*nervures 7. Segment 8. Spiracle 9. Trochanter 10. Coxa 11. Femur
12. Tarsus.*

I turned the note over but there was nothing obvious on
the back. The toilet flushed so I folded the diagram back up
again and stuck it in the pocket. What on earth did he want
with that? I so wanted to ask him, but I didn't want to admit
I'd been rifling through his clothes.

'I've been thinking about all you've just told me,' he said
as he walked back in. 'Amazing. And you're so modest
about it.'

'It didn't occur to me there was anything to show off
about,' I shrugged. In truth, it had always been a millstone
of shame around my neck.

He smiled. 'You're a dark horse, you.'

You took the words right out of my mouth, I nearly said.

*

'Are you tekkin' Katherine's pram? Only I'll hev to put t' back
seats deahn,' Vince whispered from the doorway.

I jumped. 'No,' I said. He went away for a bit but then he came
back with a bag full of clothes.

'What about her sterilizer?'

'No,' I hissed. 'No, none of it.'

He stopped trying to zip up his holdall. 'Well, how're you goin'
to manage?'

I just looked at him.

'Oh,' he said. 'Reet.' He wandered off and everything went
quiet. After a minute or two, he stuck his head round the door
and said, 'I'll go and unclip t' baby carrier an' bring it in again, then,
shall I?'

I went over to the cot to say goodbye but I didn't kiss her in case I woke her and the screaming started up once more. I didn't want to leave to the sound of that. Anyway, we were trying not to alert Poll. I can honestly say I felt nothing except relief that I was leaving my baby.

In the car, before we set off, I tried to explain to Vince how I felt. 'Do you know that story about Sinbad, where a little old man tricks his way onto Sinbad's shoulders and then won't get off? And he rides him like a horse, and turns Sinbad into his permanent slave? And when Sinbad gets angry, the old man beats him with a stick and throttles him with his thin little legs? And Sinbad has to get the old man drunk to escape?'

Vince was staring at me as if I was mad. 'You can always go back for her when you're feeling more yourself,' was all he said.

He turned the key in the ignition and we drove off into the night.

# Chapter Fifteen

The phone on the sideboard rang at eleven the next morning.

'Kat?'

'Yeah?'

'Guess who.'

'God, I don't know.' I didn't either, not straight away. How was I to know Callum would phone me at home. Then light dawned. 'Oh. It's you, isn't it?'

'I can't deny it, it's me.'

'How did you get my number?'

'Rang Directory Enquiries, bozo, how do you think?'

'Oh, yeah.' Obviously. 'What is it?'

'I can hardly hear you, you're very faint. You sound like you're in outer space. Can you speak up?'

It was force of habit. Even when Poll wasn't in, as now, I still felt I needed to whisper if I was up to anything personal. Not that I had a lot of intimate phone calls to my history. 'Sorry. Is everything OK?'

'Yeah, fine. I thought I'd let you know, I've been doing some research and there's a train goes from Bolton at half-past midnight.'

Standing where I was, I could see straight through to the

front-room window that looks out onto the street. Some boys of about ten were walking past up the hill, throwing gun caps on the pavement and shrieking when they exploded. I heard a dog bark from a distance, and some adult voice shouting, then the boys' jeering and swearing and more bangs.

'Well done, that's terrific,' I said to Callum. 'Goes where?'

'Crewe.' He sounded impatient.

'And the reason you're telling me is?'

There was a rapping sound from down the line. Then Callum came back on again. 'That was me banging the receiver against my head. Listen, I mean I can go to that party, I'll just have to leave early. Probably about ten past, quarter past twelve, depending on how far away the station is from the club.'

'It's pretty close,' I said before I could stop myself.

'Great.'

'But, Callum, look, I'm not going.' I leant against the sideboard and knocked a piece of paper to the floor. When I bent to see, it was a postcard from Rebecca that Poll must have picked up and neglected to tell me about.

*Having a great time checking out National Trust properties. Going to see a garden tomorrow landscaped by Capability Brown! Counting the hours till Results Day!!! Becks X*

Becks?

' – thought it might be a laugh,' Callum was saying. 'I'm always up for a party.'

'I don't like clubs,' I said, hoping he wouldn't guess I'd never been in one. The front of the postcard showed blank-eyed Poseidon in marble.

'Shame. It would have been a laugh.'

'So you said.'

'Hey, is Poll there?'

'No. She's—' I thought quickly; 'having her dinner at the Working Men's with Dogman.'

Poll doesn't go visiting much, because in general people put furniture in stupid places. But the truth was, Poll had gone round to Maggie's with a bunch of magazines and some bottles of Guinness because Maggie had fallen in our kitchen and sprained her ankle. The reason I didn't want to tell Callum was that Maggie had slipped on one of my Poll-traps, which he'd seen me setting up. 'Why, exactly, are you trailing a line of wash liquid across the doorway, Kat?' he'd asked, sliding the last box of antique Robin starch back in the cupboard for me. 'Mice,' I'd told him. He didn't ask again, so I suppose he believed me. Well, he'd effectively lied to me about the cockroach drawing.

'Dogman?' Callum snorted. 'What a name. I'm going to have to see this bloke some time. Does he actually look like a dog?'

'No, he smells like one.' And given half a chance, he'd clamp himself to your leg.

'Nice. So, you're definitely not going on Saturday?'

'No.'

'OK. Well, I'll, er, I'll be in touch. Is it all right to ring you here?'

'Not really. If Poll picked up the phone and it was your voice, a male voice, I'd never hear the last of it.' I could just imagine the sort of things she'd say, my life wouldn't be worth living. And if she found out who he really was, my God.

'And you've not got a mobile, have you.'

'No.' No point: no one to ring.

'Have you got a Hotmail account? I could email you at the library.'

'Sorry.' How crap is she, he must have been thinking. 'It's OK to send messages through Miss Dragon. So long as you don't call her Miss Dragon.'

Callum made a noise that might have been a sigh, or simply an extra-large breath. 'Right. Fine. I'll be sending you a message, sometime.'

After he'd rung off I felt utterly flat. I went upstairs and tried on the basque again – now too loose – and the black skirt, with the boots. Then I put some make-up on and wetted my hair down so it wasn't quite so sproingy, then I twisted it up and fastened it with a jumbo slide and teased some strands down on either side of my face. I got the nail clippers out and snipped off some of the madder hairs from my eyebrows. Before I took it all off again, I pulled the curtains to, so the bedroom was in semi-darkness, and tried to imagine what I'd look like in a club. Stupid, was the answer, so I drew the curtains and put everything away. I left my hair up, though, and also I did put a couple of stitches in the back seam of the basque, because it seemed a pity not to. I could still detect Callum's male scent lingering by the bed.

'Hoy, Katherine.' I heard the front door bang open and Poll clatter in. 'Are y' up there? Katherine?'

'Katherine,' shouted Dogman in a particularly stupid voice. 'Katerina!'

She reached the bottom of the stairs and yelled, 'Are we gettin' our dinner on? Dickie's fetched a big box o' beefburgers, and Maggie's sent you one of them giant

Toblerones. Next door brought it her off their holidays but she says she han't the teeth to cope with it.'

Dogman started up, I don't know who ever told him he could sing.

*Well I was there, so were you*
*The mayor and the vicar and the council too*
*All the wives and ladies on full view*
*The night John Willie took his ferret to a do.*

I checked my watch. Time for a binge.

*

The night before Donna's party, I had a funny dream. I was in a stone tower, I saw it first from the outside and then I was in it, trapped on the top floor. I'd laid an egg, and Callum was there. He said, 'I'll look after it, your egg. Trust me.' He put it inside his underpants to keep warm and then started to climb out of the window, holding on to my hair to stop himself falling. My head was hanging over the sill and I heard him say, 'I know a great recipe for Spanish omelette.' Then I woke up and found my plait was fast down the side of the headboard.

So I was in a foul temper all day and Poll, for once, insisted on coming late-afternoon shopping, and that was probably why the Great Row happened. We'd been sniping most of the morning, through dinner, and all the way up to Spar. Then, round the aisles, she kept putting daft things in the basket and I kept taking them out again and slamming them back down on the shelves. It was like taking a naughty toddler round.

'We don't have a dishwasher, well we do, it's me, but

we don't need dishwasher tablets,' I snapped, snatching them out of her wrinkly hand.

'They're for t' washin' machine,' she argued. 'I've seen 'em on t' telly, big white tablets. You know nowt, you do.'

'At least I can read,' I said nastily. An elderly woman I didn't recognize glanced across the freezer cabinet, saw Poll's white stick and frowned at me. Heartless teen attacking disabled grannie. 'Who put these crystallized violets in? As if I didn't know.'

'They looked like cotton buds,' she said, glowering. 'They're in t' same sized container. And you've finished t' others off and never towd me.'

'I did not. I never use cotton buds.'

'Well, you've shifted 'em, then. You know how important it is for me t' have my toiletries in one place. Otherwise it could be disastrous.'

It was Maggie who'd once stopped Poll at the last minute from rinsing her hair with Toilet Duck.

'Yeah, but how am I supposed to clean when there's clutter everywhere?' I threw two bars of Galaxy in the basket, and a multi-pack of Milky Ways. 'You can't stick a pin between the bottles on that bathroom ledge. Sometimes I have to move your bits and pieces because they're thick with dust. There's all dead flies and moths behind them on the windowsill. *Don't* put that packet of baby food in.'

'It's rice, it says; see.' Poll shook the yellow box aggressively in my face.

'*Baby* rice. Not proper rice, Put it back.'

She did, and knocked a load of rusks onto the floor. 'Now see what you've done,' she said.

'God.' I scrabbled the rusks up and shoved them back

where they'd come from. 'Can we get a move on? Because I'm really beginning to get fed up.'

Poll turned to me, her mouth small and pious. 'You're fed up? You are? You should try going blind. It's a ruddy picnic.'

She pulled away from me and tottered off down towards the checkout, only she went off at a tangent and crashed into a revolving stand of cards. I saw her keel over, and birthday greetings spill across the tiled floor. Several customers ran to help.

'Can you stand, love? Are you feeling dizzy? Did it knock your shoulder? Daft place to put a carousel, in't it? You could sue.'

I let them rush in, do their St John's Ambulance routine, while I leant against the chilled desserts and tried to take some of the weight off the wire handles that were digging into my arm. Watching her being pulled onto her skinny legs, her headscarf askew, I thought how harmless and pathetic she must look to an outsider. The manager came out from the back and offered her a wet wipe.

She mopped her brow bravely and made to hand them back.

'No, no, keep them,' he said, staking a £1.59 packet of moist tissues against a call from the Accident Helpline. I knew, by the glee on her face as she stowed them in her bag, that she was perfectly all right.

'Eeh, I think I could walk if I had a sip o' Bailey's,' she said hopefully.

Once outside she dropped the dying duck routine and laid into me.

'Them people in there, they care more about what happens to me than you do. Standing there like you're simple while your own flesh and blood writhes in agony on t' floor. It's not on. And you can stop pulling faces. Just because I'm blind doesn't mean I can't see.'

'Tell me something I don't know.' I gripped the carrier bags tightly and the Bailey's chinked against a jar of pickled onions.

'If you brek that bottle—'

'Oh, give it a rest.'

'Don't speak to me in that tone of voice, lady.' She wagged her stick at me.

'It's not like you're my mother,' I said, and waited for the thunderclap.

We were passing the church where the pavement's really narrow. Poll stopped dead in her tracks, so I ran into her. 'Oof! Your mother?' She steadied herself against the wall and glared into my face, breathing hard. 'I should damn well think I'm not. I'm sane, for a start. I haven't run off and left a helpless infant to fend for itself. I haven't wrecked a marriage. I haven't – ' pause while she pulled out a hanky from up her sleeve – 'I haven't tekken anyone's son away from them.' Blowing of the nose, dabbing of the eyes. 'So, no, I'm not your mother, and you should be bloody grateful for it. God only knows what sort of a mess you'd be if she'd had owt to do with your upbringing.'

I'd heard this speech before over the years so it didn't have the force it should have had. I gave her a little dig in the small of her back to start her moving again and pushed in front of her, desperate to get home. We were still in the public High Street and, yes, there was Mrs Threlfall across the road, waving. Too late to pretend I hadn't seen her.

'Maud's out of hospital,' she shouted to Poll, in between traffic. Poll swung her head round to locate the speaker. 'Maud Eckersley. She's to wait on some test results.'

'Did you hear that?' I grumbled, half-turning.

Poll ignored me. 'Tell her Get Well Soon from me,' she yelled in Mrs Threlfall's general direction. Much nodding and waving, but we managed to carry on moving down the village.

Where the footpath widened, by the Indian, I slowed so I was level with her. We walked in silence for thirty seconds while I tried to get the words sorted out in my head. 'Yeah, well, you say all that about my mother—'

'Because it's true.'

'But you've always told me what to think, you've never let me decide for myself.'

'Decide what? What's to decide? The woman killed your father, oh, hell fire.' She got out the hanky again and stood still while she wiped under her eyes. Now we were almost outside Porter's Newsagents and I just knew someone was going to come out the door and march straight into the melodrama. I touched her arm with the intention of pulling her along, but she jerked it away irritably. I'm not going to let this conversation drop, I told her silently; doesn't matter what sort of feeble pose you strike.

'It's not that simple, though, is it?' I went on. 'Up till now, I've always swallowed your version of events. No one's ever told me the story except you, so I've only ever had your side. But I've been thinking recently, and some things don't add up. Like, if my mother really was a murderer, an actual murderer, how come the police didn't arrest her straight away? How come she isn't mouldering in prison somewhere?' I suddenly remembered a book I'd read as a child where that had been the twist. 'Oh my God, she's not, is she?'

Poll spat against Porter's wall, all tears gone, and wiped her lips on her cuff. 'Don't be soft. Of course she's not.'

'So is she on the run? Did she have to change her identity to escape the law?'

'Escape? That's the right word for it. No, she feigned madness so they let her be. She should have been put away, anyroad. I'd have had her strung up, a life for a life.'

I stared down at the top of Poll's headscarf, at the little interlinking horseshoe pattern round the border. 'Look at me, Poll. Look at me, this is important.' She raised her chin very slightly so I could see her sour mouth, but not her eyes. 'I thought you said she *was* mad. Are you telling me now she was putting it on?'

'Hello, ladies,' said a cheerful voice. Oh bloody hell, now it was Mr Ashcroft from the Over Seventies, stepping out of the newsagent's with a *Chronicle* and twenty Player's. 'Nice to see a bit of sun out.'

'Aye, it is,' said Poll without enthusiasm.

'We were due some.' He checked me up and down and shook his head slightly, but I'm used to this treatment. I gawped back rudely and he turned to Poll. 'Where's your little dog today? He's not poorly, is he?'

'He's resting at home. He gets tired.'

'Don't we all?' Mr Ashcroft chuckled. 'I say, don't we all?' He stopped laughing when I scowled at him. 'I'll let you get on, then; I bet them bags of Katherine's are heavy, aren't they? Just as well you're a big strong lass.'

He may have sensed some violence in me because he

shuffled off pretty quick, considering he's got emphysema, and Poll and I plodded on.

'So are you saying my mum wasn't really mad?'

Poll shrugged. 'Do I look like a doctor? All I know is, she went mental when it suited her, that's all. She recovered fast enough, after.'

This was good news, because I'd always worried she might have passed insanity on to me.

'I don't know why you're smiling,' said Poll. 'It means she was sound of mind when she decided she didn't want you any more.'

Poll's the sort of woman who enjoys dropping salt on slugs. I wish you were a slug, I thought; I'd season you to death. As we hovered to cross the road, the temptation to guide her into the path of a speeding van was enormous; to sing out, 'All clear,' and watch her get splatted against the tarmac. Her bloodstained headscarf left flapping in the gutter. Then the van and the moment passed and the road was empty except for Mr Boardman's electric bicycle, and no good pushing her out in front of that. I made sure she walked through some dirty great puddles on the way to the other side, though.

'I still want to know more about her,' I persisted as we turned down the Brow. 'Whatever she did to me. I want to know, *things*, like, where she went to school, what sort of music she liked, her favourite film. I've never even seen a photo.' (Fingers crossed behind my back.) 'It's crazy, she's my mum.'

Poll stumped on with her head down. 'She doesn't matter, I've told you. You're better off without her, you always have been. Forget her.'

'But that's for me to decide. Isn't it? My right? I'm her daughter.'

A car horn blaring feet away made us both jump: Maggie's Dawn sweeping past in her silver Jeep, waving like a lunatic.

'Godfathers.' Poll clapped her hand to her chest. 'Who were it?'

'No one. A dog ran out. It's all right, though. It's gone in Aspull's garden.'

'That's a relief. Listen.' Poll stopped again and drew herself up straight, facing me. 'Let me ask you summat. Think back. Who was it sat up with you all night for weeks when you had croup and couldn't breathe? Filling bowls of boiling water for the steam and putting them all round? Who was it went trailing up to school that time they took you over t' fence and rolled you in a cowpat and you needed a change of clothes? Who was it gave that headmaster a good hiding, and convinced the education officer to leave you alone for a year? Who's shelled out for your fancy uniform all these years, blazers sixty pound a time, and we can't get second-hand because there's no one in your size?'

Yes, and I've paid you back for it, every penny, haven't I? Waiting on you hand and foot, your unpaid servant. I just gritted my teeth and said, 'I know. But I still wish I knew where she was.'

'Well,' said Poll, flashing me an angry glance, 'I'll tell you what I think. The sort of creature she was, she's almost certainly at the bottom of a canal somewhere, or tekken an overdose or thrown herself off summat high. You go rooting about, you're going to find stuff you wish you'd never known. Sometimes it's better to live in ignorance.'

'Oh, well, this is the place for it, then. This whole damn village is founded on ignorance. I'm getting sick of ignorance!' I erupted. 'I'm sick of your take on the world, this hide-under-the-table attitude. I'm eighteen now, for God's sake. I could be married, all right, stop sniggering, I could be moving out and living in a place of my own with a job and everything.'

'You? You'd never cope, not on your own. It's dangerous out there, I've told you often enough.' We'd reached the house. 'Life's all about tragedy; you don't believe me now, but you'll know about it when you get to my age.'

Like age means you're wise. You are so full of shit, Poll Millar.

I badly needed something sweet so I hauled the shopping through to the kitchen and located the Milky Ways. I unwrapped two to be eating while I threw the duller items in cupboards, so my mouth was crammed with chocolate when I heard the cistern flush upstairs.

'Poll?'

'What?' she snapped, and her voice was too close.

I put my head round the kitchen doorway and she was sitting on the sofa trying to lever a shoe off.

'Hang on.' I gulped the chocolate down. 'There's someone upstairs, using our toilet.'

'Oh, aye, that'll be Dickie. He said he was coming round.'

'Did you leave the door open?'

'No need,' grinned Dogman as he walked into the room, cool as you please.

'Dickie has his own key now,' said Poll, in a kind of Go on, I dare you to say something tone.

'I have,' said Dogman, holding up an enormous bunch

of keys and rattling them smugly. 'Well, your grandma thought it made sense. I'm always round here.'

You can say that again, I thought. Fucking hell. 'How come you've got so many keys?'

But Dogman just laughed.

'Are you puttin' t' kettle on, or what?' said Poll.

When I came back, Dogman was jiggling a cardboard box in his arms and looking pleased with himself. 'There you go,' he said to me, holding the box out. 'One man's shit is another man's gold.'

I peered in. A load of old tat, how kind, you shouldn't have. 'What is it?'

'Women's things. Poll's had a root through earlier, but there's nowt she fancies. Here, tek it.'

Out of curiosity I did, dropping the remaining Milky Ways in too. When I got upstairs I tipped the box out on the floor and knelt beside it. A bunch of used cosmetics fell out; it looked for all the world as if Dogman had gone into someone's house and just cleared their dressing table while they were out. Even the brush had hairs wrapped round it; that went straight in the bin. The lipsticks were worn to chisel tips and the eye shadows starting to spill from their containers. But, bless the smelly old bastard, he'd scooped me a hot tong thing that looked like it might, at a pinch, go some way to taming my hair. It was dirty round the handle and the barrel was covered in a layer of sticky brown, which I assumed was baked hairspray. I plugged it in and a red light came on to show the thermostat was working. While it heated up, I sat cross-legged in front of the wardrobe mirror and tried some of the new lipsticks.

In the end, I didn't make too bad a fist of things. There

were a couple of dodgy moments when the burning barrel caught my scalp, but the final effect was worth it. For the first time in my life, my hair hung down rather than frizzed out. I shaped a curl at the ends, and twisted the sides in like I'd seen them do at school. I remembered what the make-up counter girl had said, and wondered about cutting myself a wispy fringe. Betty-the-Mobile usually trims my hair for me while Poll's perm is cooking; she's all right, but she only knows how to do pensioner styles. See, if I had a job and money, I could go to a swanky hairdresser's and have a consultation, investigate having the kinks relaxed, maybe have some layers razored in, or highlights. Except they were very scary, those salons, and the assistants all wore tiny skirts and looked like models, and they'd probably burst out laughing when I lumbered in. I wondered where you could have your eyebrows professionally tweezered.

I put the basque on, for devilment, and the long skirt and the boots, and stood in front of the mirror. What if I did go to Donna's party? I tried a mysterious half-smile at myself. Then, like victims do in horror films, I peered into the reflected room and spotted something nasty behind me.

On my bedside table, an open tub of Vaseline, which wasn't mine or Poll's. And, eugh, gross, now I looked properly, a definitely-Dogman-shaped depression down the length of my bed.

I suppose there could have been a DIY, household-type explanation, Poll had him lubricating the sash window or something, but how likely was that, really? Sometimes, especially when I was younger, I'd imagined my dad lying there, listening to his records or reading his books. Now the picture would always be Dogman, greasing his privates.

I put my hands over my face and screamed quietly into my palms for a minute or two. Then I went over to the record player and put Ultravox on, very loud. I plugged in the phones and then lay down on the floor with my arms over my eyes, till I saw sparks. Oh, Vienna.

\*

He drove me into the centre of Chorley, I saw the road signs in the headlights. We finished up on a cobbled side street, in front of a mid-terraced brick house.

'Have I been here before?' I asked as we got out of the car. Because it looked familiar.

'No, not to this one,' Vince said, leaning on the doorbell. His face was like a skull in the shadows.

After a minute, a scrappy little man in a dressing gown answered, rubbing his face. I thought he'd shout at us for waking him, but when he saw Vince he opened the door right up and we both walked in. 'I'll just go and put some pants on,' he said, and disappeared up the stairs.

It smelt like a dirty place. The man came back down wearing jogging bottoms but no top, and his ribs stuck out like he was starving. I sat in the living room and Vince and the man went into the kitchen to talk. I heard Vince say, 'Are you sure it's still all right?' and the man reply, 'Yep, it's no problem, I owe you one.'

'You owe me several,' said Vince. 'July, August, September . . .'

'What can I say?' said the man. 'You're a saint.'

'I'm a fool,' said Vince, but in a nice way, not getting at him.

The man brought me a glass of brandy through and we all sat

round the electric fire. 'My name's Stu,' he said. I was past caring. I drank the brandy down and asked for another.

'We can stay here for a little while,' said Vince. 'Stu's on holiday next week.'

'Lanzarote,' said Stu. 'You can have the couch for a couple of nights, Vince, till I go. I'll show you your room, love. Come with me.'

He led me up to the back bedroom and I had that déjà vu thing. 'I think I've been here before,' I said. 'Although I don't remember all this.' The walls were covered in Thin Lizzy posters and album covers, and there was a table with piles of paper and a BBC Model B computer on it.

'You've never been here, I promise you, love. Honest.' He waved his hand at the computer. 'I run two fanzines from this room, it's my base. I don't normally let anyone round, in case they mess up my system. But I know you won't, will you? Good girl. Now, the bathroom's across the landing.' He pointed through the door.

'I know that already.'

He shook his head. 'You're thinking of somewhere else. There's loads of two-up two-downs round here with exactly the same layout.'

'Like Poll's,' I said faintly. It had taken me till now to see it. This house was the twin of the one I'd just escaped from.

'That's right. Now, make yourself at home, but don't touch my picture discs, OK? Some of them are worth twenty pounds.'

I meant to put a sheet over the mattress, but the minute I lay down I was asleep. I wish I could say I dreamt about Katherine, but I didn't.

# Chapter Sixteen

God knows how long I was there on the floor; certainly till it got dark out. Whenever the record finished a side, I got up, flipped it over and lay back down again. This happened five or six times until, as I was pulling my headphones off to put side two on again, I heard a tapping at my window. I dropped the phones in fright.

Tap tap tap. Wasn't there a film about a murderer who did that, just before he struck? Must be a bloody tall murderer, though; either that or he was standing on a ladder.

I pulled the corner of the curtain up a little way. *I'M A BURGLAR LET ME IN* said the handwritten placard pushed against the glass. There was the faint sound of cheering below, and the card was swivelled round on its pole. *MEET U AT BOTTOM OF HILL U HAVE 10 MINS*

I pushed open the sash and poked my head out. Callum waved at me from the front garden.

'Get out of there,' I hissed at him. 'Don't let Poll and Dogman see you.' I was praying they'd drawn the front curtains, or that they were watching TV in the back.

'Come down, then,' he grinned. He was wearing his contact lenses again, I noted.

'I can't.'

'You can. If you don't come down, I'm going to ring the bell. In fact, here I go now, here I am, extending my digit in the critical direction, I'm only centimetres away—' He stretched out his arm towards the door.

'Oh, for God's sake. It's not funny. Stop it.'

'Aw, just come down, for a minute, say hello. Pleeease.' He dropped his hand to his side and looked up appealingly.

For two pins I could have dropped my *Illustrated Dictionary* on his head, that would have shut him up. But that smile . . .

'Pleeeeeeeeease?'

'Oh, hell. All right, then. For *one* minute. And you have to put Poll's clothes prop back where you found it, and pull all that parcel tape off the end. And take that cardboard with you; she could read that and have a fit.'

He did a smart salute and threw the prop onto the ground. I hoped to God there were no neighbours watching. At least it was night time.

'I'll see you in five, then?' He flashed a palm at me, fingers spread out.

'You said ten minutes.'

'OK. But don't waste time mucking about with your hair or anything girly. You look great already.'

I glowed for a second, then realized it was something he'd said simply to speed me up. Still. 'I need to get a coat.'

'Nah, it's warm out here. Come as you are.'

I looked down at my near-bare bosom. No way could I be seen in the street wearing a basque. 'Well, something to cover up, then. Hang on.' I ducked back in but he called me out again. '*Will* you stop shouting? You'll have the whole street out if you don't quieten down. What is it?'

'Can you bring that party invite with you?'

'Christ, you don't give up, do you?' I muttered, shutting the window.

I yanked open the wardrobe door and pushed aside the woollens. Under my long navy cardigan was the white top I'd bought with Donna. I snipped off the price tag with my nail clippers and started to undo the basque. Then I thought, I haven't time, and anyway it'll only be like having a bra on. I buttoned up the blouse over it; you could see a hint of red through the white material but I didn't stop to worry. A few strokes with the hairbrush to smooth my hair at the back where I'd mussed it up, and I was ready. As a last thought I flicked the invite through the gap at the bottom of the window. I didn't see where it landed.

I crept to the bottom of the stairs and listened. *We know what you've been up to, Hastings. Your mate's told us all about it.* A tough policeman was interrogating someone at the top of his voice. I heard Poll say, 'Why don't they look in his car, there must be blood all ovver it,' and Dogman reply, 'They're daft, the police, they don't see what's going on under their noses.'

I so wanted to turn right, through the front room, and make a run for it. But my front door keys and peggy purse were in the fruit bowl on the sideboard, which was in the living room, on the left. I'd have to go in.

I tried to keep the noise down, but Dogman turned round in his seat as soon as he heard the door swoosh over the carpet. 'Bloody hell, look at you,' he leered. 'You've been busy, haven't you? No wonder you've been so quiet all evening. I like your top-thing.'

Poll whipped round too. 'Where do you think you're going?' she said as she heard the jingle of keys.

'Out. So?'

'Don't cheek me, madam.' Poll pushed herself up from the sofa and came round to peer at me, putting herself between me and the door. 'Lord above, what have you done to yourself? You look like Bette Davis in that film where them sisters were foul to each other, what were it called? And one were a cripple, and t' other went mad.'

'I think she looks tasty,' said Dogman. 'I could eat her up. Yum yum.'

'I need to go,' I said. Before I vomit, I could have added.

'You've had no tea. I did shout of you but you never answered. It was bacon grill but we had to throw yours away, it went like leather.'

'Doesn't matter.'

'You can't go missing meals at your age. Don't blame me when you're stricken wi' gallstones. Where are you off to?' Poll stuck her chin out belligerently. 'Who are you meeting?'

'Rebecca. It's a birthday party for a girl at school.'

*Do you expect me to believe that?* shouted the TV detective in the background, thumping the table.

Poll relaxed her body language very slightly. 'Birthday party? Oh. Where?'

'Harrop community centre,' I said promptly. 'Where we went to see *Beauty and the Beast* that time. Rebecca's giving me a lift there and back. I don't know when it finishes, though, so don't put the deadlock on.'

Behind her, Dogman was licking his lips. 'You scrub up nice,' he said. 'You're a bonny girl.'

I dodged past Poll and made a run for the front door.

'How come you didn't tell me about it before? And where did you get them clothes?' I heard her screech. 'You've no coat.'

I slammed the door behind me and glanced round. The street was empty, so I started off down the hill, my purse banging against my chest.

Callum was standing in the lay-by at the passenger side of a small van. He was wearing combats and a jersey top with a hood.

'Hiya,' he called when he spotted me. 'Hurry up. We've been here for hours.' He opened the door for me. 'Hop in.'

I checked inside and did a double take when I saw a redheaded lad at the wheel. 'Hey,' he said, without turning his head. Cigarette smoke streamed out of his nostrils.

'It's all right.' Callum nodded into the van. 'This is Mitch from college, he's a mate. In you get.'

Panic began brewing in my stomach. Stranger Danger, I thought. Climbing in a van after dark with two lads. It went against a lifetime's instincts. I'd be front page of the *Bolton Evening News* tomorrow, Big Fat Girl Found in Ditch. Grandmother Says It Were Her Own Stupid Fault.

'But where are we going?'

'Bolton. Mitch has got some business there. I cadged a lift. Thought we could at least have a drink, you and me, even if we don't get to that party. Oh come *on*, Kat, have some fun for once.'

I bet this is how people end up taking drugs, I thought: not wanting to offend. 'I'm not sure.'

'Look,' said Callum, coming up close and lowering his voice, 'I promise if you change your mind halfway there, all you have to do is say the word and we'll turn straight round and come back again, no harm done. So you've nothing to lose. Go on. All we'll do is sit in the corner of a nice quiet pub for an hour or so. I think we'll have a really good time.'

'Is Mitch coming with us?'

Callum laughed. 'Well, it is his van, fair dos. But don't worry, he's dropping us off in the town centre and going on elsewhere.'

I took a breath, and hauled myself up by hanging on the sides of the door. 'Shove over,' he said when I was in. So I shuffled my bum across the seats to Mitch, who still didn't take me on. Who is he, exactly, I wanted to ask, and why is he wearing so many rings?

'Belt up,' chirped Callum, clicking his seat belt into place. 'We don't want anyone pulling us over tonight, do we?'

'We do not,' said Mitch. The ignition started up and the CD player began blasting out a dance track, all bass, that went right through my jawbone.

It all felt unreal, sitting in that smoky cab with the air throbbing and the streetlights flicking over us. I realized I was gritting my teeth with fear; tried to relax; failed. I looked over at Callum and he smiled back. He'd lit a cigarette too and the glowing tip bobbed around in the darkness.

'Mitch used to live in Bolton.' Callum tapped the dashboard with his free hand as though he was playing it.

'Oh.' *DUF-DUF-DUF* went the music. 'So you're back here to see your friends?'

'Yeah,' said Mitch. 'Sort of.'

'Whereabouts in Bolton?'

'You know where there was that IRA shooting?' *DUF-DUF-DUF*.

I nodded.

'More or less next door.' *DADADADADADADADA DUF-DUF-DUF*.

'Right.'

'But that were after I moved.'

'Oh,' I said. 'I expect Nantwich is a bit quieter, is it?' I gave a nervous snort.

'Well, it was till Mitch came to live there,' said Callum. I thought Mitch looked pleased at this, but it was hard to tell in the gloom.

He dropped us at the bus station, Callum leaping out like a dancer and me landing like a sack of potatoes beside him.

'We can't go to that party,' I said at once.

'I know; way too early. Let's find this nice pub first.' He strode off down the road and I trotted after him, hugging my purse to my chest. 'Know anywhere good?'

'No,' I said, but my voice was lost in the sound of some passing girls shrieking. The street was as crowded as a Saturday afternoon, but shoppers usually wore more clothes. Poll would have had a haemorrhage at the amount of flesh on show, Dogman would have drowned in his own saliva. There were some hefty lasses among them, too.

We ended up in a tiny old pub off a paved square. Inside it was busy but not packed, and I found a seat near the fireplace and studied the beams while Callum got me half a pint of cider.

'Been here before?' he asked when he came back.

'No.' I wondered if he'd burst out laughing if I told him precisely how many pubs I'd ever been in; one, and that was only the Working Men's Club to pick up Poll's shopping which she'd left under the table.

'It seems funny,' he began, then stopped.

'What?'

'Nothing. How's your cider?'

'Fine. I have had alcohol before, you know.'

'I never said you hadn't.'

'What were you going to say?'

He pursed his lips and took a sip of his pint. 'Only that it seems funny, odd, to see you out of Bank Top. Out of context, out of your environment. It's like you belong there—'

'Christ, don't say that.'

Callum raised his eyebrows. 'Why, don't you like it?'

'Not much, no.' And yet I thought of the fields that stretched behind our house, the hazy moorland above Harrop, the quiet stones of the cemetery. 'Well, I like some of it.' Clare Greenhalgh, grown up and sleek, smirking at me from the top deck of the bus, nudging the boy beside her and pointing down. 'Not the people so much. But Bank Top's where I'm from, it's my roots. The place where you grow up is part of your identity, whether you like it or not, isn't it?'

Callum shrugged. 'Dunno. Is it?'

'I think so. It's just a shame my roots are in Bank Top.'

'It's not that bad. At least you don't live on a mafia-controlled estate, or in one of these mega tower blocks where the kids drop bricks on passers-by for fun.'

'No, but it's dull and rundown, and every bugger wants to know your personal business.'

The lights of the fruit machine played over Callum's serious face and I thought once again how great it was to have somebody who listened to me. The next time he came to my house I was going to show him Dad's ashes; he deserved to see them.

'I can take or leave Nantwich,' he said, 'it's OK, not a patch on Scotland, obviously. But I always got the impression you loved your village, really, and that was why you never went anywhere much. I reckon you're attached to Bank Top by a kind of spiritual bungee cord.'

'Oh, pur-leeeese.'

'Yeah, because you know all sorts about it, the history and that. I know you slag it off but I thought that was affectionate slagging, like the way kids moan about their mums. Sorry. Or their grans. Even though they love them.'

Good God, he thought I loved Poll.

'Well, I don't like Bank Top, for the record, and if there is any sort of bungee cord in existence, it's about to get snipped. I'm going to tell you something.' My heart started to speed up. 'A great big secret. Nobody knows this, or at least not all of it. Some people know bits, but nobody knows the whole picture . . . '

'Get on with it, then,' said Callum, taking his tobacco out. 'I'm agog.'

'Well, I might not be living in Bank Top much longer.'

He paused, mid-pinch. 'Really? What, a job or something? Oh, I get it, you're off to uni. Where you going? I've kept meaning to ask where you were headed. I really need to get my arse in gear and go to some open days. I missed a load last term.'

'I'm going to Oxford.'

'Fucking hell,' said Callum, breaking into a huge smile.

'You kept that quiet. Oxford University? Fuck me. You must be well clever.'

As soon as the words were out, I regretted it. 'What I mean is, I have a place. To read English, at University College. But I can't go, obviously, 'cause I can't leave Poll on her own. For God's sake, she's seventy and disabled, it would be really cruel. And anyway, I might not get the grades.'

'Yeah, you will,' said Callum, rolling a cigarette. 'You'll get all As, I can feel it in my water. I've got some module results to come, but I'm only predicted Ds. I don't care. Mum says my education's rounded enough, and anyway, I might take a year out. Hell, Oxford, though.'

'But it's a secret,' I insisted, 'you've not to tell anyone.'

He looked at me, puzzled. 'So doesn't Poll know?'

'No. She knows they called me for interview but she thinks I got rejected; she told me I would before I went. The teachers at school know I was offered a place because the college wrote to them and said so, but they think I'm going in October. I put it down on my UCAS as a firm acceptance.' I grimaced. 'Bit of a mess, really.'

'And has the school not told your grandma?'

'She never goes anywhere near it. In the seven years I've been at the grammar, she's never gone to a single parents' evening. She says they're too stuck-up.'

'Jesus. But why keep it a secret? I don't get this.'

'No, I don't either, to be honest.'

'Are you going or not?'

'Keeping my options open.' I dipped my head to swing my hair down defensively, but I'd lacquered it into place and it didn't budge. I knew how stupid I sounded.

'Drink up,' said Callum, 'and I'll get you another. I want to hear how you got yourself in this mess.'

'There was this wasp,' I said, as he walked away.

\*

We stayed in that house for two weeks. Vince hardly talked at all, but that suited. I made little meals that neither of us ate. In the mornings he tried to reclaim the back garden, while I had a trip to the corner shop and then did a bit of cleaning. I found the local library was only three streets away so I spent my afternoons there. I don't know what he got up to then. And in the evenings we watched sitcoms and quiz shows. We always went to bed early.

After a fortnight, Stu came back. 'See my chest,' he said, pulling his shirt up. 'Good, in't it? Mind you, all my arms are peeling. Oh, hey, look at the garden, I never knew I had a lawn.'

Later, I saw him giving Vince a wad of notes in the kitchen. Vince said, 'I think that's my cue to leave.'

Stu said, 'Only if it's convenient. I do need to do some work on my fanzines, though. I'm planning a special with a pull-out section on bootlegs.'

We went back to Poll's, but only to get some stuff I'd left behind by accident. The idea was to sit outside in Stu's car till we saw her go out with the pram, then sneak in.

'Get all your personal documents,' said Vince. 'You need to register yourself wi' a doctor, apart from owt else.' But I wouldn't go in, in case I saw something of Katherine's lying about. I'd had to shut my eyes while Poll wheeled her past on the other side of the road.

We went straight from there to Chorley again. I thought we were returning to Stu's, but Vince stopped outside a row of shops. 'I've a flat,' he said. 'Ovver th' hairdresser's. Come in and have a look.'

You could smell hairspray, I swear, but it was OK. A tiny TV, thin-legged chairs, saggy sofa. The bathroom suite was brown with palm-tree tiles. On the bare single bed was a pile of sheets and towels, still wrapped in cellophane.

'Will you be awreet on your own?' asked Vince.

'Are you not staying?' I said, then had a panic in case he thought it was an invitation.

'I've Stu's car to tek back. Then I've some business to attend to. I'll drop by wi' some groceries later. Are you sure you'll not get lonely?'

'I like being on my own these days,' I said. It was true, although the nights sometimes gave me trouble.

He appeared at tea time with some tins, a loaf, and milk. 'You've gone to skin and bone,' he said as he watched me unpack. Before he went he gave me a phone number. 'This is for emergencies. You can stay here as long as you want, but let me know if you're moving on. Get signed on tomorrow with the DHSS, and see a doctor. There's fifty quid to keep you going till your giro comes through.' He laid it on the table and put the salt pot on top of it.

It had been quiet before at Stu's, but it was quieter after he'd gone. That was all right. I just had to wait till the library opened next day.

# Chapter Seventeen

While he was at the bar I watched a very slim woman in knee boots perching on a man's knee, swinging one leg sexily. I wondered what would happen if I sat on a man's knee; he'd probably never walk again. For a second I imagined lowering myself onto Callum's knee, oh God oh God, think of something else quick. He did a thumbs-up across the bar at me and I had to look away in shame. But by the time he came back, I'd got myself in order.

'So,' he said, shuffling his chair in, 'if it's not a daft question, why did you apply to university if you didn't think you could take up the place?'

'Fear,' I answered promptly. 'I only put my name down for Oxford because Mrs Law told me to. I do as I'm told, mostly, plus she's one scary woman, she makes Miss Dragon look like Shirley Temple. Then, when I got the letter inviting me down, I said to her I couldn't go because I didn't know what train to catch or anything. I'd never been on a train on my own, and it would be December, and dark at four. I also explained that Poll couldn't be left overnight. I thought that would put an end to it, but Mrs Law just said I ought to try and Sort Something Out, and threatened to come round to our house and see Poll herself, which would have been like Godzilla versus King Kong. I was so petrified of Mrs Law that I went and asked Maggie to Poll-sit, which she said she'd do, bless her, but that still left the train problem. Poll said she'd been hearing about that route and apparently there'd been more fatal crashes on that line than any other, and also there'd been a rogue guard luring female passengers into his van by asking if they'd lost a Rolex, then showing them Japanese porn. I think she might have been making that up. But I was still completely rattled, so I went back to Mrs Law and confessed that I just didn't want to go.'

'Was she pissed off?'

'She wasn't very happy.'

She'd gone mental with me. She said I was one of the brightest students they'd had through the school in her time there, and what a total waste it would be not only of my own talents, but of the dedication and interest of the staff, if I ducked out of higher education simply because I lacked the wherewithal to read a timetable. I'd started to cry, which threw her, and her efforts to talk me round after that ended up with me sobbing hysterically. In the finish, she'd had to go and get matron to help calm me down.

'But you were still too frightened to refuse?' asked Callum.

'No, I think I'd have bottled out of going even despite Mrs Law, but then I had this stroke of incredibly good luck. Because, at the last minute, Mrs Law said she happened to be travelling down that way to her brother's to drop off some Christmas presents, and she could give me a lift. There *and* back. I mean, how lucky was that? Maggie said it was Fate, and I agreed with her. And although it was pretty weird sitting in the car with Mrs Law for all those hours, it wasn't as bad as I thought because she turned out to be quite funny one-to-one. She didn't expect me to talk at all, just told me stories while I listened.

'She told me about her childhood and going to a convent school where you had to curtsey to the nuns, and how kind they were to her when her father died suddenly. She said they were kinder to her than her own mother, who spent the wake leaning on men and drinking bourbon, and never even gave her daughter one hug. I kept glancing across and trying to imagine Mrs Law young; I couldn't, though.

'When she'd talked for a long time, she began asking me about life with Poll. I told her the practical things I have to do for my grandma, and how she can be moody with me. Then I went on to Dogman and Maggie; some of that made her laugh. Finally I found myself describing what happened with my parents. Just before I got out of the car, I asked Mrs Law if it was all in my confidential file at school and she said, "Only the basics." So I begged her not to repeat any of it and she said, in this haughty voice, "Do you honestly think I would?" and went straight back to Scary Teacher mode.'

'That's teachers for you. You can't ever make friends with a teacher, however they suck up to you. So what was it like then, the interview? Were they all dead posh?'

'I stayed in my room most of the time because I didn't know what to say to anyone. I did try, in the morning. I thought I'd go down to breakfast and listen in to what the others were saying, see if I could pick up some tips. So I went down and it's all dark wood panelling and narrow little stairs, into this sort of ante-room with a wall of carvings and a door cut into it. A sign next to it said BREAKFAST.

Students were going through the door, so I waited a minute and I went through too. But when I got on the other side, it was pitch black. The door was on springs behind me and once it had closed, I couldn't make a damn thing out. I thought it was a joke, or a test. Like, they might be watching me with infrared cameras to see if I panicked.'

'And did you?'

'Oh yeah. I put my hands out in front of me and felt around but I couldn't make anything out and my chest started to go tight as though I was having an asthma attack. It was dusty, like a secret corridor. Then, I suppose it was only a few seconds later, another door opened right in front of me and there was the dining hall, and this young man peering in at me. I barged right past him to get out into the light. When I looked back, I could see it was a sort of double wall with a space between. I don't know what it was in aid of, but they could have done with a few candles in there or something. So by the time I sat down to breakfast I wasn't in any state to listen or eat. I thought, if there's any dons in here having their Weetabix, they'll have been watching me and thinking, Christ, she's too gormless even to walk though a door.'

Callum was smiling as he took out his tobacco tin again. 'Trust you.'

'I know. If there's a way to fuck up, I'll find it. Then what happened at the interview itself, that was bizarre and surreal too.'

'Bizarre and surreal? That doesn't sound like you, Kat.'

I kicked him gently under the table (me! kicking a boy! in a pub!).

'I'll ignore that. What happened was, I got taken along

to this old room full of books and there were two academic types sitting behind a huge desk, a man and a woman. The woman had a look of Honor Blackman, and the man was the spitting image of our newsagent, Mr Porter, but without the tattoos. I was pretty strung up with nerves, not because I especially wanted to get into Oxford, because I wasn't sure I did. I just hate talking to people I don't know.'

'You talked to me all right the first time.'

'Yeah, but that was different. You were family, we were on home territory.' And there was something special about you from the start.

I looked across at him playing with his pendant and wondered what would happen if he could read my mind.

'Go on, Kat,' he said. 'Give.'

'Yeah, so, anyway – ' I took a long drink and tried to gather my thoughts again – 'I hadn't been sitting down two minutes, I think they were asking what texts I'd been studying for A level, when I felt a tickling behind my knee and when I checked, there was this massive wasp crawling up my leg. I whooped and jumped up, and Honor dropped her glasses under the desk. The wasp buzzed off and we all watched it fly over to the window, head-butt the glass a few times, and settle. Honor goes, "I've told Mr Bowman the heating's on too high, it's ridiculous. And the Porter man goes, I believe there's a nest in the boiler room, Hadrian was telling me last week, though I don't expect anyone will actually *do* anything about it." Next thing, I found myself reaching down for Honor's glasses; I'm so used to picking stuff up for Poll it's automatic. I passed them across the desk to her and she said thanks, and we had a little laugh,

although I was fighting hysteria. So I went to sit down and
– oh, God, it was awful.'

'What? *What?*'

'I felt something sting my side.'

Callum winced. 'Yow.'

'I shrieked at the top of my voice and bolted for the
door, quickly followed by Honor who caught me outside
and bundled me down a corridor into a toilet. Only when
I undid my clothes – ' I leaned towards him conspiratori-
ally – 'because when I said "side" I really meant "bottom"
– there was nothing there, no red mark or anything. So I
flapped about a bit, in case the wasp had got trapped inside
my skirt and was getting ready to do a proper sting.' I didn't
tell Callum but I'd also pulled my knickers down, to be on
the safe side. 'And that's when I spotted the plastic tag. You
know when you get new clothes and the labels are attached
with a plastic thread that you have to cut off, otherwise you
pull a big hole in the material? Well I'd had a new skirt.'
(New knickers, really.) 'And although I'd clipped the long
end of the tag off, I'd left the other stuck in, and it was that
that had pricked me. Not a wasp at all.'

Callum was shaking his head at me.

'I know, I know. Trust me. So I came out of the toilets
hyperventilating, and Honor assumed I had been stung
but that I was trying to be brave. I didn't enlighten her
because that would have made me look even more stupid
than the fight I had with the door. She was all for sending
for some antihistamine cream, or at the very least, some
vinegar, but I told her I'd put a wet tissue on it and I'd be
fine. She sat me in a side room, very plush, waspless, and
gave me a glass of water to sip. Then she said, had I heard

of the Bach Flower Remedies? I didn't know if the question was part of the interview, so I tried to sound noncommittal. She scuttled off and came back half a minute later with her handbag. "Here you are," she said, and brought out a tiny dark bottle with a bulb on the top, like a dropper. "It's totally herbal," she told me, and squirted a dose into my cup. I said, all suspicious, "How come it smells of brandy?"'

'You're seeing that cider off no problem, I notice,' said Callum drily.

'Yeah, well, it's only like apple juice, isn't it?' I took another huge swig to show I wasn't fussed. 'Anyway, Honor maintained it was only the smell, it wasn't alcoholic, and the stuff would help calm me if I sipped it slowly.'

'Did it?'

'Oh, and how. She left me on my own, which was exactly what I wanted, and said she'd be back in fifteen minutes. Then, and this part is weird as well, a little boy appeared.'

'What, like you were hallucinating?'

'No. I think he was somebody's son or something. He wasn't supposed to be there, I suspect, but then I wasn't either, technically. He sneaked round the door and just stared at me for ages, the way kids do. White-blond hair, Spiderman sweatshirt. I reckon he'd have been about four, five. Then he goes, "Does a goat wear a coat?" The Flower Remedy must have been working because instead of ignoring him, I heard myself say, "Does a bat wear a hat?" Then he said, with a dirty laugh, "Do ants wear pants?" and I said, "Do kittens wear mittens?" '

'I see a pattern emerging.'

'So we carried on like this for ages, Does a fox wear socks, Do mites wear tights.'

'Does a fly wear a tie.'

'Do shrews wear shoes, you've got it. He was sharp, I'll give him that. I started saying silly stuff—'

'As opposed to the sensible stuff you'd been saying before.'

'Yeah, and when I couldn't think of any more rhyming clothes we made up nonsense phrases, Does a hog live in a bog, Is a dove in love, Is a cheetah neater. Then Honor returned and he nipped off up some stairs. I was taken back to the interview, only by now I was high as a kite. Instead of being tongue-tied, I couldn't stop blathering.'

'You didn't try the goat–coat routine on them, did you?'

'Oh no, it all made perfect sense, what I came out with, thank God.' I'd been inspired. I could tell they were impressed, and that had made me want to talk even more.

Callum's lips made a little popping sound as he took his cigarette away from his mouth. 'So they offered you a place.'

'I got the letter three days after Christmas. Mrs Law said they're trying these days to give people from, ahem, deprived backgrounds a leg up. So the fact no one in our family's ever got a university degree will have counted in my favour. I've still got to get two As and a B, though.'

'You've got to go. I mean, Oxford. You have, haven't you?'

'Sometimes I think, how can I not? That wasp was an omen, I'm convinced of it. You don't get wasps in winter. It was sent to get me through the interview, because I'd never have managed it on my own. Then I see Poll, stumbling around the place, scraping chutney on her toast instead of jam, and I think, how could I even contemplate leaving her?' I wondered what she was doing at that moment; whether

Dogman was still with her or whether she was sitting on her own in the dark.

'Mmm,' said Callum, noncommittally. 'Tough call. Can't social services sort something out?'

'Not twenty-four/seven. And there's all kinds of rules and regs, it's incredibly complicated to apply, which I suppose is the idea. It's too depressing, I don't want to talk about it.'

We sat in silence for a while. Smoke curled up between us; in the saloon next door, someone was singing 'Lady in Red'.

'Still,' said Callum at last, 'you got a place. That's so impressive. You don't half hide your light under a bushel. You're funny, you're clever . . . '

I'm fat, I thought.

To stop myself blushing I said: 'I'm broke too, I'm afraid. I can get one round in, that's all. Sorry. I thought I had more in my purse.'

'It's OK.' Callum got to his feet. 'I got paid today, and money always burns a hole in my pocket.'

He took himself off to the bar and I went hunting for the ladies'. In the mirror I saw that my hair was still where I'd moulded it, and my face still matt. I touched up the lipstick and, unbelievably, undid two buttons on my blouse. I thought I looked nice, till a skinny girl showing her stomach came and stood right next to me. I could see the thought bubble over her head: Eugh, what a lump. But when I turned to go, I could see she was intent on fiddling with a contact lens, tears streaming down, and probably hadn't even noticed me. 'Shyness is a kind of vanity,' I remembered Cissie saying. 'I read that in the *Reader's Digest*.'

When I came back to our table, someone had taken our seats so we moved over to the side door and stood in the breeze. We started talking about teachers, and the worst ones we'd ever known – Callum had quite a lot to say on the subject – and then he outlined his plans for a year off, and which university he'd like to go to when he came back from travelling the world (Newcastle). He told me about a holiday he and his mum had spent in Thailand, and how she'd once told someone's fortune and they'd paid her with an antique necklace but his mum wouldn't wear it because she said it had sad vibes about it. He described life on a croft, and how he'd have a state-of-the-art photographic studio constructed without ruining the character of the building, and how, at night, he'd play his music at top volume because there'd be no neighbours to complain. 'That's the one thing I hate about where we live now,' he said, leaning sideways to stub his cigarette out in someone else's ashtray. 'It's a terrace and it's over a shop. That's three separate lots of people to moan about noise. I wouldn't mind, but the old woman on the left reckons to be deaf, so how does that work?'

'It's the natural state of the old, to be hacked off.'

'Do you reckon? My grandad used to be nice. Before he died. Mum was always complaining he spoilt me.'

I heard that a lot, about grandparents spoiling grandchildren. I wondered what had gone wrong in our house.

'How are you feeling?' he asked suddenly.

I shifted my weight from one leg to the other. 'OK. My back's stiff, I could do with sitting down. Shall we go into the beer garden and find a table there?'

'Or—' Callum grinned. 'We could go along to that party.'

'For God's sake. I thought I'd said I wasn't going.' I couldn't help but laugh at him. 'Ten out of ten for persistence.'

'I know, I'm very persuasive. I might go into politics if the croft falls through.'

'But I haven't got the ticket any more, so it's academic.'

'No, I've got it. You threw it out of the window; I caught it. I had to chase it right across the road.' He reached into his pocket.

'Well, you'll need to go on your own because I've only got one ticket.'

'Aha, Kat, but that's where you're wrong, because it says here, "Admits two".' He waved the ticket under my nose. 'So, are you up for it?'

I grabbed the ticket off him to check although I knew he was right, held his wrist briefly. 'Tell me why you're so keen to go. You won't know anyone.'

'Those are the best sort of parties,' he said. His face was half in shadow, his cheekbones outlined. The short hair had made his eyes look much bigger. 'I just love clubbing.'

'How does that square with wanting to live on a croft?'

'I'll be old by then, I'll have got it out of my system. Oh, go on, Kat, now I've come all this way.'

·I didn't ask you to, I thought.

'Tell you what; how about we go along, see what it's like, then if you're not keen we can leave.'

And go where? The pubs were ready to close.

'Please?' He held up an imaginary microphone. '*Come with me into the night, You never know what's waiting there.*'

' "Stellar Days"?'

'Angelhunter.' He looked pleased with himself. 'I've

227

been doing my own research into Eighties music. Was it one of your dad's favourites?'

'Yeah, it was; I mean, he had the single. I play it sometimes when I need cheering up.' Poll always complained the beat went straight through the floor. 'It's one of my favourites.'

'So,' said Callum, taking me by the arm, 'in the spirit of "Stellar Days", let's go for it, eh?'

Donna's face when I walked in with him by my side. *'And watch the ice catch fire?'*

'That's my girl,' he said. I let him take me by the hand and lead me to perdition.

Five minutes later we were outside the entrance to Steem. 'Are you cold?' he asked.

'No. Why?'

'I thought you were shivering. Oh, here we go.' He handed the ticket to one of the bouncers, who pointed wordlessly up the stairs. 'Come on.'

The people who'd come behind us were directed down, into a sort of cellar, and we began to climb the illuminated steps towards the thudding music. On the landing, a boy I'd never seen before was leaning his head against the flock wallpaper and groaning. A blonde girl was sitting nearby, scowling. We took no notice; Callum's eyes were fixed on the door ahead and his face was aglow. He was jerking his head already to the beat.

Then, as we walked through into the spinning lights, I heard a riff that sent a thrill down my spine. I gripped Callum's shoulder. 'It's "Cars", they're playing Gary Numan.' It was another sign, and my heart leapt with confidence.

But the riff slid away and the tune changed to something I didn't know, modern.

'It's a sample,' he yelled over the noise. 'Armand Van Helden. The track's called "Koochy". 'S good. Let's get a drink and go up on the balcony.'

The music was so loud it was disorientating; lights flashed in my eyes without any obvious sequence. I saw faces I knew, saw plenty of double-takes, which was good, unless they were saying, 'My God, what does she look like, silly cow.' Callum came back from the bar then went to dance, while I leaned on the rail and watched him. My head felt blurry but I didn't want to lose sight of him. Donna nearby, in the middle of the crowd, I waved but she didn't see me, somebody trying to snog her, somebody letting off a party popper over her head. A black-haired girl dancing close to Callum, waving her arms around in front of his face, showing her ribs, putting her arms round his neck. Callum laughing, throwing her arms off, moving away, moving away. The girl dancing on unfazed, turning to writhe next to someone else. My limbs had gone heavy but my brain was wired.

'What time is Mitch picking us up?' I shouted when Callum returned, stripped to the waist and soaked with sweat.

'Give us that glass,' he signed, and drank so fast that half of it went down his chin. 'Jesus. I'm fucked.' He sat down on the floor with his back to the railings. 'Come here.' He tugged at my skirt, so I lowered myself next to him. Alex and Sita sloped past, nudging each other when they saw me. Callum gave them the thumbs-up and they giggled, and gave it back.

'Why don't you dance?' he yelled in my ear.

I just shook my head.

'It's good. I'll request that "Koochy" for you, if you want. Hey?'

'No thanks.'

'Come down with me, next time something you like comes on.'

'No.' I sighed. 'I hardly look the part, do I?'

'You what?'

'Nothing. I don't want to dance, OK?'

'Suit yourself. You look fine, though. Really.' He smiled and elbowed me in the ribs. 'You should relax more. Come out more, get drunk occasionally.' His face tickled my cheek.

I felt strange; tipsy and anxious and excited and careless.

'Listen,' I shouted down his ear. 'Do you want to know another secret?'

'Bloody hell, what now, Woman of Mystery?'

I started to giggle. 'I'm gay.'

I watched him break out into a slow smile. 'Get away.'

'No, I am. I'm gay.'

'You're not, you know.'

'How come?'

The grin was very sure. 'Because.'

My heart felt like there was a live bat inside it, fluttering and swooping. He was right there next to me, his smell through the smoke, the stubble on his chin. So I kissed him.

He didn't resist. So I kissed him again, and this time he kissed back. All the blood in my body rushed upwards into my head; I thought I was going to faint. Then he pulled away, and put his palms against my shoulders to keep me back.

'No,' he said. 'This isn't going to work.'

'Sorry, sorry. I know, I'm too fat. I don't know what I was thinking—'

Callum stared at me as if I was insane. 'What are you on about?'

I started to talk in a rush, tried to stop tears of embarrassment forming; 'I'm too big for you to fancy. Everyone thinks fat people have no feelings but they do, it's not just thin beautiful people who have souls, is it—'

'Stop it.' Callum pulled me against him for a moment and I wondered if he was going to kiss me again. But he moved away again and put his hand up to show I should keep quiet. 'Kat, Kat, it's nothing to do with your shape. I think you're great. I think you're really fanciable. I—'

'What?'

'I can't fancy you, I mean, I do, but I mustn't. Shit.' He hit his forehead hard with his hand. 'Why did I get myself into this?'

I gazed at him in bewilderment.

'I'm so sorry. I should have told you from the first, but then you wouldn't have had anything to do with me.'

'Told me what?'

'Don't hate me, Kat.' He closed his eyes in pain. 'I'm your brother.'

*

I learned to live in that library. I was there outside the doors when it opened, and always the last one to be ushered out at closing time. They didn't mind because I was quiet and clean. Mostly I took out children's fantasy, Susan Cooper, C. S. Lewis, Andre Norton. But once a week I reread *Pride and Prejudice*. I wanted to climb inside that book and never come out. Wednesdays were bad because the library was closed all day, and Sundays.

It was a Sunday when I phoned Vince. I'd run out of books and it was dark outside. There were some drunks shouting outside the takeaway on the corner.

I was sitting on the sofa, holding a cushion on my lap, when I realized I was patting its back and rocking. That's mad, I thought, and put the cushion down. But my arms felt empty without it. I carried it round the flat for a while, shushing it, then I decided to call him. Just to hear a voice.

He was a long time picking up, and when he did he sounded weary. But he tried to make his voice more cheerful when he knew it was me.

'How're you gettin' on, love?'

I said I was fine. I'd got my giro, and some tablets from the doctor. I said I'd decided I was going to go to apply for college and learn how to be a librarian. He sounded happy when I told him. Neither of us mentioned Katherine.

Then I heard a baby crying in the background.

'Howd on a minute,' he muttered, but I don't know who he was talking to, because there was a woman there. I heard her say, 'I think he might be teething, see his cheeks.' It wasn't Poll.

So I put the phone down, then I called Directory Enquiries. 'Where's this the code for?' I asked them.

'Sheffield,' they said.

I couldn't find my own nail clippers, my violin ones; Vince took them away. But I lighted on a pencil sharpener in one of the kitchen drawers, and managed to unscrew the blade with a coin-edge. So that did the job.

# Chapter Eighteen

'Half-brother,' he'd said as he bundled me into a taxi and thrust a couple of notes at the driver. 'Only half-brother.' As if that made it less dreadful.

He'd steered me out of the room, 'where we could talk properly', and we'd become the rowing couple on the stairs.

'I don't get it,' I kept saying. 'You're my cousin.'

'I lied,' he said. 'Your dad was my dad. Different mums.'

I had to think about that for a few seconds, it was all cock-eyed. Then I rounded on him. 'That's crap. My dad was only eighteen when he died, how could he have had time?'

'He just did.' Callum was pulling at his necklace. 'He met my mum at uni, he met yours at school. Christ, I'm sorry—'

All right being sorry now.

'But someone would have told me – Poll, Cissie, someone in the village. You are so making this up. It's *total* bollocks.'

Callum winced, but went on. 'My mum says she went to Poll, but Poll refused to believe her, threw her out of the house. Actually tried to kill her.'

'Don't talk wet. Poll's moody but she's not a bloody

murderer. For God's sake. I reckon your mum's got a mental condition. Does she know you're here, did she send you, to make trouble?'

'No.' He hung his head. 'She's got no idea. I lied to her too.'

'So the only reason you hung around me was to find out about your – ' I could barely get the word out – 'dad.'

'No.' He jerked his head up. 'No. It was at first, I admit, but I didn't know how things were going to turn out. I didn't know I was going to like you as much as I do . . . '

'But – eugh – that's disgusting. Think, think what you're saying. It's incest, isn't it? You can go to *prison* for that.'

Callum grabbed my arms and held them, looked into my face. 'I could run, now. I could run away from you and this God-awful mess, and never see you again. But you have to hear this. We've got a link, we're connected. You've felt it, haven't you? Haven't you?' He gave me a little shake but I didn't reply. 'Admit it, you can talk to me like no one else. Or you wouldn't have told me all those secrets. And the clouds, nobody else has been interested in my cloud photos except you. You're my sister, my only sibling, it's natural I should feel in tune with you—'

I wrenched myself free and clattered down the stairs to the entrance. Callum came after me.

'Get away from me, or I'll scream,' I called as we landed on the street. One of the bouncers put his head round the doorway, watching.

'Will you just listen? Will you let me finish?' His top, which he'd tied round his waist, was starting to slide down his hips. He looked sweaty and dirty. I wanted to get away from him, fast.

'No. I'm going home.'

'How?'

My heart whirled round in a panic. 'With Mitch,' I said faintly.

Callum shook his head. 'At least let me hail you a taxi. I need to get you back safe, Christ, it's the least I can do.'

I let him follow me to the taxi rank, and sort things out with the cabbie. It made it worse, somehow, him paying the fare, but I had no choice.

I cried all the way home and, do you know, the driver never said a word to me. I suppose they get it all the time.

When I walked in, the house was quiet and the downstairs lights all off. I put my keys and purse in the fruit bowl and went upstairs to wash my face. As I passed Poll's room, I heard her call out.

I pretended I hadn't heard and went into the bathroom, locking the door. I wiped the make-up off as best I could, brushed out the hairspray viciously, then tied my hair back into a tight plait. The clothes I left in a heap under the sink. I'd deal with them in the morning; burn them, probably. When I came out, Poll was still shouting for me.

'Wait a minute,' I said. I went into my bedroom, rooted out my big smocked nightdress and pulled it over my head. It was so comfortable after the basque. I didn't look in the mirror as I passed it.

Poll was sitting up in bed, waiting, with only the bedside lamp on. She wouldn't have been able to see a damn thing. Winston breathed somewhere in the gloom.

'Thank God you're safe,' she said in a quavering voice. 'I've been imagining all sorts.'

I bet you haven't imagined an incestuous entanglement, though, I thought.

'I'm fine,' I said. 'Back in one piece. What time did Dickie go?'

'About ten. What time is it now?'

'Getting on for one.' I wondered if Callum had caught his train, or if Mitch had turned up again. Callum. I must never think of him again.

'I were frittened.' Something gleamed on her cheeks. 'Winston started barking at nowt, an' he wouldn't be calmed. They've had a break-in at Spar, Maggie were tellin' me. There's gangs roaming about.'

'Well, I'm back now.'

'It's dangerous out there.'

'Yes, it is. But I'm here now.'

*

Who else could I go to but Cissie.

It was a buzz of activity when I got there. Freddie the manager was in reception, up a stepladder, fastening bunting to the steel beams, while the women at the desk were blowing up balloons. As I signed in, Ally trotted past wearing a fox fur round her neck. 'Hiya,' she sang, and waggled the head-end of the fox at me. Its little dead paws rolled on her huge bosoms.

'What in God's name's going on?' I asked Cissie when I found her in the lounge writing numbers on lolly sticks.

'It's our fete tomorrow, don't say as you've forgotten. I thought you and Poll were coming?'

'We are, we are,' I said hastily. Poll would be well cheesed off when I broke the news.

'Well, bring your pennies. There'll be a cake stall and second-hand books, and I'm in charge o' t' treasure hunt, you'll have t' have a go at that.'

'Smashing.' I hate fairs, actually. When we had one at Bank Top Primary once, somebody stuck a label on my back saying I was the bouncy castle. I wore it all afternoon, till Mrs Kirtlan spotted it and pulled it off.

'And a dialect poetry recitation with a hamper for t' best performance. Only open to residents. Mr Poole's going to do an Edwin Waugh medley. I s'll have t' have my hanky out for "Willy's Grave".'

'I can't wait,' I said. 'What's Ally's fox fur in aid of?'

'No idea, unless it's come in a bag of jumble. She's a card, she really is. Now, where was I up to with these?'

I helped her finish her lolly sticks and then we went back to her room. While she was shifting Beanies off the armchair, I hung the Do Not Disturb tag on the door, and shut it.

'I've got something to ask you,' I blurted out, the minute she was settled.

She saw by my face it was serious. 'Ahh, love, is it Donny?'

Donny? I was thrown for a moment. 'Oh, no. It's Dad.'

That made her sit up. 'What about him, love?'

'I know,' I said.

'Know what?'

'About his other woman. The one he had on the go when he died.'

Her wrinkly lips pressed together and she sank back against the chair.

'And his other baby,' I went on. 'So it's no use trying to

pretend it never happened. Too late for that. But I want to hear your side of it.'

'Dammit,' she said. 'I knew this would happen, one day. How have you heard? Who's been talking? 'Cause you've not to believe everything you hear, you know; there's some wicked folk out there who only want to mek mischief.'

'That's why I came to talk to you.' I leaned towards her. 'I know I can trust you to tell me the truth.'

'Oh aye, the truth. It's a slippery beggar, truth. My truth, your truth,' she gave a great sigh, 'it all blurs. Have you got this off Poll?'

'No. She's no idea I know anything.'

'So, who?'

'Look, tell me your version of events, then I'll tell you how I came to hear.' Callum's face flashed up before my eyes and I felt a twisting sensation in my chest. Not to think of him.

Cissie sagged. 'I suppose you had to know sometime. You're, what, eighteen now. But it wouldn't have done any good before, telling you your father's failings. He's been everything to you, your dad, whatever his faults were. How could anyone have tekken that away from you? I never rated him so much, but I wasn't going to say owt as'd upset you.'

'But I need to hear about him.'

Her face was working, as though she was fighting back words. 'As long as you aren't angry with me. Don't go shooting the messenger, as they say. I've always tried to protect you, as much as I could, stuck in here. You've been like a daughter.' She reached out her hand and I got up and went over, to kneel by her chair. She took my fingers and held them tightly. 'You're very dear to me.'

'It's OK. Tell me what you know.'

Her voice sunk to a near whisper. 'Poll told me, a month or so after Vince had walked out. She was at her wits' end, looking after you – and you weren't an easy baby, bless you – and still overwhelmed by her son's death. Then her husband deserting her. And, you might as well know it all; it was your mother that Vince ran off with. Can you imagine? Not that we broadcast the fact. I tell you, the moment Elizabeth Castle walked into this family, she started to poison it. Evil.

'Anyway, Poll came to see me, I was still at home then, and we opened a bottle of sherry. We talked about the past, when her younger sister Mary died of polio, she was only seven, and Poll had done everything for her with Florence being ill so often. Dressed her, made her meals. They'd been very close, so it was a terrible blow for Poll when little Mary died. Jean wasn't so cut up; she was always the odd one out. I wasn't surprised when she emigrated.

'And we remembered her dad dying so suddenly of peritonitis, he was only fifty. Everyone else was celebrating the Coronation, it seemed very hard at the time. Poll thought the world of her father. Then she lost her mother in '79. It was one blow after another.

'We were putting this sherry away and she got pretty drunk. She said to me, "Cissie, I shall never care about anybody again. All that happens is, you get hurt." Because she'd worshipped Roger, absolutely worshipped him. And she thought, after his death, that things couldn't get any worse, but then this madam turns up out of the blue, with a baby girl, claiming it's his and that he got her pregnant during Freshers' Week, whatever that is.'

'Baby *girl*?'

'Oh aye, that's why Poll was so hostile. It might have been different if the baby had been a boy. She pined for a grandson. Not keen on women, in't Poll.'

Now I was really confused. God, was there *another* baby out there that was my dad's?

'So Poll told me she threw this young woman out of the house straight away because she was obviously lying, she'd got herself in a fix and was just after money, and she must be scum to go bothering a bereaved mother like that. Roger would never have two-timed like that, Poll said. But even while we sat there shaking our heads, we both knew he would. He'd been spoilt, that was his trouble. Own way and a bag to put it in, from day one. I didn't say that to her, of course. I went along wi' it, and vowed to keep it a secret. Partly I felt really sorry for her, partly I knew it was the drink talking and she'd wake up next morning regretting having told me. We've never spoken about it since.'

'But a baby girl? Cissie, it doesn't make sense.'

'How do you mean, love?'

So I started to tell her about Callum. I told her how he'd first appeared at the bus stop, then at the library, and what he'd claimed to be. 'He said he'd found me on the Internet,' I said, remembering how happy I'd been that day in Miss Dragon's office, and now it was all spoiled. 'He told me about his life and his interests, that he was "straightforward" – I remember that. Of course, I can't believe a single word in retrospect. He could have been anybody, lived anywhere. And right from the word go it was all about Dad, what sort of music he'd liked, could he see a picture, that sort of thing. Pretending his real focus was my mother.' I recalled the way he'd pored over that photo of her; God, he was a good actor.

'And you had him in the house, on your own?' Cissie looked grim. 'Eeh, I think you've had a lucky escape. He could have done anything at you.'

I remembered him palming the beetle diagram. What else had he nicked while he was there? 'He seemed nice at the time.'

'Well, they do. Have you been in touch with the police?'

For all the misery of the situation, I couldn't help smiling. 'And what would they charge him with, exactly? Impersonating a cousin?'

Cissie huffed. 'A phone call wouldn't hurt. They might have his details on their records.'

I shook my head. How to explain that, despite all the lies, he'd felt like the best friend I'd ever had and I still missed him like crazy. The summer of Callum. It had been my best time of my life. I could never tell Cissie about his smell, his laugh, his eyes. That kiss. Oh God, that awful, awful kiss.

'Are y' all right? You've gone a funny colour.'

I swallowed. 'I was still trying to work out how the two stories fit together. You say it was a girl, then this son turns up. Either Poll got it wrong, and the baby was a boy, or there's another one out there, a half-sister, by someone else again.'

I loosed my hand and stood up, feeling as heavy as if I'd stepped out of water. *Don't tell me to relax* said a poster next to Cissie's bed, picture of a hairy terrier; *It's only my tension that's holding me together.*

'Either way,' I said at last, 'my dad wasn't very nice, was he?'

'I think he loved *you*,' said Cissie, looking up at me anxiously.

'Yeah,' I said. But I thought, she could so easily be lying, couldn't she? It's all just words, in the end.

I felt as though I'd lost two people. Back in my room I stared at Dad's portrait, willing him to explain. The grin, the floppy fringe; you'd think he hadn't a care in the world. I looked for Callum's face in his features, saw as if for the first time the long-lashed eyes, though the jaw was different. Or was it? I wasn't sure any more. Through the window, the sky was mostly clear and blue, with some indefinite wisps hanging over the Pike. I watched them for ages, still holding the photo frame, but in the end they melted to nothing.

*It was your mother's fault,* I imagined him saying. *She drove me away, with her mad behaviour.*

Was it my fault too, for being a difficult baby?

*No, absolutely not. You were great. You were my little girl.*

Poll calling from next door evaporated the fantasy. 'I need a hand,' she was shouting. She sounded upset.

I went through to her room and found her with her sweater up round her neck and her bra tied in knots. Her old breasts sagged down over her blown-out stomach.

'Blasted thing,' she said. 'I don't know what I've done.'

I tried not to look as I pulled the sweater off and turned my attention to the bra. I'd never done anything so intimate for her before and we were both ratty with embarrassment.

'What the hell have you done to it?'

'I don't know. I can't flamin' see, can I?'

Normally she's good with bras. At the market she chooses ones with silk rosebuds on the front, so she can still cut the scratchy labels off but she doesn't get them inside out; or, in the event of no rosebud style being available, I sew a shirt button between the cups for her to feel. Glamorous it isn't.

'You've managed to twist every damn strap there is. God. And you've bent the hook, so it won't fasten any more. That's with yanking it. I'll have to cut it off and sew another on, unless I can force it back into shape with some pliers. Look, take this one off and start again with another.'

I wrenched open the bra drawer and threw a new Playtex at her. She caught it as it hit her chest, and started to unravel it, feeling for the button. I went round the back to help.

'I'm all right now,' she snapped. 'Go and get t' kettle on, do summat useful.'

I thumped downstairs and made two mugs of tea, then took mine to the settee so I could sit next to Winston. I stroked his bony brow but he didn't wake up.

'All he does is sleep these days,' said Poll, peering over the back of the settee as she walked past. 'Mind, it'll do him good. He dun't cough while he's asleep.'

She came in with her tea and sat in the armchair nearest me. 'Dickie says, if he's still coughing by Monday, we should tek him to t' vet's. He might have got a piece of bone fast in his throat. Or it could be furballs; he does chew hisself a lot, so it's likely. Dickie's been putting Vaseline on his nose to stop him getting bunged up; apparently it works a treat for cats. They lick it off and it lubricates their insides, he saw it on *Pet Rescue*. I'd have put it on Winston myself, except I'd probably have greased his back end by mistake.' She laughed wheezily.

'Or used Vicks, and had his nose on fire.'

'Aye, well.'

'I know; I should try being blind.'

'Well, you should. Then you'd have more patience.' Poll sipped her tea virtuously.

'That's the pot calling the kettle. You're the shortest-tempered person I know.'

'I've a lot to put up with.'

'Haven't we all.'

Winston let out a huge shuddering sigh. We held our breaths to see if he'd cough, but he only yawned and smacked his chops.

She mumbled something into her mug and got to her feet.

'You what?'

'I said, I'm sorry if I was a bit sharp with you upstairs. It's frustrating, though.'

I nearly dropped my tea on the carpet.

She went on: 'Are you having some malt loaf? I could just do with some.'

'Let me come round a minute, I feel quite dizzy.' She missed the sarcasm completely. 'Yeah, all right.' I balanced the mug on the arm of the settee and stood up. 'But I'll cut, you can butter. I'm sick to death of blood on my cakes.'

\*

A week later I paid a visit to Dad's. I had no key any more and there was no answer when I rang the bell. All Mum's pots were dead, and there was post on the mat behind the letterbox. I got in through the kitchen window at the back.

I could see straight away things weren't right. It smelt. There was food on the floor round the bin and you couldn't see the drainer for pots. And it was a shock, because Mum always kept everywhere beautiful. I thought, he's died. I'll go through and find him full length on the rug.

He was lying on the sofa and he wasn't dead. He wasn't even asleep. He rolled his eyes when he saw me. I said, 'I'll make a start on the kitchen.'

When I went back in the lounge he'd gone upstairs, so I tidied round the sofa too. There was a bottle of Luçozade by one corner, except, when I sniffed it, it wasn't Lucozade at all. I poured it down the toilet and threw the bottle in the bin.

After half an hour he came down again, and he was in fresh clothes. I carried on washing up, didn't say anything.

'I wouldn't have recognized you,' he said. 'You've gone that thin.'

'Have you any milk?' I asked.

He just looked at the floor.

'I'll pop down to Haslet's and get some. Is there anything else, while I'm there?'

I could have been a Martian, the way he kept staring.

'I heard about your feller. Where's the baby?' he said finally.

'I lost it,' I said. Which was true in a way.

He nodded. 'We're out of bread and lavatory paper,' he said. 'You'll want some Shreddies. I'll make a list. Do you have a car? You could have a run to Tesco's.'

'No car,' I said. 'And I'm off Shreddies at the moment.'

'Whatever you want, then,' he said, and shuffled out. And just like that, I was home.

# Chapter Nineteen

I didn't want him near me ever again, but I wanted an explanation. Every day that passed and I hadn't heard from Callum, I thought about destroying the wasp pendant. I imagined hurling it in the River Douglas, or burying it somewhere in the cemetery. Or laying it on the railway line so it got bent out of shape the next time a train passed. Poll used to do that with pennies when she was a girl; other children's, not her own.

Two things stopped me getting rid of the pendant, though. One was, it was the only physical reminder I had of my brother, and if I threw it away, I might as well have dreamed him. And the second was to do with my place at Oxford, in case the wasps were somehow related by luck, and junking the pendant meant forfeiting the grades. I thought I'd hang on to it till after the results came out, at any rate.

The night before, Rebecca phoned in a state; said she'd had a dream that she'd sat the wrong paper, and did I think it was too late to call Mrs Clements to check? I'd been pretty cool about results day till then, but afterwards I was like something on springs.

'For God's sake, sit down. You're mekking me weary just

watching you,' moaned Poll as I hovered painfully between the living room and the kitchen.

'Leave her alone, she's on edge,' said Dogman over his shoulder. 'Hey, Katherine, while you're up can you do us some cheese on toast?'

I made it without grumbling, ate half a packet of Fig Rolls while I watched the grill. After all, he was harmless; there was no mystery about Dogman. He was disgusting, but he wasn't about to come out with any jarring revelations. Better the Dogman you know.

That night it took me ages to get off to sleep, and when I did I dreamed I was back in the interview room with Honor asking me about my AS texts. The questions weren't difficult, but every time I tried to answer, I found my mouth was full of chewing gum. I tried to pull it out but there was more and more, great long strings of it, until it was all over my hands and blouse, and my mouth still full. Honor looked totally pissed off with me and I knew I'd failed.

Winston woke me, hawking in my ear, at six, so I went downstairs in my dressing gown to wait for the post. Two hours later, Poll made an appearance.

'Have they come yet?'

'No.'

'You've to phone Maggie when they do, remember.'

I went back up to have a wash, straining my ears all the time for the letter box.

'Summat's come,' I heard Poll shout up. I threw the towel on the floor, pulled the dressing gown on again and thundered down the stairs.

*YOU HAVE PAST, 10/10* said the note she was holding.

It had been written on a piece of cereal packet. Bloody Dogman.

'What's it say?' asked Poll.

Dogman tapped at the front window. 'I've a doctor's appointment at nine, can't stop. I'll see you later,' he mouthed through the glass. He took a good long look at my cleavage before backing off down the path. I was delighted to see him smack into the edge of the coping stone and wince in pain.

'It's a good-luck card,' I told her. 'I'm going to get dressed now.' But as I turned to go, I spotted the postman way off near the top of the brow. I could have run out naked, I was so desperate.

At last the letter box clunked and there was my future on the mat. I ran to open the envelope.

'Is it here?' asked Poll, somewhere in the background.

I let out a howl of grief and collapsed on the chair. 'I've failed! I don't believe it, I've failed. How? How did that happen? Oh bloody, bloody hell.' I buried my face in the cushion while Poll swiped the bit of paper off the arm and went to get her magnifier.

I raised my head to see her standing by the window, frowning. If only she could see something different printed there.

'I can't mek it out, it's too small.'

'It's two As and two Bs.'

'Two As and two Bs? How is that a fail? You told me it was a U if you didn't pass. Honest, what are you like? Histrionics over nowt. You want summat to skrike about, you do.' She threw the scrap of paper at me and it swooped to the floor.

'But the A in General Studies doesn't *count*. God. I was supposed to get AAB, at least. How have I got a B in English, for God's sake?'

'What do you mean, you were "supposed to get"?'

I buried my face in my hands. 'You might as well know now, 'cause I'm not going. I had a place at Oxford. I didn't tell you because there didn't seem any point. Well, there isn't now, that's for sure.'

As Poll stood and scratched her head, I ran back to my room to get dressed. I had to get out of the house, and quickly.

I must have sat for an hour or so on the war memorial. Why was my life so crap? Why couldn't just one thing turn out right for me? I knew I was clever, and that wasn't boasting, that was empirical fact based on years and years of exam results and coursework and reports and what Mrs Law had said to me, and God knows, I'd lived with the swot label for years and I wasn't even going to reap the reward, it was so BLOODY unfair.

— *But you weren't going to university anyway. You know you couldn't leave Poll on her own. You always knew that. You should never have applied in the first place.*

— I could go. I could! Now the place at Univ had been taken off me, I realized I'd never wanted anything else so badly. Poll would have sorted something out with Dogman or Maggie, or I could have had a proper go at the council to see about a home help. Just because her life was restricted was no reason for mine to be as well. I'd have done it somehow.

— *That's a fib and you know it. Never mind worrying about*

*Poll, that's a smokescreen. You're too scared to leave. That's the truth. You think you'd never cope on your own.*

— I would cope, I really would. They have college rooms for you to live in, and college parents to look out for you, and there are clubs to join, and tutors to talk to if you're feeling low. And you get three meals a day but I know how to cook and clean anyway, that side of things. Thanks to Poll, I can wire a plug in seconds.

— *And how good are you at speaking to strangers? Finding your way round new places? Have you really thought through how complicated adult life is? There are trains and buses to catch, maps to read, bank accounts to manage, doctors to register with; there are relationships to form and maintain and finish, all sorts of social events to attend. At some point you'll have to learn to drive, apply for jobs, rent a house. Can you honestly imagine yourself doing these things?*

— I can't be the only one, though, there must be other students feeling scared about leaving home. I thought of Rebecca, Donna, Nicky, Alex, whatever our results were today, all of us peeling away from our old lives and spinning off into the unknown. Terrifying. But people coped, didn't they?

— *You don't have to go anywhere. Clare Greenhalgh has bought a house two doors down from her mum and goes round every night for her tea. Better to be dull and safe. And how would Winston feel if you walked out on him? You can't explain a degree to a dog. He'd probably pine to death, and it would be your fault.*

Rainy afternoons with Winston on my lap and a box of chocolates between me and Poll on the sofa. Was it such a bad life? Being a carer was an important job, that's what the Rehab officer had told me. The world couldn't turn without carers. I'd never have to justify my lifestyle, leading Poll on my arm.

Then Dogman popped into my head; Dogman taking us to a cafe in Bolton once after a big win on the horses, me pointing out that other customers were leaving tips, Dogman shouting out, 'Tip? They want a tip? I'll give 'em a tip. Never wipe your arse on a broken bottle.' Everyone turning round to stare while he guffawed at his own wit.

I had to get to Oxford. I had to get to Oxford, or I'd die.

There were quills all across the sky as I walked home. There's irony for you, I thought, now trying to pick over the exam questions where I might have slipped a grade.

They were sitting round the table when I got in; Maggie, Dogman and Poll, sharing a Swiss roll.

'There's a Mrs Lord been on t' phone for you,' Poll piped up. 'She says summat about your "insurance", is that right? Anyroad, you've to ring her, she says.'

I knew what that would be. Did I want to take up my reserve offer at Aberystwyth. No, was the answer. I only stuck it down because we had to put something, and it happened to be the first one on the list.

I dialled the school number with shaking hands but only got the engaged tone.

'Well, Vince was a clever man, you know,' Poll was saying. 'Brilliant wi' figures. He should have been an accountant, really. Not stuck at t' loco works all them years.'

'And your Roger.' Maggie nodded sympathetically.

'Oh, now he was sharp as a tack. Mind you, I went in for th' Eleven Plus, and there were only six of us sat it.'

'Aye, I remember that,' said Maggie. 'Were it a clerical error?'

'I don't know. Unless my father demanded I sit it. He were a bit of a mard, that headmaster, he might have put me in for th' exam just so he could have a quiet life.'

'Didn't you have a funny turn, though?'

Poll laughed creakily. 'It were t' statues. All these naked statues round the room.'

'Where was it? The Mechanics'?'

'That's right. I'd never seen owt like it. And they put me bang next to a marble man, all his tackle hanging out. So the first thing I do is, I knock my inkwell ovver and there's ink everywhere, on their nice parquet and down t' table leg. I was never going to pass after that.'

Maggie tutted and took another slice of roll. 'I weren't clever at school. Do you remember the time Miss Eavis asked us which window we should shake a duster out of? She wanted me to say, it depends on the way the wind's blowing, but I said the back window, in case the neighbours see how dusty your house is. She thought I was being cheeky. And I got the cane once off Mr Marsden, for saying the Equator was an imaginary lion that ran round the world. They weren't nice like they are now, teachers.'

'I'm dyslexic,' said Dogman.

The phone rang under my hand and I jumped a mile.

'Hello? May I speak to Katherine Millar please?' My heart rejoiced to hear Mrs Law's stern tones.

I started to gabble about Aberystwyth and having a re-mark, but she stopped me.

'I've been onto the Admissions Tutor at University College and they're going to call me back. There's nothing you can do at the moment but wait. Would you be prepared to accept a deferred place, if one were offered?'

'I don't know. I'm scared that if I don't go this year, I'll never go. Do you understand what I mean?'

'Yes, I think I do.' Mrs Law was brisk. 'But you'd take it if it was the only option?'

'I suppose.'

'Good. I'll get back to you as soon as I hear from them. All right?'

After I put the receiver down I had to face Poll.

'So, did you get in, or what?' There's something about Poll's eyes; even though she can't see very well, it feels as though she's staring into your soul. Maggie and Dogman turned to look at me.

'They're going to let me know. But if I do get a place, I'm going to take it, Poll. I have to.'

Poll's face fell. I could tell she was totally shocked. Maggie reached across and patted her on the arm. Dogman shrugged and took an enormous bite of cake.

'Cross that bridge when you come to it,' murmured Maggie, still patting away.

'I'll be upstairs, then,' I said, like the coward I was. 'Can nobody use the phone till Mrs Law calls back?'

'Now don't get yourself in a state. It'll probably come to naught,' I heard Maggie say as I left the room.

It was past dinner time when Mrs Law called back. I went to tell Poll straight after. She was in the kitchen with Maggie, Dogman having gone off to the betting shop. Maggie was watching her make a cup of tea; pick up the cordless kettle with one hand, find the tap with the other and turn it on, feel up the side of the kettle for the spout and, keeping her fingers there, move it across the sink till it was under the stream and she had water splashing over her fingertips; then take her fingers away whilst keeping the kettle totally still. I saw her listening for the sound of it getting full and testing the weight of it through her wrist. Then she turned back and felt around for the little contact knob on the kettle base, and slotted it home. Her fingers crawled up the handle to the switch at the top, and she flicked it on. I slipped over and turned the tap off for her.

'Well?'

'I've got in. I've got a place at Oxford for this October,' I said, feeling queasy with fear and happiness.

'That's smashing, love,' said Maggie, uncertainly. 'Fancy. We s'll have to start talking posh now, you and me, Poll. Holding our little fingers up when we sup our tea.'

Poll's expression was one of utter dismay. 'So are you going?'

Maggie held her breath.

'I don't see how I can't. It's a once-in-a-lifetime opportunity. Some people would give their right arm for a place.'

'That's right,' said Maggie. 'You've to mek the most of your education. Although Manchester University's very good, and it's close to home. Dawn's Paul went there and he works for Marks and Spencer's now.'

'But I haven't got a place at Manchester. I've got one at Oxford. Don't you see, being clever is the only thing I've ever been good at. It's the right place for me. It'll give me time to think what to do with my life. I'll come back.'

'Aye, but will you?' wailed Poll. 'Will you come back to your blind old grandma once you've tasted the good life? Or will you be off to London or somewhere, doing some high-powered job with no time even for a visit?'

'Of course she'll come back,' said Maggie. 'Won't you, love? Yes, look, she says she will.'

'But how am I going to cope without you?'

The kettle clicked off. Poll reached for it angrily and, before either Maggie or I could stop her, she'd snatched it up and poured boiling water over the kitchen top and down her leg.

'How am I going to manage on my own?' she kept saying as we cut her tights off and bathed her shin with cold water. 'Is it blistering?'

'No, it's just red, that's all,' said Maggie.

'Well, it stings like the devil. I should see a doctor.'

'I don't think there's any need.' I left them while I went to mop up the mess in the kitchen.

'What if I'm in shock?' she shouted after me.

'I'll ring the surgery, ask Mrs Ashburner at reception, if you like.'

'Aye, do that. Tell her I'm in terrible pain.'

I'll tell her you are a pain, I thought. She's tipped scalding water on herself deliberately, Mrs Ashburner. What would you do with her?

'Tell you what,' I said from the doorway, 'I'll go up there and ask if there's anything I can get from the chemist. Are you all right to stay, Maggie?'

Maggie nodded. But she followed me to the front door.

'You have to understand, love, she lost her son when he went away to college.'

Do you think I'm stupid, I nearly said. 'I know. But that was different.'

'I'm just saying.'

I backed out, pulling the door to sharply. I needed to go to the library and see Miss Dragon.

*

'It wasn't exactly *The Corn is Green*,' I told Miss Dragon. No one to lift me shoulder-high and carry me in triumph down the street: nobody strong enough.

'I expect your grandma's proud, really, she needs some time to get used to the idea. Anyway, never mind that. You've got in, that's what's important,' she said, giving me a hug unexpectedly. Miss Mouse, standing by, touched my arm and smiled shyly. This was more like it. I hadn't felt so happy for ages.

'We've got you this, for your studies,' Miss Dragon went on, bringing out a Waterstone's bag from under the counter. 'I'd have given it to you whether or not, because I know you'll use it.'

It felt like a brick, but it turned out to be *The Oxford Companion to English Literature*. Both women had signed their names under a Best Wishes for the Future message on the flyleaf. I glanced round to see who might be watching, but there was hardly anyone in; Thursday afternoon, a quarter to two. Come half three it gets busier, when school comes out.

'I feel I have a vested interest in your education.' Miss Dragon picked up a pile of leaflets from the desk and shuffled them like cards till they were edge to edge neatly. She lined them up with the corner of the counter. 'We think you'll go on to great things. It's about time you left us behind, spread your wings.'

Then the phone rang and Miss Dragon picked up. I stood

for a while, in case it was going to be a short call and there'd be more time for singing my praises. Miss Mouse waited too, smiling all the time.

'Well done,' she whispered, twice, before drifting away.

I watched her thread her way between revolving book stands to work at the table Callum and I had used, last time we'd been here. Callum again. When was he going to stop invading my head? But I ached to tell him my news. *Fan-fucking-tastic*, I could hear him saying. I wished to God he'd call, even if it was only so I could tell him to get lost.

I looked back at stout, lovely Miss Dragon tapping the notepad with her blunt-ended fingers, her mouth showing impatience with whoever was on the other end. She was stretching herself up straight and pulling her cardigan round her. I could tell she was cross with someone. But she liked me. And whatever I'd been thinking, even if she was a lesbian, there was no gayness in that hug. It had been warm and kind, happy for my happiness; maternal.

*

It wasn't long before Vince caught up with me. I wasn't sure what you did when you left a rented place, so I'd taken the keys but left a note of my dad's phone number on top of the TV. Daft really, but I wasn't thinking straight.

We met on the Town Hall steps; I told him where I'd be. When I handed over the keys, he said, 'If you're sure. You could have stayed there longer, if you wanted.'

'Will you be coming back?'

'No,' he said. 'I've to look after her now. She's been pretty poorly.' He scratched his head like he was embarrassed. 'She took some finding.'

'Who?' I asked, because I wanted to hear him say it.

'Judith.'

'And the baby.'

'Aye; and t' little lad. Little Callum.' He'd smiled fondly and I'd wanted to slap him in the face.

'I don't need you any more,' I said rudely.

'I know,' he said. 'But I'll still send you money.'

In films they always say, 'I don't want your money', but I kept quiet. The packets came for years, all the time I was at college, and I spent them all.

Don't think I loved him, because I didn't. I realized long ago he wasn't father material; Katherine's or mine. He was just useful for a while.

# Chapter Twenty

Rebecca got her place at Bristol, Donna was off to Lancaster by the skin of her teeth. For two whole weeks I was leaving Bank Top to go to Oxford, till Fate poked me in the eye once again.

At home, Poll, Maggie and Dogman had been mounting a three-pronged attack to dissuade me from going.

'You'll have to completely change the way you talk, you know. They'll never understand you like you are. They'll think you're mentally deficient.' – Poll.

'I've brought you a brochure on Manchester University. It's six year owd, but I don't suppose t' place has changed that much. Dawn says Paul was home every weekend, and he could have stopped there if he'd wanted, and travelled in each day. It would save you a stack of money. Otherwise you end up in terrible debt, for years.' – Maggie.

'I've brought you a video, about some college girls who all get murdered one by one. Killer's in t' roof space and he comes down at night and chops bits off 'em.' – Dogman.

I spent every hour I could at the library, where Miss Dragon was compiling me a reading list while we waited on the official one turning up.

'Some of these I've had to order in from Manchester Central,' she said, scrutinizing the column of titles. 'Of course, you'll soon have access to one of the finest libraries in the country.' She looked at me over the top of her reading glasses. 'You're a lucky girl, you know.'

'I appreciate that.'

'How's your grandma?'

'Livid.'

Miss Dragon sighed and leaned her forearms on the counter. 'I gave up decades of my life to look after my father. And after he died, what was there left?'

'I don't know.'

'A bungalow in Harrop, to myself. Of course, I had my qualifications and my job, one keeps busy, there's the RSPB . . . But I like to think I could have got a little further, had I made different choices. So let your grandma be livid. You have a life to lead.'

'I've got an interview with the Rehab Officer next week, to talk through care packages.'

'Well, that's splendid. Taking practical action; good.'

'Yeah. The trouble is, she's so stubborn. They have people to train you, show you how to do ordinary household tasks with limited vision, but she won't let them in the house. She says they'll snoop. And they have all sorts of gadgets, talking clocks, embossers, brilliant stuff, but she's really choosy about what she has.'

Miss Dragon frowned. 'Why is that? You'd think she'd want to be independent.'

'Oh, she does and she doesn't. One minute she's wailing for help, the next she's shrugging you off. I can't do right for doing wrong. The objection to the gadgets is that they cost money.'

'Doesn't she get them free? She should do, a pensioner with . . . Sorry, I'm assuming she has no assets. None of my business, of course.'

'No, you're right. She's as poor as a church mouse, she's always telling me.' Which is why no computer, no mobile phone, charity-shop clothes, I could have carried on. But I didn't want Miss Dragon to think I cared about things like that.

'So what's the problem? Are social services being awkward about it? I've heard some dreadful stories about means testing.'

'Social services are fine. Well, they did lose a form once and we were waiting for ages, but mainly they're pretty helpful. It's Poll who's the obstruction. She says she won't have them going through her private documents. She says she came from a generation where your personal finances were nobody's business but your own, and she doesn't see why total strangers should see how little money she has and make mock.'

Miss Dragon tutted. 'People of your grandma's age are often fiercely proud. I don't suppose she approves of credit either, does she?'

'God, no. Not least because to get yourself a credit card you have to give all sorts of information about yourself. She's spitting fire when these researchers stop her in the street and ask what brand of cooking oil she prefers. She hit a woman once. It was so embarrassing.'

'I can imagine it was.'

Miss Mouse floated by and smiled sideways, without raising her head.

I felt like I was back in the fold again.

*

Walking back down the village, under a sky that threatened drizzle, I tried to see Bank Top as though for the first time. Imagine not living here any more. Would I miss the place? Past the doctors' surgery, with its nosy waiting room, always someone calling out some awkward question or other when you went in to collect a prescription. Past the church where I'd had to go every Easter, Christmas and Harvest, on account of attending a church school, and where Revd Rowland had once given a really good talk on bullying, which had had no effect whatsoever. Past the sweetie shop, the Methodists', the road leading to Bank Top Primary Hell. It was impossible to see this long street as just a road with buildings on it. Everything was filtered through memories.

That led me to thinking about Oxford, and what it would actually be like starting university. Would I get a room to myself? With a sink? What if there was nowhere to be sick in private, and I put on *stones* in weight?

What if I got lost on the way to a tutorial? And the don thought I was messing about, and assumed that I was lazy? What if everyone turned out to be way cleverer than me? If it came out that I only got a B, while all the other students had As? And they decided I was only let in because I was from a lower-class background? Did you have to write your grades down anywhere, so people could see? Maybe they got read out at the first tutorial.

What if all the other students had loads of mo
did expensive hobbies that I couldn't join in w.
they all had dead posh clothes? What if they really *couldn't*
understand my accent?

*What if the door had been the omen, and not the wasp?*

I don't know what I'd been thinking. Leave home, me?
Two minutes, I'd last.

I wanted to call in at the cemetery, but I'd already
been longer than I'd said and there was Winston to walk so
I carried on down the Brow, feeling thoroughly depressed.
As soon as I got in, I'd find Poll's tea tray and hit myself
over the head with it a few times.

I felt in my peggy purse for the key, then realized I'd left
it on the sideboard. I rang the bell and waited. Normally
you get a scratching of claws on wood, some snuffling or a
bark, followed by old-woman swearing in the background.
But today all was quiet. Poll must be round at Maggie's,
or in the garden. So I went down the ginnel at the side of
the house and through the gate. The garden was empty
and the back door locked.

In the outhouse, where Poll once used to keep coal
and which currently houses a broken washing machine
that Dogman's going to fix someday, I felt above the lintel
for the spare key. Then I let myself into the kitchen and
pressed the kettle switch as I walked past. I flipped up the
lid of the bread bin, extracted a chocolate sponge slice
from the plastic packaging, and folded it, whole, into my
mouth.

I only found Poll when I came through into the living
room.

It was like those TV murders, where all you see at first is

a hand sticking out. I gaped down at her curled-over fingers for a second, then ran round to the other side of the sofa to see the rest. She was flat out on her back, one arm flung above her head, eyes closed. Her skirt was up above her knees, showing the top of her tights, and her forehead was bleeding where she'd struck it against the gas fire as she went down. One slipper was missing. For a second I thought she'd been attacked. Then I spotted Winston, also motionless, near her feet. I know it sounds mad but I went to him first.

I pushed his head gently up and it rolled sideways in my hand. When I let go, it just flopped to the carpet. His flank had a caved-in look about it; he reminded me of an empty nightdress case. I couldn't see breathing.

'Poll,' I yelped in fright. 'Poll? Can you hear me?'

I turned back and knelt by her head. I reached out to touch her cheek, my arms weak with panic. Her eyelids flickered.

'Poll!'

No response, so I heaved myself up and made for the telephone. Trembling all over, I dialled for an ambulance, listened to the choices, answered some questions. I was to keep talking to her, they said. Gather any medication she needed. Don't attempt to move her, or give her anything to eat or drink. Paramedics would be there within fifteen minutes.

I should have gone back to sit with her but instead I phoned Dogman's mobile. Maggie would have been nicer but she's no car and she's not allowed to lift anything heavy.

'I'm only at t' top of t' Brow,' I heard him shout through the swish of traffic. 'I were coming round anyway to knock a nail in that bit of carpet on t' landing. Get some Bailey's down her, that might bring her to.'

I ignored this stupidity and went to sit by Poll, who was now twitching her head and moving her lips like a dreamer.

'You're OK,' I kept saying, which was a huge lie but it's what you say to accident victims even when limbs are hanging off. 'I've called an ambulance and Dickie's on his way.' I wondered whether to lie about Winston too.

Then the door burst open and Dogman was there, two carrier bags full of crap in his hands as usual. He dumped the bags on the floor.

'Have you a blanket?' he said. 'We could put a cushion under her head too.'

'I don't think you've to move the patient,' I told him. I lowered my voice: 'In case you paralyse them.' I went to get the blanket, though.

When I came back he was prodding Winston while still talking to Poll. He made a slitting-throat gesture at me and pointed to the dog, let's hope he never goes in for bereavement counselling, then swivelled on his haunches and peered closely at Poll. 'What's this in her hair?' he hissed. 'It looks like mouse dirt.'

I leaned over. 'Chocolate sprinkles,' I said, like it was perfectly normal. I knew it was probably down my front as well as round my mouth. 'Shift out of the way then I can throw this blanket over her. Did you leave the front door open for the ambulance men?'

Just before they came to take her away, Poll woke up. We watched her eyes focus and unfocus a few times before she was really with us. 'I tripped ovver Winston,' she said weakly.

'I know, I guessed.'

'He's poorly, I think.' She tried to raise her head.

'No, he's fine. Just sound asleep,' said Dogman.

She drifted off again. Then, as the paramedics shouted from the hall, she squinted at me. 'You took your bloody time, you did.'

The paramedics were upbeat about the situation.

'What's your name, love?' Pause. 'What's her name?'

'Pollyanna Millar. We call her—'

'Pollyanna? Pollyanna, can you hear me, love? You've been in the wars, haven't you? But we'll soon have you in safe hands. We'll have you break-dancing again before you know it. Can you tell us where it hurts? Can you feel this? Could you give my hand a little squeeze? That's smashing. Now we're just going to lift you onto a stretcher, so you might—'

While they got her onto the stretcher, Dogman saw to Winston, rolling him up tenderly in the blanket. 'I'll have him,' he whispered. 'You go with Poll.'

'Are you going to the vet's with him?'

'Do you think there's any point?'

'There's some money for bills in the top drawer. Take him, please. Just in case.'

'Aye, awreet, I will.' Dogman shifted the blanket against him as though he was carrying a baby. 'Give us a ring from th' hospital, will you?'

I nodded, and we all trooped out.

'Have you locked your front door, love?' said the lady paramedic as we stood by the back of the ambulance. 'Only there's scum who'll break in even at times like this.'

I ran back to check, even though I knew for certain I'd shut it with the latch on.

*

It had been a long day, but it was an even longer night. They sent me home about eight, by which time they thought Poll might only be suffering from concussion and a twisted ankle, but they said they still wanted to keep her in for observation. I wondered if her notes said, 'Pollyanna Millar: fell over dog'.

I had to get the bus back, in the dark, and I had no coat and only just had enough money for the fare. When I got there, the house was chilly and there were no lights on, and I was shaking with cold and nerves as I walked in through the porch.

I checked every room as I went round lighting the place up, in case a burglar had got in, hidden himself in the wardrobes or under the beds, or in the airing cupboard, or under the stairs with the vacuum cleaner, or behind the long curtains in the front room, or under the sink. I struggled not to think about the Killer who lived in the Attic, or rapists who shinned up drainpipes.

Our attic entrance was over the landing and, when I went to look, well covered with unbroken cobwebs, so clearly no psychopath was using it as a hideout at the moment. But the idea of a man scaling the walls and his face rising up against ·the blackness freaked me so much I had to go and make sure all the windows were shut tight. Then I re-checked the beds, wardrobes, etc. in case someone *had* climbed in upstairs while I'd been downstairs. All the time I was thinking, this is so stupid, because even if

Poll was here and an axe murderer broke in, what could she do against him?

Then I imagined Winston leaping to my defence against an intruder, in a feeble, miniature sort of way, and that made me feel so sad and lonely I started to cry. When I'd called earlier from the Royal Bolton, Dogman had said the vet thought Winston had been run over. He must have hopped through the dog-flap and then nipped out illegally through the gate, although I'd not left it open. Maybe Poll thought she'd put the bolt on when she hadn't. Anyway, he'd probably seen something on the opposite pavement and gone hurtling across. Nobody knocked at the door and said, I think I've flattened your dog, but then the driver might not even have spotted him, he's so small. There was some blood in his poo, the vet said, so that meant internal bleeding, and his claws were frayed at the tips as if he'd been pushed along tarmac at speed. Dogman described Winston staggering home and dragging himself through the flap, across the kitchen and living room, to collapse between the sofa and the armchair, where he died. I saw it all as he spoke. How was I ever going to break it to Poll?

Poll, lying crumpled on the carpet; Poll under a white sheet on a metal bed with glazed eyes, this terrible gash on her forehead. Me standing there in turmoil, waiting for the doctors to tell me what was going on. What if they were wrong and it had been something serious that affected her balance? Maybe I'd go tomorrow and they'd take me off into a side-room, like they do on *Casualty* when they have to break bad news, and say, 'Are you next of kin?'

And now back at home, alone and upset, with no dog even. I never thought I could miss her so much. I hadn't spent a night on my own ever before. Dad was no help now, of course, smirking at me from his photos, the big deceiver. I wasn't speaking to him because when I'd gone to the cemetery to tackle him about Callum, all he'd sent was a cloud-trail of Morse code. 'Sackless bloody symbolism,' I'd shouted up at the sky. 'Why do you have to talk in riddles all the time?'

I almost phoned Dogman again: I was *that* desperate, even though it would probably have been a frying-pan/fire situation. I could just imagine the sort of comfort he'd offer, given half a chance. My opportunity to see the glories that lay beneath his manky old coat.

Instead I called Maggie and brought her up to date, even though I'd in fact told her all the news from the pay-phone at hospital. 'Did I get you out of bed?' I asked, when I realized she had no teeth in. She said not, so I spun the call out for fifteen minutes. I couldn't tell half of what she said but it didn't matter.

After that I went to the kitchen, piled some food on a plate, did one more recce of the house and retired to my room with a chair against the door. I started on *Pride and Prejudice* because that's my ultimate comfort book, the one that always makes me feel better. The number of times I've hidden inside Mr Bennet's library. But the house was creaking and groaning as though an entire army of burglars was scouting the downstairs, and I couldn't get past the first page. I seemed to have forgotten how to read.

It seemed a long time till it got light outside again.

\*

There's no drug like a book. If I couldn't read, I'd die.

269

# Chapter Twenty-One

It took a whole week till Poll returned – some problem with her blood pressure and a suspected hairline fracture – and ten days to admit that I wasn't going anywhere. There was still a month and a half till term started but I knew the whole idea of leaving to become a student a hundred miles away had always been a fantasy. My instinct had been right. I would never, ever cope on my own.

Which was just as well, because Poll had turned really clingy.

'I don't know what they did to her in th' hospital,' whispered Maggie, as Poll took herself off upstairs, limping and sighing and clutching her chest. 'She keeps having these dos, panic attacks she calls them. Our Dawn had them after little Kayleigh was born. One time she couldn't go out of th' house and she'd run out of nappies. When I went round she'd put a sanitary towel on t' baby and taped it down with sticking plaster.'

I shrugged. I hated babies. Dawn could have wrapped it in Bacofoil for all I cared. 'How long did it last?'

'The sticking plaster?'

'No, having panic attacks.'

'Oh, well, she waited I don't know how long before

saying owt in case they thought she were an unfit mother and took Kayleigh into care. But she went to t' doctor in t' finish, and he gave her tablets. Psoriasis, I think they were called.'

'That's a disease.'

Maggie narrowed her eyes. 'Eh, I don't know. Summat-sis. I'll ask next time I see her. But Poll's got to get over losing her dog, that was a terrible shock for her on top of the fall. And with you going too . . . '

I got up quickly and went in the kitchen out of her way for a minute. I looked through the smeary glass at the long narrow garden with Winston's mound at the bottom, at the faint white shadows of Dogman's melted gnomes, at the saggy washing line beaded with rain. I could simply have said, I'm not now, I'm staying put. I don't know why I didn't come straight out with the truth. Maybe I didn't want Maggie to feel she'd won. Anyway, she and Poll would know soon enough I wasn't leaving for Oxford.

When the Freshers' Guide came through the post, it was with a kind of relief that I scanned it and then threw it in the bin. You had to have a medical and I always hated those, stripping off to your underwear, watching the nurse eye your rolls of flesh; the scales with their sliding bar that had to be tipped back, and back, and back till the doctor tutted in amazement. Also on the agenda were Karaoke, Bar Quizzes, Treasure Hunts, Ice-skating, all manner of crazy fun. Condoms were available in the toilets near the JCR, because who knows but in the middle of a barn dance you might not fancy a shag with someone you've only known ten minutes. My Freshers' Week would have been

a hundred and sixty-eight hours of sitting in my room trying to avoid everyone.

I did pick the envelope out of the bin, though, after a
while. I'd keep the guide, with the reading list and the original letter offering me a conditional place, in the pages of
Dad's textbook alongside the photo of my mother. I figured
it would be a good memory to have, proof that I could have
gone to Oxford if I'd wanted.

'But,' I told Maggie as we washed up together, 'if I do
stay, there'll have to be some changes round here. You know,
more freedom.'

'Tell your grandma,' said Maggie, rubbing at a slug trail
on the back doormat with her shoe.

'I will. I've been making a list.'

We went through to where Poll was sitting, hunched and
miserable, in front of *Boot Sale Challenge*. 'All the fight's gone
out of her,' Maggie had said earlier; it was true. A good time
to tell her what was what, then.

'I've been having a think,' I said, settling at the end of the
sofa nearest Poll's chair and muting the volume on the TV.

'Oh aye? What about?'

Maggie smiled at me encouragingly. 'Go on, love.'

I took a deep breath. 'Now I'm eighteen and I've left
school, I want a bit more freedom.'

Poll turned and peered at me. 'You what?'

'I'll stay under this roof, look after you—'

Poll spluttered. 'It's me as looks after you, more like.'

'Keep going,' Maggie said to me.

'But there need to be some changes round here.'

'Oh, *do* there?'

'Yes, there do. Such as, I want to come and go as I please.'

'You've got a key,' Poll huffed. 'I don't know what you're moaning about.'

'Yes, but I still have to tell you everywhere I'm going, don't I?'

'I should think so too. That's manners. I don't want to be worrying where you are all t' time. What if you're abducted, and t' police go, "Where did she say she was headed?" and I have to tell them, "I'm sorry, officer, I don't know"? That'll look good on t' news, won't it?'

'Poll's got a point,' said Maggie. 'A quick phone call to say you'll be late. Just so's she knows you're safe.'

'But not twenty bloody questions every time I step over the threshold.'

'There's no need for bad language,' said Poll. 'All right. You tell me so I don't have to ask.'

I left the point and moved on. 'I want to be able to wear what I like, not just the things you get for me off the market. They make me look like, like you. Like I'm about seventy.'

That nettled her. 'You wear what you damn well please, then, if you don't mind all and sundry looking up your skirt and down your bust. And I'm not paying out for it, you've to fund it yourself. "Vest" is all I've got to say on the matter. Dress like a trollop, see what happens.'

'Well, they do,' said Maggie. 'It's what t' young 'uns want. They all do it, show off their bits and pieces, it's the fashion.'

'I've said all I'm saying.' Poll pointed a finger in my face. 'You'll find out.'

'That's up to me. And while we're on the subject, I don't want any sarky comments about boyfriends, if I bring somebody home.'

Poll didn't say anything but she started to laugh, which was worse. I looked despairingly at Maggie.

'She's a bonny girl,' said Maggie. 'She's a lovely curvy figure. If she'd tie her hair back a bit more so we could see her face . . . ' She leaned across the sofa and lifted my hair away from my cheek. 'You want to mek the most of yourself, love. Lift your head up more, put your shoulders back. You're always trying to hide away, and you've no need. You've beautiful skin.'

Poll had carried on laughing but in a forced sort of way. 'If you say so, Maggie.'

'I want to watch more of the programmes I like,' I continued. 'I'm fed up of house-decorating and quiz shows. In fact, I want a TV of my own, in my room. Everyone at school had their own TV.'

'Everyone at your school had more money than us,' snapped Poll. 'I'm a pensioner, if you hadn't noticed—'

'Now, hang on, I think our Dawn might have an old one,' Maggie interrupted. 'She were going to put it in t' free paper, but I'm sure she'd let you have it for next to nowt. I'll have a word.' She beamed at Poll. 'So that's summat else sorted out.'

'Thanks, Maggie. Where was I up to? Oh yeah, at some point I want to do an Open University course. Miss Stockley'll help me apply, and I can use the computers in the library to do the assignments.' I had in mind a degree in librarianship, but I didn't tell Poll that. I was hoping madly that Miss Dragon would be so flattered by my career choice she'd forgive me for throwing away Oxford.

Poll just shrugged.

'And the last thing is, I'm fed up of Dickie being round

here all the time. Can't we see less of him? It's as if he lives here, for God's sake. I'm nearly tripping over him. I don't like the way he lets himself in now without ringing the bell.'

She sat upright, her brow furrowed. 'Dickie's a friend. He's good to you, I don't know why you've tekken against him all of a sudden. You used go walking with him and all sorts. You used think he was marvellous. Well, didn't you? You'd moth-eat him every time he was round. Honest, Maggie, she did.'

'I know, I can remember.' Maggie smiled fondly. 'You were a bobbin when you were small. Allus into everything, doing your little projects. I remember saving you all that tinfoil once.'

'Aye, and do you not remember Dickie building you that bird table so you could do your survey for school? You've a short memory, you have.'

That was pre-breasts, though. I said, 'He's changed.'

'You mean you have,' said Poll. 'Bread etten's soon forgetten. You ought to be more grateful for what you have, not whining for more all t' time. Anyway, Dickie's like family. Well, he is to me.'

Family; now there was a word to conjure with.

'He is harmless,' said Maggie, nodding. 'You've not to tek him seriously.' She patted me on the knee. 'So, are we straight now?'

Poll and I scowled at each other.

'Well, then,' Maggie went on, 'I wanted to show you both this in the catalogue.' She pulled a rolled-up magazine out of her shopping bag and opened it up where the corner of a page was turned over. 'Get your magnifier, Poll. Move that light closer, Katherine. Can you see?'

'Is it a penguin?' Poll cocked her head.

'No, it's a stone dog; see, it's sitting up and begging. It's the spitting image of Winston. I thought you could put it in t' garden, on his grave.'

Poll dragged the picture closer. 'I see him now. In't he beautiful?'

'*This life-like canine companion,*' Maggie read over her shoulder, '*crafted from hard-wearing resin, will withstand the harshest of British weather. Rain or shine, Westie will always be ready to play. Price slashed to nineteen ninety-nine.*'

'Oh yes, we've got to have one of those. Can you fill in the form for us, Maggie?'

We've money enough for that, then, I thought.

*

I got the TV, though, within days. That made me feel a whole lot better, because I could go up to my room, shut the door and watch decent programmes without a background of non-stop grumbling. It was mean in some ways, because it meant Poll had to try and make out the shows she liked all on her own downstairs, without me to fill in the crucial details. But it gave us a break from each other.

I'd started to rearrange my room too. I bagged up half the clothes in my wardrobe; I was going to take them down to Scope. Some giant old lady would be glad of them. I moved some of the furniture round, just for a change, and took most of Dad's posters down off the walls. I was fed up of living in a shrine. In their place I Blu-tacked some posters of my own; one of Virginia Woolf, one for *The Lord of the Rings*, and a black-and-white study of some trees on a hill. Dogman had given me these six months ago and

I hadn't even unrolled them because I assumed they'd be smut. They were tatty round the edges, as if he'd peeled them off someone's wall himself, but he swore they were from a table-top sale in Harrop.

I also repainted my door cherry red gloss from a tin I found in the outhouse, and borrowed Maggie's steam cleaner for the carpet. It came up a different colour. With tea-lights all round, a joss-stick burning, and a black lacy shawl hung over the back of the chair, the room looked nice. I'd plans for a new lampshade and a throw for the bed, with velvet cushions. Maybe I could ask for them at Christmas.

Poll thought it looked like Santa's Grotto, but Maggie was impressed when I took her up and showed her.

'You've a flair,' she said. 'Our Dawn's keen on stencilling and she's done all gold butterflies round her picture rail. You could do summat like that.'

'Look at this,' I said, holding out my hand.

'Whatever is it?'

'Isn't it obvious? It's a tractor.'

'Oh. I thought it were an old cotton reel with a drawing pin stuck in.'

'Ah, well, that's where you're wrong.' I put the collection of pieces on the dressing table and started to assemble them. 'I found it when I was clearing out; Dickie made it for me out of the *Ladybird Book of Things to Make and Do*. I remember him cutting the end of a candle off and pulling the wick out, and hunting all round the house for the right size elastic band. It still works. See. You use the matchstick to wind it up.'

We watched together as the cotton reel crawled along the top.

'It goes over hills too.' I leant a book in the tractor's way and it clambered on, and up. 'Dickie cut notches round the edges to make it grip. Clever, isn't it?'

'Very good,' said Maggie.

'And I tell you what.' I scooped the tractor up and let the matchstick spin. 'I've decided to be nicer to Dickie. Make more of an effort. He's not going to go away, it's no good kicking against the pricks.'

'I think you're very wise,' said Maggie solemnly. 'Mek the best of things, that's the secret of happiness. Not money.'

We heard a thump in the porch followed by Dogman singing a burst of 'On Mother Kelly's Doorstep'.

'Talk of the devil,' chuckled Maggie, nudging me in the ribs.

'Hey, look what I've got.' Dogman was standing at the bottom of the stairs, holding up a dripping carrier bag and looking pleased with himself. A dark liquid was spotting the carpet by his feet.

'What've you done at your leg?' asked Maggie, squinting down the steps at the stick he was holding. 'Have you lamed yourself? There's blood on your trousers, did you know?'

Dogman snorted, and strode through into the living room. When we got down he'd made it to the kitchen and was holding the bag over the sink. Swirls of red were pooling round the plughole. He'd obviously murdered somebody and brought their heart in a bag to show us.

'Blackberries,' he grinned. Except he pronounced it blegbrizz. 'I bet I've two pound here. The bushes on t' station car park are full of them. I could have filled twenty carriers if I'd wanted. Only thing is, I don't really like 'em myself.

So I thought Katherine could mek a nice plate pie out of them. Or jam.'

'Won't they be covered in chemicals off the exhausts?' I found a mixing bowl and tipped the berries into it.

Dogman winked at me, as if I'd just said something flirtatious. 'Soak 'em in salted water, get the maggots out. That's all you need to do. Do you like my bramble hook?' He tried to twirl the cane and dropped it with a clatter on the floor.

'Poll's out in the garden,' I said, to get him off my back. 'Her Westie statue's come and we planted him this morning.'

Maggie tottered through the back door and I stayed to wash my hands. 'They always remind me of Seamus Heaney, blackberries,' I said, thinking aloud.

'Is that your boyfriend?' leered Dogman. 'You're not courting a Paddy now, are you?'

'No and no. I think Poll's calling you.' I made to get past him but he blocked my way.

'I think it's a good thing you're not going off to college.'

'And why's that, then?'

'Load of ponces, students.' Dogman folded his arms. 'The ones at Oxford are the worst. You have to wear a gown all day, I've seen it on t' telly; swanking about. Then there's all the murders. It's one a week.'

'What, in Oxford?'

'Aye. All t' posh people busy knocking each other off, when they're not listening to opera.'

I shoved him away. 'Inspector Morse is a fictional character. You know, made up. He's not real, it's a cop show.'

Dogman only smiled and tapped the side of his nose

sagely. 'Anyroad, you don't want to be a student 'cause they do nowt all day long.'

'As opposed to you, who works all the hours God sends?'

He grinned from ear to ear. 'I've a job, me. Very important.'

'Oh yeah; what?'

'Don't you know? I'm a rent boy,' he said, laughing at my expression.

I couldn't get outside fast enough.

Under the streaky blue sky it was warm, with clouds of midges hanging in the air. I went to stand with Maggie and Poll, who were chatting by Winston's grave.

'You wouldn't want him to have suffered, though,' Maggie was saying. 'And he'd had a good long life.'

'Do you remember when we got him, Poll? Off that wacky woman who lived behind the church?'

Poll sighed. 'I do. I think it were a lucky escape for him. She ran a filthy house. She had about six or seven dogs and they all had their dinners out of one big trough. Poor Winston could never get his share, I reckon. We thought he were a puppy he was so small, but she said he was at least two year owd. He did eat when he came to us, didn't he?'

We'd gone to get Winston after a particularly hellish period at school. I'd suggested a dog, never for one minute thinking Poll would say yes, but she did.

'What are the eyes med out of?' asked Maggie, bending down to see the statue in close-up. 'Are they glass? Very lifelike.'

'And what about that time his claws got fast in t' rug, and we thought his leg was paralysed?'

'And when he bit that little boy who was tormenting him with a stick outside Porter's. And you told the mother, "Stop carrying on, he's learned a valuable lesson." '

'Well, he had. You've to go careful with dogs, till you know them.'

'Ooh,' said a voice at my neck, 'stockings.'

I whipped my head round and there was Dogman lifting up the hem of my skirt with his bramble hook.

'Jesus.' I leapt away from him in horror. 'What the *fuck* do you think you're doing?'

'Ooh,' said Maggie, who'd never heard me swear.

'Whatever's t' matter now?' said Poll wearily.

I took off up the path, feeling dizzy with disgust.

'That were a mean trick,' I heard Maggie say, above Dogman's laughter.

I went out through the side gate and down the ginnel to the road, where I stopped for a moment to kick the wall.

I'd thought I looked nice in my birthday purple sweater and a knee-length bias-cut black skirt that Maggie had brought me off Dawn. 'It's an elasticated waist,' Maggie had pointed out. 'Dawn says she's too owd for it. I thought I'd pass it on.' I'd been thrilled when it fitted. The stockings had been an idea I saw on a daytime makeover show. 'Black opaques really slim chunky calves,' the presenter had said, pointing at an embarrassed woman with over-highlighted hair. I thought it was worth a go, so I'd checked tights out in Boots but they were too expensive. Then I'd found some black opaques on Chorley market, except these were hold-up stockings. 'They're good, them,' the lady on the stall had remarked as she wrapped them up for me. 'Very *hygienic*.' I didn't know what she meant by that, but she was right about them being good. They stayed put and looked sort of funky.

Oh, the thought, though, of Dogman looking up my skirt. Years of him stretched ahead; poking, prodding, squeezing past, ogling. I didn't think I could bear it.

I'd go to Miss Dragon and she'd say, That's awful, I don't know how you coped with it for so long, move in with me while you train to be a librarian.

She'd say, Well, don't come crying to me, you had your chance to get away and you blew it.

I'd go to Miss Dragon anyway, whatever she said.

*

It took four years to get my full qualification. Dad offered loads of times to buy me a car so I wouldn't be mauling with buses, but I always said no. You can read on a bus.

I soon got the house nice again and, after a few months Dad started to do a little bit of gardening. That was the first sign he was on the mend. We kept ourselves to ourselves. It was a happy time.

And then, after I'd got my degree, I had this chance to be near Katherine again, and I found I wanted to take it.

# Chapter Twenty-Two

I walked slowly, under a sky of fat white taproots. *It's only water vapour, it doesn't tell the future. You make your own future.*

Not really; not in real life. My life.

I pined for Dad and his messages which I didn't believe any more. Who was I to mock Cissie for her anthropomorphism, when that was exactly what I'd been doing all these years? I never knew the man. He was an invention of my head, a fantasy friend.

I wanted to tell all this to Miss Dragon, and try to explain again why I couldn't go to Oxford, and what had happened with Callum. I still looked for him when I went out, squinted into the distance to see if it was his figure coming towards me. I looked especially when I passed places we'd been together, like the Methodists', as if I could maybe catch up with the time that had gone. In a stupid way, it was a surprise *not* to see him sitting on the chapel wall, blowing smoke rings and watching the clouds. Of course he wasn't there. And if he had been, what would I have done?

I didn't hurry. I wanted to get to the library about fifteen minutes before closing, then I might have a chance to talk to Miss Dragon in private. I had this idea that she might see how upset I was, lock the front doors and take me into her office. I could maybe ask to stay at her house for a few nights, if she didn't offer first. Logic told me there was a thin chance of that in reality, but what else was there to try?

Even though the schools had only been back a couple of weeks, the kids had been busy with autumn themes. Bank Top Primary had donated some cut-out squirrels to decorate the library windows, and some studies of leaves and poems about harvest for the notice board. Miss Dragon keeps her kingdom smart.

At first I could only spot Miss Mouse, talking on the telephone with her back to me. I slipped past her and settled myself into the children's corner, grabbing a Jacqueline Wilson and burrowing into the beanbags. You can't see this area very well from the front desk so I thought I was pretty safe. The place was empty anyway, apart from Mr Rowland, who was pinning up leaflets on the community space. Then Miss Dragon came out of the office looking glum.

The two women muttered together and I could see some kind of mild argument taking place. I wondered what they could possibly be disagreeing about. Miss Dragon looked the most upset. I was sure neither of them had seen me, so I took the opportunity to slide into my secret hiding place; that is, under the curtain which hangs down behind the end of the Early Readers' bookcase. I've used it before, when people have come in that I didn't want to see, e.g. Clare Greenhalgh. If you crouch down below sill level, then no one can see your back view through the window from outside either.

I put the book down on the floor and settled myself quietly against the wall. I knew I'd only have to wait five minutes or so till the library was officially closed, Miss

Mouse went to catch her bus, and Miss Dragon would be alone and available for counsel.

I heard Mr Rowland make a poor joke about daylight saving, then say goodbye. The doors squeaked open, shut. A calm settled.

'Go on, get yourself off,' said Miss Mouse's voice. She sounded quite authoritarian.

'But your bus,' came Miss Dragon's weak reply.

'I can catch the later one. Stop arguing, you're in no fit state.'

There was a pause and I caught the scrape of keys along the desk top.

'Are you all right to lock up? And set the alarm?'

'Yes. I'm fine. Now *go*.'

Another pause. Miss Dragon, sounding apologetic: 'I will, then, if you're positive. I must admit, I am in agony. It must be an abscess. They say bad toothache's worse than childbirth.' Feeble laugh. 'Not that either of us would know. Right, I'm going now.'

'Good luck,' said Miss Mouse. 'Hope you get it sorted.'

The doors squeaked once more. Shit, I thought. Is that not totally bloody typical. Thank you, Fate. And now, how was I going to get out without looking a fool?

There were movements across the room; books thumping into place, chairs shushing across carpet, newspapers crackling. Lights began to go out, click, click. I could say nothing, stay here all night. That wouldn't be so bad. Because if I emerged now, after staying silent so long, Miss Mouse would probably have some kind of fit. I heard the rattle of curtain along track and knew she was coming closer. Miss Dragon would have understood but

Miss Mouse was nervy at the best of times; she'd freak. She'd think I was going to attack her, or something, steal a computer. She'd press the panic button and the police would come. It would be in the papers. The whole village would read it. Dogman would rupture himself laughing, and Clare Greenhalgh would show her friends and say, I always knew she was screwy, that one.

My breath was coming shorter and my heart pounding, so I nearly died when a voice just next to me said, 'The lights are off. You can come out now.'

There was nothing for it. I pulled the curtain sheepishly to one side, feeling my hair crackle with static. She was standing six feet away, her arms by her sides and her cuffs down over her fingers.

'I was waiting for Miss Stockley.'

She nodded. 'Come in the office.'

I let her lead me there because I didn't know what else to do.

'Sit down. I'll make a drink.'

Callum was there again, in my head; sitting across the table, twiddling his pendant. It was too painful, so I turned instead to watch her. Her long skirt today was black, her baggy cardigan olive green. Her clothes always looked too big for her.

'We've no milk left,' she said, addressing the wall above the sink. 'Do you mind having black coffee?'

I thought that sounded yuk, but I didn't say so. I needed to talk to someone and scalding hot coffee guaranteed me at least quarter of an hour.

Finally she settled herself opposite me, but with her legs turned sideways as if poised for escape. She was terribly nervous, I could see. Maybe it was because I was seeing her close to; usually she had her back to you, or her head in a book. I thought I could detect darker roots at her scalp and wondered whether she lightened her hair, although that didn't seem likely for a woman who never wore make-up. 'It's me,' I felt like saying, 'don't be scared of *me*. We've never spoken much but we are friends, remember.'

'You seem – upset,' she said. 'You want to tell me about it?'

Yeah, why not, I thought.

'Oh, you know. Home life. It's not very easy living with my grandma. You don't know her, do you? She never comes in here. She thinks libraries are a waste of time.'

'Miss Stockley's talked about her,' said Miss Mouse. The surface of her coffee trembled between her hands. 'I gather she's – quite strict with you?'

'She was. Not any more, though. I've turned the tables, it's me in charge now. She used to tell me what to do when I was younger but I've told her, I'm an adult, I can make my own decisions.'

'Good on you.' She spoke quietly and carefully.

'Mmm . . . It doesn't work like that, though, does it?'

'What doesn't?'

'Life. Being an adult. You can't just do what you want. I thought you could, but you can't.'

Miss Mouse pressed her lips together and frowned slightly. 'What do you want – Kat?'

'To go to Oxford!' That was easy. 'I want to take up my place and do a degree. But I *can't* because Poll won't be able to cope without me, emotionally or practically. She poured boiling water down herself a couple of weeks ago, then a few days later she had a bad fall and had to go to hospital. And her dog died . . . I can't leave her. She brought me up. I couldn't walk out on her after all these years, it would kill her, probably. There's no halfway house in these situations either. If you stay you're a saint, if you walk away you're a rat. Nothing in between.'

Miss Mouse didn't say anything to this. She just gazed into my eyes, and the lines at the corner of her mouth tightened.

'Thing is,' I went on, 'I've made my decision and I'm happy to stick with it; well, not happy but I've come round to it, to staying at home and looking after her. I could do correspondence courses in my free time. I wouldn't let my education slide, I'd keep it up. And I'd be doing my duty at the same time so it wouldn't be so bad. Except for Dickie, this friend of hers, he has his own key and he wanders in whenever he feels like it. It's as though he's the one who has a right to live there, not me. The thought of spending more time with him. Why he can't be her full-time carer . . . He reckons he's got a demanding job, but I've never seen any evidence of it. He's always down at the bookies' when he's not with us. He's basically a bum.'

I paused and waited for her to sympathize, but all she did was blow on her coffee.

'Do you know him? Dickie Knowles? Nasty yellow hair, he always wears a filthy beige coat? He's no reader, so you wouldn't get him in here, and I know you don't live in Bank Top, but you might have seen him slouch past.'

Miss Mouse shook her head.

'Oh. Well he's horrible. He *touches me up*. I've had enough of it.'

You were supposed to feel better after you'd got something off your chest. I wished it was Miss Dragon sitting opposite, she'd know what to say to make me feel better. I thought of a film once where a woman was crying and crying during a therapy session, and all the counsellor did was wait till she'd finished, hand her a tissue and say, 'Same time next week.' Perhaps that was the way to handle problems.

I said, 'Perhaps, if I'm being totally truthful . . .'

Her eyes burned into me.

'. . . it's not all my grandma's fault. Some of it's me.'

Miss Mouse raised her eyebrows.

'What I mean is, secretly I'm sort of glad I can't go – oh, for God's sake, promise you won't tell Miss Stockley this. Don't tell anyone. You won't, will you?'

'I won't say a word.'

'You know, when I was little I sometimes used to get invited to parties, and they were always horrible. I used to sit in the corner and watch the other kids race round doing stupid tricks with balloons and teaspoons, and wish I was anywhere else. Once I took a book upstairs and hid in a mum's bedroom while they did games. You had to do something with an orange, roll it through your legs I think, and I knew I'd be crap at it. When this mum found out, she was really cross because she said it was rude to go in people's bedrooms unless you were invited. She told me off in front of the other kids and they were in stitches. So the next time I got an invite – and it was only 'cause the whole class were going – I told them my grandma wouldn't let me out. I pretended I was furious with her, and they believed me.'

Now I'd started talking it was as if I couldn't stop.

'Then, every time something came up, something social, I got into the habit of saying I wasn't allowed to go. I used the excuse all the time at secondary school. And I made out that my grandma was a bit iller than she really was, that she couldn't be left, because there was no arguing with that, I just got sympathy from the other girls. I mean, they thought I was boring, but they never made fun.

'So really, the Oxford business is just an extension of that. And I think I could have convinced myself it would all work out for the best if it wasn't for Dickie and his wandering hands.' I took a breath, let it out slowly. 'God, sorry for going on, I didn't mean—'

'But you do want to take up your Oxford place,' she said. 'And I think you could, Miss Stockley was telling me, from a practical point of view. With a reassessment from social services, and your grandmother's friends helping out. And of course, the terms at Oxford being so short, only eight weeks. You'd be back before she realized you'd gone.'

She was making it sound so straightforward. 'But there's nothing you can do about my fear, is there? There was one night, when Poll was in hospital, I nearly went mad because I was in the house all on my own. I couldn't cope at all.'

'That's precisely why you *must* go away. Otherwise you'll end up on your own permanently. Do you understand what I'm saying?' Her pale cheeks were growing pink.

A vision of myself in my forties rose up in my mind's eye; stuck in Poll's house, the furniture and decorations all still the same but scruffier, Poll's ashes on the sideboard. I'd sit in front of the telly all day and eat till I was too fat to get through the door.

'Do you understand?' Miss Mouse said again, more urgently.

'I think so.'

'If you don't go, you risk becoming very bitter. You can't go through life saying, "I could have gone to Oxford," every time you meet someone.'

'I know.'

'Would it be too late to write and tell them you've changed your mind again, and you will be coming? Is that possible?'

I giggled with embarrassment. 'I never let them know in the first place. Never got round to it.'

'Well, then. That means you always intended to go, doesn't it?'

'It means I couldn't bear to write the words down.'

'Same thing.'

'Is it?' The room seemed to vibrate around me and I thought of Callum again, his surprise and admiration when I'd told him where I was headed. He was there again, at the sink, washing mugs and grinning. 'I think this office must be built on top of ley-lines, or something. Everything seems to happen in here. It's the place where my life turns upside down.'

I started a laugh that turned into tears. Miss Mouse reached out and touched my hair very gently, then let her arm fall to my sleeve. She stroked my cuff and I stared at her fingers, surprised.

'I did a good job when I chose this for you, didn't I?' she said.

I swallowed. 'That was you? That bag of clothes on the doorstep?'

'Yes.'

'God. It's brilliant, everything was. You've seen me wearing the tunic, haven't you? You don't know, you don't know what you started . . .'

Then I saw: it was like washing the mud away from a piece of ancient pottery and the pattern coming clear before your eyes.

'I think—' I began.

'I started it nineteen years ago. Nineteen years ago, my first mistake. I wanted to begin to put things right.'

She was leaning forward and her eyes were bright.

'Are you—?'

'Although I can never really make up for going. I understand that.'

'I think I might know who you are.'

All the random moments that had been swirling around us for years suddenly coalesced to form a new future. I could make out her nodding through my tears, then her arms were round me and mine round hers, her bony body. And even then I was thinking, don't touch her, she abandoned you! But the pull was too strong and I let myself be held while the room buzzed and my brain splintered apart.

After a long time I moved away and we sat back down, though she kept her hand on my wrist.

'Could you come back home with me tonight?' she said shakily. 'There's a lot to talk about.'

When I was a little girl, I'd rehearsed this moment. It had never been here, with her, though. It usually took place when I was a grown up successful something-or-other, sitting behind a huge oak desk, or in the hall of a posh house with stripy wallpaper and a bowl of roses on the table.

She'd turn up unannounced, all apologetic, and I'd sweep her to one side. 'Life-wrecker,' I'd cry. 'Coward.' She'd slink away a broken woman with me shouting, *'Serve you right.'* I'd slam the door and draw a line under the whole business.

I'd had it all worked out for so long. Where were the words that I needed; where had they gone?

\*

Please God let me have said the right thing.

# Chapter Twenty-Three

The first thing I did, to my surprise, was phone Poll from the front desk and tell her I was staying overnight with a girlfriend. I didn't let her argue, although I could hear her chuntering on as I was talking. I *think* she heard me say I'd call back in the morning.

Miss Mouse – Mum – went round having a final lock-up, and set the library alarm, then we – Mum and I – had this surreal, spaced-out walk to the bus stop, neither of us talking, although my head was screaming with noise. *You've got no nightie, how could she run off like that, who'll do Poll's eye drops, dare I ask her if she killed my dad, does she know about Callum, where does she actually live, is Vince there, how could she run off like that, how could she run off like that?*

Some drunks called to each other from across the street. I said, 'I'll have made you miss your bus, won't I?'

'No, there's one every half-hour.'

I was thinking, whatever happens, I want a souvenir of this evening, something tangible I can put away in a box with Callum's wasp, the Oxford newsletter, her photo. I'd hang on to the bus ticket and keep it forever; if it came to it, I'd pick that manky old lolly stick up off the pavement and have that as my treasure. Anything to prove this had been real.

She was talking now, about Miss Dragon.

'My best friend,' she was saying.

'I thought so,' I replied. I didn't say I thought for a while they'd been lovers.

'She's done more than show me the ropes, she's understood my ways.'

I didn't really get that, but I smiled as if I did. 'Does she know? About you and me?'

'No. I've not told anyone. But she was very kind when my father died, last year.'

My other grandad. 'Oh,' I said, 'Miss Stockley's dad died as well, she was telling me.'

'That's probably why she was so good with me. Our households were the same.'

It was such a weird conversation to be having, not least because what we were talking about bore no relation to my loud, racing thoughts. It was like having the radio and the TV on at the same time. The bus came and we got on. I pushed my ticket down to the bottom of my peggy purse, and we sat at the front behind the disabled seats. Aside from us, the downstairs deck was empty.

'I mean,' she went on, 'that Dinah lived with just her father, and so did I. They were much closer, of course; they did a lot together, while he was still fit. Dad and I were sort of semi-detached. We liked our own space.'

'So you live alone now?'

'Yes.'

Not with Vince Millar, then.

The central strip light hummed above us, you heard it

when the bus was idling. Flick-flick-flick went the street lights past the window. I thought, I'm sure I shouldn't be sitting on the 575 having a polite conversation. It should be ranting and recriminations, and running off into the night and sobbing till dawn on the moors. Or hysterical joyous weeping and white-knuckle clasping of limbs, like the victims of *Surprise, Surprise*. Trust me to get it wrong. Bet Donna French would have handled herself with style.

'If I'm being truthful, I don't even really miss him.' Mum (*Mum*) was rolling her ticket into a long spindle between her mottled fingers. 'That probably makes me sound terrible, but we'd made our peace, and he went quite suddenly, without a lot of suffering. He had said a few times he was moving to Exmouth to be near his cousin, so I often pretend to myself that he's just gone there for a while.'

That sounded a bit mad to me, but everyone's got their own way of coping. 'So what happened to your mother?' Because if she ran off, that might go some way to explaining what you did, I was thinking.

'I lost her in my teens.' Mum had unrolled the spindle and was now pleating it into tiny folds.

'What do you mean? You got separated?' I said stupidly.

'She died of stomach cancer,' said Mum. I looked away, watched the driver's hairy forearms for a while, counted his gold rings. I never know what to say when someone comes out with that sort of thing.

After a minute she said, 'It wasn't a good time. I was ill for a while after.'

I held my breath, waiting for baby Kat to come into the story. But she changed the subject.

'I live on Windermere Crescent. Off Chorley New Road.

I get the bus in every day, well every day the library's open, because the stop's only a minute away from my front door. It's a nice house. When I was away and Dad lived there on his own, he really let it go. I had to do a lot of tidying up when I came back. You can have the spare room, it's quite a good size. I can wash your sweater and things, and tumble them for you in an hour, so you can wear them tomorrow. You'll have to wear Dad's old dressing gown in the meantime.'

Yes, I thought, because none of your stuff will fit. Why wasn't I that shape? And then a voice in my head immediately went, How can you be concerned with something as trivial as fat when this is your *mum* at last?

'You are definitely all right to stay, aren't you?'

'Oh, yeah,' I said, trying to sound as if I was in control of my life. 'It'll be fine.'

*

The house turned out to be a biggish Thirties detached with one of those porches shaped like a huge brick keyhole. A security light clicked on as we went through the metal gate, showing a paved driveway edged with neat stone pots.

'You should have seen it when it was just my dad on his own. This was all grass, knee-high.'

Inside the long hall was an Axminster carpet and a white-painted banister. I could smell potpourri or air freshener. Everything looked very clean. I followed her through to the kitchen and watched her fill the kettle.

'Tea? I'll just nip up and put sheets on the spare bed,' she said, taking her coat off and hanging it in a cupboard under the stairs. 'Go through to the lounge.' She pointed the way.

I poked my head round the door to see a very ordinary sort of living room, a bit old-fashioned, tons of books lying around, then I went back to the kitchen to brew the drinks. While the kettle boiled I took stock. The surfaces were immaculate and, in the main, bare. Apart from the kettle, a radio and a toaster, nothing else was out on show. No mug-tree, no utensils, no jars, no cleaning fluids. No ornaments or plants on the windowsill, no fridge magnets. There was no evidence of pets. Only a calendar and a Constable reproduction hung on the walls.

I opened a few cupboards to see if I could locate the tea and only found lots of crockery and pans. At last, inside the cupboard above the fridge, I found some jars and packets, half a small loaf in a bag, and a pot of freeze-dried tea. In the gleaming fridge there were some diet yoghurts, skimmed milk, and a bunch of bananas; that was it. Not even any butter. She must be due a major shop.

'That's sorted,' she said, coming into the living room, where I'd settled with the drinks. 'I'll make us something to eat in a bit.'

Like what, I wondered. Oxo on toast?

'Have you been watching me, then, all these years?' I burst out. 'All this time, have you known who I was?'

She'd been going to sit down, but at that she scooted away from the sofa and went to stand in the bay, arms clasped round herself.

'Yes.'

'Well, *why* didn't you say something to me?'

'I tried, a few years back. I did. I telephoned, and you told me to get out of your life. That's what you said. *Get out of my life.*'

My heart started to thud, because it wasn't true. 'No way. I didn't know anything about you phoning. When? What else did I say to you?'

Mum was twisting on the spot unhappily. 'I'd talked to your grandmother about meeting you – this'll have been about six years ago, a year or so after I started at Bank Top Library. I phoned her several times and she told me you didn't want anything to do with me. I said I didn't believe her, so she put you on and you told me to leave you both alone. It was you. I'd been going to speak to you about who I was, the next time you came to borrow a book, but I didn't dare after that.'

'I can't remember it at all. Poll never said you'd been in touch.'

'That I can believe.'

'And you told Poll you were working in the library?'

'*No*. I only said I wanted to see you. I didn't dare tell her where I was based. I honestly think she'd have tried to kill me if she knew. The woman's mad. She attacked her own husband, beat him up.'

That made me feel peculiar, her talking about Poll like that. 'She thinks you went off with him.'

'He helped me to leave, that was all. Then we went our separate ways. I don't know where he is now. Good God. He was ancient. It would have been like eloping with my father.' She put her hand over her eyes for a moment, and laughed unpleasantly. 'What an evil mind that woman has.'

So Cissie got that wrong too, I thought. But she had it from Poll, so no wonder. Perhaps Poll was mentally ill. It would make sense in some ways.

'So did you deliberately get a job near to me?'

Mum nodded. She kept looking up at the ceiling and taking deep breaths, as if she was trying to stop herself saying too much all at once.

'Well, wasn't it one huge risk coming back? I mean, didn't you think someone would recognize you?'

'It was a risk, yes, but one I was prepared to take. It had been ten years since I'd been in the village and I'd changed a lot. I'd lost a great deal of weight, I'd dyed my hair and had it cut short. Changed my name, obviously – and quite legally; I'm Ann Ollerton now, you must never ever call me Elizabeth. That was another life. And the only people who ever saw much of me when I was living in Bank Top were Poll and Vince because I was so ill I hardly ever left the house. Vince had disappeared—'

' – And Poll was going blind even then. Did you know that when you came?'

'I'd seen her with her white stick when I drove through once.'

Bloody handy for you, then, I thought.

'There was a woman, Maggie, Mary, I can't remember exactly; she might have spotted me, at a pinch, because she used to come round sometimes when I was still at Poll's.'

'You're lucky,' I said. 'Maggie does read, but she favours inspirational books from the church library, or romance off the market, type of books where the heroine starts off in a shawl and ends up in Brussels lace. So she never bothers with the library.' And if you're not actually looking for someone, I was thinking, if you don't expect them to be there, you probably won't see them.

Mum only stared up at the ceiling rose. 'I never thought

it through like that, I just needed to be there. You don't understand the pull I felt to be near you.'

'But not when I was a baby.'

'No. I told you, I was ill. Depression's been my baby.'

There was a silence. I wondered whether to ask her about Dad, and about Callum. It would be like blowing up mines in her face.

'Do you know what I think?' she said suddenly. 'I think we should have a drink.'

I thought so too. I needed a break. 'Can I use your toilet?'

'Up the stairs on your left. Sherry, brandy or Martini?'

I thought they were all vile. 'Martini, smashing.'

On the landing I paused and counted doors. The bathroom was on the left, what must have been my room in front of me with the curtains drawn, the light on and a dressing gown laid across the bed. Two doors on the right; hers the first one I opened.

I suppose I was hoping for a little shrine. The room was pine and pastel, unremarkable except for the towers of books along the wall under the window. The dressing-table surface was clear, no cosmetics out, and even on the bedside table there was only a pair of reading glasses and a bottle of pills. But over the chest of drawers was me; two newspaper clippings, one of me winning a book quiz in about the third year at secondary school, and an older one of Bank Top Primary's Harvest Festival, with me holding a plate of onions. Both pieces had been laminated and pinned to the wall. There was also a colour photo that I remembered Miss Dragon taking, the day after I got the letter saying I'd got a place at the grammar.

I stood grinning for a minute, remembering. Then

another memory popped up, of me screaming down the telephone while Poll held the receiver in such a way that I could only get at the mouthpiece. 'It's that flaming pervert again,' she'd said, shaking with temper. 'Don't listen to his filth. You just tell him, tell him to get out of our lives.'

I turned the light off and closed the door behind me.

When I got down there were two glasses of Martini sitting on the coffee table.

'I'm not a drinker,' said Mum. 'I can't remember when this was last out. But we should have a drink tonight. Shall I make us something to eat as well?'

That was weird, because all she had herself was two Weetabix, lightly sprinkled with milk so they held their shape, and this slug of Martini. I wanted to help her make the meal but she insisted I stay in the living room watching TV. Eventually she brought through a plate of cheesy broccoli pasta for me, the sort where all you do is add water, and we ate sitting on the sofa in front of *TOTP2*.

'I wasn't expecting company tonight,' she said, observing as my fork uncovered a little pocket of unmixed sauce powder.

'No no, it's delicious,' I said, and I wasn't lying either. I'd been ready to eat the kitchen sponge I was so hungry. On the screen in front of us Sting sang about being lonelier than any man could bear, but he didn't look it.

Afterwards she let me back in the kitchen to wash up; I felt we were making strides. The Martini was beginning to penetrate and I was feeling bolder.

I said, 'Was it awful when Dad died?'

'Yes. I was ill.'

I acted ignorant. 'From the car crash?'

'That wasn't my fault,' she said quickly. 'The coroner said so. It was a proper inquest and the verdict was accidental death. I've got the newspaper clippings to prove it.'

'Right.' I carried on swilling the sink, chasing particles of Weetabix down the plug hole.

'I'll show you.'

'There's no need.'

She put down the tea towel and took my hand. 'Yes there is. I can guess what you've been told.' Her grip tightened. 'I know you must hate me, I know that really.'

'I'm not sure what I feel,' I said, after a struggle. If we weren't honest here, we were lost. 'It was a mistake on the phone that time. I didn't mean to tell you to go away. I got confused and thought you were someone else.'

Tears started at her eyes and she began to pull me through the hall.

'I've never been far away. I wanted to help. You liked the clothes, didn't you? That was something I got right. It took me weeks, months to get them all together. I only wanted nice things for you.'

'They were lovely.'

In her room I pretended surprise at the photos of me.

'See? I've only been able to put these up after Dad died, but I've been close to you for a long time.'

I sat on the bed while she brought out the coroner's report from a suitcase under the chest of drawers. I didn't feel comfortable reading it with her there, I'd have preferred it if she'd left me alone, but she clearly wanted to gauge my reaction.

'See?' she said when I'd finished.

It was true; according to the paper, she'd been cleared. It

had been my dad's fault for driving like a maniac. I thought of Poll's lies and hated them, and understood them.

'He was so arrogant,' Mum began. 'He always had his own way, and his own rules, he never stopped to think about other—'

'Don't,' I shouted. 'Don't say anything about him. I don't want to hear. If you start slagging him off, I'll walk straight out of this house and never come back, I promise you. I did not come here to listen to bad stuff about my father.'

I stuffed the report back in its envelope and threw it back into the open case. She went out of the room and after a minute I heard taps running, over the sound of sobbing. I'm not going to feel guilty, I thought, I don't actually owe her anything. For a moment I wondered whether I should just grab my purse and go. But then I caught sight of the photo album. At the back of the case, half under a college scarf, a gold embossed maroon cover: *My Memories*.

And there they were. All the pictures that should have been round Poll's house: Roger and Elizabeth, Roger and Elizabeth. In Poll's back garden; sitting on a stone wall up on the moors somewhere; in my old bedroom; holding hands in the porch of this house. Mum with her long dark centre-parted hair, Dad with his devil-smile. And they did seem odd together, as if they were asking to be cut apart with scissors.

I sat for a long time looking at one of them in his Metro, smiling through the windscreen. The water was still running in the bathroom. It felt as if my whole identity was draining away with it.

I flipped over the last couple of pages and it was me, a fuzzy fat baby. First the three of us, then me and Mum, then me and Dad. Finally just me on my own, boss-eyed and chewing a teething ring. It was really me; Poll had the ring and the Babygro still in a bag under her bed. The strange thing was, in all the shots, everyone looked really happy.

I put the album open on the duvet and went to get Mum.

*

I leant over the sink and watched the water run away from me into darkness. I thought, what if I've lost her all over again?

# Chapter Twenty-Four

It was still dark when I heard her get up.

She was out on the landing, laying my clean clothes carefully over the banister. All she was wearing was an underslip, and my eyes were drawn to her thin arms covered all over with small silvery scars, like stretch-marks. She caught me looking, and jumped.

'I didn't know you were awake.' She pulled my sweater against herself.

'Is the bathroom free?' I mumbled, wanting to get away as much as she did.

She nodded and we fled in opposite directions.

I washed and dressed quickly because I knew she'd have to be at work. Personally, though, I was in no rush to go back to Poll's. I started to rehearse the tale I'd tell her about where I'd spent the night. Tempting to be hung for a sheep as a lamb, and tell her I'd been at an orgy in Harrop, or mainlining heroin round the back of Porter's. Even that would be nothing like the shock of the truth.

'I'm going to tell Poll I've been with my friend Rebecca,' I said to Mum over my slice of dry toast. She was sitting opposite, sucking on a cube of frozen orange juice that dripped down her sweater cuffs every so often. I kept remembering the arms under those chunky sleeves, and tried not to stare. 'I don't like to lie, but on no account must Poll find out about you. She'd go berserk, and she's unstable enough at the moment.'

'All right.' Her voice sounded flat, disappointed.

Well, what did you think I was going to do? I felt like asking. Shout it from the hilltops? Destroy my entire past at one fell swoop? I could have gone back to Poll holding the information like a flaming sword above her cowering form, and cut her version of my life into tiny parts. But what would that have done for me?

Here, in this kitchen, was a woman who had sat by and watched me struggle for years, who never even told her own father I still existed. It was in my power to take her apart as well, if I'd wanted; tell her I never wanted to see her again, that the embrace last night in the bathroom was only the product of Martini and confusion. Or I could confront her with the unmentionable, the story of Callum and his mother. Did she even know?

I wouldn't though. Hurting either of them would only be hurting myself. I'd keep the secrets, for now, while I decided what to do with them.

'We'd best run if we want to make the eight-twenty,' she said suddenly. I watched her load her bag with bananas and crispbreads, and felt sad. Why did she have to be so bloody fragile? Why couldn't she have turned out to be strong?

\*

Poll was making a show of ironing when I got in, putting more creases in than she was taking out.

'Ooh, look who's showed her face,' she said. 'Finally. You'll get a name, you will.'

Instantly I wished I'd never come home. I said, 'How lovely to see you, Kat, have you had a nice time with your friend?'

Poll only pulled a face. 'Out till dawn. Well, I don't care. I've been managing fine on my own.' I watched as she deftly ironed a ladybird flat into the sleeve of her blouse.

'Good,' I said. 'Because I'm seeing her tonight as well.'

'What, *all* night? God Almighty.' Poll rested the iron up on its end. 'Out all night with a woman? That's not normal. Dickie says you might be gay. He says he's had his suspicions for a while. I don't know what to think; there's summat shifty about you at the minute, that's for sure.'

'Actually, I'm asexual.'

'And what's that mean, Miss Clever?'

'Look it up. Hey, have you seen that nasty stain on your blouse?' I pointed to the orange blob on the sleeve and she skutched it away to hold it near the window.

'Damnation. Is it brown sauce?'

'It *was* a ladybird. Give it here, I'll put some Vanish on it.'

Poll dropped the blouse across the ironing board and sat down on the sofa, looking defeated. 'I've been worried,' she muttered. 'I hate it on my own.'

'Didn't Maggie come round, or Dickie?'

She didn't answer, so I presumed they had. I put the blouse on a short wash and brewed us a hot chocolate each. Then I cut us two thick slices of parkin and brought them through.

After a few minutes chewing, she seemed happier.

'Dickie's left you a present. To say sorry, he reckons, although he were only having a bit of fun. It's a queer do, stopping out all night up to I don't know what, but then tekkin offence at one little joke. Anyway, he's apologized. It's in a bag on your bed.'

I left the parkin and went up to see. The redecorated room still gave me a pleasurable shock when I went in. Wherever I went in the future, this would always be my home. I wondered if Dogman had managed to find me a throw or some velvety material for cushions.

But no, it turned out to be an apron. A full-length laminated apron with a cartoon picture of a scruffy dog on the front that would sit about level with your tummy. I thought perhaps if he'd got it me because it reminded him of Winston. I checked the ties and they were all intact, no dodgy marks or stains anywhere. I'd seen aprons you could get that looked like you were walking round in your underwear; thank God he hadn't got me anything like that.

I tried it on for fun and stood in front of the mirror. Something was written underneath the dog in swirly writing; I hadn't seen it before. I struggled to spell it out from the reflection: S-N-A-T-C-H. Dogman wanted me to wear the word 'snatch' written over my crotch.

'Whatever are you up to now?' Poll found me at the bottom of the garden two minutes later, with the apron and a box of matches.

'Watch,' I said, and struck a match. I held it against the offending word. There was a feeble glow, then the laminate burst into flames. I laughed out loud. 'Call that fireproof?

How could you have worn that in a kitchen? It was a complete health hazard.'

'Is that Dickie's apron?'

'It is.'

'You're mad,' said Poll. 'You'll be put away.'

\*

'Come and live here,' Mum said that evening. 'You can have new furniture, decorate anywhere you like. I'll get you a computer if you want. I'm not short of money. Move in with me.'

'I can't.'

She looked upset. 'But you hate it at your grandma's.'

'I know, but it's home. I'm, I'm not sure how I feel.'

'About what?'

About you, I nearly said. 'Everything.'

'I suppose it's a lot to take in all at once.'

I thought, you don't know the half of it.

\*

I told Maggie first.

'I've got to go,' I said. We were shelling peas in the kitchen while Poll had a nap upstairs.

Maggie seemed to know at once what I meant. 'I know, love, I think you have. Will they still tek you?'

'Yeah. I've to be in Oxford next Sunday, for Noughth Week.'

'Is that when they show the northern students round?'

'No. It's a week for the new ones from all over to settle in, sort out their accommodation, meet their tutors.'

'Ooh, hey.' Maggie nudged me. 'Tutors. You will be grand. You'll not want to know us common folk.'

'Don't be daft.'

Peas plopped into the bowl between us and the weak autumn sun shone through the kitchen window.

'I presume you've not said owt to your grandma?'

'Not exactly.'

Maggie nodded. 'You will tell her, though? You won't just tek off? Because that would be very upsetting for her. I've a book she might find helpful.'

'I'm going to tell her this afternoon, when she wakes up.'

Maggie looked grim. 'I should have some Bailey's ready, if I were you.'

By the time Poll appeared the peas were shelled and Maggie and I were watching *A Place in the Sun*. Bob and Carol from Leeds were examining an apartment in an Italian village. 'It's all very well,' Maggie was saying, 'these foreign places might be warm but no one speaks English, do they? And all them steps up and down.'

We got Poll sitting with a drink, Maggie standing by with her lavender cologne stick, then I explained to her that this time I was definitely leaving home.

'Get away,' she chuckled. 'We've heard that one before. Shift out o' t' way, I can't see the screen properly.'

I stayed where I was. 'No, this time it's different, I've decided.'

She scratched her side and yawned. 'You're not capable of mekkin decisions, you. Well, you aren't, are you? Chopping and changing. I'll believe it when I see it.'

Maggie came in at this point: 'She is going, Poll. She's bought her ticket and I've seen it.'

I gaped at the lie. But it was a canny thing to say, because it seemed to dawn on Poll that I was serious.

'But you wrote and told them you weren't coming, didn't you? They'll have given your place to someone else.'

'No, I never did.'

Poll was beginning to look really alarmed. 'You'll never manage. You're one of life's square pegs. It doesn't matter where you go, you'll never fit in. I bet you'll be back in a fortnight, won't she, Maggie?'

Maggie kept quiet.

'What'll happen to me? I'm nearly blind, you know. How will I cope when my sight goes completely?'

'It won't, will it? It's not got any worse for two years now. They said at the hospital, you never go totally blind with dry macular degeneration.'

'You do.'

'You don't. I was there, remember.'

Poll stood up, trembling with rage. '*Them as calls their grandmother a liar Is in danger of hell fire,*' she chanted, jabbing me in the chest for good measure.

I made the mistake of laughing, and before I knew it, she'd slapped me hard across the face. I couldn't believe she'd done it. I put up my hand to rub away the sensation of her cold bony fingers on my cheek, and to relieve the stinging. 'My *God*.'

'Now, Poll,' said Maggie, trying to draw her away from me, 'I know it's hard, but there are these stages you need to go through. Reeling, Feeling, Kneeling and Healing. No, not Kneeling, Dealing. That's how you cope with a big loss. It's in a book I've got. So you're at the Reeling stage at the moment, which is natural, 'cause it's been a shock, but then you come out of that and go into Dealing, I think, is it? But don't tek it out on Katherine, she's only doing what the young ones do. I wept buckets when Dawn left and she were only on t' new estate round the back. It's nature, flying the nest.'

'I'll get a new care package sorted before I go,' I said. 'I know I've left it late but Maggie'll help out till it's in place. The Rehab Officer's coming on Monday for a chat, and you know she's a lovely woman.'

'Is it that lame one with the long fair hair?' said Maggie, letting go of Poll's cardigan. 'Oh, she's smashing, in't she? She knows what it's like to be crippled.'

But Poll was still in a fury. 'Oh, oh, my heart,' she cried, sinking onto the sofa. 'You've killed me.'

I stayed where I was, but Maggie bent stiffly to help. She patted Poll's forehead and took her hand, then straightened up, half turning to me. 'It's hard for her. She loves you, you see.'

'No, she doesn't,' I said, 'she just wants to keep me here as an unpaid carer. She's frightened of having to cope on her own.'

'You're the one as is frightened,' Poll moaned from her sickbed. 'All I've ever tried to do is protect you.'

'Shall I telephone for a doctor, do you think?' asked Maggie. 'I can feel her heart pounding away and she's very pale. What do you reckon?'

I started to walk to the door. 'I'm sorry, Maggie, I'm not staying around for the performance. Do what you like, call a whole fleet of ambulances if you want. The Bailey's is on the sideboard. I'm off.'

'That's right, run away,' called Poll, raising her head briefly.

'That's exactly what I am going to do,' I said.

*

'It's Maggie I feel sorry for,' I told Cissie as we sat by the picture window watching the gardener hoover up leaves from the lawn. 'Too much falls on her shoulders. She'll be cursing me before Christmas is here.'

'No, she won't,' replied Cissie. 'She likes it, fussing over Poll. It meks her feel important. There are some people in life who need to be needed; Maggie's one of them. Soon as her daughter left home, she was on the lookout for someone to mither. She'll enjoy stepping into the breach till social services get themselves into gear. And really, Poll doesn't need that much practical help, does she? There's plenty worse off than her.'

'It's more emotional support she needs at the moment.' I sighed. 'You don't think people'll criticize me for going away and leaving her?'

'They'll be clapping you on the back and cheering, more like. Eeh, love, you've your own life to live as well. Get on, enjoy yourself while you're young. It soon passes.' She looked mournfully down at her own body. 'Then you end up like this. Just look at them ankles.'

Ally stumped across the lawn in front of us and shouted something at the gardener, who laughed and switched his hoover off. They stood chatting happily for a minute, and I saw him glancing down her blouse a few times. As she walked off she wiggled her bottom at him and he put his lips together like he was whistling. Where did she get that kind of confidence from?

'Can I ask you something?'

Cissie stopped scrutinizing her legs and turned her face to me. 'What, love?'

'Tell me honestly, what was my dad really like?'

She made a noncommittal noise and stared into the middle distance.

'No, tell me. I know you didn't like him; I know about his affair. But what was he like as a person?'

'The trouble with you,' said Cissie, 'is that you see people as either all good or all bad. Nowt in between. When, in reality, everyone's mixed up nice and nasty. That's the way humans are. Some are nastier than others, of course.'

'Like my dad?'

'No, love; no. Being absolutely truthful, I never took to him especially, but he weren't a bad lad. Well, he were, but not really *evil*. Spoilt, of course. That were his mother. But not a cruel boy. You can't blame him for loving life. I'm sure he never meant to hurt anyone's feelings when he took up with that other woman, he probably just didn't think it through.'

I pictured Mum and Jude, side by side, smiling hopefully. 'So who did he love, in the end?'

'Himself, chiefly,' said Cissie. 'Poll had always taught him the sun shone out of his own backside. How was he to know any better?'

Afterwards, I wondered if I'd ever tell her about finding Mum. One day.

Over my head there were white railway tracks in the blue, guiding me off into infinity.

'Oh, fuck off,' I shouted into the air. 'There's no such thing as sky messages. There never was.'

\*

My dad used to say, when I was little, Softly softly catchee monkey. I didn't get it at the time. But I know now it means go slowly. I'll have her, if it takes years. What else have I got to do with my life?

# Chapter Twenty-Five

The postcard had been sent to the library, but it was Miss Dragon who handed it to me, not Mum.

*Kat*
*So so so so <u>sorry</u>. I HAVE to talk to you. Midday Friday?*

The front showed a portrait of Charlotte Brontë and there was no signature, but I knew who it was from and where he'd be.

Miss Dragon raised her eyebrows as I put the card in my coat pocket. 'I don't mean to interfere, Kat,' she said. 'But if you don't want to see him again, I can field him for you. Pass on a message.'

I glanced round the library to make sure no one was listening in. No sign of Mum, anyway.

'You didn't like him, did you?'

'Since you ask, no. Much too charming. I thought he was lovely, for about ten minutes. Have you two fallen out?'

'You could say that.' I replayed his face coming towards mine through the half-light, and it was like a kick in the chest. Mrs Dragon watched me with concern. 'Listen, have you told anyone else who he said he was? I mean, *anyone*?'

'Absolutely not.'

I could have kissed her for her old-fashioned rectitude, her bobbly check skirt, her brogues.

'Thanks. I'll really miss you when I go.'

'Of course you won't, you'll be far too busy having an interesting time. But thank you.'

'And there's no need to worry about Callum. I'll face him. It's something that has to be done.'

She gave me a long, fond look. 'If you say so. But I'll disembowel him if he does anything untoward; tell him that from me.'

*

He was sitting outside on the library bench when I saw him again. Too chicken to go in, I thought. His hair had grown slightly but the glasses were back, and he had an army greatcoat round his shoulders.

'Where do you want to go?' he said, standing as I approached. 'I don't want to stay round here. Too many people.'

For what? 'Let's go to the cemetery, then,' I said, my mouth dry with nerves and anger. 'Oh, and I've got this for you.' I held out the little paper bag to him.

'Not the pendant? Please don't get rid of that.'

'No. This photo. You might as well have the original. What would I want a picture of my dad's mistress for?'

He looked mortified as he recognized again the pregnant woman leaning on the Metro, but he didn't say a word. I wondered whether I should have ripped the photo up in his face; too late now, though. The bag went in his pocket and we set off down the village.

I'd intended not to talk till we got there, but I couldn't

stop myself. 'I feel like I'll never be able to trust anything you ever tell me again,' I said bitterly as we walked past the school road. 'I don't understand why you had to deceive me like that. I thought we were friends, that you liked me. So why couldn't you have told me the truth from the start? Or keep up the deception, one or the other. In fact, why did you have to go rooting around at all?'

He hung his head. 'It's important for boys to know about their dads. I've always wanted to find out about him; Mum would never give.'

No bloody wonder, I nearly said.

'So I got fed up with it and took matters into my own hands. I posted on a Web site that tries to match up people who've lost each other, adoptees mainly. Not that Friends Reunited, this one's called Lookup. The day after my posting appeared, three people emailed and told me there was only one person called Pollyanna Millar registered in England; two of the emails included your address and phone number.'

'Why? Why would complete strangers send you that sort of information? I don't believe you.'

He shrugged. 'Try it for yourself. They're Internet fiends with nothing better to do, maybe. One of them said she was a private detective, and for a small fee she'd gather information on you, or facilitate a meeting. I didn't reply to any of them. But what would you have done, this phone number sitting in front of you, begging you to ring it? I came and had a look at the house before I met you, you know.'

'Freak.'

'I wanted to take my time. Get it right. Ironically.'

We'd drawn level with the Methodists' when a voice

called out: 'Ooh, hello again.' It was old Janey Marshall, carrying bunches of flowers into the Methodist church. 'You two still doing your, what is it, research?' She gave a huge, ugly wink.

'We've finished all that,' said Callum. 'Thanks for asking. Now we're just going off for a shag. See you around.'

Janey's face froze.

'Let's hope the old cow has a stroke or something,' he said loudly, quickening his pace. 'Can't you walk a hundred yards in this God-forsaken place without someone poking their nose into your business?'

I was stunned. 'What the hell was that in aid of? Jesus, Callum. I have to live here, you know.'

'I thought you were going to Oxford. Or didn't you get in?'

'Yes I bloody did, actually. I'm going on Sunday. Poll says it's fine and she'll look after herself.'

'Well, then. Bye bye, Bank Top.'

'It's still my home. God, the terms only last eight weeks. I'll be back in no time.'

'Eight weeks and the Methodists'll have forgotten all about it,' said Callum, thrusting his hands into his pockets. 'It'll all get lost in the excitement of knitting toilet-roll covers for the Christmas Fair. Stop getting so agitated. There's more to life than Bank bloody Top, Kat.'

I was so furious I had to stop myself speaking for a minute, in case I said something I regretted. I wanted to ask him so much stuff, get it straight in my mind, before I told him to disappear forever. I didn't want to start the row too early.

We made it to the wrought-iron gates before I really turned on him.

'Go on, then, explain; why the story about being my cousin? Why didn't you tell the truth from the start?'

'Because you'd have hated me. If I'd burst in on the scene and announced your dad had kept a mistress that you knew nothing about, you'd have been livid.'

'I'd have been shocked. But I'd have come round. I had a right to know.'

Callum shook his head and carried on up the gravel path. 'Well, you know now. I'm *sorry*, OK? It was my chance to find out something about my dad. If you'd flown into a rage and said you'd never wanted to see me again because of who I was, I'd have learned nothing. I'd have blown my one opportunity. I had a right as well.'

'You should have asked your mother.'

'I did, last week. We've been talking about it. I told her about coming here and meeting you, and she was pretty gutted. She threw a cup at me. But when she'd calmed down, she told me a load of stuff. It's been great, we've got really close.'

'Bully for you.'

'Yeah, all right, all right. Anyway, back then, all she'd tell me was that Dad had died in a car accident and that he was already with someone. And there was a baby.'

'So when you found me, back in July, did you already know about my mum running off?'

He stopped under a yew tree, screwing up his eyes against the sun. 'Yeah. It was in a letter I found, how she went when you were less than a year old. Of course, I didn't know whether she might have come back in the meantime.

But I thought, if you did suddenly whip a mother out of the hat, I'd say I'd got confused and that it was Miller I was searching for. Something like that. I've usually got an idea up my sleeve.'

'You shit,' I said. 'I don't even know whether you're telling me the truth now.'

'I am.'

'And what was this letter? Was it your mum's? Who was it from?'

'Your paternal granddad. Vince.'

'Fuck.' I walked away from him a few yards, then came back. 'And *why* was he writing to your mum?'

Callum kicked at the gravel with his shoe. 'Because he was giving us money. He gave some to your mum too. I think he felt responsible; Mum says he was one of those people who likes to go round trying to put things right. After he left your grandma, he traced Mum through the university, and came all the way over to Sheffield to look after her. She let him stay for a while, because she'd been so ill. Then, after about six months, he left us. God knows where he went after that. But he always sent money, every month. We wouldn't have managed otherwise.'

'Where did he get all this money from?' I thought of how Poll had struggled for cash all these years.

'Dunno. It's stopped now, though. We haven't had anything from him since I was about nine, ten, Mum says. He just disappeared. He might even be dead, I suppose.'

I found myself scanning the sky, but all there was in the air was my cold breath. 'You are such a huge fucking liar.'

'I'm telling you the truth now.'

'So that makes it all right?'

I stalked off round the back of the chapel to the war memorial and sat on the icy stone steps. Who could you trust, really? If I'd had a gun, I swear I'd have shot him as he came, now, round the corner; blasted a big hole in that stupid greatcoat of his. I'd have stood over him as he died, and laughed.

'How many more times can I say it?' he called. 'I'm sorry.'

Don't you dare sit next to me, I thought. He must have picked up the vibes, because he leant against the chapel wall a few feet away and stared at his boots.

'Did she ever get married, your mum, like you said?'

'No. I think our dad spoilt her for another man.'

Your mother and mine. 'You don't especially look like him, you know.'

'Neither do you.'

'It was a mean trick to play with the photo, letting me think it was Elizabeth. That was really low.'

Callum spread his hands. 'You said it was the only picture you had. I couldn't take that away from you. I couldn't destroy your illusion like that.'

'God.' I struck the stone column with my fist. 'You've an answer for everything. Why does everyone think I need protecting all the bloody time?'

He said nothing, and the white skin on my hand flushed and welled into tiny beads of blood. Below us, Harrop stretched away into moorland and sky. I can leave all this behind, I was thinking. Two days.

'Listen,' he said, coming closer, his voice gentler, 'there's another reason I came back to see you. As well as to tell you the truth.'

'What?'

'You know, in the club, right, when we, when I—'

'Oh no, don't start that again. You're either a liar or a pervert, one of the two. I don't want anything to do with it.'

'I wasn't lying about the kiss. You need to know. You're lovely, you're like Blanche Ingram.'

'*Blanche Ingram*?' I almost sniggered. 'She was a scheming cow, wasn't she?'

'No, not that way.' There was a sort of smile on his lips that made me angry and warm at the same time. 'Lookswise. Tall, curvy, strong. You glow.'

'Fuck off.'

'You do. All right, never mind that. I'm not about to leap on you, I've got a new girlfriend, actually. So you're not in any danger. But I hate the way you think you're ugly when you're not. If I wasn't your brother—'

'Which you are.'

'I know. Didn't you feel like you were in tune with me, though? That there was a sort of pull between us?'

'No.' I stood up. 'Have you any more revelations for today, or have we finished?'

'Kat.' He took my fingers in his. 'Jesus, you're like ice. Look, I wanted to say, nothing funny, but you're my sister, I don't want to walk away from that. Now I've found you.'

'People walk away from their families every day,' I said, withdrawing my hands and putting them behind my back.

'Yeah, but it doesn't make them not exist. They're still there. You might as well close your eyes and expect to go invisible.'

'I don't know. I need time to think.'

'Kat.' He went to put his arms round me.

'Get off. I told you, I need time. I need to stop hating you.'

He looked miserable at that. Good, I thought. I bet you assumed you could talk me round with a bit of charm and flattery. Well, you were wrong.

'I've got your number,' I said. 'I'll be busy for the next eight or nine weeks, but I'll give you a call before Christmas.'

'That long?'

'That long. But I will call. Promise.'

He walked me to the gate and tried again to hug me, but I ducked away.

'I turn right here,' I said. 'You're going left, for the station.'

'OK,' he said. 'Fair enough. One last thing, though. If you hate me anyway, I might as well say. My mum reckons your mum was mentally ill. I mean, really bonkers. Sectioned at one point. So, if you ever do find her, if she ever does come out of the woodwork, watch yourself. Go steady. Be careful you don't end up looking after her instead of after your grandma.'

I watched his tall grey figure walk away till it was out of sight.

*

This time I was going to get it right.

# Chapter Twenty-Six

So in the end, my policy of cowardice and inaction paid off. Oxford has turned out to be brilliant, because everyone here's a bit weird so I don't stand out. They all call me Kat, at any rate.

This is where I'm up to now: six weeks into term and I'm technically in college but spending most of my time round at the flat Mum rents in Summertown. She moved in two weeks ago, after she'd worked out her notice at the library. When she finds a job, she'll put her Bolton house on the market and buy a place here. Then I can move in. That's what we've said, anyway.

She's easy enough to live with. We have our own kitchen cupboards, and I've accepted the fact she doesn't eat just like she's accepted the fact that sometimes, after a meal, I lock the bathroom door and play the radio loudly. But even that's not happening as often as it used to. Food's not the same in her house, somehow.

One day I saw her standing in silhouette by the window and she was so slim it took my breath away. 'Why don't I look more like you?' I couldn't help saying. She laughed. 'That's a fallacy, children always looking like their parents. Children aren't clones, they look like themselves because they're new individuals. You wouldn't want to be me, I promise you.'

I'm still finding out about her. Once, as she was unpacking, she showed me a ring box containing a dried-up old conker, like a little brown brain. 'Your dad gave me that,' she said. Last of the big spenders, I thought, but I didn't say so. It obviously meant a lot.

Another time I was looking through her box of Everyman novels and I found a folder full of hole-punched sheets and dividers to mark off the years. I flicked through the pages and they were just lists of books. I wondered why she'd kept them, then I began to recognize some of the titles. Turning to the most recent, I could see they were the ones I'd taken out from Bank Top Library. She'd catalogued every single book I'd ever borrowed.

Other surprises we keep hidden. She's never mentioned Callum, except once to say she was sorry I'd fallen out with my boyfriend. I didn't reply and the conversation went no further. One thing about my mum, she certainly gives you your space.

Although I don't call her Mum. I call her Ann. If anyone asks, I say she's my friend. I don't encourage a lot of questions because I'm frightened of tying myself in knots. I certainly haven't told anyone she's my mother, because I'm not sure she really is. Oh, I don't doubt she gave birth to me, but it's not the same thing.

So far I've had postcards from Becks (*I went to a club last night!!!*), from Donna (*Saw this and thought of you* – picture of Clever Cat from Letterland – *keep rolling the tubes*), and from Maggie (*We are all free from colds here but dickie has put a nail through his foot hope you are wearing your winter coat*).

Nothing from Poll, but she does have difficulty writing. I'm not too worried, I'll see her at Christmas and we'll make up. I've not heard anything from Callum either. Perhaps I'll ring him when I get back, perhaps I won't. Perhaps I'll invite him on a Trisha show, 'I Temporarily Fell for my Lying Love-rat Brother'. Christmas is also when we're planning to tell Miss Dragon; Dinah, I'm going to have to start calling her.

Maybe we could all get round the table and pull crackers together.

There are parts of my dad's story, and therefore mine, that only I know; parts that only Poll knows, parts that only Vince would know, parts that only Ann and Jude know. Only all of us together would stand a chance of seeing the whole picture, and maybe not even then. I know that every time I leave the flat, Ann turns my photograph of Dad to the wall, but there's no way I'm going to take it down for her.

One thing I've learned in my short life is that no bugger's who you think they are. That's OK, though; you just have to keep on your toes.

# CHRISTMAS POSTSCRIPT

I had vaguely meant to go and see Poll back before the end of term, but there hadn't been time. They work you really hard at Oxford. I like that.

Ann had a job interview so I travelled on my own. I managed the changes and everything, and no one stole my luggage or pulled the communication cord or showed me their penis. I got off at Bank Top and hauled my bags up the Brow to Poll's.

Oddly, there was no one in and, by the looks of the post on the doormat, there'd been no one for a day or two, at least. And yet I'd written to say when I was coming home. Where was everyone? I used my key and went through to the living room. There were two free papers and a slip from the window cleaner on the table, but everywhere else looked unnaturally tidy. Most of the ornaments and pictures were gone. The kitchen had been cleared out, though not cleaned, and when I went upstairs to use the toilet, all the soaps and bottle had disappeared off the window-sill. My room was more or less as I'd left it, but Poll's bed was stripped and her quilted dressing gown absent from behind the door. The place *smelt* empty.

I didn't know what to do. Was Poll in hospital again?

Had she died? But no, Maggie or someone would have phoned and told me, surely.

I hunted for a note or a letter to tell me what was going on; nothing. I phoned Maggie and Dogman, but there was no reply from either. Finally I called a taxi and went to see Cissie at the home.

Mr Poole was in reception, wearing a Santa hat on his head. It was jingle all the way. 'I'll fill your stocking,' I heard him say to Ally as I signed in.

'Honest,' she rolled her eyes at me, and her face was the colour of a cricket ball, 'they're like a class of infants. There's still three weeks to go, you know. Come here if you want that tinsel sticking on your Zimmer.'

I found Cissie in her room. She was looking distracted.

'Thank God you've come,' she said when she saw me. 'I've had a message from the Railway.'

'How do you mean?' I was thinking I'd left something on the train, maybe.

'The Railway Arms. Maggie gave them my number to get in touch with you because she thought you'd come here. She was supposed to meet you off the train, but she's fell on some black ice and they had to carry her into the pub. They think she might have broken her cheekbone. She's been tekken to the Royal Bolton, anyroad. They're like glass at the best of times, them cobbles down to the station. They want tarmacking.'

'Oh God, poor Maggie.'

'I know, it's a shame. She's a kind woman. Too kind. She were bothered about you, they said.'

I sat down on the bed. 'Yeah, what's going on? Is Poll all right? The house is deserted.'

'Cissie pursed her lips. 'All right? I should say she's all right. She's flitted, that's all.'

'*Moved house*, after all this time?'

'And how.'

'She didn't think to tell me. Typical. God, that's my home.'

'Not any more, it in't. That's why Maggie were meeting you, to bring you up to speed. Poll decided, a couple of months back, she wanted a new bungalow. She came to see me last week. I thought there must be summat up. Brought a box of Roses and delivers this bombshell.' She reached for the chocolates and shook the carton. 'Oh. I was going to say have one, but they've all gone.'

'Never mind. So where is she?'

'Well, you know Coslett's farm? Right at t' other end of the village, on t' way to Ambley? There, in a bungalow for the disabled.'

I was following the route in my head. 'Next to the white farmhouse?'

'That's right. John Coslett built it for his mother, and then she died, and then a chap from Harrop had it awhile. And it's come on the market again.'

'So Poll's sold our house?' It was unbelievable.

'No. Not yet.'

'So how's she funded it? Is it a social services thing? You're going to have to talk me through this, Cissie, 'cause I don't get it at all.'

'No, well, you wouldn't. It was a shock to me. I'll tell you what she said. She reckoned, if she was going to have to live on her own, she wanted somewhere easier to cope with. Hand rails, no steps, a special bath, big windows.

It's very deluxe, she showed me the details; a beautiful garden. That I've no problem with. "But," I asked her, "who's paid for it?" And she said, "Me, I have." So I said, "How have you done that? Have you come up on t' lottery?" And she said—'

'What?'

'She's been collecting money from Vince for years. Or should I say, Dickie has, on her behalf. He had property, Vince. I don't know how many houses he owned, but he'd been buying to rent since his grandad and then his mum left him their houses. He'd used the rent to buy others, and so it went on. Nowt flash, just little terraces, but it all added up. I knew he'd owned a couple, way back, but I thought they'd had to be sold to pay off a debt. Turns out that was completely wrong.

'Now, when he went, Poll couldn't get at these houses because they were in his name. But six years ago he wrote to her out of the blue and said she could have the rent.'

'Bloody *hell*. Does she know where he is, then?'

'No, he didn't say. Just sent this parcel of keys and deeds. So Poll med Dickie her rent man and handyman, he's been going round collecting the money and doing general maintenance. She pays him a wage, you know. Cash in hand.'

'And where is all this money?' I thought of our threadbare sofa and the flaking fridge. 'Christ, Cissie; how much is there?'

'She refused to say. I told her she'd get done for not declaring it, but she said it's all legal. She says, get this, that she's got an accountant.'

'No way.'

'It's what she said. I don't know whether to believe her or not. This bungalow's real enough, though. You'll be amazed when you see it, if it's owt like the photos.'

'Oh, Cissie.' We sat in silence for a minute, then I said, 'Why would Vince have given her all that money, though?'

'He probably felt guilty, I should think. Perhaps he heard she were going blind. Or maybe he'd bought some more houses since and thought he didn't need them all. Or he could have hooked up with a rich widow, or gone on the streets, or topped hisself. We'll never know. But he were never very interested in wealth, weren't Vince. I think property was more of a hobby.'

'Some hobby. And where's Dickie now? Has he moved in with her?'

'He's in an annexe, apparently.' She raised her eyebrows. 'I don't know how they carry on aside from that. I don't ask. So there you are. Oh, she's going to employ a carer, she says, in the New Year. Someone she can boss about properly. I pity that person, I do.'

'Who wants a mince pie?' called Ally from the other side of the door. 'Come on, boys and girls, get them while they're hot.'

Neither Cissie nor I had any appetite, but we had three each.

'Will you be seeing Poll now? I've her new number written on that pad by the bed.'

'I'm so angry, Cissie, I don't know what I'm going to do.'

She picked an escaped raisin off her skirt and ate it. 'It's going to be a rum sort of Christmas for you,' she said.

*

Christmas Eve found me in Oxford with Ann. We went to Midnight Mass together and walked home under sparkling frost. Where the pavement narrowed, I had to step in the road.

'Steady,' I said, my voice loud in the quiet street. I felt drunk.

She looked at me and laughed. 'We are all of us in the gutter, but some of us are looking at the stars.'

'Oscar Wilde?'

'The Pretenders. But I think they stole it from him.' We craned our necks back to see the constellations. 'Do you know their names?'

'Most of them. I had a Ladybird book on it. Do you?'

'Yes,' she said, pointing, 'Big W, the Saucepan, Mini Saucepan, the Bow-tie.' Her breath came out in little spurts of cloud. I wanted to catch hold of her hand and run all the way back to town, keep the magic going.

'Doesn't a night sky make you feel small?'

'No,' she said. 'Shall I show you why?' And she came up close and put her arms round me. 'Watch the stars.'

She turned me round slowly, as if we were dancing, and the sky moved.

'What are you doing?'

'We're the axis of the universe,' she said. 'You have to believe that.'

\*

I didn't want it to be Christmas Day.

But it wasn't as bad as I'd thought. We listened to Radio Four and unwrapped our presents to each other; a velvet tunic and a professional hair-shaping set for me; an antique brooch in the shape of a basket for her. Then I was busy getting the dinner on, and Dinah Dragon arrived saying how quiet the motorways were, and Ann put the BBC2 opera on, and we were all grinning with nerves because our relationships had shifted round and nobody was quite sure how to behave any more. But then I took Dinah next door and showed her the guest room, where Ann was going to make me a study, and she asked me whether I was truly happy with the way things had turned out, and I said, I thought I was as near to it as made no difference. Then she said, was I missing Poll.

'Yes,' I admitted.

'Give her a ring,' she said.

I looked doubtful.

'Go on, because whatever she says to you, you won't settle till you do.'

'Won't Ann mind?'

Dinah said, 'I'm going to take her out for a walk now. We'll be gone about half an hour.'

I'd so wanted to go and see Poll, even if it was just to give her a good slapping, but I hadn't had the courage. After the interview with Cissie, I'd gone back to Ann and stayed there. I hadn't seen Poll now for nearly three months.

The phone rang and rang, till Maggie eventually picked up. 'Hello?'

'It's Kat. What are you doing at Poll's? I thought you'd be at Dawn's.'

'I've only popped round to give her her present, I'm off in a minute. Oh, love, it's good to hear from you. Poll's been missing you. Are you all right? Did your tutors let you stay in Oxford, in the end? You're not on your own, are you? Are there a few of you?'

In the background I could hear the music to *The Snowman*, and Dogman's voice shouting, 'What's this bloody rubbish? Bloody snowmen? Who's on t' phone?'

'Dawn,' Maggie told him promptly.

'Yeah, everything's fine; can I speak to Poll?' I said, my heart pounding.

'She's just on t' lavvy. She'll only be a minute.'

'Has she been to Cissie's?'

'We went this morning. She's looking very well, ankles a bit thick. Sends her love.'

'Look—' I was losing my nerve. 'Tell Poll happy Christmas from me, OK? And I'll see her in the New Year. We'll talk then.'

'She says – ' Maggie lowered her voice – 'it's all coming to you when she dies, you know. Every penny.'

'Not to a dog's home, or Dickie, then?' I could hear the bitterness in my own voice.

'She says not. She says it won't be long now, she's tired of this world.'

I could make out Poll yelling something about Bailey's. It sounded serious. 'What's going on, Maggie?'

'Oh, she's got a new puppy, that's all. Tilly. Dickie give it her this morning, she were ovver t' moon. It's another Westie, but it's not like Winston. This one's a little demon, I think Dickie got it from a home. It's knocked her glass and her drink's gone on t' floor.'

'I towd you not to get cream carpets,' Dogman was saying. 'Every mark shows. Come here, I'll have a go at it.'

'Let me put her on,' said Maggie. 'I know she'd love to chat.'

'Not now,' I said quickly, and put the phone down.

Explanations, apologies, recriminations; it could all wait till after Christmas.

Later, I watched Ann chase a lone turkey drumstick round and round her plate, while Dinah told us stories about her father's time in the army and I tried not to panic about feeling full; there was no way I was going to make myself sick on Christmas Day. I imagined a stranger walking in and seeing us sitting round the table with our tissue hats. Hearty Dinah, with her ruddy cheeks and faint moustache; quiet Ann, with her skeletal arms; me. We must look a pretty strange party. But this was the family I'd chosen, for now.

My life as it stands is a web of deceit. Not just my own, either: I've taken on other people's too. But then, whose isn't? What family isn't held together by a cartilage of lies? In these fractured times, these days of spin, you have to make the family you can.

Bring on the New Year; I'll be ready.